KU-215-312

TWELVE TIMES BLESSED

Jacquelyn Mitchard is a journalist and the author of two previous non-fiction books. *The Deep End of the Ocean*, her first novel, was a runaway *New York Times* bestseller, as well as being Oprah Winfrey's first Bookclub choice. This was followed by *The Most Wanted* and *A Theory of Relativity*, also major international bestsellers.

Jacquelyn Mitchard

Twelve Times Blessed

HarperCollins*Publishers*

HarperCollins*Publishers*
77–85 Fulham Palace Road,
Hammersmith, London W6 8JB

www.harpercollins.co.uk

Special overseas edition 2003
This paperback edition 2004

First published in the USA by
HarperCollins*Publishers* 2003

1 3 5 7 9 8 6 4 2

A catalogue record for this book
is available from the British Library

ISBN 0 00 716469 6

Typeset in Sabon by Palimpsest Book Production Limited,
Polmont, Stirlingshire

Printed and bound in Great Britain by
Clays Limited, St Ives plc

For Pam, my rock
And Franny, my light,
And for the crew, bless them all

The author wishes to thank the many people who helped make the writing of this book honest and possible. They include Jane Gelfman, for nineteen years agent and best friend, for her exquisite taste and unwavering advocacy; and Sam Cohn, for his intelligence, friendship, and belief in me; Jennifer Hershey, editor of light hands and heart; editor Marjorie Braman, heir to the impossible, who still managed to find this book inside itself; and the Ragdale Foundation, where much of this book was written during 2001, especially Sylvia Brown, doyenne of the colony. I thank Cathy Hemming and HarperCollins for their faith and my growing relationship with the best of all publishers. And to Patti Kelly, who has worked tirelessly for seven years for my success and my sanity, gratitude and a hug.

I am also grateful for answers to Patricia Staats, M.D.; William Bonadio M.D., ER physician and author; friends and teachers Kitt Foss and Nancy Thurow; Anne D. LeClaire, sister writer, for her generosity, wisdom, and knowledge of Cape Cod, and for her example as a prudent shopper. I thank Michelle Jewell and my friend John for being willing body doubles, and my dear and only niece, Esa, for her name and her love. For their insight into the customs and cuisine of Louisiana, I thank Louisianne's Restaurant in Middleton, Wisconsin, Wynston Estis.

For their tolerance I thank my sons Robert, Dan, and Martin, my daughters Jocelyn, Francie, and Maria, my darling granddaughter, Sydney Ellen, my son-in-law Bryan, my husband, Christopher, for his even keel, and many beloved friends and kin, including Laurie, Patty, Larry, Peg, Emily, Jan, Brian, Lance and Rusty, Jeanine, Rebecca, Jane, Deb, Joyce, Dulcey, Andy, and Clarice. Forgive me my absences and trespasses, and know you are close to me and my heartbeat.

FEBRUARY

MY FUNNY VALENTINE

We challenge you to find more soul-satisfying chocolates than these, packed inside a red satin keepsake box (maybe to hide those first lost teeth, after the Tooth Fairy comes?). That's for you alone. Baby will snuggle in a white-and-red striped hooded pullover, suitable to the season, and each of you will sport a size-appropriate pair of seasonal socks, edged with golden arrows for boys, and hearts and beads of pink and red (impossible for even the most curious little fingers to remove) for girls. Romance missing in your life since the advent of you-know-whom? Not after you relax to this CD. 'Bolero' is only the beginning.

A FAMILIAR PLACE, when you have gained heft of life, can feel as confining as a familiar pair of pants when you've put on weight. True Dickinson has gained both, and her discomfort is as much the pinch of regret as the bitterness she feels when she has to suck in her gut to fasten her buttons.

As the crow flies, which is how people like to put it, True Dickinson lives only a mile from Nantucket Sound. But recently, and with regret, she has been unable to see the pewter of its winter billowing with customary awe, just as she has stopped looking at her friends with gratitude, at her success with pride, at her small family with surprised contentment. Not since she came from her birthplace in Amherst to the Cape, first as a sitter during college summer breaks, then as a bride with her husband, a pilot for the commuter airline, has she felt such unaccustomed restlessness. Stray and strange thoughts of moving away sometimes escape her purposeful days like

1

loose strands that occasionally escape from her tight and sensible French braid, which True is so accustomed to plaiting every morning she could do it in the dark. She catches herself thinking, I'll blow town, light out for the territories, just my son and me, leave the Cape altogether for a someplace with more oxygen and more sky.

Her consternation, of course, is misplaced.

It is situational, not locational.

For just as crows don't really fly straight – they are so curious, always swooping off on avian tangents to explore something shiny or smelly, that it probably takes a crow longer to get anywhere than it takes a human being in a car obeying the speed limit – True feels trapped not by the lack of space in the life around her but by the profusion of empty space of life within her. She is lonely. The ends of her life are working their way loose. Her son, whom she is accustomed to thinking of as a little child, is nearly ten, middle-aged, in kid years. Thus, True can no longer pretend she is a 'young widow.' Her mother is growing older; her longtime assistants speak of plans to relocate, to take on new adventures.

She is beginning to see herself as the point from which other things depart.

Would she describe herself in this way? Perhaps under hypnosis.

True knows that she's suffering from seasonal lag. And 'tis the season for *that*. February is no less lonely a month in a resort community, where every view is a watercolor landscape, than it is anywhere else, and may be more so. The closed lids of shops shuttered until summer are depressing to those who pass them, even to locals who rave about having their streets and churches all to themselves. It's a common misconception that people who are inclined to take their own lives do so at Christmas. The truth is that fingers itch for a strong piece of rope or a stash of sedatives starting in February, when the holidays have failed to deliver on their promise, and when the unbearable renewal of life brims just around the corner.

It is a particularly bad month for True. The month of her birth, it is also the month of her husband's long-ago death. Peter Lemieux, who flew eight-seater Cessnas through rowdy coastal weather for a living, died ironically, struck by a motorist on an icy night very much like this. Pete had stopped to help a woman whose car had blown its radiator. A moving van had mowed him down. For years, True has been unable to remember the sound of Pete's voice, and she has no idea whether the image of him she can summon to her mind is a mental snapshot of the wedding photo that she dusts along with her lamp and her hand lotion, or a true memory of the way he looked. True's mother, Kathleen, also widowed young, also by a car accident, nods in solemn empathy when True keeps refusing to bring out and watch the few videotapes she and Pete made during their son Guy's babyhood. Kathleen periodically suggests watching the tapes together, as if an erased life were something to be reveled in, like a great exfoliating bath. True knows that, even after eight years, the sight of Pete's platinum crewcut and square-cut face with its pilot's crinkled tan, perpetually young, will shatter her complacency, which she maintains by carefully separating *before* from *after*.

But more than this, she reckons intuitively that what she really cannot bear to see is the infant image of Guy, the only child she likely will ever have – miniature, mirthful and trustful, his cheeks drooping, round as peach halves, wider than his forehead. That velvety baby touch True *can* remember, and it grieves her to think it will quite probably be a touch that, for the rest of her life, she will only borrow.

She also knows that, while not quite the merry widow, she is not like her mother, not like the other young widows at the group she attended briefly, who had vied with each other to claim which limbs and digits and months of life they would trade for an hour in the arms of their husbands.

She also thinks she knows why, but keeps that thought folded carefully away, as mute as her bridal veil that lies folded in her cedar chest. No one but True had known about Peter's difficult nature, his cheerful assumption of control over her and everything else in his well-boundaried life, down to the strict allocation of True's lunch money, his utter self-centeredness, transformed by one fatal moment of heroism. Nor does anyone realize that, with his work and his military service, he and she had spent very little real time together as a couple.

Most people simply assumed True Dickinson was a princess of pluck, a game gal, a sturdy New England pragmatist with her long-legged stride and her soulful gray eyes, a widow cut on the bias of old Margaret Sullavan movies. And this has suited True very well indeed.

For some years after Peter's death, she had reveled with an almost

3

unseemly pride in others' perception of her as a woman of boundless courage and optimism, boldly stepping forth onto life's moving sidewalk as if it weren't laid out with sharp turns and periodically strewn with ball bearings. After her business took off, True had donned suits with short skirts and lectured to women's groups in New England and beyond on the benediction of hard work as a salve for grief, on her unwavering vow to cast off the temptations to cling to friends or succumb to self-pity. From some magazine article, she had borrowed the phrase 'When the going gets tough, take more risks.' The business, started with nothing but her own strong will, her experience at her previous job, and a business plan crafted from nightly study of reference books at the library while Guy played with his toy ambulance at her feet, had been the object lesson, the proof of her plum pudding.

But this heroic self, stalwart at cheering others even through her own bereavement, has begun to go aft agley.

True is changing, and it is not 'the change of life,' but something subtler. She fears she is becoming both a carp and a sap. She hopes no one else has noticed this, and in all honesty, she has done little more than notice it herself. To her friends, to her family – to you, if you asked, she would quip that she's fed up with the sameness of things, and, after twenty years, with a place that seems no longer to permit her a full breath. She'd say the Cape is so hidebound she can't set up a child's trampoline without petitioning a joint session of the legislature, for fear of disturbing a Pilgrim bone or, more likely, a billionaire's view of the bay. And though this is the least of the forces that constrict her psyche, nothing in her being – in neither her breeding nor her upbringing – has given her a tool to work at that lock.

Tonight is True's birthday, her forty-third. She is piloting her trusty Volvo slowly through what the radio announcer has called the worst nor'easter anyone but the oldest fishermen on the Cape can remember. She is driving to her 'birthday party,' a phrase that itself makes her wince, at a new restaurant far out in Truro. Isabelle Merton, once True's live-in nanny and now an office assistant who still lives with True free of rent in exchange for some childcare chores, is riding shotgun. And though True and Isabelle never lack for things to natter about, she feels the unaccustomed need for silence and solitude. Professional wrestlers and structural engineers might not reflect,

4

on their birthdays, on the substance of their lives, and on the time that remains to them, but everyone else does.

Yankee politeness, however, dictates that she make cheerful conversation, and so she tells Isabelle, 'Guess what Kathleen did tonight. She came around behind me and pulled my sweater down over my rear. She said, "You're getting a little shelf there, dear." Nice of her, huh?'

'Oh, True, how can you be surprised by anything your mother does?'

'I know. But I still am. Do you think when you're sixty-whatever you'll still get a kick out of being skinnier than your daughter . . . ?'

'True, you know what they say, if it's not one thing, it's your mother,' Isabelle says with a wave of her saffron-fingernailed hand. 'At least you *have* a mother, one who cares more about you than about her Harley.' But, True thinks, she sometimes wishes Kathleen were as distant, at least geographically, and as blasé as Isabelle's motorcycle mama. Not only does Kathleen work with True, but she lives in a guest cottage on True's property. She breezes in and out of True's own house at will. No phone call nor letter nor card tucked into a bouquet escapes Kathleen's sharp eyes. True sometimes wonders what it would have been like had it not seemed logical for Kathleen to move to the Cape after True's husband died. She wonders how privacy, as distinct from solitariness, might feel.

And yet, since it is a sorrow to Isabelle that she springs from roots that run pretty shallow, she sympathizes, 'I suppose you're right.'

'Give her a little credit,' Isabelle urges. 'After my mom left us, my grandma reswept every floor I ever swept and rerinsed every dish I ever washed, for ten years. Kathleen doesn't really interfere much, and she's a rock in other ways, for Guy, at work . . .'

True sighs, 'I know. I know.'

They drive past the dry sculpture of the marshes under ice, through a landscape where it seems impossible that commerce could take place, and then suddenly, there is the sign: THAT ONE PLACE. The parking lot is jammed. For an instant, True suspects her friends of foisting a surprise party on her, an event she has vigorously protested many times and would secretly adore.

Wet snow instantly frosts the contours of True's hair and

5

Isabelle's cloche, in just the few steps between the car and the door. The rosy glow of the windows make the place look to be on fire.

As soon as they are inside, True realizes that she has mislaid the significance of this day to other people. She has done this often, over the years. The tables are lit with red tapers because it is Valentine's Day. For people with romantic lives, it is a night to make new vows or to recall old ones – no matter the weather, so long as we're together – not a holiday cherished by widows, and a special irritant to a widow whose mother has named her in honor of it. It has taken True Dickinson decades to come to terms with her name, which she once thought made her sound like some beset virgin thrown on the charity of her mysterious third cousin after the death of her missionary parents. She blames her mother for this, her father having seemed to True, even at the age of eight, to be a cipher in this and most domestic matters. A prep-school librarian most of her life, Kathleen not only tended to take on literary airs, but was proud of her children's traceable relations to the reclusive Emily, the belle of Amherst – True's ancestral cousin. At least, True does not use her middle name, Harte, a family name from her mother's side, which, combined with the first, only sounds more ludicrous. However, it could have been worse. Her middle name could have been Love, or, like one of the little girls who lives at The Breakers, in Guy's class at school, Passionette.

Now she sees the usual suspects, her best friends, waving from the bar. They are Franny Van Nevel, True's college roommate and crony, who'd met her husband visiting True one long-ago summer on the Cape, and Rudy the assistant she'd stolen these seven years ago from Elizabeth's Heroines, the famous toy company they still always refer to as 'the doll cannery.' Everyone else in the place is seated two by two, some with fingers entwined across the marble tops, in defiance of the candle hazard. True tries to muster a hooray-we-made-it grin for Franny and Rudy, but the hopeful tension that had been bubbling in her breast expires with a sigh. More wine and madder music are definitely worth a try. She pauses to feed quarters into the jukebox, choosing three different versions of 'Thunder Road.'

The song currently playing is Tony Bennett, 'The Way You Look Tonight.' True wants to kick the jukebox in its neon jaw.

6

Franny (who first attracted True's attention freshman year at Amherst College, in part for romantically and deliberately changing the spelling of her name to match that of the wistful Glass girl in the J. D. Salinger book) and Rudy wrap her in a three-way hug with Isabelle. He gives her a kiss on each cheek. 'Long time no see, boss,' he says tenderly. It has been all of twelve hours since Rudy had stopped by True's house on the way to his yoga class to bring her a bagel with a candle. 'Happy happy, baby. You don't look so happy.'

'I'm happy,' says True, 'I'm just . . .' she gestures around her. 'It's just . . . look at everyone else in this room. You guys are to be commended for giving up the romantic dinner you should be having with your significant others for my not very significant . . .'

'De nada,' Rudy says. 'Keith had to work anyhow. He's planning a midnight dessert.' With his toothpaste smile and broad-shouldered altar-boy good looks (Franny often says, 'I'm so glad Rude's not the short-shorts kind of gay guy, more the North Face kind'), he explains that he, too, was late, having had to catch his two Jack Russells, Nick and Nora, after they gave chase to a couple of Jehovah's Witnesses. 'I kept telling the lady, who was perfectly nice, that the dogs were Unitarians. And, I swear to God, she kept saying, "Now, you know dogs don't have religion. And it wouldn't hurt you two" – she gave Keith and me the fish eye – "to have a look at these pamphlets. It's still not too late."'

True smiles, her chin on her hand. 'Half the women in this room probably wish it still weren't too late, Rudolfo.' Women tend to sigh around Rudy.

'Steve's got a bottle of Cristal for later,' Franny chimes in, 'and I got chocolates from the kids for breakfast.'

'Oh, well, in that case,' True sighs, then grins, 'I feel much better about being the only person in this room who's not only single, but too old to die young. I thought you might share my tristesse.'

'That kind of talk does not become you, True,' Isabelle points out, with an admonitory finger, 'and we agreed not to go to age land tonight.'

'You don't have to go to age land for twenty years,' True pleads, 'Esa, be real. This whole room reeks of passion and devotion. And except for the Altruzzos over there, who have probably been married for seventy-five years, practically every person in it is probably younger and thinner than I. That's not self-pity. It's clear vision.'

Isabelle replies, 'And I'm sure they're all saying to each other, isn't that True Dickinson, the one who started that fabulous business all on her own, who just got her picture in *Fortune* as One to Watch, who bought that gorgeous place near the lighthouse, who has a darling, talented son and a face like Catherine Deneuve but is unfortunately much fatter and older than she appears to the untrained eye.'

'You tell her, Esa,' Rudy says. 'Any more of this talk and you're going to make me wish I'd have cooked.' Everyone falls silent for a moment, imagining Rudy's macro kitchen: a birthday dinner of miso with a side of miso.

Esa tosses back her tumbled mass of auburn hair. 'I, however, will share your bereftitude,' she says, 'since I am once again an archaeological widow.'

'I'm not sure that's a word,' True cannot help laughing. 'What do they teach you in the journalism department?' Isabelle's beau is a professor at Lowell College – but not, she hastens to remind everyone, *her* professor – where Isabelle has been earning a degree for eight years. She'd answered True's ad for a sitter on the second day of her first term, and has since become so much, ever so much more to True. Since The Professor is so often off on digs and gigs, if she did not live with True, Esa often insists, she would have long since succumbed to her genetic predisposition for degenerating into a wastrel.

'I know a joke,' Franny says experimentally, her slender face, freckled as cinnamon on cream under its cap of black curls, as deceptively innocent as an Irish angel's. 'How do you get an old lady to say "fuck"?'

'I'll bite,' answers Rudy. 'How *do* you get an old lady to say "fuck"?'

'It's three old ladies,' Esa explains. 'Otherwise, it's not . . . you know, a joke. I've heard this one, Franny-O, but go on.'

'Okay, okay, one old lady, three old ladies, whatever. We're three old ladies here, except for you, Esa,' Franny says, out of deference to Isabelle's peachy twenty-fiveness.

'And me!' Rudy cries. Rudy is thirty-three.

'Well, you're not old, but you're also not a lady,' says Esa.

'There's that,' Rudy agrees.

'Everyone just shut up now,' Franny, a social worker who is accustomed to having her orders taken to heart, instructs them genially. 'How *do* you get three old ladies to say "fuck"?'

Fuck, True thinks. Fuck. I say it every day when some order goes haywire. But I did it last, what, eighteen months ago? *Eighteen months* since she'd broken up with Evan, giving Guy's unconcealed hatred of him as a feeble excuse, the real reason being her tendency to fall asleep as he read to her from the Norse epic poem he worked at, when he wasn't recapping movie actors' teeth. When True and Evan met, at a mutual friend's medical school graduation lawn party, the epic, nine years in the unfolding, had thrived like a grove of locust trees, to three hundred pages.

'Get a fourth one to say "Bingo!"' Franny concludes triumphantly, and though True chuckles along, she thinks: pretty soon I'll be looking forward to bingo in the gym at Saint Thomas More, every Friday night except in Lent, driving over with my mother and Mrs. Harkness and Mrs. Coffin, complaining the whole way about those terrible, rude, off-Cape drivers with their fancy sports cars. I'll have spent the whole afternoon making sure my ink markers haven't run dry and counting up all the little red discs in my string bag to be certain I won't run short in the cover-all. I'll have volunteered twice that week at the Episcopal resale shop. I'll have written a letter to Guy at college, reminding him to wash his boxers and socks in hot, because hot disinfects . . .

'Should I get a bottle of wine?' Rudy asks.

'I shouldn't drink,' says True. 'It turns straight to sugar.'

'And I can't drink, I'm driving,' Esa says.

'Well, Steve's picking me up, so I can drink, but if nobody else is going to drink, why the hell did we drive all the way out here?' Franny asks, annoyed.

'Okay,' True sighs, 'I'll have a glass or two. Actually, I should toast my . . . birthday. But this is the end. I'm on the wagon. No more Kir Royales. Before alcohol, I had a waist . . .'

'That is the gospel,' Esa whispers, sotto voce. 'Whatever trivial amount of weight you might have gained is probably directly attributable to me and my enlisting you in my slide toward early alcoholism . . .'

'It is not. I'm not just chugging Merlot. I'm chugging mocha lattes.

9

Now, when I walk down the street, I feel like my ass is a little dog I'm walking, and when I turn the corner, I have to wait a few seconds for him to catch up.'

'You are impossible,' says Isabelle.

But Esa has a point. Both of them had grown to like a tipple and a nosh. Even when Isabelle was only seventeen, nowhere near legal, when the business was in its hysterical start-up phase, they had ended each fifteen-hour day by melting like wax to a flame toward the liquor cabinet. Guy was only a tot then, and Isabelle nominally his childcare provider, though she also did a dozen other tasks to help True keep her head above water. The little boy had obligingly learned the drill, and when True came out of her office, which had been, in her old house, a converted walk-in closet, he would open the break-front to remove three crystal wine glasses and insist on drinking his apple juice from the third glass. 'Oh God,' Isabelle said on one of these numb, weary nights, as she and Guy clinked glasses in a toast, 'I'm really the poster child for nannies, aren't I?'

'I don't think he'll remember this,' True assured her. 'How much do you remember from when you were two?'

Guy, of course, has vivid memories of the wine-glass clinking.

Isabelle now, however, confines most of her thumping to nights with her college friends. She dances on the resiny floors at fishermen's bars like Danny's Galley and the Stiff Bore. To open the door of one of these places is to set free a musk of smoke and sexual hunger so strong it can stagger you in your tracks. True doesn't venture into them. But since Isabelle's lover is in Chile on sabbatical for five months – '*Five* months!' Isabelle yowls, as if she has been condemned to a life of celibate contemplation – Isabelle has been 'almost entirely, technically' faithful. 'And it has not been easy,' she often points out. 'When you are both pining for the person and pissed off at him, and there are all these sailors with cute butts telling you they might never come back from their next voyage . . .'

'Jesus,' says Rudy. 'It's not like they were shipping out to Pearl Harbor.'

'It sounds that way, though,' Esa reflects, 'when you're smashed.'

True has no idea what a phone call to Santiago costs, but her business phone bills have spiked sharply, and after a call, Isabelle, always moody, grows so fog-bound that even Guy can't engage her full attention.

10

'At least you *had* a life,' she'd told True a few weeks earlier. 'I'm never going to have one. Answer me, when you watch the Discovery Channel, do you ever see archaeologists wearing baby backpacks? No. Because either they don't have babies, or they stop home only long enough to impregnate and then get back to . . . civilization. Like, Inca civilization. Dead peoples' eating utensils mean more to Douglas than any intimate dinner I could ever cook over candle-light. Do you think he really wants me? On the phone, he can only talk sherds. He gets upset if I call them shards.'

After one of those long, long transcontinental conversations, Esa came wandering into True's bedroom, threw herself down on the bed, and asked, 'Do you think you can get carpal tunnel from mastur-bating?'

'Get the Rabbit Pearl,' True had advised her, remembering the name of a vibrator she'd heard about from a business acquaintance. 'Women in California swear by it.'

It had never occurred to True to actually buy one of these contrap-tions for herself, though there are plenty of nights when her longing for sexual release is as insistent as the sore throat she gets when she wants to cry herself to sleep and even Patsy Cline won't get her started. But Isabelle actually went and ordered one, and now True finds herself straining to hear, through the wall that divides her bedroom from Isabelle's, the humming bee noise that lets her know Esa is romping with Douglas The Professor, once removed.

It is Isabelle who suggests they play darts.

'I don't want to,' Franny complains. 'Darts are for drunks.'

But darts, unlike tennis or backgammon, is the only game at which True can beat Franny, who is casually, comfortably athletic. 'Yep. I've decided. Let's play darts,' she says too loudly. 'It's my birthday and I get to pick the games.'

But before they do, the three pull out from under the table True's gift, and when she opens it, she is astounded.

It is a True doll; and though Franny is a whiz with a needle and Rudy wildly inventive, she cannot see how they have managed it. The doll wears blue jeans, has a sweep of blond hair tucked behind one ear, and carries in one hand a teeny million-dollar bill, and in the other a basket of teeny teddy bears and baby bottles, a refer-ence to True's company. The doll wears a sweatshirt with a stamp-sized picture of Guy silk-screened on the back, and is embroidered

'Gee's Mom,' a nod to the correct (and only-at-home) French pronunciation of her son's name so sweet it makes True catch her breath. Rudy has drawn the card. It says 'You're our Heroine!' and features a naughty caricature of their old boss, an austerely slender and beautiful woman with a personality as daunting as her looks, brandishing costume dolls like samurai swords, a wicked on-target jape on their former employer.

'You guys,' True begins, genuinely moved. 'How did you . . . ?'

'Well, we didn't *make* the doll,' Rudy says. 'Elizabeth let us have a model – she was sort of in on this, True, and you should drop her a note – I think the model was a discard. I think she was going to be Chris Evert until Elizabeth realized nobody under thirty-five remembers who Chris Evert was.'

'But all the rest of it,' True breathes, cradling the doll, admiring its detail.

'Franny really thought of it,' Rudy admits, with a tinge of sorrow.

'But you did all the work, except the costume,' Franny offers generously.

'And I tramped up street and down alley finding the miniature teddy bears and stuff . . .' Esa adds.

'But why not a . . . bottle of perfume?' True asks.

They fall silent.

So they have noticed.

'We thought you needed to be reminded what you do, what you've done, where you've been, and that you're, oh True, you're a . . . we meant the card,' Franny says.

True's eyes spill over.

'Don't get all weepy,' Rudy remonstrates, glancing around the room, reminding True that, fey or not, he is, after all, a guy.

'And that you're a good mother,' Esa puts in. 'No matter how hard you work, and no matter how much Guy guilt-trips you for every date you have, you're the best mother I know.' Isabelle's chin juts forward. 'To him . . . and to me.'

'If you don't want me to bawl, you'd better stop saying things like that,' True instructs them. She studies the kaleidoscope of revolving sympathy and affection in Franny's green eyes – Franny and her builder husband, Steve, have two girls, Angelique and MacClaine, but she has mentioned in passing that they may try to scrape up enough dough to adopt a baby boy. And every one

12

of them knows how True yearns for another child. They have braided together all her parts except the missing one, and they all know it. 'You all went above and beyond. I'll treasure this all my life.'

'Enough slobbering. Let's play,' Rudy says stoutly.

They all buy their three darts for a dollar at the bar and each deposits five dollars in a clean plastic cup. 'We'll have to let True win,' Franny gripes. 'It's her *birthday*.'

'No, play as if your life depended on it,' True says. 'I'll win anyhow. I'm in the gifted-and-talented bar-darts program. Let's play Cricket. The object is aim for the fifteens and twenties . . .'

'No, let's play Three-Oh-One. It's easier,' Rudy says.

'You have to have paper for Three-Oh-One,' True says. 'To subtract. And a bajillion darts unless you want to keep running and getting them.'

'No, you don't,' Rudy says. 'Just three at a time. It can even be the *same* three. Truly Fair, you need to get out more.'

'Tell that to my needy customers and equally needy distributors,' True mugs.

'Let's just throw the damn darts at the board, one at a time, and the most bull's-eyes wins,' Franny says.

'And then are we going to eat at some point?' Rudy asks nervously. 'It's not letting up out there.' They all gaze out the rosy-tinted windows. The snow is horizontal. Drifts are banked against the wheel wells of parked cars. 'Maybe they serve breakfast,' Rudy continues, with a shrug.

'After the game,' True says, testing her wrist, lengthening her stroke. She and Rudy often play darts on the board they've made in their office at True's house. The bull's-eye is Elizabeth Chilmark, their former boss, and instead of the traditional numbered wedges, there are twelve wedge-shaped targets to make up the circle, each pasted over with a color photo of one of Elizabeth's Heroines – Joan of Arc, Cleopatra, Clara Barton – the elegant costume dolls from which Elizabeth, who dislikes children and who is so severe and driven True is certain she never owned a doll herself – has made a czar's fortune.

But Franny nails the first round, easily, and does a little entrechat in the middle of the peanut shell-strewn floor, pumping her fist. Rudy and True tie in the second round, their darts needle-width apart on the bull's-eye center, so they have to tack on a fourth, medal round to be fair.

'I'm going to be serious now,' True warns everyone.

First, she glides – she thinks of it as 'sashaying' – up to the bar to get another glass of wine. This night has not been so bad; on the barometer of birthdays, it's striving for a solid seven out of ten, the best two having been the night she saw the clear outline of Guy's baby fist under the drum-tight skin of her pregnant belly and the one when her mother brought home her part-schnauzer puppy, Posy, who lived seventeen years. Drink a little, drink a lot, she thinks; the bad weather corrects for the alcohol hazard. On impulse, True buys a whole bottle of relatively aged Merlot, and catches a glimpse of herself in the long, shelved mirror. Her buttermilk hair is wavy from the dousing of snow, and her milkmaid complexion shimmers with a rosy ribbon of color along each cheekbone, gift of heat and wine. Because the mirror is old, like wavering water, her lips look bowed, plumped and vivid, about to be kissed. At least her poundage and gravitational challenging hasn't got to her face yet.

As she whirls away with the uncorked bottle, a man's voice, a voice that is soft, but somehow carries not over but under the murmur of conversation because of its pitch, its Southern tang, says, 'I'll take you on.'

She cannot see the person who spoke. The voice seems to have come from beside her, but there is no one at the bar except a few necking couples. She does not know whether whoever spoke was speaking to her. Again, she hears, 'I'll take you on.'

There. He is wedged between the bar and the wall, in the little gap where servers wait impatiently with their trays for their drink orders. Though he is at least six feet away, and speaking softly, she can hear him.

She answers, 'What?' And then, she thinks – did I step on his foot? Does he know who I am? Is he drunk? If he is drunk, he is beautifully so, his languid posture so relaxed, so . . . wide open that his shoulder invites her head. His thick black hair is nearly shorn to a buzz. It has made sculpture of his shapely skull, and his eyes are the faultless blue of True's hydrangea, with lashes long as burnt grass. 'Darts?' he says. 'Because I saw you can play.'

True looks for Rudy and the others, and sees that all her friends

14

have given up on her, and are now fighting over the bread basket at the table.

Well, True thinks, sitting down on a convenient bar stool to still the quivering of her inner thighs, okay, okay. This isn't a flirt; this is a friendly. This guy is . . . probably twenty-five. Perhaps she or her mother knows his mother. 'Are you from Chatham?' she asks.

'No,' he says.

'How do I know you, then?'

'I don't think we know each other. I just thought you might like to throw darts, because I don't let anybody in here who can beat me.'

A regular, True thinks. A clammer during the day. So are those forearms accounted for. Forearms she dares not look at, because she fears her eyes will cross. She laughs then, which is when she realizes she hasn't drawn breath for more than a minute. The man hands her three darts – 'On the house. I know the owner . . .' and extracts his own from behind the bar, from a velvet case with embroidered stars.

'Not fair,' True says. 'You have your own, so you must be a ringer.' The Sinatra from the jukebox has receded, grown tinny and distant, and the conversations seem muted. There is the sense in the room that something is afoot, as when a crowd of dancers draws back by mutual assent to spotlight a couple whose solo will be a ballet of love or war.

'I'll be gentle,' he says.

'What do you play?'

'Three-Oh-One if it's fine with you.'

'You need . . .'

'I have paper.' He shows her a cribbage pad.

Three-Oh-One starts with that many points, three hundred and one, as anyone who has ever grown bored in a bar knows well. It's played three darts to a try, and you work for the circles with the highest numbers, the numbers on the outer wedge base-value, the small outer ring double, the small inner ring triple. The little ring outside the bull's-eye is twenty-five points, and the bull's-eye, the tiniest inner ring, the plu-prize, is fifty. It gets dicey when you work your way down to fifteen, then ten, then two points, because to hit a higher number than you have left to subtract is to go bust.

15

True hits the outer bull's-eye ring, a triple, and the inner ring with her first three. 'Birthday luck!' she says.

'Happy birthday,' the man tells her softly. 'Big one?'

'Yep,' True says, 'forty,' inwardly wincing at the alacrity and ease of the lie.

'Hmmm,' says the man, 'I'd have guessed . . .'

'What?'

'Oh, probably forty,' he says. He nails doubles on all three, so she's still way ahead on the path down to zero.

'Is it me again?' True asks, thinking, I've lied, well, so I've lied . . . I'll never see this man again in my life. 'I'll try to finish up quickly. My friends are hungry, over there . . .'

'Let's go, then,' he suggests. 'Don't want hungry people.'

They begin again. But True's arm seems to weigh as much as her leg. Her first throw doesn't even nick the board, and hits the floor with a dull ping. A nod from the man signals he'll let her have a gimme. Her second lands far out on the outer wedge. Gathering herself, she aims slowly, like a golfer lining up a putt. Double ring. And then another bull's-eye. She extracts her darts and they total their points.

She's still winning. Skipping over to the table for her glass, she winks at Isabelle, who gives her thumbs up. And then she watches as the young man nails three straight. He is down to thirty. He is down to ten. Each of the real feathers in his custom darts quiver, like the tip of a warrior's spear. He is going to kill her. She feels like a kid who has just sat on Santa Claus's lap and then caught him in the alley behind the mall, having a smoke.

'Why didn't you do that right off?' True asks, stung.

'It wouldn't have impressed you as much.'

'Okay, so I'm impressed now. Good night. Thanks for the game.'

'But you still have a chance . . .'

'I don't think I'll take it.'

'No, come on. I saw you before. Get that look in your eye. Be the dart.'

True does that. Her darts sing . . . she can think of no other way to say it, true. Outer edges. She has tied him at ten. The young man steps up next. His first two shots are masterly. He is down to two. His last goes just enough astray that it makes True suspicious. Hardly even bothering to aim, she nails her ten. She's won.

'You won,' he says.

'You let me,' she pouts.

'I didn't let you.'

'You let me,' she says flatly.

'I swear on my mother's grave I didn't let you.'

'I'll bet your mother isn't even dead,' True retorts, thinking, now *there's* a way to impress a new acquaintance.

'No, she's alive and well with my pop in Metairie, Louisiana, but I would swear on her . . . her dear head that I missed that last and you won, fair and square.'

True finally sighs, 'Okay, I give up. Guess I still have my eyesight.'

'What are you having?' the man begins.

'We're drinking wine. We have a bottle.'

'No, for dinner. I highly recommend the crawfish étouffée. It's not a cliché. Adapted from Grandma's Creole recipe. One of many.'

'Cajun or Creole?' She has never heard food described as a 'cliché.'

'You know the difference?' he almost laughs, delighted. 'Most people think they're the same thing. But I do both. My grandma grew up in Haiti. Well, that's not true. She was a child in Haiti. They moved here when she was about twelve. But she learned from her grandma, and she from her grandma . . . you get the picture.'

'You . . . are the cook?'

'I am the cook.'

'Then why aren't you cooking?'

'I'm not the *only* cook. And not all the time. And it's late. Almost everyone else has gone home, you see.' Indeed, all but three of the tables now stand empty, the festive red tapers guttering. 'So, your real birthday is on Valentine's Day?' He looks directly and openly into True's face.

'My real birthday. It's a little annoying. Though not so much as the kids who had theirs on Christmas. My son's is on Saint Patrick's Day.'

'A theme family.'

'How?' True asks, puzzled. 'You mean holidays?'

'Saints,' says the man.

'Oh, sure, right. He'll be ten.'

'So you waited until thirty.'

It is a peculiar conversation. Men do not usually ask about her age at gestation.

17

'Ahh, right, thirty. Though we were married when . . . just after college. My husband was . . . not around so much. We had no money. We waited. He was in the service, a Marine flight instructor, then getting his pilot's license.'

'He's a pilot?'

'He's dead.' This never fails to provoke some reaction.

The young man's eyes widen and grow bright with an unfeigned sadness. 'He crashed?'

'No. He was hit by a car.'

'That's ironic.'

'So they say.'

'Tough on your boy. Just one?'

'Just one.'

'I was born in October,' says the young man, wandering over to collect his darts, gently polishing each on his flannel sleeve. 'A Scorpio. My grandmother reads the tarot cards. Said my birth cards predicted a jack-of-all-trades.' Enough about you, lady, True imagines him thinking, let's get back to me.

'But instead, you're a jack of one. A chef.'

'Chef, carpenter, mountain-climbing instructor, year of law school. I majored in dance in college. And tried to do a little of that for money . . . what do you do?'

'I run my own business,' True says. 'I have a catalogue company.'

'Like Orvis? I applied once to teach at their fly-fishing school . . .'

Jack-of-all-trades and full-time show-off, True thinks. 'Not hung up on completion, huh?' she asks, turning to leave. 'No, my business is about as different from Orvis as it's possible.'

'How?'

'I sell baby gifts. Not just one at a time. It's a service. The baby gets a gift, all handmade things, once a month for the first year of its life. And the grandma or the auntie gets the joy of knowing it arrives every month, and gets the credit, with the one purchase.'

'Only grandmas?'

'No, best friends, godmothers. Sisters. Anyone with the plastic.'

'They order off the 'Net?'

'Or the 800 number.'

'What d'you call it?'

'Twelve Times Blessed.'

'That's pretty.'

18

'Thank you.'

'It fits. A baby is a blessing, and the gifts are a blessing.'

'That's our thinking. We tried a million names – oh you don't care about this.'

'No, I do,' he smiles and steps closer, urging her to say more.

'Well, we thought of Baby Business, but it sounded . . . well, like bowel movements, and Once a Month,' True feels her face heat with a spreading blush, 'but my best friend said *that* sounded like, you know . . .'

'Getting your period.'

'Right,' True continues quickly, thinking that this is among the strangest conversations she has ever had with a stranger. 'And we thought of Gift of the Season, which sounded to all of us like those boxed grapefruits from Harry and David. We all got so frustrated.' She remembers the long August nights in the tiny, non-air-conditioned cottage where she had lived then, a few months after the police had come to her doorstep and told her what had happened when Pete stopped in the breakdown lane on the way home from an ordinary island run. 'Then, I think it was Rudy, he just said, it's a blessing. And we knew it was the right one. You know when you've hit it.'

'You do indeed,' says the young man, with an unwonted intensity. 'But you only have one baby.'

'Didn't plan it that way.'

'I plan to have kids one day. I love being around kids.'

'Be hard with all that cooking and dancing and mountain climbing.'

'You have a sharp point. I reckon it would require some settling down. And some growing up. But settling down with this place is the first step toward that. I reckon in some things I will be stead-fast.'

'I hope with our dinner.'

'Mais yeah. Certainly with that. Tom will be at his best.'

True notices Franny beckoning. They're all whispering, laughing, thinking she's making a pass at this guy. 'Well, we look forward to it . . .'

'It feels good to win, doesn't it?'

'To win?'

'To win. Darts. Anything. Feels good to be the one to take the dare, knock it out of the park, jump off the highest rail. You feel it with your whole body. Down to your fingertips. Like you feel . . . well, like you feel an orgasm. You're like that, aren't you? You like to win?'

Yes, True thinks. I like to win. And as she thinks that, the young man, whose hands will touch food she will soon eat, reaches out and holds her shoulder for an instant. She inhales sharply and smells him, a smell that puts her in mind of a Christmas tree just felled, as if, before the mesquite smoke and pepper and sweat and cooking oil accumulated on his clothing and hands, he had been laundered and line-dried. And then, with a butterfly's touch she is almost certain she has imagined, he lays his thumb above her breast, not with impropriety but with surgical intimacy, as if to measure the beat of her heart.

THE STORM IS in earnest, and True feels the crawfish, which had gone down like an inhalation of perfume, now squatting in her gut like a bullfrog. The wind tears her scarf from her neck, and she sees it uncoil, airborne, serpentine, into a cluster of locusts across the road. True always rushes out of the house ill-prepared – Cape weather is usually temporary, and forgiving – without gloves or sometimes even a coat. Tonight, in the interest of fashion, she has worn a long, heavy, black-wool sweater. It feels now like a screen door, each loose stitch a window for stinging air that has come all the way from Canada to remind humans of its clout.

All their good-byes have been hurried, nearly panicked. True is not drunk; she's glad of that. Franny, at nearly six feet tall, can handle her liquor like a longshoreman. Rudy could walk home from here, though no one can see five feet through the blizzard; he'd probably lose himself and die of exposure on the way. Rudy's little van is weighed down with inventory, though. He'll make it. It's she and Isabelle who have a far and twisting route to travel, back up the Cape Highway to Route 28, until they are home safe at the big white house where she knows her mother is faking a mini-stroke. She hopes Guy is fast asleep. Like all children who are half-orphaned, Guy is a worrier. He worries about his book reports, his jump shot, his falsetto, his short legs. But especially, he worries about his mother.

So, they take it slowly. The headlights are sufficient only to the approximately five feet in front of the car that the beams illuminate.

20

True reaches over and switches off the radio. Storms like this demand silence. They leave people in Vermont and Connecticut, and even Boston, incredulous. They only hit the Cape, but when they do, they paste it across the chops with the best right cross Mother Nature can muster. True sees the sign for Route 28.

All is well. They are, at normal driving speed, about fifteen minutes from home.

'He was very cute,' says Isabelle.

'The guy at the restaurant, the cook,' True agrees.

'I think you should date him,' Isabelle goes on.

'Okay,' says True, the way she answers Guy, when he asks if they can buy an Ultralite plane or a submersible motor scooter for snorkeling.

'I mean really; you should date him.'

'Well, Esa, I could probably adopt him. He was your age.'

'No, he's older. I could tell. Maybe not as old as you, but older.'

'And he's too cute, Esa. He's probably gay.'

'Rudy said not. And his gaydar is infallible.'

'Okay. Well, how about we figure this out after we survive the drive?' True asks.

She has not quite finished speaking when her car seems to take wing, its solid heft lifting off a delicate crepe of ice on a curve. True does not falter; she turns slowly in the direction of the skid, but they are past zero point, wallowing head down into a culvert and the stunning thud of the impact, when they plow into a twisted clump of alders and willow. They burrow in so slowly that the airbags are not activated, but their torsos rock, their necks arch with a thrusting pain, like Guy's bendy superheroes, farther than they should.

They sit staring forward, like dolls, stunned into immobility by the impact of tons of inert metal slammed through crusts of icy snow. Trees, real trees, not just saplings, around them, have been snapped like matchsticks.

'Are you okay?' Isabelle finally asks.

True is . . . fair. She has knocked her mouth on the steering wheel and can taste blood over the immediate pillowing of her swelling lip. She cannot see a house, or even a light, but as nothing in Cape Cod is very far from anything else, they must be within walking distance of something. It is her first thought to roll down the window, but the windows are banked solid with snow. They must have gone off near the edge of the marsh. True feels a quirt of pure fear. How close are they to the actual crust of the marsh? 'I'm thinking I should open the window, and push the snow away, so we can dig ourselves out of here, but I'm afraid the snow will fall in, and we'll lose whatever heat we've got in here,' she tells Esa. 'But don't be afraid.'

'I'm not afraid,' says Esa. 'Why don't we just call a tow truck?'

'That's why I love you,' True answers, whipping out her fine and fully charged Star-Tac. She dials her auto club number. No Service, the tiny green monitor informs her dolefully. Okay. She tries again. She dials Rudy. He will be home by now. No Service. Esa pulls out her own cell phone. Dials 411.

'Got it! It's ringing!' True can hear only Isabelle's side of the conversation. 'Any towing company . . . I see . . . well, just switch me over then . . . I thought you guys were all connected, aren't you? I see . . . well, we're really stuck here . . . Can you do it for . . . she hung up.' She scrooches around in her seat to show True her woeful child's face. 'The bitch hung up. She said, call 911.' True waits. 'I can't get 911,' Esa says. Both of them spend the next couple of minutes trying valiantly to dial any number they can think of – True's, Holly's, the restaurant, Danny's Galley, the Chocolate Swan, the fire departments in Chatham, Dennis, and Brewster, the Unitarian Church, St. Thomas More, True's brother, Isabelle's mother – who lives in Kentucky – and Isabelle's ex-boyfriends Karl and Manny. Then they stop, thinking that they had better try and conserve the battery. True's phone is hot to the touch.

'It must be the signal's blocked by the snow, the snow we're in and the snow we're . . . in,' True finally admits. The interior of the car is still warm, but there is a pungent, comforting smell, which reminds True of summer Saturday mornings, her earliest and nearly only memories of her father, the ritual of the trip to the gas station – in the days before seat belts or any kind of safety, True perched on her dad's lap, tiny hands on the wheel of the big Chevy station wagon. 'We should turn the car off,' she tells Isabelle. 'That's what they say, if you're stranded? We're . . .' True does not want to scare Esa, 'pretty blocked in here. We could asphyxiate ourselves.'

'What if we can't turn it back on?'

'It's a Volvo.'

'Well, what if we can't turn it back on even though *it's a Volvo*. They'll find us here in the spring.'

'This won't stick. You know this will melt off in a couple of days at most.'

'A couple of days? Days? We'll still be dead, True Dickinson. We didn't stop for death. It kindly stopped us by itself.'

'Don't be so melodramatic, Esa. Someone will come along in a minute.'

And yet, no one comes.

Prudent people are long since home. 'My mother will call the cops pretty soon. I never stay out this late.' As she speaks, they make out lights, and both of them begin to shout and wave, True laying on the horn, as a truck slushes past, seems to slow, and then moves slowly on. 'Why were we yelling?' True asks herself aloud. 'They can't hear us. They can't even see us. We're fifteen feet below the road.' As if on a command, silent and compelling as a dog whistle, both of them again reach for their cell phones. True's still has no service. Esa's works, but she cannot hear anything over the static. True flips on the radio. Crackling and popping, an authoritative voice – no disc jockey – reports winds in excess of sixty miles per hour at Nauset Light. 'I think it's time we try to just push our way out,' True says. Owing to the cant of the car, the snow is less deep on True's side. But on the passenger side, it's buried up to the roof. True musters all her strength and shoves open her door. It budges, no more than an eighth of an inch.

But so does the car. It shifts slowly. Isabelle's side has settled lower. 'Slide over!' True cries. 'I think we could sink in something.' Esa is next to her in a moment. They grip hands. True's love and protectiveness for Esa is like a torch in her sternum. If only they had not driven together. If only Esa were home now, with Guy, and safe. There is . . . she can see lights again. The same truck? Someone is searching for them. She pounds on the horn, which bleats like a newborn lamb under the bulk of the snow. Isabelle turns on the radio. It is The Zombies, the old hit 'She's Not There.' They sing along, at the top of their voices, True taking the backup.

'I have to pee,' Isabelle says.

'Good, pee,' True answers. 'You're supposed to drink your own urine if you're stranded.'

'There's a Diet Doctor Pepper in the back seat.'

'It's empty. It's Guy's. I tell him not to drink Diet, but he thinks he's fat.'

23

'He's not fat. He's perfect. He's like a little fireplug. Guy will be all right, won't he? After they find us in the spring?'

'It won't take until spring. They'll probably find us by . . . Wednesday. My mother will live forever. And there's Dog. My brother would just stick him in between the girls like he'd always been there. Guy will be fine. He'll probably be a genius. All geniuses have tormented childhoods.' She thinks of her mother, the consummate Yankee, wiry as a monkey, crawling over the stock boxes in the barn to reach the ones in the back.

'Since we're going to die, I should tell you, we're getting married,' Esa says.

'Oh honey,' True says, pulling Esa against her shoulder as tenderly as she would a nursing infant. 'That's wonderful! When?'

'When he gets back. April.'

'Oh, where?'

'I don't know.'

'The Unitarian Meeting House is beautiful, and so is Saint Thomas More . . .' Icy gusts, and sharp slivers of snow drive through the tiny crack True has opened and now cannot close, and she is thinking, like some moron on her deathbed planning to be cryogenically preserved to see her great-grandchildren, that the forsythia will be in bloom in time for Esa's wedding. The forsythia will still be in bloom when Esa leaves her, when she takes her Chinese robe, and her bottles of berry lip stain, and her Forties hats, and her mirror with the border of shells and plastic pearls they hot-glued together, and leaves. Tears fill True's eyes. She must concentrate all her will in the moment. Her butt has frozen solid. Warm thoughts, she summons. Hot showers, thick dry stockings, mashed garlic and spinach, mocha with a double shot, her duvet.

'We're atheists,' Esa reminds her.

'Doesn't matter.'

'No, he'd never go for it.'

'How about your mom's house?'

'Hello!' snorts Isabelle. 'My mom and Harley Hob are hardly going to host a spring wedding at the roadhouse.' Isabelle's mother, whom she sees rarely, is what True's mother would call 'rough.'

'My house then!'

'Oh, I'd hoped so! You can give me away!'

'But I don't want to give you away.'

They sit in silence for a long, painfully cold moment. True wants badly to sleep. She thinks of the poem by her Amherst ancestor, first shock, then stupor, then the letting go . . . Isabelle leans over and kisses True, briefly and tenderly, on the lips. 'If I were gay or something, or a confirmed celibate, I'd stay and just live at your house, True. I love you best. But I have to have a life . . .'

'I would never ask you . . .'

'I know, but it makes me sick to leave you. To leave you and Guy. Who'll take care of you? Who'll find your keys and tell you when your blush isn't blended so that you go out of the house looking like a German tourist?'

'You're not my mother, Esa.'

'But you're mine,' says Isabelle. They're both crying now. Isabelle tucks her head under True's chin, as Guy does when he sneaks into her bed at night. Guy, she thinks, my baby, my boy.

Pete is gone. Pete was some boy who was so cute True couldn't help marrying him when he was home on one of his leaves. She'd thought he might die in the Persian Gulf or something. They'd had ten years of marriage, during which Pete flew six days a week and played softball on three teams. Who had Pete been? All Pete's relatives live in Montana. They send Guy cowboy boots in ascending sizes every Christmas. He has once been to visit them, and came home burbling with tales of mountain hikes and creels of trout, but not nursery rhymes or cocoa at bedtime. And there is Dog, her dear brother the kids used to call Augie Doggie, he has his own girls and his girls do everything from gymnastics to Kundai Math. He's so busy. He's so spacey. He'll never be a good enough surrogate father to Guy. If she weren't already in these straits, she would hasten to her lawyer and transfer guardianship for Guy from her brother to Esa. It is Esa Guy knows best, and she has come a long way since her orange-haired teenhood, and will soon be married. But Esa will also soon be a Popsicle. Neither Isabelle nor True has to tell the other that their situation is harrowing.

True can no longer feel her toes.

'Do you have a blanket in the trunk?' Isabelle asks. 'Because we can pull down the back seat . . .'

'No,' says True. 'I have jumper cables. And lawn chairs. But no blankets. I'm never prepared.'

Neither Isabelle nor True says anything more. First Isabelle, then

25

True, falls asleep. The clock on the Chatham Baptist Church tolls midnight.

IT'S A BRANCH, a rope with something, a loop . . . bumping against the window.

'Shut up,' True mumbles. 'Guy, shut up now. Let Mama sleep.'

'Hold on!' calls a voice from somewhere above. 'I'm going to try to pull the door open first, so you can climb out. Then we'll hook the chain on the truck! Tie the rope to the door!' True reaches out, jamming her arm through the open crack. The lock mechanism scores her arm deeply, and she sees her blood crimp into frosty little crystals at the edge of the scrape. Her fingers immobile as numb mittens, she uses one hand as a spatula to mold her stiff fingers around the rope. In the glare of the headlamps from above – the snow has abated – she sees a man with a yellow mackinaw thrown over a parka, all but his jaw is jammed under a black knit cap. 'Come on!' he cries. 'I can't get down there! We'll both break through.'

'Okay, okay!' she cries.

He snaps the rope, as if to draw her attention to it, and it slips out of her hands. She tries to wiggle down onto the floor to reach out for it where it lies in the snow, but can't fit herself between the seat and steering wheel. She fumbles for the power switch, but . . . the car is not on. 'Esa,' she gasps, 'turn the car on.' But there is no response. True turns the ignition key herself, her arm bent back at a tearing angle. Movement is restoring bloodwarmth, and indescribable pain, to her fingers. She grabs the rope and makes a clumsy knot in the door handle, clumsy, but a sailor's clove hitch. Who knows whether it will hold? There is a roar and whine of wheels on snow from the road above, and as the truck tugs, the door groans open, and True falls facedown, out the door into the snowdrift. She scrabbles to her feet, hip deep in snow, and the man begins to pull her as she struggles upward, on her hands and knees, then her knees, then finally her feet. When she finally sees his face, and sees that it is him, the cook, the man with his own darts, she is not surprised. She gasps, 'My friend is down in that car!'

At his signal, True climbs into the cab and guns the engine of the truck. He has waded back down, the rope attached to the bumper now tied around his waist. Heat, blessed, redemptive, pours from the vents. True has never felt more physically vulnerable. The man is hauling Esa up the grade; her shoe has fallen off. He hefts her into the cab of the truck. 'Esa!' True screams. 'We're okay now! Wake up.' Isabelle's lips are the palest violet. 'Esa,' True screams again.

'Slide over,' the young man says. 'We're going to the hospital.'

'SHE'S RESTING,' SAYS the doctor, a young auburn-haired woman. 'We've got her under warming blankets and we're running fluids. She's young and strong . . . and I don't think there will be lingering effects from whatever frostbite there is, except she'll feel the weather like an old lady when it gets cold!' The doctor laughs; she actually laughs, fingering her stethoscope. 'Filthy night,' she says, glancing out at the black beyond the glass doors.

'Frostbite? Will she really be all right?' True asks. 'Will she die?'

'No, but you're lucky, both of you,' the doctor says sternly. Doctors always seem to do this, True thinks suddenly, to behave as though whatever has befallen you is your own fault. They are like rigid parents, doctors. Like her mother. 'I'm going to give you a sheet of instructions about your stitches, and you should make an appointment with your own doctor to have them removed . . . in about a week. It's your left arm, so if you're right-handed try not to use it. And now, you'd better get home before we have to start an IV in you . . .'

'No, I'm staying until Esa wakes up,' says True, turning to their rescuer, 'you can go home now. You have to. I'm so sorry to have kept you so long. I can't thank you enough . . .'

'I had to stay to see if she was going to be fine, didn't I?'

True stops and regards this young man, the caked dirt and mud on his white khakis, the rip in the cuff of what appears to be a fairly new parka. Is this young man not only a Good Samaritan, but also . . . simply good? Has she encountered so few – her mind almost stumbles over the antiquated term – gentlemen in recent times that she must stifle the shameful urge to offer this one a tip?

'Well, you didn't have to, no,' True answers, 'but I would have, and I'm glad you did.' She thinks of the two of them stumbling through the door, Esa white and still as a marble angel in Hank's

27

arms, then past the swinging doors into the emergency room, the wheeled cart, the shock at being turned back from following Esa because True was not, in fact, immediate family. It seems years ago. It has certainly been hours ago. A watery yellow streak of dawn underlines the paling sky.

'And if I leave, how will you get home?' he now asks her.

'I'll wait until morning, and then call Rudy.'

'Don't be foolish,' Hank says, 'I don't live far from you. Nothing in Chatham is any more than ten minutes from anywhere else. And you live in the big house by the light. I know where you live. I'll drive you.' He strides away and returns with a few small, soft hospital blankets. 'Here, you can wrap these around you under my big blanket.'

When they slide together into the truck and the heat begins to thaw her wet and throbbing toes, True begins to cry, and she sobs the entire distance, in pain and relief, babbling, chattering, every muscle in her legs and chest in unsynchronized tremor, despite the rough rug, which smells strongly of dog, that Hank has tucked around her soaking sweater coat with the hospital blankets tucked inside that, so the worst of the cold will be kept from her skin.

For the rest of her life, she will remember the oblong light from her doorway thrown onto the snow as they staggered up the walk. It was, by then, four A.M., and the first terns and black skimmers were taking flight, their lonesome cries, two, then four, rising from the beach. Her mother, her dear and irritating face wild with anguish, gathered them both in – True caught her involuntary look of dismay as the snow melt puddled on the polished wood of the foyer – and Guy came running down the stairs, his too-small tiger-striped boxers agape, his silly, oversized balls and olive-sized little-boy's penis plain to see, and flung himself on her. She had clung to his warm hefty small body with a grasp like a prayer. Then, True had taken Guy with her upstairs while she dried off and pulled on Peter's huge old robe. Vanity had not bowed even to catastrophe, and she had paused to sweep her hair up into a white towel – having read somewhere that all women look beautiful with their hair turbaned in towels – and to wash the mascara off her face. Hopeless, it had been, in any case. Her lip had swelled to the size of a bagel, and her neck and cheek were scored with dried blood and raised welts.

28

But when they had come back down, True in a dry robe and Guy now decent in a pair of soccer pajamas, he was gone.

When True arrives back at the hospital the next morning, the man named Hank is already there. Curiouser and curiouser.

That day she'd called the restaurant, That One Place, to find and thank him, and it was only then she even learned his name, which is Bannister, and learned as well that he was not only the cook, but the owner. It is not he who tells her, but some woman who answers, and she is ashamed to have thought him conceited. Sore and swollen, too much in pain even to apply her moisturizer, True almost does not enter the room when she sees Esa asleep and Hank lounging in a chair, reading an ancient *People*.

But he looks up before she can slip away. 'Wow, Tom and Nicole were still swearing on Bibles they were having steamy sex twice a day when this was written. I was always more a Nicole fan, weren't you?' He smiles. 'Boy, you sure look like you were rode hard and put away wet.' Hank smiles so easily True can take this only as fact, not an insult. Isabelle sleeps on. Since she is asleep, it is logical that he is not here only to see Isabelle. He is here to see True.

'Well, you could put it that way,' True answers, thinking of that skidding, flat-out race through the dark to Cape Cod General in Hyannis, as Esa's waxen face swayed back and forth between them in the cab of the truck.

'You,' True whispers suddenly, another chunk of that icy darkness handed back to her by memory. 'You were the one in the truck. The one we saw pass.'

'I closed up after you guys left,' Hank explains, 'and you were going so slow I saw you go down. I had to find a place to turn around, which took a while. Then, I couldn't find you. I figured you'd gotten out okay. I started home. But I had a hunch. Must be my Creole blood. Maman, my grandmother, calls it the "seeing blood." I was all the way to Chatham . . .'

'I thought you said you weren't from Chatham,' True interrupts, conscious of her ragged Harvard sweatshirt and too-tight woolen leggings.

'I'm not from Chatham,' Hank says slowly. 'I'm from Metairie. But I live in Chatham . . .'

'Your place is in Truro.'

'I couldn't afford to live in Truro and anyhow, it's too dull. I have a house on Bobby Lane.'

'That's six blocks from us,' True says. 'Well, I cannot thank you enough. I will have to figure out a way to thank you.'

'No thanks necessary, ma'am,' he says, and True winces at the honorific. 'I feel good. I feel like a paramedic.' Hank shrugs into his black leather jacket, waves her into the seat he has vacated, and, with a glance back at Isabelle, leaves. Trying to quench musings about whether she will ever see him again, True glances over Isabelle's chart, noting that only one finger may be permanently damaged, nerve-numbed by frostbite, though Isabelle's temperature had plummeted below ninety degrees. But she also cannot help allowing her eyes to flicker again over Hank's body, a cowboy body, and the translucent blue of his eyes, which, like a baby's eyes, seem never to blink.

On the third day of Isabelle's hospitalization, she finds him there again.

'I'm glad you came. I'm so glad to be able to tell you myself how great you . . . I mean how grateful we are. You were such a good neighbor,' True says, as they both smile down over Isabelle's bed. She has given him the highest compliment a New Englander can give, but it sounds prissy even to her ears. 'We ought to do something for you. Pay you back in some way. Besides our thanks, which you have forever. And that we'll tell everyone we know to come to your restaurant.'

'Not necessary.'

To the sound of the voices, Isabelle awakens, and True and Hank beam like new parents.

'Got any babies?' Isabelle asks. 'True runs the most amazing baby business in the world.'

'So I hear. But, nope. No babies,' says Hank. 'My sister's expecting. Number three.'

'Well, you can count on a full certificate from Twelve Times Blessed for that baby,' True says. 'And that is so little. You saved our lives, really.'

'How about a beer?' Isabelle asks, sitting up in bed.

'Now?' Hanks asks. 'Do they let you have beer in here?'

'Maybe you should rest,' True reminds Isabelle, thinking this is the sedative talking.

'I didn't mean now,' Isabelle says. 'A beer, sometime?'

'I don't drink,' Hank explains, and blushes. 'If you own a restaurant and you drink, pretty soon you own a bar, and then pretty soon you own a vacant lot.'

'How about coffee?' Isabelle persists.

'Don't drink coffee . . . well, not northern coffee. Nobody ever heard of chicory here.'

'Well, what do you do?' Isabelle is exasperated. 'Do you eat?'

'I eat. Not my own food, though. Or I try not to, anyway. It gets boring.'

'Well, want to go out to dinner?'

Hank levels a look at True, and she shrugs; she doesn't know what to make of this. She thinks Esa is a little hallucinatory, asking Hank for a date. Three telegrams from her own beloved, her betrothed, The Professor, are tacked to the cork board on the wall, over the massive potted hibiscus Rudy and Franny have sent. Though the telegrams have clearly come through Chilean operators – 'Your danger for me is distressing to a hot degree' and 'My love for you is over wires in a deep kiss' – they are fervent. The Professor has cut his trip short by two weeks to fly, well, not exactly fly, but rush a bit, to Isabelle's side. Well, True thinks, her mouth literally going slack as she watches the balletic grace with which Hank lowers himself into the cheap metal hospital chair, at least if she falls in love with him, it will keep her around.

'What I really like to do is bowl,' Hank says. 'Me and my brother-in-law bowled all the time at home, and nobody much up here under the age of forty or fifty seems to want to do it.'

'Okay, bowling,' Isabelle says brightly. 'You can bowl, can't you, True? You can go to Kings and Queens, in Dennis.'

'Me?' True is stupefied. 'You're talking about me?'

'You, you and Hank, you can go bowling. For friendship's sake.'

'Oh, Isabelle, go back to sleep, honey,' True says hurriedly. She is humiliated, as she is when Guy does something like ask her in public why she sleeps with a gel mask on her face.

But Hank looks up at True from under the tangle of those cinder lashes, and she sees some genuine shyness and none of the dashing toothiness people drag out when they're put on the spot. 'Ma'am, do you want to go bowling with me?'

'Uh, really . . . really, maybe we can have you over to dinner some Sunday . . . Isabelle makes a crazy risotto . . .'

31

'I work Sundays.'

'Monday, then.'

'I got to tell you, I'd rather bowl than eat,' Hank says.

True wants to haul poor, sick, quick-thawed Isabelle out of her white bed and smack her around with her IV bag.

'I'm busy for the next . . . six weeks,' says True, thinking, I will eat only fruit, only fruit and tofu, steamed, not fried.

'You are not, True,' Isabelle says. 'She'll go on Monday. I get out tomorrow.'

'MOMMY,' GUY SAYS on Monday night, 'I'm off the score now. I don't need my music anymore. Want to hear me sing the murder song, the one before they kill Aslan?' He is in the play, *Narnia, the Lion, the Witch and the Wardrobe,* at the Harwich Junior Theater, and he plays the Evil Dwarf, a big role for a small boy.

'Okay,' True says. She is sitting on her bed, surrounded by many pairs of pants, red, purple, pleated, elastic-waisted, denim, wool, corduroy. There are also new pants, drawstring numbers, in three colors, in a J. Karol bag near the door. Esa has gone power-shopping on her behalf. She has been trying on pants for an hour, and is sweating profusely. 'I gotta rest anyhow, and you can help me.'

Guy stands up, draws in breath to his diaphragm, and begins, 'Creatures of darkness, goblins and ghouls! Murder today! A murder today!' He has a fine, strong alto voice, and True is thinking of getting him voice lessons, since acting seems to be something her formerly timid son actually enjoys. When he sings, he abandons himself. He gleams. She gets up from the bed and kisses Guy's soft, domed forehead. He has a streak of platinum, a birthmark the size of a thumb just above one temple. 'Kiddo,' she says, 'you keep on doing that, I'm going to be lining up to look at posters of you on Broadway.'

'Cut it out, Mom,' Guy says. 'You have to have a really good voice for that, and piano and everything.'

'You could do it. It would take a lot of work.'

'Do they have a school for that?'

'Lots of them.'

'Here?'

'No. Other places, California, I guess, New York . . .'

'Would I have to stay over every night?'

'You'd be big. You'd be eighteen.'

'Well, I don't want to then.'

'Why?'

'Well, I would go, but I wouldn't want to sleep over.'

'You'd feel different about it if you were . . .'

'No, I wouldn't leave you. I don't want to ever move. We . . . we just got this house like two years ago . . .'

True begins to cry, suddenly and unreasonably. She flops on her back, because she has already applied five coats of mascara, and this way, the tears will only smear her cover-up cream.

'Mom. Mommy!' Guy cries. 'I said I wouldn't go. Don't have a nutty!'

'I'm not, Guy,' True explains, 'I want you to go. I mean, I don't want you to go anywhere until you're ready, but then you can go anywhere you want. And I would want you to.'

'I *said* I wouldn't . . .'

Isabelle pops in without knocking. 'Rudy says no worries about the little-boy swimsuits. They're on the way, hey.'

They have been readying the June baskets, and one of the items that will go into the boxes for baby boys who are six or seven months old are these miniatures of the black-and-white-striped turn-of-the-century bathing costumes with straps, the kind musclemen wore in old daguerreotypes. Everyone's excited about them, since baby girls' suits are easy to keep on, but baby boys' suits either fall off or make the little boys look like dwarfs. Since True uses only independent contractors, on a cut-and-sew basis, it means her staff has to locate the right material and provide it months in advance for her seamstress to fill the order. Luckily, the model was perfect, with a nice, roomy bottom and a snap-bottom closure that didn't spoil the design line. The rest of the June blessings box will be easy – sunscreen handmixed by a naturopathic wizard from New Hampshire, the graduated beach funnels that were such a big hit last year, and hats that close with a button and come with a back flap to protect tender folds. True glances at Guy, who has not stopped singing, though he looks annoyed, and remembers him at two, in his sky-blue Sherlock sunhat and the sunsuit with fish buttons, the one Peter said made his son look like a baby fag.

'Only two hours until . . .' Isabelle slouches, draws back an imaginary bowling ball, and lets it fly, 'Strike time! What's the matter, True? What's going on?'

'She's crying because I said I *might* be going to music school,' Guy rolls his eyes. 'And she won't listen when I tell her I'm not going.'

'Are you going to music camp or something?'

'No!' Guy yells. 'All I was doing was singing and she started crying. Why don't you just put some more pants on, Mom? What is this bowling thing anyhow?'

'Just going out with a friend.' True sits up, motioning frantically to Esa for a tissue and pressing a finger on each eyeball. 'I'm okay, now, baby. I'm fine, see?'

'Are you sure he's a friend? Just a friend? That's what you said about Evan. Are you flirting with this rescue-truck guy?'

'I think she is, Gee,' says Isabelle, using the French pronunciation with special tenderness. Her late husband Peter's family are French-Canadian, and he'd believed that naming his son after the Canadiens' hallowed Number Ten would point his son toward a future as a forward for the Bruins. At least, True is grateful that Pete had not insisted on his first inspiration, Maurice, for Maurice Richard. Though she would have considered it sacrilege, True would have then changed their boy's name after his father's death, to something like Dave or Don. When Guy entered kindergarten, and until second grade, True had tried valiantly to explain to teachers how her son's name was pronounced. But the best any of them had ever done had been 'Jee,' which led kids to call him 'Gee whiz,' or, worse, 'Gigi,' until True finally gave up and used the American way of saying it, which kids seem, oddly, to love. *'Hi guy, Guy!'*

Isabelle is now going on with her pitch, 'Wouldn't it be good if she were flirting? Wouldn't it be great if Mama had a boyfriend who had a restaurant? Free fudge-bottom pie?'

'I am not flirting with this guy,' True explains firmly, and sits down on the bed, laying aside all pants until Guy has practiced his song, twice more, with the dance steps, to her and Esa's applause. 'He is just a nice guy and he likes to bowl, and he has his own business, so it's kind of like a business meeting.'

'All she does is work all the time anyway,' Guy grumbles. 'She said she was going to take every Monday and have our date, one hour every Monday night. We were going to go to Aladdin's Castle and play Skeleton Kombat, and get Ben and Jerry's . . .'

'I'll take you,' Isabelle says.

'Don't bother,' Guy snatches up his music and stomps out of the room, his back a ridge of fury. 'You cry over me, but you're going bowling anyhow.'

'Gee, you know I hardly ever miss our Monday, and plus, that wasn't nice to Esa,' True calls. She has abandoned all her own pants now, and is delving into the J. Karol bag. 'These are a ten, Esa. I can't get one leg in a ten. That's what it's come to. *Tens* are too small.'

'They're made by Glad Rags,' Isabelle says. 'They're generous. That's why I got them.'

'I'm sorry, Esa,' Guy calls, heading downstairs. 'I'm sorry that my mother doesn't pay attention to me. Maybe when she's old, I'll put her in a home. Granny says that's what Mom's going to do to her when she's old.'

'I'll bet she did. But you know I wouldn't do that. That was rude, too, Gee,' True chides him absently, 'and I'll be the one in a home before Granny.'

'I said sorry to Esa,' Guy answers, 'I'm not going to say sorry to you. I'm a little mad at you now.'

'Gee, come on . . .'

'A person has a right to his own feelings. My teacher says that's in the code of honor to yourself.'

'I will take him to the arcade,' Isabelle promises.

'It is our date night,' says True. 'And I've broken my word to him, which is probably about the worst thing you can do to a kid, and all over a guy who's too young for me, or probably wants to ask me for a loan or business advice. *Très* stupid.'

'It isn't stupid,' Isabelle says, 'and if you did everything Guy wants you to do, instead of what he actually needs you to do, you'd spend eight hours a day just watching him bounce tennis balls or pucks against the garage door. If he was the one who had a sleepover tonight, you think he'd be bellowing?'

'He wouldn't have made plans,' says True, though this isn't true. Guy jumps at every invitation from a pal. Still, she isn't going to let herself off so easily. 'He would have kept his word.'

True makes herself a promise to wake Guy up tonight, when she

35

gets home, no matter how late, and make the two of them hot chocolate from the bar of real cocoa Dog brought from the West Indies.
Guy loves being awakened by his mother at night. He says it feels
like Christmas Eve or a snow day from school. She will make it up
to Guy, this coming Monday and all the Mondays thenceforward.

But now she must give all her attention to her own state of disgust.
'What man, what handsome, younger-than-me man would want this
body? Come on, Esa. This was a stinky trick you pulled,' she moans,
staring into the mirror, doing what she so often does, mentally
sculpting her body.

'True, if I really thought so, I wouldn't have done it.'

'I know.'

'And plenty of men like . . .'

'Large women? You were going to say that, weren't you?'

'No, older women. In this magazine I got a couple of weeks ago,
a guy's magazine, it said twenty things to do before you die. And
number one was, fall in love with an older woman. And anyway,
he can't be that much younger.'

'I told him I'm forty.'

'All the better.'

'But if it goes anywhere, I'll have to fess up.'

'Why?'

'Because you . . . just can't lie about your age. By a year maybe,
if you were this magician who could always keep your driver's license
out of sight, but three?'

'He called a few minutes ago.'

True's stomach surges. 'He did? What did he want?'

'Just to know where to meet you, what time . . .'

'What did he really want?'

'He wanted to know if you still wanted to go.'

True falls back on the bed, pillow over her face. 'See, Isabelle?
He doesn't want to do this! He's being *polite!* He probably has a
girlfriend who looks like Audrey Hepburn. The *young* Audrey
Hepburn. He probably has six girlfriends.'

'That's what I thought you'd say. I thought you'd make some
dumb joke and beg off. So I told him you'd meet him at Kings and
Queens at seven-thirty.'

AS SHE DRIVES, True thinks back to her encounter with Guy. She is damned if she does and daunted if she doesn't. The last time her son got out of the car at rehearsal, she had noticed his shoelace dangling, and instead of her customary irritation, had tried to recall the last time she had been asked to tie up his laces. Years ago. She will probably never again be asked to tie a shoe, unless her lithe mother breaks a hip. Guy's childhood is rocketing past her; he already glances around him to see whether the other kids have noticed when she kisses him at school. And now, she has given up her date with him for a foolishness, for a guy to whom she, under most circumstances, would probably be invisible.

And yet, there must be something for herself. Guy will grow up. He will go away to school. Rudy will move to some more glamorous place, and Esa already is on the way out of her life. There is a shaft opening down True's center faster than her accomplishments, in business and in life, can fill it. Behind her locked bathroom door, before she dressed, she had performed the now-customary inventory of flaws that have proliferated like mushrooms. She'd contorted into acrobatic angles on the lip of her bathroom sink to get full benefit of the pitiless fluorescents, examining the starbursts of violet vein behind her knee, lifting the heft of her hair to examine the wealth of gray strands nestled beneath the buttermilk blond, more each day, like nettles under a hedge.

When she wakes in the morning, she leans both hands on her windowsill when she steps on the scale, removing first one, then the other, before daring to open her eyes. She's carding herself, as the bartenders at Danny's Galley once carded her, far into her twenties. She's bent on proving to herself, for reasons probably perverse, that yes, her strong hands with their tapering tips now have greenish vessels like stubborn worms, which don't vanish when she holds up her arms to let the blood flow south, and that these veins are not just the result of the strength she's gained from lifting weights.

But as she does, she's also searching for an antidote to this fact's significance. A cure. A way into a locked box, the contents of which will render this data insignificant. Do other women her age, who are loved by steady men, scrutinize themselves so ruthlessly? Does Franny? Is she prospecting for the love that would be the key?

Isabelle's gusty young voluptuousness, like a windblown rose, probably contributes to True's dismay. Isabelle makes size twelve look like a million bucks. She glorifies True's castoffs and her own secondhand-shop finds; can twine her handfuls of dark hair into a scarf and be Nefertiti, or pull on a ski cap and be Pippi Longstocking, pin a Forties blue gown with rhinestones at the neck and be Kate Winslett. Her breasts under her Grateful Dead T-shirts scorn a bra for propping, her legs with their lathe-turned calves have no need of slimming stockings. And yet True loves Isabelle as a kid sister, as . . . a daughter. She cannot imagine life without her Isabelle, and the knowledge that Esa will soon belong to someone else – more than she belongs to True, slices her deeper than the joy she feels for her . . . employee. Isabelle is her employee. It is True who has converted her to kin. So absorbed is she that she misses the entrance to Kings and Queens and has to pull into a driveway to loop back.

TRUE'S ATTITUDE TOWARD bowling alleys is near-phobic. They are like truck stops, places where vulgar practices are not only unleashed but advertised, like the machines on the walls even in the women's bathrooms that offer multihued condoms with names like 'Black Steer' and 'Pussy Willow.' It was funny, when she was seventeen, to pretend to be so delicate she could not manage to pick up an eight-pound ball, it felt sexy to have Jonathan Martin fit his leg against hers to teach her the rudiments of the approach. Now, these are places for young marrieds out for a night away from the relentless demands of their two-year-olds. Teens searching for a safe first date, something that will make the boy feel manly and keep the girl's hands from fussing with her hair.

It is no place for a forty-three-year-old, unless she is a forty-three-year-old with another of her kind, surrounded by little boys and girls in birthday-party mode. Twice, she has dutifully carted seven of Guy's friends to Kings and Queens for a birthday party. But, she believes, even the cake and hot dogs served resentfully by an angry harlot, stank of lane wax and cigar smoke. She does not want to be here. What if Hank does like her? Will she feel like a fool if they kiss and knock teeth? What if Hank, more likely, only wants a buddy or a mentor? Will her disappointment render her nasty? She winces. It has done so, on occasion.

Hank is late. This makes her feel even more conspicuous and absurd. She is wearing a pair of drawstring pants in lightest wool, which fit her well except for being two inches too long, corrected by her cowboy boots, the highest heels she could find in her closet.

She also wears a sparkly red tunic Esa bought at the hospital auxiliary. She has given in to Esa and let her hair hang down, instead of binding it back into its usual thick braid, and the eye makeup Esa insisted on makes her eyes look so huge and sunken she could pass for a chorus girl in Berlin, circa 1938.

'Well, hi there,' Hank says easily, cat-footing up behind her so quickly he makes her jump and step on the hems of her pants. He has his own ball, of course, in a bag.

'If we'd been going scuba-diving, you'd have brought your own tank, wouldn't you?' True asks.

'Of course,' he says, not understanding.

They line up for shoes, those punch-line shoes. In bowling shoes, with these pants and these eyes, she will look like Charlie Chaplin. This is a huge part of her rue for bowling. As she sees the brute behind the counter dutifully dust them with a squirt of disinfectant spray, True thinks, that is what the real smell is. Dozens of feet. Fisherman feet and truck-driver feet and overheated bar-girl feet and unwashed senior-citizen feet. Thousands of feet have loosed their germs into these shoes.

'Size . . .' Hank glances down. 'Six for you?'

'Eight,' True sighs.

'You Northern girls,' he smiles.

'What?'

'Big feet,' he says.

'We walk on them. Can't wait for our menfolk to carry us around, honeychile,' says True.

They find a lane, and select a ball – teal, with starbursts – for True. She thinks, all I am required to do is be good-humored and get this over with and not trip on these pants, which I should probably return tomorrow. Be good-humored, and optimistic and adult, and take it all in the spirit in which it is offered.

I am in good shape, and this is a game, not a sport. Thank heaven he has not suggested racquetball.

On her first roll, she gets a decent spare. Seven pins. On her second, she catches herself thinking that Hank, seated at the banquette behind the scoring table, is measuring the vast expanse of her ass, and she lets the ball go on the backswing and hears a thunk which she knows must mean she has broken his shin.

'Oh my God!' she cries.

39

'It's okay. I'm okay,' he's wincing. 'It's kind of like being kicked by a horse.'

'So, were you a cowboy, too?'

'No. But didn't you ever ride a horse in your life?'

Of course she has. It was an elective at college. She had been rather good at it. 'I'm sorry,' True says. 'I tend to get a little touchy. When I feel guilty.'

'That's okay,' Hank says. 'I think I can stand now.'

'I'm really sorry.'

He hobbles up for his own try. A strike. Of course.

'Lucky,' he says.

Her next ball flies straight as if a sextant had been used to chart its course down the middle of the lane, just as her godfather, Sonny, a Boston Italian who'd grown up with her father, had taught her: to hold the ball level with his eyes, as their priest held a chalice, before lunging forth with knightly elegance. She does this, and knocks down eight pins. And grins.

Hank takes down their scores with a grease pencil. As he does, True studies the members of the mixed-doubles league in the next row over, all couples in their thirties; all the wives wear bowling shirts, tucked in; all the men are just ripe enough to begin to seed – she can see one, a devastatingly handsome guy – already has had plugs done. He has that thatchy look of the recently hairstored. They all look so festive, so companiable. True can imagine them going out later, for pizza, getting a foaming pitcher . . . as she watches, one of the women looks up at her. In that glance is everything, from her to Hank, and then back to her; she is wondering, True knows, is this True's nephew? Surely, she does not think he is her son.

But the woman knows something is out of kilter . . .

'Look,' True says pleadingly to Hank, who has returned to the seat, 'let me tell you something. I'd rather you'd have left us freeze to death in the ditch than do this.'

'I thought you liked games of challenge.'

'I do. Well, some. But I hate bowling.'

'Why didn't you say so?'

'I thought I was over my bowling aversion. But apparently, I'm still not. I'll have to go to a class or something, where they first just let you hold the balls, then try on the shoes. Then you go to the

40

bowling alley just for pizza.'

'Do you like pool?'

'I love pool. But I can't face the smoke of a bar tonight, okay?'

They drive, separately, to Comfort and Joy's, where True orders a double mocha, since caffeine does not keep her awake, and Hank orders water and an apple.

'Tell me about how you got the idea for your business,' Hank begins, after taking a gargantuan bite of the apple.

'Well, it started with the idea that everyone's busy, but that everyone wants to give a new baby a glorious beginning. Grandmothers, for one, are young now; they have careers; and sisters live across the country from their sisters. And the biggest generation in history is about to become the elder generation. It seemed as though, no matter if the economy hits the shits, the only thing you'd still pop for would be a baby.'

'That's brilliant. So they can buy a gift a month if they want to do it that way?'

'No, they have to buy the whole year. That's the thing of it, that's what makes it pay. Twelve wonderful surprises, and we keep computer files of each baby's age, so that the gifts are appropriate to their sizes – people e-mail us if their grandson is a real monster, wearing 2T at five months – and we stick in little surprises for the mom, soothing music, a moisturizer . . .'

'You know,' Hank says then, while True is distracted, noticing Joy Hook, the owner and a friend of hers, spying on them through the pass-through window of the café kitchen, 'you have really beautiful hair. Is it real?'

'It's not a wig, if that's what you mean.'

'No, I mean, is the color real?'

She wants to kick him with the metal toe of her wrangler's red-tooled boot.

'Yes, it is real. It is very blond, and up close, very gray in a couple of little places.'

'It is practically not at all gray. Do you do that stuff because you think somebody else is going to do it first? How old are you really?'

'What do you mean? Are you suggesting I was lying about my age?'

'A little,' he says.

'How old are you?' she asks.

41

'Thirty-eight,' he shrugs, his shoulders moving under his shirt like a cat's muscles as it finds its feet and aligns its spine.

'Okay, well, I'm actually forty-three.'

'Well, I'm actually thirty-three.'

'Oh, to hell with you,' says True.

'What's this?' Hank holds up both palms in surrender. 'Who started the age thing?'

'You did,' True says, knowing even as she speaks that she is about to blow. She is feeling that prickling along the margin of her hairline that precedes those incidents that make Esa call her The Red Queen, when, as sometimes happens, a mistake in addition or a breakdown of one of the computers makes her lose her temper to a degree even True finds shocking. She is always profusely apologetic about a minute after one of these spells takes place, once giving Isabelle flowers after Isabelle had dinged the door of the old Toyota they all use as a company car and True gave her a stinging lecture on equipment and accountability, a lecture that made Esa cry. 'Hank, Hank, I'm sorry. I'm sorry I swore at you. I just feel like an idiot, and when I feel like an idiot, I get mad.'

'I refuse to speak.'

'Well, I wish I'd refuse to speak. And so does everyone who knows me.'

Now, so that she doesn't have the chance to say even one more regrettable thing, True gets up to leave, slings her jacket around her shoulders, and throws a twenty on the table. 'That's more than this cost,' Hank comments, rising slowly.

'I always overtip when I'm mad.' True suddenly bursts out laughing. 'I guess it makes me feel like all that, as my son would say, c'mon, be nice. Let's go.' She figures the door is three good strides away. She prays she will not catch her heel or do anything else to mar her exit. Hank catches her before she can close her car door.

'Wait a minute,' he says. 'This isn't how this was supposed to go. So we both fudged a little. So what? It doesn't matter now. I don't care if you don't.'

'Well, I do care. How was it supposed to go? Is this what you always do? Flirt with older women who come into your restaurant so they'll go all ga-ga and order the lobster instead of the codcakes? Play darts with them and let them win so they'll spend more money?

Horse around with somebody who might have some influence in the business community you want to be part of? Wait. Stop. I didn't mean any of that, either. You see? The longer you stand here, the worse things I'm going to say.'

'Are these the worst things you've ever said to anyone?'

True stops to consider. 'I don't think so,' she admits.

'Wow,' Hank marvels, 'I was thinking it was a sort of momentary event.'

Faint with shame, True wants to rewind the tape – record a new version of this conversation, in which she and Hank chat companionably about restaurants and mail-order being risky businesses, about reliable help and seasonal business, and part with a tender handshake.

'Wait, about the darts. I have a confession to make. I have a dart that's weighted. It gives me an edge,' Hank says. 'I'm not that good. I made up all that stuff about trying out for the fly-fishing school. I was just going to get a job selling stuff over the phone to get the discount on the clothes.'

'So there you have it. We all have flaws. And just why did you tell me such a whopper?'

Hank shrugs slowly. 'You're not the only person on earth who's insecure. I wanted to make a big impression on you. You're an attractive, successful woman. I didn't want you to think I was just this . . . dumb kid with big shoulders . . .'

'And then you played rescue ranger, and acted like the concerned gentleman from the South, helping out the clumsy Yankee, and when I went upstairs to dry off, you just left . . .'

'There you go again. You just said you were sorry. Who made you like this?'

'Who?' True has never thought of a 'who,' in these terms. Certainly not Peter. She's simply always had a ferocious temper that surfaces . . . that surfaces only when she feels she's being . . . what? Fooled? Made conspicuous? *Who made you like this* is actually an interesting question. 'I mean, look, True. That's so unfair! You think I drive around looking for people to pull out of ditches? Wouldn't you have done the same thing in my place? And I left because your mother was looking at me like I was the Boston Strangler or something. She didn't say one word to me. Where I come from, someone comes in, middle of the night, somebody who just helped out your kin, you say, want a glass of water? Want a towel?'

'Yes,' True says, unable to help laughing again, 'that's how she is. That's a pretty fair observation of the way a New England lady of her age would treat a stranger.' Except, she thinks, Kathleen would consider saying nothing at all politeness. 'I guess you're right . . .'

'Don't take it all personal. I have a mother, too. She'd have got up in her kimono and started cooking gumbo for everybody and playing Reba on the tape player, which would have been just as bad.'

'No, it wouldn't have been as bad. I'm so grateful, really. I shouldn't have talked to you this way. It's just . . . you know, I took an hour getting dressed tonight. This is my fault, because I had expectations I shouldn't have had. I feel like a big goon. I was . . . I didn't mean to, but I was regarding this as a date, which was absurd . . .'

'Listen, True, I knew who you were when you came into That One Place. I even knew you were coming, from the reservation log, so I came in, even though it was my night off.

'I get *Fortune* magazine. I saw you, and I thought, this is a woman with guts. I thought I would like to get to know you, because you're an entrepreneur, like me, except you're way further along than I am . . . I don't own that place myself, you know. There are two of us . . .'

'You wanted a mentor, then?'

'No, I wanted a friend. To talk about ideas with.'

A friend? True thinks, her mercury rising yet again. A *friend*? For this I tried on twenty pairs of pants?

'A friend you could sort of slip your hand down the front of her sweater a little . . . ?' *Am* I nuts, she thinks? Is he right? Am I going over the top because he was cheeky, or because I'm miffed that he didn't mean to be?

'I didn't slip my hand down your sweater. I wondered at the time if you thought that. It was a little error. It was just meant to be a friendly touch. We actually touch people in the South without them thinking we're rapists.'

'I have no idea why I'm so mad. I have no idea where it's coming from,' True says, and then straightens her back and locks Hank eye-to-eye. 'No, that's a lie. I didn't even ask you what your reasons

44

were for coming out tonight. But I had other ones.' And they sprang, she thinks, from the bottom of the teenage girl's perpetually hopeful heart in this middle-aged woman's body, from the wronged cry of the stubborn memory of the woman who, not so very long ago, used to stop conversation simply by entering a room. 'I thought you . . . I hoped, I guess, that you liked me. *Liked* me, liked me. Not just as a friend to talk things over with. And now, even if you say that you do, you really will never understand how difficult it is for me to say that right now.'

'You know,' Hank says, 'when I saw you come barreling up out of that ditch, crying that your friend was in danger, I thought you were maybe one of the most beautiful women I ever saw. And I still think that. And what I wanted to do, right then, was kiss you. That wasn't an act.'

True sways. She reaches back for the side of her car; it will hold her up. Hank steps closer. He smells of violets and pine. She lifts her chin, knowing that Joy is probably glued to the picture window with half her staff, staring. True does not care in the least. Let them look. Let them see that this man wants her. With a tremendous exhilaration, she parts her lips, just slightly, and allows her eyes to flutter once, and then close.

Hank smiles at her, and lifts a strand of her hair from her forehead.

'What?' True cries. 'You said you wanted to kiss me.'

'I do want to kiss you. I did and I do. But then you started this . . . you scared the hell out of me. Now the time isn't right.'

'Oh, to hell with you all over again, then!' True says, and gets into her car, mortified. 'Who's nuts?' she asks as she rolls up her window, ignoring Hank's tap on the glass. She peels out of the parking lot.

At home, she half-lifts the solid, inert bundle of Guy's sleeping body and cradles the upper half of him, which is all of him she can still hold on her lap. 'I'm over four-seven,' she has heard him tell his friend Fenn. 'That's almost five feet tall.' Tears break and run down; one pops Guy in the eye, as a raindrop falling will waken a sunbather at the beach. She sings a phrase or two of 'Scarlet Ribbons,' which she sang for him when he was a baby, and still sings now, whenever he is sick, and he smiles in his sleep. 'Go to bed, Mama,' he says without opening his eyes.

45

The house breathes in the rhythm of its sleeping young, which is when houses are at their most replete, most content. In her guest cabin, fifty feet from True's front door, she can see her mother reading, moonlight glinting on the triple deck of Yale key locks Kathleen has fitted to the door of the fairy-tale cottage of a tiny, kindly witch. This is life enough. True makes circles in the sweat of the glass on the long window next to the door, but none of them will stay moons; all of them weep. When the telephone rings, True lifts it, and then gently, so it makes no sound, replaces it in its cradle.

MARCH

THE LUCK OF THE RAINBOW

March comes in like a lion and goes out like a lamb, and our hand puppets of both friendly animals are washcloths, can go in and out of the tub as easily as changes in the weather. Soaps in a cluster of four-leaf clovers come tucked in a mesh bag made of all the colors of the rainbow, for storing bath toys or keeping small pairs of socks from separating in the wash and running away on their own!

'HE CAN'T DO it, True,' Rudy says, slamming down the phone in exasperation.

'Why? Why? Did you tell him we don't need the actual cats until June?'

'He can't get the Michigan black cherry in time.'

'Then have him use the blasted red cherry. Or red oak.'

'Whistle Cats are made only from black cherry.'

'Oh, for heaven's sake, Rudy. Like babies are going to know the difference if the Halloween kitty they're slapping on the rug has a black cross grain or a gold cross grain!'

'Well, he says that if they're not made the way he makes them, they don't go out.'

'He can just forget the spring duck-families then,' True says bitterly, gnawing her pen.

'That would be biting off your nose to spite your face, True,' Kathleen stops to warn, using a phrase which True never has understood. 'If you're talking about Larry Sornberger, his Walking Duck Family is the state of the art.'

'They're the über ducks,' Rudy sighs.

'And three toy companies have had duck families recalled for dangerous detachable parts . . .' Kathleen continues.

'I know that,' True, who does not, retorts.

Rudy temporizes, 'He's an *artisan*, True. They're all daft. And we don't want to lose the duck families.'

'This all could have been avoided if we'd done what I suggested in the first place . . .' Kathleen points out.

'Which is what?' True and Rudy ask in unison.

'Give every vendor an agreement to sign, setting forth our lead-time policy.'

'That is a good idea,' Rudy admits.

'It really is a good idea, Mom; you're completely right. We *should* have done that years ago. Simply in terms of hours lost bickering, we'd be ahead. Nonetheless, Mister and Missus Smarty Pants, what are we going to use for hand rattles for the Halloween boxes?' True asks.

'Keith has a friend who does polymers, actually,' Rudy explains, 'mostly cup holders and office equipment. But I was thinking, if he made one mold for kitties, we could make them black cats and put little orange sparklies in them. We'd have to pay for the die casting, but it'd be a one-time expense . . .'

'Wouldn't that violate the whole premise of handmade?' Kathleen intones.

'No, because they'd be original, and American, but just not wooden,' Rudy answers.

Kathleen sniffs and turns to True. '*Plastic* is not what we stand for.'

'Well, Mother, it would be *rubber*, and we don't have sand shovels made of wood, either, or CDs, or lotion bottles . . .'

'Suit yourself,' Kathleen says, smartly hiking up the flannel slacks, of which she has a dozen pairs – black, white, gray, charcoal, off-white, off-gray, off-black. Holding in her hands an infant's bunting fashioned in the shape of an ear of corn for Halloween, True rises to glance out her window. Down on Ridgevale Beach, a pair of eccentrics in tweeds is romping with their golden retrievers. By the time the rattles and other gifts are actually stuffed into these little buntings or the pumpkin snapsuits for bigger babies (later useable for sleepwear: 'Nothing Wasted' is sacred canon at Twelve Times Blessed), it will actually be summer. True tries to summon the hot massage of Nauset sand under her back, the embracing darknesses heady with lilac and viburnium. But that is asking too much on this early March day, in one of the last weeks when the Cape is held fast in its stopped landscape, the sculpted silence that seems so holy in December and so lead-locked by February.

She will keep floating, floating on her back. She is too busy to roll over and swim. Or drown.

Take these molds. If they're going to negotiate, they'd better get hopping, and while Rudy is still around to be her link with the polymer man. Rudy and Keith have been making serious San Diego plans. Rudy has a calendar with photos of the California coastline, and he pointedly leaves realtors' letters lying about on his desk, as if they were telegrams.

His California dreaming reminds True that the people with whom she works may be her touchstone, but she is not theirs. She has gathered them 'round her, surrogate aunts and uncles for Guy, siblings and pals that fill the space left by a missing father Guy scarcely knew. But her cozy clan has other lives, expanding lives. Social lives, she corrects herself. *Romantic* lives. She has an abundant life, with her work and as quintessential sandwich between Guy and Kathleen. She is a sole layer of filling, yet substantial, she flatters herself, like a tuna melt. It is more than enough to keep her more than busy – busy? Harried is more like it.

There is no room on the menu for mooning about. None.

Hank has called twice. That she knows of. True has noted and crumpled the tiny slips of paper, complete with dates, that her mother left near the telephone after listening to the messages on True's machine – something True has told Kathleen she needn't bother to do, but which her mother persists in doing anyway. He has written a note on a postcard with a picture – a bowl of cherries, which Kathleen left on True's bed stand, facedown. The message reads, 'I think I struck out. Your friend, Hank Bannister.' True has not been able to throw it away, though she has carried it twice to the tall wicker trash hamper in her room.

Kathleen is probably relieved, True thinks. She pictures Hank's lazy cat's face, and imagines what Kathleen might call him: A rake? A barn burner? A hustler?

Is he, in fact, True thinks briefly, a rake, a barn burner, or a hustler?

49

But even if True adored Hank, might her mother, who believes that she and her daughter have parallel lives, consider it a sort of slap in the face if True found true love? 'I understand, honey,' Kathleen said once, when the shot clock began to run down on one of True's few and brief romances. 'No one else could ever be half the man my Bert was.'

Now True asks, 'How can you leave me, Rude? How can you leave me alone with Kathleen? I love my mother but I need a layer of bubble wrap between us.'

'I love being the bubble wrap in your life,' Rudy says.

'That's just one thing. How will I replace you? You have half my institutional memory. And all my creativity. Want a raise? Want a car?'

'Truly Fair, don't do this,' Rudy warns, busying himself with looking up the polymer man's phone number.

'But come on, we're a team, aren't we?'

'We sure are, but so are Keith and me. You know you'd do the same thing.'

'Would not.'

'Would so.'

'Would not.'

'If crawfish man were to ask you to tie the knot, you'd hasten your way South with him in a Lou'siana second.'

'I so would *not!*' True yells.

'Don't you think I'm going to miss you?' Rudy yells back. 'God, I'm like Guy's half father!'

'Esa's leaving. Guy'll grow up . . .' True pleads, trying for a special quaver in her voice.

Rudy grins. 'My mother does that a whole lot better than you do, honey. True, this is the part where I should say, get a life . . .'

'I have a life. This life.'

'This is work, True. Life is life.'

'Oh you mean that! I can always get that!' True says, and wonders, can I? 'You leave it when you go home at the end of the day. I have it twenty-four-seven . . .'

'*You* have a million dollars. I have a salary . . .'

'But no matter what person I hire, he's not going to know me. Who's going to talk to me about Elizabeth's? Who's going to talk to me about Cleopatra, asps sold separately?'

'We've had so much fun,' Rudy admits. 'Nobody ever had so much fun at work as us.'

True's last project with Rudy at the doll cannery had been Kristi Yamaguchi. She remembers the day she told her pal that she so loved the touch of the tiny leotards and spangled outfits and figure skates that actually laced that she was beginning to mull an idea, even before Peter's death, about tiny, exquisite things for tiny, exquisite living people, like the stunningly beautiful blond baby Guy had been. Rudy thought, even then, it was a spectacular idea, the largest generation in American history about to become affluent first-time grandparents.

'Elizabeth caught the wave right before it crested, just like you did,' Rudy says now, tapping his teeth reminiscently with his pen.

'I wouldn't have known enough to do that except for her,' True demurs. 'She thought girls needed role models. Way before Girl Power hit. And she was obsessed with her work, with every detail of that place. Do you know I never once saw Elizabeth eat?'

'But you were the only one who ever did anything with her,' Rudy says suddenly. 'I never even saw her go to the bathroom.'

'She had a bathroom in one of her closets. She didn't think the whole floor had to be alerted every time she was going to flush. I never really went anywhere with her. Like, we didn't do lunch. We went to Encore Encore.'

'The resale store?'

'Don't you know the rich buy used? I mean, used Chanel, used Anna Sui, for dimes on the dollar? The clothes are perfect. Those people only wear the things once.'

'You don't.'

'That's because I'm *nouveau* riche. I buy *new* Eileen Fisher and then see it a month later on sale and I want to kill myself. I still think I have to buy things at garage sales. And anyhow, I'm not rich, Rude.'

'You are, in my neck of the woods.'

'And no one cares about rich, in a woman, except . . .' True says suddenly, 'Guys who court old ladies who rattle with rubies . . .'

'Have we changed gears suddenly here?'

'Maybe.'

'I don't think we're talking about Elizabeth having the hots for Stefano in production . . .'

'Well, you have to admit, a man picks a younger woman, everyone thinks he's a makeout artist. If it's the other way around, everyone thinks he's invisibly disabled.'

'Keith's younger than me.'

'So? It doesn't matter.'

'And it shouldn't matter for heteros, either. If a woman wants a younger guy, so what? That steed-and-mare shit is so medieval,' says Rudy, and adds, abruptly, 'speaking of which, you know, I'll never have a baby.'

'You could, though,' True says, her love for Rudy breaking the crust of her self-absorption. 'You and Keith could adopt.'

'He doesn't want one.'

'Maybe not now. He's awfully young, Rudy; you don't think about that stuff so early, if you're a guy. But, Rudy, if he doesn't after time passes, you shouldn't give something like that up because the other person doesn't want to. It's too . . . it's not like let's get a Toyota instead of a Nissan.'

'I know. But . . . what if I had to give him up, then? It's like . . . you know how it is . . . what I did for love . . . and let's not talk about babies anymore. Jesus, I'm steeped in babies. I'm probably going to want to breastfeed,' Rudy answers. True sees that he has drawn a delicate pencil sketch of a newborn on his note pad, with the gift box exploding stars and teddy bears, surrounded by the ring logo of Twelve Times Blessed.

She must steel herself to imagine how her office will feel without Rudy's wry, energetic presence. How will she find another office manager with Rudy's style, his dear singularity that allows him to give her not only so much work, but so much of his life? Who will goof with her on frivolous suggestions for the blessings? Caramel Espresso Pudding, Baby's First Pesto. Hoodies with all seven of the Ivy League Colleges outlined on a primary-colored map? And who will come up with real jewels, for which True awards bonuses, such as the newest special separate offer: pieced quilts that can be commissioned, made by Kentucky grandmas from squares of baby's first outfits?

Who will be left?

Kathleen.

Oh, there be a fresh hell, True thinks. She and her mother already are perilously on one another's toes. How has it transpired that her older brother refers to 'Mom and you,' as if True and Kathleen were a married couple? Certainly, Kathleen *had* been overwhelmed by being alone, long after the death of her husband and long before the death of her son-in-law. And Dog (real name Augustus, for his August birthday) had lived up to his frat-house nickname, Augie Doggie, not interrupting his film-buff weekends and hockey tournaments to help his mother negotiate her bafflement over computers at the school library or the stop signs in the new subdivision that went up around her old house. After living in Amherst all her adult life, Kathleen felt, she'd told True, that the town was reconstructing itself all around her while only she remained the same. True's brother, barely five miles from his mom's house, sympathized, but it was left to True to take action when Kathleen confessed that the couples from their shabby-but-starched white-collar crowd, the same couples who danced with Katie and Bert at the Moose, and went camping at Monomoy, had moved to lawnier suburbs or retired early to small cottages on the Cape, that she felt stranded.

Kathleen remained a sort of librarian emeritus at Amherst Prep elementary school, never realizing the slow climb to the middle class that her friends achieved. True *had* forced Dog to help her mother sell the modest brick Georgian, the only house she'd ever lived in except her parents' (Kathleen had been so grateful to Dog that she gave him a cut of the profits from the house). True got her mother's thanks, and the job of driving about with Guy in his car seat for a month of Sundays until Kathleen found a cheery condominium near the school.

And then somehow, suddenly, decisions were made in the swirl of True's early days of widowhood, when the loss of Peter's presence if not his person left a rent in her life True could not mend alone. Then the business started, and Guy needed his grandmother's reassuring sameness, a bridge to Esa's new presence, as True's ear became welded to the phone receiver. Almost magically, and True is still not entirely certain that with her consent, Kathleen was on the Cape for good. The condo was sold. The new house, with its guest cottage, was purchased. Kathleen had a nice nest egg.

True is happy that her mom remains versatile and active at her age, without a speck of self-pity, busy with her cluster of friends from Saint Thomas More, the Episcopal church; her little gig selling the beach-and-dump sticker concession for the town of Chatham;

her job supervising the packers at Twelve Times Blessed, with a fine eye and her librarian's precision. At the community center, she meets everyone, including movie stars, and hears all the gossip. And because of True's sleight of hand at payday, Kathleen also draws a substantial salary, more than the actual job would pay anyone else. She lives the life she might have lived had True's father survived to retirement.

And yet True has never fully grasped why Kathleen has chosen widowhood as a way of life rather than a phase of life.

Kathleen's admiration for men is extravagant. Every Hallmark card Dog sends is treated as if it were parchment illuminated by monks. She praises men in general for their strength, their knowing, even – during one excruciating college conversation, when she had advised True to always use feminine-hygiene spray – the acuity of their sense of smell. A man, Kathleen pronounces grandly every time Dog turns down one of his wife's mild requests, such as her taking a part-time job, should be lord of his own castle.

And she flirts. She flirts with the mailman, the UPS guy, the crafters. She flirts, in fact, with everyone except the men True dates. Her remarks about True's short queue of suitors have been tiny, spare, and frosty. *More downstairs than upstairs,* said Kathleen of the landscaper with whom True shared a few months of bumptious romps at his beach shack. *Won't fall over in a stiff breeze,* Kathleen commented when she watched the orthopedist (a blind date courtesy of Franny) duck-toe his way up True's walk. And everything about Evan, the cosmetic dentist, was wrong. 'Little long in the tooth,' Kathleen said, casting a sideways glance at Evan's silvery fringe and slight paunch, at the gifts Evan quite decently brought to Guy and to her – floss in neon tones, a chattering set of windup dentures that pleaded, 'Brush me!'

But Evan gave True a great porcelain veneer to brighten the incisor that had dimmed steadily since a childhood skating accident, and long, lovely orgasms – after a mutual trip, at his behest, for blood tests at the Bluebird Free Clinic – though he rarely had orgasms himself. Don't, he'd once gently warned True, make it a requirement. He would come, in time.

Evan hinted that he and True would, after a decent interval, marry. He had considered that interval to comprise . . . oh, seven or eight years – it didn't take a mathematician to recognize that Evan was planning their union to coincide with Guy's departure for college. True went along, giving herself small pep talks: Evan was a good man; Evan was a kind man; Evan might be her last chance. Dating, in her generation and at her stage of life, she has come to believe, is not so much a matter of succumbing to the fever of operatic passion, but more like an exclusionary diagnosis: She has caught herself waiting for fatal symptoms. Would a man chew with his mouth open? Make an anti-Semitic remark or a serious grammar error? Say 'tits' in front of her son? Confess an attraction to mud wrestling?

Evan had done none of these things, but Kathleen remained cool toward him. Here was a stable, wealthy man, a man who could be counted on to take care of Kathleen's only daughter. Why had a woman once so happy in her own marriage been so blasé about the years of True's remarriageability slipping away?

True usually puts it down to Kathleen's own desire to keep True her twin in bereavement.

Not that she and Evan would ever have worked. Guy abhorred Evan with a hatred that grew in force until her kind boy turned into a rude little savage. It brought True to her senses. And brought the interlude to an end. How long otherwise might she have gone on essentially masturbating with a man she didn't remotely love or even much like?

After Rudy leaves for home, True can hear Guy's stereo pounding out the Latin rappers he and his friends suddenly favor. She has found a signed picture from a fifth-grade girl in his jacket pocket, and Guy has asked her, entirely innocently, whether his birthday this year can be a sleepover and whether this girl can come, too. 'We'll all wear pajamas, Mom,' he had promised.

True has cooked up a birthday for Guy she thinks is going to knock his socks off. Next Monday, on their pizza date, she decides she will spring it on him. Guy's birthday will fall on the weekend after the three-day run of his play is completed, and True has been on the phone with a dear, funny, cadaverous man who's one of the permanent members of the theater company, and who played Captain Hook in *Peter Pan* two years before. Ellery has agreed to show up in full Hook regalia at the Skull and Bones, a restaurant partly built around an old schooner, and make up all Guy's little guests as pirates, even teaching them the rudiments of swordplay as actors do it on stage. Harmlessly, but with great panache, like an impressive dance. How would *that* go over on the playground at Chatham Comprehensive, True wonders with pride?

Though she still hasn't completed her buys for fall, she thinks she'll slip away from the office early, run upstairs, and tell Guy her idea right now, instead of waiting.

But when she does, Guy's face looks like a September sky over the Sound, clouds chasing sun won over by clouds.

'That's neat, Mom,' he says simply, manfully.

Something's wrong. True knows that Guy will accept this birthday party. But he will be doing it for her.

'You don't like it.'

'I do! It's great!'

'But? Do we ever lie to each other? Lie to our most best friend?'

'Well,' Guy looks miserable, 'it's baby.'

'Baby?' True's astonished. 'Sword fights? Real pirates?'

'It's like having clowns or something.'

'No, it isn't!'

'Well, it practically is. It's like you used to have Santa Claus come over when I was little . . .' You still are, True pleads silently, you still are little, 'and you'd pretend you didn't know he was coming. I mean, even I knew he was coming. I could *read*, Mom! I was six! I could see, right on the big calendar. Six-thirty. "S.C. Here."'

'I . . . don't know what to say, honey.'

'And it wasn't even the *real* Santa Claus! As if!'

Oh, my God, True thinks, please don't let him ask me now . . . Guy has always been a bit . . . slow in these matters. Perhaps because he has lost so much already, he has been reluctant to give up childish things, though he is equally and desperately avid to become a midget preppie gangster, like his pal Fenn Bourse. He has maintained a stalwart lack of interest in the Santa matter, though True can tell it's costing him.

Guy would never have it known, but until he was seven, he would creep into her bed each night, at three in the morning, like some stealthy night watchman. She would find him, arrayed along the footboard under the Hercules sleeping bag Kathleen had given him. And though she gave due diligence to the inevitable worries about whether she was fostering an unhealthy sexuality or a damaging dependence in her fatherless child, she privately thought that theory pure bunk, even in two-parent families.

When Peter had complained about the infant Guy sleeping in their bed, True had, for once, stood up to Pete, telling him her own opinion, that every night of touch Guy received as a baby would be one less night he'd go looking for it in some Galley Girl's bunk when he was sixteen.

Now, she regards her boy, sympathy and shame sparring in her breast, and finally asks, 'Well, do you blame me? About the Santa visits? Wouldn't you have done that for your little kid?'

'Yes, Mom, but that's not the point,' Guy continues with a trace of irritation. 'It's that you don't want me to grow up ever. You want to keep me a baby, like in your catalogue . . .'

'Oh, Guy, no!'

'Well, a little.'

'Okay, Mister Clint Eastwood. What do *you* want to do for your birthday?'

'I got it all planned. I want to have a sleepover, and give everybody flashlights, and stay up all night and rent movies like *Excess Chainsaw Massacre* . . .'

'*Texas Chainsaw Massacre*.'

'And *Scream 2*.'

'Those are R-rated movies, Gee. I won't have it. Fenn's mom would throw fits.'

'But, okay, run outside at midnight and play Ghosts in the Graveyard.' True can see her mother's anxious face, at her cottage window, as a dozen boys run screaming through the cedars and red maples, shrieking.

'Okay, Guy, so be it.'

'*Really?*'

'Really.'

'It won't hurt your feelings?' he asks.

No more than having my intestines extracted slowly, True thinks, and says, 'Heck no! I won't have to pay Ellery to do the pirate gig! Flashlights and cheap horror movies! I'm there, Teddy Bear.'

'And no stuff like that.'

'What now?'

'Teddy Bear.'

'Okay, Grizzly Bear.'

'Mom, no bears, period. It's okay in the house. But I want you to tell Granny and Esa, too. I'm in the double digits, Mama.'

No kisses good-bye in the car at school, True wonders? No reading aloud at bedtime? 'You can still kiss me any time you want,' Guy offers, with his preternatural ken of his mother's thoughts. 'But don't say things like "Why don't you have Fenn over to *play?*" Boys my age don't play . . . well, we do play, but we call it hanging out. And we don't call us boys, we call us guys.'

'I've got it,' True says. 'Ten-four.'

Turn around, turn around, turn around, she thinks. Even Guy. Guy is not yet on the porch, but he has turned the handle on the door.

Later, True is lying on her bed, her ears full of tears, again, having cried more times in weeks than she has in years, when Isabelle opens the door. She sits down on the bed.

'Puppa,' she says.

'I'm just mourning . . . something or other.'

'Hank called. He wants to know if you'll have lunch.'

Hank.

Again, this subject she has managed not to think of.

She has managed, with womanful will, to not think of Hank almost around the clock. She has not thought of Hank as she drives far out of her way, while visiting a new craftworker, to pass his restaurant and sees his truck with the BORN AGAIN PAGAN sticker, not thinking of him when Franny asks if things got spicy with the Cajun cook. Not thinking of Hank has cost True her appetite. She picks at her morning bagel, forgoes her lattes in favor of water. The thought of food wrings her gut. She does not need the scale to tell her she has lost flesh. Her cheekbones now truly top hollows; her jeans meet easily. True has never felt such abominable and hopeless lust. She doesn't know there are many such wanton women, under changeable March skies, all across America and the free world.

'Esa,' she says now. 'He, all he . . . we're both in the business community and he wants to make . . . amends. Jesus, he's a nice guy. I just, you know, I wanted him. I'll, like, pass out with shame if I ever see him again.'

'So why would he call more than once? If he's making the effort only for networking, or sheer politeness? And do you know how often he's called?'

'No,' True admits. 'How do *you* know?'

'I just color over the ripped-off pages on the phone page to see whose number is there,' Esa grins, the apple-farmer's daughter.

'I have no secrets.' True flops backward onto her bed.

'Do you want to have secrets from me?'

'Just this one. Just this one dumb one. Please, Esa. Leave it alone and I mean it.'

'But you don't. When I say, leave me alone, I mean, *don't* leave me alone.'

'Well, *I* mean leave me alone. In the nicest possible way.'

'You don't. You're just being . . . Kathleen.'

'I'm not at all. I'm being practical.'

'That's almost exactly what your mother would say, but with a True affect.'

'Affect? Is that a word you learned in psychology class?'

'There, you see. That's totally Kathleeny. It was downright nasty.' Esa's chin is dangerously close to trembling.

True is surprised. 'It was. It was wicked bitchy. I'm really sorry. Do I do that all the time?'

'No, but when you do, you do.'

'How?'

'Scratch you where you don't want to be scratched, and you get a full Kathleen.'

'Shit. Forgive me. I don't mean it. It . . . scares me when people care too much.'

'And Hank did call.'

Am I becoming my mother? True thinks.

To divert herself, she flips on her laptop.

An e-mail informs her that the Rabbit Pearl is on back order.

RUDY AND KEITH, Kathleen and True and Franny pile into True's car for the opening night of 'Narnia.' Dog and his wife have come down, with True's nieces, Merit and Alyssa. They all gather in the lobby of the Cape Family Theater, a space built on donation by an anonymous Cape actor – True suspects it is the lovely and gracious Julie Harris – and throng around the photos that deck the walls. For his role, Guy has been transformed into a minute and terrifying creature,

59

with a long red beard ('It kills my face, Mama,' he says) and shoes wired to curl up in double loops.

The lights dim, and True is dumbstruck. Her boy is, he is gifted. His voice is sure; his gestures are deft and sly. The audience roars in all the right places, and gasps when he hands the Witch the knife to slay the noble Lion.

She cannot wait to get her hands on him. Dog has brought a bouquet of chocolate roses. They wait, after three curtain calls, for Guy to emerge from the dressing room in costume, cameras at the ready. Rudy and Isabelle lag behind, chatting with one of Rudy's friends, a local actor, stunning in the grandeur of his massive twisted Aslan mane, his face burnished in greasepaint gold.

She sees Hank just as Dog throws his arms around his nephew, lifting Guy off the ground and swinging him around, 'Way to do it, pal!'

He is leaning against one of the pillars, seemingly unsure of whether to join them, his leather bomber jacket open over a soft gray sweater. They make eye contact. She nods. And Hank approaches. True draws a deep, wavering breath.

'This is Hank Bannister,' she tells her brother, who lets go of Guy long enough to grasp Hank's hand. 'My brother, Dog. Well, Augustus. Dog to us.' Next to Dog, True notices, Hank is tiny, slight. He cannot be more than six inches taller than True's woeful five feet and four inches, which she daily wishes she could stretch on a home rack. 'Hank owns a restaurant in Truro . . .'

'Truro! That's a ghost town this time of year,' booms Dog.

'We do okay,' Hank smiles. 'People must consider it an adventure.'

'What's the accent?' Dog asks.

'Louisiana,' says Hank. 'Guess I still have a trace. Though Louisiana by way of Colorado and Florida and Vegas and New York . . .'

'World traveler,' Dog comments, a trace wistfully. Linda, his wife, pinches his arm.

'Itchy feet.'

'Do it while you're single,' Dog advises, hugging Merit to his side.

'Well, I think this is pretty much home now.' The look he sends True is imploring, pained. 'Did your sis tell you about the time we went bowling?'

'You're . . . dating?' Dog asks. True thinks, shit, he didn't have to gasp.

'It was an unfortunate detour,' True laughs with genuine goodwill, and Hank turns to address Guy, who has been accepting congratulations from his public.

'I'm Hank,' he says, extending his hand. Guy proffers his left. They look as though they're holding hands to cross the street. 'That was some nutty performance, Guy. I mean it. I did a little acting once . . .'

'You're an actor?' Guy is suddenly all there.

'No, I'm a cook,' Hank says. 'But a long time ago, I did a couple of things.'

'Movies?'

'No. Stage.'

'Broadway?'

'Not hardly. More like college theater. I was a dance major, because I was kind of dumb to be a science major and kind of short to play basketball. So I figured . . . okay, you like to jump around, what can a guy who's not too smart and likes to jump around major in? I only did one play I ever got paid for, and it was summer stock, *Oklahoma!* You got to be more of a jumper than a dancer for that. But you know what? It was out here, and it was the first time I saw Cape Cod, and boy, after that, I always knew I was coming back someday.'

He is gay, True thinks. Amphibious, at least. And here I was wondering, had he noticed that I'm thinner? That I've been layering on this firming cream, which seems to hold the skin under your chin taut at least until you get out of the bathroom?

'I have to learn to dance,' Guy says mournfully. 'I have to take lessons. You have to learn to dance if you're going to be a real actor. I don't have any sense of my body center. That's what the choreographer says. Mama, can I get this beard off? It feels like I have ticks.'

'Go ahead and change, but wait, let me get a picture first,' True says. 'And when you go in there, don't just maul it off, Gee. Use the spirit-gum remover.'

'Basketball helps,' Hank puts in.

Guy turns back. 'I play dee,' he says. 'On the town rec.'

'Well, it helps a lot with dancing, you know, having them strong thigh muscles,' Hanks says, and True's throat squeezes. 'In fact, I

61

thought you looked like a guy who might play, so I brought you this.' He holds out a piece of paper, slid inside one of those glassine sleeves used to hold wallet photos.

Guy examines it. 'It says . . . Scottie Pippen.'

'Yep.'

'It's his . . . actual autograph?'

'Yep.'

'How'd you get it?'

'A buddy of mine got it for me during the last playoff Michael was in. Sportswriter buddy.'

'But it's got to be worth a lot of money. You don't want to really give it to me. I'm . . . a kid!' Everyone laughs.

'No, it's really meant for a kid. I just didn't know the right kid. All my kids are girls, my sister's kids. So far.'

'You don't have a boy?'

'Nope. Not yet.' Hank does not try to disguise his straightforward look at True.

What Hank has given her son, True thinks, is much more than a card. It's a ratification for her son, who still has the small, round fireplug body of a little boy, as an actual guy. She would not be able to find words to tell him what this means to her, how she has suffered as she watches Guy barreling along, trying to keep up with Fenn, who already has the triangular shape of the teen he will be, with Fenn's lightning feints and fakes on the court. How she has feared that, after all, he will end up a lonely, chubby Mama's boy.

As Guy begins to bustle off, True whispers, 'Haven't you forgotten something?'

Guy looks confused.

'Oh, you mean thank yous! Thank you, Uncle Dog, for the chocolate rose. And thank you, Mister . . .'

'Hank.'

'Hank, obviously, this is the coolest thing I ever . . .' Impulsively, Guy opens his arms and hugs Hank around the waist, his cheek against Hank's leather coat. True does not imagine the surprise, then the softening in his body as he slowly places his hands on Guy's shoulders. Dog and Linda are suddenly overtaken by an outbreak of coughing.

Guy says, 'You know why you're coughing? The costumes all

stink! You can't wash them or they will all fall apart, they're so old! We have to spray them with Febreze or you like stink to death. The guy who played this part before me was an eighth-grader, and you know, he already had hormones? And you should have smelled this coat when I first put it on . . .'

'That's about as much as we want to know,' says True.

'It's sweaty work,' says Hank.

'Can I change now, Mama?'

As Guy bustles away to change, his velvet dwarf-pants now drooping to reveal his butt crack, between white halves, like two peeled hard-boiled eggs, his family smiles and shakes their heads. Rudy and Esa shrug into coats and bid everyone farewell.

'That was so very, very, very sweet,' True tells Hank, as they take a few steps away from her family. 'And I have been meaning to call you and apologize for my stupid, awful behavior, you know, middle-aged crazies.'

'Come to my restaurant with your family now,' Hank says urgently. 'Let me cook you dinner.'

'Thanks so much, Hank, but we have reservations at The Old Turtles. It's Dog's favorite . . .'

'Then come to my house, after.'

'My family's staying overnight . . . what? What for? Why?'

'Come to my house after they're all asleep. I don't care what time it is. Come to my house, please, True, please come to my house.'

'Look, Hank, you're a nice guy. I didn't mean all the stuff I said. You don't have to explain . . . anymore. I got the card. It was sweet. You are sweet.'

'That's not why I want you to come. I want to talk to you, yes, but touch you, too. That's all I can think about. All the time.'

There are no two ways a face feels at such a moment. A face feels as though it has caught fire, as though this blazing face is visible to passersby outside the windows, to ships at sea, to cosmonauts idly peering out of the portals on the space station Mir.

She will not go to his house. She will see how she feels after she eats.

No, she will definitely not go.

ON THE WAY to the restaurant, Guy's favorite doo-wop song comes on. 'Sing the backup, Mama,' he insists, still sailing from the performers high, ' "Why do you build me up . . . Buttercup" . . . you didn't sing "Build me up." '

'I'm having a thought, Guy,' True says.

'This autograph he gave me,' Guy tells her. 'Do you think it's okay for a stranger to give a kid a thing like that?'

'You don't have to be afraid of him. Mom was right there. And Unkie. And Hank is . . . Hank is a really good guy, Guy.'

'And you have a crush about him.'

'Of course not.'

'That's good. Because, no offense, Mommy, he's like, not old enough to be a father.'

'I think he is, Guy.'

'Well, did you kiss him?'

'No.'

'Are you going to kiss him?'

'No.'

'I hate to have to say this again, Mommy, but you know that's what you said about Evan the Terrible.' (Thanks, Esa, True thinks. Esa thought up the nickname.) 'You said, oh, we're just grown-up friends . . . but then he started coming around all the time, and . . . you . . . and you . . .'

'I what?'

'I don't want you to get mad if I say it.'

'I won't get mad.'

'Promise?'

'I promise.'

'I think you sexed with him.'

True grips the reassuring, grooved-leather wheel. 'What makes you think that?'

'Well, now you're really going to get mad.'

'I'm *not*, Guy! Except if you don't just out with it already.'

'You have one of those things for sexing.'

'What things?'

'Those things like a big rubber thimble.'

He is talking about her diaphragm. It lies under its casing of dusting powder in what looks to be a ring box in her sock drawer.

'Guy! Why did you go through my stuff? You don't like it when I mess with your things . . .'

'I was looking for a pair of white socks, Mom! That's all. And I just opened it up, and I didn't know what it was, so I asked Brendan Frederickson . . .'

'You asked *Brendan?*' The Fredericksons are such strict Christians they can't find a sufficiently fundamentalist church this side of the Sagamore Bridge, so have to rent the VFW hall to host worship services.

'He said that his mom had one, too,' Guy says easily. 'They're all right for married women.'

'Well, when I got it I was married, to your dad.'

'So you wouldn't have any more babies. You only wanted me, I guess. If you have the best, why bother with the rest?'

'That was my thinking,' True says dryly.

'But you might have had more kids, if Daddy didn't die.'

'I expect so.'

'What if you got married again?'

'What if I did?'

'Would you have more kids?'

'Probably not.'

'Too old, huh?'

'Not really, Gee. I'm not *that* old. I could have a baby. Would you like a baby? A baby brother or sister?'

'Depends.'

'Depends on what?'

'What kind of kid it was.'

'I thought maybe I'd adopt a baby from China.'

'Would she speak Chinese?'

'Probably not. Not unless we did. Babies speak what their parents speak. You're French and English. Do you speak French?'

'Yes, I do. Un, deux, trios . . .'

'And?'

'Quatro, cinco, sex.'

'You must be Spanish, too.'

'Well, if she couldn't speak Chinese, what's the point then? She'd just be a regular old baby.'

'Just, well, there are a lot of babies in China who need parents.'

'Where are their parents?'

'They were poor, or sick, and couldn't keep them.'

'Well, if you got married, would you have sex?'

'I thought we were talking about adopting babies.'

'If the guy with the restaurant kisses you, and you get married, does it mean that I'll never be able to come in your bed again, even if there's a hurricane? Or if I puke?'

'Guy, Guy, think about what you want to order for dinner,' True says, ruffling his rough, red-streaked, stage-dyed hair. 'Do you want clam strips? Or Caesar salad, since it's so late? You know, when you were little, you used to call it Cesarean salad, because I guess somebody told you that was how I gave birth to you.'

'Pizza,' Guy says, seeming as relieved to be done with the subject of sex as True is. 'Pizza Margherita. With extra tomatoes. And don't say that stuff about what I said when I was little outside the house, Mom, okay? It's embarrassing.'

'You say stuff like that about me. Like you said once I weigh more than what's on my driver's license.'

'But I was mad at you when I said that.'

'Oh. It's only okay if you're mad and if it's you, not me.'

Guy sighs.

They enter the restaurant, and True sees that half the cast members' families have chosen the same place, so they all push the tables together, and the kids take over one long ten top and order pitchers of green pop slop and slabs of pizza. True sits with her brother and sister-in-law, Linda; Franny and her daughter Angelique, while Franny's younger daughter, Clainey, who often performs with the troop, and has many friends in the cast, runs to hug Guy. Kathleen has pleaded weariness, and Beatrice, the director of the theater, has dropped her off at home.

As they order their second round of drinks, True suddenly asks her brother, 'Doggy, do you ever wonder why Mom never married again?'

'No,' her brother says, tearing into the mozzarella sticks.

'Because she practically gloms on Judge Hammersmith, and the UPS guy, and the court clerk . . .'

'I assumed it was because she worshipped Dad so much.'

'There's that,' True admits. Beyond True's shortcomings, about the only subject on which Kathleen will give an impromptu lecture is the merits of Robert Dickinson, True's father, whose modest car spun on the ice and overturned in a culvert when True was ten and Dog twelve.

Robert Dickinson had sold encyclopedias, when such things were still sold door to door, and had apparently been wildly successful at it, from the spate of plaques Kathleen has displayed on her cottage wall. As a result of his absences, and his silences at home, Robert not only sold but read the encyclopedia, including each year's year-book, cover to cover, and once told his children he couldn't wait until they were old enough to do the same thing, so he could quiz them at dinner. Dog and True recall little of their father. They do not grieve for him. In fact, they call the accident Chappaquiddick, since it had happened at roughly the same point in time, and Kathleen has never been forthcoming about the details. They have always wondered if their father was on his way home from a tavern that black spring night. What Kathleen will point out, at the drop of a hat, is that her Bert was a man who could come home from ten days on the road, go into his shop, and put up a porch in a single afternoon and still have enough energy to dance the tango at the Saint Dunstan's dance that same night.

'Maybe she never found a guy who could tango,' Dog adds. 'Remember how she always said, "He wasn't one of those men who look like a sissy when he dances?"'

'Yep,' says True, thinking of Hank's arms, wondering how *he* dances. 'She'd say, "He knew how to lead so that you felt light as a leaf in his arms."'

'Pretty hard to top,' Dog says.

'I wish I'd known your dad,' Linda puts in. Both brother and sister look at her blankly.

'I guess she knew him in a way we didn't,' Dog shrugs. 'God, she was fierce after he went. "Eat every pea. I *paid* for those peas." Remember how ashamed she was of having to work?' True does, and how their mother often reminded them, when they complained about their dowdy plaid uniform skirts or vests, that they were getting a better education than they would have had their father lived. Dog says it now, teasing his own daughters, who also go to Amherst Prep on reduced tuition because their father teaches there: *Do you know,* he says, *you're getting a better education than you would have if I had lived?*

'But if she loved being married so much . . . they say it's the people who love being married who get married right away, and I always hear her tell Ellen, *I have not had a single date since Bert died.*'

'Imagine Mom on a date.'

'Well? Can't you? A nice church supper? I think it's odd.'

'Well, Sis, you didn't exactly jump back to the altar, either, did you? And you had a decent marriage,' Dog replies, and orders more fried oysters.

FROM CRUISING IT so many times, after looking it up in the phone book, True knows exactly which house is Hank's: the quirky A-frame on Bobby Lane. She would have known even if the lights on the porch, at the curb, and in the living room hadn't been turned on, in sharp contrast to the rest of the neighbors, lost in long winter's naps. It is one A.M. Everyone in her family is asleep.

He has the grace, the touching grace, to turn off the living-room lights the minute she enters the house. She kisses him before he has a chance to reach out for her, a high-school kiss with a flick of tongue. His lips are soft as a girl's. They kiss again, this time both of their hands clamped on the smalls of each other's backs. True slips her coat off her shoulders; she can feel Hank, in the dark, open the snaps on his shirt. Through her blouse, he reaches for what he imagines to be the clasp of her bra. He reaches for a front closure, the kind a young girl with breasts like perky pups would wear. When she feels his hot hands on her breasts, lifting them, her breath deserts her.

'Soft skin,' says Hank. 'Exquisitely soft skin.'

She hears his zipper open, feels him fumble, with one hand, for the buckle of his belt, and reaches down to open the button of her long skirt, wriggling out of her hose, kicking away her cowboy boots. Hank leans one hip against the door and closes it.

'You are so skinny without your clothes,' she says, 'like a child.'

'We call that wiry, ma'am. I can't keep weight on in that kitchen. But a child,' he says. He places her hand on his satiny groin hair, and he is only slightly hard. 'Give me a moment, sweetheart. Sweetheart,' he says. 'It's been a while for me. I'm nervous . . .' But then it grows, blooming, a good, thick root, a viscous tear on its petal tip.

They kneel, embracing, True thinking, he will feel my belly, my butt . . . they lie down.

'Do you want to use . . . ?' Hank asks.

'I don't, do you?' she answers, her breath hard to find, ragged.

'I don't want to use anything. Pregnancy?'

'I don't think so,' she says.

'But I'm not afraid of that. If that happens, it's okay,' he tells her.

'Or if you have a terrible tropical disease and are going to die, I want to catch it and die, too.'

She really does feel this. It is something she has never felt before, except for Guy, a devouring, utterly uncontained emotion. She adores him. She is losing her mind. So she wrenches her mind open and lets it fly loose. This one moment she will have rapture. If only this.

Hank says, 'That is how I feel, too. Exactly like that.'

She lies down beneath him on the carpet in front of the door. 'Carpet burns, on the knees,' he says. 'They're the worst. They don't get you 'til two days later.' This breaks her heart. It reminds True that there have been other explorations, as urgent as this, which cannot wait for the comfort of a bed. But he says then, 'You're so wet, so wet. I smell you, and you smell like vanilla. Like a cookie.'

'That's because . . .' True says.

'Because you love me,' Hank finishes. He puts one of his fingers against her mouth, in her mouth. 'And I reckon I'm yours.' And she is lost.

SHE SITS UP half an hour later and slips into the closest thing, Hank's flannel shirt, and wonders in how many places around the world at this very moment in time women are sitting up and, from a combination of modesty and the desire to appear tiny, putting on their men's shirts.

'That . . . was fun,' she says.

'That proved to me that the possibilities are endless,' Hank says.

True thinks this is an eccentric way to put it. 'How do you mean?'

'Sexually.'

'I figured sexually, but . . . how?'

'That we can have fun together, over and over.'

'You wondered?'

'I wondered, since . . . I'd never been . . .'

'With an older woman.'

'No,' Hank says deprecatingly, his glance gone wider and cloudy, but True can see right through those deliberately opaque eyes.

'And you thought, like, I'd have those flaps under my arms that swing back and forth . . .' True laughs out loud. True's arms have always been splendid – she has always been able to wear a sleeveless dress without walking like a penguin.

69

Hank smiles, too, but says nothing.

'So, is that what you thought?'

'No, of course not.'

'But you thought something.'

'Well, of course, I wondered . . . what would be different. But it turned out, the whole general effect was . . . it was perfect.'

'The whole general effect.'

'Woman, why do you seize on one word? Let's change the subject.'

'You were the one who used the one word. No, you mean the whole general effect, but specifically . . .'

'True,' Hank says, running a thumb along her neck, down her breastbone. 'You are beautiful and wonderful and sexy and quick and older than I am but not much.'

'And you thought it might make a difference,' True is ready to cry. 'You thought you wouldn't think I was sexy.'

'I knew I would think you were sexy. But I wondered what would be different.'

'What was different?'

'Only that, well, necessarily, a woman, even if she isn't overweight at all, and you're not . . . if she's younger, she's just more . . . I don't know . . . she's . . .'

'What?'

'Her flesh feels different.'

'Toned, you mean.'

'You said it. I didn't. And I didn't even mean exactly that. I'm a verbal idiot.'

'God help me. Toned,' says True, using her feet to search for her own scattered clothes. 'Ouch! Yikes, there's a thought. Why'd you have to be so honest?' She does not want to stand up and display any errant part that might waggle.

'Don't go, and don't get a package on,' Hank pleads. 'Are we going to have to end every encounter we have with a fight?'

'No,' says True. 'But I don't want to be a mercy screw, either.'

'*What* are you saying, woman?'

'I mean, if you did it to make me feel good.'

'What would be in that for *me*? Think about it. I come to your kid's play; I try to be a good gentleman caller . . .' This is a good sign, True thinks, he's said this in a way that lets me know he's quoting from a play; but she then thinks of her friend Jersey in high

70

school, whose boyfriend wrote in a card lines that began with 'Shall I compare thee to a summer's day . . .' – only later she was told by four other girls that he knew just that one sonnet.

She thinks of Isabelle's dimmest boyfriend, who broke up with her by sending her a haiku.

'I'm sorry,' True admits. 'Let's start over. Let's talk about what people talk about on dates when they do them frontwards instead of backwards.' She blushes. 'That is, talking before sex. I don't count the bowlus interruptus as a date.'

'Okay. So, where'd you go to school?'

'Amherst.'

'Smart girl.'

'No, townie. I grew up there. I moved here when I got married.'

'What about your husband? Tell me about him.'

'He came from Montana. But he went to Embry-Riddle. Always knew he'd be a pilot. My brother went there, for a while, too, until he realized the asthma attacks he got whenever he went up in a plane were really panic attacks. And now, my brother's an English Lit teacher, so go figure.'

'Yeah, I have a sister who wanted to be a doctor but fainted and gave herself a concussion the first time she saw a cadaver.'

'What does she do now?'

'She's a ballet dancer. Good thing it didn't impair her coordination when she hit the floor . . .' This is all good news, True muses. He comes from brains. He comes from arts.

'So that's it,' she says.

'But you didn't even tell me half the middle! I was just settling down here for the rest of the biography, and you go and change the channel.'

'I can't imagine why you want to hear this. Well, okay. Pete came home with Dog a few times. They went out to the Cape. He loved the Cape. I knew the Cape really well. I'd been a summer sitter out there . . .' She thinks of those long, open-ended summer days, when her employer had treated her, a seventeen-year-old girl, as an adult, offering her vodka-and-tonics just as she did her own, grown-up friends, the other beach mothers, in their discreet bikinis, who sunned away the days while their husbands worked the weeks in Boston and tooled up on Friday nights. There was no thought of skin cancer, or even, yet, of the impropriety of offering liquor to a minor. It had all been so innocent, if so . . . unhealthy. True thinks of it as a time of drenched sunny bliss and freedom. Night parties on the beach. The twins, Paulie and Mikey, on whom she'd had an equally-divided crush, the lush nights she'd allowed one or the other of them access – hands only – to the secrets under her halter tops, as a beach fire cast shadows. 'Lots of girls from off Cape did that. It was a great job. I worked in Harwichport, in this little neighborhood that looks like the Jersey Shore, little cabins with funny names like "O'Reilly's Folly" all scrunched up against each other. I worked for a couple who were cousins of the Nickersons . . .'

'Which Nickersons?'

'*The* Nickersons. Who own everything in town. The fish market. The housing businesses. Look at the names in the cemeteries. The Nickersons *are* Chatham.'

'So that meant . . .'

'That meant they paid me well, and I only had two little boys to look after, and my brother could bring his friends to stay over at their house. Mary Anne, that was the mom, would cook these big breakfasts, blueberry waffles. I think it was Mary Anne's waffles Pete fell in love with. Then he went on to graduate school, courtesy of the Marines. Air Corps. An officer.'

'That's impressive.'

'Oh, Pete could do anything. He could run all day and never get tired. Lift *anything*. Boot camp must have been like a beach party for him . . .' She sees Hank shift uncomfortably, pull a corner of a couch throw across his body, and she wonders how he could possibly be self-conscious. And yet, it amuses her that this guy is thinking of her late husband as a Greek decathlete and feeling nervous about the comparison. Probably the only time in his life he's ever felt as though another man might best him, True thinks, with a secret smile, and says, 'It's a longer story, but he ended up as a pilot for Cape Air.'

'Because of you.'

'And because he wanted to fly the small planes. I'd already decided I wanted to live here, not that it would have mattered.'

'You'd have gone anywhere for him.'

'No, he would have insisted I go anywhere he wanted, and what-ever I said wouldn't have mattered. I was lucky. Once I'd come out here, and gotten a job as a teacher, that actually wasn't so great.

72

But Franny had married Steve then, and I had that friend, Mary Anne, who I used to work for, and in time, she introduced me to Elizabeth, and I ended up leaving my teaching job and working for Elizabeth.'

'You miss him a lot.'

'Pete? It's been eight years. So, of course I do, but less and less. For Guy's sake, all the time. But we . . .'

'What?'

'We . . . he was a good man. He would have been a pretty good man. But he never . . . got there. Grown up, I mean.'

'That's what I keep hearing about me.' Hank stretches, pulls on his jeans over his naked butt with a shrug that flips True's heart like a poker chip. 'I keep hearing I just get bigger clothes.'

'No, Pete loved me. But he was a child and . . . to be honest, I was a child . . .'

'In a kingdom by the sea . . .'

A literary allusion. True files it. She can move him another square ahead, from the Hank of All Trades with his face, not to mention his ass, for his fortune. His giving Guy the card has proved that he is not a rakehell, or at least, that he is a rakehell with a sentimental heart. 'You were twenty-three, you got married. My generation.'

'What'd you major in?'

'English Lit. Very practical. But you see, I thought I would teach forever. Like my mother, and later, my brother. We're genetically bossy.'

'And your business?'

'Well, it started with Pete's insurance money. We didn't have a lot, but we didn't need a lot. The military takes good care of widows and orphans. So there were expenses we didn't have. Veterans benefits.'

'How does it work?'

'I had some marketing experience from where I'd worked. But basically, they're packages of presents, all handmade . . .'

'All?'

'Every single present is handmade, or handsewn. That's part of the appeal. It's all . . . natural, I guess.'

'And how do you find them?'

'Well, you know, Cape Cod, all of New England, is crawling with artists. And a lot of these artists, they make big things, oil paintings,

73

furniture. But you can't live on that. So they make little bread-and-butter things, too, that they sell at shows. Say if you make wooden tooth-boxes . . .'

'A tooth-box, like, for dentures?'

'You goofer.' They both laugh. 'No, for the first tooth your baby loses.' True smiles, with a rueful shake of her head, 'I know, I know. But people do this. Say you make wooden, carved and painted tooth-boxes, and over a summer, you sell a hundred of them at ten bucks a pop at the county fair. Now, if you could sell a thousand of them at five dollars each, and know next year you could sell a thousand more . . . it works for the artists and it works for us.'

'I see. It's ingenious.'

'Thanks,' True says. 'I'm proud of it.' She thinks of her mother's downturned mouth, her mother admonishing her that the insurance money should be put in investments, bonds not stocks, for Guy's future, that the business was a pipe dream, though even Kathleen has come around, she has never said a word of apology for having so little faith in her daughter's acumen.

'Who's Elizabeth?'

'She's famous. And I don't mean on the Cape. Everywhere. She makes dolls. It's like this amazing success story. This woman started making real-life-looking dolls that were based on well-known women of history, and then hired writers to make these wonderful books, and she would sell them together, the doll and the book, the story of the real person the doll was supposed to be. They cost a hundred dollars each. Without armor . . . I mean, without accessories. And they use the books even in schools. She gets offers all the time to sell it to Fisher-Price and stuff.'

'That'll happen to you next.'

'Oh, no, I'm not at that level, and if I ever were, I would never sell.'

'Never sell?'

'No. Not really for any amount, unless I was going to do something like retire and buy a villa in Ireland and home-school Guy.'

'That doesn't sound half bad . . .'

Hank moves one square back. Keen industriousness is a trait True admires in people, even kid people. But then he says, 'So tell me about this Elizabeth and her baby dolls. You were a teacher and then you got an interview with Elizabeth.' True is astonished. Most men she has known make a cursory inventory, with what seems like a considerable effort, to find *something* to ask about a woman. But this man wants dates, details. She has never felt so explored, so, well, fascinating. Is he truly, genuinely interested? Does he actually, impossibly feel what she *thinks* he said the moment before they'd torn off one another's clothes? Or is he merely picking her brain, small-business owner to small-business owner? With a view to picking her pocket? Is he going to ask her, after a polite interval, whether she'd like to invest in a second restaurant?

'They weren't *baby* dolls,' she says, giving him the benefit of the doubt and pleased to talk about something she genuinely knows. 'You weren't listening. They were grown up . . .'

'I'm sorry. I'm Southern. We call all dolls "babies."'

'Okay. They were all women like Cleopatra (*asps sold separately*, she thinks sadly of Rudy) and the books weren't all that came with them. Like one of the most popular dolls was Isak Dinesen . . .'

'The lady who wrote about Africa!'

One square forward.

'Right. Now, I don't think most little girls had any idea who wrote *Out of Africa*, but she was, in some ways, our greatest accessory package.'

'How?' Hank asks, leaning back, pillowing his head on his arms, as if he has no idea how beautiful he is, how natural his pose, like the male equivalent of a calendar girl.

'Well, these things were carefully researched and crafted to look as much like the real McCoy as possible. There was a lady's rifle, a little bush-baby whose paws you could bend so it could sit on the doll's shoulder, and a safari kit with canteens and a tent that could be set up, and that cost about eighty dollars on its own, and all these outfits, from jungle khakis with boots to this purple flapper's gown with beads. That was so beautiful I bought it for myself, actually.'

'Like Barbies, but politically . . .'

'Correct, exactly,' True continues. 'That was the trick of it. Great clothes, no guilt for moms.' She stops for a moment. 'You don't want to know all this, Hank. You don't have to be polite. You've gone well beyond your required quota of postcoital conversation.'

Hank, however, says exactly the right thing. He says the right or the wrong thing, never the middle thing. This, True will come to realize, is a trait. He says, 'I do want to know, and I seem to recall treating you to my whole résumé one night, when you were starving for dinner . . .'

'You did that all right!'

'What was the best seller?'

'Oh, Joan. Definitely Joan.'

'Joan?'

'Joan. Saint Joan of Arc.'

'Another saint.'

'Well, every girl can identify with her. Just fifteen years old, poor, beautiful, leading an army on her tall white charger.'

'I don't know. You'd have to be a certain kind of girl . . .'

'Well, Joan was the franchise,' says True. 'And we were all awful behind Elizabeth's back about it. Especially Rudy – you know Rudy, he's my assistant now, I stole him from Elizabeth – and Carter Berman. He was this marketing guy. We had a suggestion box. And she'd always be yelling at us, "Accessories, people! Think accessories!" Like, and don't tell anyone this, the Sojourner Truth doll was beautiful, but Elizabeth went on a rampage. She said, "Where are we going to go with this, people? More head turbans? More pencils and paper?"'

Hank laughs. It is unfeigned. It could not have come from politeness, because it comes from his toes up. He snorts.

'I apologize,' he says. 'We are laugh snorters in my family.'

'It's okay,' True is laughing, too. 'She'd say, "We need ethnicity and diversity! *Product* diversity!" So Carter and Rudy wrote a plan for Joan that went beyond her sword and her suit of armor – that was so gorgeous. Rudy said, "I'm thinking a stake, nothing with a sharp point, of course, and a pyre, something simple, two AA batteries, a nice revolving light under some really good composite modeled wood . . . "'

'She must have freaked.' Hank claps his hands.

'She never said a word! But we *saw* her read it. The only time she reacted aloud, and we got a talking-to, was when somebody suggested we sell . . . this is humiliating . . . the pink suit for Jacqueline Onassis, blood capsules sold separately.'

'There was a Jackie Kennedy doll?'

'Oh, she was right up there with Joan. And Amelia Earhart. Even Guy, my son, has an Amelia Earhart. Those were the top shelf.'

76

'So these were dolls for, like, tomboys. Or at least girls who had ambitions. Girls who didn't just dream of being mommies.'

'I guess.' True gets his drift, but wonders how any normal little girl could resist Jackie, her dozen silky gowns with tiny sparkling chokers and suits with pillbox hats, or blond brave Joan, the early figures with long hair, the later ones cropped short, in her scarlet prison gown. No girl she'd ever have had, that's for sure, True imagines. 'Well, they weren't all hits. There was Eleanor Roosevelt. In market surveys, little girls all admired her, but we couldn't get them to want a middle-aged lady doll in orthopedic shoes, with glasses.'

'What did you do?'

'When a doll failed? Elizabeth raised hell.'

'No, what did you *do*?'

'Well, I supervised the writers who wrote the histories, the biographies.'

'How'd you come to do that?'

'I'd been an English teacher, like I said . . . I mean, as I said,' True thinks of herself, twenty-four and unfortunately permed, running screaming from a year of teaching rich puddings at a Cape prep school. 'And I started out writing catalog copy. Then I got promoted. Rudy said I was the heir apparent, that I'd have taken over someday, because Elizabeth has no children of her own . . .'

'Why'd you leave?'

'Well, Pete died. And so I had a tiny bit of insurance money. Benefits, as I said. And I wanted the adventure. And I'd soaked up so much of Elizabeth's experience, or I thought I had.'

'You wanted to challenge her.' His eyes are shrewd now, narrow with confidence, and True feels something not unlike fear. She does not want to be known so soon. And falsely – or is it falsely? And does she, in fact, welcome his guesses, right or wrong, his attempted excavation of her life? 'That's how you are,' Hank says, satisfied.

True protests, 'You have no idea how I am! I never thought of it like that, but maybe, maybe a little. Not that I have. Twelve Times Blessed is no Elizabeth's. And there was also, and this is more important, I wanted to make a future for myself. We were paid fairly, at least after we'd been there awhile, but she was the queen bee. Elizabeth was . . . well, parsimonious. We got a *reduced price* on dolls at Christmas. We didn't get *free* dolls for our children. I remember the Christmases. She'd come stalking in – and this woman is almost six feet tall – with some movie star's name on a slip of paper, and say, "Send her the whole bloody line for free. Two. She has twins. Though she could probably buy and sell me ten times over." But she knew that having Cybill Shepherd's kids carrying around Joans was totally top-of-the-rock advertising. And, come to think of it, I read *People*. God, now I do the same thing. Rosie O'Donnell's babies got Blessings.'

'You do,' Hank says. 'That makes sense.'

'Sure. She tells her staff; they tell their friends . . .'

'So was Elizabeth mad when you left?'

'You couldn't tell. She was never exactly Missus Cuddly. But I think on some level, she . . .'

'Respected you for it.'

'Mmmmmmm . . . . And you know, I do my job interviews just like she did mine. I talk to everyone the person ever worked for before I even meet him or her, so I don't let personality get in the way. And then I ask one, two questions. Like Elizabeth asked me, I'll never forget it, "Can you write a good English sentence?"'

'And you said yes.'

'She said, "Can you start Monday?" So then I had a job, and Pete and I played house, and it was fun. See, pilots don't really grow up. I guess they're like rodeo riders or race-car drivers. Forever young. It would be great now, for Gee . . .'

'Why do you call him that? Gee? With a hard "G," the French way?'

'Yes. I like it,' says True, with satisfaction. 'He was named after a hockey player for . . . I don't know, the Canadiens. Guy Lafleur. They called him "The Flower." Pete was an athletic man. He played on three softball teams, and he flew. Once, I counted up all the months we'd actually spent together in ten years of marriage. Less than half.'

'But there must have been lots of nights you just stayed up all night and talked.'

'No,' True says honestly. 'Peter Lemieux was more a do-guy than a talk-guy.'

'Private jokes,' Hank urges her.

'No,' says True. 'He called me Shortcake. Because he said I was short and round. Although I wasn't, then. We . . . got along. We never fought, except when I tried to do things some way that wasn't his way. He was very stubborn.'

'You don't seem like the type who'd back down from a good fight.' True remembers Pete's set jaw, the times he'd simply left the house, for hours, returning still mute, mute for a full day after she'd committed some minor infraction, choosing crushed shells for the drive of their tiny cottage when he'd specifically requested stone, though the shells were on special. How cowed she had been by his departures.

'I never wanted to argue with him,' she shrugs. 'It was the way I was raised. My mom obeyed my father, at least she'll tell the world she did, now, though I never remember my father saying much of anything, and he died when I was not even as old as Guy . . .'

'But you loved him?'

'My dad?'

'No.'

'Peter? Sure,' says True, then admits, 'no. But I wasn't miserable, either. I saw friends be literally miserable. He didn't drink or screw around. Or hit me. We had our own house. Then, we had Guy, and he was a great father . . . and now, I like being on my own. It works better,' says True.

Is she disingenuous? Has this deliberate watercoloring of her past become a habit? She thinks not. She has tried to imagine catering to a man, in terms of sheer minutes lost, and has decided this would be impossible given what her business and her boy command. True cannot imagine anyone ever again asking her to remove a stain from a shirt collar or get him a beer while she's up. Her eccentric faux-family unit in the rambling, vastly overpriced Cape that True bought after ten years of longing for it, so that her nieces now think an auntie with a beach house is the coolest grownup on earth, has seemed enough. Since Pete's death she has never allowed a man to sleep overnight in her bed. She has never allowed the woman-of-passion piece of her to overwhelm her intellect and make her pitiable, like her friend Ronnie. Ronnie moves aging surfers and grad students in and out of her house with breathtaking regularity, swearing to her daughter that every one of these losers is good for the long haul.

Even Evan had spent his rare overnights in the lower-level guest room, with no midnight rambling. The counselor True visited with Guy insisted that Guy's reaction had nothing to do with Evan personally (though Guy ranted nightly that Evan was 'an old fart, with his phony nicey-nice way of talking to me') but with Guy's awakened fear that Evan might become a permanent fixture, that the son might one day have to share his mother. True explains this now to Hank. It seems important for him to know she has had a rakish – well, at least a PG-13–rated past.

'He's a little stuck in his Oedipal phase,' the counselor had explained. 'Do you know what that means? Oedipus was a king . . .'

'I understand the term,' True had told the woman. 'But he's only eight years old.'

'This is five-year-old stuff,' the counselor went on. 'Guy is a little stuck.' They had not returned to the counselor, and Evan had not returned to True's house.

Now, she glances at her watch. It's two A.M. Kathleen is probably still up and on patrol, but True thinks that she may as well hang for a sheep as a lamb.

She asks the inevitable question: 'Where were you when Kennedy was killed?'

'Right here,' Hank tells her. 'It was the first time I'd come out here. There was this woman . . .'

'Of course. You know, that's how every story starts. I don't mean just yours, but isn't it? There was this guy. There was this girl.'

'But it wasn't just the girl. And that didn't last. It was really, I was with my buddies Jake and Tom, to look at the place I – well, we, three of us – eventually bought, the restaurant. Jake sold out, quick. That was in ninety-nine . . .'

'I mean the real . . . I mean President Kennedy,' she explains softly.

'Well, bébé,' Hank says, his accent suddenly pronounced, 'I guess I wasn't born.'

This is what True's friends call a senior moment.

They have nothing to say.

True opts for cheer. She asks about Hank's context. His sisters are Win, Tannie, and Reed. ('Really, their names are Mary Winston, Mary Tannifero, Mary Reed. Family names. I'd have been Mary Henry if Mama could got away with it,' says Hank. 'Tannie is the one who's expecting.')

'What do you think is the best thing in the universe?' True asks.

'Other than the obvious?' asks Hank, predictably.

'Other than the obvious,' True answers, rolling her eyes.

'Okay, I think the best thing in the universe is popcorn, triple-buttered, with brewer's yeast. No contest.'

80

'Get out of here.'

'No. What?' Hank sits forward.

'Get out of the room. I am the only person I know who thinks popcorn without brewer's yeast is a waste of calories.'

'Everyone eats it!'

'No one I know except for me,' True says, yearning to hear more, more magnificent similarities.

'What's your favorite song?' she asks.

'Ancient or modern?'

'Modern.'

'The one by Tom Petty. The one that says, she makes me want to live like I want to live.'

'That's mine.'

'I figured. And that *is* what I want,' Hank says.

'What *do* you want?' True asks desperately. 'A loan? A few romps? I'm up for that. Come on, really. What?'

'I could tell you,' Hank says slowly. 'But you wouldn't believe me now.'

'Try me.'

'I'll tell you a part of it,' he says. 'All the relationships with women I've ever had, though they were, in some says, pretty great, they ended.'

'And?'

'I don't like things that end,' Hank says, and looks up, and in his eyes she sees two perfect Trues, magnificently rumpled. 'I want, what I want, is a life. Here. With a woman.'

'I'm sure you'll find one,' True smiles. He is, after all, sensuality made flesh, canny but not manipulative. She wants him to her liquid core.

'Don't disrespect me,' Hank says suddenly, with molten intent, taking her hand. 'Don't. Don't play coy.' He runs his index finger up and down the back of her hand, then turns it over, and does the same thing with her palm.

'This is thin ice,' True says.

'Are you afraid?'

'Uh, yeah. I'm sane.'

'I'm not.'

'That's clear.'

'But no one is, who is in love.'

81

'Are you in love?' True asks. 'Don't answer. Don't tell me.'

'Okay, then let me tell you a story,' Hank says, his blue eyes avid. 'It's going to sound stupid, but give me ninety seconds.'

'I'll give you ninety *minutes*. You just ploughed through my entire history. I don't think your stories are stupid.'

'Well, I have this friend. Perry. He's my best friend since we were so high, younger than Gee. And Perry, he's built like my cooler at That One Place. I mean, this man's head is the size of a fire hydrant. My sister Win could do pull-ups on one of his forearms, and that was when she was a *teenager*. Perry and me – and I, that is – we went to Florida once when I was on spring break and he was, well, he didn't go to college. We just went, and one day, we decided, hey, we never been fishing in Florida. Let's us go fishing for a swordfish, and then grill it. You ever have grilled swordfish?' True nods. 'Okay, so we went out with this great guy, really more like a sort of buddy than an uptight boat captain, off Key West. And the things are rare down there, these days. It cost a bundle. But both of us wanted the experience. By then, by the time we actually got there, we didn't intend to keep it.'

'I'm sure . . . you have a point here,' True says, perplexed.

'I do, but I have to get round to it,' Hank makes calming motions with his hands. 'Well, for three hours until the sun was high, we couldn't catch cold. A couple little redfish. Then, just as we were about to turn back, we saw all these birds acting crazy, and the captain sort of motored over there more out of curiosity than anything else, and we put out the baits, and wham! The line is going out so fast it's literally hot. And Perry and me . . . I . . . we took turns in the big chair you strap yourself into? Because we were only going to have this one experience. True, it took us two and a half hours, and even Perry, who's as dark as a cast-iron skillet, was burned to a crisp on his face. His lips swelled up that night, I thought I was going to have to take him to the hospital . . .'

'But . . .' True prompts.

'But for that two and a half hours, that fish, and the pain in our backs and our arms, seeing it leap and dive for the bottom, how beautiful it was, like a . . . like Pegasus or something mythic, no, like . . .'

'I know what you mean.'

'That was it. I could *feel* the fish's panic and its strength, and

82

nothing, nothing could have turned my eyes away from it. It was as if I was inside and outside the fish at the same time. I was giving everything I had to give. I could feel the muscles in my arms quivering, and I'm strong. I wanted to let go, but I couldn't let go, even to wipe the sweat out of my eyes. There was nothing else in the universe,' Hank is breathing harder. 'And finally, he was worn out. And we gaffed him. The hell was, that hurt him, and we had to keep him. He was mortally wounded. I sat on that boat and, a grown man in front of two grown men, I cried about it.'

'I see,' says True. She does not. 'That's . . . compelling.'

'Because he, the fish, had given me this incredible experience, this incredible focus, this challenge, and I didn't really want him to lose. I wanted both of us to win.'

The fervor in his gaze is undeniable. 'So you're probably wondering how this relates to the relationships between men and women,' Hank finally says.

'It crossed my mind,' True admits.

'I think it's possible for . . . two people. With most women – you're going to think I'm some pig, but I'm not – I'm there. I listen. But with half an ear. I appreciate their . . . charms, and their humor, and their dreams, if they have dreams. But none of them has ever had it all. None of them has ever been that fish. You see? None of them has ever engaged me on every level. It's not like I'm some great shakes, or anything, as a man. But I knew I was never going to give up everything for a woman until I felt that way. As if I couldn't look away even if I wanted to.'

'What were you going to do?'

'Go it alone. Just go to the snack bar once in a while.'

'That's what I was going to do, too,' True says. 'It's not so bad. And . . . it's not so great, either.'

'That's right. But it's better than settling for less.'

'And you're saying, based on knowing nothing about me, you feel that way about me?'

'*You* feel it, too. I'll bet you that you've never gone this far in your life so soon with anyone, have you?'

'Sexually?'

'No! It's possible to do that like shaking hands. I mean every way.'

83

'No,' True admits. 'No. I'm a careful person. I tend to weigh my options.'

'Well, I'm not rash to jump into things with both feet. I get enthusiastic and then I cool off. But how I feel is, you're not an option to me, True. You're my destiny. You're the one I knew would come. But I didn't know you'd come walking right into my restaurant, with your wet hair loose around your face, and your cheekbones like some . . . statue, and look me square in the eye, and basically challenge me. As if you were saying, *Boy? Here? Now?* I mean "boy" in the Southern sense, not the literal sense. I don't think it could have been any other way.'

'So you would base a consuming love on a hunch?'

'Well, in the end?' Hank asks. 'What else is there?'

She wants, suddenly, the comfort of her two-hundred-and-forty-thread-count sheets, her vast and clean and quiet bed. Hank looks to her abruptly greasy and wild, like a guy who would know how to fix motorcycles. She fears where he will take her on his.

'So you leaving someone behind for me?' Hank finally says, breaking the silence.

'I'm not saying I'm leaving anyone behind for anyone,' True says softly. 'I feel . . . a great deal, but this was a thing that happened, we didn't plan it.'

Backpedaling now, she wants him to put on her brakes, because she will not. She fears that she cannot.

'You know better,' he says. But now past her moment of combustion, she fire-walks with caution. Still, pulling back from such potent attraction is like leaving a magnetic field. She wants so badly to see all this as he sees it, to never let her eyes waver from his vision.

But because she must, she says, 'We'll see. What about you? Is there someone who's going to be hurt that you did this?'

'No,' Hank says, too briefly. 'Listen, I have a secret vice. I smoke a cigar every day. Put this coat on and let's stand on the porch a moment.'

It's bitter out there, but at least there's no wind, and the cigar's perfume is faint, like the residue of spilled wine. 'Who have you dated, True? Lots of people? A few but significant?'

'A few and insignificant,' True tells him, 'a builder, a baker . . .'

'A candlestick maker.'

'And all, and I do mean all, the orthodontists in Massachusetts.

I have a friend whose husband is a divorce lawyer, and she sort of considers it one-stop shopping. A decree, a settlement, a date with True, you know.'

'*Mon dieu*,' Hank says, 'is what we say back home. For any purpose.'

'Do you speak French?'

'*Mon dieu. Laissez les bon temps roulez. Je t'aime.* You call your sister "*chère*," but meaning "my dear," not the singer. You call a guy you don't like "*cochon*." That's about it.'

'I speak more French than that.'

'*C'est la guerre*. I should have picked up more. My grandparents spoke it at home. My father's folks.'

True's again aware of the hour, and asks, 'Do you have . . . my car is locked and I'm barefoot, and I don't want to walk over the gravel. And my hair is sort of a rat's nest in back. Do you have a hair brush in there? I don't want to go home looking like I've been wrestling.'

'Though you have,' Hank smiles. 'I use a sort of plastic thing, like a dog brush on this mop, but I'm sure my housemate has one around.'

'I don't . . . uuugh, want to use some other guy's hairbrush,' True shivers. 'Forget it.'

'No, she's very prissy and clean. She has pretty hair.'

'*She?*'

'My roommate. My housemate, that is. We share the house.'

'You live with . . . a woman?'

'Platonically.'

A small door taps and opens in True's belly. 'You're only friends?'

'Now. She works at the restaurant.'

'Now . . .'

'We were . . . we were together for a while. We both knew it wasn't going anyplace.'

'Does she know you're not together anymore?'

'Yes,' says Hank. 'No. I mean, yes. Theoretically. I've just never had eyes for anyone else, so I haven't dated anyone. And we, well, sometimes it seemed compelling that we . . .'

'You've slept with her? Recently?'

'No.'

'No?'

85

'Not for . . . a long time.'

'How long?'

'Months. At least two.'

True glances around her, panicked, as if a fanged Doberman will leap from the rosa rugosa. 'Where is she now?'

'She's asleep, I guess.'

'We did that . . . with your . . . roommate in the house?'

'She's a very sound sleeper. You could drop a brick on her foot.'

'I'm leaving.'

'No,' Hank protests. 'Wait, wait, wait. It isn't like it seems. We just share this house. What we did, together, for both of us, it was just . . . a little pleasure, a little touch, a little life . . . it was never as though we were going to be in a relationship.'

'I know what you mean. I've had that sort of experience. But you do *live* with her.'

'Not in the sense you mean, True. I swear. We aren't that way. We share a space. We're basically pals. We don't even go to the movies together.'

'And yet, she's here, now, and I don't think she'd like it.'

'I don't think she'd give a darn. Nor would I if she brought a guy here. For all I know, she has. In fact, I know she has a crush on the bakery guy,' Hank tries to reason, taking True's hand. But she is shell-shocked.

'If I didn't need my bra and my keys, I'd already be gone. In fact, just throw them out the door, the bra and the keys. Or keep the bra. I just need the keys,' True whispers, backing toward her car. She hears noises in the house. The dry, edgy shakes she remembers from college all-nighters begin to overtake her. 'Please, Hank. I don't know what I think about all this. But it's not good. Please, go get my stuff for me. I have to go home. It's the middle of the night. No, it's practically morning. I've got the jits, and this isn't helping.'

She drives home, glancing in the rearview mirror. Her face doesn't look the way it feels, her chin rubbed raw, an abrasion of some sort on one cheekbone. True thinks back to nights coming into the house after a makeout session with one of her high-school boyfriends, how she'd gaze in the mirror before bed, regretting that she had only sleep to look forward to, mooning over her engorged lips and flushed cheeks and tousled hair. Back then, erotic heat had made her beautiful. Perhaps it still does. But there has been so much confusion, so much emotion, she *feels* as though she has been dragged behind a car. She washes away mascara fans with a fingertip, then applies lip glister. She stops at an all-night gas station and buys two quarts of orange juice. She drinks one immediately.

In this grayling light, it is difficult to make out the package or bundle on True's porch swing. Then her headlamps swing over it, and she sees Guy, parka hood up, comforters top and bottom.

'What in the heck are you doing?' she asks, leaving the car running, askew across the drive.

'I woke up, and you weren't there.'

'I went to . . .' True holds up a bottle, 'get this orange juice. We didn't have any, and people are staying overnight.'

'You think I'm stupid?'

'Yes, I do. It must be thirty degrees out here.'

'Not to mention the windshield factor,' Guy mourns, as sorry for himself as a stockier version of the little match-girl. 'I know very well your bed wasn't slept in. It was cold, for one thing. And made, for another thing.'

'Well, I was out.'

'Out until the middle of the night?'

'Yes.'

'Talking?'

'Yes.'

'To that dancing restaurant truck guy?'

'Yes.'

'So you do have a crush about him!' Guy stands up and sweeps the comforter about him with a gesture worthy of Shakespearean aplomb.

'What's the windshield factor?'

'The windshield factor, Mom! The windshield factor! Why it feels even colder to you than it really is, like it would feel if you didn't have a windshield on your car! Don't tell me you never heard of it! And that's changing the subject!'

'I'm going to change your subject unless you get in that house!' She smacks him on the rear as he scuttles indoors.

'Can I sleep on the end of your bed?' Guy says. 'Uncle Dog told us the Lucky Hans story.' This is a Cape legend Dog delights in embroidering to terrify his daughters and her son.

'Yes,' True says sleepily, and then thinks of lingering aromas of bleach and cigar smoke. 'No. I have to take a shower and I'll wake you all up.'

'Okay,' Guy looks downcast. He has dropped his parka and the comforters in the upper hall. 'Will you make pancakes in the morning?'

'Yes,' True says. She is standing in the hall transfixed, the image of Hank's dark head between her legs like a restraining hand on her shoulder.

'Will you make waffles?' Guy asks, alert to something, and so closing in, like a wild dog scenting blood.

'Ummm, yes,' True says.

'Go to bed, Mom,' Guy tells her. 'You look like you're coming down with something.'

'NOTHING?' FRANNY ASKS, incredulous. 'You mean nothing, nothing? Not even pulling out?'

They are sitting outside, on a mild afternoon, as slender slips of crocus peep through melted snow, a day True's ancestor Emily would have called a day of purple shoes, at the big harvest table where crafters sometimes display their wares for True when they visit, in the belief that natural light shows work off to its best advantage.

'No, nothing,' True replies, bending busily over the work she is doing, avoiding Franny's eyes. She has known Franny long enough to realize that Franny's Greta Garbo brows will have hitched up under her ruff of black bangs.

'Do you know this means you've slept with the last ten women he's slept with?'

'I know I've slept with him practically in *front* of the last woman he slept with,' True says.

'You could get pregnant.'

'That wouldn't be the worst thing on earth. I could be secretive about his identity. Hollywood stars do that.'

'They just keep the guys secret because they're, like, gardeners or something.'

'You know more about this than I do,' True says dryly. She is willing to shift gears, not for the sake of reticence but to keep her evocative memories unbesmirched by the fingerprints of gossip.

Talking about Hank while a ceaseless current of Hank quotes and images courses through her mind makes her feel giddy, as if she is

88

watching two movies at the same time, one a Western and one a mystery, both featuring the same actors. What she and Franny are trying to do is to craft grapevine wreaths that they will bedeck with streamers of real ribbon, purple and gold and green, for Esa's wedding. The wedding is set to take place in three weeks' time, but is still embryonic, more a concept than a plan, a situation that drives True crazy.

'I know this much,' True says, her mind on the night before, when she and Hank had parked in the Nauset Beach parking lot and listened to the man who is always there, playing calypso on the garbage can lids, who seems to have two wives and at least four kids. 'We do nothing whatever, and when I'm with him, the world falls away. I feel as though I'm . . . riding in limousines. But also like I'm sixteen again. I'm happier than I've been in a thousand years.'

'That a lot of lifetimes,' says Franny. 'So, what if it turns out he's serious?'

'What if he is?'

'That would be a first for you – no offense, a second.'

'No, Franny,' True says seriously. 'You knew Pete. It would be a first.' She adds, 'He compared me with a fish.'

'Oh, *well*, if I'd known about the fish analogy . . . I guess that explains it.'

'It was locational. It made sense at the time.'

'Huh,' Franny says. 'Well, this grapevine makes great wreaths. A little tulle and these will look like *Matha* herself made them, though I do wish Isabelle would hurry up and figure out the rest.'

At this moment, as if announced by a cue, Hank's truck rattles into True's driveway. True looks down at her occupied hands. Hank has a way of swinging out of a seat that is like swinging out of a saddle. She has persistent trouble breathing in his presence, and even controlling her voice on the telephone.

He leans down and kisses True, catching her lower lip in his teeth. 'Come live with me, and be my love,' he says, then adds, 'Hey. You're Franny, right?' He puts out a hand. 'I have the whole cast memorized now. Franny is the best friend on earth. Isabelle, the darling from the ditch, who lives here. Kathleen, Rudy, the idea guy . . .'

'Right. Good Christ,' Franny exclaims, making a parody of fanning herself after they shake. 'What a line. Are you Irish?'

Hank drapes one leg over the bench on True's side, and places his palm on the back of her neck. 'I am, on my mama's side,' he says.

'And this is what is called blarney,' True interjects. 'Come live with you and Lucy and be your love?'

'True, be fair and decent, huh?' Hank pleads, embarrassed. 'Franny, listen to this. Lucy came to work at the joint. She had a place and the girl who lived with her moved out. I jumped at it. Not necessarily at her. I was sleeping on Tom's rollaway. You've lived here twenty years. You know how it is to find a place on the Cape in the summer. People would sign a sublet with Jeffrey Dahmer if he looked like he didn't have much of an appetite. When I moved into that house I never knew there would be you, True.' He turns to Franny beseechingly. 'That makes sense, doesn't it?'

'I'm not getting in the middle of this,' Franny replies mildly.

'Nonetheless,' True says, taking a piece of tulle and making a parody tie, with a proper Windsor knot, around his neck.

'Honey, my only other option is a tent, right now,' says Hank. 'But if you want me to pitch a tent, I will.'

'Should I go inside?' Franny asks. 'I feel like I'm watching you two . . .'

'Make love?' Hank asks.

'Sort of,' Franny replies.

'Well, we are. I think that this is how you *make* love from acquaintance. It's like a process.'

'Hank,' True admonishes. Her face is on fire. 'Look, you have to go to work and *we're* making a wedding.'

'Okay,' he says, 'I'll call you in a little while. Then I'll call you back. Then, when you're asleep, I'll call and wake you up.'

Franny watches the truck depart. 'Shit,' she says, '*I* want to marry him.'

'Let's please get back to the task at hand,' True says. 'You can't imagine what a distraction he, and all this, is.'

'I could try,' Franny says with a lascivious grin. 'But I see how it must drive you nuts that he lives with someone he *ever* did the wild thing with. I guess I also see his point. I mean, what's he supposed to do? Move out and live in his car on the basis of your knowing each other, what, two weeks?'

'Well, in the biblical sense, even less,' True concedes. 'Maybe ten hours. Total. Great hours. Hours talking about everything. And yet nothing, because it seems as though there will be time to talk about everything, and by the same token, that there's no reason to talk about anything at all, because it's all understood. I can't quite explain.'

'You don't have to,' Franny says. 'That's why they call it love.'

'But still, it's utterly presumptuous to even think of saying I'll no longer see him unless he moves out. People can't change their lives on the basis of something so new.'

'People have.'

'Nuts people. Single people. I mean, I'm single,' True carefully amends her statement, 'but not really. I have a child. And they are only housemates now. But yeah, it does get under my skin. I can't even feel comfortable calling him. And when we go anyplace . . .' she thinks of the places they have gone – the back of the truck, the floor of a friend's yoga studio, 'it's ridiculous. I feel like we're a pair of teenagers running around trying to find places to make out. And I won't bring him home, with Guy here . . .'

'I could conveniently have Guy over for dinner and swimming.'

'Could you have my mother, too?'

'That's harder,' Franny sighs. 'It must be wacko to have to hide your private life from your mother at your age. At our age. Why do you?'

'*Hide* it? There's no question of hiding it. Why? I have no idea why. She's just so damned disapproving. I couldn't handle it. And after Esa moves out, I'm not even going to have her to run interference. My mother opens my mail, Franny.'

'She *opens* your mail?'

'Oh, don't get me started. She opens my business mail routinely. That's part of her job. And she opens my personal mail routinely, because it just never seemed like a problem for her not to. Hey, my mother used to open my mail and *read* it, when I was a teenager.'

'Did you want to kill her?'

'Of course, but I couldn't actually kill her. When I was a minor, if it was, like, my report card, she had a right to open it anyhow. Kathleen is the nosiest woman on earth, and she's hip to this, Frannywoman. She doesn't miss anything.'

'But you have to sympathize, True,' Franny says softly. 'She has no real life but yours.'

'The fact is, it was sort of convenient, in a way, until now. She was the designated call-screener. All I had to do was make the throat-cutting motion and she'd say I was in a meeting.'

'But now you want your secrets.'

'Well, I want my space.'

'It's a tough one. He's got his roomie . . .'

'His housemate.'

'Okay, his housemate, and you've got Kathleen . . .'

'So I don't even want to think about it until I figure out how things are. I know I'm crazy about him, or just crazy, but I don't want to make any big moves until I know where it's going, and until I have a change to get Guy used to it; and I sure don't want anything to trip up Isabelle's big day.'

Isabelle is, after all, True thinks, her dear, nearly her child. The person in all the world, excepting Guy, she has allowed closest to her core. Necessarily, at least for now, she has to concentrate on Isabelle, and the fast-approaching wedding. Out of deference to her intended's profession, Esa wants a theme and food that savor of something ancient, medieval, but at first refused to take any money from True to create this atmosphere. Franny and Rudy have suggested bone spoons for the buffet, shrunken heads, and a black-chicken slaughter; but True thinks she knows what Esa has in mind – a royal wedding with mists of the river Avalon, recreated above Ridgevale Beach. And on a budget of approximately nothing.

To achieve this, she has had to overrule Isabelle's prides. They have all gone to work on the preparations, even Rudy. He and Keith arrived, breathless, last Wednesday evening to report that they'd found a farmer who would give them a bargain on the meat for the outdoor roast.

'We can get a quarter of a steer for three hundred bucks!' Rudy cried.

'They make such bad pets, anyway,' Keith added.

True has insisted on paying for the food and helping to hand-craft the decorations, although she is hopelessly ham-handed at that sort of thing. She also has consented, at Esa's request, to perform their 'spiritual' ceremony, after the couple tie the legal knot at the Barnstable County Courthouse. She is struggling to create something appropriate to the occasion – encompassing archaeology, friendship, and the sea – searching the Psalms. She must also bear in mind that Isabelle's mother is roaring over with a contingent of her Harley pals, though not – as Kathleen has reminded everyone – contributing a nickel toward the reception. True has talked a pal of hers into donating a striped tent, it being the off-season for Cape nuptials. The local funeral director, who has always had a letch for True, will haul over a few dozen folding tables with chairs in his hearse, if he and his squeeze, the librarian, can come to the feast. She and Franny are decking the hall – which is to say, the yard. The backbone of the decorations are these wind-sock things, tulle-wrapped wreaths onto which Franny and True will hot-glue lengths of fabric and pieces of mirror and then pray steadfastly against a squall.

Periodically, she and Franny go back to the hedges with shears and not an inconsiderable amount of scrapes and bruises, trying to wrest really big grapevines from the fences and foliage around True's house, where the wild grapes have licked up even into the highest branches of the beech trees. They will use these larger ones to build a nuptial arch, bending and securing the vines with their own tendrils to a plastic trellis. Completed, and especially from a distance, it all will look supremely festive. The candleholders will be seashells; Guy is on this detail with his pals.

'You know,' Franny says of one particularly symmetrical wreath, 'what would be cute is if you made these into little door hangers for the business. With little painted plaques on them with the babies' names. Kathleen could do it. Guy could do it. Even Angelique could do it. Even Clainey. You could pay them peanuts. Save a lot of money. All Angelique is doing with her life is majoring in tanning, anyhow.'

'I have to write that down,' True says, and yells, 'Esa! Can you come out here and take down a note?'

Isabelle emerges on the porch. True and Franny glance up. Their mouths open simultaneously in awe.

She is yet again trying on her wedding dress, a vintage find, richly embroidered with silver roses, featuring fingertip-length sleeves twice the size of Esa's waist. Isabelle has not been good for much except mooning and modeling since The Professor (it has taken True some effort to call him by his real name, which is Douglas) said yes. They have chosen a Guinevere wedding band, which will fit Esa's finger above the second knuckle, and which Esa also often displays at dinner. True's admiration for it is cleaved only by her abiding sorrow at losing Isabelle. Only Hank is compensation for that sadness. It

93

does not take a postdoc to reckon how fiercely was Isabelle's supplication to her pagan gods for True's infatuation with Hank to take root.

It has taken not only root, but flight. Too close, True already thinks, to the sun. There is the faint smell of scorching. Her yen for him is horrible, unremitting; there is no time of the day when she would not touch him, and thrills even to the sensation of walking to answer a call knowing that it is he. It's a fact. Hank must find his own place. Soon. But he has so little time to search, and finding even a semidecent single on the Cape that is not squalid or outrageously expensive, is next to impossible. And it is a full-time job, akin to searching for a particular drop of water in a bucket. Hank's partner, Tom, is an able, plain chef; but it is Hank who knows instinctively how a quarter-sized soupçon of red powder tossed into the cream sauce from his palm (he never measures) will glorify the whole dish. True has wandered in to watch him cook (she now feels like royalty walking into That One Place, to be wined and dined for free), and she marvels at his skill.

Isabelle pirouettes. They applaud, but continue to gossip.

'Still,' Franny whispers, 'it's kind of thrilling and romantic. The teenager hiding-out business.'

'Kind of,' True agrees, but it irks her how neatly Hank manages to avoid the subject when she, ever so obliquely, raises it. There's always something else, something minor and enchanting, to discuss. 'What's the saddest song?' he'd asked her recently, when she'd suggested the need to *really* talk.

'I think "Brothers in Arms" is the saddest,' True answered.

'I think the saddest song is "Waltzing Matilda." It makes me feel Australian. I wish I *were* Australian.'

'So move to Australia,' True had suggested, with a tang of pique in her voice.

'Can't,' Hank smiled. 'Got my foot stuck in the door.'

Which comment had made her subside, as perhaps it was intended to. Does Hank have something up his sleeve, she wonders? Will it stroke or sting her? Or is his avoidance of difficult logistics simple men-tality, the blithe gift of putting off anything pressing? Her brother, after all, has been constructing the same screened porch for three summers.

True leans on her hands at the picnic table, trying to picture what

94

she and Hank would do if they had time to do anything except search for screwing venues – the movies they might see, the places they might take Guy. She and Guy are going for three days to Florida at spring break, to a place where ordinary humans may swim with trained porpoises. How would Hank like that? Should she ask him along? Is it far too soon?

'I think we're meant to pay tribute to the goddess of the harvest. I think she's feeling ignored,' Franny says now, louder, interrupting True's reverie. They put down all their wares to fully regard Isabelle and offer applause.

'No, of the spring,' Esa instructs her. 'I'm Persephone, not Demeter.'

True raises her hands in a ballet pose, in praise of Esa, but her mind takes a long and solitary stroll.

Only last night, Kathleen made it clear that she was wise to the situation. When True simply could not even wait for the solution to the crime on *The Three Detectives*, her and Guy's sacred weekly Disney show, Kathleen gave her daughter a glance that would have withered – well, wild-grape vines. She followed True to the back door.

'I am not going to give you advice because you would not take it,' Kathleen said. 'But I know you're not going to a Shape-Up meeting or to play volleyball with Franny's team.'

True blushed. These had been two reliable lies – good for a handful of absences over the course of ten days.

'No,' she admitted.

'This man, this boy, True,' Kathleen whispered. 'Ask yourself. What does he want?'

'I imagine he wants what he says he wants,' True told her mother. 'To be with me. It's hard to believe, but he really does. He's as crazy about me as I am about him.'

'You know what I mean.'

'I'm trying my best not to know, Mother. Give me a break. Give us a break.'

'I think he wants your . . . position.'

'Which position?' True asked wickedly.

'True!'

'I'm sorry, Mom. Little teeny bad joke. You mean my money.'

'Call it what you will. Those are not my words. They're yours.'

95

'Trust you, Mom. Why didn't you say that about Evan? Though you had enough to say about Evan without that.'

'Evan was a dentist.'

'Hank is a restaurateur.'

Kathleen made a face that hinted of a hot afternoon downwind of baked seaweed. 'True, I am not being cynical here,' Kathleen said gently. 'But this man is essentially a drifter . . .'

'No. It might seem like that. But not anymore. He's put down roots. Has put everything he has into making his place work.'

'But such a young man with no ties . . .'

'He's lived here two years . . . and he has ties, with his family in Louisiana. They're very close.'

'I don't want to discuss this any longer,' Kathleen said then, with the ineluctable knack she has always had for making the other person feel as though she has been harassed into a contentious debate, though Kathleen herself began the conversation. Still, True did not need Kathleen to plant such bitter seeds. Everything Hank says about the struggles of keeping That One Place capitalized set off deafening alarms in her head, though she knows that even great restaurants are notorious for succumbing in the first, dismal year. Cooks are fractious; staff often unreliable and light-fingered; state rules exacting. With anyone else, she'd have simply sympathized. But with Hank, her guilty mind has to wonder if he's making a touch. This is one of the reasons she has told no one, except Franny and Esa, how far this fling has flung. Last night, on the telephone, Hank said, 'It could be that I really am in love with you. I've only been in love, really, once before, and even that, I see now, was nothing to this.'

And she said, 'Well, I know I love you. As to what that signifies . . .'

'Don't wreck it, True,' Hank admonished, cutting her off. 'We said it. I meant it. I have not said this too many times before. Let it just be there, between us.'

True reruns this moment, and gashes her finger on a thorn.

'You're distracted, True. Mind wandering?' Franny asks. 'Now, tell me, since Esa's gone back inside. Is he a big man?'

'I have to look up,' True smiles, and they begin humming the old girl-group song 'Here Comes My Guy.' They both know Franny is not referring to height, but True is more diffident than many about such matters.

'And do you have big feelings about him?'

True grins, '*Big,* big . . . feelings, that is. But there's also the fact that I don't know a damned thing about him . . .'

'That's why God made the Internet . . .'

'I don't mean I think he's on the run from prison . . .'

'No, I mean credit checks, bad debts, suchlike . . .'

'I mean I don't know a thing *about* him. I don't know what food he likes. Or his favorite movie. Or whether he moves his lips when he reads. Or if he would fart in front of me.'

'You could learn all that.'

'Yeah, too late.'

'True, what do you want to happen?'

'I'll give you three answers. I want to give it a year or so, and see how we blend, get him to know Guy, see if we could be partners, go slow. He always says, in effect, let's take it day by day. He's right. Everyone who says that is always right. Second, I want him to shut the business, move back to Louisiana, and write to me occasionally. Third, I want to be so crazy in love with him that we get married next week, and we live in utter bliss for forty years.'

'Which is the real answer?'

'They all are.'

Guy comes pounding up the drive from the school bus, his backpack open, spilling papers. 'I got a letter!' he shouts. 'Look, Mama! I got a letter from Grandma and Grandpa L. It's to me, not to you. They want me to come out there for part of spring break!'

'You can next year. We're going to the dolphin place this year.'

'But they say I can ride their horse Polo all by myself, without you. Can't we go to the dolphin place next year?'

'I made reservations six months ago, Gee.'

'But I'll probably be a better swimmer in a year. And they're going to get me my own fly rod, and send me a plane ticket! It's for my birthday! Because I'm ten now!'

True has visited the Lemieuxs exactly twice, once on her honeymoon, once just after Guy's birth. She has seen them about ten times in her entire life. She knows the checker at the Super-X better than she knows her former mother-in-law. She would no more let her child fly cross-country alone than she would allow him to go down in a shark cage on a school field trip. From her considerable experience with horses, she knows them to be both dumb and stubborn,

97

big enough to crush people and pea-brained enough to be terrified of butterflies.

On the other hand, the Lemieuxs raised Pete and his brother to be strong and healthy men. They are principled and decent, if not exactly warm and salt-of-the-earthy. On still another hand, she would have eight full days and nights to explore the meaning of her and Hank without the constant insistent tug of Guy's needs. They could go away . . . they could go to a little inn and . . . On still one more hand, what if the plane crashes? But as a pilot's wife, she knows this is less likely than the school bus careening into the ocean on the bridge over Bitter Creek. The real question is, does she want a whole week free to see Hank? To have Hank . . . maybe even, if she dares, in her bed? To ask questions – unasked questions – and hear answers?

'You would miss Esa's wedding!' she tells Guy, smoothing his sweaty hair back from his brow.

'No, that's on the Saturday, and they said I would go on the Sunday and come back on the Wednesday.'

True casts Franny a helpless look. Franny casts her eyes down, deep into the intricacies of her grapevine wreath. There will be no help here.

'Cool,' True finally says. 'What an adventure! Write Grandma and tell her you can come.'

'Don't say "cool," Mom,' Guy remonstrates. 'Say, "Dude!"'

'Dude!' says True, and sighs, her sigh rising up like an exhalation of smoke, through the trees, across the sand, up over the Sound, and into the clouds, beseeching any chance open hand of providence to give a fool such as she a break.

98

APRIL

SPRING THING!

*April showers may bring May flowers, so we've concocted
a surprise mix of bulbs you two can plant together, packed
in a tidy green container of round-edged baby garden tools.
There's also a rain hat covered with bugs (not the real kind!),
and a puzzle featuring all kinds of charming crawlies, with
pegs for easy placement by small fingers. Since we really
spring for spring around here, there's also Larry Sornberger's
handcarved wooden pull toy, The Ducklings, along with our
duckling slippers, in yellow and white, to match. And don't
forget Bountiful Blessings, our cologne, which will make a
muddy mom smell like a goddess of the rain.*

ONLY THE HARLEY riders had not fretted about the previous night's
downpour. Inside the house, everyone else obsessively monitored the
weather channel, and Rudy placed calls to pals of his, local fishermen, begging for auguries of a burn-off by midday.

Thankfully, temperatures overnight had remained in the sixties –
much like Esa's mother, Franny remarked when she arrived late Friday
afternoon to deliver the cake. Franny had made the cake herself and
carried it like Limoges in an Apple computer box.

'Woodstock,' Franny said. 'Minus the music and the drugs.'

'Don't be so sure,' True muttered anxiously. Isabelle's mother and
her best friends had arrived provisioned not only with beer kegs
strapped across the luggage racks of their massive hogs, but with
chickens to spit and roast on their campfires. These people clearly
would have been at home on any range. True was reduced to the
silent repetition of affirmations about the brevity of the whole event.

99

They kept away visions of a double-truck spread in the *Herald*, prominently featuring the gang in full leather, brandishing Budweisers. Mickey, Esa's mom, strode across the yard in her chaps beside husband Hob, who looked to True like some mythical creature capable of uprooting temples. 'The eight of us never go anywhere without each other,' Mickey explained, offering a hard hand, 'births, vacations, cruises, showers, court appearances, chamber-of-commerce dances, and you don't have to mind about feeding us.' She extolled the skill of making pepper-laced corn bread in ancient cast-iron skillets over open fire. 'The trick is,' said Mickey, 'you never wash the skillet. All the oils stay in.' True, who had observed the fingernails of the chief cook, an accountant called Howard, confessed herself too full from a late lunch to try even a nibble.

On Cape Cod, land is something that even the Lord can make no more of, so houses tend to be close-togethers. Neighbors ignore or anticipate predictable events, such as spousal Friday-night fights that bark through summer screens, or stifled yelps of passion that sound as though they come from your own bedroom closet. Such events can be, in their way, inspirational, and in any case, no one but the madly rich, with their white rock–walled compounds, can expect anything else.

This all being true, Esa's mother's clan still was harder to ignore than a school of washed-up Portuguese man-of-wars broiling on an August beach. 'I get that retiring, reflective side of my personality from my mother's branch of the family,' Isabelle said. True smiled nervously.

True's house sits on a wide, pie-shaped lot. No one can look into her windows, and the only house nearby is forty feet tall and has a rotating light which, magnified by its Fresnel lens, shines eleven miles out to sea. This privacy has always been a blessing – now it is a rescue.

'Gasoline,' Kathleen suggested darkly, poking her nose out True's front door. 'They're dousing those fires with gasoline to keep them going. We'll have the police here.'

'Try not to worry, Mom,' she counseled. 'I have to write my ceremony, and I can't get all frazzled. Remember, it's Isabelle's only wedding.'

True had been by now scouring poetry texts from college, and various volumes of plays. Deep in a paean to Maud Gonne by William

Butler Yeats, she hears the guitar twang from outside, and is thereby so apprised that this train is bound for glory.

'I don't think I can stand it,' she tells Hank on the telephone. 'Your restaurant is quieter.'

'Then come here,' he suggests. 'I'll set you up all nice in our sacred little banquet room.' She takes him up on it, the inspiration of his presence itself, his easy artistry with the flowers and napkins, the scent of braising from the kitchen before opening, reviving her spirits. By the time Isabelle, Douglas, and Rudy arrive with Guy, True feels she has made real headway.

'I want to make sure everything in this suits you two,' she tells Isabelle. 'So don't think you'll hurt my feelings if you want something left out.'

Rudy, who has strong feelings about the removal of archaeological treasures from their countries of origin, opens by suggesting the part in Exodus that, he recalls, promised punishments for removing 'the emerald, the sapphire, the diamond, the beryl, the jasper that were to be the memorial for the children of Israel.' He adds, 'Remember? If a thief be found breaking up, and be smitten that he die . . . I've always loved the word "smitten," and "smote" isn't bad, either.'

In a graceful distraction, as he tosses the salad tableside, Hank suggests Psalm 11: 'Say ye to my soul, flee as a bird to your mountain? That would tie in with the whole archaeology thing . . .'

'You're all such Bible scholars!' True says, genuinely shocked. 'Where did I miss out?'

'I took it as a literature option,' Rudy admits.

But Douglas is not sure the frank deism of Psalm 11 suits him, and True finally retreats to the comfort of Ruth, verse 16: 'Entreat me not to leave thee, or to return from following after thee, for whither thou goest, I will go; and where though lodgest, I will lodge. Thy people shall be my people . . . if ought but death part thee and me.'

'Even if you said nothing else, the "thees" and "thous" would be enough,' Isabelle sighs. 'They remind me of Gregory Peck.'

'Alan Ladd,' Rudy corrects her.

'Isn't there any part in English?' Guy asks.

'This is special-occasion English,' True explains, as everyone finishes their coffee. 'It makes people sit up and listen.'

No one, True sighs inwardly, would have to be more sanguine about following around her mate hither and yon than her Esa, playing Ruth as Douglas roams the earth in search of campfires from nomadic tribes of the fifty-thousand-year-old equivalent of Esther. They all go home spent, True ruefully opting out of more than a quick kiss from Hank for the sake of the beneficence that a full night's sleep would bestow on her face. Lucy, she of the sassy boy's hips and Barbie bosoms, watches from behind the kitchen galley doors, her face, visible to True over Hank's shoulder, a crumpled moue of disgust. True stuffs crumpled paper cocktail napkins scrawled with speech scribblings into her bag. Everything, including the housing dilemma, would have to wait until the wedding rolls by, a caisson laden with soggy grapevine windsocks, tarp-draped motorcycles, tenderloin and foccacia for thirty arriving at two, with True just one of the tambourines stuck on the side of the wagon, in her seafoam linen suit with her wide-brimmed, silk-ribboned hat.

TOWARD DAWN, JUST as the rain let up, True hears the Harley folk singing 'Give Peace a Chance.'

And just as the clock strikes seven-thirty, the Sandersons from down the beach road call.

'True dear,' shy Quaker Sylvia Sanderson says softly, 'I know it's far too early to call. But these poor, wet people, on your lawn . . . are they . . . well, they seem to be very . . .'

'They're not staying,' True hastily assures her. 'It's my assistant's wedding day. They'll be gone by sunset, Sylvia.' Esa shook her head. 'Well, they'll be gone by midnight.' Esa shook her head again. True shrugged madly. 'Well . . . by tomorrow morning at the latest. Tell Luke I'm so sorry. We imagined they'd stay at a motel . . .'

'Oh, it's certainly no inconvenience,' Sylvia tells her, her voice obviously unruffled by gratitude that Mickey and Company have not settled in for the summer. 'We simply worried, with the rain and all, whether anyone was in need of . . . some kind of first aid. Or shelter. There is our barn, and it's warm and dry.' True's throat tightens with tender pride for the grace of Yankee manners.

Not an hour later, as True, Isabelle, and Kathleen are brewing coffee, Isabelle's father shows up. When Kathleen opens the door, a big-beamed blond man in jeans and a leather windbreaker asks, 'Is this the place?'

'That depends,' Kathleen answers.

Then Isabelle cries, 'Daddy! You said you couldn't come. You said you were disking someone's field!'

But he has, all the way from Annenberg, Wisconsin, and stands turning his field cap in his hands. 'I'm here to give my daughter away,' he announces. 'I won't stay the night.'

'You're welcome to,' Kathleen says suddenly. 'You may use my small cottage. I can stay in True's, in my daughter's, house.' And True is again touched, by how suddenly Kathleen can slip the locks and throw wide the doors when civility demands.

Esa's mother, who has not seen her former husband in twenty years, whoops and leaps up onto the porch. 'Kellen!' she cries, throwing her arms around him. 'Look at you. You're big as a house! You must go two-eighty, easy!'

'Nice greeting, Ma,' Esa comments.

'You look the same, Mickey,' Kellen Merton says with a sigh. 'You look beautiful.'

'So how did you manage to get away, Dad?'

'Damn near didn't,' Kellen Merton explains. 'Convinced Johannsen to do the back spray with Eddie. Stuffed myself into one of those dwarf plane seats, my rump's still aching like it got stuck in a gas-station toilet.'

'Dad, it's my wedding day,' Esa says. 'Spare us the physiological extremes.' Isabelle made proper introductions to Douglas, who says he has heard many good things about Isabelle's farm childhood.

'She learned to work, I'll say that,' Esa's father asserts.

'Where are your things? We can help you bring them in,' True offers.

'No need. I'm going back tonight,' Esa's father explains.

'She means for the wedding,' Isabelle offers. 'Your suit.'

Kellen Merton holds up a duffle. 'You wrote "informal."'

'I didn't mean . . . that informal, Daddy.'

'Is there a store open?' True calls to the room at large. It is eight A.M., the wedding scheduled for noon.

'I'm not spending any money on a monkey suit,' Kellen Merton declares. 'The flight alone cost me . . .'

'I might have one of Bert's jackets at my house,' Kathleen says softly. 'I'm sure I do. And would it fit? I think it very well might. My late husband was a big man. Do you like a gray tattersall?'

103

'Ma'am, I've never owned a suit in my life.'

'Well, I'm sure you'll like this just fine. Not a moth hole anywhere in it, after all these years,' Kathleen tells him, leading Kellen out the door. 'Now, my Bert, he towered over most men. But not an ounce of fat on him . . .'

'There is a God,' Esa says.

The sun makes a watery appearance by ten, and frail daffodils tentatively raise their battered heads. Franny coils Esa's luxuriant hair into a French braid, interlacing a silver cord. Hank comes early, resplendent in a dark gray suit with a red tie. True cannot help but relish her finger's memories of the topographies under the fabric. For the first wedding in the dozens she's attended over a decade, True will not feel envious and bereft.

Just before noon, Mickey emerges from her rubber tent in a violet suit, with clean, brushed hair, looking twenty years younger, and helps position the arch of grapevine and bittersweet. In a mighty heave, her husband, Hob the Giant, lifts the rain-soaked tent to drain off the heavy pockets of water.

It is time, and Isabelle's father, natty in True's father's old coat and pants, holds out his arm.

'Daddy,' says Isabelle, who indeed does look like a lady of legend. 'I figure you gave me away a long time ago, when I went off to college. I want you to walk with me, but there's another man in my life who has to come, too.' Rudy self-consciously straightens his tie, but Isabelle holds out her hand to Guy. 'Come on, shortie. Walk your old pal down the aisle?'

True bites her lip as Guy draws himself up to his full four-foot-seven, and takes Esa's hand.

Only Hank's steadying touch at her elbow keeps her from dissolving so thoroughly she would be unable to negotiate the thirty-foot walk from her door to the arbor.

Her voice trembling, True begins, exactly at noon: 'I am not a minister, of course, only Isabelle's boss for eight wonderful years, so I'm humbled that she asked me to share this moment with her and her Douglas. With all great respect to the parents who raised this remarkable young woman, I take some credit . . .' A knot of tears caught under her voice interrupts her, and she takes a centering breath, ' . . . for how Isabelle, true to her name, has grown from a bud of a girl to the most beautiful woman.

'Nearly seventy-five years ago, the playwright Thornton Wilder wrote that marriage is something nearly every human being does. With few exceptions, he wrote, people are made to live two by two. He said that once in a million times, it's interesting. This is a marriage,' she adds, steeling her eyes away from the rubber tents, 'that is particularly interesting, since Isabelle and Douglas have chosen not only to spend their lives together, but to spend a life that will certainly include adventure. We know why they're here. Why are we all here? We are here as witnesses. We are here to promise that whenever this young couple falters, we will offer our support. Whenever they lose sight of the absolute love that brings them here today, we will give our advice if it is asked, and our silence if that is what is needed. And as Thornton Wilder said, don't forget all the other witnesses at this wedding – the ancestors. Millions of them. So, Douglas, who spends his professional life learning the ways our human ancestors lived and died and married, and Isabelle, who has for the past few years worked in a business that helps welcome people to the world, you stand here today in good company.' True glances at Hank, expecting a proud smile . . . *atta girl*. But there is something else in his eyes, something so profoundly intimate that she nearly forgets her place, and between them passes a concentration of emotion so dense and intense that it is nearly frightening. It is the closest thing to telepathy True has ever known with another adult. She can read exactly what he is saying: *You are my heart. You are my woman.* Something is sealed.

The red marsh reeds sough like off-key violins as True reads the Bible verse, and she listens to their music as she asks the questions every woman somehow knows by heart before she is twelve: Do you? Will you?

THEY DO. OF course, they do. And they will.

HOURS LATER, TRUE sits alone at her kitchen table, Franny's magnificent cake, which depicted the Stage Harbor Lighthouse, where Douglas and Isabelle met now a crumpled and tottering heap before her. She has made herself a strong cup of tea. Hank has taken off, back to the 'store,' as he calls it, where he is, tonight, front of the house, the one who will greet and flirt and suggest wines. Esa and Douglas, she hopes, are not asleep in the colossally expensive hotel suite, which has been her gift to them. In return, tomorrow they will escort Guy to Montana, where they had long planned – unbeknownst to True – to head for their honeymoon.

'We'll do horses, the ancient-fossil kind and the real kind you ride,' Esa said earlier. 'And search for evidence of humans and mammoths in cohabitation.'

'That's something I've always suspected,' Rudy was quick to comment, his head on Esa's shoulder in a prolonged farewell hug. Even Rudy hadn't been up to much levity. If Keith's business plan went forward, Rudy and he could be gone by May. He might not see Isabelle again, for a long while. 'Maybe you can go to Little Big Horn, too, Esa. Kind of the Niagara Falls of the Northwest.'

'Doesn't sound too romantic, for a honeymoon,' True had ventured, sotto voce, as Douglas loaded Esa's trunks into his battered van.

'Oh, when you haven't seen your guy in six months,' Esa had told them dreamily, 'it will be romantic just sitting in the car, just singing with the radio.'

This True believes. She thinks of Keith and Rudy, listening to their Betty Buckley CDs, heading west toward the sunset. All of them, following their own paths. All those paths leading . . . away. But Hank is here. What they have felt is more than sexual entanglement . . . isn't it? Despite having examined every incongruity that pertains to them, there is the splendor of the well-being she feels every time she sees him, the intoxicant contained in the peppery smell of an article of his clothing, their eye language over the heads of others, the silly yet utterly significant fact that, though they come from different worlds and generations, they love the same game – making up stories about couples who pass by – and invariably making up the same stories.

Isabelle and Douglas had seemed an unsuitable match, and yet, now off they have gone together, stupefied by their good luck.

There is no stencil for her affiliation with Hank. And True has always done personal things as a good girl, or if not so much a good girl, then one at least determined not to draw negative attention to herself.

She does not want to draw negative attention to herself now. But she would rather draw lightning than let Hank go without knowing what force beyond the obvious compels them together, and why, after so short a time, they feel together, at least alone together, like a conspiracy, a fraternity, a sect of two. Hank has said this. He has called them 'soul mates.' True knows this is a banal term, but from Hank's mouth it is clover honey. She cannot think of a better description.

She drinks another cup of tea, so strong she knows she will not sleep all night. She then finds Guy sprawled across his bed still in the First Communion suit he'd stuffed himself into for the wedding; his clothes for packing, from underwear to cowboy boots, strewn across the floor. True is grateful for the chance to make some visible order at least here. She will find a suitcase, and lay in Guy's clothes in some semblance of order that will impress her former mother-in-law. She must also prepare a kit of allergy medicine and a list of insurance numbers, permission slips for medical treatment. Like a zombie, she accomplishes these tasks, and then climbs into bed beside Guy, and smells his wet-dog hair, the smell of every little boy who's spent the day running like a hyena beneath the level of radar at an adult event.

She puts her arm around his barrel chest and sleeps.

They are awakened by Kathleen, in a righteous panic. Beside her is Kellen Merton, Isabelle's dad, washed and combed, in a fresh, snapped, flannel shirt. Kathleen had not, True realizes with an inner tickle, stayed over at her daughter's house. Kathleen's little house has two bedrooms, but . . . this could not be. Could this be? True's urge to speculate is so strong she can barely concentrate.

The plane leaves in two hours, Kathleen insists. Isabelle and Douglas are at the door. True barely has time to process that this will be her longest separation from Guy since the day of his birth. 'Don't forget, Katie,' Kellen Merton is saying, 'May's the best time. When the trees bloom.'

'I've never seen that part of the country, though my husband traveled there,' Kathleen says, her arm around Guy's shoulders.

'I'll really miss you,' True says to her son, trying to keep her voice even and hearty.

'Oh, I'll miss you, too, Mom,' says Guy, with a cursory hug. He's already given Douglas his duffle. Douglas gives Mister Merton a hand into the rear seat. He waves at 'Katie.'

And then, Guy is running back. 'Remember when I was a baby and went to Monomoy Sea Camp overnight which I hated and never want to go again, though it was a nice place?' True admits she does. (Guy hadn't been a baby. He'd been seven.) 'Remember when I gave you a plastic bag I said was filled with . . . it was dumb . . . kisses, and you could take one out whenever you missed me?' True remembers. 'Well,' he shows her a closed fist, 'this is a handful. I know it's a baby thing to do . . .'

And you're doing it for me, True thinks. 'Thanks, Gee,' she says. 'I'll hold on to them.'

'I thought it might make you feel better,' Guy smiles.

The hug, this time, is in earnest. True feels that now that she is letting Guy go, they are crossing into territory in which they must accept their distinct identities. She doesn't know if she likes it.

Esa-less, childless, and at least temporarily loverless, True throws herself on Guy's rumpled bed. Hank must be home now – at Lucy's, perhaps sleeping in. Perhaps he is being considerate of her own exhaustion. Perhaps he is distancing himself. She could drive over. But, no. This man who has entered her body and her life with such assurance and speed is also withheld from her. Perhaps this is how he intends to keep the . . . all the rest of it, which he knows comes with True, at bay.

Perhaps his real-estate dilemma is a handy dust jacket for his ambivalence.

She will not think this.

Still, the house is cold and feels cored of its lifestock. Outside, a late-spring snow has begun to fall, quickly reducing the beribboned branches to sticks hung with wet rags, as if the trickish spring had trailed away in their Cape Persephone's wake. Silence clamps down like a hand over a mouth. True has never been so utterly alone, nor felt quite this unthought-of, as if she, too, is frozen, a remnant left behind. Another woman might tackle a good novel and pop open a bottle of Merlot. But True is morbidly enthralled by the silence. She wraps herself in her son's comforter, folds herself small in a corner of his bed, and sleeps. When she is awakened, it is dark.

The phone . . . she thinks it will be Hank. But it is Guy, calling from Montana, and it seems to True as though her son has vanished into one of those disintegrators beloved of shows such as *Star Trek*, and been teletransported to Montana. The call is short. He's going with his grandfather to see a cow give birth or something. True cannot get up even to adjust the thermostat or flip on an orange,

108

restorative light. She plunges back into sleep. Sleep may remedy nothing, but there may be something at the other end of it.

IT IS HANK who suggests New Hampshire.

'There's nobody there,' True says. 'Why not Nantucket? At least they have food.' They are parked in her car in Harwich, on the deserted road to a mansion under construction. This twenty-roomer, which will house a developer who has only one child, and that one only three years of age, will displace the whole historic harbor, which has launched fishing boats for one hundred and twenty years. Hank is having his daily cigar, and True is reassembling her blue jeans.

'My point,' Hank tells her. 'Do we need to have people there?'

'We could go to Strawberry Banks,' True suggests. 'It's pretty. And they have historic inns. One has to be open.'

'I was thinking we'd hike up Mount Washington,' Hank tells her. 'I've always wanted to get to the top of that. I don't know much of New Hampshire.'

'Well, it's very green,' True says, thinking of her dozens of trips to visit what she estimates to be the approximately one in three New Hampshire residents who are woodworkers. 'Though not now.' She thinks of her own rhododendrons, still furled in their shining winter sleep, all but ready to burst into foamy jungle flowers in just a few weeks' time.

'I was thinking we could hike to the top to say we'd done it.'

'That would be . . . exhilarating. They have snow up there still, Hank, you know. They just had that big ski rally thing a few weeks ago. We might not . . . you know, summit.'

'Well, we could give it a try. And then, maybe we could go to Canada. Do you have your birth certificate? You need that, don't you?'

'I have my passport. Do you have your birth certificate?'

'I needed it for my driver's license, or my liquor license, or something. So, yes, I do.'

'I can't just up and leave, Hank, either. And neither can you. Or can you?'

'Tom can do for me. His brother will help. And Chris'. They said they'd do. I took Chris's shifts when he went to New Jersey for his sister's wedding. He's got to dig in deep, if he wants to buy in. We're okay with staff, at least as of today. The new cook is a prince. I know he'll leave when the season starts. I just know it.'

'But I have fall orders to process. I'm short, without Esa.'

'You told me Rudy said the new woman taking over Esa's job is smart.'

'She's not even on full-time yet.'

'Well, okay . . .'

'I suppose Rudy could run things for a few days. Kathleen knows everything but the computer.'

'When was your last vacation, True?'

She has to think. 'Well, it was in ninety-eight,' she says gamely, 'the Toy Expo in New York.'

'That's not a vacation. Look, Kathleen's fine. You're worn out from the wedding, and I could use a break. Guy is fine. We've never been anywhere together in the entire . . .' He cannot help but laugh, 'nearly a month we've been together!' The laugh is contagious. It is all so silly, and still so sublime.

Because of the possibility of slippery weather, they take Hank's truck. True notices in the back what appear to be tent stakes. If there is anything True fears and loathes more than bowling, it is camping. Peter had been an avid camper, and True had evolved a theory that camping for men and camping for women were opposite experiences. For men, camping involves manly feats of food kill, and chest-thumping draughts of piney air. For women, camping involves the internment-camp experiences of pit toilets and group showers, as well as of hauling water for washing every dish in the picnic basket four times a day.

'We aren't going to camp, Hank,' she says. It is not a question.

'For emergencies,' Hank promises.

As mountains go, Mount Washington is no K-2; but True's new boots, which the clerk at Shoe Biz had assured her would feel just like bedroom scuffs, feel instead like the shoes she remembers from her prom and her wedding day – dainty-looking things like miniature guillotines that punished with blocks and straps and invisible interior ridges like little knife edges. Hank points out the birdsong – a cardinal, he thinks, or a red-eyed vireo, but True would not be interested in the king's nightingale, she is in such pain. She knows her fitness level despite her weight gain is such that she could be sprinting along this pebbled trail – if she did not have feet. As a result she is angry at Hank, who seems to be trying to do Sir Edmund Hillary. She stumbles and tries to conceal her agony. When she feels a blister open, she bites down on a scream. The peak of Mount Washington, crowned in its aureole of sunlight, looms as distant as the top of the Washington Monument. Pebbled mud slides like gravy from under her boot toes. She also feels grouchy and crampy, though her period, thankfully, is not due for at least a week, a blessing on this trip.

But she is reminded by the combination of the setting and the tightening in her abdomen of the only foul moment in the only trip True and her mother had ever taken alone. When True was a girl, they had climbed Pikes Peak. Kathleen had always been vigorous, a walker before everyone walked, a scourge with her big hickory stick to all neighboring dogs, but True was surprised when her mother suggested doing something so frankly outdoorsy and extravagant. It had been a celebration, a celebration of True's having been chosen valedictorian of her high-school class, a trip that began with Kathleen going wallet-wild in Denver on European sweaters and pleated pants that made True an astonishing exemplar of fashion the following fall at Amherst. She cannot recall a time when Kathleen ever was more tomboyish, more impulsive and confiding, more the mother True had always believed lay buried beneath the dutiful penny-pincher, the sipper of single gin-and-tonics, the stalwart organizer of the four food groups on the daisied Melmac.

She tries now to think of that trip, of her and Kathleen belting out show tunes 'Shall We Dance?' and 'Happy Talk,' as they strode with their sticks in the group of six, which included Pam and Suzanne, two of True's closest high-school friends, their mothers, and one of their fathers. She had not minded camping then – the mothers had brought delicious freeze-dried concoctions purchased through L. L. Bean and homemade cranberry bread for their breakfasts. The mothers, not the girls, had cleaned the dishes. It was not until she'd gotten her period, unexpectedly, on the descent, that True had descended into a misery of humiliation, cutting up her extra sweat-shirts for makeshift sanitary napkins, slipping away to burn them at night. She was, and still is, so shy about personal hygiene that she'd been unable even to ask her girlfriends for help. When Kathleen confronted her, demanding to know whether True was smoking ciga-rettes in secret, she had confessed that yes, she was, and submitted to a tongue-lashing from Kathleen rather than own up to the truth. She had not, in fact, told her mother about that part of the journey until Guy was born, in one of those dozy, confiding, nursing moments when it seems permissible, even imperative, to tell another woman any intimate thing. Kathleen had not even remembered the accusation until True reminded her of Court O'Malley, her friend Pam's father. Of him, Kathleen could call to mind every detail, his broad shoulders and shock of auburn hair.

The path is steeper now, and True and Hank sit down to eat their low-carb coconut bars. True's feet are blazing stumps. She cannot feel her toes as distinct digits. But when she bends surreptitiously to examine them, she notices a ring of blood around the ankle of her white socks. Quickly, she unlaces her boots. Blisters on her big toes are oozing, and the bottom of one foot is a half-moon of abrasions, but her ankle?

The blood is running down her leg. True lies face-up on the morning-hot shelf of rock and moans. Her life is impossible. There are no sweatshirts to cut up. It is at least a week until this event would ordinarily happen. Her gynecologist hadn't been fooling – these things get wacky in your forties.

'Are you okay?' Hank asks. 'Are you sick?'

'I'm sick,' True agrees. 'I have to go back down right now.'

'It's only another few hundred feet. It was so important to me that we get to the top.'

'You go ahead. I'll lie here and bleed.'

'Your feet are *bleeding?*'

'They're new boots. And it's not just that.'

'I'd take them back. That's outrageous.'

'I have funny feet,' True explains. She will not use the word 'bunions.' She wants to pound the rock until it cleaves, and creep into the cleft.

'Are you sure you can't make it?'

Is the man insane?

'In fact,' True says, loath to get up, desperate for a way to distract Hank from her for a few moments so she can see whether blood has soaked through her khakis and her white shirt, and if it has, whether the jacket will cover her rear, 'I'm not sure I can even make it down. Is that a house over there?' She points to a stone cottage where an ancient Ford pickup slumps in the yard. 'Could you please go over there and tell whoever lives there I'll give him fifty dollars to drive me down this hill?'

'I can carry you down, True.'

'Oh, sure.'

'It's not that far.'

'I'll start walking back. You go on ahead up to the top. I don't think I'll get so far you won't be able to catch up to me.'

'But that's not the point.'

'What's not the point?'

'I wanted us to experience the view together, I wanted us to pretend we could see the whole world from the top of this mountain, a whole world down there that both of us could explore, together.'

'That's very sweet,' True is genuinely touched. 'You go on and tonight, at the inn, you can tell me all about it.' She feels as though she is talking to Guy.

'You still don't get it,' Hank continues, with the hint of a pout. 'I had this all planned. To me, the top of a mountain is the real estate just one floor below infinity. Anything is possible. The only thing above you is the sky. But we're nearly there. I can make my little speech.'

True watches him, as he reaches into his pocket and extracts a waxed-paper envelope. 'I made this ring in college. It's only silver, and it's very plain, and the seam isn't what it should be. But I've kept it for more than ten years, waiting to meet the woman whose hand I would want to put it on.' Hank takes True's hand. There is blood under the nail of her index finger. He slips the ring, which is artfully light and slender, strands of silver braid, onto her fourth finger. It's at least four sizes too big. He laughs, running his free hand through his black Indian hair, and slips it onto her thumb. 'I want you to wear it.'

'That's so loving, that's so wonderful,' True manages, her throbbing feet a distant percussion of pain. 'Does the design have a meaning?'

'A meaning? A meaning? Are you deliberately being dense? You're fooling, right? It's a wedding ring, True, you goof. I want you to marry me. I want you please to marry me. I would be honored if you would marry me.'

'Marry you.'

'Yes. I love you, *and* we have fun. We have better fun together than I've had since my best friend Perry and I went fishing for gar in the swamp outside Taloochee. We could have fun forever. I'm asking you to marry me. I know we haven't even been to a movie, and I know you won't like the ones I like. But that won't matter. There's more to it than that. It's a sealed deal. It's an arranged marriage. When I saw you the first time, I knew that.'

In the space of the seconds before she answers, two eagles alight and begin an elaborate, noisy hop-dance on the rim of their ragged nest. True sees only the birds, and imagines from the flap and tangle of wings that they are mating. She does not think eagles mate for life.

She thinks of what a decade means, beyond ten years. Ten fingers on a healthy pair of hands. Ten dimes to a dollar. Ten years to a decade, a decade being defined, True has often heard, as a generation, the span of years that separates one age group from the one that comes after. When she looks at forms, the sheaves of forms she's required to fill out each year, for Guy's Social Security, for matters as trivial as magazine subscriptions, she studies how close she is edging from the 35–44 box to the 45–54 box, presumably comprising an entirely different echelon of priorities.

There are decades of history – the Roaring Twenties with their desperate charm and dangerous glamour, the Fifties when life and employment seemed so abundant that any man with a job could hope for a Cape with four bedrooms. Decades in a human life. Turning twenty and stunned that you are no longer really a kid. Turning thirty and pledging that this is the time to figure out what it is you will be doing for the rest of your life. Turning fifty and vowing that there is still time to do it. True has read that the span of childhood is ten years, that a baby grows to be an adolescent in ten years, and this troubles her; she feels instinctive kindliness toward anyone who still refers to Guy as 'a little boy.' When True's own mother was forty-three, True was already in college. When True was in college, Hank would have been in fifth grade, as Guy is now. When True was ten years old, Hank's mother would not have trusted her to care for him. She would have been too young. But when he was three and she thirteen, she'd have been the perfect age to baby-sit him. In a big family, they could have been siblings. In an old-fashioned family, she could have been his aunt.

In a movie that featured two actors her age and Hank's, the central conflict could be nothing except the issue of True's age. In a movie that featured an actress Hank's age and a male star True's age (or a good ten years older than True), the central conflict could be anything: the threat of bioterrorism, the pursuit of the man who's been mistaken for the mobster who stole the gold bars, the vet intent on saving the gorillas.

In mere instants, True thinks of the intense and yet healthy bond she and Guy have formed, the risk of the intruder, the risk of the betrayal, the certainty of diluting her most basic devotion by adding another person. Then, she thinks of the inestimable benefit of a father still supple enough to pitch the curve ball and make the layup, a father who also knows the *pas de chat* and the *relève*.

Guy could grow up with a father, the only father he will ever have a memory of knowing.

Guy could grow up with an interloper he will resent all his life.

People could consider True a middle-aged dizzy, sexually hypnotized by a barn burner. People could envy True and wonder what sensual secret she possesses that drives a man like Hank, who could have a woman ten years younger than he instead of ten years older, mad.

The eagles are not mating, True recognizes. They are spatting. The female has prey, and the male wants a taste. But the mother brandishes a serious claw; this limp mouse is for her young. They tear the mouse between them, the male lofting himself in one swoop to a lower branch to pin his share, the tail portion, between his claws and rip into it with gusto. The female tries to apportion pieces of furred flesh among striving, scrabbling nestlings. There may be a bite left for her. It is, after all, only a mouse. There are probably more mice where that one came from.

True looks at Hank's face and feels her own face open to match it, her cheekbones lift, her eyes fill. She has felt such love only once before, and that was safe. It was for Guy. So she will not rebuke her instinct. She will take Hank inside her, be damned anything else around them, and within her, she will build another self, which is cherished, and see the world through those eyes.

'Yes,' True says. 'Yes, yes, yes, yes, I do. I never imagined saying this. I do. I will. I do, I do.'

'That's for later.'

'I do now.'

'Okay! Suits me!'

'But why? Why do you want to?'

'Because you're remarkable . . .'

'No, you are remarkable. You could have anyone.'

'If I can, then I am.'

'We'll be just fine.'

'It'll be a walk in the moonlight. I think we'll be just fine.'

'Guy will be fine.'

'Let me take care of Guy. I know I can handle it.'

'Okay! Suits me!'

'God!' Hank yells, face turned upward, fist raised. 'I'm marrying her! Let's get down this mountain, then, and celebrate.'

This maneuver occupies the better part of three hours. First True hobbles in stockinged feet, ignoring the pinch of pebbles on the tender balls of her feet, then Hank supports her, one of his shoulders under her armpit, holding her partly off the ground. They sit down often. Family groups pass, and offer help. True does accept an icepack from one nice older gentleman, but nearly faints from the pain of it applied to her toes. Finally, Hank carries her, first in both arms, then as a firefighter would, over one shoulder. This is the manner in which they arrive at the inn at the foot of the mountain. The proprietor gives them a level look. 'This is part of a tradition in my family,' Hank explains. 'We just got engaged.'

In the merciless light of the hotel bathroom, True surveys the wreck of her lower limbs. She looks like a horror dummy in some B-film.

'Let me watch you undress,' Hank says softly, from outside the barely open door.

'Hell, no!' True cries.

'You're my fiancée!' Hank points out.

'You come in here now and I call the whole thing off!' True threatens him. She strips away the muddy, sticky layers of her slacks and underwear, balls them up in the trash and runs a bath. The moment the hot water touches her feet, she cries out. She cannot help it. Hank opens the door.

'No,' he says. 'I'm not listening to your objections because they're silly.' Surveying her feet, he disappears for fifteen minutes and returns with the only things he can find in the village: water and baking soda. With a paste of this, he bathes True's feet, taping on gauze

116

pads. Then he washes her hair with the inn's soothing soap, and helps her into a robe. True lies stiff on the bed, trying not to allow her body to move vertically. Hank lies down beside her. 'Feet hurt too much to consummate this new thing?'

'It's not that.'

'What's wrong?'

True makes a gesture that encompasses her pelvis. And Hank nods.

'How could I mind anything like that?' he asks. 'You're not someone I picked up. You're my girl.' They make love with ferocity of isolation that blanks True's mind. Or rather, it seals her mind from the relevancies of her real life. She is only a female, or all females of all species, grasping and begging, needing this ripple of muscle more than food or breath, as she imagines an addict craving crack over safety, as if this minute-long contraction will cure and absolve her if she can only make it there. 'Will you always be my woman?' Hank whispers, 'and always my whore, too? Like the Cajun girls who wear beads around their waists, that roll and slip when they move their hips? I won't finish you until you tell me. I'll leave you right where you are, *chère*.'

'I will always, as long as I can, always,' True whispers to him. As she comes, she imagines the sight of soot-streaked walls, a dream of flickering copper light, a gleam of teeth. Hank is somehow crouched, his feet planted flat, half standing, as he tugs her, hips first, along with him. The moan sings in her skull, in her spine.

For the first time in her life, True falls asleep after sex. When she wakens, the room is so dark she cannot see Hank or her own hand.

'I have to eat,' she says, 'but I can't leave this room. I can't put on my shoes.'

Hank cajoles the innkeeper to let him bring up dinner on a tray. True eats as if she has never seen food, bread and salad and some kind of stew heavy with parsley and mushrooms. Hank has asked the wife of the couple for tampons, which endears him to True more than the satisfaction of the dinner. How many men would ask?

'So this wedding,' she finally says, 'when were you thinking it might take place?' True imagines fall, a luxurious warm and golden Cape autumn. In her yard, like Esa's wedding, for luck.

'What's today?' Hank asks, gazing out of the window.

'It's . . . it's Monday.'

117

'Okay, then how about Thursday? Thursday was always my lucky day. My dad worked late and my mom and I sat up and ate pretzels with mustard and watched *Bewitched*.'

True sits up on the bed, where she has lain down, feeling sated in every muscle. 'Thursday when?'

'Thursday, two days from today.'

'What?'

'Why did you think I asked you to bring your passport? Did you really think I wanted to visit Canada?'

'What? Now?'

'Now. Before I change my mind.'

'If you're going to change your mind, we'd better forget it altogether.'

'No, not because I'm going to change my mind. Because we love each other now. And we could love each other in three months, or a year, but time is only more time, and besides, I can't find anyplace to live.'

'You want me for my house.'

'I want you for your son, actually. I have a feeling about Guy.'

'A feeling?'

'That there's still time left for him, to take me . . . to take me as his father. If he were only a little older, I couldn't be sure.'

Guy, True thinks. Oh, Guy. She has not thought of her son, out somewhere on some plain she has never seen, birthing cows, falling from horses, stepping on rattlesnakes. 'I couldn't possibly marry you or anyone without telling my son,' True says. 'Losing his father so young, he depends on me in a way you probably can't understand.'

'I understand. But I have a notion that if you ask him, he'll talk you out of it. He's used to having you all to himself.'

'He is.'

'And it's not good for him.'

'It's not bad for him.'

'But this will be better.'

'How can you be so sure?'

'I can't. I'm acting on instinct. I know he needs a father, though. Anyone could see that.'

It is this, True decides before she falls asleep, Hank curled with his spine just touching hers, that she will give people as the reason, when they gasp.

She phones Guy in the morning, at his grandparents' house. She and Hank have concocted what they think is an elegant scheme. They will marry, here and now, in New Hampshire; but arrange a tiny church ceremony for the Saturday when Guy comes home. Being in on it, a part of it, Guy will not feel so disenfranchised, they reason. Before the telephone even begins its long-distance *brrrrr*, True has already decided that she will not even tell Guy about this premarriage marriage, that she simply will raise the subject of an upcoming marriage. She loves her boy far too much to betray him, and this feels, any way she turns it, like a betrayal. It feels like a cheap trick.

Her former mother-in-law answers, 'True! Good gracious! How are you? Your boy just tried to call you, before he went out fishing.'

'Hello, Mary Ellen,' True says cordially. 'Can you find him? I really need to talk to him. Are you and Pete well?'

'Dandy as can be, at our age,' It never fails to shock True that Mary Ellen, whose child is dead, can always manage to sound so casual. If it had been Guy who had died, True would have opted for a persistent vegetative state, if not something permanent, involving barbiturates. 'You know our Dennis made us grandparents again a few months back.'

'I do. Congratulations.'

'Well, how about if I have Guy call you when he gets home? It could be night. Let's see, that's . . . five-oh-eight . . .'

'No, I'm in New Hampshire, Mary Ellen. I'll call him later, myself. Okay? Can you make sure he's home around five?'

'Well, when Grandad and he get fishing, specially considering he's only got a day or so left.' Mary Ellen says, 'I'll do my best.' She clears her throat. 'I want you to know, True. You have done a fine job raising Guy. Peter Junior would be very proud.'

'Thank you, Mary Ellen,' True says, thinking, You will think this for about the next half hour. She tries again. He's still not home. True cannot shake the guilt she feels, which is like an ink stain on something as white as a cirrus cloud.

She attempts another call again later Tuesday, but it is Wednesday afternoon when True finally reaches her son.

'Whatcha doing, Teddy, uh, dude?' she asks.

'Teddy dude?' Guy's belly laugh crushes her heart. She can feel his outsized little hand, his fingers entwined in hers, their game of bumping shoulders and hips when they walk down the street.

119

'Momeeeeee!' Guy whispers, lowering his voice, 'I miss you so much!'

'I miss you more!'

'I miss you more!'

'But you're having fun?'

'Big-time. I'm going fishing today and camping out tonight! Are you having any fun?'

'Kind of! I got to climb Mount Washington and I really hurt my feet!'

'Who's with you?'

'Hank,' True says.

'Hank, the dancing restaurant guy?'

'Yes, Hank the dancing restaurant guy,' True smiles at Hank bravely, as he runs a finger under his collar. All clichés are realized, she thinks. Hank feels tight under the collar.

'Did he go climbing with you?'

'He sure did!'

'Did he get hurt feet?'

'No, he had the right boots. I had some crummy old boots! Crummy new boots.'

'Well, I'm glad you're not just sitting around crying . . .'

'No, in fact, guess what? When you get home, I got a kind of a surprise for you.'

'A dog?' Guy cries.

'No, not a dog. Better. Way.'

'A horse?'

'No, I have a surprise, it's sort of an idea . . .'

'Are they doing *Oliver!*?'

'I'll tell you when you get home.'

'Now.'

'I *can't* now.'

'Is it a secret?'

'Yeah,' True whispers. 'It's our secret. But I wanted to hear your voice and tell you that I had a surprise for you when you got home.'

'Okay,' Guy says. 'Not very long now. 'Member when I used to say "only one more sleep 'til you're home," when you had to go on a business trip?'

'I remember,' True says. 'You used to say that, duh, about six months ago.'

'It seems longer,' Guy says.

It certainly does.

'I love you more than anything in the world,' True tells him.

'Me, too,' Guy says. 'Bye, Mom. Don't get so missing me now.'

'Okay,' True says. 'I'll try.'

She closes the telephone and hands it to Hank.

'You didn't tell him.' Hank is stupefied.

'No, and I'm not.'

'You mean, you're not going to tell him now, like we talked about?'

'I mean I'm not doing it.'

'Not . . . doing it?'

'Not doing it now. Without sitting down with him and telling him. I won't. I can't. I won't break trust with him. It's cheesy.'

Hank looks past her, at the mountaintop. 'You're going to say no if he doesn't want you to.'

'Sweetheart, my Hank, don't think that,' True tells him, enfolding his arm, holding his hand against her cheek. 'It's just that the love of a mother for a child, you don't know it. You don't feel it. Yet. I could never hurt him that way.'

'Why do you assume it will hurt him?' Hank leans forward, turning her bodily toward him. 'Why do you assume that something you want so much, and that will be right for him, too, will hurt him? Just because it's soon? Just because it's me?'

'Not that,' True says. 'He's never had to share me. He's never had to wonder whether anyone in my life came before him. He's thousands of miles away. He'll feel as though I'm sneaking around behind his back.'

'*Bébé*, you're the parent,' Hank insists. '*You're* the parent. The only reason I can think of you wouldn't tell him is that either you're ashamed for your former in-laws to know you're getting married, or you think I'm not good enough for your son.'

'No,' True objects, thinking, he's right. He sees. I am in doubt. If I am in doubt, I will lose him as sure as the moon rises. So, as much in panic as in sturdy insistence, she says stoutly, 'I don't think either of those things. It's just too soon.'

'What would be creepy,' Hank suggests, 'would be *not* to tell him, not to give him any warning at all, and then spring it on him at the airport or the next day. You're not giving him much credit.'

121

'What are you afraid of if we don't do it right now?' True challenges him suddenly, nearly angrily. 'That I'll back out? Or that you'll back out?'

'Do you really want me to tell you?' Hank's hands tighten into fists.

'I do.'

'I'm afraid you're so used to doing what everyone else wants you to do that someone will get to you and convince you I'm a gold-digging piece of shit, and though you won't really believe that, you'll think enough other people will that you'll chicken out of it altogether and want to see me on the sly until someone more suitable comes along.'

True gasps. 'I'm not that shallow. I'm not an idiot.'

'Well, then we have to tell Guy. And you have to give value to the fact that I planned this, as the most romantic gesture of my life, and it hurts the hell out of me that you'd gut it like this.'

'But how, Hank, how will I . . . ?'

'We'll make it up to him. We'll make him the best man at our wedding. Our *real* wedding. And we'll go on our honeymoon, all three of us, after Christmas, maybe to that place in Florida where they let you swim with the dolphins . . .'

'Did I tell you about that?'

'What?'

'That the dolphin place was where I'd planned to take him this week, before it turned out to be Isabelle's wedding, and before his grandparents asked him to come? And that we were going to do Disney afterward?'

'No.'

'Mmmmmmmm,' True bites her lip. 'Did Esa tell you?'

'No. I just thought it would thrill a kid. It would thrill *me*, to tell you the truth. We'll do the whole thing, Disney World . . .'

'He's never been.'

'Well, True, he's only ten. He's not too big for it.'

'I don't believe in signs and stuff.'

'Neither do I,' Hank tells her. 'What do you mean?'

EARLY THURSDAY MORNING, before they enter the church in Norris, New Hampshire, for the appointment they made by telephone, True says, 'I'll call him now.'

'Suits me,' says Hank, though he looks panicked. 'I'll talk to him, too.'

'No, I'll just talk to him this time,' True says, thinking, fat chance Guy talks to me at all, steeped as he is in the past of his real father, surrounded by what she imagines will be her in-laws' faces aghast, their stilted attempts to try to explain why adults sometimes do surprising things, all the while unable to disguise their loathing. She tries once, and gets an answering machine.

They phone a quick excuse for a half hour's lateness to the amiable Episcopal priest, buy coffee, and True tries again. Her mother-in-law answers. Needles of nerve course along True's neck. 'Guy is being just as good as he can be. I don't know if he's come inside twice since he's been here . . . we've had such good weather, a real spring . . .' Mary Ellen natters.

'Well, I'm on this cell phone, Mary Ellen, so please, let me have him before I lose the line,' True says. 'I'm with a friend of mine. The connection could go out any minute. I'd love to talk more, but can I speak to Guy?'

'Well, of course, True, he's right here.'

'Hi honey,' True says.

'Hi honey,' Guy answers saucily.

''Member that surprise?'

'Yup.'

'Well, I'm about to tell you.'

'That's good, because I was going to have to tell you off when I got home, because you said we never do that to each other.'

'You mean, not tell,' True agrees.

'Right,' Guy says. 'Okay, Mommy, I'm ready.'

True feels a horrible spike of pity and regret. Oh, my baby, my boy, she thinks. Out playing in the wide Montana sunshine, unsuspecting of his mother who cares so much for herself she will shuck off the only life they have known, behind his back . . . Oh, this is wicked wrong.

'Hank's here,' True begins.

'Are you going to let him hear?' Guy asks conspiratorially.

'Yes. He's in on it.'

'He is?'

'Yep. Yep, he is,' says True and breathes deeply. 'Because we are going to get married.'

123

'We are?' Guy asks reflexively.

'Yes.'

'To who?'

'To Hank.'

'Mommy! You don't even know him and plus he's too young to be a dad and he's probably irresponsible and only wants you for your money.' True imagines Mary Ellen's sharp ears. She also imagines, with relish, stomping on the delicate arch of her own mother, whom she suspects Guy is parroting.

'No, he doesn't, smartie,' True controls her voice. 'He wants Mommy for all the good reasons. And I love him. I don't know how! I just fell in love with him. And he says he really wants a boy to grow up with . . .'

'That means me? Or a baby of his own?'

'That means you, Guy. He wants . . .'

'Is this going to be before I'm twelve?'

'Yes,' True says.

'Before I'm eleven?'

'Yes,' True says.

'Well, when is it?'

'We were thinking Saturday,' True whispers.

Either the phone gives out at this moment, or Guy hangs up.

Mary Ellen answers when True dials back. 'He's gone outside,' she says in the cut-glass tone True remembers from her courtship with Pete. 'I'll fetch him.'

Guy is silent. True can only hear him breathing.

'Well, listen, Bugdust, did you hang up on me? I forgive you. And I sure love you. Guy?'

'What can I do for you?' Guy asks. He could be a CPA.

'You usually say, "I love ya more!"'

'Well, obviously I love you more than you love me. I didn't do this crappy idea.'

'Guy!'

'Well, you did!'

'You'll be home in two sleeps. I miss you. Granny misses you. Hank misses you.'

'Right,' Guy says. 'I'm so sure.'

True hands the telephone, which is hot with the extensive conversation or the pressure of her hand, to Hank.

124

Hank says, 'Guy, look, I don't expect you to take all this in overnight. But at least give me a chance, right? Nobody thought you could do the Dwarf role because you were too young. Your mom told me. Everyone said, he couldn't do it. But you got a tryout, didn't you?' He waits while Guy evidently gives a reply. 'Well, that's all I'm asking for. A tryout. Then we'll take it one day at a time.' Silence. 'Yes, I do. I said that. You were a big part of it. Why would I lie? What's in it for me?' Silence, waiting. 'I don't want her money. I have my own money. Listen, Gee, why would I lie to you? Why would I lie to someone I'm going to know my whole life?' Silence. 'Okay. I thank you for that.' Hank closes the phone and gives True a watery smile.

'He's going to wait and see,' Hank explains.

'Well,' True answers, her lips clamped in sympathy, 'I'm proud of him. If he were afraid of losing my love over you, he'd have lied and said he was happy.'

LATER THAT MORNING, for her wedding, True wears a white satin shirt and velvet pants they found at a secondhand store, and rubber garden clogs, size ten, the only shoes into which she can force her swollen size-eight feet.

When asked whether she, True Dickinson, will take this man, Henry Bannister, to be her wedded husband, she finds herself unreservedly, despite all, willing. The black-and-white portrait by a local photographer that arrives two days later shows True looking utterly soft and imperious – she suspects retouching – reclined against Hank's shoulder, her white shirt draped as if she'd intended one shoulder's fabric to droop low over her breast, while the expression on his face reminds her of looks she has seen on men who have won the biathlon or brought down vicious beasts on safari. He looks proud, possessive.

This picture will always please her.

Outside the church, True finds that she cannot stop hiccuping. Hank finally has to stop and buy a ginger ale. He teaches her to lean over and drink from the can both upside-down and backwards, ten sips. Works like magic. Then she asks for his cell phone. 'I have to call Guy,' she says. 'I have to. He'd never forgive me. And this way, he'll have a little while to adjust. You know he hung up on me before.' Hank nods in reply. 'Well, I could hardly expect him to do

125

anything else,' True murmurs. 'In fact, just hanging up on me was actually pretty reasonable. I mean, we're . . . strangers.'

'*We're* not strangers,' Hank objects.

'To him we are. To anyone else, we would be. We just have a hunch.'

'Well, like I said to Guy . . .'

'Yeah, but it's too late for a tryout. You already got the part. It's opening night. What is your middle name?' True whispers.

'It is Rogan. Henry Rogan Bannister. My mother's maiden name.'

'What do you like to eat for breakfast?'

'Hamburgers. Leftover pizza. Apples. Always apples. And muesli. You know that.'

'What sport did you play in middle school? What street did you grow up on? Did you call your folks? When I was asleep? What's your father's name again?'

'Gus. He used to tell us Gus was short for Henry. Or for "Henri." He always hated the name. I played basketball, but I was too short. I was on the track team, and I was really fast, but I broke my ankle.'

'What does he do?'

'Who?'

'Your dad.'

'He's a surgeon.'

'A . . . surgeon?' True slaps herself mentally. What had she expected? That Hank's father fished in a shrimp boat? That *is* what she has expected. She has thought, and it has been her comfort, that Hank is marrying up, because she should get some tribute for what she sees as their unequal complement of physical gifts. Actually, she is the one who is marrying up, ancestrally at least. And in what the world might call every other way. She has snagged a big bass; people will compliment her.

My land, she thinks, people will compliment her.

Okay, well. She can do that.

They are quiet for an hour, then, holding hands, awed by the enormity of their act.

'Do you think . . . you've never been married before, the dailiness of it . . . you'll be bored,' True ventures, as they cross the state line.

'How could I be bored?'

'And I'm *older*. Older. Get it? Have you thought about how you'll

126

feel when I'm fifty and you're forty? When you're a young man by anyone's definition and I'm on the cool side of middle age, a younger old woman?'

'I know I've never met a woman I thought I would never be bored with, for all my life.'

'Not for lack of trying.'

'I'll admit to that. I searched. I fell in love for a week in Galveston. I fell in love for a month in Boston. And a woman in France. I saw a woman from around here on and off for six years, until she moved to Boston, because there was so much about her I loved . . .'

'Who was that?'

'It doesn't matter.'

'I still want to know.'

'She wasn't you. She didn't keep me guessing all the time. She didn't make me admire her every day, that she could run a business and raise a child and do a wedding.'

'But don't all men . . . all men, not just you, want the perfect thighs, the thong body . . .'

'I've had that.' True's heart makes the long elevator drop, broken cables springing like snakes. 'That usually comes with a personality as deep as a sunburn. A man, after a while . . . I don't want you to take this the wrong way, but he tires of young women, the makeup, the blunt cut, the French manicure. They're *so* young. That's not perfection . . .'

True abruptly remembers feeling the hot wetness on her leg, the thumping of her feet. She is not perfect. But he is *saying* that physical perfection is not what he wants. He is saying what he wants is distinction in his woman.

He may be dead on the level. He may be one in a million.

Or this may be the biggest ration of bullshit since time began, True thinks. *All* men want the living realization of the Swimsuit Issue. All men. They settle for less, but they don't choose it. She watches men's desperate, glazed eyes in the parking lot at the Pick 'n' Save, as they stride along beside women who are wearing the same capris and horizontal stripes they would have worn forty pounds before, when they were nubile and volatile. She has thought to herself that these men would kill these women if they could, commit murder for supermodels.

But this cannot be. She has so little real experience of men. Her

127

lawyer's wife, Holly Bourse, the mother of Gee's friend Fenn, is easily a size fourteen, and her husband, Addy, dotes on her. Her doctor, Rollie Guinness, is not older than her husband, but she looks older, and the man adores his mate, asking at parties, doesn't his missus look beautiful, isn't she something, particularly since Rollie survived a killer virus the previous year.

'What I mean is, that the curves and the . . . changes,' Hank says, 'it's interesting.'

'Well, you're the only man on earth who thinks so.'

'Then you're lucky you found me.'

'I am lucky. I'm so lucky.'

'True,' he says. 'Do you know how it feels to a man, at least this man, to be loved by an older woman? A beautiful, sexy, alive, older woman? It feels like being a ninth-grader who gets to go to the dance with the queen of the prom. It feels like this woman of experience, this woman of the world, actually wants you.'

'You do? You feel that? I've never heard anything the like of that.'

'And later, I'll be older, too. I worked this out. A woman in the United States outlives her husband by an average of twelve years. So, actuarially, you're the same age as I am.'

This is hopeless. She nods.

'Like a guy I know said once, I'm yours,' she says.

FOR WHAT SHE hopes is the last time in her life, True is boundlessly grateful to drive herself home alone.

She does not want to leave Hank. And yet she would like to pass a wand over him and freeze him in place for a couple of hours, until she can sort out the entire rest of her life.

They kiss chastely across the front seat, in the parking lot of his restaurant. Hank advises True, husband-like, to wash her bloody hiking boots in the machine. He thinks they will come out all right if she puts them in the dryer along with a tennis ball.

'I'm going to put them in the trash, along with the receipt,' True tells him.

'Well, I'll be home later, honey!' Hank says with phony joviality. He is pale. True notices a dusting of freckles on his nose.

'Oh, tonight?' True asks.

'Well, I can't very well stay over on Bobby Lane. It would be just weird, too, True.'

128

'God, it would, wouldn't it? We're married.'

'That's what the paper do say.'

'Well, I'll see you later, then.'

'I'll just bring a . . . a little bag with my shaving stuff and you know, tomorrow . . .'

'Fine, oh fine,' says True. 'If I take the truck, who'll bring you?'

'Tom or one of the servers.'

'Not Lucy.'

'Not Lucy, though she would, you know, True. She's a good friend.'

'I don't think you know women as well as you imagine you do, Mister Bannister. I don't think she's going to react the way you think she will.'

'We shall see, Missus Bannister.'

'Miz Dickinson still. But yes, Missus Bannister, too. Wowie.'

'I love you, *ma chère*.'

'I love you, Hank. I'm not a bit sorry.'

'Neither am I.'

True is not going home, though. She determines that as soon as she pulls out of the parking lot. Her mother, she is certain, will blow an aorta. She prays to the Episcopal God that Franny will be home. As she pulls into Franny's driveway, she sees the ruby crystal lights in Franny's living room, clear as fruit jellies, and nearly sings in jubilation. Franny's husband, who is a builder, and who is in the beginning of the hell of his busy season, will not be home yet, and Angelique would not notice if True and Franny were belly-dancing in the kitchen.

'Help me,' she announces, opening Franny's door. Her friend is at her computer. She lowers her reading glasses on their beaded chain.

'Did you have a good trip?' Franny asks.

'We got married.'

'Well, True,' Franny says seriously, opening her arms to True's collapse into them, 'he's a sweet man, and he's an adorable hunk, and this is one of the three happy endings you said you wanted. And it's true that at our age, we know in, like, fifteen minutes if there's any hope at all.'

'But maybe I've ruined Guy's life.'

Franny goes for the coffee-bean grinder, then switches gears and gets out her brandy glasses.

'He'll probably do okay,' she finally says.

'Okay? Probably? You're supposed to say he'll be fine!' True takes a burning gulp of her brandy.

'He'll be fine, in time,' Franny says. 'What, do you want me to lie to you? It's going to be a shock. What did Guy say?'

'He had nothing to say.'

'Nothing?'

'Nothing besides I changed his whole life behind his back, and I didn't even tell him we were married; I told him we're getting married Saturday, which, if I can talk Father Tierney into it, we are.'

'Well,' says Franny, 'you must be sure. As sure as you can be.'

'I'm sure I love him. I'm not sure I should have married him.'

'Well, dolly, I can say this. You don't really know a person until you're married. Not even if you live together. I remember the first six months I lived with Steve I was afraid to go to sleep because I knew I snored.'

'So you would be embarrassed by a thing like that?'

'No doubt!'

'So I'm not nuts, then? I keep thinking, what if he comes in the bathroom when I'm going? I know couples do that in front of each other, but I couldn't ever. I haven't gone to the bathroom in front of anyone over the age of four since . . . since I *was* four.'

'All that,' Franny adds, 'and there's his parents. He has both parents, right? Well, that's a whole other thing, and if he's the only brother with three sisters, no one's ever going to be good enough . . .'

'Oh, swell, I hadn't even thought of that,' True says. 'Well, pallie, I'm going home.'

'Not to the Chatham Bars Inn? What about the wedding night?'

'We had the honeymoon. Then we got married.'

'Very mod-ren.'

'Why don't you come with me?'

'Where? Your house?'

'Yeah, to tell my mother.'

'You haven't told Kathleen? I'm glad I'm not the one who has to tell her.'

'Thanks! Thanks a big, fat bunch!'

'I love your mother, True – she is a genuine original. But she is a little strict about some things . . .'

'A little strict! She'll try for an involuntary commitment to Martingale.'

'I think you underestimate her, True. She could very easily have married again herself. She still could.'

'Oh Franny, and the sun will rise in the west tomorrow! At least then let me stay here overnight. No, I can't. I have to go. If Hank gets there before I do . . .'

'Actually, that would be rich!'

'Thanks, Franny. I'm glad my fear perked up your evening!'

True hugs her friend, leaning on her and quaking with absurd and jittery giggles, and promises to call tomorrow. She drives home and, with exquisite care, parks the old truck in her driveway.

Kathleen is bustling about the kitchen, clearing up small paper plates and plastic drink cups. True spots a lime, neatly sliced in eighths, on the sideboard. 'Been playing bridge, have you, Mom?'

'Gin,' says Kathleen. 'I have the most wonderful news!'

This is not in the script.

But perhaps Kathleen *is* going to remarry. Fly to Wisconsin for apple-blossom time. True would pay for her one-way ticket, first class.

'Well,' says True, 'I've got news, too. What's yours?'

'Okay,' says Kathleen with a conspiratorial smile. 'I personally convinced the business manager at *Today's Child* to include the blow-in cards for Twelve Times Blessed.'

'Mother! That's wonderful.'

'They have a million subscribers, True.'

'It's going to cost us.'

'Yes, but think of the demographic spread.'

'Listen to you!'

'Well, I didn't just lick this off the grass, True.'

'*Today's Child* shows clothes that are kind of young-mother stuff. That's not our primary market.'

A mere five years ago, Kathleen hadn't known any more about marketing than she knew about slicing prosciutto in a deli. Now she bubbles, 'Oh, but they do grandmother articles, too. And how-tos. Very extensive. Appliqued things. I think we're going to get some very interesting bounce.' True could scream with joy if she weren't on the verge of a meltdown. She feels a surge of admiration for her mother. It is precisely the wrong time for this.

131

'Do you think we'll be overwhelmed? You know, I have this fear – the J. Peterman disease. Using last season's revenue to buy this season's stock. Pretty soon, you're building a store in Grand Central Station.'

'I think we can handle a little expansion. I discussed the financial picture with Jeanine at the bank. And had a talk with Rudy. By the way, the new woman called in sick the second day on the job. And True, it was rather sinister. Something about her brain hurting. I don't think she's going to be able to fill Esa's shoes.'

'Mmmmm. Well, she's not the only fish in the aquarium. So Mom,' True begins, 'I noticed you and Mister Merton occupied the same quarters on Esa's wedding night? Any footsie going on there?'

'True Dickinson,' says Kathleen, stopping dead with a half-filled Hefty bag in one hand. 'I would no more . . . that man has got to be twenty years younger than I am. We did talk quite late. He's had a very interesting life. This Mickey was apparently quite a handful. Left him and Isabelle several times, with Kellen's . . .'

'It's Kellen, is it?'

'With Kellen's mother the only one to help, before she finally settled on this Hob. Seems they were very young. Flower children, you might say.'

'Isabelle's lucky she didn't end up getting named Sunlight or Tulip.'

'Indeed. So what's your news?' Kathleen asks.

True literally girds her loins, which are not only cramped but a trifle tender. 'Remember when we hiked up Pikes Peak, Mom?'

'Yes.'

'And I got my period . . .'

'I remember the incident.'

'Well, that happened to me on Mount Washington. Plus, my new boots totally ruined my feet. I'm going to have to wear the moose slippers Guy gave me for Christmas for a week.'

'He called.'

'What did he say? I talked to him a couple of hours ago.'

'He said that he was having fun. Sounded a little homesick, though, didn't you think? That's to be expected.'

'Mom, I want to tell you. Hank's going to spend the night here tonight.'

Kathleen misses not one half a beat. 'Well, that's none of my business, True. Ellen and Mary did ask, tonight, a little bit, whether you and this boy were actually seeing each other. Of course, I said nothing about it.' True nods sagely. 'I hope you understand what you'd be getting into, being involved with a man so much younger than you, and with such a disparity of income . . .'

'Mom, That One Place is very successful.'

Kathleen sniffs, 'I suppose I should go there. Given your involvement. But the food is very, very spicy. Very outlandish. I think it might be hard on Ellen's stomach. You know, last year, she was this close to having a perforated ulcer. But Mary was there last week . . .'

'Well, he'll be spending the night here, at this house, quite regularly.'

'I thought,' Kathleen says, setting down her Hefty bag and pulling out a kitchen chair, 'that you had strong feelings about exposing Guy to that sort of thing. Not that I question your need for a personal life. I did not experience those same needs myself – being married to Bert Dickinson was quite enough fulfillment for my own personal life, and women didn't leap in and out of bed . . .'

'I've hardly leapt in and out of bed . . .'

'I'm not suggesting you have, but the effect on Guy of an unmarried man . . .'

'He's not an unmarried man.'

'He . . . is not an unmarried man?' Kathleen asks. She stops, looks down at her splayed hands for a moment, and then looks up at True. 'I was thinking of a nightcap.'

'I would like one, too, actually,' True sighs. 'You better make yours a double.'

Kathleen skillfully makes the drinks. True figures she will be sloshed by the time Hank arrives, and that this is probably just as well. The two women sit down, facing each other across True's handmade cherry table.

'So he's married,' Kathleen says. 'That's a nice kettle of fish. Is he at least separated? Is she in town? Or wherever he hails from? Alabama?'

'He's married to me, Mom.'

Kathleen is speechless.

'We got married yesterday, in New Hampshire.'

'Can that possibly be legal? Isn't there a . . . waiting period?'

'No. I'm forty-three years old, Mom. I didn't need a consent form.

133

I have in my bag, along with my bloody rotten climbing boots – in which I hurt my feet horribly – a signed and perfectly legal marriage license. And, come Saturday, if I can work it out, we'll get married again, in the rectory, by Father Tierney. Hank's folks will be mad. They call the Episcopal Catholic Lite.' Kathleen sniffs and waves a hand, as if an insect has taunted her.

'I suppose you will expect me to move out,' she says then.

'Move out? Of your house?'

'Well, I'll expect you'll want your . . . own privacy.'

'Are you intending on sleeping with us?'

'True!' Kathleen rises as if to dump out her drink.

'Sit down, Mom, I would never expect you to move out.'

'And what about this . . . what about Hank?' She says his name as though she is holding something away from her that has been kept too long in Tupperware on a refrigerator shelf. 'And Guy?'

'Well, we figured we'd get rid of Guy. Send him to boarding school in Switzerland right away. Mom! Don't be silly! How can you ask such a thing? Nothing will change, except I fell in love and got married. A little hastily perhaps . . .'

'You can say that again.' Kathleen is becoming quite the slinger of slang, True thinks, which reminds her she is slightly tipsy.

'Okay. A little hastily. But I feel it was the right moment. He planned it, and asked me beautifully.' True holds out her hand, with the ring still on her thumb. 'He made this ring. For me.'

'How nice.'

'Well, now your part is to say, my dear daughter, I hope you will enjoy every happiness.'

'I hope that, of course. I hope this will end better than the last time.'

'That's a whopping endorsement. Mom, that's not fair.'

'I suppose you think this will all be easy?'

'No, I think it will be terribly hard, and I'm scared to death. And I also hope you'll do everything you can to help me not feel so scared to death. I mean, you told me all my life about how you and Daddy had the perfect marriage. And I didn't. With Peter I didn't,' True continues, over the beginnings of a protest forming on her mother's face, 'you know I didn't. Oh, on some level, you knew I didn't. I want my chance, Mom. I want to have fun, and love someone, and give Guy a daddy.'

'I'm going to bed,' Kathleen says abruptly. She gets up, then turns back to face True. 'Do you mind if I sleep in the spare room? It's blowing out there. My bones are chilled.' True suspects the liquor is more the cause, and considers offering to walk her mother across the yard, but realizes even before she speaks that this will kick up a whole new dust storm. However, the fact is, True does mind, mightily. And she thinks Kathleen's request verges on vengeful, if not downright bizarre. It will be awkward enough, Hank's first night in her home. In *their* home. But she says, 'No, of course, that's fine.'

TRUE HAS FALLEN asleep on the couch when she hears someone knocking softly at the front door. Hank is standing on the porch, with his duffle bag, looking sheepish. 'Hi, honey, I'm home,' he says. They both giggle weakly.

'My mom's upstairs, asleep.'

'She's here? Why in the hell?'

'I think to make me feel uncomfortable. I think she is taking a tiny revenge.'

'For what? How did she take it?'

'She was a little surprised. I think most people will be a little surprised, Hank. And maybe she's jealous. Not of my being married, but of my not being all hers now.' True leans her head against his chest, and breathes deeply. He smells of smoke from the bar, and Parmesan cheese.

'Well, my feeling is, there are about five people, your mom included, who absolutely have to approve of this. And as for the rest, well, joke 'em if they can't take a fuck.'

'It was probably best we just did it, rather than wait. People would have had a chance to talk, and talk us out of it.'

'And now, they can't say anything. We've stuffed their words back into their mouths, you see?'

'I guess.'

'I called my mother.'

'How was she?'

'Well, she said it was high time. People were fixing to think I was gay.'

'Come on. You're thirty-three.'

'We marry young back home, and me being a dance major and

135

all. And so many girlfriends, none of them really took. She's not the first one to have had the notion.'

'Well, I can sign an affidavit.'

'You more than anyone.

'She said, welcome to the Bannisters. The few, the odd, the Bannisters. They can't wait to meet you. In fact, they're threatening to all come up here next week.'

'Oh, dear. It's just . . . the wedding, then our wedding . . . I'm sort of overwhelmed. I want to lose twenty pounds and have my face sanded and redecorate the house first.'

'Good. It's nicer here later on, and we'll have the fall gift things done that I know you're worried about all ready. Maybe Thanksgiving.' He does not say, *Darling, you don't need to have your face sanded. He does say 'we' about True's business.*

'Your mom thought I was the local gigolo, huh?'

'Why do you say that?'

'Hunch.' They are going up the stairs to True's room. She is imagining sweeping away one side of her hell of cosmetics from the double sinks, so Hank can have a place. She is also imagining what to hide. Her sleeping pills. The progesterone cream she rubs into her belly. The Rabbit Pearl, still in its pristine box. The Rabbit Pearl is going into the Dumpster. Until then, she is glad her office has a safe. She is having conniptions over photos of her pregnancy, of her senior prom. 'Your mom will get on fine with me, True. Trust me. Never met a woman I couldn't charm.'

'Well, you may have your work cut out for you. Kathleen's about as earthy as the Queen Mother. And she's worried about Guy.'

'You'll see. My mom said to give you a big, smacky kiss.' He does. 'And tell you that you have a true Bannister name. You could almost be a Southerner, with a name like that. And now, I have to sleep, True. I'm not a trooper like you. I can't get married, cook for sixty, and do the tango all in one day.'

They shower, one at a time, in turn, door ajar between them. True puts on her only pajamas, striped flannels, with cotton underwear beneath. Hank puts on sweatpants and a T-shirt. 'You don't mind,' he asks, 'if I'm not naked with you?'

'Do most people mind?'

'Actually, yes . . . I've gotten in a lot of trouble for not staying naked, and for not wanting, well, not being able to sleep with my

136

arms around the woman, speaking of which, do you manage to work other women into every conversation? It's like you think I've been the playboy of the western world.'

'You have, a little. But you're right. Why do I do that?'

'I'm not mad at you for it. For asking. But it doesn't become you.'

The sting finds its mark.

'What doesn't?'

'The insecurity thing.'

'Well, I . . . ,' True thinks she may cry, 'I'm not insecure. I'm curious, is all.'

'Sweetie, if you think I've had my share of adventures, you have no idea. You should meet my friend Perry. Well, like it or not, I sleep in pajamas. And I do snore.'

'I have no idea if I snore. I haven't slept with anyone long enough to have them complain. I don't have dentures, though.'

'That's good. I like a woman with teeth. If you snore, I won't mind. It'll be like having my dog, Sully, around again. I miss that dog.'

'Teeth. The better to bite you with, my dear.'

'Been bitten before. Survived.' True falls silent. Hank rolls her over onto his stomach. 'Does that hurt you, too? Come on, sweetheart. You've never scratched a man with your nails? In a passion?'

'No.'

'Well, I'll have to get you to scratch me then. I'll have to make you scream. Maybe not tonight. Maybe not with your mom next door. Now, see, I can understand that face. You don't like to think about a woman biting your new husband, y'know? It's like finding condoms in his shaving kit . . .' The instant regret on Hank's face tells her there *are* condoms in his shaving kit.

True sits up and puts her hands over her face. 'It's just hard to get used to. It's been so sudden, the time between when you were . . . free to do whatever and when you were . . . well, mine.'

'Look, True. Want to get it all over with right now? I've never had sex with a man. I've never had sex with two women, but I've come close, on two occasions, no, on three occasions. I've had anal sex, once; it was awful, and it was my idea, and the girl was so furious afterward she offered to shove a cucumber up my butt. That's it.'

137

'Okay.'

'Wanna compare score cards?'

'No cucumbers on mine, alas.'

'Okay, then. Now, let's get back to real life. Think we should get Guy a dog? I think we should get him a dog, as a coming-home present. I never gave him a birthday present.'

'One world at a time, Hank.'

'Who said that?'

'Saint Augustine.'

'This is one hell of a house. True, God. I never imagined living in a house like this,' Hank says. 'It's a mansion.'

'Well, your house must have been nice.'

'It was nice, but my daddy was always running off to cure kids' brains or guts in Guatemala or something, so he wasn't the richest doctor. And it was all on one floor, like all tropic-type houses.'

'Well, *mi casa es su casa*, as they say,' True says sleepily. Through the wall, True hears her mother cough. She wonders if it is a warning. No headboard banging tonight. Like children lost in the woods, Hank and True hold hands and fall asleep. Dreams of dogs and little boys running dance like a shadow border along the crown molding of the ceiling.

ON THE DAY before Guy is due home, True and Hank drive to Boston to visit Addley James Bourse III, True's lawyer since Peter died, and the husband of her neighbor, Holly. Addley has directed True to the right investment firm, helped her form a corporation, and establish Dog's guardianship of Guy. Now, this will need to change. She wants to make wills, feeling an urgency she can't quite name. She wants to feel ordinary, to put her affairs in order, give this union weight. Word is spreading through town. Franny says she has become something of an information clearinghouse for people afraid to call True and ask whether the rumor is fact. True has finally agreed to take the picture and put an announcement in the *Herald*.

Franny has made an announcement, too. She will host a reception, at True's house, in May. 'Mine's too small. And we're calling it a celebration, not a reception, *but* we are not adding "Please, no presents." I like presents,' Franny instructs True.

True would not dream of bickering. She also likes presents. And she suspects that, although she has a blender and a nest of mixing bowls, enough wine glasses and, courtesy of her grandmother, enough napkin rings and salad forks to last several lifetimes, her friends will think of charming things to bring, and many guests will show up only to be able to say they saw the man True Dickinson married. She is considering renting a karaoke machine.

At the offices of Bourse, Bentley and Lynn, Addley offers them tea and apologizes that he hasn't had the foresight to purchase champagne. 'Our True is full of surprises,' says Addley, which, until True met all six-feet-five inches of his squash-playing self, she had considered a silly name for a man. 'Starting her own business, taking herself a . . . husband.'

True knows Addley has stopped just short of saying 'a bride,' and she knows Hank hears it, too. Well. They had better get used to it. In Oriental tradition, a spicy rumor lasts eighty days. And so they are in for it. Addley's comment is just the first of many they will receive. True and Hank grin at each other.

'Well,' says Addley, 'we have business before us. It's too late for a prenuptial agreement, so what we need to make is a marital property agreement, before we get to wills. That means what will happen to the assets each of you brings to the marriage now, what will happen in the event of the death of one of the partners, what will happen if the marriage ends, and so on.'

'We didn't think of doing anything like that,' True says. 'We're married. That means what's mine is his and what's his is mine.'

'Right, of course,' Addley agrees. 'But we're not describing a marriage in which both partners are in their early twenties and they're starting out together with just beans, and planning to have children together . . .'

'That's the kind of marriage we want,' True says. 'Right, Hank?'

'I think he's talking about the disparity in our income,' Hank says softly, 'and protecting your assets for Guy.'

'Exactly,' says Addley.

'But you would do that,' True says.

'Of course I would,' Hank says. 'But he means, what if we divorce, and I've lost my business, and worst case, you've died and I want to use up all the money you've earmarked for Guy . . .'

'You wouldn't do that,' True says.

'You two have discussed this?' Addley asks.

'Not really,' True admits.

'I'm going to leave the room for a little while, then, and give you a chance to work this out, and then we'll proceed,' Addley says.

They sit alone with their bottles of SoBe Tea, and regard each other guardedly. Finally, Hank clears his throat. 'I don't mind having an agreement like that, True. After all, we don't really know each other. I could have been a bank robber and you wouldn't know it.'

'Were you a bank robber?'

'No.'

'What's the worst thing you've ever done?'

'You want me to tell you this now?'

'Does it spring to mind?'

'Well, it's pretty bad.'

'I'm ready.' He's molested his sister, True thinks. They can get an annulment.

'When I was a teenager' – True's stomach clenches – 'I found a wallet in a washroom at a gas station. It had to be some other poor kid's wallet. I took all the cash and left the wallet in the sink.'

'And?'

'And that's it. What do you mean?'

'That's the worst?'

'Yeah. I still dream about it. It was like, a hundred dollars in singles, you know? Probably all he had. And I looked right at his face on his driver's license and I did it anyway. What's the worst thing you ever did?'

'Well, once I decided to be a novelist. I wrote like, fifty lousy pages of this story about a girl with some name so stupid, like Lydia Lincoln . . .'

'Or True Dickinson . . .'

'Right. And my brother, my dear brother, once when we were home on break, he decided to give me a surprise by cleaning out and washing my car. It was around my birthday. He threw out the pages, which I had stuffed under my car seat. And I . . .'

'What?'

'I slugged him.'

'And?'

'I hit my brother! Hard. For nothing.'

'That's it?'

'That's bad enough. And I also once told him a blouse he gave

140

me for Christmas came from a cheap store. I still think about that. I'm going to write to him about it one day.'

'Well, okay, we've never done jail time,' Hank says, then adds, 'Do you have a lot of money?'

'Not for around here.'

'Well. Counting my share of the restaurant, and some teeny investments, my net worth is about seventy thousand.'

'That's not hay, Hank. That's pretty good, given you've knocked around a lot.'

'And been an ass. Given away great bikes I built because I wanted to leave town and didn't want to bother selling them . . .'

'I have about . . . two point five,' True says then.

'Million?'

'Counting the house and the business. Maybe a little less.'

'That's what he means then. You have almost three million dollars?'

'Believe me, you could throw a stone out that window and hit ten people with twenty times that much . . .'

'No wonder your mother thinks . . .' Hank is nearly speechless.

'But I don't. I thought we would have this ordinary marriage, where we share everything . . . And have one checking account . . .'

'Except Tom and I have a business account,' Hank reminds True.

'And I do, too, of course. And I have money in trust for Guy's college, and, though I guess we haven't really talked this out either, Hank, I didn't think we were going to necessarily prevent having more kids . . .'

'I'd love a child with you. It's still possible, right?'

'Theoretically. Or we could adopt a baby. I've thought of that.'

'That would be fine.'

'And it's basically an insult, isn't it?'

'The contract? True, I swear on my mother, I don't take it that way. Do anything you want.'

'Well, I thought I would make you my heir, and I would be your heir, just like ordinary married couples. It's not like we're sixty-five and we decided to knock out the walls between our condos at Sun City . . .'

'A lot of people don't get married at all until they're forty.'

'And you want to be Guy's guardian, don't you?'

'If that's what you want.'

141

'Well if you're going to be his father, his stepfather . . . are you going to adopt Guy?'

'Isn't that up to Guy?'

'Yes, I suppose.'

'If that's what he wants, I thought that would be the case more or less anyhow, since he hasn't got another father.'

'No, you'd have to be his legal father,' True murmurs.

'I see. Well, that's fine. I guess. Whew, this is all a lot to take in.'

When Addley returns, Hank has moved to True's side of the table and taken a chair by her side. True sits up straight and says, 'What we want to do is just . . . this is the kind of state where everything is joint property if you're married?'

'Everything that comes after the marriage.'

'But if we just waited and it all got mixed up, eventually everything would be both ours, right? The house and all?'

Addley is quiet. Then he says, 'Yes.'

'Okay, then,' True says. 'Draw up the papers. We want everything just mixed in and my will changed to Hank as my next of kin and his – do you have a will, Hank?'

'Yes,' he says, 'somewhere. With my mom as beneficiary. It's not much. A little retirement fund. My life insurance.'

'Well, all that, I guess. We'll mail it to you. And then we'll come back.' True looks out the window at the Boston pier, where all the touristy shops and oyster bars sit boarded and still.

Finally, after long moments, Addley says, 'I don't think I'm the one to do this.'

'Why? You do wills, Addley.'

'But I'm primarily a corporate-type guy.'

'You did my will.'

'True, I mean no disrespect here. But I would have to say that I think this irresponsible. You started your business on fifty thousand dollars of insurance money, and it was all you had. You worked like a slave. And though I respect the spirit in which you two come here . . .'

'You don't respect what we want to do.'

'I don't think it's wise, at this point, no. And an attorney is not supposed to be an objective factotum. And even if I were, I'm your neighbor, True. I've seen you struggle. Mister Bannister, trust me. I don't mean any disrespect to you or to True. But perhaps I'm not

142

as detached as I might be if she were not an old family friend . . .'

Ultimately, it takes them four lawyers to find one who will do what they wish. True tries not to care, but a stone forms in her throat when she thinks of all their smooth, concerned faces. They remind her of the undertaker who showed her a $4,000 casket for Peter, explaining that some people want the reassurance of protective covering that 'will last throughout the ages, protecting the remains from the changes that otherwise might intrude on the body of their loved one.'

Finally, they visit a small converted house in Dennis, where they find a gnomish, yet somehow fetching bald lawyer, who has never had a partner, who offers them only water in paper cups from a cooler, but who tells them, 'I have not met personally, but I have heard of, people who have chosen to leave their considerable fortunes to Pomeranians. There is nothing in the legal code of the Commonwealth of Massachusetts that prevents that, though the human siblings of these Pomeranians tend to take considerable offense. I observe that you are not a Pomeranian, Mister Bannister, nor an indigent drifter from Southern California, and Miz Dickinson is not Ivana Trump. And you two seem relatively sane. Though judging people's sanity is certainly not my forte. And though we lawyers consider every document graven in stone, they are not and can be changed if you so desire.'

The wills, over a period of weeks, will be duly prepared, with trusts for Kathleen and Guy and any other children who might be born or adopted by the couple. More than two months will actually pass before they return to the frame house in Dennis to sign the documents. It will be a humid, gusty day, and they will be caught up in the midst of a dumb fight, a dumb fight over a motorcycle. They will have been repeatedly astounded that their providential, predestined, mystically encircled love also has ample room in it for defensive positioning, prideful silences, and nights falling into bed like two pillars of stone, but also for Guy watching reruns of *Andy Griffith* between them in their bed, and learning the merengue in the living room from a tape they bought on impulse through an 800 number.

They will have had sex forty times, not the ninety-nine times they'd expected.

They'll also have spent time with each other's parents and realized

143

they are not biological anomalies but approximate products of them. And though this will shock each of them privately, neither will confide in the other. At the lawyer's office, True will be forced to reflect that she can envision circumstances under which she and Hank might end their marriage, but not circumstances under which she would not want Hank to be Guy's father, Guy having – at last and at length – admitted Hank past the invisible perimeter.

But more important, they will have seen sidelong glances and heard flabbergasted congratulations that will have hardened them into a nation of two. They will have spent nights together huddled over an idea called First Year Away, have begun to call certain behaviors 'going Kathleen,' and found how to unloose the knots in each other's spines, hers at the base, his near the heart.

A New England bard wrote that something there is that does not love a wall; and something, perhaps the same something, in True's Yankee nature is loath to admit a mistake. As for Hank, there has not been a divorce in the Bannister family in two hundred years. So if both of them are humbled, they will still be resolute when they march in together to sign, and will laugh when their lawyer smiles and tells them, 'Your wills come with our guarantee of immortality. Now that your affairs are fully in order, you need feel no obligation whatever to die.'

MAY

MAY WE PLAY?

Scatter the seeds inside our spring blessing, and see Baby's first vegetables spring up by June. Then soften your hands with Blessings Balm, a magical potion that transforms hard-working Mommy hands into velvet gloves. That way, you won't snag what comes next. Baby animals are coming to the world, and to your house. Inside a soft-sculpture barn with a handle are a baby lamb, a chick, a cow (and its Mama, of course!), a foal, and a farmer to take good care of everyone. Every Blessings toy, including the baseball cap with our stars-and-bears logo, is carefully made without detachable parts and with safe dyes, in case anyone wants to do some chewing!

'YOU SHIT BITCH snot!' Guy yells from the top of the stairs, 'I couldn't say that on the phone, but it's what I really think!'

It is the first day of May, and Guy has just arrived home from Montana.

Things have not gone as True and Hank had planned.

True has gone alone to the airport, to pick up Guy, intending to slowly bring up the subject of families, perhaps siblings, the need, since Esa's departure, for more of a family around them, and then why she is doing this, for both of them. Tolerant Father Tierney after asking skeptically, 'A mini wedding? That won't lead to a mini marriage, will it?' has agreed to perform the religious rites at two P.M. on Saturday.

But Guy is pale and closed and silent as a mussel.

True's heart pommels her. She has fifteen miles – four exits – to introduce a Nagasaki moment into a life that has already had, in

145

its one decade, a Hiroshima. It has left its impression, if not its memory. How has she fallen for Hank's blithe assurance that this can be 'made up' to Guy? Or is she simply being overprotective, as she was when Guy was an infant and Pete accused her of following the tot around with a thermometer in the blue-jeans pocket.

She has been hoping Guy will be intrigued by having a man around the house. Now she sees this is as likely as winged monkeys picking up the car and flying them home. Hank, she thinks in sudden alarm, should not even be in the house when she and Guy arrive. He should leave. For a couple of hours, or a week. She has, quite literally, fucked up her perfectly decent existence, the luminous center of which sits strapped in the seat beside her.

Guy is her own, her only, her being, his every word and gesture branded on her identity.

How can she have thought of Hank in the same way, even in the throes of the most dire enchantment? True cannot conceive of having lived without Guy for these few days, which seem to have been extended by circumstance into decades of both their lives. Guy seems to have gained an inch in height and shoulder; he is golden, burnished, like a boy in an advertisement for climbing gear. True wants to devour him. She wants to do all the secret, smothering things mothers do, rearrange a mythical cowlick in his hair as an excuse to expose his brow, drop a kiss as a ruse to check for fever, tweak his shirt to once more observe his navel, the place where they once were joined, in the way the mothers of infants may do without permission. She wants to go back to the way they were before, each other's best pal, each other's image. They will lose this, now.

They would have had to, eventually. But the pangs of this new life throb like a new burn.

She imagines her grandmother's clock ticking at the big house with the wraparound porch on Stage Harbor Lane, where Kathleen and Hank wait in what True imagines must be an unpunctuated silence.

Kathleen can hold a silence like a hound on point.

'Are you sure you don't want to go for a root-beer float before we go home? Just you and me?' True asks.

'That's okay, Mom. Grandma L. says that stuff's not good for a boy,' Guy says, gazing with penetrating interest at things he has seen for his entire life. 'It's all that soda from the office machine that's making me fat. Water. That's what I do now. A gallon of water a day.'

'Oh, good.'

'Well, I put lemon in it.'

'And how are Grandma and Grandpa?'

'Fine. Mom, why are you going so slow? I want to see Granny and Ed.' Ed is Guy's goldfish, who has survived, statistically, years beyond his predictive carnival-lifespan. Guy has trained Ed to follow his finger.

Ed! True thinks. I haven't fed Ed! What if Ed is belly up? But no, please God, her mother will have remembered. Gee will not have to mourn losing his only pet and sole custody of his mother on the same breezy afternoon.

They crunch into the drive. There is a construction-paper basket of flowers on the doorknob, courtesy, True suspects, of Tenny Retton, the little girl two houses down, who makes bead jewelry and says that she wants to work for True when she grows up. Her big brother, Lane, is a summer packer for Twelve Times Blessed.

May Day, True thinks.

Mayday.

'Granny!' Guy bursts in the front door. 'I saw a cow get born! We saw a whole wad of elk in the mountains! I rode Polo the horse without a saddle . . .' He sees Hank at the moment Hank's and True's eyes meet in mutual plea. 'Oh, hi . . . uh . . . I forgot . . .'

Guy is not the only one. Hank seems to have forgotten his name as well. He flaps his hand.

'Mister Bannister,' Kathleen finally says, smiling serenely, gathering Guy into a hug, tugging every curve of his hefty self onto her tiny lap. Not for years has True recalled how she and her brother would bite their toast into the shape of revolvers and point them at their mother behind her back as she nattered at them, 'I pay the same taxes as anyone else for that bus, and I'm not driving you two just because you can't get yourselves out of bed at a decent hour . . .' All this even though she and Dog were both headed the same place as their mother, for Amherst Prep. She cannot imagine why she is reminded of this now. Except that Kathleen (though she is doing absolutely nothing to indicate this) seems so righteous, so poised to pick up the pieces . . . to call this an error in judgment that she understates the situation.

147

The kitchen light is so bright True feels someone is about to have a heart transplant. She steps over to the dimmer and turns it down.

'Well, you know what,' she says smoothly, 'Hank wants you to stand up for him.'

Guy stands up.

True says, 'I mean stand up for him at the wedding. Like you did for Esa.'

'To be my best man,' Hank says softly. 'You can't be the legal one, 'cause you're not old enough. So Tom will have to sign the paper. But I want you to hold the ring.'

'Right.'

'You mean you will?'

'I mean "right" as in "duh." I'm not even sure I want to go.'

'Oh.' Hank asks conversationally, 'Why?'

'Because you decided to marry my own mother without even damn asking me!'

'Hold on, there! I got the impression your mother was grown up! I didn't think she had to ask your leave to do things she thought were good for both of you.'

Guy, tears threatening: 'Only kids do stupid stuff like this. I'm embarrassed of you!'

'Gee, wait,' True pleads, as Guy snatches up his duffle bag and his new fly rod in its case. 'We never meant to hurt you. We were just so much in love we couldn't stand not being married. That's the right way, Gee, you know. I could have gone around like Ronnie and brought guys home . . .'

'I'm still embarrassed of you!' Guy cries. 'Guys don't want to hear how somebody is so much in love with their own mother they want to sex and stuff!' He whirls to head up to his room.

'Lemme see that fly rod first,' Hank interrupts.

Guy glowers, then slowly and carefully unpacks the rod from its case.

'Sure, now this is a beauty,' Hank says. 'I could never fly-fish. Now, my daddy, he can really fish. My uncle tried to show me how. I'd get the damn string all over the trees.'

'Well, that's because you're not supposed to do it under the trees,' Guy says sternly. 'You *stand* in the water and cast under the trees, to the banks.'

'Well, I caught gar on a bamboo pole with a breadball.'

148

True looks at Hank with surprised admiration.

'That's not like trout,' Guy points out.

'No, trout is the prince of fish.'

'My grandpa said that. That exact thing.'

'Your grandpa must be smart.'

'Yes, and he gave me all these pictures of my daddy when my daddy was little. His baby picture looks completely, exactly the same as me. He died when I was two. I have his flight-school hat, and when I'm older, I can have his leather jacket from Embry Riddle. He was a pilot. He was in the war. Were you in the war?'

'No, but my daddy was. He was in the Korean War. He was in the Big Red One. He was a medic. That's the most dangerous thing. He's very brave, my father.'

'So was mine. He was trying to rescue a lady when he died. He got hit by a car, a drunk-driving car.'

'I know. That's something most kids don't ever go through. You must be pretty brave, too,' Hank says.

'Do you want a toasted cheese, Guy?' Kathleen asks, as Hank experimentally whips the rod, testing its tensile strength.

'Okay,' Guy says. 'Hi, Ed, old man.' Ed is still swimming sturdily around his Neptune castle. 'Mom, can I get a horse?' Oh, please heaven, True implores, let him have done the thing kids do – switch gears in the midst of a crisis and get caught up in the ordinary.

'No. Where would we keep a horse, in the garage?'

'How about a dog?'

'I think that's a pretty great idea,' Hank says. 'Wish I had a dog.'

'Bet you wish you had one on you right now,' True says.

'Indeed I do.' Hank takes True's hand. Guy flinches, but seems unruffled, and asks, 'Do you have a dog?'

'My old dog lives with my mama, in Louisiana. She's sixteen years old. Too old to move up here. She likes just sitting on the porch. Playing with my mom's cats.'

'What kind?'

'Sully? I don't suppose she's any kind. Part shepherd, part lab, part hound.'

'What's Sully short for?'

'Sully.'

'Oh. I thought it was like Sully for Sullivan.'

'I have no idea why we called her that. Maybe my sister meant "Sally." She named her.'

'What I want is a border collie. They're the smartest. I'm going to call him Gypsy.'

'They're really good dogs. One-man dogs. I should take you fishing there.'

'Where?'

'Down where I grew up. You can see gators.'

'I know you're lying,' Guy says, almost kindly.

'I swear on my mother's head I'm not. You see whales and stuff around here.'

'Not just swimming along . . .'

'Seals!'

'Well, yeah,' Guy admits grudgingly.

Kathleen delivers a sandwich, the way Guy likes it, a slab of cheddar 'grilled' only by placing it between two slices of overdone toast. He smiles up at her. Utter, unfeigned trust. How could True not have pictured this moment and not made a prior plan? How could she have been so hormonally juiced that she had drowned her own intellect? This is how stories that end up in *Good Housekeeping* begin, stories with headlines like 'I Kidnapped My Son From a Crack House': 'Despite the early loss of his father, Guy Lemieux was a happy, well-adjusted, and talented boy . . .' This is not the right time to tell him. This is the only time there is to tell him. Pay no attention to that man in your kitchen, Guy. Everything is perfectly okay. I still love you best. Does she still love her son best? There is no question. Even the question is absurd. She loves Guy more than her own life.

She loves Hank. She loves him as much as she can love a man, and, she suspects, more than most women ever do. And she is his wife. And she owes both of them better than this eye-rolling, hand-twisting pantomime that would look, to a casual observer, as though she is choking, like a gar on a breadball.

'Gee,' she says, 'it's time for bed. We're all tired here.'

'Is he staying over?' Guy asks.

'Yes, it's okay because we're almost married.'

'Right,' Guy says.

'In fact, we did the law part in New Hampshire . . . so we could do the real part here. Just like Doug and Esa did. So, legally, we're already married.'

'Huh,' Guy says. 'Well, I think I'll go over and stay at Granny's tonight.'

'That would be fine,' Kathleen says, reaching for her coat.

'That would not be fine,' True replies. 'You belong here. With me. And Hank. From now on.'

'Okay, now I can't even stay at my own granny's?'

'If we're out or something, but not tonight.'

'Well, I'm not calling you "Dad,"' Guy says to Hank.

'You don't have to unless you want to, if you ever want to. I like my name,' Hank replies.

'You do? It sounds like a fart to me,' Guy replies.

'Guy, that's enough of that,' True warns.

'Oh, Mom, like you know anything . . .'

'I think you're overtired,' True says.

'I think I'm just pissed,' Guy says. 'I want to go with Granny.'

True says, 'No.'

'I *want* to go with Granny!'

'I told you, not tonight.'

And the battle is joined.

TWO HOURS LATER, Hank and True are sitting cross-legged outside Guy's locked bedroom door. He has not answered any of their questions for the past hour. The sounds of his crying have subsided. They think he may have fallen asleep. 'We have to get this lock off,' True says, 'and it's going to be a bitch. It's the good kind.'

'Could wreck the wood,' Hank says.

'Well, I can't just leave him in there all night.'

'Maybe it's best. Give him his privacy. Can't be easy for a boy to cry in front of a man he hardly knows, who just married his mom.'

'He's ten, Hank. He doesn't know real men don't cry.'

'I didn't mean anything by that. I just know how it was for me, when I was a boy. You'd get a hook stuck in your hand, or cut your foot on bottle glass, and you'd try as hard as you could not to go crying in front of . . .'

'I'm not trying to raise him to be Steve McQueen.'

'Don't take on, honey. What are you mad at me for?'

She is ambushed by her love of him; her Indian-haired poem of a man. 'I'm not mad at you. I'm just so pissed at myself. I know what you mean, but I can't leave him in there alone.'

151

'Let's just lie down awhile, and see if he gets up. He's got to go to the toilet sometime.'

'Once he peed out the window when he was mad at me.'

'Let's give him a little while.'

They lie in the bed that True has known as hers, side by side, careful not to touch, as if a line has been taped down the center, the way she and Dog used to tape a line down the back seat of the car when they went on drives to visit their two unmarried aunts in Salem. And these are the precise positions they still occupy when morning comes. She tiptoes down to check on Guy. He is gone. When she looks out her bedroom window, she can see him through Kathleen's window, earnestly waving his hands as he inaudibly emotes over breakfast. She grabs her robe and clogs.

'Hi, Mom,' she says. 'I'm taking Guy home now.'

'You are not!' Guy's face is beefy with rage that puffs his cheeks and makes his eyes disappear behind raw ridges. She had taken minutes to fall asleep, she now realizes. Her son clearly had cried long into the night.

This is the kind of mother she is.

'True, don't be so stern. It's as if you're acting like this is his fault,' Kathleen says. 'How would you have felt if you'd come home from a trip and found a stranger in your mother's bed and your life totally turned on end?'

'His life is not totally turned on end!' True shouts, balling her fists, then opening them to rub her arms. Guy's life *is* totally turned on end. She will not admit this because she is . . . embarrassed. No, more than that, deeply ashamed. It is why she will not call Dog and confide in him, as she customarily does when their mother does something wacko, or ask Franny to come over and give Gee one of her practiced jokey talkings-to. She will have to wheel around, go back into her own house, and talk about this with a total stranger whom she knows only in the biblical sense. She takes Guy's hand and, leaving his oatmeal on the table, all but drags him across the yard. She can feel the Sandersons' eyes as they observe, quietly, in the nonjudgmental Quaker way.

ON SATURDAY, TRUE dresses early in her best suit, squeezes her still-bruised feet into heeled sandals, and stuffs a hundred-dollar bill for Saint Thomas More's Church into her evening bag, along with the

152

solid-gold lighthouse earrings she has chosen to give Franny in thanks for her being True's matron of honor. Esa is still on her honeymoon, and Rudy somehow can't be located. She finds Guy lying on his bed in jeans and a dirty T-shirt. 'Get dressed, honey,' she says.

'I am dressed,' he replies.

'Get dressed, Guy,' True orders him. 'Nice.'

'Go to hell,' Guy advises her slowly.

'I am at the end of asking you to be good, and I am at the end of apologizing, and I am at the end of understanding sheer brattiness. We might have to work out stuff between us for ten years because I married Hank too fast, but right now you're going to get your butt up off that bed and move it into a pair of chinos and a nice shirt, or I'm going to slap you on it, and I'm going to take away your boombox and donate it to the resale.'

'Why? Because I have my own ideas?'

'No, because you are being rude as a pig, and you aren't that kind of kid. And even if you hate Hank's guts, he did bring you the Scottie Pippen card and he did come to your show and he tried to be nice to you.'

'That was all to suck up to you. Go ahead and take the boombox then.'

True sits down. 'Would you like it if I did this to you? If you wanted to be in wrestling or something and I didn't want you to so bad that I refused to come to your games?'

'They're called matches, Mom, and it's not the same thing.' Guy has a point.

'Well, I'm going to ask you once more, and I'm going to ask you out of love for me to do something you don't want to do but that someday, I would bet you fifty bucks, you will be glad you did.'

'You would really give me fifty bucks if I hate him all my life?'

'I'll give you fifty bucks if you still hate him by the end of summer.'

'Get out of here. That's so a sucker bet,' Guy grins, getting up and heading for his closet. 'I can get like two great rookie cards for that, signed.'

Bribery under her belt, True phones her mother and asks if she is ready to leave, and learns that Kathleen plans on keeping up with her hours at the dump-and-beach sticker concession that afternoon, otherwise she would unfairly put too much work on Mary and Ellen.

'You're not coming to my wedding?' True asks, genuinely

stunned by this new move. 'You're going to sell dump stickers instead of coming to my wedding? Even Dog is driving over for my wedding.'

'Shucks, I went to the first one,' Kathleen says. 'I'll come to the party Franny's having.'

'How do you know Franny's having a party?'

'She called this morning.'

'You didn't tell me.'

'She asked what you were wearing. I told her. I didn't think you wanted to be disturbed. Your bedroom door was closed.'

'Mom, I ordinarily close my bedroom door when I shower and dress.'

'Well, I didn't feel I had permission . . .'

'Don't do that! Don't, please! I beg you on my knees to come to my wedding. If you don't come, it's going to hurt my feelings, and it's going to hurt Hank's feelings, and it's going to hurt Guy's feelings, not to mention making him think he can mouth off to me even more than he already does, which is in itself breaking my heart.'

'Well . . . I . . .' Kathleen equivocates, clearly not wanting to hurt anyone, and yet clearly not wanting to give out even tacit approval of this union, by the mere fact of agreeing to participate.

So True plays the trump card: 'Do you know how it will look to Father Tierney if you refuse to come to my wedding?' Kathleen falls silent, pondering. 'Not to mention that you'd just spend the time talking about it with Mary and Ellen anyhow.'

'Let me get a skirt on,' Kathleen mutters, 'and a decent pair of shoes.'

When True is later asked to repeat that with her body she will honor Hank, and with her spirit cleave to him, that she will cherish him with all that she is and with all that she has, in the name of God, she promises she will. Hank repeats the same words, having told his mother and grandmother earlier on the telephone that 'Catholic Lite' was better than nothing, and that he was sure God would be somewhere in the vicinity. When Guy hands Hank True's ring, and the ring she has purchased for Hank – which he will, it transpires, never wear – her son shrugs. Since Franny actually is planning a party for Hank and True later in the month, there is no need for a luncheon or a dinner. There is nothing left to do but to go home, so they all kiss, and do just that.

154

'Little sis, happy at last,' Dog whispers into True's hair. 'If he takes that grim look off your jaw, he's my best friend.'

'Does it show? And did it ever show that I wasn't happy?' True whispers back.

'Yes and yes,' her brother replies.

FOR THE NEXT few days, Guy punishes True by acting as though his grandmother is his mother.

One day after school, just before the tide comes in, True hears him ask Kathleen if he can walk out onto the flats. Kathleen gives him permission. True interferes, the Eva Braun of mothers. She knows that Kathleen has known all along True would interfere, and so has risked nothing by giving Guy the gate to do something Kathleen would ordinarily forbid; and this infuriates True further. The tides are notorious this time of year, and could sweep a husky adult under. Guy is a sturdy little mustang, and would probably do okay; but it is a rule that he never walks out alone at low tide. It is as though Kathleen is abetting Guy's determination to see True as a neglectful parent.

'You treat me like a baby,' Guy mutters and stomps off to shoot baskets with Brendan.

Hank wanders in on his way to work and kisses True so thoroughly that her crotch mutinously tightens. Rudy sighs.

'Guy hates me,' True tells Rudy after Hank leaves.

'Yep,' Rudy agrees. 'He does.'

'Gee hates me,' True tells Franny over the telephone, 'and he'll hate me forever.'

'Forever's a long time, True,' Franny says, terribly helpfully.

'Now, here's the essay question. What do I do?'

'I would ask him out formally to dinner, you and he, for your Monday-night date, and let Hank cook and serve you. Then, the next week, I'd take him on your Monday-night date nowhere near Hank, so that he can see his whole life isn't going to revolve around this guy, and that he'll still have a piece of his mother's attention no one else can own.'

'That's my Franny,' True croons. 'How come you're so smart?'

'Well, I usually don't follow my own advice, if that matters.'

'She *what?*' screams Isabelle, who has dropped in at this moment, having returned the previous day from her honeymoon. Rudy and she huddle with their heads together. True smiles and makes a big 'okay' sign to Esa, as she continues to listen to Franny, who concludes, 'It would be different if he'd run away or swallowed a bottle of aspirin or something. This revenge stuff is fairly minor and obviously symbolic.'

'Well, I'm fairly miserable and obviously psychotic.'

'Leave him alone and he will come home, and don't be such a drama queen,' Franny advises. 'You're just throwing fuel on that side of Guy. Go have a nap. Or better yet, have a nap with Hank.'

But True knows, as she hangs up, that she cannot go and take a nap, or have a glass of wine, or anything else similarly soothing. She has work to make up that the new girl somehow cannot grasp; perhaps there really is something wrong with her brain, despite her Harvard degree. She is so unsuited for the job and so obviously not up to its myriad demands and multiple tasks that she and Rudy have discussed offering her two months' untaxed severance in exchange for not suing for unemployment. Then Rudy and True will work seventeen-hour days to make shipment until they find someone they can count on – even if they have to raid Elizabeth's staff for it, though they have sworn they will never do this again. Once Rudy leaves, True has said, she figures she will have to fold, since there will be no one left on the planet who understands the company, except Hank, who will learn by osmosis, but who has his own business and has never expressed more than a passing interest in involving himself with True's.

However, after she has let Esa twirl her around, and listened to her repeat how she, Isabelle, had told her so, that this was the guy, she knew it all along; after she has swallowed her pride and given an honest answer when Esa asks how Guy is taking this; a miracle unfolds.

'Here I thought I was going to be the one with the surprise,' Isabelle begins, with a pretend pout.

'You're expecting,' True guesses.

'No,' Esa says.

'You're moving to Utah,' True tries again.

'No.'

'What then?'

Douglas, Esa announces, has been offered a postdoc at BU. Esa has no intention of moving to Boston or paying for the privilege.

156

They will buy or rent a condo or a cottage just over the Sagamore Bridge, perhaps in Onset.

Isabelle has come not only to see True, but to get down on her knees to True and beg for her old job, or any job at Twelve Times Blessed!

If True needs her to, she will even stay over once in a while and help out with Guy, since Douglas, true to form, will still be out of town so often with students.

It is True who falls to one knee in relief, taking one of Esa's hands in hers.

Eyeing True with a raised eyebrow, Rudy asks Vivien, the new girl, to come outside and down the road with him for a smoke, since he has something to discuss with her (True allows no smoking anywhere near the merchandise). 'I didn't know you smoked,' Vivien says, extracting her pack.

'I've decided to start,' Rudy explains.

TRUE FEELS HANK slide naked into bed beside her, making her nose wrinkle to the strong pine soap they use to wash the seafood reek from their arms. Without a word, he slides down her flannel athletic shorts and begins to tickle her with his tongue. She reaches out, reflexively, to stop him, then realizes that sooner or later, they are going to have to relax and stop shoving a chair against the locked door. She should not be reluctant to have ordinary sex with her legally sanctified husband and her (their?) son asleep down the hall. But she cannot concentrate, and Hank, whose tongue is not robotic, notices that his gentle gymnastics are having small effect.

'Why don't we just carry on?' Hank asks, 'to the next step?'

'Why don't we sneak out and do it in the car? Or be celibate until Guy's out of high school?'

As she lies across Hank's thighs, first pulling her T-shirt down and her boxer shorts back up, Hank directs her, 'Don't you know about the vein on the outer side?'

'I thought the point was just to get as much in as possible.'

'No, the outer side is the key.'

'You tell everyone this?'

'Most women don't know it.'

'Most?'

157

'Well, one did. But I think she had a little too much practice for my liking.'

'You want us to be practiced as Japanese courtesans and still innocent?'

'You talk too much.'

Neither of them hears the lock pop. True is dressed, but Hank is naked.

Her life is over. Guy is standing in the doorway, in his Bruins jersey. The look on his face lasts forever. He is giving her up. He will never trust her again. Turning with a sob, he barrels down the hall.

'I'm sorry,' he yells back, 'I'm sorry!'

'Relax,' Hank advises her.

True can hear Guy still calling, 'I'm sorry! I'm sorry!'

'Relax?' she nearly shrieks. 'That would be as if we didn't give a shit about him and went right back to fucking our brains out. Don't you see? He was coming to . . . to accept us, or something, and here we were.'

'Well, why didn't you get the good kind for *your* lock?'

'It was never necessary.'

'God, he's probably out the door by now. Over to Kathleen's. My grandma always said things look better in the morning.'

'Everyone's grandma always said that. And what do you care? He's not your kid.'

'I'm going to ignore that. I think. Though I didn't deserve it. Let me rub your back.'

But True knows she has to go to her son. Stiff as lumber, she waits until Hank begins snoring lightly, then slips on her long pajama shorts and a T-shirt and tiptoes down the hall. She sits on the edge of Guy's bed, and literally shoves him over.

'I know you saw,' she says.

'Why did you do that?' Guy asks.

'To have a baby,' True says, fabricating a reason on the spot. 'So you could have a little brother or sister.'

'I was going to come and *talk* to you,' says Guy, tears rolling over her hands as True cups his face.

'I'm not a bad lady, Gee. I love him. Married people in love try to have babies.'

'You love him *more*.'

158

'No, I'll never love anyone more than you. It insults me you say so. It hurts my heart. You know better.'

'But you're going to sleep with him every night. Even if I puke.'

'It's not going to be so different. You can still come in.'

'Oh, yeah, and see stuff that makes me nauseous. Like crummy stuff naked boob stuff in Brendan's dad's bathroom under the sink.'

'Don't say that. What about me getting married gave you permission to have a mouth like a truck driver?'

'He's not like a dad.'

'How do you know?'

'He just isn't.'

''Cause he's too young?'

''Cause I can tell he doesn't know kids come first to their mom! Otherwise he wouldn't do this! That's what you said, you always come first.'

'You do come first.'

'Then why did you do *that?*'

'That's how moms and dads make love. It's how they show they love each other. Like you learned in health class.'

'Like I said! What if I puke in the night?'

'Well, you just knock on the door.'

'What if you're . . . making out?'

'I'd stop.'

'Oh, like you could stop.'

'Of course I could stop.'

'Once you start doing it, you can't stop.'

'Who says?'

'Brendan.'

'Look, Guy, Brendan doesn't know anything more about making . . . love than you do.'

'He says once you get locked together, you can't stop until morning.' Oh, precious Lord, True thinks. This is what her son has put together from a pastiche of Body Changes class, mares and stallions in Montana, and Brendan's vast expertise.

'Baby, that's not true. It takes about fifteen minutes, the whole thing, and you can stop any time you want.'

They both look up as Hank, in pajama bottoms, enters the room and sits down at the foot of Guy's bed. 'Tell him to leave,' Guy instructs True.

159

'He wants to talk to *me*,' True explains to Hank.

'What I reckon,' Hank says slowly, 'is that this concerns all three of us. Me, too. I mean, I'm the man around here. The other man, right? And we're going to have to get used to each other somehow, right?'

'Wrong,' Guy says, his face muffled in his pillow. 'You're not my father.'

'I didn't say I was.'

'And you won't ever be my father.'

'That's up to you.'

'Well, I won't ever want you to be my father.'

'How come?'

'Well, first, you're ugly.'

'Gee!' True sputters. 'Take that back.'

'No,' says Guy.

'I'm kinda ugly,' concedes Hank. He inches up a notch farther on the bed, and puts his hand on Guy's hip. 'Look, old fella, this has gotta suck big-time. But one thing I want to tell you before I leave, and I'm not going to make Mom come with me, is that I love your mom. I love her and I'm going to take care of her . . . and you and Granny, too, if you let me. You can think of me like Unkie. Or you can think of me like a bigger friend. Or maybe like a dad. But I'm not going anywhere, partner. I'm here. And there's gotta be some good thing about that.'

'Name one,' Guy challenges him.

'Well, I can jump a stunt bike twenty-five feet.'

'That's bullshit.'

'Watch your mouth!' True is as tickled as she is appalled. 'That cussing has got to stop.' Hank shoots her a look that says clearly, back off; he's only trying to impress me.

'Nobody can do that,' Guy smirks.

'I can,' Hank asserts. 'At least twenty.'

'I bet you ten bucks.'

'I take it.'

'I mean, really ten bucks. Not like adults say, oh, okay, I'll bet you ten bucks the first elevator that comes is the left one and then they say they never shook on it. I don't have a stunt bike. *Mom* says I'd break out my singing arch,' he points to his teeth. 'But Fenn does. Brendan does. Can I call him? You'll probably break the bet by the time I call him.'

160

'Southern men don't do that.'

'Are Southern men better or something?'

'Only at making bets. If you welsh on a bet in the South, you have to fight a duel.'

'Get out,' Guy says, sitting up.

'My great-great-grandpa had to fight a duel.'

'Get out,' says Guy. 'He never did.'

'He did. With horse pistols,' Hank persists.

'Gee, all I ask,' True interjects, 'is for you to accept my apology for doing our marriage like this. I would have married Hank anyhow, Guy. I love him. I really do. He's not like . . . stupid Evan the Terrible. And I married him as much for you as me.' Guy snorts. 'No, really. You'll come to see, now you're older, it's good for a . . . boy to have a . . . dad . . . a guy around, who's older. I can't do all the things a man can do, Guy.'

'Unkie can.'

'But he lives in Amherst.'

'Rudy can.'

'Rudy might move.'

'Are you sure?'

'No, but he really might . . .' She realizes she is making Hank sound like a household appliance. 'I don't mean he's going to take the place of your father, or anyone else we love. But it never hurts to have more love around you.'

'What was the duel about?' Guy asks.

'Honor,' says Hank.

'I don't mean, like, honor. I mean, what was it *about*? Like a *girl*? Or a cow? Or a ranch?'

'I can ask my daddy.'

'You call your father Daddy?'

'I do. That's a Southern thing, too.'

'Up here it's a baby thing.'

'You can call me . . .' Don't go too far, True prays. 'Anything you want. Start with Hank, or if you think that sounds like a fart, then Henry. Or Old Man. Or Butt Brain.'

Hank rises and leaves the room, fading noiselessly as a shadow. True sits beside the bed. 'Lie down with me,' Guy says, and grabs hold of her arm with a grip she cannot break. 'I could make sixty bucks off you guys,' he says sleepily. True lies down, and he turns

161

his rump to nuzzle against her stomach. In what seems like seconds, he is breathing deeply and sonorously. True thinks that he is, after all, a guy, her Guy, a small man. She and Franny have often spoken of men, and of how their chromosome structure, X and Y, must account for so very much of the differences between the genders, no matter how liberal the interpretation. You break up with a guy, Franny and True and Esa have agreed, and you spend days listening to 'Clair de Lune' over and over and drinking white wine and sleeping until eleven in the morning. In the same situation, a guy gets his car detailed.

There's only one thing, Franny never fails to remind her. Guys wrote those songs. I've got sunshine on a cloudy day. Look at me; I'm as helpless as a kitten up a tree. Oh, my love, my darling, I hunger for your touch. Maria, I've just met a girl named Maria, and suddenly that name will never be the same to me. Memory haunts my reverie, and I am once again with you . . . those were written by men. Franny insists, if they can do that, they cannot really be eight-celled organisms.

When she finds her way back to their bed, Hank is also snoring, that key place on the nether end of his member forgotten for the night.

True leaves the door open.

In the morning, they wake to find Guy curled in his sleeping bag, on the foot of their bed.

'Don't,' Hank cautions her, as she points. 'Don't say a word. Just get up and go make an egg or something. Don't embarrass him.'

OVER A COFFEE date in celebration of the tenuous reunion of her new tri-bond family unit, True meets Franny for a planning session. 'Let's see. What we're after is a public expression of joy. Gifts. Flowers. Legitimacy. Who should we ask? For all three of you?'

'The neighbors and Esa and her groom and the gang from work and the Bourses and the Sandersons, I guess. Though I can't imagine wanting to see Addley Bourse's face. But Holly's okay. And their kid Fenn is on Guy's basketball team. My mom's friends, and Joy and her husband. Beatrice and Laura from the Chatham Family Theatre. Elizabeth, do you think? Unless you think that's a little . . . much. For a second marriage?'

'You mean for a marriage to a younger man? And remember, it's not *his* second marriage, True.'

'There's that.'

'And the presents!' Franny exhales in a girlish rush. 'Wine of the month, blown glass, gift certificates to quaint country inns, you know?'

True allows herself a spark of amusement. She always has loved presents. That is perhaps why she is in the present business. And for eight years, she's had few. Rudy and Esa never fail to come up with darling things, and Franny gives her the very best books. But Kathleen gives her gift certificates, and Dog always forgets. Widows, especially mothers, become accustomed to knowing what is in every box under the tree, even the ones with their own names on them, though Esa has pulled off a few pacts with Guy, including once inducing him to save six months' worth of allowance for the garnet cross True wears around her neck.

Franny continues, 'And you'll want to ask all Hank's family . . .'

The flame goes out. 'No.'

'Do you think you can remain a secret bride forever?'

'I thought we might ease into it. By . . . Christmas maybe. Christmas, 2005.'

'No, you must face the music and dance, True.'

'His mother is very young. She had him in like . . . middle school.'

'True . . .'

'Well, college.'

'So she's at least as much older than you as you are older than Hank. No, twice as much older. Maybe.'

'This is a fact that makes me want to heave, Franny. If you're trying to be comforting, you're failing. God, can you imagine having a mother-in-law only ten years older than you are?'

'No.'

'Well, then why are you putting the curse on me of having to face that fact?'

'Because you have a mother-in-law? No changing that now. You could have married an orphan.'

'Oh, Franny, Franny, Franny, be serious now; what's to be done? How much can I change in three weeks? What if I eat only fruit . . . ?'

'Stop being silly. You've lost enough weight. Lose more and you'll look wrinkly . . .'

'What if they look at me funny? Please take me outside and drive over me, Franny.'

'I don't think that works to flatten you out.'

163

'No, I would expect it to be fatal or disabling at least. Esa's back. She'll run the company until Guy grows up.'

'What would I be liable for then, assisted suicide? Car-a-kiri?'

'No *jokes!!!*'

'I'm not joking, True. You're the one being an ass. I mean that in a nice way. When you worry, you don't just worry, you circle the drain.'

'Why is that?'

'I think because you've been through so much in your life. But that's over now. So back to the future. Now, if we're going to have music, we'll have to have tapes. Angelique's cute fella Rob can do that. Now let's do wording for the card, then . . . a celebration, hosted by . . . I've got it, by Guy Lemieux . . . for the marriage of his mother, True Harte Dickinson Lemieux Bannister . . .'

'A little long.'

'By Guy Lemieux for his mother, True Dickinson, and Henry Bannister.'

'I like that.'

'And poetry. Ummm, maybe some Edna St. Vincent Millay. Or the ever-popular Bard. How about this? "Escape me? Never – Beloved! While I am I and you are you!" How about that?'

'Sounds like I had to chase him and get him in a leg trap.'

'Okay. How about Lennon and McCartney? How about, " . . . I know I'll never lose affection/For people and things that went before . . . In my life, I love you more"?'

True says, 'You know, I think that's it. Sure, perfect.'

'And how about, say, Memorial Day? When the lilacs are in bloom, and the cotton is high?'

'And so is the seaweed's stinking up the beach . . .'

'You'll wear lavender . . .' Franny suggests, 'and go barefoot.'

'"Scarborough Fair"? Or "Sunset Boulevard"?'

'What do you want to wear? Alençon lace and a corselet?'

'No. I just didn't see it this way.'

'True,' says Franny softly. 'You didn't see it at all. I guess I'll have to take you shopping. That's what I should be. A personal shopper for the rich and deliberately woebegone. You'll get a sleeveless dress to show off your gorgeous arms, and a beady shawl, and I'll put up your hair and you'll glisten.'

'What would I do without you? Franny, huh?' True asks.

'Wear jeans every day and dress jeans for special occasions,' Franny answers honestly. 'Be a beautiful frump with the best hair on the block.'

ON THE MORNING of their wedding celebration, True and Hank have their first, raw, guts-out marital fight, and things go downhill from that point. A wedding, though a union, also is always a collision of conflicting interests, a competition of the most basic sort: Whose family is more visibly normal? Whose has produced the most accomplished picture?

She is dressing, in lavender rayon, a beach-glass necklace and earrings in deep amethyst, with strappy sandals, when Hank, his face half-shaven, asks, 'What do you weigh?'

'A hundred and thirty-nine,' True answers, honestly, or as honestly as a human being can, shaving only five pounds.

'What's your normal weight?' he asks then.

'A hundred and twenty-nine,' she answers. 'Why? Do I look fat in this?'

'You look wonderful.'

'You brought it up for some reason.'

'Just because you're always going on about your weight. Not that all women don't.'

'Do all women? Because you clearly know.'

'Every woman I ever met. The same way all women love pickles. Because they taste good but they don't have calories. Even my mom. My sisters. And that even though my sisters are as skinny as twigs.'

'Well, they'll probably think I look like a hot-air balloon in the Thanksgiving Day parade.'

'Mom,' Guy says from the door, 'this shirt won't stick down.'

'Here's how you do it,' Hank offers. He instructs Guy to stand with legs apart and pants at half-mast, how to batten down the shirt before zipping up. 'Works every time.'

'Cool,' says Guy.

'About my weight,' True continues.

'You're the perfect weight for you.'

'There's a big but in that. Or should I say, a big butt with two *t*s?'

'I didn't mean to start anything,' Hank tells her, finishing his shave, pulling down the ironing board to give a final touch to his shirt, which has just returned, still in its bag, from the cleaner.

'Why do you do that?'

'There's a corner sticking up.'

'Do you iron everything?'

'I iron everything.'

'They have a name for that.'

'What?'

'Obsessive-compulsive disorder.' Guy, shirt smartly tucked, sits down on the bed, clearly interested.

'I call it neatness. It matters in business. A bad collar means a sloppy restaurant.'

'What do unironed boxer shorts mean? Or an unironed pajama top? A bad date?'

'Don't start with me, True.'

'Guy, go see if Esa's here yet.'

'I know what you're doing,' Guy says. 'You're fighting, and you don't want me to see. But I'd like to see, 'cause you're normally so ooey-gooey nicey-nicey.'

'We've only been married a month! What do you expect?' Hank asks.

'And plus, we're not fighting,' True says tightly. Her lipstick is feathering. She feels a desperate longing to smear it all over her jaw.

'Grown-ups never admit to fighting,' Guy offers. 'You and Gram fight all the time. I can tell. You get this big smile on your faces with all your teeth showing and you say "please" and "if you don't mind."'

True takes off her dress, throwing it in a corner of the closet, and pulls on jeans. 'I have to go over to the office and check on things. I'll get dressed later. I'll put on a muumuu.'

'Shut up, True,' says Hank. True is so shocked, she sits down on her closet floor.

'Shut up? Shut *up*?'

'I'm not one of your summer employees. I'm not a field hand. Don't bully me.'

'And I'm not one of your Playboy-bunny knockoffs. Don't bullshit me. You're worried about what your parents and your willowy sisters and their husbands . . .'

'They're not married . . .'

166

'One is . . .'

'She's not coming. She's about to give birth.'

'Which one is that? Flora? Fauna? Fiddlehead?'

'Tanniferro.'

'I declare, Rhett, those surely are colorful names.'

'Not tight-assed Yankee names, that's for sure. Jane. Brinn. Fenn. Luke. Dob. Y'all afraid you're going to run out of syllables up here?'

'You shut up.'

'Kit. Fran. Holly. Whoops! That's two syllables. She must be a foreigner. Lynn. Chip.'

'You are afraid!'

'I'm not afraid of anything! Except your big mouth. True, you're so insecure you put it all over everybody else like paint. Why are you like this, on our day? I'm proud of the woman I married. You just don't want to face today because you're afraid people will notice the inevitable and think . . .'

'The inevitable?'

'Forget it.'

'The inevitable what?'

'The inevitable. The difference in our ages.'

'You think that because you act like you're in college, you *look* like you're in college. Hello! You don't.'

'Okay, okay,' Hank rounds on her, towering over her where she sits. 'What do you want me to say? You don't look thirty-five, True. You don't look forty-five. You look forty-three. Actually, you look forty. A perfect forty. I look a little younger than I am, probably because I haven't had your weight in life . . .'

'You mean my responsibilities . . .'

'However you want to put it . . . to shoulder. Deal with it.'

'I'm an adult, Hank. And I have dealt with it, for eight years, by myself, thank you kindly. Welcome to my world.'

They both hear Isabelle calling from the lower level, 'Where's my guy? Where are you, Gee?'

'I'm up here; they're fighting,' Guy calls.

Hank reaches down and pulls True to her feet. 'We're both nervous,' Hank whispers into True's hair. 'It wouldn't be natural not to be nervous. I haven't ever done this before. I haven't ever faced my parents as a grown man. You haven't ever done this before. Not this way. We have to stay linked. It all comes from us.'

'You're right. You're right,' says True. 'You and me. Birth to earth.'

'Womb to tomb.'

'Promise?'

'I promise.'

And then Esa and Guy are upon her, Esa's very cologne enough to make True weep with joy, from the memory of how the scent of White Linen once permeated their peaceful mornings. She holds Esa close. 'Here's the nanny! Where's the professor?'

'Oh, downstairs, flirting with your mom. You know, she and my dad write every week. E-mail!'

'She's a dickens. Kathleen pretends she can't touch the computer without it blowing up.'

'It's quite a romance. At a delicate remove, of course.'

'Give me a break,' True shakes her head. 'What do they talk about?'

'Books, says my dad, and widowhood and stuff.'

'Your dad's divorced, Esa. He's not a widower.'

'You've met my mother, True. For him, it might just as well have been being a widower.'

'I'm going down to see Rudy,' Esa says. 'I'll let you guys . . . do whatever.'

'Oh,' says Hank. 'We're not planning on doing whatever.'

'We're nervous,' True says. 'We're having a fight.'

'Oh, God, who wouldn't be?' Isabelle flings back her hair. 'Douglas and I fought like boars on the morning we got married.'

But True and Hank kiss, wholly and impulsively, the moment Esa closes the door. Somehow, both of them feel safer.

'That's a weight off my back,' True says, 'knowing it happens to normal people.'

'And speaking of weight, I don't know why such blockhead stuff comes out my mouth,' Hank says. 'You look like the queen of the May in that dress, True. I swear on . . .'

'Your mother's grave. Or head. Or eyes. Yes, well, she'll be here before you know it. I'm just going to pop down and get a little work done before I come up here and reassemble my finery.'

'I'm just going to work on my shirt collar some more . . .' Hank grins and makes a popgun gesture at True, 'Gotcha!'

But late that morning, which is a Friday, something happens that has occurred only once before in the history of True's company. A baby dies. A baby who is six months old, a boy in Chicago, dies in a car accident. It is the grandmother who writes, terrified that the gift packages will go on arriving, taunting the heartbroken parents. Rudy comes to True, his pallor making True wonder whether he is well. They FedEx lilies to the family, and refund the entire amount of the twelve-months purchase with a discreet letter of condolence. 'Love,' True writes, tears of her own brimming, 'is never wasted. Thank you for letting us be a part of Duncan's life.' When she finishes the letter, she closes shop for the day, at only two o'clock, and tells everyone to go home and dress for the party.

Hank has offered to pick his whole family up at the airport in the Volvo, but his father has insisted his son mind his own roost, and has hired a car.

It is quite a car. When the car pulls into True's drive, those guests who have already arrived pause.

It is not a stretch limousine, but it is a limousine, and the sisters, when they jump out, are just as Hank described them, twigs, gorgeous twirly-haired twigs, all legs and black ringlets. One of them, True guesses the younger, wears harem pants, wraps both legs around Hank in what she must suppose is the sisterly style of Southern greeting. He all but tosses her into the air. His mother emerges next, tall and large and what Kathleen would describe, to her bridge friends, as 'blowsy,' a knowing silvery woman who looks straight up at the window where Franny, on her knees, is frantically whip-stitching True into her foundation garment. The older woman looks up, catches True's eye, and winks. Hank's father emerges last, leaping out of the limo and kissing Hank on the lips. The hair is the same, so dark as to be crow-blue in the sunlight. The hips are the same. But Hank Senior, called Gus, is much taller and heavier than his son. He also is obviously, though laced with cream, a black man.

Franny cracks up, nearly gouging True's bare thigh with her needle. 'Guess who's coming to dinner?' she asks.

TRUE AVOIDS THE canapés and the lobster salad, the goat cheese baked into individual tiny pie crusts, so as to get decidedly, quickly drunk on Chambord and champagne. Her father-in-law has kissed her on both cheeks, to the unabashed delight of Holly and Addley

169

Bourse; her mother-in-law, Clothilde, has taken her by both hands and hugged her, given her a long, white box she conspiratorially asks her to wait 'until this shindig is over' to open, and has told her she is lovely, soft, round, and sweet, which True has no idea how to take, and soon doesn't give a shit. She has sorted out which sister is Reed and which is Win, which one is a dancer who used to be a medical student and which one still is a medical student. She is sitting with Isabelle on a blanket under a tree, while the men toss a football around. Even her neighbor Luke Sanderson, who has not moved in a gait faster than a saunter since True has known him, is showing off his old Princeton moves. Gus Bannister has taken Guy to sit beside him on the Adirondack chair, insisting he call him 'Grand-père,' and is showing him the contents of his pockets, which include a pocketwatch that signals with a train whistle, a scalpel fashioned to close like a pocket knife, and a preserved human eye.

'Are you blotto?' Isabelle asks.

'Not as blotto as I want to be,' True tells her.

'Aren't you happy? You married the cutest guy in town? *And* I'm coming back to work? You have the perfect life.'

'I'm happy. But I'm scared. I'm scared that this is a little too much for little old Chatham me.'

'Oh True. You're the risk-taker type . . .'

'With parasailing. With entrepreneurism . . . not with life.'

'Come on. This is such a blip, all things considered. Do you care?'

'Of course not. Would you?'

'Of course not. Would anybody normal care?'

'Do you think of my mother as normal?'

'In a sense,' Esa answers truthfully. 'She's not . . . unusual.'

'What this does,' True points, using the stem of her glass, 'is give my mother gigolo-ammo galore. Not that she needed more.'

'Your mother isn't prejudiced.'

'Not Boston-bussing-wise. Not even next-door-wise. But marrying-into-the-family-wise? She's a Democrat, Isabelle. That doesn't mean she's a liberal.' Franny joins them, pulling the blanket out a little so as not to grass-stain her white rayon.

'First time I've worn white this season,' she says. 'Feels great. Feels like summer.'

'We were talking about white, and not so white,' True points out.

170

'And how my mother is going to react to my having married a *Negro*.'

'It's actually other people I'm more worried about,' Franny confides. Someone has put in a CD of a zydeco band whose members went to school with Hank. It's bouncy, peppery music, and Hank's father and mother rise up as one and begin a sprightly and complicated two-step, Clothilde throwing back her silvery hair and swinging her large and unrestrained hips as she minces and glides.

'They're lovely,' True says.

'That's you two in thirty years,' Franny smiles.

'Actually, in thirty years, Hank will probably be wheeling me around the dance floor while I hold my IV pole.'

'True, give it up. You're becoming boring. And you have the genes of the ancients. Your mother's as flexible as my yoga teacher.'

'She goes to your yoga teacher.'

As the tempo slows, Gus makes a wide-eyed scan of the crowd and then lightly, gallantly holds out his arm to Kathleen. Neither True nor Franny exhale. Will she accept, True thinks? Will she make an excuse of the heat? No, she has manners. She'll accept. Someone will take a picture. All the pictures will be in black-and-white. The photographer has said these are more timeless; that colors, for example, that will one day look out of style always hold up in black-and-white photos.

This had not been what he'd had in mind.

Kathleen rises, a ghost of a smile on her face, and takes her place at precisely the right remove in Gus's arms and they waltz on the platform laid across the grass. 'She can really dance,' Franny says.

'She and my father danced all the time,' True tells her. 'At the Moose Lodge. She was senior regent, or something.' Holly Bourse, balancing her ginger ale, comes to join them, as Esa rises to go find Douglas and force him to dance. 'I've only seen pictures of them dancing. I never saw them actually dance. Just like, though I know I was at my father's funeral, I feel as though I've only seen pictures of that, too.'

'You know that the second stage of drunkenness is becoming philosophical. Watch out, True. The third stage is thinking you're invisible,' Esa admonishes.

171

'He is so handsome, your groom,' Holly says. 'We're all jealous. We want him to marry us, too.'

'Holly,' True touches her friend's cheek. 'That's so darned sweet. He is a doll, and his looks aren't the half of it. His looks are the least of his goodness.'

'Do you think his father will be offended that the groom on the cake is white?' Holly asks, and True's hand hardens into a slap she must retract.

'Stuff a sock in it,' Franny tells Holly.

'But you knew,' Holly goes on.

'In fact, I didn't know,' True says.

'But it doesn't matter to you.'

'Would it matter to you, Hol?'

'No, True! Only if I were going to have children, and you're not, right?' Holly says nervously.

'Wouldn't you, Holly?' True asks, iron entering her voice, ignoring Franny pinching her arm.

'No,' Holly answers, 'because to be perfectly honest, life is challenging enough, without that . . .'

'Without what?'

'Without being mixed.'

'Well, judging by Hank, they wouldn't look very mixed. I'm guessing his pop is already pretty mixed,' True says.

'You might have *children*?' Holly's jaw genuinely drops.

'I'm healthy. He hasn't and he wants them. Guy would probably like a baby sister. You're not *that* much younger than I am, Hol. You're, what, thirty-nine?'

'Thirty-eight,' says Holly.

'Lots of people in their forties do it,' True continues.

'Right,' Franny says. 'Steve and I might adopt.'

'But the baby could turn out . . .'

'What . . . ?' True begins.

'Well, black!'

'Black?'

'Black . . . black.'

'Only if we adopt an African-American kid. Which I guess we could, now I think of it. But no child can be darker than the darker of its parents,' True says.

'How do you know that?' Holly persists.

'I listened for five minutes in freshman biology, Hol. Jesus. Is this a big topic? Do people think he . . . can pleasure me more or something?'

'I don't think anyone thinks that,' Holly says, oblivious. 'Although, True, honestly, it *is* sort of exotic.'

'It *is* sort of exotic,' True admits, motioning to the caterer for a refill. 'I like that. I like it a lot.'

'Might as well hang for a sheep as a lamb,' Holly says gaily.

'My sentiments exactly,' True smiles.

HANK IS DANCING with his elder sister Reed, a slow swing, darling both for the grins on their faces and the practiced ease of the touches and twirls. Only siblings can dance this way, or fathers and daughters, mothers and sons. This is how she and Dog can dance, True thinks, catching his eye, after an adolescence spent trying out on each other in the living room what they would use to thrill others in the world. Dog catches her eye, inclines his head. True gets up and, to applause, they join Hank and Reed, as the waltz ends, and the tempo picks up, some riff on an old Chuck Berry song about a teenage wedding. Isabelle and her husband are bobbing up and down, dancing in the way of their twenties generation, as Dog grins and takes True's hand and says, 'Let's show them how it's done downtown, Sis.'

It is almost outside the range of her hearing, over the music and the clink of glasses, that True hears Hank's mother ask him, '*Est que ce ta maison, aussi?*' and True sees him pinch his mother playfully. She stores this and looks up at her brother.

'Aren't you going to ask me if I knew his dad was black?' she whispers, as Dog enfolds her for the first spin.

'I assumed you knew. And what the hell. Nobody gives a damn. This is Massachusetts.'

'Home of the free and the brave.'

'And the BoSox.'

'And the Patriots.'

'And the Constitution.'

'Where no one mentions the Portuguese, except to praise their sonnets.'

'Well . . .'

'But it could be worse. It could be Mississippi.'

173

'Right.'

'And everyone will approve, once it gets around. They'll find us very millennial.'

'Whether or not they approve, well, honey, only shitheads will disapprove. Like I said, nobody will give a damn.'

'I thought the age thing was the big deal. Shows to go you. You think Guy will?'

'No, he'll be fine. I know my girls wouldn't believe it when their history teacher taught them about lynching. They kept asking me, they made that up, didn't they, Daddy? Our kids might have a lot of shit to face, but not that shit.'

'You mean that, Unkie?'

'I do, sweetie.' True forgets, sometimes, the utter comfort of knowing she has an older brother in the universe. With all his lapses, Dog is a gem. Not a diamond, rough-cut. Something bigger and healthier, like amber.

'Even though you remember,' she goes on, as a slow song begins and she slips closer into Dog's arms, noticing that Hank now is dancing with his own mother, 'that fight you had in The Squire that summer with the guy wearing the full Cleveland . . .'

'About the tone of the town changing? The *kinds* of families moving in? Since his family began coming here in the Sixties?'

'Right, and you were going to deck him?'

'He was about six-twelve, True. If there was going to be any decking done, it was going to be me going down. But, yeah, I remember. Stupid-assed bastard.'

'So it'll be okay,' True begs, and her brother smiles, and leans her back gently in a graceful dip.

'Just keep checking in with each other. That's all you have to do. Don't let anything weird get to you. Or between you. The quickness of you two getting married, the fact he hasn't been a parent, it's a lot to face. Be on your toes. You seem very much in love, and he seems very much in love, and he's a very nice guy, to all appearances, and his family seems as though they're behind him, and I think he'll be able to get around Guy once you two get settled down,' says Dog. 'I'm surprised you did this. But I'm not like Mom! I thought she was going to stroke out on the phone. She was, get this, Augustus, get this. This takes the cake. And, oh my God, she's throwing it all away . . .'

'Did she really say that?'

'Well, not in those exact words.'

'I got a feeling she used those exact words, Doggy Doo.'

'Pretty close, and she compared it to the time you . . .' he begins to laugh and cough, and takes a sip of champagne from a passing tray, which has only the effect of making him spew through his nose, 'she compared it . . .' Dog struggles for composure, 'she compared it to when you were eleven and you Naired your eyebrows . . .'

'She did?' True now cannot stop laughing, though laughing makes her feel nauseated, and then as if her stomach is rising, bubbling up through her throat like a balloon. 'She brought that up? How she wouldn't let me pluck them because only tramps plucked their eyebrows, and so I ended up looking like a baking-powder biscuit through half of sixth grade?'

'Mom said, "She has your father's luck and head for business, but she doesn't have the common sense God gave an angleworm."' Dog spins True round and round, and the bubble that has been making its way up her throat pops, and she throws up, vermillion on lavender.

'NO ONE EVEN noticed,' Clothilde reassures True, after helping her clean off her beautiful Franny-braided hair. 'Let's look in this closet. Mighty pretty things in here. How about this cream suit?'

'Too hot, I'd faint,' True murmurs, humiliated that it has been her mother-in-law, whom she has known two full hours, and not her own mother who'd whisked her up the stairs and into her room, as if brides routinely puked during familial celebrations. Kathleen, though only for a moment, had covered her face with both hands.

'How about this sleeveless yellow . . . ?'

'I'd look jaundiced. I don't know why I bought that. I hate it.'

'You should give it to me, then.'

'Okay,' True agrees, surprised.

'I'll have to take the waist out a little, but it has a full skirt . . . I like this, then, with the white fish on the white background.'

'You can have that, too,' True offers uncertainly.

'No, I mean for you to wear now, chère. It's sweet. Bridelike. Moves like on its own.'

175

'Okay. This is so awfully dear of you . . . Missus . . . Clothilde.'

'I would be honored if you'd call me "Ma." That's what I expect my boy would want.'

'Ma, then. Sounds so strange to say that to anyone. Honored was the word he used when he asked me. "Honored."'

'Then I am proud of him. I brought him up well.'

'You did indeed.'

'He surely looks proud and happy.'

'Right now especially. With the sight of his bride throwing up on her dress.'

'Honey, where we come from, it just ain't much of a party if two or three people don't toss up in the ditch or the bushes . . . and furthermore, if the police don't get called . . .'

'Well, it's a scandal here. It's a revelation of bodily functions.'

'That's Yankees for you, I guess.'

'I guess.'

Clothilde smoothes her own brow, lifting one of True's silver-backed brushes in her long white hands, their melon-polished oval nails with hints of gilt. As True slides her dress over her head, her mother-in-law asks, 'May I use this?'

'Of course,' True answers. She wonders if her mother-in-law has heard the tiny beat of hesitation. It is only reflex. She is as affronted as she would be had someone asked to use her toothbrush. But Clothilde brushes through her wavy hair and gives it a few fork pinches with her fingers. 'There now. We both of us look beautiful. You go brush your teeth, and dab on some eau de cologne . . .' True is wondering whether anyone has hosed off the dance floor and whether black-and-white film is best for action shots involving vomit; Guy is banging on the locked door hollering to find out whether his mom is all right, when Clothilde asks, 'So what was it that first attracted you to Hank? His butt?' She smiles conspiratorially but benignly, her big beautiful face opening to reveal oval dimples, and calls out to the hall, 'Don't worry, Gee.' The Bannisters are the only people True has ever met, besides her former in-laws, who seem to have no trouble pronouncing his name. 'Everything's just fine. Mom's tummy got upset from nerves. She'll be right out, *chèr*.' True is trying to come up with something adequate enough to deserve being called an answer. It is the toothbrush all over again. With her husband's mother, to trade views on the merits of his rear end? 'He was voted

176

Best Butt in high school, you know. He's always been – how do they say it? – a chick attractor.'

'A chick magnet,' True says. 'That's what my son would say.'

'He is just adorable. Handsome and strong. Your boy, I mean, not mine. I would like him to come to us and visit.'

'Thank you. He would like to know you think that. He's a little insecure right now.'

'Is he adjusting? This was kind of sudden for him.'

'I think he will. He was pretty . . . shocked for a while. He was angry. He pitched a fit, if you want to know.'

'That's to be expected, no? A hissy of the first order?'

'I guess. It still has us pretty worried,' True admits. Us, she thinks. Us. We are an 'us.' Hank and Guy and me and this nice lady and the man downstairs who looks like Adam Clayton Powell with a lot of au lait. She turns her courage two twists to the right. 'So, were you pretty shocked?'

'I was surprised,' Clothilde says, dabbing at a smear of mascara under one eye. 'But only at the suddenness of it. You should have seen my Irish mama when I married Gus. We had to run away, though you can get married when you're twelve, practically, in the South. My father was like to kill him. But after thirty-eight years, I can say honestly that my husband is the finest man I ever knew. And I hope that my son takes after him. One thing I knew for sure was that when Hank made up his mind, it was going to be like Hurricane Bob; he wasn't going to be stopped.'

'Would you have stopped him if you'd . . . known?'

'Known?' Clothilde looks genuinely baffled.

'Known I'm . . . older, a lot older, a widow with a child.'

'May yeah.'

'Pardon me?'

'It's "*mais* yes." M-A-I-S. The mixed-up French for "but yes." We say "*Mais* yeah." Creole French. I'm not, myself. I mean, look at these freckles. But Gus is. We always knew Hank would marry an older girl.'

'You did?'

'Oh *mais* yeah. Every little dove he brought around, I'd think, no sir, he'll be bored by the weekend. And he always was.'

'But he loved a girl in Florida. Who moved up here. That's the one he won't talk about.'

177

'Ain't nothing to say. She was a spoiled girl. Very upper class. Met in college.'

'What did she do?' True is hot now, fevered by the champagne and the detective lust. 'What did she look like?'

'She was short and dark-haired and not fat, but big, like me, well, not so big as me, broad-shouldered, strong,' Clothilde explains. 'She was very pretty. He must have pictures of her. They were on and off for a century. But come to think, I imagine he left his pictures home; he has so much stuff still stored in our garage. I only grabbed a few things for him when we came up. There'll be boxes still I'll have to send.'

'But she was pretty?'

'Lovely. Smart, too. She writes books. Her name is Adele. Adele, I think of a hat . . . no, Cabot. She writes children's books, which she also paints. There's one about a mermaid child . . .'

'I know them! I use them for the Blessings.'

'The blessings?'

'For my business! The gifts I sent your girl who's having the baby! I put the one in about how the mermaid mother loves the naughty baby . . . in the basket for the first birthday! I looked at so many, many books and picked that one!'

'Small, small world,' Clothilde says. 'Small indeed.'

'I can't believe this! Adele Cabot lives right over the border. In New Hampshire. That's how come he knew so much about New Hampshire. He *did* know about New Hampshire.'

'Well, as for Adele. The important thing to know is though I think they did love one another, they never got to the top of things, because I don't think she could keep Hank from getting bored. He tends to be easily bored. It is a character flaw. You see, all the jobs, that is boredom. But I said to my husband, "That girl will never keep that boy challenged," and my husband, Gus, was the first to say, well, you were right, Ma. His sister, Win, she thought the same thing. She and Hank are the closest in age. She said Hank was running after the ninth-graders when he was ten.' She puts her arms around True, enfolding her in the kind of full-breasted, slightly damp, and lingering hug True has always wanted from her own mother, and still does, and has had to settle for from Esa and from Franny. True's eyes ache with the effort not to cry, or with the onset of her hangover, or both. She takes two aspirin and uses her fennel toothpaste.

Together, they return to the porch. Everyone is careful not to look up.

But True curtseys, made bold by the woman beside her, and says, 'The gastronomical fireworks portion of the program is over. I apologize.'

'It was the dip!' True's brother calls out, amid soft, sweet laughter.

'And now, if I may,' Hank calls, bounding up on the porch. 'Put on something slow, very slow and sappy, please, so I may dance with my bride.'

It is 'Moon River' they play, and the flat sheet of waters beyond the crust of Ridgevale Beach twinkle and wink.

'YOU COULD HAVE told me, is all,' True says.

Guy is downstairs, determined to beat *Grand-père* at chess. Gus has beaten him three straight matches so far, though he clearly is under the influence. The rest of the guests have retired, except for Hank's sister, who has taken a drive to view Chatham Light with one of the summer packers, a drive Isabelle has described as 'hopeful or suspicious, depending on how you look at it.'

'I did tell you,' Hank insists, stroking her nipple. 'I told you I was Creole.'

'You told me you *cooked* Creole. Which is a different thing.'

'I told you I had learned cooking from my Creole grandmamma, and you said you knew the difference between Creole and Cajun. After all, you're Canadian.'

'I'm not Canadian; my son is,' says True. 'I'm English. I'm like the tombstones here. And I swear I thought Creole just meant it had more peppers.'

'You were right. But it also means the people are part African. Just like all calico cats are female. I told you my grandmamma came from Haiti.'

'Well, then you'd better pleasure me, like in those novels about plantations. I'm the raven-haired planter's wife with flawless porcelain skin. You're the buck from the field. Lucifer, or something.'

'*Laissez les bon temps roullez,*' Hank replies.

'And I heard your mother ask you if this house was yours, too.'

Hank's black head bobs up from its tender work, and he feels rigid under True's hands in all the wrong places. 'Or maybe I was mistaken,' True offers.

179

'No, she said that. I thought you didn't speak French.'

'I speak that much French. I was married to a French Canadian.'

'Another theme,' Hank says, rolling away from her. Suddenly chilled in her nakedness, True self-consciously tugs down the silken hem of her sheath nightgown. Night sounds, car doors closing, the growl and shush of the waves, are magnified by the immensity of their personal silence, because the subject of money, raised on a bed, or any plane of love, cannot be anything less than a stake of ice.

'It is your house,' True whispers. 'I've told Rudy, and everyone, it's all yours, too. The money, all of it.' Hank says nothing. True waits ten heartbeats. 'You could write a check for ten thousand, twenty thousand. No one would care. Do you hear me?'

'I hear you,' he says.

'Do you believe me?'

'I believe you. And I'm worn out. I need to go to sleep, *chère*.'

'Okay,' True murmurs. She is not sleepy. But Hank cannot sleep with a light on. Her book lies on her nightstand, facedown. ('That is no way to treat a book,' Kathleen will not ever fail to tell her, when True breaks spines and turns down page corners or *whole pages* instead of using a bookmark. Kathleen says anything will do for a bookmark, even a tissue. When True buys hardcover books, she buys an extra copy for Kathleen, so her mother will not have to suffer the indignity of reading a book after True has mauled it.) The unread two-thirds beckon her. It is a good novel, one she skated over in college, *Anna Karenina*. She'd once thought Anna silly and vain, just shy a prostitute, and could not imagine love so desperate it could end under the wheels of a train. She wants to read more about that now, and wishes she could wander down to the living room. But her house is a hotel tonight, an open house of ceremony. She and Hank are expected to perform in a certain way as part of this ceremony, or, if not, contrive to conceal it. People would see her, and wonder why, so newly wed in bed, she is anxious to read antique novels.

Esa, in one of the guest bedrooms, laughs once, a lover's trill. True wishes Isabelle was still unmarried, for now she could go to her, curl up straight against the headboard, pull her nightgown down over her knees, and chat out everything in the world, as they used to do. But she must not go. She must close her eyes and concentrate on the customary comfort of sleep's dark folds.

True dreams of the eagles, falling and grappling, clasped in flight. Sometime during her dream, someone grasps her own wing and she falls into wakefulness. It is only Hank, having pulled her arm around his chest.

JUNE

SUMMERTIME, BABY, AND LIVING IS EASY

Especially if you have pint-sized and comfortable swim shoes that protect tiny feet, sunglasses with a band that slips around the back of a tiny head but doesn't bind, and a straw hat that really stays on. Baby's straw hat sits right inside yours, and both can be rolled up to take up no more room than a magazine. There are matching red bandanas, too, with lady-bugs aplenty, and a book about a baby mermaid who wants to slip up on shore to see fireflies at night. Everything is gently packed in our summer diaper bag, which is fully water-proof and has compartments not only for the essentials, but also for novels, snacks, and a cooler compartment for an icy can of root beer.

SOMETHING IS CHANGING.

The black-ink drawn trees of April, the soft, mist-limed trees of May have all been banished, overrun by the green tenacity of June. And within the house, the barometer is also rising, the forecast fair.

The sight of Esa's battered Toyota in the drive each morning makes True feel rock-steady and relieved, like a cove-bottomed boat after a tip. As the old fishermen say, she has come close to zero point and not made a circle. She sits low in the water, with Isabelle at her side.

She had underestimated how split-off Rudy would feel after Esa's departure. So briefly parted, the two now seem to have a new sense of purpose. Rudy's California brochures get buried for days under more urgent papers. A crew of black-cat rattles filled with sparkly moons hangs from the window frames in the office, like a string of

182

out-of-season snow globes. They shiver and display their orange winks when the breezes steal in through the screens. The July Blessings – with their red, white and blue shorts and shirts sewn from the same material used to make actual American flags, along with twin packs of the Sun Blessings a local chemist has concocted, have been stowed into clever, soft-sided, rubber sand-pails with zippers, and sent. The August Blessings, with the nineteenth-century boy muscle-swimsuits, are in packing; the September gatherings under way.

Hank becomes more and more a part of the internal compass, by the day. When he opens the refrigerator, he no longer glances at True first, nor does he any longer ask, 'Do you have any Tabasco?' He is settling into his life, walking downstairs in his T-shirt and pajama pants.

True has gifted herself with a Monday morning to go over her finances.

In preparation, she has purchased the best coffee and a single almond croissant to comfort herself.

Because hers is an Internet-based company, True has felt duty-bound to invest in kindred companies. But her natural prudence had held her back from the heat of the frenzy, even as she read mouth-watering accounts of kitchen-table investors becoming Learjet rich overnight.

When the boom busted, True's advisor began dumping tech stocks left and right. He keeps talking long-term and patient persistence, but True still cannot be the kind of person who truly believes that a six-figure loss is 'on paper' or 'a correction.' It is a loss, and it deflates her comfort cushion to a coarser pad, through which she can feel hard times. She has a Yankee's mortal dread of paying this month's wages with last month's profits, and, while she is relieved when prognosticators say dotcom bloodbath has slowed to a trickle, her own orders also have leveled off, if not dipped a little, as luxury purchases always do when people's chains are jerked by fate.

Still, she is terribly grateful she has not taken the same risks as others.

Articles about surprised Young Turks whose vervy mountains of dough deflated were daily fare on the ordinary news pages. They were wiz kids with no degrees, and single lines on their resumes. These dreamers now sit on a loaf gone flat as matzoh. They now face real life, far less prepared for it than True ever could be. 'Get a Job . . .' one headline read the previous week.

True has resources, skills. If her business bottomed, she'd still have her portfolio of evergreens – well, much of it. She would have her house – well, at least some equity in it. But the whole idea of 'stocks' still feels a little funny to her. A part of her believes that her portfolio would better be cashed out and transformed into a neat little savings bank with a porch on the front – in other words, beach property she could rent and rely upon to rise slowly in value. Security she could *see,* that didn't depend on the disposition of some telephone magnate in Japan.

For so long after Pete's death, the stock market seemed like a benign giant who, every few months, tossed down a few more magic beans into True and Guy's kettle. 'Crashes' were momentous, but momentary, in her adulthood, and the best advice always was to hold on. She has always held on, and always been rewarded.

This doesn't seem to be the case any longer. The bounce back seems to be as sluggish as the arc of a soaked tennis ball. True puts her faith in her holdings in biotechnology companies and the like (people will always need mammograms). She will watch her purse strings carefully. She will not expand or create more specialty options, as she has been urged to do. Push may come to shove. If it does, she plans to be stoic.

She is good at stoic.

But she also has become used to a certain kind of leeway, a carelessness with the odd hundred dollars that has nothing to do with her basic nature or the way she was raised, nor even the way she raises Guy. It is wicked easy to become this way, and she has become this way wicked quick. She thinks of what she now uses cash to buy. Ice-cream cones. Coffee. Not clothing nor groceries nor even a new blender – and it hadn't been so long ago she'd done just that.

Though she always said she would sell the house before the business, she would feel it as the loss of a family member: She has become accustomed to the generosity of its contours, the neat aquarium of her office, where every desktop faces a window. She appreciates it anew through Hank's still-awed eyes. One day, he brought home enough cartons to fill a refrigerator box and announced he was putting in a stereo system, so music from a single player might glimmer through the halls on each floor. As he installed it, with a calm capability for finding ways to snake wires and conceal cables she finds deeply erotic, True was tempted to take a glance at the receipt. But her bliss has no room in it for such stingy second-guessing. When she wakes, in the mornings, to Vivaldi or Patsy Cline, she wonders how she has not known life always could be this way.

Now, pining to be outside in the first real soak of the season's sun with her husband and child, she turns up 'The Brandenburg Concertos' and determinedly spreads her projections and her budget out on the bed, picks up her reading glasses, and hunkers down for two hours with a sharp pencil.

For a long while, she does not notice the sounds of the morning from below. After a time, they intrude.

Happily.

School has ended, and Guy and Brendan are down on the lawn with Hank, who has, over the faintest of objections from True, bought Guy a Redline stunt bike. With lumber from the Sandersons' barn (True has observed Hank's way of taking a short walk and coming back with almost anything he wants), they are building a jump, a hollow isosceles triangle from which they will fly at great speeds any moment now.

'Whoo-hoo!! Mom! Come down, Mama!' Guy calls, now. 'We're gonna do it!'

True throws herself out of bed, and runs outside, spilling her coffee on her T-shirt.

Correction: on Hank's T-shirt.

'Sit down,' Hank instructs her, guiding her to an Adirondack chair.

Guy warns, 'This isn't girl stuff, Mom.'

'I'm ready,' True says.

'It's not going to be me first,' Guy says, patting her arm. 'It's going to be Dad. It's going to be Hank, I mean.'

'Okay,' True says. She and Hank exchange raised eyebrows, secret smiles. Neither of them would dare comment on the slipup. But True must bite her tongue, otherwise she'll cry out with joy. Though Hank is wiry, his T-shirt is so filled with his rack of muscle True cannot help but hope neighbors are watching. He begins by spinning on the verge of the driveway, doing wheelies with only the strength of his shoulders, glancing at her from the corner of his eye. He is showing off for his girl, and impressing his son. Who could, who ever would have imagined, only a few short weeks ago, that from the wildly scattered deck she, True, would draw a royal flush, all hearts?

She relaxes into the warmth of the chair's back. The sky is a stainless-steel blue, a breeze with no threat and no wet in it, and True's contentment is pure. To hell, she thinks, with numbers. Numbers don't add up to this.

'Set the course, now Guy,' Hank calls, 'because I have to get a head up to jump it. I haven't done this in fifteen years. I mean, since I was fifteen years old.'

'That would be even more than fifteen years,' True points out gaily.

'Thank you, darlin',' Hank doffs an imaginary cap.

Suddenly, here comes Hank, barreling up the street at an impossible speed, helmetless, high on the pedals, steering straight for the middle of the wooden platform. True begins to rise from her chair, but there is no time for caution; he is in flight, suddenly, sailing, landing without even a wobble on the grass, coasting to a stop. Guy runs to the landing mark with a roll of string, Brendan stepping on the other end (this evidently having been planned in advance) and the three of them use a metal tape measure to calibrate the length.

'Twenty-two feet,' Brendan cries out. 'It's a miracle. He has a gift!'

'It's not twenty-five feet,' Guy beams. 'So you don't win the bet.'

'I said at least twenty,' Hank reminds him.

'You said twenty-five.'

'You know I said at least twenty. I won.'

'Okay,' Guy agrees. 'I owe you ten bucks. Mom, do you have ten bucks?'

'Whoa, sir,' Hank says. '*You* owe me ten bucks. Not Mama.'

'I don't have ten bucks,' Guy explains, 'except in my bank. Which you have to break once it's filled to get the money out.'

'Fine, you can work it off in chores then.'

'Chores?' Guy asks, as if Hank had spoken in Urdu.

'Like picking up the clothes you drop on the floor and your mom has to pick up. And unloading the dishwasher even before Mom or Grandma asks, and especially when they do. You don't always do that now.'

'I'll just wait until school when I get my allowance. I'll be in fifth, so I'll get five bucks,' Guy tells Hank easily.

'What do you get your allowance for?'

Guy is confused. 'It's *my* allowance.'

'But for what?'

'For nothing,' True admits, 'but he doesn't get toys or games except at holidays, or only rarely, and he doesn't have a motorized Razor scooter or a Nintendo, and he didn't have a stunt bike until you . . .'

'That was because we weren't married when he had his birthday,' Hank tells her. 'This is my birthday present to him. Well, this chore situation is clearly going to need a review. From now on, you have to put away all your own clothes after they're washed and bring all your dirty ones downstairs to be washed and unload the dishwasher every night.'

'Nuh unh!' Guy cries.

'Yup!' says Hank. True reflects on whether this is too much, too soon? Yet, she does hate the way Guy doffs everything he has on, wherever he removes it, even if it's on the mat in front of the toilet.

'Mom?' Guy turns to her. True shrugs her shoulders. Present a united front, she reminds herself, the first commandment of parenting.

'I've got to agree with Hank. I think he has a point,' she says. 'I shouldn't always have to be picking up after you.'

True then watches the battle in her son, as he first lifts his foot to stomp off into the house, then realizes what a spoiled baby that would make him seem. Not for nothing do they call it acting, she sees, as Guy bodily masters himself and restores apparent geniality to his face.

But when he puts on his helmet and makes his own approach for his jump, True abruptly and with a sting of adrenaline realizes how angry her son still is, and how determined to prove himself a man. Guy comes pedaling at a furious pace, wobbling, extending himself to the full length of his short legs, and he does clear the jump and sail, far, at least ten feet, but when he lands, he does not get up. And then he screams.

Hank reaches Guy first. 'He's all right, True, he's all right,' he calls to True, who is standing on the porch, who must consciously pull her hand down from her heart, lest she look like Scarlett O'Hara.

She looks at Kathleen's cottage and sees that her mother is standing, rigid, outside her own front door.

*   *   *

'COLLARBONES,' SAYS THE emergency-room physician, 'break very easily in a growing child. The good news is, they heal very easily, too. Decide to jump out of a tree, did you?'

'I was trying to jump my stunt bike,' Guy murmurs, blurred by the Valium they have given him. 'My stepfather made me.'

Hank reddens. 'It wasn't quite like that. We were playing . . .'

True interrupts, 'He certainly didn't *make* him jump. Guy wanted to jump.'

In the car, on the way home, Guy falls asleep, carefully cradling his sling.

'It was my fault,' Hank begins.

'No, it was my fault, for letting it all get out of hand,' True says, 'the bet and all.'

'True, a boy might do that a hundred times, and one time get an injury.'

'But this was the one time. Now, he'll miss piano, and dance . . .'

'Well, maybe he ought to ease off on some of those things for a little while anyhow.'

'How do you mean? You were a *dancer.*'

'Well, I think Gee wants to be a guy right now. Do guy things.'

Hank switches topics, as they curve into the beach round that nestles against Cape Cod Bay. It is low tide, and out on the common flats, they can see tiny figures, a half-mile distant or more, walking toward the water. He asks, 'Look yonder. What do they do out there?'

'Well,' True says, 'they dig clams for one thing. Razor clams and steamers. And they pick up shells and driftwood . . .'

'For art?'

'Some people. Others just to start fires in their fireplaces or their campfires. And they metal-detect.'

'I always thought metal-detector people were nerdy.'

'Well, a guy found a woman's waterproof Rolex out there last summer. Not engraved. Brand new.'

'Might have to get us a metal detector,' Hank laughs. 'Must be some walk.'

'You've never done it?'

'I've never swum in this ocean. This isn't my kind of ocean. Cold, man.'

'Well, it's not the Gulf, that's for sure. But if you went out

188

there, you'd find that water's as warm as any pool. It warms because it's shallow. But if you have a kid with you, the tide can come in, and it's fast, and even a child who's a strong swimmer can get overwhelmed quicker than you could imagine. Adults have.'

'Do you let him walk out there with his friends?'

'With me.'

'And his friends.'

'Yes.'

'How old will he have to be before you let him walk out there alone?'

'Thirty, Hank,' True laughs. 'What are you getting at?'

'It's just you . . . overprotect him a little.'

'Were you overprotected?'

'I don't know.'

'Well, you were pretty cherished.'

'I know I was.'

'The firstborn and only son of a doting mother, a doctor's boy.'

'All I know is when I was Gee's age, I swam in water holes with barracuda at the bottom. I never wore a life preserver. They let me bike-jump. I never wore a helmet. I've got pictures.'

True is silent.

'Don't get mad,' Hank says.

'You're proud of that? You want Guy to not use a helmet? What if he hadn't had a helmet on today? We might be looking at lines on a brain monitor.'

'My parents didn't make such a big deal out of every move I made.'

'Well, all that proves is that it was a different time . . .'

'I just want you to take this accident as a result of a good try gone wrong, not as a tragedy. Not as a reason to make Guy a bubble boy. I want you to take it as progress, of him allowing me a role in his life.'

'Hank, I am,' True answers. 'I was thrilled to see you down there. Can you imagine how I felt when my boy, my son said "Dad" for the first time since he was a baby?' Hank takes her hand.

'Then don't make him a mama's boy . . .'

'Wait! That's not fair! It wouldn't have happened, Hank, if he wasn't mad at you, if he wasn't trying to prove his *honor* to you.

189

But hey, he isn't you. To take a role in his life, you don't have to remake him in the image of what you think a boy should be, or even what you were. Or what boys were twenty years ago.'

'I can see your point. I want him to wear a bike helmet. I know it's safer. But he does look like a doofus in it.'

'Sweetheart! All kids wear bike helmets, or at least they do if their parents catch them.'

'Well, we turned out all right.'

'I'm sure not everybody did.'

'Everybody I knew did.'

'Well, you were fortunate. I knew a kid who had to wear a helmet with plates in it his whole life from diving into a shallow pool on a dare . . .'

'Sounds like a damn stupid kid.'

True is exasperated. 'It wouldn't have mattered to him so much if you hadn't introduced the whole subject of what manly men do, shoot each other over their womenfolk . . .'

'You got a tongue on you like a snake.'

'You got a mind like a mule.'

'Take that back.'

'You first.'

'Well, I take it back too. I almost shit when he fell. I'm not mad. I'm scared, me,' Hank admits.

True puts her head on his shoulder. 'Me, too.'

But she is not accustomed to having to adjust her opinions to suit another's, at least another's with whom she shares a life. Though True has never considered herself anything but the kindest of employers, she speaks her mind without caution. Within her small dominion, she has been the ruler. She wonders, now, how many times she has been resented, as Elizabeth was, gossiped over, mocked. She simply must explain to Hank that he doesn't know much yet about parenthood. He has been only a son, not a father. 'I don't want him to avoid all risks,' True begins quietly.

'And I want him to avoid stupid ones. And you know, True, maybe I don't remember. Maybe I got away with more than I was allowed, and that's what I remember.'

THAT NIGHT, AS Guy moans faintly in his sleep, flattened by painkillers, True and Hank make love with the door open. In the moment of

190

her climax, True bites Hank's shoulder, a little harder than passion would demand. He flinches. She feels grim, satisfied, as the shuddering within her subsides. Now he has seen how a woman bites. But when they make ready for sleep, she in her silk nightgown, Hank carefully twines himself around her, in his chaste drawstring pants, and she feels, though she knows this is not the earth's newest emotion, that she has known her husband's soul since souls were first minted, and that the world can take a flying leap.

Despite the unloosening of her every muscle, True cannot sleep. She curls her spine; she wedges a pillow between her knees.

She checks Guy. At the sight of his sling, she begins to cry. She has no idea why, and she cannot stop.

So as not to wake Hank, she tiptoes down and curls on the sofa under her cashmere afghan. The tears continue. Fear. Relief. Gratitude. Forgiveness? She is not a habitual weeper; she doesn't know where the off handle is on the spigot. Just as she begins to drop off, she startles to a feeling that, at first, seems both ancient and unfamiliar. Hank has lifted her and is carrying her to bed.

The next morning, True visits the CVS pharmacy to buy cotton pads for her toner. She tosses a pair of rubber thongs into the basket, and an ovulation kit and a pregnancy test. She buys a bundle of emery boards and adds a second pregnancy test, just to round out the number. She makes sure to read the back of the ovulation kit to be certain it doesn't require drawing blood. But no, all she needs to do is what she does in the bathroom every day, anyhow.

THE FIRST TIME Hank and True appear in public as a married couple is at a benefit auction for the Cape Family Theater. The first person they meet is a much older man, a retired judge who is an acquaintance of her mother's from her Amherst days. True has not seen the man for years, since Guy was a baby. Guy has run off to show all his friends his sling, and the judge, red-eyed and corpulent, makes his way through the crowd to greet True. 'This can't . . .' the old man peers at Hank, 'this can't be your son? So big already?'

'This is my husband,' True replies miserably, as Hank snorts helplessly, unable to stifle his laughter.

'Oh, of course, I'm so sorry,' the man reddens further. 'I'd heard you'd married.'

'Yes, and robbed the cradle. But he's not so young as he looks,

Judge Hammersmith.' The judge shakes hands with Hank, who still cannot control his mirth.

'This is a fine young woman you've won, son,' he says with gravity.

'I'm very aware of that, sir.'

'You're not from here. I've got an ear for accents. I've got the hearing of an old coon hound.'

Good thing, True thinks, since you have the eyes of a bat.

'I'm from Louisiana. I own a restaurant in Truro. You must bring your wife.'

'Alas,' sighs the judge. 'My wife passed four years ago. And I have not yet been able to convince this young lady's lovely mother to take me up on my many invitations to dine with me.'

'Perhaps she'll change her mind. I had to do some powerful arguing to change her daughter's mind.'

'Well, I wish you only good things.' Judge Hammersmith departs, his stiff progress interrupted by many who wish to shake his hand. His wife, Greta, had been a substantial donor for the theater; and it is True's suspicion that the director, Beatrice, has her eye on the judge's estate, as he has no children of his own.

'You didn't have to do some powerful argument, you big stinker. Anyhow, aren't you hot? Let's go home,' True teases, as soon as the judge is out of earshot.

'What? We just got here. If you think this is hot, you'd never survive in Louisiana.'

'Well, I'd have a portable air conditioner made for my head. And it really isn't the heat. It's that you laughed. When he said that. About us.'

'What did you want me to do, punch him? It was funny. True, the man saw the outline of a male, and he assumed . . .'

'Maybe this *is* against nature. Maybe everyone here thinks the same thing. Look at that old fool. Look at True, hanging all over that young guy . . . maybe you should just leave me, run off like Heathcliffe.'

'In point of fact, you are not hanging all over me, *chère*. I wish you would.' True takes Hank's arm. 'True, you have to get over this. And toute de suite. Because it's dangerous. True, you have to believe that every time I look at a woman, I'm not thinking to myself, gosh, I wish that were my wife. I wish my wife were younger. I wish True

192

looked like her. Glancing is not coveting. Now come on, Miss Cape Cod. Let us greet the populace. And I want you to hang all over me please, like the doting wife you are, True Dickinson Bannister.'

He has not even finished speaking when Beatrice throws her arms around his neck, chattering that he *must* get involved with the acting company, that if he does not act she can teach him. He *has* to act, because he surely has the looks for it, and Beatrice has heard that he is a dancer, and there's such a great need to coach the little ones in movement. 'I'd be glad to do anything I can, given my own work and . . . teaching our son.' True stares up at Hank in astonishment. 'I'll be teaching Guy some ballet and jazz, just rudimentary things.'

'Lucky Guy. He's so gifted, True, really. The dance is all he needs. And to slim down. And they're the same thing, aren't they?' Beatrice whirls away gaily, her costume of many scarves floating and flittering as she goes.

'She's very nice,' Hank says.

'She is. She's wonderful. She's so strict. Once Guy tried out for a production of, oh, I don't know what, *Peter Rabbit*, with another theater, and he got the lead role, but he refused it, and it was his first lead . . . he's always been the utility infielder for Beatrice. But he told me later, "They're too nice to the kids, Mama. They never stop and yell at you."'

'That's preparation for real theater, though I hate to think of her being hard on him,' Hank pauses, tips up True's chin, and kisses her lightly. 'Feel better?'

'Yes, I don't want to book a same-day facelift anymore,' True admits. 'But I have to tell you, I don't feel *good,* and it has nothing to do with what people think. I feel, you know, queasy.'

Hank takes hold of both her shoulders. 'Do you think that you're pregnant?'

'No,' True answers. 'I just had . . . no, I'm not. But would you be excited?'

Hank seems to exhale visibly.

'Sure,' he says.

'You don't sound too convincing.'

'Sure I would, but like you said, one world at a time, you know?'

'This sucks,' Guy remarks, coming up behind them. 'I can't play because my neck is killing, and no one can sign a damned sling.'

'Don't curse,' True reminds him absently.

'Hank says "damn" is not a swear.'

'Oh. Well, there's a dad for you.' And so they glide, Hank easily, True on the lookout, through the rest of the humid, settling day, its vapors growing heavier and heavier, vowing a storm. True's nausea worsens, and she wonders if this could indeed be a weird signal of gestation, then remembers the congealed crust on the potato salad. She'd had only a few bites.

At home, she lies on the bed and tells Hank to send Gee over to her mother's.

'No, let me take him along with me,' Hank suggests, and Guy, overhearing, begins a chant of entreaty; he wants to put the cherries in the drinks; he's never been at the restaurant the whole night; he'll be good and not get in the way; he'll clean off the tables; chores, remember? And True relents. 'It'll be a slow night anyhow, if it storms,' Hank says. 'This is the night we close the cash register.'

'What does that mean?'

'We take in the money off the arm, to pay the taxes.'

True sits up, her stomach lurching. 'That's illegal!'

'It's a little illegal, True. It's as illegal as hiring a Mexican busboy without papers.'

'You do that? You can't do that! And you can't do the other anymore either.'

'We have to.'

'No you don't have to! Not anymore! I'll pay the taxes! Don't you see? If you do this, I'll be colluding in it. It could ruin me.'

'I didn't think of that. I think of our work as separate. I guess it isn't.'

'Oh, Hank, how many times did we go to lawyers to get our things to be *not* separate?'

'Okay, I'll talk to Tom. Now, don't work yourself up. You're white as the bedspread.'

'Okay, okay. Have fun with Gee. Don't let him . . .'

'I won't let him burn up his other arm or fall into the Broaster or drink a fifth of scotch.'

'Go away,' True says, relieved. 'You are a rascal. But, at least, now you won't be a rascal and a federal criminal.'

The storm breaks with a fury, and in one icy-blue bolt True sees one of her trees go down. The very ground shakes. True rises and throws up down to her organs in her clean oval toilet, and stands

194

up, feeling icy-blue and sweaty and relieved. Then, she sees in a flash of light her mother coming across the yard, in a mackinaw the size of Maine. She loudly unbuckles her boots, then drips her way up the staircase. 'Jesus Christ, True! Are you okay?'

'Jesus Christ? Mother, I never heard you swear like that.'

'I never had a damn tree fall ten feet in front of my door!' Kathleen peers at True. 'What's the matter with you?'

'I have the flu. I have, I think, some rotten bug I got from the yucky potato salad at the picnic for the theater.'

'I'll get you some ginger ale.'

'You don't have to.'

'I don't mind. I'm not going back over there and have a tree fall on my bed!'

They sit together on True's bed, Kathleen sipping tea and True dozing. When she wakes, she sees that her mother has been re-arranging the stack of wedding presents that still sits on True's grand-mother's old chest. 'One of these isn't opened,' Kathleen says, holding up the white box from Clothilde.

'I just never got around to it. Let's open it now.'

'Shouldn't you wait for Hank?'

'He won't mind. That's not the kind of thing he minds.'

'Is Guy asleep?'

'He's with Hank at work.'

'Okay,' Kathleen replies with real devilry. 'Let's open it.'

Inside, True finds a beautiful photo album, handmade, blank. And beneath that, another beautiful album, also sewn at the seams. As she flips it open, she sees it contains every atom of a firstborn son's life: Hank's birth certificate, his lock of dark hair, his first photos (in a tiny tuxedo), a snapshot labeled *Walking! Only Ten Months!*, another of him dancing on stage (in a larger tuxedo and a top hat) at about six, glorious summer pictures of Win and Hank, holding Tannie across their two laps, the big kids brown as horse chestnuts. Hank with a parrot on his shoulder, skinny as a child in a Dickensian etching, every rib outlined, then Hank, filled out, older, so lazily sexy and beautiful, with his hooded blue eyes about to wink at the camera that True hears her mother's involuntary intake of breath. Hank, shirtless, in a kayak. Hank battling some kind of game fish. Gus and Clothilde and one of the three girls – True thinks it is Win – both she and Hank wearing mortarboards and gowns. Hank holding an old woman, whom True imagines to be his grandma, on his lap. Hank on skis, with a woman True cannot see, who might not have a body for all the layers she is wearing; Hank in a sailing craft with a man True recognizes as a much younger Tom. Report cards and birthday letters: *Son, you're sixteen now, and though you've made us proud in many ways this year, especially at State, it's time to start applying yourself in school. I'll love you even if you're a bum, but don't make me. Pop.* As True tenderly closes the album, thinking what a full-hearted gift this is, virtually giving Hank's life into his wife's hands, a tiny glassine envelope, like an earring bag, falls out. Inside, the rusty pearl of a baby tooth. She folds it gently back into the pocket of the album, where she spies a baptismal candle, and more. She can't wait to show this to Guy, for them to compare this with Guy's own life-album.

The enclosed note says, *You didn't get to know Henry's past, so we give it to you. This other is for you to make your future together. With all our love, Clothilde and Gus.*

It is the baby tooth that turns her heart. She has an earring box in her own bureau filled with Guy's. She thinks a team of gladiators might not tear it from her hands. But here is Hank's, given with grace and an amplitude of trust, to a daughter-in-law who still is basically a stranger. True holds the album to her chest, hugging it as if it were warm, magnolia-scented Clothilde. Something quenching washes across a dry plain within her. True wonders, guiltily, tipping her face away so that Kathleen does not glimpse the beatitude, if this is the family she has watched for all her life, like a passing stranger glancing in at a glowing window. A family in which people don't move over stiffly to make room on the bench, but get up and offer you the softest chair, insisting that they were tired of sitting anyhow.

But Kathleen has not noticed. She is inspecting a find from the bottom of the box, a large, padded envelope, labeled 'Hank.' It is sealed. Kathleen, one eyebrow arched, hands it to True. 'It's already loose,' her mother says softly. 'Don't you want to open it?' She holds the steam from her tea mug first under one, then the other corner of the envelope, and slowly, slowly pries open the flap without even the tiniest tear.

'No,' True says. 'It's Hank's.

'I thought all that was his is yours.'

'Mom, you'd think you worked for the CIA. Let's . . . maybe we shouldn't look at it.'

'But you want to, though, don't you?'

'Not particularly,' says True. She would give up her right forefinger to look. Her nausea has been replaced by something she can only call an adrenaline rush. She glances at the clock. It's only nine . . . but the storm. They could close early. She opens the envelope. There are many letters. And some pictures. True lifts and peruses them one by one. Hank in a sport coat, with a woman whose long black hair falls like a cape over her long black dress. Hank in a silly nightshirt. Hank, naked but covered, reading in bed. A woman in a business suit making a kissing moue of her mouth at the camera. College-party photos. A postcard. *Don't miss me too much. I'll be back soon.* A particularly thick envelope, the kind the drugstore sends back with full rolls. True dumps it out. Adele. Adele as she remembers Adele from her publicity photos, head tilted as she looks up from a desk, Adele lying on a bed, sitting with her face lifted to the sun. Beautiful Adele. There's a letter stuffed inside, *I can't believe it, honey! Two Books TWO BOOKS!* Adele and Hank with another man, standing flanked by hawthorn bushes in bloom, she, as tall as Hank if not a bit taller, in corduroy shorts and boots, a sweater thrown around her neck in the way all Cape women except True can manage. Adele on a rocky path, with a huge walking stick. Adele against a stormy sky. Adele crawling out of a pup tent, her two winged hands a protest against the photograph. Adele sipping wine on a wide rock. A wide rock. Adele and Hank on Mount Washington.

True begins to stuff the photos back into the envelope, not even pausing when she glimpses one in which a girl in jeans, fully clothed, is straddling Hank (also fully clothed) in a mock wrestle on the floor.

'Wait,' Kathleen whispers, in an odd tone, as the thunder booms. 'Put them back the way they were. Take a moment.'

'Mom, what the hell does it matter?'

'You knew that he knew Adele Cabot.'

'Seeing is different.'

'They're just old pictures, but . . . True, stop. Put them back as they were. You don't want him to know you rummaged.'

'You think I'd lie to him?'

Kathleen looks at her daughter for a long moment, her face composed. 'Better not. Maybe he'll show you them someday. Maybe

197

he won't. Maybe his mother knew you wouldn't want to see them. She was kind enough to seal them. Just put them back in the exact order.'

'Why are you so set on this?'

'Just do. People have . . . private things. You have private things. People are funny about them.'

'Well, you've got me all worked up now! I want to read the letters. I want to see if he lied to me when he said he was never really in love before.'

'True, why would you feel that? Everyone falls in love more than once. Maybe you should never have opened it.'

'It was *your* idea, Mother.'

'Well, now, yes it was. So that's why we should put it back, and seal it with glue stick, and leave out the other albums, and tell him we opened them together.' True looks into her mother's gray eyes, with their aureole of tiny wrinkles, and sees a young woman's gaze, keen and explicit. 'He will respect you for your reticence, instead of feeling ashamed or invaded.'

'You know this.'

'I know.'

And True's mother covers her daughter to the shoulder with the comforter, as she has not done since True was pregnant, and before then, since True was a child, and picks up her mack. 'I've left a puddle on your carpet, True. I'm sorry,' Kathleen says.

'It's only water.'

'I'll go to bed now. In the guest room, if it's all right with you.' The trees are still boiling, heaving. Kathleen takes the padded envelope with her, and in the morning, when True checks, it is lying, innocent and sealed, at the bottom of the long white gift box. When he comes home, Hank glances at it, lifts it, replaces it. 'Probably my old bills,' he laughs.

LATER THAT NIGHT, she and Hank and Guy get out Guy's baby book. 'I think he looks like me,' Hank insists, and they all laugh – Guy and Hank are like a photo and a negative, light and dark – 'No, look at the chin, and his shoulders. Yep, he looks like me.'

Then they have a ball with Hank's childhood album, laughing at his striped polo shirts and Billy the Kid bell-bottoms, at the pink lapels on his prom tuxedo (and Grandpa Gus's lemon leisure suit),

198

giggling as Hank groans when they find the inevitable shot with shoulder-length hair and bandana.

Guy ceremonially pastes the first picture of Hank and True as husband and wife in the new, white, beribboned book, and then signs it, 'Mom and Hank/Dad eloping.' He says the two of them look as though they'd been up all night. 'I hope the party pictures will be better, Mom,' he says seriously. 'I'm going to write in that I was the one who gave the party.'

True places it in the dry cedar closet, on top of the rosewood box her father made for her mother as a wedding gift, in which lie the wedding gloves Kathleen had shown True when she was a child, and packets of letters, from all those months her dad traveled the country with his crates of books, A to Z.

The next night, when she is alone and Guy is outside, watching a handyman saw the fallen aspen into fireplace logs, True goes looking for the padded envelope. But it and the white box are gone.

JULY

SPARKLER, SPARKLER IN THE SKY!

It's time for fun, fireworks, and fashion. Crafters who actually sew flags, with stars and bars in all the right places, make our red-white-and-blue short set. Find it in a watermelon basket, with a brand-new twist on the monkey puzzle – picnic ants that fit together, all in a row – to keep little fingers busy. And don't forget to pack the Sun Blessings, our own deliciously safe and scented concoction, to protect new skin, and grown-up skin, too.

CONDITIONS SEEM IDEAL.

The barometer rises.

Then, it reverses.

Fair weather predominated in June. July is squally, unpredictable. Owners of beach cottages begin demanding death certificates when the renters who pledged their eternal gratitude in March find themselves unable to honor their promises just a few months later.

'I'm an uncle!' Hank shouts, late one Monday night, as True is getting out of the shower. He picks her up and swings her around the bathroom, as drops fly. 'You're getting light as a twig, darlin'. And you're a godmama!'

'What?'

'Tannie wants us to stand godparents for her new baby. In a couple of weeks. We do it early, swamp superstition being the baby's got to be dipped in case he dies. But this one's a keeper. Eight pounds seven ounces of Bannister boy! The first boy in the family! Carr Bannister Swallow. Pretty name, huh?' True grabs for a towel. Guy, attracted by the ruckus, peeps in at their bedroom door and then reverses his direction, backing away when he realizes True is undressed.

'Back in a minute,' Guy calls from the hall.

'It's a nice name,' True ventures.

'What's wrong?'

'Well,' True improvises, 'I'm not sure I can be godmother. I'm not a Catholic. Not a Roman Catholic.'

'Oh, that's okay,' Hank says easily. 'One of Tannie's girls' godfathers was my buddy Perry, and he's a Baptist. You just have to be something or other.'

'And,' True nods at the hallway, 'he's not the first boy in the family. There's, you know, our boy.'

'You know what I mean,' Hank tells her. 'In my family. The Bannister family.'

'You know what I mean, too,' True retorts. 'We're in the Bannister family, too, huh?'

'Why do you have to be so goddamned difficult about everything?' Hank pouts. 'Am I not supposed to celebrate the birth of my nephew? Is that going to *offend* someone? Why do you try to make trouble where there is none?'

'Forget it,' True sighs, and then asks, 'Do I do that?'

'You do. You look for the ice chip inside the snowball. Sometimes it's just a snowball. But you can find something to hurt you if you try hard enough.'

'I don't want to hurt. I don't want to take offense. Maybe I'm just made that way. But you have to admit, first boy in the Bannister family . . .'

'Okay, okay. That was a little much. I'm glad Guy wasn't here.'

'So now we're okay, right?'

'And that. Do you have to know before I leave the house every day if some little thing is on my mind that's going to make me think about you during the day and get irritated?'

'I guess. I like to stay in . . . what do you say? I like us to be in grace.'

'We'll talk about it at dinner, okay, *chère*?' Hank asks. 'I'm just new to thinking of Guy that way. I'm clumsy.'

You're clumsy; I'm brittle. Together, we make one perfect bull in a china shop, True thinks.

'Okay,' she, however, agrees, knowing Hank is, at least, not lying.

They plan to have dinner together tonight, one of Hank's rare nights off, at The Bistro. So as not to ruin that in advance, True adds, 'We don't have to have a big deal about it. It's just that . . . don't tell him they're his *grand-mère* and *grand-père* and then make it like this new baby is a better Bannister.'

'They won't think the baby's better,' Hank says. 'In fact, if I know my folks, they'll think of that ahead of time and get him something to spoil him.'

'You know something I don't?'

Hank lifts her chin. 'Maybe I know a slew of things you don't.'

Still, she knows she's got his goat, with the discussion of Bannister Salic law, and that he'll head down to the beach, where he'll swim for half an hour, trying to stroke away his irritation with her. But the strokes will only carve off so much of his chagrin. He'll emerge with his hair seal-slicked, his skin bluish under the beige, and his shoulder chip intact. She already has heard the opening notes of the refrain. They will enter what True has begun to describe to herself as The Grand Silence. She will ask Hank twice, or eleven times, what is on his mind. He will not reply. He will appear deep in concentration over newsprint pictures of antique Trans Ams, or books of recipes. She will repeat her queries. He will finally offer, 'Nothing is wrong. Why should anything be wrong?'

Why? Is this my man, or men in general who are prone to this behavior? True ponders.

She thinks, I must ask Franny, is that trait on the Y chromosome, too? Can they not talk about a thing directly, but only slant? And too late to remedy it? Hank had presented himself as the open man, a chatter, a puzzler, an asker of questions. He had not, early on, displayed the side of him that withdraws, that is so like Pete, and that frightens True into a seething, timid retreat, much how rabbits must feel under the shadow of wings – both outraged and cowed.

Now, True will begin the guessing game. He is angry that she has injected Guy into his celebration over Tannie's baby boy, but this is not sufficient grounds for The Grand Silence. There is some issue, or trouble, with business, that he has been waiting to discuss with her. Perhaps he has had a row with Tom. Or perhaps he is anticipating, and he is correct, that she will bicker with him about driving to Louisiana, even though he has no reason to want to drive except that he likes to drive, though a thousand-mile drive through muggy summer air, with Guy whining and Hank complaining that kids in his day didn't whine, will be an exercise in masochism. Any of these things might be the cause for her husband's unannounced plunge into the sixty-two-degree Atlantic. But she wills herself to hold back. Asking Hank what the problem is elicits nothing but confusion and resentment, she has learned.

He is, Isabelle suggests, a muller. Douglas is this way, she points out, and she has learned to flip it off. When he has finished with his mulling, maybe he will be forthcoming. Maybe he will not.

They have been married four months, and she has failed to pinpoint a root source of Hanks's vague restlessness, if it can be called that, which informs all their days, like a low-grade fever, or a draft through a sagging screen. They can be caught in bliss; but let her put a foot wrong, brush off a caress, corner him on a mistake anyone could see, and he's off. And lately, once he's off, it takes days to reel him back in. The result is that True, who is not used to equivocating, finds herself measuring out all her words in teaspoons to keep the peace. She must negotiate, is what it amounts to, with cluelessness.

It is at this moment that True stops where she stands and realizes that her patience with Hank's mulishness is thin; it is not like Isabelle's casual confidence in Douglas's abiding love. Her tolerance for Hank's reticence is thin, friable, about as deep as a sunburn.

It reminds her of . . . her.

There simply cannot be two martyrs in one family. That is territory True has herself claimed long ago. Legitimately. It is so . . . not merely unpleasant but nearly brain-scorching to even entertain the notion that she has married her mirror, that she sticks it in her mind's back pocket as sheer fancy. After all, she, True, has struggled. She has faced wicked odds and overcome them. Hank has had a fair pass since the birth canal. What is his excuse for grumping around so eloquently? She considers, instead, Hank's lapses, which are real, whether or not the result of his inexperience. There was the time last week, when Guy, overcharged over some athletic feat or other, a three-pointer or a flip on his skateboard, had come barreling up the drive and attempted to jump into Hank's arms.

But Hank, while offering a brief hug, had held Guy down.

'Whoa, fella,' he'd said, 'you're way too big for me to pick up. I'll be in traction!'

Guy's shame gushed across the hundred feet of air between him and his mother, as she sat in her office. Hank did not realize that he had made Guy feel exactly like what a ten-year-old boy cannot bear to feel like – a baby, even though, in his hunger for the cumulative remediation of fatherly affection, he has been acting exactly that way: curling up next to Hank on the couch, making excuses to touch him on the shoulder or bump into him as he passes him coming into a room. To these gestures, Hank has seemed receptive but bewildered. He pats Guy; he punches him playfully; but he stops short of kissing him. She would like Hank to kiss Guy, and hug him, unasked. She has had no idea of how to bring this up, until the jumping incident. That night, in bed, she'd said, 'You know, today, it humiliated him.'

'What did?' Hank asked, absorbed in ironing his next day's clothing.

'When you refused to pick him up.'

'He shouldn't want to be picked up. That's what I'm talking about, True. It's not right for a kid his age to want that kind of –'

'Does your dad kiss you?'

She can see Hank's wish to prevail struggle with what is, after all, the best of him. He does not lie, not outright. 'What's that got to do with a ten-year-old acting like a baby? Of course, my daddy kisses me, but that's a Southern –'

'That's the grown-man equivalent of picking you up.'

'I don't mind once in a while, but he's all over me, and he takes everything I have. You know, my hair brush, my hair gel, my clothes . . .'

The clothing has been a longstanding beef. Since the night they first made love, True does not have permission to borrow Hank's shirts. He rightly points out he never borrows hers.

And he has complained vocally that his T-shirts have come up missing. Guy *has* been taking them deliberately, wearing them in order to feel both closer to Hank and more grown-up and stylish. But now Hank has bought a separate hamper, and does his own washing – a habit, he says, of his destitute bachelorhood, when taking care of each pair of slacks, each long-sleeved shirt, was economic necessity. True suspects it is more, that he feels he is being consumed by her household, his identity absorbed in the flush and flow of common possessions, but she is afraid to give that voice. She might be accused of armchair psychologizing.

Still, why is it that a grown man cannot become accustomed to such a small thing? He reprimands Guy sharply when he finds a shirt of his lobbed into a corner of Guy's bedroom.

And now True honestly tries to explain: 'The reason he takes your shirt is the reason he tries to jump on you. Not because there's something wrong with him. Because he hasn't had a dad for so long. He wants to be like you. He wants you to want him.'

And Hank replies stubbornly, 'Well, True, the kid has to weigh a hundred pounds. I can't toss him up in the air and catch him like he was a two-year-old.'

'That's just the thing. Nobody *has* tossed him up and caught him like he was a two-year-old since he *was* a two-year-old. You have to make allowances.'

'I do make allowances. The kid has wrecked two of my good shirts with ketchup.'

'We can replace shirts, Hank. He needs your love. All your love. Even shirts.'

'But they're *my* shirts.'

'Well, in a family, things get mixed up.'

'They don't even fit him. They hang down to his knees. I think he's just used to taking whatever he wants. I saw him messing with my pocket watch the other day. My daddy gave me that for high-school graduation, you know?'

'Maybe you should give him some things of yours, little things, so he'll feel like you're . . . taking him as your own.'

'I don't feel that way yet. I'm . . . I'm getting to. I'm trying to. But I don't.'

True cannot believe her ears. 'You don't feel that way yet?' How can anyone not love Guy? Not just from her point of view, but objectively? She tries again, 'Can you sort of . . . fake it until you do?'

'I'll do things in my own time and my own way,' Hank says, but gently. 'It's not that I don't want to.'

'Oh, I see. Touching your stepfather's things is getting your own way. It's being spoiled.'

'You don't have . . . you know what you don't have in this house?'

And then, her best intentions stretched tight as violin strings by the whine in his tone, she snaps. She grows spines. And asks, too softly, 'What? Pray tell.'

205

'Boundaries. You don't have boundaries. The kid walks into your room whenever he wants. He walks into your office and starts talking even when you're on the phone . . .'

'All kids do that . . .'

'And Isabelle walks around like she owns the place. Kathleen doesn't even knock . . .'

'Do you knock on your mother's door?'

'That's not what we're talking about . . .'

'No, listen. Did you knock on your mother's door?'

'Her bedroom door. We had boundaries. I had three sisters, and I had to respect their privacy, and I wasn't allowed to touch their things without their permission.'

'Well, he has no sisters. The closest thing he's ever had to a sister is Esa, and she has had the run of the place for eight years.'

'Then we need to set some rules,' Hank says, thumping away firmly on the fabric with the iron. 'Some boundaries. You want to use something, you ask first. You want to come in, you ask first.'

'You want a hug, you ask first.'

'There's no dealing with you, True.'

Another of the Grand Silences. After two days in which their conversation has consisted of good nights and good mornings, True has called Hank outside for a walk. 'I know I've offended you. Tell me how.' Hank, hands in pockets, shrugs. 'Come on.' No answer. 'Please. I'll listen.'

'No, you'll interrupt me.'

'I won't.'

'Okay.' True then waits. A minute. Two minutes. 'So, what's wrong?'

'See? You interrupt.'

'You weren't *saying* anything!'

'I was about to. I was getting ready to.'

'Okay.' Another two minutes pass. True sits down on a stump, determined that not a single word will pass her lips until Hank offers up his thoughts. Finally, she breaks down. 'I'm accustomed to pauses that are fewer than two minutes in length.'

'Don't rush me. You'll hear things you don't want to hear.'

'There's nothing I don't want to hear less than this nothing, Hank. It feels like a weapon.'

How do men learn this? To draw a silence like a gun? Why cannot

True learn it, too? It is a great weapon, so much more effective than nagging. She waits another minute, counting one, a thousand, two, a thousand. She waits two minutes. She has never imagined she could see Hank as anything but beautiful; however, his sulky little boy's pose suddenly is cloying. If they were in a boat, she might hit him with an oar.

'Okay,' he says, finally. 'I feel like . . .' A minute. Two.

'What?'

'I feel like . . . I'm being eaten alive.'

'Oh.'

This is how you get an old lady to say 'Bingo.' Fuck.

Hank goes on, 'Guy wants this. You want that. You're always watching me. I'm used to my space, True. I'm used to time for . . . contemplation. Now, before I go to work, Guy always wants me to play with him or help him with his homework or to show me something he drew or listen to him sing, or you want me to fix something or . . . I feel like there's no time to just be me.'

'That's what family life is.'

'It wasn't in our family.'

'Oh.'

'I'm thinking of taking a few days off, go off by myself, just to think.'

'To think about what?'

'I . . . don't know if I'm made for this, True. It's like you want me to be this all-at-once-no-assembly-required husband and father.'

'I don't want that. I knew it would take adjusting. I had no idea how . . . put-upon you felt.'

'I suppose that, if I'm honest, I didn't know that was what I was buying into.'

True feels a cloud of panic cross over her head, and cowers under its chill. 'Are you thinking of . . . leaving me?'

'No, not really.'

'Not really?'

'No.'

'Well, we're married. Did you mean when we got married that we'd be married for life?'

'Yes. Of course I did. And I do. I just didn't know what forever meant. I didn't know how hard it would be to go from being a guy who, and I know this sounds lousy, set his own time and his own

207

agenda to having to live my whole life by somebody else's. I didn't know how hard it would be to adjust to being a husband and father, all at once, and in such a short time.'

'So you're thinking of leaving me, but not now.'

'I didn't say that. You're putting words into my mouth.'

'Well, I wouldn't, if you said something unequivocal for once. Something without an "I guess," or a "maybe" in it.'

Hank has begun pacing, in and out of the shadow of the street lamp, his face working. It is like watching an old movie, with bad effects. Man. No man. Man. No man. 'I just don't know if I can take the constant pressure of . . . people expecting things of me. Especially Guy. I know the poor kid wants a father, but I can't stand having anyone all over me . . .'

'You ass,' True says softly.

'What did you say?'

'I said, "You ass."' I should have said, "You selfish ass." You're a grown man, Hank. You had a father all your life, there for you, listening to you, guiding you. You still talk to him, what, every week? Didn't you think Guy would want that same thing?' She adds, 'And when you asked me to marry you, don't you remember you said, "I have a feeling about your son. I know he needs a father"?'

'I thought it would be easier. I thought he would be an easier kid. And I didn't think he'd glom on to me so quick.'

'But he is an easy kid,' True insists. Guy is in the dictionary under 'nice kid.' He is polite; he gets good grades. He does most of what he's told. 'What I think you mean is he's a kid, period, and you're not used to kids, period. Not day in, day out.'

He does not get it, she thinks, that in child time, days were weeks and weeks were years. In July, Christmas seems impossibly distant. At Christmas, it seems your birthday in March will never come. How has he forgotten this? He, who reminds her, with his bike jumping and general playfulness *that it wasn't so long ago* that he was a boy.

'Hank, I want to ask you something. Did anyone ever break up with you?' True begins.

'I don't know.'

'You don't know if anyone ever broke up with you?'

'I don't know anyone ever broke up with me in so many words. I guess it was more a matter of I just stopped seeing so much of a woman, but I wouldn't be able to tell you, here and now, who initiated the idea of seeing less of each other. But if this were anyone I dated for any length of time, we'd still talk and . . . I don't know, why?'

'Did any of your lovers ever intrude on you?'

'No.'

True feels as though she is talking to one of the recorded books Guy had owned as a little tot; you press a button and each page plays a song, the same song every time.

'You really don't know whether any of your girlfriends ever intruded on you? Did you ever have a fight with someone because she got on your nerves?'

'No.'

'Did you ever have any kind of fight with someone?'

'No.'

'Why not?'

'Why not? Why would you?'

'Well, what did you do when you disagreed?'

'We didn't disagree.'

'Even about, like, politics?'

'I think somebody once said I was a closet monk.'

'A closet monk?'

'Because I said I liked the idea of monk clothing. You know, just these long robes. Women put a dress on, and you're dressed. Not having to match your belt to your shoes. Women have it easier.'

True lets that pass, knowing that this is not an opportune time for a debate on plucking eyebrows, makeup, and pantyhose.

'Well, did anyone ever take one of your shirts?'

'No.'

'Why? What about Lucy? You lived in the same house. You slept together . . .'

'Not every night. I had my own room. We did our laundry separately . . .'

'Well, I think you've just had it your own way your whole life, and when you didn't have it your own way, or it looked like you might not have it your own way, you split.'

'Maybe I did.' He looks at her, his eyes static with concentration. 'Maybe I did do that. I didn't like . . . I liked to set the limits. But every single person does.'

'But you can't do that now. You can't set the limits, not all of them, and you can't split now,' she says. Hank says nothing. 'You're married. We promised. And we promised for good. In front of everyone.'

'Are you worried about what people would think? Or worried about us?'

'Us! I don't give a damn what people think or I wouldn't have done it in the first place. I wouldn't want to live without you. Not the same way.'

'Neither would I. Which is what makes this so horrible. True, I love you. I care about Guy. I even, hell, I'm even getting used to Kathleen. But I go around worrying about whether I'm going to let you down.'

'Well, you're not. You're not.'

'Are you sure?'

'I'm sure for one of us. I don't know if I can be sure for both of us.' Hank puts his arms around her.

As THEY LEAVE The Bistro later that week, Hank's night off deferred by their tiff, a squall is blowing in steadily. True's arms pimple with the sudden chill, and Hank, who insists it is just his blood, not he, that is thinner, enfolds her from behind.

'Just when you think you got you a summer, it goes cold on you,' he says, shaking his head. Truer words were never spoken, True thinks in puzzled dread. Drops begin to fall, huge and slow.

'Let's run for the car, at least!' True cries. 'What are we standing here for?'

'Wait,' Hank demands. 'Just wait a minute.' They huddle under the two-foot-deep porch roof of the Chamber of Commerce, as rain sluices over them, as if a shower curtain holds it around them. 'True, I want to ask you something serious.'

'What?' True asks impatiently, shuddering.

'Do you always wear underarm deodorant?'

'What?' True stumbles out into the rain, and is instantly drenched. 'What? How dare . . . ?'

'I was kidding,' Hank pulls his sweater over his head and drops it over True's. 'I really wanted to ask you, may I have your permission to ask for Guy's hand in adoption? I didn't ask him the first time, which was a violation of his manhood, and I got in a world

210

of trouble. But I want him to know, before we go home to my folks, that he is the first boy in the Bannister family. I want that very much, and I suspect Guy wants it, too.'

'Are you serious?' True is touched, but perplexed. 'How can you mean this after what we just talked about, how hard it's been for you, all that?'

'You pay too much attention to me, is all. You got to learn to be like everyone else I ever met, and not take me seriously.'

'It's serious to adopt my boy.'

'My boy,' says Hank, and his eyes have never been so molten.

'When, then?' True asks, as their lips part. His taste of salt, as if the rain were blood.

'Well, what's today?' Hank asks.

THEY MAKE THEIR way back to the lawyer with the sweet, Cheshire Cat smile, the one who drew up their wills. Not to discourage them, but because it is his duty, he duly warns them that he has, in his time, seen horrific cases in which parents marry, adopt a spouse's child, and then split, causing heartbreak compounded by a child's bewildered sorrow. 'How many?' True asks.

'Six or seven,' their lawyer says, pursing his lips sadly. He is a handsome man, with his great blue eyes and speckled pate, and yet he still manages to have the secretive, ironic look of a creature that lives in a hole in a tree.

They are silent, and exchange looks, neither aware that the other finds this look both searching and unsettling.

'We're confident,' Hank finally says. 'We think it's important for Guy's feeling of security.'

'It is,' the lawyer concedes. 'But it also could hand him an extra helping of insecurity later on if things were to go wrong. There's no statute of limitations on when you adopt him.'

'Well, we're here, and we've had the home study,' True sighs, 'and blood tests and TB tests and psychological tests and there is a limitation on those.'

'You're thinking practicality then,' the lawyer says.

'No, as Hank says, security,' True answers. 'This is real, not a gesture. As I told you when we drew our wills, there isn't any circumstance under which I wouldn't want Guy to be Hank's son.'

'Well, then, this is a simple matter.'

211

Still, she worries, whenever she catches sight of one of Hank's glances into the impenetrable distance, whether they are doing the right thing, whether, in doing this, which True assumes is a gesture meant to reassure her, they may harm Guy. A few days before the formal proceeding, however, something happens to convince her. It is, she believes, a sign.

Early one Sunday morning, True collars Guy as he bounds down the driveway. 'Where are you off to so early?'

'I'm going with Dad to make his deliveries.'

'Deliveries?' she asks. 'What deliveries?'

'To the poor people who speak French. In The Breakers, that's two. And in the trailers. That's three.'

'You talk like you've done this before,' True says.

'I did, the day we had teacher's institute.'

'What did you do?'

'Talked, goofed around. Hank asked me if I would want to call him "Dad" after the adoption . . .'

'And . . .' True prompts.

'Well, we went to this one lady's. She had thirty cats, Mom, and she was really nice to them, and she had fifteen litter boxes. It wasn't a mess, but the lousy apartment people took them. All but one. She loves cats so much, she even named her daughter Kitty.'

'What did you say about calling Hank "Dad"?'

'Well, I'm trying it out. I'm seeing if I like it. He says it's okay either way.'

'Did he ask you how you really felt about the adoption?'

'Yeah.'

'Well, what did you say?'

'I told him, the first night you asked me, I sort of almost cried about it in bed, because . . . you know, Mom, it's not very loyal to Dad. But Hank said Dad would know, and he would say it was in addition to him, not in place of him. Hank believes in heaven.'

'Did you think that was baloney?'

'No,' Guy says thoughtfully. 'Not really. I don't want to be the only kid in school who doesn't have a dad all my life. I figured since he was living here anyway, I might as well let him. Having a stepdad is stupid. It makes it sound like you got a divorce.'

'What'd he say?'

'He said he was . . . he said "thank you."'

212

'Can I come with you guys?'

'I don't know. I have to ask Han . . . Dad.'

True has planned to spend the morning catching up on paperwork, trying to further untangle the skein of misfiled addresses and size cards the girl who briefly replaced Esa had left behind. She has no business leaving the office, but she yearns to sit with her son between her and Hank in his truck. Instead of waiting for Hank to pick Guy up, they drive out to That One Place, where Hank is loading an aluminum hamper with fragrant packages, some foil-wrapped, some in Styrofoam. 'What are those?' she asks innocently.

'They're food,' Hank answers. 'You didn't have to drive him out here, darlin'. I was headed back for him.'

'I wanted to come. To come with. I know they're food. What are they for?'

'People I know.'

'I'm on to you, Hank. Guy told me. You're your own little Meals on Wheels?' Hank says nothing. 'Do you take these to poor people, Hank?'

'Only poor people who speak French,' Guy chimes in. '*Comment ça va? Bon jour, Madame Le Chat.*'

'That's good, Guy,' says Hank.

'Don't forget me,' True says.

'No, you don't really want to come, True,' Hank says. 'It's not noble. It smells. They smell, to tell you the truth.'

'I want to come.' Hank's face works, like Guy's when he is trying not to laugh or to cry. 'Okay. Hop in.'

They drive far down into Hyannis, to a street behind the bus station. This is The Breakers, an assisted-living complex that does not deserve the name, because the elderly or disabled people who live here get no assistance except the ambulances True occasionally sees parked in front when she drives Guy to a master class or to a theater space for a full-sound rehearsal. The place is a dirty, flaking scandal. Its lusterless windows have not seen an outside sponge in years; but pathetically, there are smeared attempts by some of the residents to clean them from the inside, the way a child makes a frost porthole after exhaling on the glass.

Their first stop is the crone of a woman Guy (and Hank for all she knows) calls Madame Le Chat.

'*Allo!*' Guy calls. '*Bon jour, Madame Le Chat! Nous aves steak avec lager et tarragone.*'

'*J'avez . . .*' Hank corrects gently.

'Right. Javvey steak orange lager.' Guy glances at Hank. 'Lagery lala! Yum!'

'*Bon jour, Gee,*' says the tiny woman, whose limbs are foreshortened, perhaps from birth, perhaps from disease, and wrested into shapes that reptiles would find voluntarily impossible to sustain. She scoots across the room in her whizzy electric chair. The room is stifling, thick with odors True would never attempt to identify. '*Bon jour, Henri. Qui est la belle femme?*'

'*C'est . . . ma fille,*' Hank answers, kissing one gnarled, bluish hand. True is touched and confused. He has called her 'his girl,' not his *legitime*, his wife. But perhaps that is not Creole, which has its own idiom, not French as Parisiennes speak it. Perhaps *legitime* is old-fashioned.

'*Elle ce belle,*' whispers Madame, shaking one witchlike finger. From under the furled orange boucle shawl she wears in the suffocating heat, a tiny, black-and-gold furred head peeks.

'*Le chat!* Madame, you're not supposed to have cats! You'll get in trouble again,' Guy says.

'That fat fook,' says Madame. 'He take all *mes bébés. J'ai une seule.* Well, *trois.*'

'*Ou est Kitty?*' asks Hank, arranging her steak and a tiny plastic glass of wine, and a cloth napkin, on the table that glistens with dust and grease and cat hairs. Madame shrugs elaborately. Hank motions True aside, and whispers, 'Kitty is a little . . . loose. Like Madame's cats. She ought be spayed, too. She's cute, though. About twenty-five. She looks in on Mom. Which is more than I can say for most of these folks' kids.' Hank returns to the elderly woman's side, stoops to give Madame the two-cheeks kiss, and they drive on. True has never loved her husband more than she does at this moment, as he matter-of-factly gives of himself.

The next stop is a trailer that True has seen before. She has always assumed it was abandoned, leaning like an unhinged gate in a vacant lot near the airport. She has never noticed the string of Chinese lanterns that hang, all of them lit, despite the hazy sun. 'Hank, *batard,*' cries the old mulatto man in the limp and sweat-stained fedora, who comes to open the door, leaning heavily on his cane, 'And *Henri fils. Comment va tu?*'

214

'He's a flirt,' Hank warns.

'He says tits,' Guy contributes. Hank puts his arm around True.

'*Cette femme est ma* wife,' he tells the man, whose name is Claude. '*Q'est que tu fait, Claude? Tu avais biblios? Je bring cuisine, mais delicieuses,* man. Ce Ce the ponies, eh?' Claude is from Bayou Forche, Hank whispers to True. He spends his disability on off-track betting, but thank Christ, he is lucky, and doesn't drink it up. The old man's face lights as he catches sight of the meat. 'He thinks seafood is sissy,' Hank continues, as Guy gambols around the room with the old man's ancient Springer spaniel.

'Did you ride, Mister River?' True asks.

'Riviere,' Hank corrects.

'Yes. I have twelve horses. I teach . . . what . . . *equestrienne, dressage, l'air* above *la terre.*'

'He means Lippazaners. I don't know if he's lying or not,' says Hank. 'I know he trained horses, from the pictures.' These, prominently displayed, show a dapper and erect Claude Riviere, a shining chestnut stallion against his cheek, a beautiful Spanish or Indian woman sitting on a fence behind him and the horse; Claude accepting a ribbon with bowed head; Claude on a gray Arabian with a braided mane. True ponders: If only a portion of a life might be foreseen, to reckon the final, desolate outcome, would it be possible to recalibrate, make a single adjustment, that would keep a person just one level above rock bottom? If it were possible, would people believe it, and choose to change before the steep descent, or would they be too arrogant? Would they believe that such a fate as Monsieur Claude's could await them?

'How did you find him?' True asks, when Guy and Hank have shouted 'Au revoir!' and Claude has made some indecipherable comment about True's anatomy, as well as told her that the lights signify '*Mardi Gras, tout le monde toujours.*'

'Well, I read about Marie, that's Madame, in the newspaper, when they took her cats, and I thought it was hysterical that her daughter was named Kitty. But then, I thought I would go over and see her, because the article said she was frightened because she didn't speak much English. She's from . . . I don't know, Belgium or something. I can barely understand her. So I went over, and she told me about ol' Claude here, and then I just stumbled across Blanche, who's the next one, at a bookstore, in her chair. She has arthritis.'

215

'She's your age, Mommy, the poor lady,' Guy adds, 'and she has a big, fat crush on Dad.'

'I don't blame her,' True murmurs. 'Hank, don't these people get . . . food from . . . the county?'

'Yes, but it's shit. It's institutional crap. White bread in sealed wrappers, so wet you could make a ball of it in your hand. So, I decided once a week, I would, you know . . .'

'That's . . . why you make extras on Saturday?' True nods. 'I thought it was a bennie for the staff. Hank, you make me feel guilty. Should we give them some money to fix up their . . . homes?'

'No, they wouldn't take it.'

'Why not?'

'Well, I wouldn't ask them. They love the food, and the chance to bullshit a little. It's not a big deal, True.' They next meet Blanche, whose face would be beautiful except for the ravages of her disease and her medication. Hank has rigged a kind of stand for her to hold open her books, since she cannot hold them with her rootlike hands. Books are stacked atop every table; they crowd the shelves and even the drainboard on the sink. Next time, Hank vows in pidgin French, he will bring her some new books (True puts in, 'I have a ton. We'll bring her some new novels') and the dish will be crawfish. Blanche beams, giving True a crosswise gaze.

When Hank explains that True is his wife, she sighs, *'Mon dieu.'* Blanche's walls are blanketed with posters: Some are the kind anyone could have, such as Toulouse-Lautrec's 'Absinthe Drinker,' but others are the kind not many people at all would have, such as a poster, framed and glassed, of a 1982 Monet exhibit in Barcelona.

'I think Blanche was a teacher or a student of art,' Hank says. 'She has her own pictures, the ones she made, rolled up in the bedroom.'

'We could pay to frame them.'

'That would be nice, True. She'd like that.'

The last visit is back at The Breakers, to an old man who is absent. He is nearly constantly at the doctor, because he has spinal cancer, which is killing him, but since he is eighty-eight, it is killing him so slowly he will probably die of something else. At present, he is being treated for a fractured arm because he ran into a mailbox on his motorcycle. 'I'd have loved for you to meet Jean,' Hank says, 'but I just always leave his food, because he's never around. Gee,

216

get the bones.' Guy hops into the truck cab and brings back a paper bag. 'For Sweet Sue. His dog. No one knows she lives here. She's a border collie, like Gee wants. She knows how to lie silent.'

True can't get over the idea of an octogenarian motorcyclist. 'Oh,' says Hank, 'Jean will ride again. You should see the cycle. It's around back.' The bike has to be forty years old. It shines like a silver button on a new blazer. 'He takes good care of it.'

'He rode me on it the other time,' Guy crows, to True's horror. 'Can he see?'

'Not much,' Hank says. 'He only rode him around the parking lot.'

'Why didn't you tell me about this thing that you do? You drive all over ... have you been doing this since you started the restaurant?' asks True, as they rumble toward home. He nods, and makes a dismissive gesture. She adds, suddenly, 'You need a new truck, Hank.'

'I'll tell the world I need one. This old baby is about to roll over into the double hundreds. But the way you been squinting at the books, I guess we can't afford one now,' he replies.

'Yes, we can. Let's look for one together. Let's go looking now. Just window-shopping. With a back seat for a dog and Guy and ... other things.' Hank smiles; he thinks she means midnight trysts, but she really means a car seat. 'Let's look for a truck.'

'Red!' Guy calls. 'I vote for red!'

'No, green!' Hank teases. 'Green is for geezers. Like me.'

'You know you like red best.'

'Okay, red,' Hank agrees, and when Guy hops out, Hank brushes Guy's cheek with his lips.

If True prayed, she would pray now. She would pray for the jealous gods not to be offended by Hank's beatitude when he finds the perfect red Ford, and to leave the three of them alone.

THE SOCIAL WORKER who came to their home for the cursory second interview of the home study had asked Guy, 'Is this what you want? For Hank to be your legal dad?'

'He can't be my real dad,' Guy answered. 'But I don't remember my real dad, so I guess it's okay.' The social worker then spoke to Guy alone in his bedroom, later whispering to True not to be concerned, that Guy was more worried about Hank loving him than the reverse. True told Hank this.

'I'm going to set aside a special section of my closets of shirts for him to destroy,' Hank told her, his mouth a moue of ruefulness and pity.

Several days later, on the night before the court proceeding, True awakes in the night and instinctively goes to Guy's room. There is no sound, nothing that alerts or summons her. It is only a hunch. His eyes are closed. Moonlight has made him an alabaster child, a tomb ornament. She is about to creep away, when he says, 'It's okay, I'm awake.'

'What're you doing?'

'Praying.'

'Oh.'

'I'm apologizing to Dad.' True's throat tightens.

'Sweet, I don't think he'd expect you to apologize.'

'I'm apologizing because I never knew him, and I don't want him to think I forgot him, and that I'll see him in heaven someday and introduce him to Hank. Do you think that they'd get along and stuff? They both liked to fish . . .'

'Yeah, I think they would.'

'Do you think Hank is as good as Dad?' This is the trick question.

'Yes,' she says seriously, 'I do. I wouldn't pick a dad for you that wasn't as good as your own, first Dad. And if you believe in heaven, don't you think maybe Dad helped pick him? Considering how he just showed up all of a sudden and all?' She is almost willing to believe in divine intervention, based on this sudden inspiration alone, which she has not considered until this second. 'It's possible.'

'I guess it is.'

True takes Guy in her arms, holding him as she did when he was an infant, face up. 'I think that you are very brave to do this, Guy. I think that you must really trust Mom, no matter how bad you think I did at this.'

'Well, actually, I love you, Mommy. I still love you. But I trust Hank. He said on his honor he would always take care of me. I get to hit him in a duel if he doesn't.'

'Oh, I see.'

True pauses, and then says, 'You know more than you know anything in the world that I love you best, Gee. And to tell you the truth, I don't know if I want to share you.' This is abruptly, awfully true.

'I didn't want to share you either, Mama. But, you know. That's life,' says Guy.

THE FOLLOWING AFTERNOON, True rises from a long and excruciating conversation with Larry Sornberger, during which she must salve his bruised emotions and plead for him still to provide them with the holy walking ducks next spring, to realize they are nearly late for the adoption.

'Bloody hell,' says True to Kathleen. 'Do you know where my cell phone is? I have to meet Hank at the courthouse at three P.M. And I still have to call Franny to stop by the auto mall. You're going to bring Guy, right?'

'You're sure about this?' Kathleen asks.

'What?'

'This adoption plan? This means Hank will be his legal father.'

'Oh? Does it? Shucks. Now you tell me! Are you sure of that?'

'True, be serious. This is an even bigger commitment than getting married as you did. This is a child's life.'

'He loves Hank, Mom. I know it's grown quickly, but they've both changed. A child is malleable, and Hank is trying his best.'

'What if you two parted?'

'He'd still love Hank, Mom. And I would still want him to be Guy's father. How many times do I have to go over this? I mean, what if you and Dad had gotten divorced? He'd still have been our father.'

Kathleen is silent for a beat. 'He already was your father.'

'Look, Mom, come or don't come. Just give me a decision. I'll ask Franny to pick him up if I have to. Even if she has to leave the office early.' Kathleen sighs, and shuts down her computer.

At four P.M., as his last act of the day, Judge Clark Halliwell pronounces: 'It's my privilege, then, sirs, to inform you that you are now, officially and forevermore, father and son.' The gnomish lawyer from Dennis, the same one who has made their wills, offers to trot across the street and file the papers.

'Are these all in order?' he asks.

'Let me look,' Guy says. 'No. I want it to say Guy Lemieux Bannister.' Hank lowers his head, and reaches for Guy's shoulder. 'That's for both my dads.'

Everyone swallows.

True speaks up: 'What about me? What about your other middle name? Dickinson?'

'Mom, I'll have to have two driver's licenses,' Guy whines.

'You can use initials,' the lawyer whispers.

'Okay. Let's do it,' Guy says. The judge summons his clerk, who returns swiftly with the corrected documents.

'Can he do that?' True asks.

'If you want him to,' the lawyer replies. 'There is, as they say, no law against it. He could change his name to Howdy Doody if you let him. Or Batman. Or The Artist Formerly Known As Prince.'

'I think this will be fine,' Hank says. 'Come here, Granny,' he says, hugging Kathleen. 'Should I adopt you, too?'

'You get her with me,' Guy explains proudly. 'It's a package.'

When they walk outside, Franny is waiting at the curb, leaning against the big red Ford, its green-for-geezers bow done up in yards and yards of ribbon they'd purchased, cleaning out their local florist.

'Your coach awaits, Monsieur Le Papa,' Guy says, bowing. Hank grabs Guy under one arm and swings him around. He can pick Guy up after all, no trouble.

AT FRANNY'S POOL on the following Sunday, True watches dumbfounded as Franny butters her naked breasts, belly, and arms, and offers herself like a sacrifice to the sun. Franny, fearless black Irishwoman, is the only woman True knows who still sunbathes.

'I think Hank is having doubts about having married me,' True finally says.

'I think you are out of your box,' Franny answers. 'He just adopted your kid and he looks as happy as the cat who swallowed the canary.' Franny is now anointing her throat with Sport 20 Plus. Franny's pool is so far down in a ferned and tree-lined bowl that she and Steve have hosted skinny-dip barbecues there, with Angelique and Clainey safely stowed at Steve's mother's in Mashpee. Today and always, as regards the sun, True is protective. She wears a broad straw hat and is considering a turtlenecked bathing suit. She does no more than flip her towel back for a couple of minutes each hour, like a flasher in Boston Gardens park. She has only once, and in the pitch dark, stripped down at a barbecue. But she had loved the wonderful feeling of swimming untrammeled, floating through the dark blue water dolphin-like, brushing bodies in a sensual but not at all sexual fashion.

220

'That's all well and good, but I wish he'd stroke me the way he does that new truck,' True whispers.

'Hello!' Franny says. 'Nobody does it every day after the first two months.'

'We *never* did it every day. But he's younger. He should be teeming with hormones.'

'You're probably peakier sexually than he is. Men sort of droop in their thirties.'

'That's swell,' True grouches, hunching her hat further over her eyes. 'I'm peaking and he's drooping. Should I have married an eighteen-year-old? When we were dating . . .'

'That *whole week* –' Franny puts in, giggling.

'Well, early on, he said, "All I need is half an hour and I'm ready to go again."'

'But . . .' Franny tries to interject.

'Well, it seems that all he needs is half an hour and he's ready to go to sleep,' True is bent on pouting and will not be dissuaded.

'He's not used to all the stimuli.'

'I think he got a fair amount of stimuli during his life, judging by his portfolio.'

'True, get over yourself. You're obsessed with his past. I mean really obsessed. Aren't you glad he shopped the whole produce counter and then chose the right peach? I mean, he's not used to living with a mother and a child – much less a mother-in-law. And now a new son.'

'God! If I hear that again!'

'So you know what's wrong, and yet you're asking me?'

'I know that's one thing wrong, but I don't know what's wrong beyond that. That stimuli stuff. Geez, you'd think he was brought up under glass.'

'Not entirely, because you're a little more challenging than the average bear.'

'How?'

'Well, just your household, the bustle, the overdrive. He's probably used to a beer and CNN after work.'

'He doesn't have to be so . . . wimpy.'

'Well, he'll get used to that. But you said something else was wrong.'

'And I can't put a finger on it,' True says.

221

'I could venture a guess.'

'And what would that be?'

'You watch him like he's going to . . .'

'To what?'

'Like he's going to run off with the first Irish waitress he sees.'

'So?'

'So, stop. Ignore that. Just because a man looks at the menu doesn't mean he wants to order. You look crazy when you watch him, like you're waiting for him to do the thing you don't want him to do. Like it would satisfy you.'

'That's crazy.'

'My point.'

'No, you're crazy. It would be the last thing on earth that would satisfy me.'

They lie listening to the cardinals conversing like chimes in the pines above.

'I think I should get pregnant,' True suggests.

'You mean, unannounced? There's a surefire way to seal a marriage. As in, seal its doom.'

'Well, he just about practically went bananas when his sister had a kid last week . . .'

'But so soon?'

'Well, Franny, I ain't getting any younger. If he wants it with me, he's gotta step up to the plate.'

'Would it matter so much to him if it wasn't his child, biologically? You could wait until the marriage is established and then adopt.'

'Since when does a marriage have to have a root system like a sequoia? Lots of people who have to get married stay married. Judging by the hollering he did over the last chip off the old Bannister . . . I guess it would matter.'

'What's the baby's name?'

'Carr.'

'That's nice. What are her other kids . . . she has other kids, right?'

'I don't know. Probably Roof and Boat.'

'You're a meanie.'

'Yes, I am. I'm jealous. I know that much. I don't need a psychologist to know he'd love a kid we had more than Guy. The one's the rock and the other's the soft spot, you know?'

'It's human nature,' Franny says with maddening logic. 'He'd have that baby from ground up. Or maybe not. I mean, really maybe not. As for me, I don't think the genetic connection is so important. Put a baby in front of me, I'll be all over it. Plus, I think Angelique is an alien, anyhow.'

'Easy for you to say.'

'Yeah. Did I tell you we filled out our papers last week? We're going to go to Texas if we do it, not China. You have to *live* in the country for six weeks! And Steve, sensitive soul that he is, reasons that Latino boys are better suited genetically to baseball. True, don't worry so much. Hank, he's a good-hearted guy. Give him time. He'll get over his bachelor selfishness. He'll figure out marriage is one big scramble at the light. Guy's such a sweet little bear. He'll win him over. It must be hard for Guy to get how an adult needs space. You've never been much of a space-needer.'

'I've never had the chance,' True says. 'I guess I might need . . . time for reflection and junk; people are always saying they do. But what was I supposed to do? Tie Guy up until I was finished reflecting?'

'Single parents have to be flexible. Single men don't.'

But there are people who will cut jigsaw bits to fit and True, as a child, was one of them. It was a habit that drove her mother to near-foaming wrath. She decides that she will do *two* things to help Hank settle down into family life. She will get pregnant, and she will get liposuction on her chin. These two decisions seem, in True's calculus, linked. By having what she perceives as her wattles vacuumed and stuck back into youthful contours, she will look more like the kind of woman Hank might have impregnated had he married one of the denizens of the brown envelope, who have no names but who all have piquant chins. This is what a therapist would call magical thinking, but she doesn't give a damn. And since they have never used birth control, pregnancy cannot be something Hank will find unexpected.

Then the women in the brown envelope will go away from her dreams as they have from her cedar chest.

And so she makes an appointment with Holly Bourse's face doctor, for two weeks prior to the planned trip to Louisiana (Hank has thankfully consented to fly). And she visits a fertility specialist who tells her the kit she has already purchased, and a sperm analysis for her husband are all she needs. So True waits as expectantly as a seventh grader for her period to arrive, that she may begin counting days.

Then, she drives back to Boston for the in-office liposuction procedure. The doctor administers, intravenously, a drug he says will allow True to forget the pain she experiences at the instant she experiences it – so that she will, having had no memory of pain, virtually not experience it all. She wishes such a drug was available over the counter, so she could keep a quart on hand at home. As the solution dripping into her wrist begins to gauze over her vision, she asks the doctor, 'Now, how will I look after this?'

'Well, there'll be some slight bruising. Nothing a little pancake can't cover.' Clearly, this is not a man who keeps up with terms for cosmetics.

'And how long will it last?'

'A matter of days. Do you bruise easily? No? Well, then probably not long at all. Zinc helps healing, and avoiding tobacco.'

'Well, I don't smoke. I take zinc.'

'You should be fine.'

'In two weeks?'

'Mmmmmm,' the doctor says, and True hears a swooshing sound, and is unaware of anything else until she awakens, lying on a reclining bed, her jaw bound like Marley's ghost. 'Missus Bannister,' asks a nurse, 'is your ride waiting in the waiting room?'

'Outside,' True fibs. No one has come with her.

'Okay, because you could feel a little muzzy for a couple of hours.'

'Okay.'

'So, whenever you're ready, you can get up.'

Hank's own jaw needs binding when she arrives home. 'It'll be gone in two weeks,' she tells him apologetically.

'True, True, why?' he asks.

'I . . . wanted a firmer jaw. For meeting your . . . whole family. On their turf.'

'They aren't going to inspect your jaw. You're not a racehorse.'

'I'm so scared of this trip,' she owns up, holding out her arms, but to her shock, Hank's arms don't open to enfold her against the cleft of his collarbone.

'What do you think they're like, True? That you'd mutilate yourself! They'll all love you as you are, the way I do. Because I do.'

'I kept thinking they'd like the new, improved version better.'

224

'There can't be an improved version.'

'For real?' True asks.

'For me,' Hank answers.

'I'm still glad I did it,' True answers. 'It was more for myself than you. I think I'm really going to like it once it . . .' As they walk into the cool hall, True catches sight of herself in the hall mirror, 'Oh Hank, oh mercy . . .'

'Let's make the best of it.'

True makes a pass through the office, collects her binder for the December's Blessing, which includes two new items. Everyone, especially Rudy and Esa, stares down diligently at the countertop. She takes two of the whomping painkillers given her by the cosmetic surgeon and then tries to work out in her mind whether the red-and-green slippers with turned up toes are too frankly Christian. She settles on the seamster's alternative, a slipper embroidered with snowmen, a firmly sewn, crocheted blue snowflake on the toe. One of the other office staff will call him: She leaves a note for Krista, the girl who does the books and answers the phone when Kathleen isn't around. True is not aware at what point she falls asleep, but she does know that when she awakes, her TV is tuned to a newscast delivered entirely in Russian. Hank wanders in with a cup of green tea. 'Don't you have to go to work?' she asks.

'I've been and come back, True,' he laughs. 'It's one in the morning.'

'Well then, I have to get back to work,' she mumbles.

'You're not going anywhere, Zsa Zsa,' he tells her. 'Come on. Free your radicals. It's okay to let someone take care of you once in your life.'

And the clouds recede again.

'TRUE! YOU MUST be True,' says Tannie Swallow, two weeks later, when all the sisters, the little sprongy-curled nieces – who actually are named Dana and Melanie – the baby, the husband, and True's in-laws meet her, Hank, and Guy at the airport. 'And this is Gee. Gee, I think you're gonna like our tree house,' Tannie continues. Unlike the other two sisters, Tannie is both darker and more curvy, a woman more on the configuration of True herself. In a whisper, she asks, 'Honey, what in God's name happened to you? Did you get in a car accident?'

Despite what she fears may have been an overdose of zinc, and generous applications of pancake – the doctor knew what he was talking about – and even pink-flesh stage makeup bought at the suggestion of Beatrice from the theater – True looks as though she has gone ten rounds to a split decision with Leon Spinks. Her chin is swollen as though her diet never included iodine, and her bruises have progressed through Technicolor passages from purple to blue to their current yellow-lime.

'I had my chin . . . done, sort of done,' True confesses. 'Not a face-lift, but I wanted to have, you know, a nice firm chin line. The damned doctor – excuse me, Clothilde . . . Ma, I mean, no, it won't hurt to kiss me – assured me this would all be healed and perfect by now. If you don't want me to come to the christening, I'll totally understand . . .'

'I'd never do that!' Tannie is genuinely shocked.

'You'll be the floor show!' Hank giggles.

'Shut up,' True tells him, but she has to laugh, too. 'Vanity, thy name is woman.'

'You look fine to me,' her father-in-law tells her. 'Now, what you need here is some dragon's blood. Some other herbs, too. Bruises will be gone by morning. I'll ask my mother. And this man,' he says to Guy, 'has grown a foot. Think you can take me at chess now? We play it different down here. We cheat.'

'Well, I don't know how to cheat, but I can try!' Guy says gamely.
'Can I see the baby?' Tannie holds Carr down for Guy's inspection. 'I know how to hold them. I held my other cousin, Dennis, in Montana.' Gently, Tannie places the infant in Guy's arms. 'He's so, so, so cute. But he's not black!' Everyone glances around. 'I thought he would be blacker. I like black babies best. Because their hair is so cute.'

'I can try harder next time,' says Tannie, whose husband is white. Gus is the first to laugh.

'My genes don't seem to make much difference in this family, Gee,' he confides. 'My missus is too bossy.'

'Oh, my grandma is bossy, too,' Guy smiles. 'And my mom is extremely bossy. She's even a boss of a business.'

'But so's your dad,' Gus adds.

'Oh, no, Dad's nice to everybody.'

'I'm nice to everybody!' True objects.

226

'But you don't play Van Halen. Dad, he just goofs around at work. And all his people at the restaurant goof around all the time. It's not like at my mom's office. They have to stay at their desks. Or be out in the warehouse. And not smoke. They can smoke at That One Place.'

'Well, don't you smoke,' Gus concludes. 'By the way, Gee, I hear I'm your official grandpapa now.' Guy nods, glancing at True for affirmation. 'In our family, that calls for a little ceremony.' He reaches into his pocket. 'Now, this here ring was my daddy's. He wore it in the Second World War. I wore it during the Korean War. That there's a diamond, and that's a ruby. It was meant for my first grandson. Thought I might give it to Carr, the first grandson, but you got there ahead. It's yours, now. Little big for you. Your mama and papa can keep it in the safe until you're bigger.'

'Or I can have it made to fit now!' Guy cries.

'No!' They all cry, breaking the unbearable tenderness of the moment. True reaches up to kiss Gus on both cheeks. 'Thank you.'

'You're welcome, dear. But it's not a big thing. Tradition is tradition,' Gus answers solemnly.

'I'm not going to wear it in the Third World War, though,' Guy says quickly. 'My mom and me are pacifiers.'

Everyone is laughing as they pile into the cars.

The Bannisters' home is a Spanish half-moon of rooms arranged around a pool and courtyard with a fountain. True has never seen such simplicity. All Cape Cod houses seem to draw knickknacks like a magnet draws iron filings as soon as the walls go up. There is one work of art, a pastel-and-glass sculpture, an orange rabbit leaping into flame, on a single white wall. The rest of the walls are devoid of decoration, except for dozens of arched windows. The couches and pillows are white; but the carpets a deep burnt umber. 'This is magnificent,' she tells Clothilde.

'I like to relax,' Clothilde says. 'Relax and cook. I don't like messing with dusting.'

Guy and the little girls run for the pool, while Hank curls up on one of the white sofas and falls instantly, deeply asleep. Because she cannot breathe in the heat, True stays indoors, watching Tannie nurse the baby. Tannie's husband has gone back to his office. 'He is so very beautiful,' True says. 'Hank and I are trying to have a baby.'

227

Clothilde is at her side, offering iced tea, insufferably sweet to True, but at least cold. 'You are? Now, that's something our son hasn't mentioned.' I'll bet, True thinks, suddenly wanting these women to know, beyond doubt, that this is a real marriage, with sex and plans and all these things entail. She wants to be a part of them, with their secrets and their scents. 'Are you sure . . . well, of course, it's okay. I know my friend Elise, she had a baby when she was forty-six. Took her all by surprise. And he's a dickens, too.'

'I want Guy to have a brother or sister. And I don't want to run out of time.'

'And what does my son think of this? You know, it wasn't so long ago, he was only worried about whether he could get across the bridge to the right place for his haircuts. God's gift to women, you know.' She snorts. 'Or so he thought.'

'I think he'll be glad, once it happens. He's very excited about Carr.'

'Have you talked it over?'

'I kind of want to surprise him. Like in old movies.'

'Well, you wouldn't be the first woman to do that. And he looks very well. I was concerned, I must admit. Hank has never been . . . how shall I say . . . very big on sticking to . . . well, on commitment.'

'You mean with girlfriends.'

'I mean with girlfriends, jobs, cars, houses, colleges, stereos. Every time we'd see him, he'd have some new plan. Once it was the . . . what was that, Tanniferro? The air vacuum?'

'Right, the air vacuum,' Tannie laughs, settling Carr over her shoulder to burp. 'Hank sold everything he had, motorbike, stereo, to buy into this company that cleaned the air in your house with ozones, or some such thing . . .'

'And of course, the fellow was a scoundrel,' Clothilde goes on, 'and he took off with every cent of that poor boy's money. We had to prop him up enough so he could even go back to school.'

'Then he was going to be a monk, not a Catholic monk, you realize, just a monk in a group of contemplatives . . .' Tannie says.

'He's idealistic, but not practical,' Clothilde says. 'But that's all changed, I reckon. The restaurant is going well, I hear.'

'There he is, sleeping like an old dog,' pipes up another voice, reedy and yet piercing.

228

Hank sits up instantly. *'Grand-mère!'* He opens his arms to the tiny black woman, her hair still hazelnut-brown and bound in a skewered bun, slow and erect, her light, brightly colored wooden cane seeming almost a fashion accessory.

'Henri, you look fat and healthy,' she says, settling herself next to Hank's knees.

'This is my mother-in-law, Winston,' says Clothilde, 'after whom we named Hank's sister. Maman, this is Hank's wife, True.'

'This is a beautiful name. A beautiful girl.'

'A long time since I've been called a beautiful girl,' True laughs. 'Especially this way.'

Maman Winston moves closer. 'I see, ah, face improvement.'

'Eventually.'

'Maman, you have to read the cards for True, come on,' Tannie urges.

'Give me a moment to kiss this boy.'

Guy walks in, dripping. 'Please?' he says. 'I can't find a towel.'

'That's because *Grand-mère* forgot to give you any. Let me get you all towels, and would you like sweet tea?'

'Yes, please.'

'This your boy?' asks Winston.

'My son, Guy.'

'Gee, come closer,' the old lady demands. As he does, she reaches out, quick as a cat, and grips his chin. True sees her son startle. 'This is a singing mouth. Are you a singer?'

'I am! How did you know?'

'I don't know! I just know!'

'Are you eighty?'

'And more! Will you sing for me?' Guy glances pleadingly at True, who shrugs.

'Now? In my swim trunks?'

'What if I should die, later on, and not have heard you sing?'

'Okay,' Guy agrees, 'but I have to go in the bathroom first.'

'To piss?'

'No,' he laughs. 'To vocalize. To warm up my throat.' When he returns, wrapped in a towel, Guy asks True what he should sing, old or new? Old, she suggests. And so he sings, in his sweet beginner's vibrato, 'Scarlet Ribbons.' By the end, all four women are weeping.

'This boy,' Maman Winston says to Hank. 'He is an important

boy.' Hank smiles lazily. True thinks, this is the kind of fuss he's used to having made over him, not over a child. She decides she loves this family, the generosity of its expansion. Gus comes in the door, with an ancient springer spaniel on a leash.

'Sully!' cries Hank. The old dog bangs its tail heavily on the floor and white hairs glisten in the air. 'Sully, old gal.' Guy, throwing off the towel, reaches for the dog. 'Be careful,' Hank warns him, 'until she knows you.' But Sully noses Guy gratefully, and he runs from the room to return with a green Ziploc bag of liver treats. 'I got these from Fenn for you, Sully. I knew I would see you.' The old dog gulps happily.

'Don't feed her too much,' Hank warns, then chuckles, 'Awww, go 'head, feed her too much. Her belly's practically down to her knees anyhow.'

Sully slowly licks Guy's face. True has never been much for animals licking people, but she cannot bring herself to interrupt her son's bliss.

Clothilde has made a glorious sea bass, simply basted, for dinner, and when Tannie leaves, Win, recovered apparently from the wedding photographer, arrives with her beau. 'So, Hankie, gonna take your lady to the Quarter? We don't go, but tourists like to.'

'That's dangerous, Win,' Clothilde puts in.

'But she has to hear the music, Mama, and see the strippers and the penny dancers and drink a Hurricane.'

'She'll be here a week. Let her get settled.'

'No, tonight!' Win insists, all but stamping her foot, and True thinks, yes, indeed, one of the daughters who always knew their boundaries.

'Tomorrow night will be fine,' Clothilde says imperturbably.

Tonight, the women will visit *en seule*, Clothilde says. And Hank and Gus will ride over to the home in Bayou Fourche where Hank's old friend Perry grew up, and wet a line by lantern light, and play cards.

And indeed, moments later, Hank is jumping up and bear-hugging a giant of a black man, his best pal, the legendary Perry, and just as suddenly, they are making their good-byes.

'What?' True asks. 'Wait, Hank!' But he is gone, and Win's boy-friend, begging leave, chases the two.

'Well, at least it's just us,' says Tannie, entering the room. She lives just a few blocks away, and has walked back without the baby. 'He is the best sleeper, this boy. And it's so cool and beautiful out.' True doubts whether the temperature has fallen below eighty. 'Where are my wild girls?'

'Dana! Melanie!' Clothilde calls.

'*Grand-mère*, can we stay? Can we stay with our nephew?' They are jumping up and down, in oversized T-shirts True imagines belong to Gus.

'He is your cousin, and yes, you may stay. Go in the big room, where the futons are.'

'And I will come and tuck you in,' says Maman Winston, 'and tell you of the two sweet lovers who walk hand in hand at the Kenilworth Plantation, *sans têtes,* and of the tree that weeps pearls, and then you will go to sleep and I mean sleep.'

'Without heads?' True whispers.

'But very affectionate,' says her mother-in-law, 'not like some ghosts.'

In minutes, Maman Winston is back, with a blue velvet bag.

'The cards!' Win says, clapping her hands. 'My grandmamma is the original Mojo woman.'

True, exhausted, excuses herself and slips into a T-shirt and Hank's old jogging shorts. No sense wasting time on frilly gowns; Hank's gone and the stick on the kit says tonight is not the golden moment. In the living room, she finds Clothilde reclining on the couch, now dressed in a satin caftan. 'How does she keep going?' True asks her mother-in-law, referring to the older woman, who is shaking out a deck of large, lurid-colored cards.

'I am old, and so I don't waste time on sleep,' Winston explains. 'Sleep is for the young, like them those in there.'

They gather around the table on the screened porch, True listening to the night cries and chirps of unfamiliar insects and birds and glorying in the breeze. 'Now, do you have a question for the cards?' Winston asks.

'I . . . don't know,' True says, suddenly recalling that her husband had not even introduced her to his best friend, much less introduced their son. 'How do you ask them?'

'You don't know the Tarot?'

'No.'

'Then I do a simple reading. Seven cards. First, you feel and touch the deck. Place both your feet on the floor. Bare feet.' True does as instructed. 'Now, you shuffle them, and I will hold them and you draw seven cards, which you lay out this way.' She points out a pattern on the table, roughly in the shape of a cross. True does as asked, trying with all her might to feel any summons from any of the cards in front of her, but feeling only foolish. Finally, she has drawn out and lain seven, hearing Win's involuntary gasp at one, and Clothilde's sigh at another. When True accidentally inverts one of the cards, so that its name, Fortune, is at the bottom, upside-down, she puts out her hand to fix it, but Winston corrects her. 'If it is meant to be inverted, it must stay that way.'

One by one, Maman Winston points out the cards and explains their meaning. At the top is the card called The Fool. 'This is the greatest among the sacred of the cards in all the Tarot,' Winston says in her thin voice, dropped a notch so the children will not hear. 'Its meaning is the wise man, the one of great heart. I think it is clear that in this life, this is your man, this is Henri.' She points next to the card, Fortune. 'This is among the Major Arcana, and its meaning is obviously,' she gestures to the jewels and chains of gold emblazoned on the card's face, 'great wealth and prosperity. Its showing in this setting also means that change is inevitable.'

'Oh,' True cries. 'It means I'll be financially ruined?'

'No, it means that change is inevitable. This,' Winston next points out, 'The Five of Cups. This is a card of danger. Of preoccupation with regret. It is in the mental realm, of anguish. It can signify illness.' The Five of Swords, she continues, 'is struggle. Struggle to do, with, how do you say it, getting your head together . . .'

'Right on, Grammy,' Win giggles.

'Fool child,' Winston reproves her. 'It can mean a defeat, lasting or momentary, but a triumph by using the head and heart together for strength.'

'All that in one picture?' True marvels.

'The cards never lie,' Winston tells her. The next card, the one True has laid upside-down, is the Queen of Pentacles. 'This is the card that is associated with the unfaithful woman, the mistrustful. It is the card that signifies the fall to temptation, to discord. And yet, it is reversed, so we may hope that it will, in this sense, deal with physical trouble, some sort of physical trouble, which may be temporary.'

They have all been waiting for the next card; True can feel it. It is an ugly portrait, a Judas in a tree. The Hanged Man. 'This card does not mean what it seems to suggest, True. It is the card of surrender, of a willful surrender to circumstances that are beyond the control of us as human beings. And this last,' she concludes triumphantly, 'is the One of Pentacles. This is the card of birth, and of blessings.'

'Blessings,' True says.

'Enough for one night,' *Grand-mère* Winston tells her, sweeping the cards into the blue bag with its silver stars. As True leaves the room to kiss Guy good night, she hears Maman behind her, walking softly, as if in ballet shoes. 'If you would keep your man, take a real silver coin to the cemetery and throw it in the tallest tomb, through the grate.'

'A cemetery? Any cemetery?'

'One here. I doubt it will work in a northern cemetery. A woman's grave is best.'

'I'll remember that,' True whispers.

THEY DRESS FOR dinner early the following evening. It is Hank and True and Win and her beau; Perry and his newest girl will join them in the Quarter. Guy and *Grand-père* will go in the evening boating by lantern in Barataria Reserve, in Bayou Fourche, looking for ten-foot crocs Gus swears often surface, and then fishing at 'a spot only I know, from a boy.' By the time True is ready to leave, Guy has learned to call Win and Tannie *tante,* and has confided in True that 'this is as good as Montana.'

Tante Win, her coat-hanger collarbones floating beneath lapis and silver, her arms banded in bracelets True couldn't fit over her wrists, has standards for what she wants from True's night out. She warns Hank, 'I want her to see the big house, too, when it's light.' She means, True later learns, a house from 1858 reputed to have been the home of a family of 'sous-sains' – actors and mimes by day, vampires by night. It is, in fact, a beautiful Greek revival, where marble has been laid with the abandon of seashell in Cape Cod.

'And you thought only your country was old, huh,' Hank whispers to True.

'Well, this was not *our* country, then, was it, Hankie? This was France,' Win says, asking the carriage driver to drop the four of them close enough to Magazine to walk. True has never listened to names of streets so lyrical – Felicity, Bourbon, Tchoupitoulas, Royal, along with the customary Calhouns, Washingtons, States. Milan is pronounced 'MY-lan' by Win.

'There really is a street named "Desire,"' True marvels. 'Who would name a street that?'

'Someone,' Win comments softly, 'who was too hot to get up and work.'

'I have to stop,' True says suddenly. 'Are quarters silver?'

'I think they're mostly copper,' Hank answers.

'I have to go into this cemetery,' True replies. It is called All Saints. 'Hank, please, go in that cigar store and see if the man has a half dollar.'

'Nobody has half dollars, True, what's this about?'

'Just this once.' True is counting on the luck of Maman's draw. When Hank crosses back the intersection, she sees him hold up a silver coin, a Kennedy half-dollar.

'I have to go in alone,' True tells her in-laws and Hank.

She walks among the graves, a shiver under her shift despite the heat, where all the crypts above ground, all gorgeously sad and sinister, weep stains of gray moss, their cornices and cupolas scraped by the listless papery fingers of the live oaks that shelter them. No one can be buried below ground, here, Win has told her; the ground is a mere crust over the living river, and to bury a body below ground is to meet your ancestors sooner than heaven. True wonders which grave will speak to her; but is distracted by the lines of all-too-small marble boxes, too like bassinets – Joyeux, Claudine, Imogene, Byron – four children, all dead in one year, 1919. She recalls something about the influenza epidemic. Her attention is drawn to a tomb with the carving of a hat and cane atop it. GRANDFATHER EMILE is graven on one side, 1888–1978, and on the other side, GRANDMOTHER SAPHINE, 1898– . This is a woman who now must be more than one hundred years old. She hears Hank call her from the sidewalk, and looks back, and is astonished how far she has come, on the spongy ground. Hank is small and faint in the distance, Win a lively puppet, waving both her hands. She wants to hurry, but not to err. She finally finds a crypt all made of the deepest sapphire granite, the bars, through which she peers, shined brass. The plate reads only MARIE LANDRY: SHE WALKS IN BEAUTY, LIKE THE NIGHT. True holds her breath, closes her eyes, and hears the dull clatter of the coin as it lands on the ceramic floor of the woman who True imagines may turn her eyes, pale as oyster shell, toward a stranger's destiny. Even the birds' chatter falls silent.

True turns and runs.

'What were you doing?' Hank asks. 'Haven't we got enough cemeteries in Cape Cod?'

'These are prettier,' True explains. 'They're more exotic. I saw that blue one . . .' she points, but the tomb she'd chosen isn't visible from where they stand, 'over there somewhere. I wanted to see it. Don't you come here and look at the graves?'

'They're too sad,' Win says. 'Too many babies.'

'I saw that,' True admits.

'I don't want to,' Hank shudders, 'but they say the voodoo queen is buried there.'

'Oh, Marie Leveaux,' Win scoffs. 'If she was buried everywhere they say she is, she'd have had more roommates than Al Gore had in college.'

'We used to go searching for her tomb,' Win's boyfriend, Matthew, puts in. 'They said if you could touch the corner of her coffin, you would have . . .'

'What?' True urges him.

'You know . . . with women,' he smiles.

'You better keep looking, honey,' Win tells him with good-humored guff. 'All I can see is you wasted a good half hour of shopping time,' Win complains. She hustles True toward Magazine Street, which she swears is sheer hell for women with budgets – 'but you and Hank don't have that' – and before True can protest, she adds, the street is called 'MAH-gah-zahn,' nothing like the name of monthly publications.

It is hell.

True wants every single thing she sets eyes on. Four-poster Greek Revival bedsteads, sculptures of rabbits in flight against a burning sky, mixed-media pieces that look like *Grand-mère* Winston's cards, made from punched tin and wood and glass beads, often embossed with the skulls in top hats. Win says these are the emblem of Baron Samedi, the Lord of Death. 'We worship death in Louisiana, because we think that way she'll forget to be noticing us,' Win says. 'All these dripping vines, and the deeps of the swamps, the stories of the fevers, and worse than the fevers, you grow up thinking Death is like your next-door neighbor.' She introduces True to Simone, her dance master, who also runs a shop of exotic, ancient laces and skirts and *petites choses*. While the men wander off for a burrito and coffee – True has never drunk so much coffee, and finds it to be the consistency and flavor of kerosene – Win forces True into a bustier with triangular shoulder pads and a ball skirt of faded amber. Simone sweeps True's hair up off her neck and wraps it around her hand, securing it with ancient combs of real tortoiseshell ('Don't worry,' Win says. 'These tortoises died a long time ago . . .'). After two days' application of some greasy potion *Grand-mère* Winston had given True, in a little jar jammed with a wine cork, the bruises and swelling have all but died away. What remains indeed can be covered by pancake.

'This is how you should look,' says Simone.

'I'll take it,' says True, as Simone drapes a triangular lace shawl across her breasts, front to back. The outfit costs eight hundred dollars. True, heart galloping, offers her credit card, ashamed that she has made such a foolish error. But, like a little boy with new shoes, she shoves her sleeveless shift into a bag and wears everything, right out of the store.

'You look like a lady from the 1800s,' says Win. 'Hank's gonna blow his mind. He won't notice anybody else.' Something in True's face makes Win stop her chatter. Notice anyone else? Whom would he notice? Then Win says, 'True, he doesn't love anyone but you.'

'Why do you say that?'

'You don't have to be a clairvoyant like my gram to know you worry. You watch him every move he makes.'

'But there were so many girls. When we got married, he got seven messages on the answering machine, with people crying. Well, not crying, but saying, "Oh, sweetie, I'm so happy for you."'

'That's because my brother is such a coward he never finished breaking up with anyone.'

'What do you mean? I shouldn't ask this, Win, I'm prying.'

'No, it's okay. You're family, *chère*. He just . . . he left them all thinking they were the one, huh? He left a trail of broken hearts, like they say in the movies.'

'Did you all . . . ?'

'Good, True. That's how you say it!'

'Did you think he'd ever get married?'

'I thought he would get married when he was real old. I thought he'd keep moving around forever and falling in love and falling out of love. "Winnie," he would say – isn't that mean? Sounds like a pig . . . my real name is Mary Winston, you know . . .'

'I know, Mary Winston, Mary Tanniferro . . . Hank would have been Mary Henry . . .'

'He stole my joke! That boy. Anyhow, he would say, "Winnie, there's too much good stuff out there." But Papa, Papa thought Hank was gay. He was all worried.'

'Would he have cared?'

'*Mais* yeah! So when he met you . . .'

'Everyone was happy?'

'Too, too happy. And he just thinks the stars go up on you, True. Honest, on my . . .'

'Mama's head.'

'Right!'

And when Hank sees her walk into the late-afternoon sun, with Win beaming and pointing, he whistles, and the look on his face is feral, so hungry that True thinks, this was money well-spent; this face is beyond price. She thinks also she has never had a better time in her life. She thinks that this city is enchanted. They drink lemony, pink concoctions with flowers, in the tall glasses, and, at the Martinique Bistro, Hank orders pompano and grilled eggplant in French, conferring seriously with the server, food snob that he rightfully is. Just as their appetizers, oysters sizzled in goat cheese, arrive, so does Perry, with a stunning coppery woman whose beaded dress seems to be an extension of her small, sinuous curves. 'You remember Jacqueline?' Perry nods, and Hank rises, kissing the beautiful woman, who wears masses of tiny amber-beaded braids, on both cheeks. She throws her arms around him, True seeing that she also thrusts her hips forward.

'I didn't know you were dating this big old wet dog,' Hank tells her, as she squirms into the banquette next to Win's date.

'Just for a while now,' Jacqueline smiles. 'But he's a pretty nice old dog, huh, Perry?'

'You know what Perry's name is?' Win asks nervously. 'Peridot. 'Cause he's got the green eyes.' There is a look, which no psychiatrist would have to glimpse twice to decode, flowing between Hank and his best friend, a look that plainly says, *You don't mind?* and *No, it's okay.* True does not have to ask if Hank has relished the body underneath the copper dress; and she promises herself, vows to herself like a knight on his honor, that she will not speak one word of her suspicion to her husband.

'You look good, but you look fat, *bébé*,' says Jacqueline to Hank.

'I eat my work in the winter,' Hank tells her. 'And married life.'

'I heard you was married. I don't believe that for a second. I want to meet your wife, sometime. I want to see this lady,' Jacqueline laughs harshly.

'She's . . . right here. This is True.'

'Well, I don't believe it,' Jacqueline insists. 'What is your name? True?'

'Yes,' True says, extending one ignored hand. She instantly feels, under the playful malice of Jacqueline's big black-cat's eyes, as though her getup is some kind of crude joke Win has played, that she looks like Princess Margaret decked out as Martha Washington. She feels the rolls of flesh that discreetly overlap the tight bra of her sleek top, and knows this is why Simone has offered her a shawl, despite the heat, for concealment, to fool the eye. She holds out her hand, and the shawl falls away, grazing her plate. 'Believe it,' she says, more flatly than she intends.

'Oh grease! Let me get a cold cloth!' Win cries.

'Well, congratulations,' Jacqueline says softly. 'I didn't think you would be . . . blond.' True knows that what Jacqueline means is, *I didn't think you would be old.* The ornate room seems a stunt, a dusty, fusty bordello stage set with swoops of tattered red velvet – frayed, on inspection. She longs for the clean, dry lines of That One Place, of her own cool, white-white room. She has left Shangri-La, and is withering by the instant. Rising, she excuses herself to the bathroom; Win following, quickstep in her stiletto heels.

'Don't you mind her,' Win tells True fiercely. 'That girl's been rolled in clover by every man in this parish . . .'

'That's not a big comfort to me, right now,' True says, fighting tears. She pulls the combs out, over Win's murmured *True, no,* and lets down her soft, waved, forgiving hair. She tugs the bustier up like a girdle, and stuffs all she can of her breasts and their extremities into the bodice. She and Win refasten the shawl, this time with a knot. 'I should just grab out my old dress . . .'

'No, she'd know you'd done it for her. And it's too East Coast. True, a moment ago you held yourself like Marie-Antoinette . . .'

'I can't stand to see the women he's . . .'

'Well, don't say loved, because he never loved her.'

'Is she going to be with us all night?'

'I imagine.'

'Then I'm going home after dinner . . . Win, don't try to understand; you can't, because you are as beautiful and tiny and young as the blue heron below my deck. You don't know what you don't know. You are the sweetest girl, but you're a girl. And if I watch *that* girl, for example, dance with Hank, I'm going to end up in a fight with Hank, and this has been one of the sweetest days of my life, and I don't want to spoil it. I'd rather he think I have a headache, than that I'm jealous. Please, Win, please forgive me. I'm your sister-in-law, and I'll be back here a dozen times. Hank says we're coming for Christmas . . . so please . . .'

'I *don't* understand. The bitch,' Win grimaces. 'But I do, yes, I do understand, too. You know, skinny girls get jealous, too, True.'

'I don't believe that.'

'Like, I'm a dancer. Big deal. I'm a dancer. I'm no Maria Tallchief. I'm lucky, I'll get a job teaching with a regional company, and maybe I'll do a summer show with Alvin Ailey in an outfit with a hood so only my nose shows. I'm never going to be rich. Best I can do is get married. I don't have my brother's nose for business, or my sister's brains . . .'

'But how can that mean anything to you, I mean, how can it mean anything when you get to wake up in the morning, every morning, and just be you?'

'It matters that I never eat a bite of food before six at night. It matters that I haven't had a piece of bread in seven years. That I smoke my breakfast. And that my feet look like horse's hooves . . .'

True tries to put her mind around the joy she feels when she eats hot bread set against the impossible bliss of having Win's body. 'I can't make it,' she says. 'I want to believe you, and I could have once, about ten years ago. Now, I feel like I'm . . . what? Fragile? Like I'm holding on to what I have with a thin thread? I used to feel like I would have forever, stay up all night and have forever, drink a whole bottle of wine and have forever.'

'I think my mama is beautiful. And Daddy thinks so, too. You don't believe that,' says Win.

'I do for them,' True says, and thinks of the clink of the coin on the tiles.

She is about to beg off, and mentions that she may return home in a taxi, Hank pleading with her to stay, when something rears in her nicely gathered-up bosom, and she turns back to the table. She has asked Hank to fake it until he feels it; she can do no less. And as soon as she decides that, remarkably, the highbrow carriage that had possessed her in the shop on Magazine Street claims her again. She tosses back her hair.

'*Je me désolée*,' True says, 'but I thought I felt ill,' she places her hand on her abdomen with elaborate import, 'and I am fine now.'

Hank and True share a plate of icy shrimp, and order ornate fruit drinks.

And then the four-piece band shows up, and they dance.

Jacqueline writhes, up and down, her long bangled arms a nest of seductive snakes. She slides and shivers and parodies a hump and grind. She is beautiful. And she is trying far too hard.

Hank and True dance as they did at their wedding, like lovers and also like sister and brother, like one body, born to one another's motions without the need to look, the music extraneous. Then Win dances with Hank, and True with Perry. Then, the music picks up and Perry leads True in a two-step. Sweat rolls down her brow. She grabs for her combs and twists her hair up. At some point, True throws off her shawl, throws back her shoulders and lets the twin moons of her white breasts swing. Perry bows her back over his arm, and says to Hank, 'This wife can move . . .'

Long before midnight, Hank whispers, 'Let's get out of here. Hot and smoky.'

'And,' True says, loudly enough for anyone to hear, 'this kind of food is so much better when you cook it.' True kisses Win on the mouth and accepts her strong, secret hug, and kisses Jacqueline on both cheeks. 'You must come up north, you and Perry. I know my husband would love Perry to see his restaurant; it's smaller than this, but so exquisite.' Hank's dark skin reddens. 'And we would like you to meet our little boy. We have plenty of room. The house is huge.'

They run out into the street, hand in hand. When he sees them kiss, a saxophone player strikes up 'Stardust,' and Hank throws him a ten-dollar bill and the other half-dollar.

Through the screen door, when they reach the house in Metairie, both of them see Guy and Gus, hunched in a circle of light in the bay window, and through the screen door, True hears Guy shout, 'Check and mate! I beat you, *Grand-père*. I beat you fair and square that time!' Hank takes True's hand, and kisses it. 'Wouldn't have wanted to miss seeing that, for some more mediocre music and syrupy drinks.'

They walk indoors.

'You did,' Gus admits, 'and I don't like to be beat.' They get up, and Gus says, 'Let's go check on your pal.'

Pal? True thinks grimly, he has given the child an alligator, for which I will slay him with my bare hands. Guy skips out of the room. I must teach him not to skip, True thinks, or jump up and down when he's happy. It's babyish. She then hates herself for even allowing the thought. Guy is only a child.

'My husband wasn't lying. He doesn't like to be beat,' Clothilde says to True, opening the door. The house is blessedly chilled. 'He's one smart boy, that Gee. I love that he isn't some pretend teenager like the fools around here let their boys be. And you? You look like the queen of the Mardi Gras. Mary Winston took you to Magazine Street. She burned a big hole in your pocketbook.'

'A big hole,' True says.

'But she does look fine, for a Yankee, *non?*' Hank asks.

'Well, turn around once,' Clothilde asks. 'I'd say you got your money's worth. Why are you home so early?'

'Too damn hot and dirty down there, Mama. And we never get a chance to be alone,' says Hank, obviating her need to explain, and True hears a lilt of pride in his voice.

'Well, better to put on something comfortable, and have a lemonade with mint,' her mother-in-law says. 'It is ugly hot out. You made the right choice. Win will dance all night.' I could dance all night, True thinks. But enough does not have to be all night.

Then suddenly, Clothilde turns serious. 'Now True, we have to apologize for something . . . no wait, we really do. We have done something with Gee that grandparents will always do, and it's always wrong, but you must forgive us, because he is so happy . . .' she says.

True braces for the alligator; but it is, oh, worse and better. Wonderful. Tenderly, as if he is holding the infant Carr, Guy carries

241

into the room a squirming black-and-white puppy, with preternat-urally wise green eyes, which say to True, *you're stuck.* 'Well, well,' says True, 'this what you fished out of the bayou?'

'Oh True, we're sorry . . .'

'I told her, *chère.*'

'But a boy needs a dog, you know. And this is a border collie, True. The smartest dog known to man. I bought him from my old friend, who breeds these dogs for show . . .'

'Look, Mommy, look at him,' Guy pleads.

True gathers the pup, which smells of milk and sweet hay, into her arms. He licks her tender neck, as if sensing where it hurts. 'Is he . . . weaned? He's awfully small.'

'Weaned, not fixed,' Gus says proudly, 'but they can fix them young now. Four months. He's ten weeks.'

'You planned this, you stinker,' True accuses Gus, who makes wide white eyes, his hands spread innocently. 'So how're we going to get this hound . . .'

'He's a border collie, Mom. His name is Gypsy, Gyp for short. Gypsy Carr Bannister, the First.'

'He will never let anyone hurt Guy,' Gus tells her, 'and he'll guard your house with his life. These are wonderful dogs . . .'

'They're the best,' Hank adds.

'*You* were in on this!' True cries. Hank makes an identical gesture of surrender, palms up. 'I can't help but forgive you. Heck, darling, thank you. The first thing you said was . . .'

'I'd get him a dog,' Hank smiles. 'And I keep my promises.'

'You kept this all to yourself! All these weeks!' True accuses.

'They shed about a whole dog a day,' Clothilde explains, 'and they make the vacuum cleaner scream "Wheeee!"'

'Oh well.'

'He goes pee pee outside,' Guy points out. 'Want to see?' And indeed, Gypsy daintily does his little squat. 'I have to tell him, "Go pee" in the same spot every day. And then I have to teach him "Sit," with just my hand going up, not saying it, and I must never say his name in anger, so he'll always come to me.'

'Well, who's going to fill his food bowl and pick up . . . ?'

'Oh me, Mommy. You know I'm very responsible. And *Grand-père* got him a little bag, so we can take him right on the airplane, under the seat, and a little bed, and two rawhide chewies, and he can never chew anything that looks like a person's sock or shoe or he'll think it's okay to chew all person's socks and shoes, and he can only have chicken-and-rice dog food, because lamb and rice makes doggies fart . . .'

'Well, he's pretty darned adorable.'

'I knew you would let me keep him. *Grand-père* said moms are pushovers.'

'I did not!' Gus protests.

'Don't lie, you did, too,' Guy admonishes him.

'Well we don't have to worry about what your dad is going to say!' True shoots Hank a look of mock fury.

'Oh, he knew all along. I mean weeks before we came!'

'Come *on!*'

'He did, well, not weeks, True. I told Henri last week. But we didn't want to . . . spoil the surprise.'

She and Hank and Guy fall asleep in the same bed, while Gypsy lies in his crate, softly and politely whimpering. After a few moments, True hears, and goes to gather the pup into her arms. In an instant, he is gratefully asleep under her chin, trusting as a baby. She thinks of a fence for the front yard. That at least. The road is busy . . . and perhaps an outdoor house, for when there is no one home . . .

'Like him?' Hank whispers.

'He's adorable. You devil. I can't believe you. Once Guy saw him, you knew it would be all over.'

They kiss, and it is then True remembers earlier that night, the table with its embroidered cloth, the girl with the golden scales of a mermaid. That he could have had; this he wants instead. They kiss again, and Hank's tongue swells against the roof of her mouth, his lips softening, sucking.

True feels her heart wrench. He loves her. He loves Guy. Hank says, because they cannot do what they feel, with Guy beside them snoring, 'Slide over there, Gypsy little buddy, and let me get between my wife and my son. So I can hold you both.' Something ratcheted tight in True's stomach loosens, and she slips into sleep, one hand over Hank's, one over Gypsy's tiny silky head.

ON THEIR NEXT-TO-LAST night in Metairie, the night before the baptism, True catches Hank and Perry giggling in the foyer. They are having a boys' night out. A part of her is relieved. True has seen

243

so many boats and buildings, heard so many songs and stories, she wants only to lie on her back on a rubber float and look at the stars through the glass panel over the Bannisters' pool.

'Good night, *chère*,' Hank kisses her. 'You want me to bring you anything?'

'Hope you don't,' Perry chuckles, and Hank looks at him, suddenly stern.

'This is my wife,' he says.

'I'm sorry, True,' Perry bobs his head, like a big, abashed six-year-old.

'Just a big child, him,' says Grandmamma Winston. 'They go to the haunts, the nasty places.'

'You mean . . . whorehouses?' asks True.

'No,' the old woman laughs, 'just the places where the drinks are all water and ginger and the pretty girls dance naked. They eat the boudin and pickled eggs, the honky-tonk.'

'Without me?' All the women chuckle.

'Girls don't go to the roadhouse,' Win says. 'Or ever see strippers. Except down in the Quarter.'

'Really,' True says coolly.

'If you don't like it, hit him,' Win laughs. 'We used to hit him all the time. Reed would beat the tar out of him. She's little, but she's rough.'

True and Guy spend the night swimming, languidly, their arms leaving arcs of phosphorescence in the starlight. 'Do we have to leave?' Guy asks.

'We do, but don't you want to show Fenn and Brendan your new baby?'

Guy grins wickedly, since Holly won't let Fenn have any animals. 'Yeah,' he says.

'And we'll come back. We'll come back lots.'

'Okay,' Guy says. 'You mind if I go to bed, Mom? Gyp is tired.'

True is tired. As she makes her way from the kitchen with her glass of sweet tea, she does something on impulse that startles her. She drops a kiss on Clothilde's head, and her mother-in-law reaches up to touch her cheek. 'Have you enjoyed our home?'

'Very much,' True says.

'It is your home now too,' Clothilde says, with a plain tenderness that makes True's throat hurt. And she decides then, that, if during this trip, if the kit says green light, go, she will go. She will, if she can, make their baby in this house of love and languor, which is so much like the home she wishes she would have grown up in, grown up calm and unguarded and accepting.

She visits the bathroom. The oracle says that tonight is the night. So she slips into her wedding-night satin gown, which has grown loose on her, and waits, coiled, for her man.

SHE HEARS HANK stumble slightly as he enters the room and switches on the bedstand lamp. The whole household is long since asleep. He grins sheepishly and shrugs. 'Where did you go?' she asks.

'River Annie's, where we went as boys,' he tells her. His breath and clothing stink of cigar smoke, clothes, and mouth.

'Is it a stripper place?'

'Did Win tell you that?'

'Yup.'

'Well, it's not much of a strip joint. Two strippers.'

'Tell me what they did.'

'True, don't get all riled.'

'No, tell me what they did. I'm interested. For other reasons.'

'I'm interested in falling asleep for twelve hours straight, but I need four aspirin. Is there any in the cabinet?'

'Sweetheart, how do I know? It's not my house. Can I go looking in the cabinets? I don't think I should.'

'Go ahead. Sure.'

She brings him four aspirin and a glass of water, and sees him notice her body float and slide beneath the fabric. 'Your granny said that all they serve is ginger water there. That the girls are the big attraction.'

'Well, Perry had something along with him that weren't ginger water. Perry said tonight, by the way, that you are hot.' Hank begins to laugh.

'Why are you laughing? I am hot.'

'It was just how he said it. Like such an Eighties guy. At least the house is air-conditioned. When we were growing up, Daddy thought it made you weak.'

'No, I mean, I'm hot, not temperature-wise. I'm sexy.'

'Well, miracles happen. I never heard you say that.' Naked, Hank climbs into bed.

'Now, tell me about the strippers.' And so, with many pauses and great gaps, Hank describes a pink satin bed, on which a 'yellow' girl lay in bra and stockings, which she removed. 'And then what?'

'And then she spread her legs, to leave nothing to the imagination.'

'Is that against the law?'

'Probably.'

'And then what?'

'And then she put a pillow under her butt, to leave even less to the imagination, and she, well, True, she mimed . . . you know.'

'Did she do . . . like this?' True slides up her own virginal gown, and spreads her legs, tucking one of Clothilde's immaculate lacy pillows beneath her. Though his eyes are red enough he could bleed to death unless he closes them, True sees from a stirring of the sheet that she has caught his interest. Slowly, excruciatingly slowly, she begins to move her hips up and down, sliding herself backward and forward against the pillow. She licks one finger and points, 'X' marks the spot. As Hank raises himself on one elbow, True lifts her gown over her head. 'Am I pretty like her?' she asks.

'You're prettier, to me,' Hank vows, as he rolls over to enter her. 'There is no one more beautiful than you. Do we need this?' He begins to remove the pillow, but True has read in a magazine it helps the sperm swim to their appointed rounds more speedily.

'In Hemingway books, the girl always had a pillow underneath. They said it . . . increased the friction.'

'Well, who am I to argue with Hemingway?' Hank smiles, then adds, 'Wait. I smell like a swamp. Let me shower first. Or at least brush my teeth.'

'Just teeth. I can't wait.' Hank actually runs to the lavatory.

As she arches, Hemingway having been right about something for once, True thinks, the One, the One, The One of Pentacles. This, she figures, is surrender. She imagines she feels a lock turn, and click.

AT THE CHURCH on Sunday morning, True, pancaked as a mannequin and wearing a beautiful silk mantilla Clothilde thoughtfully has provided, holds Carr Bannister Swallow against her linen suit as he is blessed and sainted, as her husband, stunning in his blue suit and red tie, stands erect beside her, as they promise to discharge their duties, raising this child in the knowledge of his Savior. A small

246

lunch party of tiny sandwiches with delicious fillings is provided, small Carr is feted with silver spoons, a name bracelet, savings bonds, silky buntings, and, from Perry, a miniature and probably quite costly leather motorcycle jacket.

The party over, Hank's family and True retire to the house to nap, which they do not, Hank having vivid memories of True's last night's performance. There are virtues to Catholicism. Sanctified, they righteously incandesce with sexual heat.

The next morning, True, Hank, Guy, Gypsy, and yet another passenger fly home to Chatham.

TWO WEEKS LATER, True takes the little white stick into her bathroom. Isabelle waits outside while True carefully pees over the appointed place on the rod.

'Come on, True, this is by far the least embarrassing thing we've ever done in a bathroom,' Esa complains.

True knows to what she is referring. Fully nine months after Pete's death, she and her then-new helper Isabelle had driven to Nickerson's Funeral Home to collect what were euphemistically called Peter's 'cremains.' They'd been shown a variety of urns, modeled on everything from the Sphinx to Rodin's *Thinker,* until True said, 'I intend to scatter Pete's ashes on the flats, which he loved.'

'You need a permit for that,' the natty funeral home director told her quickly, 'and most families like to keep . . .'

'Well, we don't,' Isabelle had said, 'and I'm *so* sure you need a permit.'

But when they examined the contents of the can, it looked grim, like archaeology instead of sweet sand. True could see pieces of bone, as long as infant Guy's fingers, and bits of what seemed to be black plastic. 'That's the body bag,' Esa had told her. 'That's what they put the person in to . . . you know.'

'I can't let people see this,' True has said. 'It's gross.'

And so, fortified by many glasses of wine, they had taken the can up to True's bathroom, and used a spaghetti colander to strain out the bones until all that remained was a soft, whitish dust, which stuck to their sweaty faces and hair as if they'd dropped an opened can of baby powder. True remembers laughing hysterically, 'That's Pete all over!'

And a week later, to the sound of bagpipes, the family soberly

247

scattered the ash. Then, by night, like pirates, Esa and True buried the bones under a tree near the Chatham Light.

True is giggling fully as hysterically now as then.

'I'm waiting!' Esa says, tapping her foot.

'I'm waiting, too. It takes three minutes.'

'Well, open the door. You don't have to keep your pants down while you wait!'

They sit side by side on the bed and stare at the stick as if at an oracle. Stubbornly, it remains virginally white. 'Maybe you peed on it wrong,' Esa suggests, as they near the two-minute mark. But then, miraculously, a strong line of blue appears boldly across the window into the wand. 'Listen, listen, True. "While it is possible that if you have performed this test too early in your cycle, a false negative result may occur, a blue line is a virtually definite indicator that you are pregnant. See your doctor for . . . "'

But True is jumping on the bed, waving the stick. 'It was the One of Pentacles! It was the One of Pentacles,' she is crying, as if Hank's nut-brown Maman had not revealed the messages of seven cards, but only one.

AUGUST

BABY, IT'S HOT OUTSIDE

The centerpiece of our August Blessing is a zipped rubber sand bucket that can also be used as a tote, complete with safe and sturdy shovel. For girls, we've got a one-piece tankini in mellow yellow, and for boys, a swimsuit modeled after nineteenth-century men's suits, with comfortable shoulder straps (because don't those boxers always fall down and leave a sandy diaper?). And since nights start to chill in August, one of our star-covered Bedtime Blessings, a sleeper that doesn't need a rocket scientist to snap it up. And did we forget the fish socks? One goofy pair for you and one for your babe? They look great with blue jeans, or cashmere.

WHY OTHER PEOPLE flock helplessly to the Cape in August is a mystery to those who live there. It is always hot, but it can be soggy hot or hot as a box of wooden matches left untended on a stove.

Hot weather gets people in trouble.

The cops in Chatham are always breaking up fights between drivers with plates from Ontario and plates from New Jersey. If visitors' one shining week features a three-day blow, everyone takes it personally. Those who roam in the bookstores and antique shops are stingy and surly, liable to pinch the odd pen or saltshaker. Chefs have been known to throw full buckets of grease out the door at the backs of departing waitstaff who got better offers from desperate owners just up the road, and disputes break out between college-age lovers who have never known more erotic nitroglycerine than among the dunes on Memorial Day. By August, those memories are like the speckled white marks sun blisters leave behind

– visible but numb, undeserving of the pain they must certainly once have caused.

They grow angry at clammers, resentful that the same shellfish they see being shoveled out of the packed sand, which should, they reason, belong to anyone, are instead served up to them for seven dollars with a sprig of arugula and a dash of horseradish sauce at That One Place. Hank has always said that people think they are paying for groceries, but are actually paying for seasoning. If they knew that seasoning, even Sysco – a good brand of spices Hank buys religiously – and others that come in bags without names he imports if he must, cost wholesale only fifty cents the half pound, they would lose their minds altogether.

On one such August night, a night that feels as dangerously hot as burning sugar, True thinks she is losing hers.

She and Guy go out to play miniature golf, with Gyp on his leash, but the no-see-ums are killing, and they decide instead to go bother Pop for a bit. At least, the drive to Truro is an excuse to cruise with the windows open and the air conditioner on, a minor sin of the flesh they both love. But in the parking lot, before Guy can throw open the door, True spots Hank standing under the cornice over the front door.

He is . . . kissing a woman.

Hank is kissing a woman, a woman, kissing a woman. She cannot see the woman's face, though there is still plenty of sunlight left, because the woman's face is turned away, upturned and veiled by her wing of blunt-cut hair, as she reaches for Hank's cheek. At least it is not his mouth. She is giving him the Bannister kiss, on two cheeks. Her hands grip his forearms. For an instant, they part. True does not know whether to cover Guy's eyes, or jump from the car, her hands splayed and upraised, howling like a wraith, or to slide under the dashboard and hide. Hank and the woman separate briefly. True's breath is ragged, by seconds more and more ragged, as if she is running uphill pursued and cannot stop to rest.

Hank places both hands on the woman's shoulders, lifts her chin and wags a finger at her, and kisses her on the forehead. He holds her against his chest briefly and releases her. Head down, the woman makes her way to a sporty car.

'That's a Passat,' Guy says. 'I love them. I'm going to get a Passat when I'm famous.'

'Okay,' True gasps. She does not want to open the door and lean out to throw up. She does not want to throw up into her hands. There is, for once, not even one empty coffee cup nor soft-drink container in the Volvo, normally a trove of such sticky items. True leans forward to place her mouth against the acrid blast of the air conditioner. She inhales, breathes out slowly.

'He's done kissing, can we go in now?'

Okay, okay, okay, okay. Wait, wait wait wait, True thinks.

'I . . . I think . . . who's that?' True asks. 'Who is that lady?'

'I don't know.'

'Did you ever see her?'

'No.'

'Well, maybe we'd better go for a float instead.'

'Why? He's already done. It could have been, no, she has red hair. And she's going out with Tom's brother now, did you know that?'

'I didn't. Who, Lucy?'

'Yeah.'

'We have to go, Gee. We have to go right now.' True is almost sure she can drive. She is only sweating now, no longer nauseated. Breathing does help. She breathes more deeply, fearful she will black out from breathing, breathing, breathing. True begins to laugh. Guy, at first puzzled, laughs along with her. She presses down hard on the accelerator and pulls into the opening of the National Seashore Park. She yanks off her outer shirt, leaving only her tank top, which is plastered to her skin. 'Isn't it hot? It's so hot, isn't it?' she asks Guy. 'I want a float. I need a float, huh?'

Something about the woman is so familiar True loses her way on the way to the Sundae School, and ends up behind a machine shop; but finally finds her way to the roadside stand, where she and Guy shamelessly consume dollops of coffee mocha with marshmallow sauce. 'That's better, isn't it?' she asks Guy, who stares at her puzzled as she rakes her hair and applies, wipes off, then reapplies her lip gloss. 'I'm going to go back and get Dad now, okay? I'll be right back, okay?' True tells Guy, 'I'll bet it was an old friend of his sister, of Tante Win or Tante Tannie. Don't you? That's what I bet.'

'Who?' Guy asks.

'The kissing lady.'

'Oh, okay,' Guy pats her arm, unconcerned.

Leaving Guy with Kathleen, to watch some show about twin teen

251

witches – 'It's Disney, Mom,' Guy insists, anticipating a faint protest True is too spent and distracted to make – she drives back to That One Place. She sits alone in the parking lot. As soon as she sees Hank step out the back for a puff at his cigar, she realizes who the woman had been. The woman had been Adele Cabot. Adele of Florida, New Hampshire, Massachusetts, Adele here and now. She cannot compose her face to meet Hank's. She cannot think of what to ask or not to ask. But as she begins to back away, Hank hears the crunch of the gravel, and comes running. 'Hi, you! I was just thinking I'd call you up and tell you to come over. We serving the dead here tonight. I thought you might want to play darts or something. At least you'd be out in front where there's air. God, it's so hot back there. Tom's working nude almost.' Hank isn't much more than that himself. He wears a strapped T-shirt and ragged cutoffs under his white cook's smock.

'I'm bored, you got that right,' True says. 'The greenheads are awful. And the no-see-ums; well, we saw 'em. Are you bored? Boring night?'

'Sitters. Come in and sit over the bread for forty-five minutes. Order one drink.'

'No one else came in? No regulars? No out-of-towners?'

'Nah.' Hank kisses her lightly on the nose – True studies his mouth, the tender wetness of his inner lip, his chipped tooth, the fourth from the back.

She waits, a long moment.

If Hank says, *That author you know, the woman I used to see? Adele? She came by here. She was down on vacation* . . . she will not explode. She promises not to, by everything she holds dear. Hank was only comforting her. True sees that now. That's all. He had not been trying to cop a feel, nor conduct a tryst, not in plain sight, not in the parking lot. Anyone could have driven up. *She* could have driven up. She *had* driven up. Adele had suffered a loss . . . a contract, a job, a series of lectures, something, or . . . broken off with a boyfriend, or, even better, found her own true love. She was saying good-bye to Hank. There, that was it. Saying good-bye and wishing him well with the same fond gestures True would have employed herself. With someone like . . . Evan. That's all. If it had been more than this, Hank would be saying now, *Adele dropped by. Adele's in trouble; you know Adele.* But Hank says nothing. True walks into the smooth dim coolness of That One Place, so, in its bangles and spice, like a joint in the Vieux Carre, like the inside of a geode. She waves at Tom. Tom's guilty look is transparent as Saran Wrap. He disappears into the back. Lucy, popping out of a satin halter top, is trying out as front of the house tonight, and shows her teeth to True. True wanders into the steaming kitchen, where the two men work silently, side by side, with their new assistant, pouring cups of milk over the shrimp in the sauté pans, tossing in handfuls of red pepper, deftly grabbing tongs to remove the steaks from the row of big Blodgett ovens where they have been shelved to cook through after searing. Everything cooks at once; nothing is spoiled. True feels as though she is watching the workings of a watch. 'Remember, I need triple the shrimp Tazo,' Hank reminds Tom.

'Roger, three or four?'

'Ummm, lemme think. Four. And something, the mousse cake, we can freeze so it won't melt when I take it out,' Hank says, 'and bread.'

These must be for Madame Le Chat and Mister Riviere. This is Hank, Hank, her good and gallant.

Hank kissed Adele.

She has imagined this. She has seen this through the kaleidoscope of hormones.

She watches transfixed, her feet drawn up on a plastic milk crate, as Tom uses a blow torch to crisp the crème brulee, which is chocolate tonight, the kind of confection True once would have scampered over a nest of angry water moccasins to taste. Now, however, it and the whole notion of a roomful of strangers outside the tiny confines of the kitchen, obstinately and strenuously troughing their way through the bouillabaisse and the mashed sweet potatoes with sweet tarragon they have come for and will consume, despite the heat, despite the gastric throes they may experience in their beds that night at Hawthorne's Inn or the Gilded Gull, feels barbarous. When she looks out of the swinging door, she expects to see snouts and horns.

'You don't belong back here, *chère*,' Hank says, mopping his neck with a clean napkin. 'You look kinda green, you.'

True walks out into the restaurant, sits at the bar, asks Rose the bartender for an iced tea, and puts both her hands around the glass, then both her hands against her cheeks.

Any wife would ask. No wife with any sense of her own mastery, of her husband's love, would be so passive, so meeching. Is she a mouse? Is she a harridan? Why doesn't she say anything?

At closing, after Hank has mopped the floor – a wall sign reads THE FLOOR WILL – That Is WILL!!!!! – BE MOPPED FIVE TIMES EACH WEEK,' and showered himself in only his cutoffs under the outside hose, he suggests they leave the truck and drive home together. She can drop him off tomorrow.

After a mile, his skin has dried. 'Can you believe that? I'm as hot as if I never showered.'

'You must literally lose weight in the kitchen when it's like this,' True tells him.

'Five pounds this summer so far,' Hank scoffs.

'And you act like it's not hard work. It's like working in the bottom of a ship, shoveling coal,' says True.

'You shouldn't act like your work is hard,' Hank says thoughtfully. 'My daddy says that makes it seem like you do it for the money.'

'I do it for the money,' True says.

'Bull, True,' Hank chides her. 'Nobody would work as hard as you do for the money. Talk about work. You don't have to take the heat literally, but you take the heat. I hear you on the phone.'

Hank steers toward Nauset, and they get out to walk. The air is finally at least moving, though a person could hardly call it a breeze. True knows she is scorned for owning one of the only central air-conditioning units in her neighborhood – Cape Codders despise air conditioning, though they will come to blows in the parking lot at JC Penney's over the floor model of any fan during a heat wave – but True excuses hers by pointing out that her house is not only a house, but a place of business. She also air-conditions the warehouse, with window units, as much for the sake of the stock as the packers. She has horrors when she thinks of some Mainline Mama in Philadelphia opening a Blessings box that reeks of raw cod from the fumes of the plant upwind.

'What are you so glum about?' Hank asks.

'Hmmm. I'm just under the weather. You know? I don't know what's got into me.'

'Let's go home. I'll see something gets into you.'

'Okay.'

254

'I'd say let's rest here, but I notice you're not much of a beach girl . . .'

'I love the beach, Hank. I just hate the sand.'

'Why'd you move here, then?'

'It was where Nature put me. If I could, I'd have the beach paved over with, like foam court, like a basketball floor. I can't stay out of Franny's pool, but I just . . . I hate sand.'

'Guy loves it. He loves being buried.'

'Every time he does that,' True says, gripping Hank's arm as they turn to walk to the car, 'it makes me twitch.'

'And he's always wanting me to do it, too.'

'Just tell him to leave off.'

'I do, but then he just does it all over again. But that's kids. You want to go for an ice cream?'

'Been there. Done it. With Guy earlier.' Shit, she thinks. Will Guy ask about the kissing woman? No. Guy forgets the business of adults, unless it directly affects him, as quickly as he forgets his shucked boxer shorts on their bathroom floor.

'Then let's hit the sheets, woman. There's something I want to show you.'

'Forget the sheets,' True says suddenly, slightly shrill. 'We have a blanket in the trunk.'

They walk back, far back, into the dark, where the beam of the lighthouse and the scattered fires of the teenagers can't find them. Even the no-see-ums are no-shows. And True, with what she hopes is a sort of seductive skill, stands in front of Hank as he lies on the blanket, then lets drop her drawstring-waisted pants, under which she wears nothing, and lies down. The water is flat under a metal moon, with clouds in lines that seem too symmetrical for nature, clouds like lead bars over a bronze sky. 'I've never seen it like this,' True says. 'I know it means some kind of weather, but it looks like another planet.'

Hank produces a double-bagged pint carton from his back pocket.

'That's not dope,' True giggles.

'It's ice,' Hank tells her.

'Ice?'

'It's just ice,' he insists. 'Plain, ol' ice.'

'We having martinis?'

He extracts one of the bar cubes, with their delicate thumbprint pock in the center, and places it over one of her nipples, which stands to attention first in shock, then delight, as the meltwater trails deliciously down her ribs, Hank leaning forward first to lick, then suck. 'Cooler?' he asks.

'In a sense,' she answers.

They lie together as Hank absently strokes her belly and her thighs with his forefinger, drawing feathers, then circles, then moons and stars. He lifts himself slightly to slide out of his jean shorts, and then reaches over his back to pull his shirt off, a gesture that, having seen it hundreds of times, is still so redolent of sheer shotgun maleness it makes True want to kneel. She has never seen another human being so carelessly formed expressly for sex. As Hank nudges his shaft home, True hears young, stifled laughter and part of a sentence, drifting back over the thud of bare feet on sand, the way a line of a song would trail away from an open car window as she lay in her girlhood bed trying to fall asleep, ' . . . so cute.'

He is holding onto her shoulders, his face contorted, his purr lowering an octave, to a groan, to a grunt, to a growl as he drives her, too hard, her shoulder blades carving an indentation in the sand below the blanket. She hurts; the mind that governs her comfort longs to throw him back, off her, to signal a restraining hand. But to disturb this exquisite collision of the burning physical and emotional planes, telescoping to a single point of heat, she is too far gone to interrupt such symmetry. It would be sin. Heedless of the presence of stragglers nearby, she cannot stifle a wince of rapture, quickly followed by the sensation of tears.

Yeah, she thinks. He is cute. He's cute across generations. He is mine. 'Are you ready?' Hank asks her, a growl.

'More than ready,' True tries to make her breath come in orgasmic pants. Hank arches; True arches. For the first time in their marriage, she fakes it.

'You wish on stars in Louisiana?' True asks, when Hank has rolled away, the cooling sweat from his skin making her shiver.

'We wish on stars, just like here.'

'What'd you wish, when you were a little boy?'

'For a McClaren,' he says. 'What'd you wish?'

'To be a famous actress.'

'Well, you got closer.'

True waits a beat. 'Know what I wish now? It's kinda morbid.'

'What?'

'I wish that my children will live long lives, that my children will outlive me.'

'Huh. Figures. You'd put a way to worry in a wish upon a star.'

'I didn't used to wish that,' she confides.

'What'd you used to wish?'

'That I'd meet a man from Louisiana, who was in the restaurant business . . .'

Hank flaps his shirt at her. 'What a line . . .'

'And that we'd get married, and we'd go down to Louisiana, and one night we'd make love and I'd wake up in the morning and lo and behold, we'd be pregnant! And nine months later, we'd have a bouncing baby girl, or a bouncing baby boy, who looked just like this man from Louisiana . . .'

Hank has gone still, looking out at the lunar sliver of the horizon. 'Are you telling me something, True?'

'I reckon I am, Pops,' she says, and crosses her fingers beneath her thighs.

Hank still sits motionless. 'True, I . . . True, to be honest . . .' True's heart begins to deflate, 'I want to say I'm the happiest man on earth. But it's more than that. It's just that I feel so lucky I don't dare say a word lest break the spell.'

'So you're happy?'

'I'm happy, happy? Shoot, I'm . . . I thought we'd have to go through shots and thermometers and . . .' We did, True thinks, loosening her fingers. 'My daddy warned me about that. But we didn't need it! All we needed was a little hooch and a little hoochie and the famed Bannister sperm!'

'Well, don't go buying cigars yet, Hank. I'm about ten minutes along and way not out of the woods, and the doctor says there's a chance of prematurity at my age, and all sorts of things.'

'Nothing's going to happen to our baby!' *Our baby. Our baby. See, see? All is well!*

'Well, I just want you to know, it's by no means a sure thing yet . . . but in about six weeks, we can start being cautiously optimistic.'

Hank jumps up and begins to brush the sand from True's lap. 'Oh, holy shit, True. Did what we just did . . . ? Did it hurt him? Her? Do we have to be . . . like on good behavior?'

True laughs, 'No! Only with . . . some things. I'll explain. Watching out for introducing air into the . . .'

'I get it.'

'Are you sure you aren't too overwhelmed? I mean, one new son, a new marriage . . .'

'No, *mais* no!' cries Hank. 'I'm scared. I mean, I'm scared it won't be okay. But that's all. I just didn't expect this so soon. This has been quite a lifetime, these six months. No, I want this more than anything. More than anything. It's just ironic.'

'Ironic, how?' True asks.

'Never mind,' Hank says. 'Stupid. I'm just knocked on my butt is all. Didn't anything ever knock you on your butt because it was so unexpected but still make you happier than you ever thought you could be? Something you didn't even really think you could hope for?'

'Only once, when you asked me to marry you.'

'The perfect example,' Hank concludes.

He reaches out to cup her shoulders, to kiss her. And she turns her face away. 'Sand in my . . . my mouth. See? That's why I hate sand,' True laughs, giddy. She will not let his mouth touch hers, not with Adele's essence still part of him.

They climb the wooden stairs to the truck, Hank still only in his cutoffs, now supporting her as if she were not only pregnant, but disabled. True sees the low-lidded looks on the faces of the young twentysomethings, who have paused in the parking lot for a smoke of what may or may not be tobacco. Well, oh well, she thinks. Sorry, girls.

True lectures herself. Surrender all doubt. Doubt is the drag weight of an anchor on smooth sailing. Weight is decline. Think, *mais* yeah, he's cute. And I am his one and only. Which is why I have to treat him like a mate, not a child, nor even a lad, not ever again. *And someday, perhaps after the baby is born, he will tell her, remember that one night? When you told me you were pregnant? The stupidest thing happened, and I just couldn't ruin that moment, but you'll never guess who showed up, a total drag . . .*

'I love you,' she tells Hank.

'I love you, too,' he says.

'Then we're okay.'

'We are more than okay. I should be calling my folks, renting a banner to fly from a plane . . .'

258

'We're okay, and . . . there *is* something I want to talk to you about.'

I will forgive him, True thinks. Whatever it is. He is going to tell me about Adele, and that it meant nothing, and I am going to believe him.

'I . . . I have an idea,' Hank says, catching her so entirely off guard, she forgets to be angry that he seems to have forgotten their child. 'I have another idea . . .' True braces herself. 'I have an idea for a company, not exactly like Twelve Times Blessed, but kind of . . . just listen . . . I thought, what if we had a kid like Guy, older than Guy, who was going to go away to college in a couple of years, and yet it's still your child, so you want him to think of home, and know you're thinking of him.'

True, despite her whirring brain, hears a single silvery tinkling in her mind's ear. 'What would you do?'

'Well, my mom called them care packages, but you'd send one every month . . .'

'With cookies in tins, and music, and handknit socks.'

'Exactly,' Hank drops back onto his knees, 'and vapo-rub.'

'Vapo-rub! That's brilliant. How did you think of that? For the first cold you have when your mom isn't around . . . but our own kind, our brand.'

'And more. Coffee. Gloves . . .'

'You're right, Hank, you're right. And an eye mask in case your roommate stays up all night studying . . .'

'Or earplugs, if he stays up all night playing music, or fucking.'

'This,' True says slowly, 'could actually work . . .' She gets up suddenly.

'Well, of course it could work, True,' Hank says irritably. 'I'm not an idiot. I'm not a child. You sound like I was Guy.'

'I don't mean it that way. That's just how I talk when I'm thinking.'

'So you'd pack these things up like we do your, well, our things, in stuff you could use later. Like a book bag. Or a . . .'

'CD case, a big one. I get it.'

'And we'd call it – are you ready? We'd call it First Year Away. Like Twelve Times Blessed all grown up.'

'Don't say one more word about it,' True tells him, running for the truck. 'We need paper. We need to write all of this down. Don't

259

say a word except say to yourself, I'm an idea man, I'm an idea man. Repeat this as a mantra.'

'Wait! Why shouldn't I tell you the rest? You said you liked the idea!'

'I love the idea. That's why we're going home. We're going to get out the notebook and make lists. If you're the idea man, you have to have a person who executes the idea. That's what I am. I'm the one who makes it happen.'

'But I want to be the one who makes it happen, too,' Hank objects.

'Hank, are you giving me this idea, or would you actually want to do it with me? Do it together?'

'I never imagined we would do it together. Or that we wouldn't. True, I really didn't think further of it than tossing it around. And I would have brought it up sooner, but your news obviously, well, that took first place. That blew me away. And sure, I thought all my time would be taken up by the restaurant, but I think I could learn to do this with you.'

'I'd like you to, but I don't see how you can unless you let someone else buy in with you and Tom, a real partner, not a manager, because you don't know how much work and time it takes to plan a proto-type, and do market research.'

'True, it's my idea, and the more I think about it, the more I would want to be involved. Make it perfect. Like Twelve Times Blessed. All the right touches. Plus, I even thought, beyond that, you know, you could do a version of it for seniors, too.'

'Wait, wait, wait! Let's leave! I'm afraid I'm going to forget one thing by the time we get home . . . let's go!' Hank grabs her hand and they run faster. And then True stops, abruptly.

'I don't mean you'd have to give up your independence, Hank. Your business. And that sweet volunteer thing you do for people. But if you really wanted to be involved, you'd have to spend more time with me, and learn about this kind of business.'

'And we'd fight. I know that.'

'That's what I mean. We'd fight, because you'd think that you knew how to do this better than I do, and it would offend you if I said . . .'

'But those wouldn't be personal fights. They'd be like you and Rudy bickering. So let me think about it. A little. But I think I can

260

manage to swallow my pride. After all,' he sighs, 'you're the boss, boss.'

True begins, 'Only when it comes to experience with this. It's your idea. We'd be partners. Up here,' she taps her head, 'down here,' she taps her belly, 'and out there, and we're going to . . .' Then, observing the sharp intake of Hank's breath, she thinks, wait. Take it slow. One world at a time. There is a healing symmetry to it. She has given Hank a surprise. He has given her one. She looks up at Hank, literally and figuratively, for the first time. She would not have thought of anything that could expand so neatly on the idea of Twelve Times Blessed, and so beautifully, seamlessly.

That night, passersby trying to take advantage of some small night breeze notice a light in the topmost room of the big house that backs up to Ridgevale Beach burning until the small hours, like a lantern on the beam of a ship.

True laughs often, as they plan, and she offers praise often, and Hank chuckles and makes self-deprecating motions to hide his pride, and, even so, around and around, like a frightened mouse, a thought capers in the cage of her skull.

WHEN TRUE RISES, late, still languid from the sweet, salty sex, energized by the balm of collaboration, and only laterally annoyed by the memory of the chance encounter with Adele, she approaches her mother making tea in the kitchen, on the way into the office. 'Hank has had the most astounding idea,' she tells Kathleen.

'Yes?'

True launches into a description of First Year Away, to which Kathleen listens patiently, nodding and occasionally shaking her head. 'It is a good concept, True. But is this the time for new ventures?'

'I'm not sure. I don't know if it's bold or foolhardy. But I also think this is surefire.'

'That's what Blooms by Dawn thought,' Kathleen puts her hands on her slight hips.

'Blooms by Dawn? How the hell do you know about Blooms by Dawn, Mom?' True demands.

'I hear things.'

'Heard from Bono lately, about his efforts for world peace?'

'True, I mean, I hear things about Internet-based business. I read and study. And what I hear is, as you know, utterly discouraging.'

True musters more bravado than she feels.

'Don't be such a wet kipper, Mom. It's a swell idea. Let's see if we can do a market sample; we can afford at least that much.'

'But what about capital?'

'Well, I've been approached by venture capitalists before.'

'All of whom wanted a controlling piece!'

'Well. Maybe they'd get a piece. For the right price. I just have a hunch.'

'You're sure it's not just hormones?'

'What do you mean, hormones?'

'I'm not blind, True.'

True inadvertently glances down at her abdomen. 'How did you know?'

'A mother knows,' Kathleen says.

'A mother knows by searching the trash.'

'No, True. A mother knows by whispered conversations that aren't so whispered, with physicians, right in the office, and by the fact that Esa simply had to tell Rudy, who swore he wouldn't tell anyone, except I personally heard him tell Keith, and also his mother . . .'

'Oh, dear. Now I have to tell Guy. And I wanted to wait until I was sure nothing would . . . happen.'

'Well, anything could happen anytime. And I'm sure nothing will happen.'

'You are, Mom? That's like trombones and flags waving, from you.'

'Naturally, I'm glad for you. If this is what you want.'

'It is.'

'And I'll hop on the 'Net and scope around and see if there's anything out there like that for college students. I saw one site for seniors that was getting a lot of hits.'

'How do you know about hits? I thought you couldn't use the computer. It just blows up if you touch it! I'll bet you could hack into the Pentagon, by now, Mom.'

'I'm learning,' says Kathleen, with serene indifference, as she dips her teabag, once, then twice, then hangs it on the little wooden rack she keeps, for later use. 'You're never too old to learn. Some things. Kellen writes that . . .'

'Oh, Kellen. The apple-farmer genius.'

'He's a very bright man. We're book-clubbing *Anna Karenina* together.'

'I'm reading that, too,' True says, amazed. She's lying. She's been too tired to read anything but product literature for weeks.

'Fancy that,' her mother smiles.

THE FOLLOWING MONDAY, True gets a startling phone call, from the *Today* show.

On the heels of a cancellation, they want to feature Twelve Times Blessed, the day after tomorrow, an Internet company going strong, and to hear her philosophy and secrets. They want to fly her to New York, and for her to overnight samples of five or six of the Blessings, so their designer can decorate a set. True has actually had dreams in which something like this happens, dreams of herself and Rosie O'Donnell, heads bent together over the surprises in a Blessings package. True goes wild, stands up, while still on the telephone with the producer, waving to Rudy, pulling her hair up into spikes. *Call Franny*, she writes on a pad, and sees Rudy begins dialing.

The first thing Esa and True do, before Franny arrives, is to purchase the name *firstyearaway.com* on the Internet. When Franny gets there, the three women ascend the stairs to the really important task: deciding what True will wear to New York.

'Do I have anything I can wear? It doesn't have to be fancy. It just can't be black or white. Or black-and-white. Or striped. That strobes.'

'I'm still hopeful. You can't wear a short skirt, because you'll look like you have piano legs, even though you don't . . . True, do you have any earrings that wouldn't look out of place at a rodeo? Beads and feathers, sheesh!'

'Hank says that, too. He always says, "How long do you have to wear them?" And I say, "For what?" And he says, "To win the bet." He says that about my cowboy boots, too.'

'Well, fortunately, I have better earrings. You need gold and big, but simple, and close to the face. I read that, for TV, you look simple; you talk simple and slowly; but you get a lot in. Just like when you do a speech. Whatever the host asks you, you say what you want to say. You just say it over and over.'

'What do I want to say?'

'Come on, True.'

'What do I want to say, for real?'

'You tell the nice blond lady that Twelve Times Blessed is unique, absolutely unique, because it offers the customer the magic of giving that special baby a new surprise *every month for the whole first year of the baby's life!* And then the blond lady will say something like, oh, like the Book-of-the-Month Club? And you'll laugh, just lightly, and say, "No, no. Every single item in our Blessings packages, except our wonderful books chosen by children's librarians . . . "'

'Me and Kathleen!'

'She's a librarian!'

'Okay.'

'Every item is handmade by artists and craftspeople, so each one is a little bit different. Why, we even have our sunscreens and lotions specially mixed so that Mother and Baby can use them together. All our products are cruelty-free, and we make them sensible. Tell them how the sleepers are like idiot cameras. Make a joke. Tell them how you could never make all the snaps match on Guy's sleepers, especially in the dark, so you decided to make yours with one big panel over the crotch and only two snaps, one at each hip,' Franny continues.

'And why the bibs slip over the baby's head like a turtleneck, so no knots.'

'Okay. I get the talking points . . .'

'No, not all of them, not the big one,' Franny wags a finger.

'What am I forgetting?'

'You announce the new company!'

'But if I announce the new company then I have to actually *do* the new company, and soon! I'm not sure I'm ready for all that!'

'I thought you said boldness was all,' Franny reminds her. 'I thought you said, when the going got rough . . .'

'Take more risks, right. I was on drugs,' True says.

'Well, you'll never get a bigger, better chance than this one.'

'That's right,' True agrees. 'I'll have to find a way.'

'And, oh, True, I forgot, drive this home, True, each one is sized for the individual baby. Even preemies. You get a lot of preemies these days,' Franny says. 'Old mothers with money, y'know? There'll be more of them.'

'Speaking of which . . .'

'What?' Franny is wrinkling her nose in distaste at a striped orange tank-dress the size of a backpacker tent.

'Don't throw that out. I might need that.'

'For what, an umbrella, at a garage sale?'

'No.' Franny looks up. 'True Dickinson!' she says, and takes her best friend into her arms, and murmurs into her shoulder exclamations usually reserved for disasters and miracles, instead of the most ordinary event of human life. 'Will you be safe? Flying?'

'That low, yes. Just a hop.'

'One small hop for womankind, one giant leap for . . . oh True, I love you so,' Franny says. 'You deserve this. Is Hank over the moon?'

'Yep. And a little shocked. And over . . .'

'Overwhelmed, probably,' Franny answers in synchrony with True; they both laugh. 'Well, he's going to have to learn to ride the surf. Wait till he sees her.'

'Oh, it's a boy. I know for sure.'

'You know already?'

'No, Hank says.'

'It's a girl, True,' Franny says seriously. 'And I am her godmother.'

In the end, True chooses to wear the seafoam linen suit she wore to marry Douglas and Esa.

'WISH ME LUCK, baby,' True says, as she leaves for New York, and both Hank and Guy answer simultaneously, 'Break a leg!' True takes Hank aside at the last moment and whispers, 'See? Talk about meant to be!'

'Don't even think about that. Just keep your jacket tucked under your butt and smile pretty,' he says. She is reassured to see that, as the plane backs out, Hank has put his arm around Guy.

Franny and True check into a bed-and-breakfast in a brownstone on the East Side, which is clean but rendered slightly creepy by the wall art, alternating stitched and framed samplers of psalms, interspersed with photos of blond children. These photos are handcolored in pastels, as photos have not been colored since True was a girl. The hostess had described in detail the necessity for low-volume television at night, because her four-year-old would be asleep after seven. Paging through the guest book, Franny reads aloud, '"The perfect religious getaway . . . praise Our Lord Jesus for City Sanctuary." Here's someone from Peru, "What a surprise to find Our Lord thriving in the middle of a city of sin and violence." I don't think she really even has a four-year-old, True. Those pictures are thirty years old. Maybe she *had* a four-year-old, and she . . .'

'Cut it out, Franny, you're scaring me,' True says, her hand firmly over her abdomen. 'I'm going to lock the door.'

Still, they brush their teeth, and settle in, side by side. The television actually has rabbit ears, and summons only one station, a wavering black-and-white vision of what appears to be some sort of British news. 'Let's call home on my cell,' Franny says. 'If Steve answers, we can be sure we haven't slipped into a time warp. The baby seems to like it, though. Maybe she'll be an Anglophile. You haven't thrown up.'

'Go to sleep,' says True. 'I have to look thirty years old in six hours.'

They both jump as they hear a door slam and lock a few feet from the headboard. Franny giggles, 'I'll give you fifty bucks if you bounce on the bed with me and start moaning and screaming. I'll give you a hundred bucks.'

'Shut up!' True chides her, but they laugh so loud, it probably has the same effect. Franny has to rush out of the room and pee. True finally does have to throw up.

Amazingly, the next morning at the TV station, True is so bewitched when the stylist quickly unravels her braid and remakes her hair into a straight pageboy that suits her better than any other hairstyle she's ever had, she forgets to be nervous when she's miked and on the set. She chats and displays the new Teddy-in-the-Box, a gift box that opens gently with a lullaby to reveal soap and a sleeper within. The host is so charmed she orders a Blessings package, on-air, for her sister. And when Jane (True thinks her name is Jane) asks what's in store, True hints broadly, 'Well, we think about all these babies growing up and leaving the nest. About that time when a kid first leaves home and a parent, the kind of parent I am, wants to send a piece of herself along with him; but she's too busy to bake cookies and knit socks . . .'

'Big kid blessings!' the host crows.

'That's what's on the horizon,' True smiles.

'But that's fantastic!' Jane tells all America, as True's heart quakes with fear or elation, which could be the same thing.

266

When they arrive home, Guy has bannered the porch, STAR MOM OF THE UNIVERSE! GO, 12 X BLESSED! GO 1 X AWAY! and Hank excitedly tells True that she has already been on the six-o'clock news in Boston.

The appearance makes the pages of 'Lifestyle' in the *Boston Globe*, and a reporter visits the warehouse for an interview. True is getting more orders than Esa and Kathleen, with all the lines and e-mails on full-barrel, can handle. She considers placing ads for more packers, with benefits, to make the job more attractive. Still, the stock market has probably bottomed, the tightrope still quivering, but things are settling down. When Hank comes home, she is still at her desk, e-mailing off confirmations to new customers, and fails to notice, until she sees the mark on the wall, that he has kicked off his boots and left them lying sandy at the foot of the stairs. It is so unlike him that she goes looking for him and finds him staring into the mirror in their bathroom. Amazingly, he is drunk.

'Hank?' she asks. 'What's wrong?'

'Nothing,' he says.

'I know something's wrong. You don't drink. Not like this.'

'Well, 'times I do things I don't do. I have things on my mind.'

'Like what?'

'Like my good old buddy Tom borrowed ten thousand bucks from our escrow and invested it in some stupid-shit phone-service company his brother helped start.'

'And . . .'

'And it went belly up.'

'Oh, Hank.'

'And he swears he's gonna pay it back right away, but I told him he can just take half his salary until he does, and now he's pissed . . .'

'*He's* pissed; he didn't even ask you.'

'And I can't make payroll.'

'Well, I'll help you.'

'No,' Hank says roughly. 'No.'

'Hank, we're partners, remember? Birth to earth?'

'You're not going to pay my staff.'

'Would you pay mine?'

'Yeah.'

'Well?'

'Well, it's different. I don't want Tom to know I had to go running to my rich wifey and get my lunch money . . .'

True's hands turn cold. 'Is that how you see it?'

'No, but that's how everyone else sees it.'

'What does anyone else matter? You're the one who said that. And who has to know?'

'I'll know. I'll feel like . . . you own me.'

'Hank!'

'Well . . . I'm a man, True.'

'And I'm your wife. For better, for worse, in good times and bad, with all that I am and all that I have.'

'Okay.'

'Okay.'

'Okay, okay, *okay!* Please help me over this.'

'Fine. Now, let's forget it.'

'It's not just that.'

'What else is it?' Hank has begun to wash his face, over and over, as if he can wash something away. 'Hank?'

'It's nothing.'

'It's not nothing,' True has no patience for this; she bites her tongue, literally.

'It's nothing you have to be concerned about. Just leave me keep thought, okay? I'll tell you sometime.'

'Hank, are you sick?'

'You mean, to my stomach? No. I'm not sick,' Hank tells her. 'I'm not.'

'Don't worry about money, sweetheart. Try to sleep,' True soothes him.

''Kay.'

'Well, okay. Good. We're going to be one of the ones that make it.'

'But what if we don't?' Hank's voice is slurred.

'We'll . . . adjust. We'll think of something. Just sleep on it. Come on. We've had a stroke of luck with this TV thing. One thing balances the other. And the stock market is as low as it can go . . .' True recognizes how little she really knows of her husband, that even the sunniest of all men have haunted hollows, and that Hank's is linked somehow with his fear of dependence, on a woman, which would ordinarily make her angry, but now the air is too charged with hope

268

and danger even to entertain the possibility of combustion. She wonders about her own father, about Franny's husband, Steve. Is there any man who doesn't hold his cards so close to his chest?

'I want to brush my teeth now. Give me a little room, please.'

'Okay. Do you want four aspirin?'

'Yep, I do. And I'll let you get them for me.' Hank takes the aspirin from True's open hand. 'I'm gonna sleep now, and do what my mama used to tell me when she shut me in my room. I'm gonna meditate on my sins.'

She remembers then. Adele. Her upturned face. He has still not told her.

'I GOT ADELE's new book,' True says carefully a few days later. 'God, she's a wonderful artist.'

'She's pretty good,' Hank answers. *He will say it now. She came by. We visited. I felt so sorry for her, because of all that you and I have, now . . .*

'Is she . . . okay? Do you hear from her?'

'Once in a while. I did a little while back. Her mom is real sick, and has been for years, and she never had a dad.'

'Like me,' says True. 'I did, but I don't remember him.'

'I guess that was why she was so . . . she was very, overwilling to please . . . but she wasn't aggressive about it. She just wanted to be loved. I think she dated a guy I knew. That's how I met her. It was a party for her first book, I think. The book about the baby mermaid who thought the mom was a . . .'

'A dolphin.'

'Right.'

'And I could tell he treated her like crap. So one day, I called her, and asked her to go to a movie with me, and you'd have thought I gave her a check for a thousand bucks. And after that, we just never stopped. Until we stopped.'

'Why did you stop?'

'I moved.'

'Why did you leave her?'

'I moved here. And I didn't want a long-distance relationship.'

'Was she sad?'

'Yes. Very sad. So was I. But it was the end of it anyhow. We were just going around in circles. A little touch. A little pleasure.

A little life. No future. I could never figure out why a woman with so much promise, with so much going for her, was so . . . timid and self-conscious. I wanted to . . . build her up. Make her see herself as she was. She had a beautiful body, like a real model's body, though not skinny. And she thought she was ugly. How could that be?'

'That was it? That was what you didn't like? That she didn't believe in herself?'

'It . . . didn't help.' She sees from his face, and the way he rapidly switches on CNN, that Hank has caught the resonance of what he has just said to his own wife. If I take a sleeping pill, True thinks, will the baby just go to sleep too, or grow another limb? She will not take the chance. Everything, she has realized, from cough syrup to vitamin B, has a warning on it for pregnant women. But the prenatal vitamins and the hormones have thickened her hair and made it lustrous. She loves to fluff and feel it. She has taken a tape of the show to her hair stylist and had her hair cut blunt, and loves how its heavy angles swing past her cheek.

'Do you worry about her?' Hank has switched over to VH1.

'Kind of. That might be why I didn't leave her for so long. She really needed me. Wait a minute, I love this song,' Hank says. It's Van Halen, 'Jump.' Hank jumps, up onto the bed and begins to strum the neck and body of an invisible Stratocaster. 'Sing the backup, True. Don't you think air guitar is a real instrument?'

'No,' she pouts. 'I don't want to just sing "Jump! Go ahead and jump!" and "Respect, just a little bit, respect, just a little bit . . . "'

'Well you can't sing the melody.'

'Why?'

'You're not a guy. And you can't play air guitar.'

'But you don't know the old songs. I do.'

'Like The Beatles. I do so. I know all of "The Ballad of John and Yoko." I know that "Something's Happenin' Here" is really called "For What It's Worth."'

'I mean old songs. Parents' songs. Like my mother used to sing when she cooked. Like . . . like "South of the Border."' Why are they talking about Forties pop?

But Hank sings 'South of the Border,' word for word. 'Don't underestimate the boy, True. My mama sang, too.'

'Okay, I have a great and original idea, too. See, whenever we're going to fight, let's sing. It'll be our signal. I'll sing the high parts. We'll sing.'

'Who do I have to blow to get the air turned on around here?'

'It's not even hot. It's about seventy out. And Hank, what do you think of it? The singing cure? Any time we fight?'

'I think it's fine. Great. But I can't sleep, True. We *live* in air conditioning in the South.'

'You go shut all the windows then.'

'You. I'm tired.'

'I'm tired, too, and I don't want to change my position. I have my legs just right over the pillow.'

'Why'd you get so many windows? Jesus, this house must have two hundred windows.'

'It has sixty.'

'Well?'

'Well, first of all, before we built the addition, they were already here because this house is beautifully designed for cross ventilation. So you don't have to have *air conditioning*.'

Hank gets up, grumbling, high-stepping across the Berber carpeting. Having grown up on silky parquet, Hank thinks Berber is not only ugly, but unnecessary torture. He says it has the consistency of nails, and that he will install parquet and Orientals the first time True has to take a trip of more than three days' duration.

It will take him half an hour to shut every window, and even the minor yen and vast tenderness she feels for Hank will not keep True awake that long. Sleep is a narcotic to her now. A sacrament. She sleeps at her desk, in her car while she waits for Guy at school orientation, curled on the sofa before dinner. She loves her sleepiness, further proof that her pregnancy is progressing. True falls asleep to Boy George, in the belief that, though she deserves neither Hank nor her good fortune, she is the queen of the world, or at least of the immediate vicinity.

ONE SUNDAY MORNING, Hank makes waffles from scratch. The kitchen is as silent and waitful as the inner surface of a bell.

'Gee, come here,' True motions, and settles Guy's head on her shoulder. 'Gee, Hank-Dad and I have something to tell you.'

'What?' Guy asks, his hands greasy with turkey-frank bits. He is

271

trying to teach Gypsy to sit, but every time he makes the hand motion, he jumps a foot into the air.

'Hank?'

'Yeah?'

'Hank?' True repeats, with more urgency, as in, *sit down over here and join in the Kodak moment.* 'We . . .'

'We're going to have a baby,' Gee finishes for her.

'Gee! Who told?'

'I deduced it.'

'You deduced it,' Hank laughs. 'You don't even know what "deduce" means.'

'Yes,' Guy says.

'How?' True asks.

'Well, there's a big old fat bottle over there that says, "prenatal vitamins." I know what "prenatal" means.'

'Are you happy?'

'Sit, Gyp.' Gyp finally sits. 'Good puppy, good boy. He did it, Mommy!'

'Are you happy?' True asks again.

'Uh, yeah.'

'Do you think I'm going to love it more than you? Is that it? Because I'm not. Any more than Granny loves me more than Dog. I'll always love you the same.'

'Nooooooo.'

'Well? Then? You always wanted a baby sister or brother.' Guy cuts his eyes at Hank. True clears her throat and Hank glances at her. She telegraphs the question.

'Don't worry about me, pardnuh. I got me a son. This one here's going to be great. Lots of fun. But, hey, you know for a while they can't do too much. Not like us. Yep, you're my firstborn. Didn't you get the ring from *Grand-père?*'

'Yep,' Guy looks up measuringly at Hank. Then he asks, 'Can I pour the batter in?'

And that, True sees, is how that is done.

SEPTEMBER

SWEET SEPTEMBER

What became of summer? One blessing it left behind is apples; and we're in the mood for the tang and sweetness of apple time – every baby's first treat and one of the first recognizable symbols in human language acquisition. A big, juicy one, of smooth wood and painted in bright, nontoxic red, splits into four sections and magically sticks back together again, a hoody sweater with (guess what?) for buttons, and Michigan's most glorious apple butter, for you and the apple of your eye. Curl up with a good read, too. We favor Mimi Mermaid and the School of Dolphins.

ONE SWEET PINEY morning, suggestive of the coming fall, True finds a rusty dot of blood in the lining of her underpants.

Hysterical, she calls her Boston doctor, and demands to be put through, despite the gentle protestations of the nurse who patiently listens to the symptoms.

The doctor finally does take the call. 'No, Missus Bannister,' the obstetrician assures her, 'a tiny, tiny amount of spotting is normal, sometimes as the cervix changes. If it gets redder, or more profuse, call me. But don't worry about what you've seen here.'

'Hank,' she whispers that night, as she lies in bed, from which she has not risen all day, having spent the day phoning Esa and Rudy and writing them e-mails from her laptop, 'I'm having spotting.'

'Where?' he asks, searching her face.

True cannot help laughing. 'I don't mean I'm breaking out in dots! I mean, little drops of blood . . .'

'The baby? Is the baby okay?'

'The doctor doesn't seem to be worried. She says the likelihood of a miscarriage at this stage is about two percent . . . if the fetus is normal.'

'Is it?'

'Hank, I don't know! It's too small for that! And I don't have X-ray vision.'

'Then just do what the doctor says,' Hank tells her casually, reaching across her to grab the phone. He calls home; and Gus ratifies everything the obstetrician has told her, which gives True greater solace.

'Try to stay off your feet until it stops completely, True,' Gus further adds, 'and put a nice ice pack on your lower belly.'

True lies supine all one Saturday, with her ice pack, her feet suspended on her lap desk, finishing her reading of Anna's downfall, until she feels she could chill martini glasses on her abdomen.

The bleeding stops.

On Monday, she goes back to work. Still, she is anxious, and visits the bathroom so many times she cannot believe her colleagues don't offer her Kaopectate. She prospects with squares of toilet tissue for menstrual blood with more avidity than she ever did in college, when her period was late despite the fact that she and her few lovers never failed to double-rubber.

She worries especially knowing another trip is in the offing; that she must soon take this uncommitted baby and somehow fly to California.

All the media attention over Twelve Times Blessed has attracted a serious venture capitalist ('He has to be rolling rich; his stationery says Bel Air, not a street address, just Bel Air, as if he owns it,' says Rudy). The moneybags man, father to three college-age children, is 'charmed' by the idea for First Year Away.

He has discussed the concept in e-mails and multiple conference-calls with True and Hank. To be honest, mostly with True, because when Otto Karp calls, he is often in Hong Kong or Berlin, where it is business time for him, but kitchen-cleaning time for Hank. True is the only one at home when he phones. Still, now he is ready to make medicine, as he puts it. And his urgency is contagious.

True visits her Boston specialist. The doctor is optimistic. 'If the spotting stops for a period of a couple of weeks, you may feel pretty safe flying in the second trimester.'

'It has to be sooner than that,' True explains.

'Then it has to be someone other than you flying,' the doctor tells her. 'I can't overemphasize the seriousness of this, Missus Bannister. Changes in pressure in the first trimester are simply not the way to go.' Together, they then watch the mothwing heartbeat on ultrasound. It is idiotically obvious to True that she would not harm, not even threaten this flutter, even if Donald Trump were to offer her one of his towers in exchange.

'It's real,' she says with primeval inevitability. 'It's really, really real.'

The doctor, a common-sense woman who once delivered babies in igloos in the Alaskan outback, smiles in tolerant jubilee, as if this vintage story were brand new. She says, 'That's a good strong heartbeat. Your lining is a little thin, but no cause for alarm, I guess. Once you've seen the heartbeat, as I've said, the likelihood of miscarrying goes way down. Relax, Missus Bannister. Many elderly gravidas – older mothers – have babies all the time, and they always have. Especially very poor and very rich women.'

True had carried the word 'elderly' around with her like dump stink for a week after her appointment, and for some reason, she also keeps the evidentiary underpants, in a plastic bag stuck in the cedar box like the Shroud of Turin. She knows that high-risk reproductive specialists use the term 'elderly' only in the strictest medical sense; but she has not been able to stop thinking, I am the elderly mother of young Hank's fingernail-sized child. Which means I'm old enough to know better, and yet I cannot behave any differently than a young gravida. She wishes on stars. She tosses salt over her shoulder and avoids the sight of the new moon through window glass. She will not step on a crack. She watches Hank and Guy elbow each other on the living room floor, shouting themselves hoarse playing Skeleton Kombat, and she feels plates in her brain slide and shift. Their masculine consciousness, their oblivious confidence in her, for all things, is a weighty source of two-fisted bliss. It makes her feel keenly that she is cartographer for much, perhaps too much, of the route this family will follow. That this baby is not only precious but somehow necessary.

Saint Anne, Saint Therese, Saint Anthony, prays True, who trusts

275

saints, mostly because they all seem to have had messy lives on earth. Please let this baby persevere. Please let this be a promise, not an insinuation. All I ask is for us to remain the same. *Clink, the coin strikes the floor of the shining tomb.*

Planning the meetings with Otto Karp – whom they have all, unfairly and helplessly, begun calling The Big Tuna – as if they were an MTV video or a television commercial, have helped, because they distract her. The momentous decision is that Hank will go in True's stead, with Isabelle ('as second chair,' Rudy says). Hank will sell the new product; Esa will sing the ballad of Twelve Times Blessed's history. The meetings will take place in a suite, over lunch, at The Beverly Hilton, a cliché, yes, but not an insulting one. A waiter will serve sole and fresh fruit. The room will have two vases of freesia. Together, Hank and True have visited The Pilgrim to buy Hank a linen suit (another cliché, Rudy suggests; they ignore him). Isabelle will wear True's raw-silk peach suit with a lacey camisole; and Franny has shortened the skirt to display Esa's splendid legs to their best advantage. They all believe Esa's legs will be the equivalent of subliminal advertising for popcorn at a movie. 'Unless Otto is gay,' Rudy points out, 'in which case I should go, and also get a new suit. I like gray.'

Kathleen will take over the computers and the mail. Krista will replace Esa in customer service for a couple of days.

Guy is allowed to miss school on Friday to stay over at Doug and Esa's the weekend before the trip so Hank and True can double-check every detail. Hank comes home early on Friday and takes Saturday off altogether, with his and Tom's management 'trainee,' their dazzling new sous chef, taking Hank's place as the back of the house.

Hank and True make an impromptu boardroom of their bed comforter.

'First things first. You don't say a thing while you're eating,' True instructs Hank. 'You act like eating is the only thing you ever think about. You talk about the sole, and how ours is superior in Cape Cod, and how eventually, he must come and we will cook for him. Talk about the restaurant you have an *interest* in . . . now, Hank, can you put it exactly like that?'

'Don't ask me stuff like that, True. It makes me crazy. It's like you're coaching Guy what word to emphasize in a monologue, and you don't even necessarily know whether it's the right word! If you're not sure I can handle this, send Franny,' Hank admonishes her. He whistles, and models his suit pants, wondering whether his pants are a trifle too long.

But True, though she does not want to offend Hank's pride, knows they will need all their combined wits and skill. She tries not to overstep: She has never understood nor accepted the difference between male and female pride, but she knows women are more practical about indignities. This is where the phrase 'to bend over backwards' truly originates. Eager as Karp seems, the deal they have discussed could very easily end up costing him hundreds of thousands for nothing, though it could also make him a great deal of money. Only True knows how optimistic The Big Tuna really is. And how their risk, though measured, is substantial, given the shambles of the stock market, and how, even with the new popularity of Twelve Times Blessed, her portfolio is taking massive hits. Without ever saying the words, they all know the failure of a second venture could swallow up her house, at least, and even That One Place. She cannot calculate whether Hank would choose to give up his restaurant first, or their home. She cannot predict to which she would agree.

It will be only days later that True realizes this: She has never considered that her own company might be the sacrifice.

'Don't lead off with an apology for my not being there,' True cannot help reminding Hank. 'If he asks, tell the truth. I'm . . . *enceinte*, but, in any case, *this was the original plan,* for you to come. Don't even mention the failure of other dotcoms. Don't talk about what you read in the papers and try to contradict it. Emphasize demographics, the population group we're targeting – the largest number of children in history leaving home for higher education, many of them with still-working, affluent parents . . .'

'Bulls, bears. Up, down. To me, the NASDAQ sounds like they should be sponsoring Formula One racers. I don't read that stuff and I don't want to,' Hank tells her. 'Just explain to me how I charm him without taking my shirt off.'

'Hank, this is serious!'

'I am serious! I got you to believe in it, didn't I? It's a great idea.'

'But I'm your wife.'

'Are you saying you wouldn't have believed in it if you weren't my wife?'

'No, of course not, but you have to feel the timing of these things, when and how to be open-handed with that box of the prototypes . . . be easy, spread them around, so his secretary and his partner can have one . . . give him time to examine the box. Ask him about his kids.'

'I know that, True. I'm the original Big Easy.'

'And then follow up with the market survey . . . the people in Chicago, seven out of eight, who said . . . well, Esa could do that . . .'

'*True!*' Hank bellows. 'Enough!'

Still, in the few days before Hank leaves, her worry over the pregnancy and money and Hank's still-unconfided 'problem,' which he says that he ponders as he swims, claw her nerves to a shredding place. She catches him on the way up from the beach one evening, his brow furrowed.

'What is it? What is it?' True asks. 'What's sticking in your craw?'

'Don't worry about it,' he diverts her when she tries to jolly him out of one of his silences. 'It has nothing to do with you . . . or us or the baby.'

'If it has to do with you, it has to do with me,' True stoutly reasons.

'No, even husbands and wives can have strictly personal problems,' Hank replies.

'Are you trying to decide something?' she tries again.

'No,' Hank answers. True marvels again at how men can say 'No' or 'Yes' and feel not in the slightest compelled to follow up with even one supporting sentence.

He is as open to this as an oyster would be to a discussion of magic realism.

So True marches ahead with determined cheer. She breathes in and out to Enya records, walks Gyp until the puppy's legs are shambling. She gains weight, eight pounds. Sometimes, she thinks about the turning point they have reached, so very soon in their marriage, in their business life. They cannot see around the corner. The new startup will simply be too much, the leaf that collapses the whole house of cards. Yet, to pull back on Otto Karp's offer would not only be senseless, it would be the sure scent of an animal wounded. She feels she is treading in deep water, when, for the good of her health, she should be back-floating on the pillow of the waves. And yet, each night, she gazes at the blown-up and

278

framed picture on her bedroom bookshelf of their last beach picnic, when both of them had allowed Guy to bury them, twin mounds under which he has scraped the words MOM and DAD. When True hears that the mezzo-soprano Kitt Reuter-Foss is coming to Cape Family Theater to sing the role of Nancy in *Oliver!* she phones Beatrice to ask whether the renowned singer from the Midwest would be open to giving private lessons to any of the children. Delighted, Beatrice has called back to tell her that Kitt has agreed to teach four students – and that Guy is one! The eighty dollars an hour will be well worth whatever True has to give up to afford it. Hank has taught Guy a *tour jeté*, over much strenuous protested stretching and bitching from Guy, proving to him that real men can leap by showing him videos of Mikhail Baryshnikov and Gene Kelly. Guy is growing slim and supple. When he stands at arabesque, Hank glances at True as he did in their wedding photo, with an unconcealed pride that verges on lust. There are still sweaty nights, back-front-and-side, and mornings when Hank wakes with his old zest, demanding her, stripping her, even before she's had a chance to tickle Gypsy off the end of the bed and run to the bathroom to surreptitiously pee and slake her nausea. They are well. They are fine.

But there are mornings when Hank wakes as though he is a blade of grass frozen overnight, outwardly perfect but so brittle she knows he would snap at her touch, which she therefore withholds. He avoids her eyes. He is silent when Kathleen tells him hello. He is abstracted, on such mornings, even with Guy, who glances away when his hug is returned with a desultory shrug. True sees her son's hurt and confusion and hates her husband for his childish inability to fake good cheer. Faking good cheer is a Massachusetts specialty. Letters from Win – now in New York and scheduled to visit in just a few weeks – are a unique source of cheer for Hank; but they make True unreasonably unsettled. She wonders whether the baby makes him feel caught between his life with True and the next open door. There has never before been an open door Hank couldn't rush through if he chose. *I didn't know what being a forever kind of guy would really mean.* She listens for the gold ring of forever in the pitch of his voice, the hard grasp of his hand, so large it strains her splayed fingers. She watches for sketches of their shared future in his lust. But the leaves have begun to yellow and fall, and True feels old, old and desperately tired of trying to feel young. Her waist and ankles have already begun to thicken. But she does not look pregnant. She looks only frowsy.

On the last evening, but one before Hank is to leave for California, Guy barges into the bathroom and catches her in a crotch check.

'Didn't you ever hear of knocking?' True asks, annoyed to the point of blushing.

'I'm sorry. But what the heck are you doing?'

'Fixing my unders. My pants are too tight,' True tells him. 'I've got a grundy.'

'You even wear underpants under your jamas, don't you? I never do. I like to fly free,' Guy shouts with delight.

'That's how Granny taught us,' True replies honestly. 'She said dressing for bed was like dressing for anything else. I just got the habit. Now I feel funny if I don't.'

'Hey, you know what?' Guy then asks, True's underwear forgotten. 'I'm going as Gene Kelly for Halloween.'

'That's good,' True says, perking up, as Halloween costumes have always been a big doings between them.

She wonders then, what a Gene Kelly costume would look like. Cuffed beige pants and a white T-shirt? She wonders, how will anyone know?

'See, I'll wear a sailor suit,' says Guy, reading her mind. 'Not a baby one. A real sailor suit, from the Army-Navy store.' Hank and he have been watching old movies with Gene Kelly and Judy Garland and Leslie Caron, and trying out some of the combinations, so that Guy can see how a *pas de bourée* or a *chine turn* is not just a step for little girls in pink ballet shoes, but a manly and athletic feat. Hank admits that, in a year, Guy will have mastered everything he can teach him.

'People will think you're a sailor,' True tells her son.

'But I'll know,' Guy says. True thinks of his first Halloween costume, a floppy bunny with red satin–lined ears, stitched by Kathleen; and his last year's getup – when, for some reason known only to Guy, he decided to dress as a waiter. True scoured the town for a used tuxedo top and then cut off half the sleeves. His friends were yelling for him at the door as she was trying to hot-glue a plastic olive into a martini glass on a foil tray.

But Guy has now also forgotten Halloween, and is jumping on

the bed, shooting the lighted Nerf basketball into the hoop Hank has installed on the crest of the vaulted ceiling so he can shoot lying down; and Gypsy jumps up on the bed and bounds along with him until True thinks the lights downstairs must be about to dislodge from their housing. She shoos them away. She wonders how he will be with Chloe or Brewster. Or Annie Laurie. Or Morrow. Eudora or Jesse. Paul or Mimi. She wishes she could tell Guy that her bathroom trips are only to check on the little lass or lad, but that would be 'gross,' and an unnecessary worry for a child.

She waits for Hank to come to bed; but he does not. She creeps downstairs, and sees him hunched in his office, his face lighted only by the computer screen. He is furiously typing an e-mail; a long one, by the pace of it. She hears the aspens outside, their rustle a mournful clatter. She does not go in.

Despite her anxieties, True's underpants remain as white as whipped cream as September in Cape Cod dances forward.

By day, it is a pitilessly gorgeous month, as if nature has shaken out of the box her every bright button in anticipation of the cruel shabbiness of November. No one can remain immune. The burning bushes riot along the driveway, and the big maple, despite the often-warm nights, has gone fully and shamelessly red. Against True's white house, with the yellow birches sunny behind it, the postcard effect is nearly painful. This, says True's neighbor, Luke Sanderson, is what tides him over the wretchedness of January. Standing on her porch, True is summoned to hope by the kindly breeze with its bright pin of underchill, by the new life she knows may even now be learning to swim and swirl inside her, by the sound of Guy from the window above her, 'My Gypsy is a good dog, he's the best dog, he has the softest dog-ears in the world, my Gypsy.' True knows that Gypsy, who is not stupid, will lie against Guy's feet until he is asleep, then hop down and pad his way over to the open door of the alpha wolf. The pup follows True everywhere she goes, even into the bathroom, and True has to nearly laugh when Gypsy, stretched out asleep in full doggy languor, hears True make a move from her desk and lets out a sigh, as if resigned to the fact that he has to struggle up and follow. True is still awake when Gypsy noses open her bedroom door, and settles himself in his niche formed by True's bended knees.

THE MORNING COMES when she rises and is not ill. She does not feel as though even oatmeal or dry toast will bomb her digestive tract. She looks into the mirror and sees a face no longer yellowed by nausea, but smoothed by the hint of extra fullness and an under-tint, faint and glowing as apricot. Her hair is . . . glorious. She scoops up double handfuls of its honeyed thickness, feels as lusty as a lioness, energetic as a college girl, and she craves huevos rancheros. Leaping on Hank, she pins him for twenty minutes, which, she realizes later, result in her biting a nick in her bottom lip. But it matters little to her; her sense of singular power and well-being is unslaked, as is her desire for more Hank, more food, and the bright chat of the office.

If this is the hormonal bequest of pregnancy in the forties, True decides, she will be going back for a second helping as soon as phys-ically possible.

THE MORNING BEFORE the day of the meeting, True wakes from a blissful and solid sleep to Hank brusquely shaking her shoulder. There is shouting from the television; is it still night? She is for an instant resentful; has he interrupted her languor to share some wacky moment from an early Bruce Willis movie?

But no, he has only awakened her to the first morning of the end of the world.

It takes days for all of them to fully acknowledge that what has happened is neither a dream nor an elaborate put-on, a millennial version of Orson Welles's Halloween prank. They sit huddled on True's bed – Guy and Kathleen and Isabelle and Rudy, because no one else comes to work, nor even bothers to call – and watch the footage over and over, watch the World Trade Center towers deflate softly, like gingerbread castles, in fountains of floury dust, watch the fiery silhouette of the second huge passenger jet outlined neatly as a child's cutout in the side of the second tower. Over and over, True reminds herself that she was awake and actually witnessed the second jet shear into the building at the moment that it happened, that she saw it with her own eyes, that it was not a program about special effects on the Discovery Channel, revealing the secrets of pyrotechnicians whose job was to make painted plywood models implode for Arnold Schwarzenegger films.

Hank, shocked into talkativeness, spends the entire afternoon calling his sisters, his parents, searching in fear of learning that one of them, his brother-in-law, a cousin, knew someone on one of the airplanes, in one of the buildings. He e-mails furiously, and checks his e-mail five times an hour. Win, who lives in Chelsea, is tearful but safe. As soon as she can leave the city, she will come to the Cape. She is trying to rent a car. True offers to buy her one if she can find something, anything that runs.

It emerges, finally, that none of them, or anyone – except Addy Bourse, who had a fraternity brother who got out of the Pentagon unhurt – at first knows of a single soul who was directly in harm's way.

'This violates the law of six degrees of separation!' Hank cries on the third day, shaking his fist at the flawless, oblivious blue sky outside their window. Dog has called. Neither he nor his wife know any of the injured or the dead. How can this be? As Massachussans, they believe they have a nodding acquaintance with everyone in the Commonwealth. But Amherst is a small place, and so is Cape Cod, and Chatham only the middle of that small place.

Had it been August, when everyone celebrity-spots movie stars on the Cape and denies it, more household names might have been turned into big, black headlines.

But school is back in session; summer is over. The big names have all gone back to New York or L.A. And none of the little names, at first, is anyone's they know.

'We should be glad,' Kathleen tells him, 'glad that no one in it was a friend. We should be grateful to God.'

'To God?' Hank asks her, incredulous.

Slowly, however, as word seeps through town, as people venture out to the post office, and school resumes after a two-day recess, they learn that the Redforts, from Dennis, who have attended Saint Thomas since True can remember, have a son who worked on the sixty-eighth floor of the World Trade Center. He is missing. The Sargents' daughter, her husband, and three children had taken off from Logan that morning bound for Disneyland on the doomed flight, as had T. J. Karavos, the beloved and amiable star pitcher for the past year's Chatham As, the one with dimples so deep they showed even when he wasn't smiling, the one they called the next Nolan Ryan. He had been on Flight 11, headed home to Pasadena, with an engagement ring in his pocket, to propose to his high-school sweetheart. True thinks of Guy and his friends screaming 'Teej! Teej! Teej!'

in the summer twilight. Logan is their own airport, impossibly slack at the best of times, but no one could have dreamed ... the knives must have been ceramic, Franny says. Art supplies, the kind they keep in the warehouse. The United States, tucked between friends head and foot and protected by the moat of its seas, was pierced at its heart without a single shot fired, or even a gun brandished. True wants to block her ears and eyes. She wants to whip back the clock hands to July, when the talk of the town was whether the tough mom or the skinny guy would take home the prize on *Survivor*, when Jennifer Lopez's all-but-not outfit caused a tiff between True and her husband because Hank chanced to mention she resembled slightly the Hispanic girl he'd once dated in Texas. Her jealousies, her silly chin tuck, all of this seems ludicrous. It is not over, say the radio announcers. There will be more terrorist targets. The Sears Tower in Chicago. The Statue of Liberty. Symbols. She thinks of memorial services ahead, of suicide infectees – nostrils and throats teeming with typhoid, coughing in subway trains, packages gaily gift-wrapped (like her own Blessings) primed to puff forth anthrax spores, human bombs checking their detonation devices and then gleefully donning their numbered vests for the Boston Marathon, buying hot dogs at the World Series. She cannot ignore the 'American Pride' signs and shirts, the flags on every doorpost, including her own. She cannot ignore that Dob, the elder brother of the little girl next door, has just turned eighteen, and has now said he will join the Navy. When Otto Karp phones ... *everything has changed ... the markets ... surely, she understands ... perhaps next year ... we must all keep our expectations low* ... she is all but unable to concentrate on his words, and simply mumbles replies. All business seems irrelevant, even as the stock market plunges down a crevasse the gloomiest bears could never have foreseen, and they have lost more money, great quantities of money. But interest rates will plummet also, she thinks; and they will ... they will buy cottages, beach cottages young New Yorkers were barely able to afford and now will need to sell. Everything will change. They will cling to essentials. True crosses both hands over her belly and thinks again of Luke Sanderson's favorite saying, about land, that they aren't making any more of it. They will remortgage the house at a lower rate, and the restaurant, and ... buy cottages. And rent them. Or something. Nothing matters but their small band, and its blessed survival.

On the fourth night, Guy wakes up screaming, 'That was Dad's plane, Mommy! That was going to be Dad and Esa's plane!' Hank carries him into their bed, Guy's ninety-eight pounds wrapped around him like an oversized cub, and True assures him, over and over, that it had not been their plane. Their plane was to have left much later in the day. Finally, Guy falls asleep, but he whimpers and moans for the rest of the night.

On the fourth morning, when her employees have drifted back into the office, glazed, True is doing her toilet-tissue review when she comes up with a stain of brownish red. She rushes into the office lavatory. She kneels and throws up, from nerves rather than morning nausea. There is more blood on her underpants, suddenly, more and redder. Telling no one, not even Isabelle, she gets into her car and drives to Boston, where she sees her obstetrician. By this time, the bleeding has slowed to an occasional dot and dash.

Her brow furrowed and her manner curiously off, the doctor tells True that she is indeed 'threatening' a miscarriage; but that the fetal heartbeat is still strong. She tells True that she could admit her for observation; but that the best course would be for True to lie down as her 'ride' takes her home, and then stay on bedrest for a couple of weeks.

'If you like, we can do a blood draw and make certain you're producing all the hormonal . . . well, whether you need supplements . . . tell you what, I'm going to give you a few progesterone suppositories anyway, though your own placenta should be . . . well . . .'

'You're so matter-of-fact!' True cries. 'It's like it's just any old thing! I don't mean to be hysterical, but you're so casual . . .'

'I don't mean to be.'

'I'm very worried. I'm heartsick,' True says.

'Well, so am I, Missus Bannister. It's because, I guess, things are so abnormal and out of the ordinary that I seem so distracted. Because, oh, these are awful and sad days all around. I had a patient who was five months' pregnant on that plane from Logan, Missus Bannister. Not your age. But she'd tried so many, many times.'

'On my God, I'm so sorry. I'd never have said this if I had known.'

'But that doesn't excuse my seeming to be matter-of-fact . . . I know yours is a very wanted baby, and we'll do everything we can to make sure this baby gets here just the way he or she should.' The

285

doctor taps her teeth with her pencil. 'After all,' she adds softly, 'that's what this is all about, isn't it? Life is the best revenge.'

It is five P.M. before she begins the drive home, a pad between her legs thick as a night diaper. Route 6 is deserted. The sound of no planes overhead is like a roar in her head. When she pulls into her driveway, Kathleen meets her, frantic. 'You disappeared! Where did you go?'

'I had a doctor's appointment, Mom.'

'Couldn't it have waited? Were doctors even back at work? So many have gone to volunteer. And why didn't you tell us? I was worried sick. We all were.'

'I don't know. Things seemed so strange, I guess I thought no one would notice.'

'True, are you ill?' True knows that her mother is thinking, a lump, a mole, an unhealed sore.

'No, I'm not ill . . . I . . . could be having a miscarriage,' True admits, as tiny Kathleen, shaking her head and tsking with rueful understanding, opens her arms. 'I have to go to bed, Mommy.'

'At your age,' Kathleen murmurs, in precisely the same tone of voice she would have used had True spilled a full glass of milk at the age of six. 'Well, get along with you. I'll bring you some tea. I'll stay here until Hank gets home.'

'Will you bring me a cold pack, too, Mom?'

'Of course.'

'When this happened before, I used a bag of frozen peas. It worked, because it was flexible.'

'This happened before? Cramps?'

'No, bleeding . . .'

'Quite a lot?'

'I guess it seems like more than it really is. That's what the doctor says.'

'Well, best to be on the safe side. True, you know you haven't been pregnant for eleven years.'

'I guess it's like riding a bike, though, Mom. And I'd been feeling just great.'

'I'm going to call Hank right now. You look shattered.'

'Okay. Tell him not to hurry, though.'

'He's not going to have a soul at the restaurant tonight, True, the way things are.'

'You're probably right. Thanks, Mom.'

'And I'll have a gin game with Gee when he gets here . . .'

'He'll be really worried.'

'I'll explain in a not-very-worry way. I mean it, True. I can do that.'

'Okay.'

'I'll get that tea now.'

Despite his grandmother's assurances, Guy comes and sits with only half a bun on the edge of True's bed. 'You're not going to break me, darling,' True says. 'It's okay if you and Gyp climb in here and watch the awful news on TV with me.'

'I care about the news. A girl-in-our-school's mom died. But I'm more sad about our baby.'

'Now, don't go getting all sad yet. The doctor said the baby is hanging tough . . .'

'Good, I'm glad it's a tough baby.'

'So there's no reason to worry yet. Mom just has to lie in bed for a while. You can bring me . . . let's see. Lots of yogurt with marshmallow-cream sauce . . . and tacos.'

'Gag.'

'Well, you know what pregnant ladies like. Weird stuff. Ice cream and pickles.'

'That's not weird. But marshmallow and tacos!'

'Not together!'

'Gee!' Kathleen calls, 'want a toasted cheese? I'm tired of waiting for this card game here.'

'Thanks,' True says when Kathleen brings the tea. She is genuinely grateful for Kathleen's ministrations, meager as they might seem to another daughter, almost relieved that Kathleen has not lost her marbles with presumptive fear, as many another prospective grandmom might have done.

Before she leaves, Esa comes to sit on the bed. 'Well,' she says, 'I've done the research. This sort of spotting is entirely ordinary in approximately thirty percent of early pregnancies; some women even have regular periods for a while . . .'

'Esa, do you think so?' True asks softly.

'I really do think so, Truly Fair. Nothing will take away our dear baby. You just have to sit down and slow down and not stress and all that junk.'

'I will. When Hank gets here, I'm not moving for two weeks. He can even wash me in bed.'

'Okay. I wouldn't even leave tonight except . . .'

'Except you want to be with Douglas. Honey, everyone in the world wants to be with the person she loves most at this particular time. Don't apologize.'

'But if you need me, call.'

'I'll call you right away.'

'Want me to take Gee home?'

'He has school. I mean, I guess he will. And Kathleen is having a good fit. She's being sort of a doll about this.'

'It is her grandchild, and you know, she's pretty excited about it.'

'She is?' True is touched.

'Yeah, secretly. Like she's proud of you. Secretly.'

'Huh,' True murmurs.

After Isabelle returns to the office to close up, Kathleen pops in again to ask whether True would like some soup she's thawed. True would, please. 'Did you get hold of Hank?' she asks, and does not mistake the way her mother's face shuts.

'He . . . couldn't come to the phone,' Kathleen replies strangely.

'They were busy?'

'I'll bring up the soup. Do you want bread, too?'

True eats her soup; and takes the slip of paper Esa leaves with her new car-phone number. Hank does not show up. After an hour, True dials her own house phone, and again asks her mother, who is down in the kitchen, 'Where was Hank when you called, Mom?' Kathleen comes upstairs.

'Well, True, Tom said he was on his way home.'

'But that was an hour ago.'

They both hear the door close downstairs.

'So, now he's here,' Kathleen says. Hank bounds up the stairs, two at a time, carrying a clothing bag from The Pilgrim. He drops the bag and leans over True, his hand covering her bag of frozen peas.

'Little trouble down south?'

True gives him a watery smile. 'Same as before, but the doctor says it's really not too much to worry about.'

'Well, thank God for that,' Hank breathes. He steps into the bathroom and turns on the shower. Both of them look at Kathleen, who has betrayed no intention of leaving the bedroom.

288

'Hank's going to take a shower, Mom,' True says.

'Should I go home, then? You're all right?' Kathleen asks.

'No, actually, Kathleen, I really want you to stay. I have to leave for Boston as soon as I get out of the shower, and I think she really needs someone to be with her,' Hank makes a parody of a stern face at True, 'no matter what she says.'

'What?' True asks. 'Why do you have to go to Boston? Who got hurt? At night? They can't be doing shipments of produce!'

'I have to go be with a friend who's in trouble, True,' Hank says, unbuttoning his shirt. Kathleen has still not moved from her chair by the bedside.

'Uh, Mom,' True says, 'could you give us a minute?'

'I'll go see to Guy,' Kathleen says, rising slowly and with extreme reluctance.

'What's wrong, darling?' True asks, beginning to get up. 'Did someone's relative . . . ?'

'No, you! You just lie there and percolate. I'm going to wash up in about three minutes and be right out there.'

And he does emerge, more quickly than True has ever seen him do – it is their joke that True is forever the one tapping her foot in the downstairs hall while Hank tries on outfit after outfit – and slips into a new shirt and sport coat.

'*That's* nice,' True says of the pale beige coat, with its shot thread of sage and red. He wears a new shirt and tie themed to pick up the green.

'Got it on sale. Sixty percent off. Now, I'll just throw my suit in a bag in case I need it, and my PJs.'

'You're staying overnight in *Boston?*'

'True, I really dread having to explain this to you,' Hank sighs, sitting down on the foot of the bed and rubbing one of True's feet. 'I'm going to be with Adele . . .'

'Adele? *Adele?*'

'I figured you'd react this way. But you don't understand. It has nothing to do with you, or with us, or with some kind of love between Adele and me. Except the love of a good friend. Her mother is dying. She's been sick for a long, long time. She's had strokes since I've known her. And now, with everything that's happened, and Marie in a coma, she called me. I'm the only one she has.'

'I thought she was with some guy. You said so. The guy from the north.'

'She was.'

'Well, then.'

'Well, he ditched her, when he found out that she was, well, you can imagine,' Hank drops his eyes and examines his shoes. He reaches down to polish away an invisible speck.

'Pregnant?' True asks. 'Adele is pregnant?'

'She is.'

'That's what you meant by it was so ironic. When I told you about our baby.'

'Only that the two women who'd been . . .'

'Wait a minute! Wait a minute!' True shouts. 'The two women who'd been what?' She notices that the door is open, and knows Kathleen must be listening to her every word. 'Close the door,' she demands. 'Close the door!'

'I don't have much time, True. Really, listen to me.'

'Close the door or I'll smash this lamp over your head, and I mean it,' True says, her voice a furious whisper.

'Whoa there, lady. You're going way over the top,' Hank says evenly, his eyes narrowing. But he closes the door.

'The two women in your life! That's what you were going to say! But one of the two women is your supposed ex-girlfriend and one is your *wife!* Me! Who is having a difficult pregnancy. Is Adele sick?'

'No, as far as the pregnancy goes, she's fine. But this could really hurt her, couldn't it?'

'How far along is she?'

'About the same as you . . . as we are. Maybe a little less.'

'How do you know?' True demands. 'How do you know how far along she is?'

'We've been in touch,' Hank says.

'You fucking right have been in touch! I saw you! I saw you kiss her outside your restaurant. Gee saw you!'

'You spied on me?' Hank gets up from the bed, shocked.

'Spied on you? We came over to see Dad at work and instead we saw Dad practically necking with some woman in the parking lot.'

'It wasn't like that. She was telling me Dave had dumped her. That she was moving to Cambridge. I tried to comfort her. That's all, True. She's a *friend.* She's an old, dear friend.'

'I don't care who she is! I need you here. Now. Especially now. This is ludicrous, Hank.' True tries for a more reasonable tone, 'The world is falling apart. I'm on doctor's orders to stay in bed. No husband in his right mind would leave his wife at a time like this!'

'I think you're overreacting a little.'

'Overreacting? If I were even reacting in the way I ought to be, I'd have slapped you across the chops! Go outside and describe this situation to the first five people you meet and ask them if I'm overreacting. Ask Esa. Ask your father! Ask Clothilde, Hank, if I'm overreacting!'

Hank sighs, long and wearily. 'Look, True, I made a promise. She has no one else.'

'She must have friends. Cousins. Siblings.'

'They're not the kind of friends you could call on at a time like this.'

'I guess not,' True agrees. 'How come?'

'She's sort of a private person.'

'Well, she'll have you,' True continues portentously.

'Not all the time. I do worry.'

'You do *worry?* Hank, don't you see you've crossed the line? People don't do this. What are you saying? You're more worried about Adele's emotional health than mine? Than our child?'

'Of course not, and if you weren't surrounded by people who dote on your every move, I wouldn't do this. But you are, and all you have to do is crook your little finger and they'll all come running to take care of you.'

'You sound like you resent that,' True suggests.

'I don't. But you're not exactly the needy type. And if you are, you have your whole crew of . . .'

'Don't say it. Don't say one word about Esa or Rudy . . .'

'Well, you have support. She doesn't. I promised I'd come, and I don't break my promises. I'm going, and you'd better handle it better than you are or you will make yourself sick. You're the one who doesn't need anybody, aren't you, True? It's easier on your own. That's what you said. You have your own little fiefdom . . .'

'This isn't all about Adele, is it, Hank?'

'Yes, of course it is.'

'No, it's more than that. It's, I don't know what it is, but there's something in this about the fact that I had a life, and a thriving life . . .'

'Right, and you just fitted me into it and it went on whizzing along like clockwork, until you got pregnant and you had to let poor, dumb Hank go represent you at your big, important meeting.'

'Shut your fucking mouth! I've done nothing to deserve this! What kind of fucked-up male-pride shit is this?'

'I'm leaving now. Give me a kiss, please, True. This isn't about us. I love you more than anything on earth. I love you, and I don't want these words between us,' Hank says softly, smoothing True's sweaty hair from her forehead, blowing gently on her skin.

True says nothing. She reaches up and slowly, robotically, removes Hank's hand.

'If you go, don't come back.'

'True.'

'If you go, I mean it, don't come back. Unless you go, make an appearance, and turn around and come back within a few hours. If you have to do that much, to suit your idea of being a good person.'

'Don't put limits on me. Don't give me ultimatums.'

'Oh, no, I am giving you an ultimatum,' True says, her voice a monotone. 'Don't come back into this house. You are making a choice.'

'I'm not making any sort of choice, except the choice to . . .'

'Get the fuck out of here.'

'True, I beg of you. Let's talk this over when I get back.'

'Get . . . the . . . fuck . . . out,' True says, and turns her face to the pillow. She feels Hank stroke her braid, briefly, hears him rummaging for his clothing, then the door closing softly. She hears him descend the stairs.

AFTER AN HOUR, during which she cries, and bites the pillow to hide the sound, True gets up briefly, splashes her face, and begins to walk down, slowly.

Guy catches her halfway. 'What do you need, Mommy? I'll get it. Go back to bed.'

'I need Dad's . . . the laptop in the little office, where Dad has his stuff.'

'I can get that. You just go lie down. Granny and I are taking care of you. She's making you tea. Where did Dad go, all dressed up?'

'A funeral,' True says. 'Isn't that sad?'

'Someone who died on Nine Eleven?'

'No, an old pal. He didn't want to go, but he had to. He'll be back soon,' True smiles and ruffles Guy's three-cowlicked thatch.

The passwords she tries are Sully1, Henri1, Thatoneplace, Clothilde, Creole, Peridot, Adele, Adelecabot, and, finally, Adele01.

This opens Hank's e-mail.

This opens her husband's e-mail.

And yet, of course, who else would he e-mail, she hopefully reasons even as she replies: His mother, his sisters, his far-flung friends.

There is a single message, several weeks old, and the trash has been emptied. She must not read her husband's mail. It is the worst sort of violation. She opens the file. 'Darling Hank,' it reads, 'You cannot know what it has meant to have your support. Even though you aren't here, I feel your strength. And it makes it easier for me to go on. I can never thank you enough.' The note is signed, 'Adele, your Adele.'

As if to hold not only the baby, but also her organs in place, True lies back down on the bed, her heart booming. She checks her pad. It is pristine.

At nine P.M., Guy kisses her good night. 'Dad will be home soon, you said?' he asks casually, as Gyp licks True's wrist, his sad, intelligent eyes imploring. 'Then why is Granny staying over?'

'I didn't know she was.'

'She went to get her stuff.'

Kathleen, of course, would not want to miss a moment of this minidrama, True thinks acidly. On the other hand, her mother *has* taken care of her. Perhaps she is only genuinely concerned.

'Mmmmm,' True promises. She has flicked on the television, and is watching a rerun of *The Mary Tyler Moore* show, only because every other station features the same footage, the black plane approaching, the plumes of flame, the tiny silhouettes, falling, falling.

Mary is remonstrating with Lou over her lack of seniority when True goes to sleep.

SHE DREAMS THAT Guy is grown. He and True are walking together on a street in Chatham, shopping for sandals. Guy is a head taller than she; nineteen, twenty years old. Square-chinned, tanned, and slender. Gypsy is an old dog, with a grizzled muzzle but a sprightly step. True does not see herself, but she feels a stitch in her hip, an ache in her shoulder. Bounteous Baby is on their right, next to Danny's Galley, and as they pass, Hank walks out onto the porch. True feels herself smile. His hairline has receded, and there are flecks of gray in his black hair, which he now wears long, wavy. He walks up to Guy and gives him a manly shoulder hug. Their mouths are moving; Guy is smiling, but True cannot hear what they say. But she does look past them, to where Adele is struggling to open the shop door and negotiate a stroller at the same time. Guy springs to help, and Adele wheels down the flagstone path their glorious baby. Adele is talking, too, and though True can hear no words, she knows Adele is telling her that the baby is called Chloe Marie, after both Hank's and her mothers. Hank is radiant with pride. True feels a wistful distant happiness for him. She reaches into the pocket of her coat – it is a pea coat, like her mother's – and finds Kleenex, and a grocery receipt on which she writes herself a note – Kathleen's purse is full of notes on the backs of napkins and receipts – to send Adele a certificate. The baby is six months old. She will have at least half a year of lovely gifts.

True wakes, a cold mist of sweat beneath her breasts. Things have turned out as they should have done.

THE FOLLOWING MORNING, up at six A.M., True first calls Hank's cell phone, which is answered coldly: 'This is Message MP Thirty-Two. The Intellicell customer you are trying to reach is not available.'

Methodically, she then calls Isabelle.

Esa answers, 'Who died?'

'Honey, I'm so sorry to wake you. Apologize to Douglas. Will you just stay home for a little while before you come in?' True asks. 'Until I call you back? I might want you to pick up something in Boston for me.'

'Okay, True,' Esa agrees, puzzled. 'Do you mean a prescription or something?'

'No, just stay there, and I'll call, honey, and I'm fine, don't worry,' True says. 'Don't leave until I call.'

'Where's Hank?'

'I'll call you right back,' True promises.

She thinks of calling Franny, but it is absurdly early. And there is no emergency. Whatever has happened already has happened. True feels no sense of untoward urgency, only the kind of seeping shock she imagines the gazelle feels when the lion takes it down. A kind of release. Though she may presently feel more torment than her mind's scope currently comprises, she now wants only information. And though she expects she will be wronged, for now she wants only to *be* wrong. She cannot cry; she cannot crumble. There is nowhere and no one to pick her up. She thinks of calling Hank's mother, and tries to forbid herself.

But her disembodied hand picks up the phone, and Gus answers. 'Are you all right, True? Is Guy all right?'

'We're all fine. I want to talk to . . . Ma.'

'She's right here. Wake up, Clo.'

'Oh, God, don't wake her up.'

They talk for an hour. True tells her everything. About the e-mail and the friendly kiss. About Hank's stubborn leave-taking and her physical predicament and her fears and her immobility.

'Has he talked about Adele?' True asks her mother-in-law.

'He has a little, True. Only in the past few weeks. We have found it odd, I must admit.'

'What's going on?'

'We aren't sure. But we gather she's had some terrible trouble, and Hank feels as though she has no one else to turn to. The man she moved up here to be with, the one who lives up north somewhere . . .'

'Not Hank? She didn't move to be closer to Hank? This guy she was with, they were serious?'

'We told him to talk about this with True, didn't we, Gus?' True hears a grunt of assent. 'He said you would feel too threatened. He said things were going too well.'

'They were. What's so wrong with her? With Adele?'

'I don't know if I should betray Hank's confidence.'

'Okay. But I'm trying very hard not to have a meltdown here.'

'Well, you obviously know her mother was very sick. Her mother lived with her. Adele is an only child. Her father left them years ago. I don't think, though I don't really know, that her father and mother ever married. She had to be in a . . . what is this, Gus? A managed-care facility. And then the man up north . . . I'm repeating what he told Gus, because he didn't really talk about this to me . . .'

'Okay, okay . . .'

295

'Well, Hank said the man broke up with her just as her mother got really ill, because Adele was . . .'

'Pregnant. Hank told me. Now, Ma, you don't think this man is fictional and that Hank is really the father of this baby?'

'No, of course not.' Clothilde is horrified.

'But he's been writing her, and I've seen he's absent-minded, almost tormented.'

'I know it's not Hank's baby. I imagine he is worried about her. That's how she kept him so long, True, dear, I'm afraid. She kept coming up with reasons she couldn't live without him.'

'So I figure. At least now. But she is keeping the baby.'

'That's what Hank said. She wants someone to love if her mother dies. I'm supposing.'

'How could Hank have told you all this and not me?' The keening in True's voice is painful to hear, even to her own ears.

'It was wrong. We told him.'

'It's just that this is so horribly, horribly timed and so horribly . . . ; it feels assaultive. In any other situation, I could even feel sorry for her. But Ma, I hate this. I hate that she called him and he went. It's like her dependence on him is . . . okay. As if it's permissible. But really it's like a piece of him she won't let go. And she's known him so much longer than I have.'

'Gus has said that to him. That this is not friendship but a sort of passive control. But Hank argues that he is trying to be an honorable man.'

'Right.'

'Well, *chère*,' Clothilde finally says. 'I have to tell you, I don't buy that.'

'Okay,' True says in a voice that is so small it squeaks.

'I don't like his going there. Her calling and his comforting her is being a friend. But her asking him to come is something else again. He is a married man now. I don't think he should have gone, and I don't think you should have agreed . . .'

'I didn't agree! I practically barred the door!'

'That makes it worse behavior on my son's part. And you can tell him I said so. His mother said so.'

'I don't think I better do that. Then he'll know I told you . . .'

'Oh, honey. He tells us all his foolishness and all his mistakes. How he feels burdened. How he loves Guy. How afraid and challenged and excited he feels about the new baby. We tell him, Henri, Henri . . .'

'What?'

'We tell him, grow up.'

'But he won't, Ma. He seems like he does, and then he goes backward, as if he doesn't know better than a child what's appropriate and what isn't. I don't mean to insult you by saying this, but it's true.'

'I believe you, True. He's a late bloomer. That's what we've always had with him. He's feckless. Sometimes. And I'm not saying this out of disloyalty to my own child.' Clothilde exhales, an echo of Hank's sigh.

True consoles her, 'I know. I'm not saying it out of disloyalty to him, either. And half of it is me. It's me. I'm so . . . for so long I felt guilty that I married him, I think I may have made him feel that way, too. At first, I went on about how my age and his made us a couple against nature, about how he was a caged bird.'

'Don't think of Hank as a caged bird, True. He chose this. He chose you. And he can't sit on the fence and still be everyone's knight and everyone's flirt, and still be a father and a husband. I love my boy with all my heart. But you know, he's had a whole life of slidin' by on his sweet talk . . .'

'Clothilde . . . Ma, what do I do? What if he feels so sorry for Adele that he . . . ?'

'He would never do that.'

'I know.'

'Go to sleep. I know it's impossible not to worry. But we all know, it does no good. That's why men don't do it. Call me later on, when he gets home. Will you?'

'Yes,' says True, and then Clothilde goes on to tell her Perry has enlisted in the Coast Guard, that Tannie is smoking again now that she's not nursing, and True watches the clock. The clock, somehow, says nine A.M. Clothilde says finally, 'Pa sends his love, too. Give our love to Kathleen and Gee.'

'I will,' True tells her fondly.

She falls asleep, and wakes when Kathleen, her mouth a line, brings her a lobster salad.

'This is nice, Mom,' True compliments her.

'I felt you might need a lift.'

'Mmmmmm.'

'I won't ask what's going on . . .'

'Okay, because you know as much as I know. Don't even bother to pretend you didn't hear. I know I was yelling my head off. It's okay.' True sits up suddenly. She has forgotten to call Isabelle. She grabs the phone.

'Esa?' She apologizes the moment Esa picks up. 'I fell asleep. What, what I want you to get for me, is . . . wait, I have to call Tom; I'll call you right back.'

'Make sure you do, True. I'm sitting here reading old *Glamour* horoscopes. None of mine came true. I was supposed to be alert to the possibility of a career reversal that would be beyond anything I'd ever imagined. Maybe it means you're going to fire me. Everything is sliding at the office. I have to get to work.'

'Tom,' she says when he answers. 'Tell me Adele Cabot's phone number.'

'I don't know it.'

'Okay, tell me her address.' He cannot recall that, either.

'True, I've tried to call him myself all morning . . .'

True hangs up and calls directory assistance. She could pound her head with her fist.

Not surprisingly, there are a fair number of Cabots in Boston.

But there are two 'A-onlys' in Cambridge. A single initial is a cue to a single woman's listing. True dials one, and reaches an indignant Janet, whose husband is Al. She dials information again, and asks for the second number. 'That is unlisted at the customer's request,' a recorded voice explains. A discussion of life-and-death exceptions with a telephone supervisor yields a refusal as flat as the recording. 'Is there an address?' The woman nasally reels off a number in the five-hundred block of Saint Vincent Court. This way, True thinks bitterly, people cannot call and threaten Adele, they can simply drive over and threaten her in person. True calls Isabelle.

'Esa, what I want you to buy is a heart monitor.'

'You're having heart trouble?'

Yes, True thinks.

'No, I mean one of those you can listen to the baby's heartbeat. A doppler thing. A special stethoscope thing. You can buy it at a medical-supply store.'

'Ohhkaay,' Isabelle says.

298

'So I can listen and make sure it's okay whenever I want to.'

'Ohhkaay.'

'And I want you to drive over to Cambridge and look for a house in the five-hundred block on Saint Vincent Court. Five-seven-oh. And ring the doorbell and ask for Adele Cabot.'

'The author? The lady Hank dated?'

'Yes.'

'You want a book?'

'No. Yeah, sure.'

'True? What in hell is going on?'

'I think, Esa . . .' True begins to cry and cannot stop; the violence of her struggle to catch her breath while lying down giving her no permission for speech, 'I think that Hank . . . I think.'

'I'll go right away, True. Don't call me on the cell phone or expect to hear from me for a while, okay? Go to sleep. I mean it. Go to sleep. The baby is all tired. Do not get yourself in a complete twist. I order you, as your most steadfast friend. Hang on. I will bring equipment, food, and information. Promise?'

True obeys. And when she wakes, it is nearly dark. She turns on her bedside lamp, and sees what has awakened her, Esa sitting silently on her bedroom chair, gazing out into the incongruent blaze of the trees backlit by the sunset.

'He was there,' True says. Isabelle says nothing. 'Did you talk to her? Or him?' Isabelle shakes her head. 'Did you *see* them?'

'In the window,' Esa says. 'Standing. Clothed. The truck was parked in front.'

'Are you sure it was his?'

'I remember the picture of the truck with the ten yards of ribbon on it. I remember the picture of him and Guy in front of the truck with the bow on the top after the adoption. I remember how you told me you all shouted, "Surprise!" I remember when I was in the hospital and I thought he was so beautiful, as beautiful as an Indian in an old print . . . like the fucking noble savage or something, and I made the date for you two to go bowling . . .' True can see the tears, golden beads in the last of the sunlight, on Esa's cheeks. 'I'm so sorry, True. I'm so sorry. I'm so sorry. What a fucking asshole. What is he doing there?' True tells her, the short version.

Then, together, they unbox the little machine True can press against her tiny mound of gelled belly, and listen to Chloe or Adam,

Drew or Francie, Brewster or Morrow, flub-dub, flub-dub, flub-dub, a steady point of life in the whirling universe.

Guy and True huddle in bed and watch a video of *Oliver!* in preparation for Guy's tryout, for the part he so badly wants, most specifically, Oliver himself. When True begins to cry – she is full sick of bawling – as Nancy sings 'As Long as He Needs Me,' she tells Guy, 'I'm not crying about Dad. I think Dad is fine, though we're going to have to have a talk when he gets home because he is worrying me.'

'I know! Like when I go to Fenn's and I don't call and I could be smashed under a truck . . . !'

'Exactly,' True tells him. 'It's just that all moms cry over this song. It's the mom-cry song.'

'I know you're in love,' Guy says, 'but Dad would never knock you on the head with a piece of firewood.'

'That's right, Gee,' True says. 'Wanna hear your baby?'

'Dude!' Guy cries out, and they get out the little monitor.

When True wakes, the Chatham town hall bell is pealing the last strokes of midnight.

SHE WAKES WHEN Hank arrives home, at five the following morning, and sits down on their bed to take off his dress shoes. True has pains in her chest she knows are the equivalent of her childhood asthma, not a heart attack. Not a miscarriage. She glances at the little monitor by the bedside.

'Well,' she says, 'I'm surprised to see you. I told you not to come back.'

'I know you didn't mean that,' Hank tells her. 'Listen, True, it was horrible. She'd had so many strokes. Adele's out of her mind. Her mother was all she had left. At least she'll have the baby. She's scared she'll lose it. I'll explain all about it after work. Tom's probably fit to kill me.'

'Adele's mother died.'

'You know about it?'

'I figured when you didn't come back that she'd died. And that it was imminent. I put it together from what your mother told me, and from your e-mail.'

'You *read* my e-mail? How the hell did you access it?' Red shame gushes over his face and neck.

'Hank, I haven't known how to reach you for two days. Do you know what that's like?'

'Well, apparently you did know,' he says, his mouth a surly moue. 'You probably didn't want to talk to me. You could have called.'

'She has an unlisted number.'

'I didn't know that. You could have called the cell.'

'It's not working. I assume it's the . . . tragedy. I assume everything's out of whack.'

'I didn't know that, either. Frankly, I had my hands full. She couldn't even make the arrangements. She was in complete collapse.'

'Fortunate for her that you weren't. You could be the take-charge guy.'

'True, I'm exhausted. Don't start. I just spent a day outside an intensive-care ward with a sobbing . . .'

'Don't undress. Speak quietly,' says True. 'Don't even suggest that I should feel sorry for what you went through.'

'And then a day at the crematorium with some stranger who didn't even know Marie. We barely got any sleep. I've basically been awake for thirty hours.'

'"Marie"? And "we"? Who are you calling "we"? Are you and Adele "we"? I thought that was you and me. What am I supposed to feel about all this? Don't you see what you've done? You don't, do you? Or you do, but you simply don't care.'

'I have to be at work. So, if we *must* discuss this, it's going to have to be later, after I've had time to get over this, and get a little sleep.'

'After *you* have had time to get over this. That tears it, Hank.'

'Tears it?'

True's voice goes dull: 'Don't undress. Pack. Pack quietly. You already have what you need for a couple of days. Send me an address where I can send anything you can't pack. Take the truck. Take the TV. Take anything but Guy and the dog.'

'What in the fuck are you talking about? Send you an address? Okay, look, I'm sorry. I know I didn't call. If I look at it from your point of view, it's piggish. I should have called you ten times. I know that. I should have apologized right away. You can't use cell phones in a hospital . . .'

'You can use them in an apartment. You can use regular phones in an apartment.'

'What?'

'Esa saw your truck parked at Adele's. And she saw you and Adele.'

'Well, we went back there for an hour or so. To grab a nap. I didn't sleep with her, or anything. I mean we slept together, in the same bed. But we didn't do anything. She made some coffee.'

'I don't care if you fucked her brains out.'

'You don't.'

'No, what I care is, you cared more about your ex-girlfriend's mom and *her* baby than you cared about our baby and about what I would be thinking, back here, about you. Not maybe even about your cheating on me. About you. Whether you were alive, or fell asleep driving and went into a ditch. Like Pete. Like my dad. You didn't call me, and you stayed away for two nights. And I was bleeding, Hank. Before. A lot. I went to Boston. I'm on bed rest for at least two weeks. We could be losing *our* baby, Hank. I'm not bleeding now, but I was.' Pale hollows appear under Hank's eyes. 'You, who never misses a day of work. You didn't even call Tom. You just focused on Adele. I've never known you to focus so completely on anything.'

'You had me followed? That's how much you trust me?'

'If you think this is only about trust, or about my paranoia, and not about responsibility, you're not following *me* . . .'

'How is the baby?'

'Okay, I think.'

'Thank God,' Hank reaches out for True's hair, but she pulls her head back. He places both hands on her belly, rounded under his shirt, which she has clutched to her face all the long night.

'Would you like to hear the heartbeat?' True asks, knowing it verges on cruelty.

'Can you do that?'

'Bought a gizmo.'

'Huh.'

She watches Hank's eyes change as he listens to Abby or Martin, Isabelle or Ian. 'That's the most amazing thing that I've ever . . . that I've ever . . .'

'Yes. It's pretty amazing. That's your child. That's our baby, Hank. These gadgets aren't all that expensive. You can get Adele one.'

'That was a lousy thing to say.'

'Yes it was. I feel lousy. I feel bereft. Betrayed. Abandoned. Everything you can feel if you are lying here knowing what I know. I hate what you did. Now, get going, Hank.'

'True, leave the house? Leave? Why? I told you that I didn't sleep with her . . .'

'Because . . . you don't get the point, do you, Hank? You don't. I hate to say this; it sounds so seventh grade. But if you don't understand why, I can't make you understand.'

'Okay,' says Hank.

'Okay?' True has not expected this. 'That's all you have to say?'

'Yep. I've had it. I'm tired, and I'm tired of this. You're right, True. I don't dare look right or left. I don't dare breathe. I'm probably as sick of you as you are of me. Adele's real problems were a relief compared to all the problems you've imagined.'

'Thanks, Hank. That was a gallant thing to say. It proves you're the honorable man you're so bent on saying you are. You consider my not wanting you to rush to the side of your ex-girlfriend while I was threatening a miscarriage *keeping you in shackles, Hank?* You think my objection to your spending two nights with her too . . . too stifling?' True pauses, and goes on, 'Okay, I'll give you some of it. Maybe once I did what you say I did. Maybe once I watched every girl as though she was the one who should have had my handsome prince. Not so long ago. But a great deal can change in a short time. We fell in love in a short time. You learned to love Guy in a short time. And in a short time, you stopped me from doing that. You made me trust you. You made Gee trust you.'

'And so what you do with that is . . .'

'No, wait! Wait. You made me believe you that it didn't matter that I was older. That our family was whole, that your silences were just a quirk. They weren't a quirk. They were a ruse. You were wondering how you could make ol' True happy while comforting dear Adele. Tapping away in your study. Telling your folks. Lying to me. We made a plan together, for a business. We made a baby. And then this.'

'This . . . what? I can't believe how you act about this. Like I killed somebody.'

'You did. You killed us. And maybe it wouldn't cut so deep if I really did believe it was such an emergency you couldn't even call your wife.'

'What? So I could hear all this bullshit? Which you would have laid on me. You wouldn't have given a shit. At a time like that?'

'So you didn't really forget. You knew quite well how I'd react. And she isn't really just your old pal. Good. Because I haven't believed that since I saw you kiss her. And it wasn't even that I saw you kiss her, you know that? It was that you didn't even tell me, like it was something to hide! I might have been over Adele, if she didn't keep popping up. And she keeps popping up because you won't let her go. Or she won't let you go.'

'It was barely a kiss. It was like I'd kiss Win.'

'It was not!'

'It was so!'

'It was not!'

'Maybe to a Puritan!'

'Don't start that! Don't you dare start that malarkey about how I have ice water in my veins because I was born north of the Mason-Dixon line. Hank. I saw you kiss her, and I'm not hallucinating, and I'm not *overreacting*. But yeah, we Puritans do have a name for that, Hank.'

'What?'

'Lowlife. Snake. More than anything, liar.'

'I can't believe you'd throw out your whole marriage over this one little thing. I can't believe it drives you so much. You sure run deep, True. You sure care a lot.'

'I can't believe you thought it wouldn't. You broke faith with me, Hank. You broke faith with me. You weren't faithful . . .'

'I said I didn't sleep with her. There was no intimacy.'

'There it is, just what you said, that's intimacy. That's *all* the intimacy. Don't you see that? More than if you'd had a quickie and then jumped up and driven back to the restaurant. I'd have been mad about that. But maybe I could have gotten over it, seen it as some stupid gesture of farewell to the single life. But this, I can't . . . or rather, maybe I can understand. You made me believe you, and it scared you, didn't it? You made me believe you'd be a forever kind of guy, and that meant you had to believe it, too.'

'Okay.' Hank holds up his hands. 'You win, True. And what are you going to do about . . . that?' He points at her belly. 'You're going to throw out your husband while you're fighting for our baby's life? Or are you going to end it, True? So it won't spoil your looks?'

'I would never do that, Hank. I want our baby. I want you to have our baby in your life, too. And especially, I would never do it for such a lousy reason as being crapped on by a guy. You're not ten years younger than I am; you're a hundred years younger than I am. Because you don't *think*. And unless you learn to think a different way, we won't make it. Maybe we never could have, because we've had whole lives before we met. Or maybe because we're both used to having our way.'

'You were always convinced I was going to fail you. It's enough. I tried. I lost.'

'You sure did lose. Even your mother thinks so.'

'You told my mother? You talked to my mother?'

'I called your mother, the morning after you took off. Even she thinks you were wrong to go to Adele. She's my mother-in-law. I can call her any time I want.'

'Yeah, but not to rat me out. Sonofabitch. She must be royally pissed.'

'Yes, she is. And see? That's what you care about. Pack quietly. We'll talk on . . . ummm what's today?' True holds her face. She can feel its angles and plates, their fragile binding. She holds them steady with her fingers. She puts her fingers against her lip to stop its shaking.

'Tuesday.'

'We'll talk on Friday, okay?'

'What about?'

'I don't know. About how the baby's doing. About how to explain this to Guy. I'm going to sleep. Get out.'

Stay forever. Don't leave me. True digs her nails into her forehead. She will not say it. 'I said, get out, Hank.'

'Give me my shirt,' Hank says. 'It's my favorite old one.'

'No,' True says. 'This is mine. This is *mine*.'

She does not believe she has ever seen a face more crumpled with grief than Hank's, at that moment. Then he walks into the closet, grabs things off hangers with a speed that sends the hangers clattering along the pole, and stalks out.

And numb with bafflement, knowing she has just done the right thing for the right reason, but that a momentum beyond her grasp has propelled her to it, True throws one pillow over her head and one under her belly and, her nose buried in the shirt, actually falls asleep.

OCTOBER

BOO, BABY!

Halloween can be exciting, but scary, too. We strive for the thrills without the chills, the softest of fleece makes our ear-of-corn and pumpkin costumes suitable later for play or nap garments. They're filled with the gentle gifts of the season: A sparkly kitty, custom-crafted to fit a small hand, a book about a mother bat and her baby who won't go to sleep (can you relate?), and a hand-dipped Vermont candle that gathers all the smells of autumn, to light your nights and soothe your spirit.

'WHAT'S THIS FRICKIN' mess? Where's Dad? Isn't he back yet?' Guy is shaking her awake. Sleep has become a tunnel down which True disappears as often as she can, more than once a day, if possible. She glances at the bedside clock. It is four P.M., on the first of October, and True's son is still carrying his backpack from school.

'Don't say "frickin',"' she mutters through chapped lips. She sounds like a drunk.

'Dad says it's not a swear.'

'I say it's a swear. I know what it means. It means the same as the "F" word. And if you frickin' say it again, I'll wash your mouth out,' True tells him, adding, 'brat,' then adding, 'come here,' and holding Guy close. He smells of wet dog, hair gel, and something sharp, like cloves.

'Brat? I'm a brat?' Guy throws down his bag like a gauntlet. 'Granny says you threw out my dad, and *I'm* a brat?'

'I didn't throw out your dad. Well, I did. He went to live at . . . Tom's, for a little while, because we're fighting too much and he did something really crummy.'

306

'What?'

'Grown-up stuff.'

'Did he sex with someone?'

'No.'

'Then what's the frickin' problem?'

'Gee, take Gyp for a walk. A long walk. And then get your big Broadway book. You have your lesson with that lady, Kitt, today. I'll drive you.'

'Are you sure you can get up?'

'I'm sure,' True says. 'I'm fine now.' She is lying. She has no idea whether she should get up. But she has decided she will stay off her feet as much as she can and hope that nature will be tolerant.

'First, you don't tell me you're going to get married, and then you don't tell me you're going to throw out my only dad . . .' Guy begins to cry, and True enfolds him. 'Gee, it is a frickin' mess. But we'll work it out. Dog and Granny and Esa and Rudy . . .'

'And Dad.'

'And I hope Dad.'

'You're not going to get a divorce?'

'No. I hope not. Maybe. I don't know. Probably not. I have to teach him a lesson.'

'Teach him a lesson? He's a grown-up!'

'Grown-ups have to learn lessons, too, Gee. I don't know if he can learn it. I think I have to learn a lesson, too.'

'You're the mother! You have to know!'

'Well, what do you think?'

'What do I think? I'm a kid!'

'Remember the time I took you and Fenn bowling and you predicted you'd get a hundred and thirty-one? And you did get a hundred and thirty-one? Well, maybe you're psychic, like Maman Winston in Metairie.'

'Does she know about this? She'd put a curse on you.'

'No, she doesn't,' True replies, thinking she must call Clothilde, and that she would rather have sinus surgery. Thinking, also, of the five of cups, the great struggle of head and heart, the momentary defeat. Was that the world foretold? Or her own selfish world? In New York, small boys the size of Guy are wearing new blue suits and listening to bagpipes at their firefighter fathers' funerals. And yet, ordinary life remains a fertile field for tragedy. Even Humphrey Bogart would not disagree.

A sea eagle, near True's house, has discovered her nest ravaged by a raccoon, which serves her right, for mating too late in the season. The eagle had acted on instinct, or impulse. Now the raccoon will winter in the home she built with her beak and her claws. The eagle does not think to kill the raccoon. She turns over the shells of her brood, which would not have hatched.

Esa comes into the room unannounced, makes a quick and intuitive assessment, and tells Guy she, not his mother, will drive him to his lesson.

'So,' says True, at the same moment, 'so what do you think? About Dad and me?'

'Mom,' Guy tells her, wiping his eyes on Gypsy's ears, 'I'm only a bowling psychic.'

'IT'S OKAY. I'M really okay,' True tells Franny a week later, at callbacks for the play, as they sit side by side in the rehearsal hall. True has bed-rested herself nearly mad, and feels exhilarated if only to be out of the house. 'I'm doing a whole lot better than I thought I would be doing.'

'You look good,' Franny allows. 'Do you feel . . .' she nods at True's belly, 'okay?'

'I *feel* terrific. Physically. But I can't remember what month it is. Or whether I'm in town or not. I wish I could get my brain to function as well as my midsection.'

'Maybe the hormones are a gift right now.'

'That's what I think. I'm going to have them distilled. An elixir. Euphoric oblivion, only from Twelve Times Blessed.'

'Are you really doing as well as you seem? You're a marvel,' Franny comments. 'I'd be a basket case.'

True pauses. 'In fact, Frannywoman, there are moments, long moments, when I wish I were dead. But I can't die. It would kill the baby and Guy. So I get up and do something. I Was a Middle-Aged Zombie.'

'You can joke,' Franny points out.

'What's the alternative? What do I do? Call you crying at four in the morning? I've already made Esa sleep over, *sleep in my bed*, twice, when she should be home with Doug, because I couldn't bear to go to sleep alone.'

'Why don't you just take him back and torture him for a few months?'

'I've thought of it, but then he'd think he was right, that he could do anything and be forgiven. He'd think I was a spineless twit. Could you live with a man who thought you were a spineless twit? Anyhow, I keep thinking he'll throw himself on my mercy.'

'Hasn't he?'

'No, he's called.'

'What does he say?'

'I won't talk to him. Kathleen usually answers the phone. She's virtually moved in, of course. And I'm actually grateful to her.'

'Then how do you know he isn't trying to throw himself on your mercy?'

'I'm afraid that if we talk, he'll say one word about poor Adele and then I'll have to have him killed. He does talk to Guy. He comes to get Guy. I hide.'

'I don't know what I'd do,' Franny muses, 'if Steve slept with another woman . . . I know I'd take him back, merely for the pleasure of forgiving every day for the rest of his life.'

'What if he spent two nights and one beautiful day in exotic Cambridge in the arms of his ex-beloved, after your begged, sobbed, and even threatened him so he wouldn't go? What if he ignored all that and went anyhow?' It is excruciating for True to admit this, and Franny both sees and appreciates it.

Franny taps the end of her freckled nose, a habit she has used to center her thoughts for all the years True has known her. 'I get the issue. Still, if he didn't *sleep* with her . . .'

'Doesn't anybody see this but me?' True fairly howls. 'It's worse than that! I might be able, like you said, to get over a stupid drunken roll in the hay, but this was . . . love, Franny! This was an act of love!'

Beatrice motions sharply at the two of them to pipe down. And there are many avid eyes among the mothers and fathers, turned inquisitively on True, who slumps in her seat.

Thankfully, the tryouts then begin, and all eyes face front. The crowd of several dozen children and parents suddenly falls so silent True can hear Franny sucking on her cough drops. Her daughter Clainey also is trying out for a part in the theater's most ambitious show to date.

Beatrice begins carefully to explain why *Oliver!* will be a bigger and more demanding production than *A Christmas Carol* has been in years before. 'For one thing, we been invited – yes – to

309

perform at the Boston Civic Opera House . . .' sussurant sounds of awe . . . 'for two nights, and we are negotiating to perform for two nights at . . .' she pauses . . . 'Radio City! Can you imagine that?' The children pipe and chatter. 'Now, now, and we have a very demanding rehearsal schedule, and we have the great honor of having Kitt Reuter-Foss, who is a renowned mezzo-soprano who has performed with the Metropolitan Opera, to sing Nancy – Kitt is here,' the lovely redhead True has glimpsed at the door of the bed-and-breakfast when she dropped Guy off for a lesson wrinkles her nose and waves at the children, 'to help us choose, so anyone who is involved with a sport or is . . . having some challenges in school, you might want to wait for next year. We will have twenty shows, not counting the ones on the road, and parents, I want you to know that a donor has provided for increased security at all those shows, and for an . . . armed, and I don't want this to frighten anyone, an armed security guard on the buses that will take us to Boston and to the school shows.'

Beatrice's great gray eyes, in their nest of gentle creases, widen with compassion. 'And these are indeed scary times, aren't they? But it is important also to remember that art is a weapon against brutality, isn't it? And so, before we begin, I would like to take a moment for all of us to bow our heads and pray or think silently about the ones who are lost and not yet found, for our soldiers, for our country's safety, and for peace on earth.' Obediently, they all lower their heads. Then Beatrice claps her hands. 'Let us hear some singing!'

Franny's little Clainey looks like a Christmas-tree angel in her scalloped lace dress and white ballet shoes. But as she sings 'I'm Forever Blowing Bubbles,' it's impossible to hear her teeny voice even over the tinkle of the rehearsal-room piano. Still, when she dances, light as the silk from a milkweed pod, True sees Beatrice scribble on her pad, and glances at Franny. Clainey will end up as one of the little ragamuffins in the chorus, thank goodness. It would have been terrible if Guy were to have gotten into this production, but not Clainey – both for Franny and True's friendship, and for True, who wants so badly to be near Franny or Rudy or Esa, or even Kathleen, that she intends to spend every moment of the next six months attached to one of their hips. She wonders how many people, in how many places on the earth tonight, have just said the same words as she, and meant them as insincerely. *I'm doing okay. Really, better than I thought.* What can that mean? That she breathes out and in? What more can she say to Franny? *I thought he would be back at the door in two days and he wasn't? I can't believe he doesn't want to go to therapy? I can't tell you how many times I've searched my body with my fingers in the night for a reminder of him to feel something of what I felt with him* . . . Yes, she could say all these things.

But she is afraid to make them real. A part of her still believes in the reunion that must come. She would not confide that in anyone. Perhaps not even, not totally, to herself.

Guy rises next.

'I am going to sing "The Lord of the Dance," which I don't know who wrote it, and a dance my . . . my dad taught me, and my monologue is "Where the Wild Things Are."' He gathers himself to sing, drawing up his chest, 'I danced on the morning . . . wait! By Maurice Sendak. I'm sorry.' Beatrice nods, raising one eyebrow. The children who have been with the company for a time all know that introducing your performance is something all professionals do, and Beatrice insists that all her cast members are professional actors, 'whose only payment is applause.'

The song is so radiant that a tall woman with long dark hair True has never met leans across two people and whispers to her, 'Is that your kid? Nice voice.'

True swivels to smile at her and sees Hank. Two rows back. She reaches out her hand, and they clasp and smile. She bites down hard on her lip so as not to cry. The first steps of Guy's dance are deft and precise, but the cartwheel turns – one, two, he's almost there – end with him on his butt. He rises up florid with shame.

'This is such a *slippery* floor,' Beatrice comments lightly. 'Thank you, Guy. And thank your father for choreographing a real challenge for you.' Gamely, Guy launches into his monologue, and is drawing appreciative laughter, when the stage manager cuts him off. He's exceeded his time limit, and there will be a hundred more children, over the next two nights, who have been called back for seventeen roles.

Sweaty and pouting, Guy slouches into the seat next to True. 'I sucked,' he says. He then spots Hank. 'Dad!' he exclaims. 'You're back.' Guy actually lays his cheek on Hank's forearm. Hank winces.

'I'm here. You did not suck,' Hank whispers. 'You did fine. They're looking for a general look, not perfection.'

'I *sucked,*' Guy repeats murderously.

From the way the woman who complimented True leans forward anxiously as the next child, a sweet, white-blond boy, takes the stage, True assumes that this is her son. To say the boy's voice is beautiful, as he sings 'Amazing Grace,' would be a crude insult. He sounds like a German choir boy, a paragon of control and breath. Flawlessly, he recites a Tennyson poem, and concludes with a few seconds of tap. Sucking in her breath, True leans over to the woman, who is nodding wildly and giving thumbs-up to her son. 'He was terrific. I'm True,' she extends her hand.

She notices the moment that Guy notices that Hank has disappeared. Guy slams out of his seat and leaves the door swinging. She rises to run after him, but the woman whose hand she shook is still talking. Politeness, and the wish to distract everyone from Guy's tantrum, stalls her.

'Oh, I know who you are. You're the baby-box lady. You're famous. I'm Genevra,' the woman says, her moonlight pale face opening into a warm smile. True now must recover a piece of what she thinks of as her former personality and make a moment of conversation.

Franny tries to help. 'My daughter tried out, too. She's the cute one you couldn't hear.'

These are never easy events for parents whose children are competing for relatively few parts. They are especially difficult, True reflects, when your father is as evanescent as Hamlet's was.

'Gen . . . what do they call you for short?' True asks.

'Genevra,' the woman answers.

'Well, your son is really something.' True does not care, but asks, 'Has your son worked with Cape Family Theater before?'

'No, he usually does commercial work,' Genevra answers. 'He's been in one film and six commercials. But he loves this musical so much, and it's not . . . objectionable to us, except for the violence, so we decided it would be all right for him to try out.'

'Well, I'm sure he'll make it,' True offers.

'Oh, I think so, too.' Franny's secretive mime of a pointy-nosed snob nearly makes True laugh.

True goes outside to fetch Guy, who is sitting on a window seat, wiping his eyes.

'You have to come back in. Those are the rules. You can't run out like that. It's unprofessional.'

'I'm not going to get in it. Why should I sit there? And why did Dad come and watch me and then sneak out?'

'I don't know, except he probably had to go to work and didn't want to make noise. You'll see him tomorrow,' True soothes her son. With Guy still on the verge of tears, she leads him back inside, and they sit bravely through another hour of tryouts, suffering and cheering for the children whose parents have to all but shove them out of their chairs, or who forget their words, clapping in relief for the evenness of the regulars. In the car, afterward, Guy announces himself 'too fricking tired' for a soda and asks why his mother keeps offering him stuff that will make him fat, anyhow. 'Take it easy,' True admonishes him. 'I know why you're mad. But don't lay it on me. It was hard for me when he left, too. I just thought you might want a treat. You put out a lot of energy up there.'

'For nothing,' Guy says.

'You don't know that,' True says patiently. She can think of nothing but Hank, despite her child's obvious pain. She has more fucking steely politeness in her spine than Emily Post and she is sick of herself. Has the man no heart?

For the next two days, while she listens to the unfolding of 9/11 events on the radio, the deaths of the firefighters, their terrible gallantry, the discovery that the terrorists lived and trained at the very university where her late husband, Peter, received his aeronautical degree, while she directs Esa's new assistant on the updating process, showing her how to send pop-up computer reminders or postcards to those Blessings buyers who forget to update the company on 'their' babies' changing sizes ('How do you ever remember all this?' the girl cries, for an instant utterly overwhelmed by the minutiae that makes the company work), she selfishly waits for the phone to ring. For mail to drop through the slot. As she did when her high-school dates didn't call her back, she even picks up the house receiver to make sure the line isn't dead. When Isabelle arrives for work on Wednesday, the first thing she asks is, 'What part did Guy get?' and True is horrified to recognize that she has forgotten to wait for *Guy's* call, which of course brings down the same curse as feeling chipper and having lunch with your friends on the way to a mammogram. Immediately, she tries to make up for her lapse in preemptive distress by indulging in an orgy of it. She promises herself to be certain that Guy will not get a speaking part, and to be appropriately comforting.

'Don't talk about it,' True warns Esa. 'He fell when he danced. I think what Hank taught him was too hard for a kid.'

'Well, he could still get in.'

'But he wanted . . . you know, a role. He wanted to be Oliver.'

'Eeeeeeek. That's . . . is he ready for that?'

'Well, you know, another year, another show . . . I'll tell him that.'

'He still might get it. No one can sing like Gee.'

'There was a kid there who could sing rings around him. A soprano. Oliver is supposed to be an innocent. Guy's an innocent, but he doesn't act like one.'

'Ummmm,' Esa says. 'Well, when do you get to know?'

'I don't know if she'll call or just send the dreaded letter,' True replies. 'And don't think I don't feel like Missus Piece of Shit for worrying about whether my kid gets in a play when the whole world is going to hell not to mention that my husband left me and I'm pregnant . . .'

'You don't have to say that,' Isabelle tells her. 'Life just goes on. It has to. It's our victory over the dark.'

'Been hitting the old movies with Douglas?'

'Yes, but you know, True, it is.'

Isabelle takes over with her assistant. Rudy arrives. He alone has not been altogether 'in' on her and Hank's parting, though he has made the appropriate noises of sympathy. True can tell his nose is ever so slightly out of joint. She decides to try for a confiding tone.

'I have my test in a couple of weeks,' she tells Rudy, 'to see if the baby's okay.'

'You're really going to go ahead with this?'

'What are you saying? You mean, am I going to . . . have an abortion?'

'Yes, True.'

'Rudy, I'd never do that.'

'Religion?'

'No, common sense. I have enough to raise a baby alone.'

'Enough what?'

'Enough money, at least for now. Enough of my wits left. Enough support. And people have done a lot more with a lot less.'

'But do you have enough . . . room? In your life? I mean, your plate is full. You're starting this new thing, and you don't have a partner now.'

'I can do it.'

'Well, you're braver than I am.'

'Do you think I'm foolish?'

'I think you're . . . underestimating what it takes to raise a baby on your own, at your age. Don't take on, now, Truly Fair. But you do have Guy and Kathleen to take care of.'

'So because Hank is being a pig I should give up something I've always wanted?'

'It could be seen, by some people, as selfish to bring another life into the world, this world . . . if you don't have the emotional resources to give him or her everything a baby deserves.'

'Who thinks this, you or Keith?'

Rudy blushes. 'Keith. I took your side.'

'Well, joke him, then, Rude. You think I wanted it this way? You think I'm not scared to death, of all those things you just talked about? But what . . . I mean, this little life has struggled and hung on, and . . . I still, I still love Hank. I hope we'll make up. I can't see how we could, but I hope so.'

'I know.'

'And he wants this baby, too, whether or not we're together.'

'Are you sure of that?'

'Keith or you?'

'Me, this time. I'm not so sure it wasn't the baby that made him book.'

'I'm glad you're saying this.'

'Why?'

'Because it's pissing me off, that's why. Not at you. It's natural to think that. And so, I'll be ready when the next five or six or ten people say the same thing, because they will.'

'True, all of us will stick by you.'

'I know you will,' True says, taking Rudy's hand. 'I know. It's just . . . don't expect that you won't hear around town your boss is crazy, when this starts to show.'

'I already am.'

'Oh, good.'

'Well, you brought it up.'

'Who said?'

'Lee Macy, and Dee.'

'What'd they say?'

'Along the lines of, what did she think would happen, what did she think a man of that age wanted . . .'

'Okay, I get the gist.'

True sighs. Then she asks Rudy, 'Wouldn't it be nice if people could get their own lives?'

'This *is* what their lives are, True. Just because you don't gossip doesn't mean it isn't everyone else's national pastime.'

'Well, I don't care what they think. So long as you and Esa and . . . well, the people who count, are ready to love me and my kids, I just don't care.'

'You care.'

'Yeah, I do care. But Guy didn't learn to act by licking it off the grass. I'm going to pretend I'm okay. I'm going to pretend my arse off. I have to. I intend to be the gay divorcée.'

'That's the first sensible thing you've said.'

'I didn't mean gay *that* way.'

'There's always hope, you know.'

'Yeah,' True says, wrinkling her nose at him. 'I like that name. Hope. Very *Mayflower*.' Rudy stands up and hugs True. She lets herself relax, and begins to tremble.

'Truly Fair, awww, honey,' Rudy soothes her.

Guy comes into the office from the bus, and drops his bookbag. 'We had wind sprints in gym. I was the second to last.' He lies on the floor.

'I was always the last one picked, too,' Rudy points out. 'Now I'm a virtual athlete.'

'You mean like virtual reality?' Guy asks.

They are laughing when they hear the phone ring in the main house, and Isabelle half-rises to answer it, but Guy gets there first. Rudy and Isabelle fall silent as True strains to hear him.

'Yes, okay,' he says, with no particular affect. 'Okay. Thanks, Beatrice.'

At least, True thinks, he has remembered his manners.

Then Guy comes barreling down across the breezeway to the office, yelling, 'Mommy! Mom! I got it! I got it!'

'What, what? Oliver?'

'No, I'm the Artful Dodger!'

True phones Hank, and a few minutes later, he comes squealing into the drive on his way to work. 'That's the best role in the play, dude! You get to sing all those great songs, about picking pockets and . . .'

'I know! I know! And . . . I get to wear a top hat! And dirt!' He begins to run toward Hank, arms open, but then stops. 'I forgot. I'm too big . . .' Hank kneels and kisses Guy on the lips, and then picks him up.

'You are the man, dude! You are the man!' he says, and they embrace again.

True gets up and leaves the room, glad she knows where the door is, because she is blinded.

ALL THE WORLD now, as described by the headlines, is full of names of countries a person would know only from a board game: Uzbekistan, Benoir. The war – against whom, nobody seems sure – has changed names in a batty way, from Golden Eagle to Infinite Justice to Enduring Freedom, the last of which True thinks sounds like the name of a pantyliner.

True phones Hank one night at the restaurant and says, 'I think we should talk about the business. About First Year Away.'

'I'm not in the mood for business meetings with you, right now, True,' Hank tells her, cupping the phone against the noise in the background. 'If you'd wanted to talk, you should have paid attention to me when I tried . . .'

'And I think we should talk about Guy,' she goes on, cutting him off. 'About your seeing him.'

Hank pauses, then answers, 'Okay. Can I drop by tonight?'

'I'll be up.'

They put down their respective receivers without saying good-bye.

When Hank arrives, Guy is asleep. True begins, 'Let's say some normal things. Let's fake how we would be acting if our world and the big world weren't opening at the seams.' This is a huge effort for her, and Hank seems to appreciate it. 'Hank, what would you like to name our baby?'

'Brewster,' he says, 'though I guess that's up to you. Like everything else. Will you call him Bannister?'

'Brewster Bannister?' she almost laughs.

'I've always liked the name of that town. And Brewster Bannister sounds . . . vaudevillian. Or it could sound congressional. Brewster D. Bannister.'

'What's the "D" for?'

'Dickinson.'

'Awwww. That's sweet. He could be a ballplayer. Like T. J. Or a hockey guy. Brew Bannister, number sixty-eight, comes out of the penalty box . . . I think of him grown up, too, Hank. No matter what premonitions I had. I have so many hopes for him. I was so happy, so happy I couldn't believe it was true. I was doing the thing I thought I could never do for you. I was so happy and so scared at the same time. It was too good to be true. And it was.'

'That's not my doing. I still want to know why in the hell you don't come to the phone when I call . . .'

'I don't know what to say and I don't think you do, either.'

'I do, but I guess you don't want to hear it, judging by how you've reacted so far.'

'I guess it's too soon to be talking about names,' True says brusquely, changing the subject. 'I'll want you to have an interest in the business. I'll want you to have a share of the profits. And you can help in a real way if you want to, getting the financing.'

'How?' Hank moves out onto the porch and lights a cigar.

'I'm thinking of approaching Elizabeth. She has pots of money, and I don't think she'd be scared off, the way Otto Karp was. I know she trusts me.'

'So where do I come in?'

'Well, some Monday, when the restaurant is closed, you could, if you would, host this little lunch, and I'll present her with the idea.'

'*We'll* present her with the idea.'

'I don't mean this as an insult, Hank, but I'm the one she knows. She's . . . eccentric.'

'Okay.'

'Okay, you'll do it?'

'Yeah.'

'And as for Guy . . .'

'I'll want him every weekend.'

'Every other weekend.'

'I don't see him all week. An hour after school, driving him to a lesson? That's not being a dad. He won't be able to play basketball this season, will he? With this show?'

'I guess not. But I hardly see him all week either. And I thought being a full-time dad was what drove you into the ground.'

'True, you live with him. And, hey, I'm a damned idiot! As you have often pointed out! I didn't know how much I would miss all the demands until I lost them! Don't that make you happy, True? I miss having him bug me. I miss having him say, "Wanna play blackjack, Dad?" every five minutes!'

'Well, do you have a place where he won't be exposed to . . . ?'

'What, nude women and pot smoking? Yes, I have my own place. A sublet of a cottage.'

'Boy, you sure did that quickly, this time around.'

'I needed a place I could have my son sleep. Got a problem with that?'

'No. I just meant . . .'

'I know what you meant. But half the reason before that I didn't get a place at the beginning was I wanted us to get married, True. Duh.'

'I'm sorry, then.'

'Why don't we split the weekends? I'll take him Fridays and part of Sundays, and bring him home Sunday early.'

'Okay. But there's the show to consider. He'll have rehearsals.'

'Well, if they go late, I can pick him up at the theater on Saturday nights sometimes. When we close. We close early now, nine.'

'We'll work it out.'

'Helluva world now, huh?' he says. 'I've thought about a lot of things, True. I've even thought about enlisting.'

'Enlisting? But you have a family . . .'

'At least in the Coast Guard. I can do a service. They'd take me.'

'But your business!'

'You can do reserves. They'll need coastal guards. Great benefits, and I'd be helping out. I should. My daddy was my age. He was in Korea. I'd feel like a pansy if I didn't.'

'Huh.'

'And it probably won't last so long.'

'Ever heard of Vietnam, Hank?'

'I don't think it will be like that.'

'I do think it will be like that.'

'Everybody has to do what he thinks is best, True.' He puffs on his cigar, then dies it out and crumbles the remains. He stops, and looks at her with an unvarnished longing. 'Where did we first lose it? I think it started because you treated me like a kid from the

319

beginning. Maybe I acted like one. I think it goes back to that picnic, where the guy thought I was your son, and you lost it.' True realizes what a monumental effort *this* is for Hank, to open a fifty-gallon Pandora's box, and admires him. She will try to match his hard work, though all he has said thus far is 'you, you, you.'

'I didn't really treat you like a kid. I didn't! I treated you like, like the man you are, right now. Someone who didn't know what he didn't know. You saw that as treating you as stupid. I think it started over being a parent, about how Guy would feel if you couldn't pick him up, that's when I think we got lost.'

'But there are a dozen other things I never told you. You would get that tight little Kathleen mouth when I'd forget to drop off a damn paper at Guy's school on the way to work. You got that look that says, this guy's a retard. But it's okay. He's my retard. He's my trophy husband.'

'That's utter shit! I never treated you like a trophy husband. I was embarrassed.'

'Embarrassed?'

'I mean, I was embarrassed by our age difference. Not proud of it. *You* never embarrassed me. Not really.'

'Even when I didn't know that FDR wasn't the same guy as Teddy Roosevelt? When Franny and Steve were over and we played that game . . . ?' True cringes. 'See what I mean?'

'And you insulted all of us by saying that the questions were the kind of stuff only older people would know about? Cut it out! When you said about my sweatpants that maybe you'd get pants like that when you were like . . . forty? How many times have I had to swallow that?'

'I didn't mean to insult you. I just went on the defense.'

'Me, too.'

'You were born on the defense.'

'This isn't going anyplace. We're just playing poker; I'll see you one insult and raise you one . . . As for my being born on the defensive. People say that. Now. They didn't use to. I . . . think you're right. I don't know why. No one ever dumped me. But . . . I don't trust . . . men. Not even you. Not really. Even before you did what you did. And I never knew that. There was no reason to know that before.' True is reaching deeper, deeper than she likes. She can hear the sound of locks flying open in her gut.

'What have I ever done to make you not trust me? Not men. Me, personally.'

'Beyond the very clear obvious?'

'I wished I'd never met Adele.'

'Me, too. Though I guess you don't now. You're probably happy as two little peas in a pod.'

'How would you ever know what I wish now, True?' Hank sighs.

'You never tried to make me feel secure, Hank. You'd say things that all women notice, Hank! Not just me. We notice when a man says, "I've gotten shit for not sleeping with women naked." That translates to, I've slept with all the sexy women in the world who all wanted to be naked with me, and then I got sick of knocking around and settled down with something reliable, the human equivalent of a La-Z-Boy. How would I have trusted you when you made dim remarks like that, right in my face?'

'But you asked for it, True! You pushed me. You had to ask for details. Like you wanted to torture yourself. And, I'm a guy, True. I blurt things out. You're never going to find a guy who doesn't blurt things without thinking, or forget things. Or neglect to call. Or get wrapped up in a game or a debate and simply forget to call . . .'

'Or get wrapped up in his ex-lover and forget to call . . .'

'If you didn't want a guy for a husband, you should have married a woman.'

True admits, 'I'd forgotten. I'd really forgotten how dense guys can be. And I don't mean that as an insult.'

'I don't take it as one. And then, just when things were looking up, when we were firing on all the cylinders, you took Franny to New York.'

'My girlfriend Franny? For the *Today* show? You wouldn't have wanted to go.'

'I really wanted to go!'

'You didn't say so! If you're so big on saying so, why didn't you?'

'What was I supposed to say? You had it all planned before I even knew about it . . .'

'Well, you could have come if I had known. I thought you'd think it was dumb. Because it had to do with my business. Or, a girl thing. Hairstyles and which jewelry to wear.'

'No, I'm very good at that stuff. I was hurt. I thought you'd want your own husband with you.'

'I'm sorry.'

'And money, money, money. Every dime accounted for. Like the sky was falling every day . . . you acted like we were going to live in a trailer! I felt so guilty I was going to sell the truck!'

'Oh Hank, the thing about money. I was brought up to worry about money. Let's shut up about money, money, money. You'd think it was your dick.'

'Which I hate.'

'What?'

'I hate my dick.'

'What the hell?'

'I think it has a point on the end, instead of being big and thick. And I used to think you were wishing, wow, I'd like it if he had a big, thick one, a big ten-inch whanger . . .'

'You're crazy. You're fucking nuts. I mean that in a nice way.'

'Well, I think that. I almost bought weights once, to grow it.'

'If I laugh, I'm not laughing at you. But, Jesus, Hank, I didn't think there was anything on earth you could say to make me laugh right now; but this . . . takes the cake. You have a perfect . . . dick. You fill me. You used to make me feel primal stuff. I shouldn't tell you that 'cause it'll just make you more conceited.'

'Yeah, I might be conceited from the waist up. But every guy feels . . . guy wants a bigger dick.'

'Only if he's trying to find a girl with a cherry-bomb ass to show it to. Only if he wants to marry . . . Julia Roberts or Princess Diana . . .'

'I dreamed once I married Princess Diana. And Madonna. In the same night.'

'Well, you clearly don't have the same ego deficits I have.'

'Didn't you ever have an erotic dream about a movie star?'

'*Hell*, no. I never had an erotic dream at all. Except about my brother.'

'Your *brother*? Now, that's sick.'

'It is not. Franny said.'

'Oh, Franny said, so it must be gospel. How come you trust the opinion of every girlfriend you have more than you trust me? How come you come back and say, you know, you were right about this or that, but only after you ask Rudy or Franny?'

'I don't do that anymore. I did at first, before I knew you very well. I was used to checking everything with them. But the idea for

First Year Away. I didn't ask them about it. I *presented* it to them, as *your* great idea. And . . . and I think if we were still married, we should be singing now,' True says, battling tears.

'Sweetheart,' Hank says, putting his arm around her. 'Maybe we should think this over. Stay together at least until the baby comes. You don't look so hot.'

'There you go, Hank! That's how you mend a marriage? Offer temporary companionship and tell the woman she looks like shit? Was that a major truth? Or a blurt? Silence. Blurt. Silence. Blurt. Hank, don't you know how that affects me? I'm always trying to figure you out. I'm trying to learn the things about you people know *before* they get married. I can't read your mind.'

'And I can't answer your million questions. How did she feel when you said that? How did you feel when I did that? It's like having my brain operated on. When I try to explain things your way, I get a headache.'

'Then we're both better off.'

'Fine,' Hank says bluntly. 'I just have one question. May I use your "studio" downstairs to give Guy some dance pointers for *Oliver!*?'

'Certainly.'

'Should I call and make an appointment?'

'No, you still have a key. Just find out when Guy can do it. Right after school would be good, before you go to work.'

'I can give you back the key if you want.'

'Don't be an ass.'

'You know, True, maybe this never would have happened if you hadn't been so preoccupied with trying to be a girl you forgot that it was a woman I fell in love with.'

'Or if you hadn't lied to me from the first word about things you should have been honest about, like that you'd been to Mount Washington with Adele . . .'

'Adele! Adele! Gosh, I wish she knew how important she was.'

'Because you probably did the whole speech with her you did with me! You probably proposed to her with the same dumb ring.'

'You don't have to keep it.'

'Okay,' True says, and tries to wrench it off her hand, but cannot, because her fingers are swollen. Hank looks pained.

'I should have got you a big, fat diamond like Holly's you could flash around.'

'Now, I can flash around my big fat stomach!'

'Why does it matter if I went there with Adele? I went there with Tom and Perry, too, and I didn't propose to them. Should I have told you that I'd been there before?'

'Did you propose to her?'

'No.'

'Did you propose to her on Mount Washington?'

'No.'

'But you did propose to her.'

'We talked about getting married. Theoretically. About a hundred times. Which is probably why we never did it.'

'I never want to mention Adele again! I'm so sick of her! I'm sick of thinking about her. I dream about her! Go ahead and marry her! I don't care if you enlist in the Navy SEALS! Go ahead!' True leans hard on the pillar, breathing as she does when she runs. 'That was a blurt. I didn't mean it. I don't know if I have the strength to talk about this, any of this, anymore. Not tonight.'

Hank begins to turn away, and True opens her front door. It is then she hears Guy's window close with a soft clap.

ONE LATE AFTERNOON, True hears music and wanders over to the workout room. Hank is teaching Guy to toe-stand in his new, size-eight jazz shoes (à la Gene Kelly) to the tune of the old Judy Garland song, 'You Gotta Have Me Go With You.' True watches with pride and sympathy – how she loves both of them. They may be in a muddle; but here is Hank still trying to do for Guy what she could not do. Here he is still trying. And as she thinks that, they spin into pirouettes, the doubles that always land Guy on his butt.

'You forgot to spot,' Hank reminds the boy.

'How the hell can you spot when you're looking at your feet?'

'Your feet will take care of themselves. You look at a spot on the wall. What you see when you come around. Well, let's do the easy part, the time step with the claps.' He starts the CD over. 'Now, remember. Syncopation is claps off the beat, listen. It's not for any reason, just to add interest to the piece.'

'I have enough trouble keeping up with the real beat,' Guy tells him.

'No, you're musical, Gee. I hear you, rappin' around the house. You have a good sense of beat. And if you take piano,' Hanks says as Guy grimaces, 'I know, I know. And I know what every parent says, "Oh, I wish I'd kept up with *my* piano lessons." Well, the thing is, you really do. Because the piano is the basis of all instruments. It's really a percussion instrument, and if you can sight-read even a little, you can sing anything.'

'Can you sight-read?' asks Guy, obviously glad for the interruption, since he is dripping in his muscle T-shirt, his face purple as a plum. Not for the first time, True wonders if he has inherited her childhood allergies.

'A little,' Hank confides. 'But it's disgraceful. I have to count the staff to start myself . . . F-A-C-E . . .'

'Every good boy does fine,' Guy continues.

'They still do that?'

'Yup.'

'Okay. I don't want your muscles to get cold. Let's do barre work.'

'I'm too sore.'

'Gotta do barre work. Only way not to get sore is to *stretch*. It don't make sense, but that's how it is, padnuh.'

'The damn barre is higher than my head . . .'

'Well, I could lower it a little,' Hank admits. 'You use the windowsill.'

What True sees when Hank crosses to the barre is something she cannot believe is not a trick of her eye. Guy watches Hank, carefully, piercingly, then deliberately reaches out with the toe of his shoe and trips Hank, who falls, unguarded, against the end of the ballet barre. His leg crumples beneath him, a perfect 'L,' except facing in the wrong direction.

'Jesus!' he cries, rolling over to grasp his knee.

'Oh, I didn't mean it!' Guy cries.

'You did, too! I saw you!' True cries. 'How bad is it? Did you bruise something? Or break something?'

'I really didn't mean it! I'm just such a . . . oaf,' Guy says.

'It's okay. I'll live. But I think I'm going to have to see a doctor,' Hank says through clenched teeth, brutally righting his knee's cant.

'I'm gonna puke,' Guy puts in.

'*You're* gonna puke?' Hank asks, sweat dripping through the rivulets beside his nose. 'You should feel this motherfucker.'

'Both of you, shut up! Gee, I saw you trip him. I saw it! If you're mad at him for leaving here, tell him. Don't try to hurt him.'

325

'So you'll have to go to a hospital,' Guy says, not particularly sorrowfully, ignoring True.

'I guess. Don't be scared.'

'Do you think it's permanent?' Guy asks.

'No,' Hank says. 'Now, you guys, if you could help me get up and get me something to lean on . . .' True casts her eyes around the immediate vicinity and locates a golf umbrella. She hands it to him. Hank looks up at her. 'True, don't be a ninny. I don't think this would support Guy's weight. I'm wicked hurt here.'

'You sound like a Cape Codder,' True murmurs. Hank flashes a grim smile, 'I'm thinking more in the nature of . . . a crutch . . . or a big stick . . .'

'I have a piece of old bannister in the garage,' True cries. 'We could tie it to your arm with Guy's old sling, from when he broke his collarbone. God, they're going to think we beat each other at our house . . .'

'How appropriate, a bannister,' Hank tells her. Limping, the piece of polished wood lashed to his arm, Hank hops as True maneuvers him to the car. As he is lowered into the back seat, he howls in pure animal pain, but though around his mouth is a ring of unpigmented white, he motions to her not to worry.

'Go to Granny's, Guy, right now,' True tells her son tersely.

As they drive, True asks, 'How did you pull your knee like that? You probably did more damage! You're so . . . don't you feel pain?'

'Chère, I burn myself twice a day. I've pulled every muscle in my body, banged every finger on my hands with hammers, lost nails. I feel pain, but I don't get stuck on it. I forgot to tell Guy to stretch,' Hank muses as they bounce over the speed bump into the hospital parking lot and he cries out involuntarily.

'Hank, I'm so sorry he hurt you. I'll punish him. I'll take away his boombox. I'll ground him for a month. I can't figure it out,' True says.

Hank has rent ligaments on both sides of his knee. 'This is a pretty gruesome X-ray,' the doctor tells him. 'But we'll watch it. And unless you're trying for the playoffs, we might, and I mean might, avoid arthroscopic surgery.'

'Surgery?' Hank pales visibly.

'If you keep off it for six weeks . . .'

'I can't keep off it,' Hank says, 'I'm a chef.'

'Well, you'll be a one-legged chef for a while. This a cooking injury?' the doctor asks, as he orders materials for a full leg cast.

'No. I was dancing.'

'In a mosh pit?'

'Teaching my son to dance. I fell wrong,' Hank explains.

'You could put a rolling office chair in the kitchen,' True suggests.

'True, the kitchen is about eight by ten. Where would we put a rolling chair?'

'Maybe a stool?'

'I'll work it out,' Hank says, meaning *shut up*.

'Well, your dancing days are over for a while,' the doctor comments. 'I don't know if you'll get full mobility . . . well, you're young. We'll see you back here in a week, okay?'

Four hours after his fall, True and Hank pull into the driveway. Guy is at the car door instantly, helping Hank onto his crutches. 'That's a big cast!' he cries. 'Is it bad? Is it permanent?'

'No, I'll be fine,' Hank says. 'Gotta lay low for a while. You're going to have to listen to me when I teach you. Did you stretch?' Guy turns and begins to tickle Gypsy's belly.

'Mmmmm,' Guy says. 'A little. Are you sure you won't be crippled forever?' True glances at her boy. Despite the innocence of his play with Gypsy, he looks . . . angry.

'Out with it, Gee. Why did you do this?'

'Because he's spoiled rotten is why,' Hank says. 'You always give in to him, or he just nags the hell out of you, and if he doesn't get what he wants from you, he goes to your ma, and she gives it to him.'

'I have given in, probably too much. It's hard to raise a kid on your own. You just give in. Maybe it's hard not to give in on little stuff when he's lost big stuff. Maybe this one will be spoiled rotten, too, for the same reason.'

'Not if I have anything to say about with it,' Hank says, in a softer tone.

'Well, it's pretty obvious that you won't have much,' True's voice is flat, like glare ice. 'It's not like he's mentally ill.'

'Well, if this wasn't an accident,' Hank taps his forehead.

'I thought you'd have to have a wheelchair,' Guy says. 'I was hoping you would.'

'Guy!' True is appalled.

327

'I hate that he got hurt so bad. But I did think he'd have a wheel-chair, for a little while. Until . . . like Christmas.'

'Haven't you got anything else to say?'

'Sure,' Guy answers. 'What?'

'That you're sorry? That you shouldn't have been such a vindic-tive brat. What if he'd hit his head? What if you'd killed Dad?'

'I knew I wouldn't kill him!' Guy begins to cry, his chest trem-bling under his rehearsal T-shirt, which reads, I WAS TRAINED TO ACT THIS WAY.

'You knew you wouldn't kill him?' True shouts.

'I didn't want to kill him! I was thinking of ways I could save your life!' Guy says to Hank.

'What in the fuck are you . . .' Hank sputters, as True shushes him. 'What do you mean, Guy? Save my life?'

'Because you can't go to the war if you're crippled!' Guy sobs. 'I saw it in the movie, with Gene Kelly! He smashed his own hand, but then he ended up being a hero anyhow, but you were going to leave us and go to the war, I heard you tell Mom, and I thought if I hurt you a little, that was why I tripped you on the barre. I wasn't trying to kill you! I . . . I love you! I already had one dad die! It's bad enough you left us! If you went to the war I knew you'd prob-ably die because you're pretty old, and most soldiers are pretty young, and you can't run as fast, well, sort of fast, but really, you'd have to be a general to not get killed, and even they get killed if they drop a bomb on them . . . I didn't want to really hurt you! I had to do something!'

'Oh, God, oh my dear Lord,' Hank sighs. 'Didn't you think you could just tell a person this? Guy, honey, Guy, first of all I am not going to the war. How can I go to the war? I *am* too old, and plus, I have a kid. I would never leave you. And now I'm crippled.'

No one knows what to say, and though True wants to put her arms around Hank and Guy, because she does not know for whom she feels more pity, she simply covers her face with her hands.

'Next time I tell you what to do in the studio, you listen, okay?' Hank says seriously.

'Yes.'

'And don't worry so much. Your mom and I have to talk about things, but I'm not going anywhere. We've got our pad, right? And we're going to decorate the bathroom with old album covers?'

'Yes,' Guy says.

'And I'll see you Sunday, right?'

'Right,' Guy says.

'I'm going,' Hank tells True.

'I can drive you.'

'Thanks, True. I've seen you drive. I'll take my chances,' Hank says, and True turns away, without telling him that she thinks that last night, for the first time, she'd felt the baby move.

IT IS GENEVRA'S son, a sweet, well-mannered boy named Conor Cahill, who gets the role of Oliver. And she has three other children, all girls, all equally well-mannered, who sit at her feet and color or sew while Conor and the other children are inside the rehearsal room.

During those times when Esa or Hank can't drop Guy off for rehearsal, True, too weary for the two-way drive, simply lies on one of the covered benches and alternately naps or watches the woman's composure with admiration. 'It's like she's got them drugged or something,' True confides in Franny, whose Clainey has indeed been picked to be the sole girl in the raggedy band of tiny thieves headed up by True's old friend Ellery, in his element as Fagin.

'I heard they're these big Christians worse than the Fredericksons,' Franny whispers, 'who go to that thing down there in Dennis?'

'That thing?'

'You can't really call it a church. It's more like a mall, with a school and a community center and a gym . . . Steve calls it Six Flags Over Jesus.'

'Maybe I should go there,' says True. 'Guy is getting a mouth on him like a dockworker.'

'He's got to be getting it from Clainey,' Franny replies, with unwonted humility. 'It's "*farg*" this and "*farg*" that. I washed her mouth out the other day, literally. And of course, *she* gets it from her big sister, who's moved on past the Disney versions of the swear words . . . I think Angelique is going to be a career criminal. She was interrupted on her way to a party the other night by the bulge under her jacket, which was a six-pack.'

'Coulda been worse,' True says, nodding at her own bulge. 'You're a social worker, Frannywoman; how could you have raised a budding delinquent?'

'You know, the shoemaker's children,' Franny says. 'I had her too

329

young. I tried to be nice to her. I won't make the same mistake with MacClaine, or if I ever have another one. Don't you either. Ground her from birth.'

They find a space on the bench beside Genevra, and True makes introductions. 'Do you stay through every one of these rehearsals?'

'Oh, yes. We only have the one car,' Genevra says. 'And my husband works nights for FedEx, so I have the time. I volunteered to help out. They really need someone backstage. The kids need some guidance. And mine don't have to get up early. A group of us home-school, and it doesn't matter really when we start.'

'That's lucky,' Franny says. 'I'm having to haul Miss MacClaine moaning out of bed every morning to catch the bus.'

'That's too bad,' Genevra says. 'Poor kid. Have you ever considered home-schooling? Or do you . . . work?' She seems to curl her lip slightly.

'I do work,' Franny says, with a sidelong glance at True. 'Helping other people raise their kids. Ironical, I guess. But I also think I'd slap her upside the head if I was trying to teach her geography and she sassed me.'

'I *know* I couldn't teach Guy,' True puts in. 'Especially in my condition.'

'Yes, he is a handful,' Genevra says, and True's ears burn. 'But it's really not so hard if you're patient. You don't have to pass any state tests or anything. You just sort of get the books from the school district and make sure they're more or less up to grade level. You can cook it up as you go along. And you can teach them what you want them to learn, and *not* teach them what you don't want them to learn, if you know what I mean. Of course, Conor's way ahead. He's had to be, with acting so much.'

'I work, too,' True says. 'All the time. And don't you think they have . . . less respect for their own parents?'

'Well, not really,' Genevra says, bending down to help her little daughter unwind a knot of yarn that is in a tangle. 'I think mine respect me more than they could ever respect anyone else. That's the whole basis of it. I respect them, too. And we have so much fun. We're doing a unit on Native Americans now, building our own tepee . . . I hope the weather holds so we can sleep and cook in it, just one night . . . it's getting so cold, and I don't have all the girls' sweaters done.'

'Done?' True asks.

'I knit them,' Genevra says, 'every year.' She laughs. 'Don't get me wrong. I use a machine. I'm not Superwoman.'

The three laugh, Franny and True nervously. 'Do you ever knit for . . . other things?' True asks then, sensing a possible craftsperson in the making. It is an effort to think of her business, as if it mattered to her; but effort is what this whole period of time is about.

Genevra replies, 'Church bazaars, things like that. And I've sold some of my mittens and so on.'

'Because you know I own a company. And we'd love handknit baby mittens. Do you want to talk about it sometime? I can leave you my card?'

'I can certainly ask my husband,' Genevra replies, with a sparkly smile. 'I think that would be neat, a little extra income and all those little mitties going out around the world . . . but Cal would have to give the okay.'

'Well, it's not quite around the world,' True says.

'Well, around the country. And I make them in animal shapes. The girls like them better, don't you, bunnies?' Three blond heads bob up and down.

Franny and True stop for tea at the little shop next door to the theater. 'She's like a Stepford Wife,' True says, 'with the Stepford Debs.'

'Maybe she's just an old-fashioned girl,' Franny replies. 'Takes all kinds.' They kiss cheeks and Franny asks, 'Got a formal debut for this act yet?'

'I wish it was right now. But in fact, it's either February or March, depending on how spaced I was with the kit. The doc says I'm a little big . . .'

'Could just be fluid. Your ankles are really swollen . . . don't they hurt?'

'They're numb. But I am glad I don't make my living in a topless bar.'

'Aren't you madly excited?'

'Tell you the truth, I'm a little scared. Without Hank. Everything has that big tag on it, honey. Without Hank.'

'Well, Esa and I will coach. And you have to hire someone. Hire a baby nurse. Hire a full-time nanny. And Jesus, True, he could still come home.'

331

'Esa helps. I'm trying to watch the dough.'

'But Esa has so much to do. Don't burn her out. Surely, you've got the money for a mother's helper a few hours a day.'

'I guess.'

'You run him to rehearsal, after you work all day. You just can't keep up the pace, True.'

'Yeah, the doc said slow down; my blood pressure's a little high.'

'You could get pre-eclampsia.'

'Don't scare me! Isn't that a sort of all-out system failure where they have to take the baby right away, because of the mother's blood pressure . . .'

'Yes. Although they don't always have to take the baby right away. But they do have to hospitalize the mom. And headaches. Do you? Have headaches?'

'Yeah.'

'Listen, True, get thee to a nannery . . . or I will! On your behalf! You need some down time.'

'Okay, mi'lady. I promise.'

'And let Hank know. He'll want to help. He'll want to take care of the baby, if not you.'

'We only fight whenever we talk. That's probably what's making my blood pressure go up.'

'That was always his effect on you, wasn't it, True?' Franny asks.

THE ACCOUNTANT WILL come Monday. True has not had time to anticipate him, given Hank's departure and various other brush-fires, but she has told Isabelle it would be prudent to have a cardiac surgeon on hand when the man arrives. She has no idea what the war will mean, atop her previous losses, and feels wretched even thinking of it in economic terms. She has set a realtor looking for beach cottages at desperation prices, and believes she's located one, in Harwichport; but it's still expensive, more than four hundred thousand even if she dickered like a . . . rug merchant. She feels guilty even thinking 'rug merchant.' There are terms no one will ever use again. True has been helplessly doing exactly what she has sworn never to do, dipping into college and retirement funds to make payroll, using profits to buy stock for only two, three months down the line. A wiser woman would simply face the music and sell the house, but True cannot, will not believe that the economy will continue to slide until there are breadlines in front of Danny's Galley. Then, if that happens, she reasons, everyone will be in the same boat; they will liquidate everything and get jobs. Guy will get jobs making pizza commercials. She has a teaching certificate, and she has taken pains to find out what would be required to update her credentials. They will move to this presumptive cottage, have the baby, and she will enjoy her summers off.

When the accountant arrives, cheerful precisely in the manner of an undertaker, it is the blue-and-white striped decor of the beach cottage she is mulling, not the mass of open ledgers in front of her; so she is not ready. And after they begin their conversation, she realizes she could not ever have been ready enough.

The meeting with Elizabeth must be scheduled but quick. The new company must be pushed out there, to make its fortune, like Jack with his bag of beans. Orders continue to pour in to Twelve Times Blessed, as if clients refuse, as she does, to honor the maniac state of the earth by dishonoring their babies. She has never had more demand than she does, right now, with two of the packers having been called up from the reserves and two others having remembered the urgency of getting their college degrees. There are still the four new full-timers, older men, come out of retirement. They neither want nor need health insurance. Kathleen commands them with glee. True has decided to hire a friend of Rudy's to take over the presentation work, Kathleen's job, since the girl, at interview, proves to be a swell dresser. The time to strike is now.

Hadn't True, after all, been the lecturer who told crowds of sad, hopeful faces, 'When the going gets tough, take more risks'? It seems now, with the world careening on its axis, that doing imprudent and venturous things is paradoxically wise. Her country is dropping bombs and packages of bandages on the same spots in the same country. Who is True to exhibit more logic or restraint?

TRUE HAS GONE to Bella Madonna in Wellfleet to buy one good maternity suit, a lush, light-cream wool-and-silk blend, for her appointment with Elizabeth, a lunch at That One Place. She tries not to think about the way Elizabeth's face will harden into a waxen smile when True asks her for money. It makes her pee seven times before she leaves the house.

For the previous few days, True has felt under the weather, and Isabelle has been ferrying Guy to his singing lessons with Kitt, and to rehearsal every night, telling True she doesn't mind the haul, that she catches up on her class reading. In fact, True knows that Esa's maternal instincts, not toward the baby, but toward True and Guy, are coming fully into flower as True blossoms. She has grown more attentive and more tender to Guy than she has been since he was a baby. She sleeps over at True's house often, without being asked, insisting Douglas works so late he barely notices her absences. With all True has on her scorched mind, this is yet another boon, a true blessing. Overhearing bits and pieces of conversation, she knows an antique bassinet is in the offing, even now being prepped by one of the crafters. She also knows Esa and Rudy have commissioned Genevra Cahill, 'Oliver's' mom, to make a white-on-white quilt for the baby, with a crocheted border and pillow edging. Though she realizes it is supposed to be a surprise, True cannot help peeking at it when she drops in occasionally, as Genevra works away during her vigils at the rehearsals. One night when Esa is staying over, Douglas away at a three-day meeting, True comments on Genevra's delicate work.

'But she is a wacko,' Isabelle tells True.

'Why do you say that?'

'It's just . . . she has this creepy look in her eyes. And she said something one night that scared the hell out of me. She said that maybe her pastor was right, that Jesus Lord . . .'

'She didn't say "Jesus Lord."'

'No, that was it. She said, "Jesus Lord," like you'd say "Franny Van Nevel." She said maybe "Jesus Lord" really was punishing the United States for being a nation that had fallen away from His teachings, and that this was the beginning of the comeuppance for all the nations.'

'What did you say?'

'Well, I felt like taking Guy by the hand and running for the car. But for some reason, I said to her, how can you think that? You have all these beautiful babies. How can you think God would want all of us to be hurt?'

'And what did she say?'

'Well, she said, "We wouldn't be hurt."'

'What do you think she meant?'

'I think she meant that *her family* wouldn't be hurt.'

334

'Because they're righteous.'

'Or maybe she meant,' Isabelle says, twisting a corner of her voluminous nightgown, 'that they wouldn't be hurt, because they'd all be taken up to paradise or something, like in Revelations.'

'Ughhh.'

'And she's snippy to Guy.'

'Snippy?'

'Well, I heard her say, "Let Con have the crayons. They're his." And all Guy was doing was drawing.'

'That's no big deal,' True sighs. 'There's always one mother who hangs around, like the ghost of Christmas past, bossing the kids.'

'I didn't like it.' Isabelle is not being oversensitive. True can tell she is genuinely on her guard. And after Isabelle had gone to bed, True reflected that she didn't like it, either. Guy has always been a friendly, sharing kid. He's only gotten in trouble with Beatrice once, for doing karate kicks instead of listening when he was supposed to, and that had been years ago.

Yet, on the morning she goes over her debts and credits, she lets her thoughts drift again to Genevra. If she is as odd as all that, perhaps True had better forget the animal mittens, though the pairs she's shown True are indeed beautifully made and adorable.

Tomorrow, she will see Hank, True thinks. She is bone-tired. Her head aches. But she gets up and showers, heaving herself sideways to shave her legs, and carefully conditions her hair.

She still wants to look fine for him. She still wants him, period.

TRUE SMOOTHS HER skirt and adjusts the gold antique pin she has borrowed from her mother.

'You look very nice,' Kathleen has told her. 'Businesslike, and yet not too formal. Now, do not crawl to her, True. That's what she expects.'

'How do you know what she expects?' True asks miserably. 'Oh, Mom, I know what you mean. I just think she's going to say, "Seek your fortune elsewhere."'

'I think she'll be expecting you to ask for your job back.'

'Maybe I should ask for my job back.'

'That wouldn't be a bad idea,' Kathleen says thoughtfully. 'Things being as they are now.'

'And what would we do with the odd several thousand zippable waterproof sand buckets and knit hats with the cow jumping over the moon on them, Mom? Have a big garage sale?'

'Well, we could, the way Elizabeth used to do with overstock? Remember? Women would camp out overnight to buy the dolls for half-price?'

'Mom, I don't want to give up my company.'

'I don't think it's a matter of want, True. You have Guy to think of. The baby. And I know that your worth isn't . . . all it was.'

'And how do you know that?'

'Rudy.'

'I have hired the biggest mouths in Massachusetts. Mother, I beg you on my knees. I'd get down on my knees if I were able to see my knees and this wasn't my only pair of good stockings, don't tell anyone about my stock. Or anyone's stock. I don't want anyone to smell blood.'

'I would never do that.'

'Not even Mary. Not even Ellen. Not even at confession. Not anyone.'

'I would never do that. I'm . . . well . . . I have told Kellen. Isabelle's father. But he's all the way out in Wisconsin.'

'Oh, swell.'

'And he's a very . . . well, he barely speaks to anyone, True. He tells me that our e-mail conversations are about the only real talk he does, except with Esa, and except about the weather.'

'So Esa knows.'

'Well, *you* told her. And she did the books, before that Vivien took them over.'

'Okay, oh dear,' True kisses her mother's petal-soft cheek. 'Well, let's all be little mice now, and keep our own counsel. Now, wish me luck.'

'I do. Don't let seeing your former husband make you forget your purpose.'

'He's not my former husband, Mother.'

'Well, not legally.'

'I love Hank, Mom. I just think it's hopeless.'

'That's something anyone could understand,' Kathleen tells her. 'But, though I'm very sad to say it, I believe you are right about Hank. He was never worth it.'

'Please, Mom. Don't make me defend him.' Kathleen shrugs.

Elizabeth, more slender and elegant than True remembers, is

waiting in the parking lot at That One Place. Hank has prepared crab croquettes with chipolite and toast points, a black-bean soup, and a salad with lobster and raspberry vinaigrette.

'I've heard about Guy's leading role, from Beatrice,' Elizabeth begins.

'I hope you get to see him,' True smiles, as they sit down.

'I should. I paid enough for that soprano. I'll be at the gala.'

'I didn't know you contributed to the theater company.'

'Only endlessly.'

'That's wonderful, Elizabeth. Beatrice does magic with a little velvet and verve.'

'She does,' Elizabeth says, nibbling a toast point. 'And you look well, True. You look well and young. I wish I could say "slender," but you do look fit.'

'You should see my dog.'

'How do you mean?' Tom wordlessly appears with hot corn bread.

'I can't really work out, and I don't want to end up as big as two shopping carts, so we walk and walk. He's the fittest dog in the Cape.'

'I see. Well, it's done you both good.' Elizabeth would never mention Hank and True's separation. 'You look beaming.'

'So do you, Elizabeth.'

'I don't look young. I look rested. I am rested. Because, and you will read this presently, if you read newspapers, I have sold Elizabeth's Heroines.'

'Sold . . . ?'

'Sold it to Short Stuff.'

'But it was . . . it was yours, your baby.'

Elizabeth gives True a look that makes her feel she is shrinking, like Alice under the mushroom. 'It was never my baby. But it was something I loved, and I brought it to the place where it can go on without my daily input. I will remain on the board of directors for a very short while, possibly. Stefano will be in charge of the company, for a longer while. But it had been seventeen years, True. You realize that. The challenge was no longer new.'

'So are you retired?'

'The easy answer is yes. But no. I'm doing some things that Roger and I have wanted to do for some time. More traveling. And I'm working with Beatrice on some things that will make a difference

337

in the community, the whole Cape community, for the arts. Like seeing that CFT has its own home space, a lovely theater, if I do say so myself, in the planning. Not only for children. And there are other reasons.'

'So you will be busy.'

'I'll be busy. And I'll be wealthy. And I'll need to take it a bit easier. Short Stuff is a mammoth outfit, as you know. Despite this awful business. Little ones will go on needing role models, now more than ever.'

'The war.'

'The repeating of history we are apparently condemned to learn again in every generation.'

Tom, silently, has brought the soup. True waits for Elizabeth to begin, but she asks instead for a bottle of champagne. Ghostlike, Tom appears with one. 'Let's toast,' she suggests.

'To your new adventures?'

'To yours. The obvious and the one you asked me here to talk over. And to your husband's lovely and successful business. And to my hope that you mend your fences.'

'You know?'

'Well, about the new company, of course. I assumed you didn't ask me here to make sure I was eating well enough. I assume you want to ask me about this college company.'

True sighs. 'Who *told* you that?'

'It wasn't Rudy.'

'Do the very walls speak?' True asks the air around her.

'You'd be surprised.'

'No, I wouldn't. Do they speak about Hank and me?'

'People say things.'

'Unkind things.'

'But I don't believe them, True. I don't know what has come between you, but I know it must not be as significant as whatever it was that brought you together.'

True takes a deep breath. 'Well, that remains . . . to be seen. So, then, Elizabeth, the long and the short of it is, I believe this company, for which I have set forth a plan,' she places her four-page synopsis, in its blue glassine cover, on the table between them, 'has wings. I believe that my generation is going to send more children to college, more children accustomed to more luxuries to college, than any

338

previous generation. And that is the driving idea behind First Year Away. It's Hank's idea and I must say I think it smacks of genius. Unlike my parents' generation, many mothers and grandmothers are still going to be in the work force when the children go off for the first time. They won't be in the kitchen, making cookies, sending care packages with warm socks and . . .'

'In other words, it is Twelve Times Blessed, grown up.'

'Precisely.'

'I like it. It's like that man who made a fortune sending kids birthday cakes at college . . . what was his name?'

'I don't remember,' says True, 'but I know the man you mean.'

'And the numbers are in here?'

'Yes, they are.'

'But surely, you could go to a bank, or refinance your home . . .'

'I am refinancing my home in any case.'

'And yet you preferred to come to me, though it must have cost you considerably in pride, because . . . ?'

'I wanted to keep it . . . quiet. And because I thought you might like being a part of it.'

'In fact, I might like being a part of it. I greatly admire Twelve Times Blessed.'

'So, if you look at this, and think it over . . . I've made a generous provision for your return on the investment.'

'I'd like to have half of it.'

'Of First Year Away?'

'Of Twelve Times Blessed.'

'No!' True says. Tom, at the pass-through window, blinks. Hank, behind him, deliberately invisible to Elizabeth, makes a throat-cutting gesture.

'Why not?'

'It's mine!'

'But it would be a better arrangement for you. Your present business would be safe. Your new business at less risk.'

'It would feel . . . like defeat.'

'Think about it.'

'I will,' True sighs. 'Elizabeth?' she then asks quietly. 'Do you hate me?' She watches Elizabeth drain her champagne flute, wishing she could have a nice long pull herself.

Finally, Elizabeth smiles. 'Of course not. I . . . try to understand

339

this, I rather cherish you, True. I was very disappointed when you . . .'

'When I left? When Rudy left?'

'Yes, in fact, I was . . . shattered. Really.'

'But you had everyone in creative. Stefano.'

'Stefano is no True Dickinson. However, I knew it would come. The point at which you realized how much talent you had. And when you realized all that you had learned, if I flatter myself, from me. I was sorry only when it had to be at the cost of your enduring the death of your husband. But that led to your fellow,' Elizabeth waves a ringed hand to include the room, 'and that, if nothing else, will lead to a beautiful baby.'

'Yes, I am glad about that. If nothing else.'

'And he is industrious. He'll be involved with the new venture. I've been to this place several times. It's delicious.'

Tom brings a dessert tray, and True begins to wave him away, but Elizabeth summons him back. True gapes. She has never known Elizabeth Chilmark to eat more than a single bite of anything containing sugar or chocolate, not even at birthdays in the office. 'I'll have the floating island,' she says.

'Me, uh, too,' True says. 'Thanks, Tom.'

'And so. Let's enjoy dessert. I will advance you . . . this sum, and I will be the half owner of Twelve Times Blessed. And when the time comes, if it does, you can offer to purchase my fifty-one percent.'

'Forty-nine percent. Elizabeth. You can't expect me to let you have a controlling interest in the thing I built with the only money I had.'

'Well done. Of course not. I'll go for it. I'll let you buy it back at a cost that the market at that time suggests.'

'I thought you would say no. Flat-out no. I didn't think you'd . . . don't you want to be involved with the new business?'

'Not really.'

'Why?'

'I have so many things on my mind. And you will do a better job. You and Rudy are a crack team. You have to admit it.'

'He's leaving me, though. As soon as things settle down, he'll be moving to California.'

'Oh, bosh. He's been saying that since dogs carried parasols. He's

340

not going anywhere. Evie won't let him out of her sight. I've known Rudy's mother for years. You mark my words.'

'This agreement. It's complicated. I'll have to consult my husband.'

'He's not coowner of your business? Surely you made a marital agreement?'

'No,' True sighs. 'Perhaps I should have . . . especially now.'

'Well, you must have had great faith. But you do need to make one, especially now.'

'Roger owns half of everything you have.'

'He most assuredly does not. He has his own holdings, and I mine.'

'I guess that's the smart way.'

'It is. But I suppose it doesn't demonstrate great faith.' Elizabeth finishes off her last spoonful with gusto. 'That was supreme! I wish I could hold another one. I'd eat it! Now, where are you off to?'

'How did you know I was going anywhere?'

'You glanced at your watch.'

'I have to meet a deadline.'

'Well, before we go, I happen to know congratulations are in order.' Elizabeth opens her purse and places a hundred-dollar bill on the table.

'This was to be on us . . .' True explains.

'Oh, of course, I know that,' Elizabeth replies. 'This is for Guy. For him to celebrate being a son of two again.' Unspilled tears hurt at the back of True's eyes. 'Because, whatever happens, he is that. He does have a father.'

'He does,' True admits, hoping Hank cannot hear her. 'And a good one. You don't have to do that, Elizabeth. I was touched when I got the bowl, with the dolphin etching, for our wedding, and the doll, oh the doll . . . I wish you would have come to the party. It all seems to have happened so quickly, rushed past me. I'm thanking you for wedding gifts on the verge of a . . . divorce.'

'I got your notes. I wasn't well. You have . . . good manners, True. Your mother has good manners.' Elizabeth rises from her chair. 'Well, partner, I will see you soon. In some musty office. With papers. Do you feel better?'

'Much, much, I can't tell you how much better.' Elizabeth leans over, and quickly, like a match lit and snuffed, kisses True's cheek. 'I'm glad you asked me. That shows faith. And the adoption and the baby . . . that shows faith. And courage. You have always had courage. It's important. Have courage now, True. Do the right thing, but remember that the most obvious path is not always the right one.'

'I'll try. I'll try my best.'

'And your best is fine indeed,' says Elizabeth, and departs, smiling more broadly, stepping more sprightly than True has ever seen her. She is aghast. Tom and Hank, who has been concealing himself in the kitchen, come out and sit down beside her.

'You gave her half of the business,' Hank says.

'I had to,' True says, 'but I'll get it back. I think she means for me to work to get it back. I think that's what she means by this. A lesson. And she'll make some money from it, once the new business is under way.'

'And we won't have to make this the next boarded-up restaurant on the pike,' Tom says. 'Fucking camel jockeys. As if shit wasn't bad enough . . .'

'Oh, let each day's evil,' True says, 'be equal to the joy, or whatever. Well, I can't have that lovely Moet and Chandon. Drink up, boys! It's on me. Tip your glasses. We're out of the woods . . . for now. I feel like a grande dame. True Dickinson rides again.'

Hank wheels on his heel and walks back into the kitchen, nearly ripping the buttons off his smock as he removes it. She hears his truck, only a second later, spray gravel in the lot.

'Why do you have to act like you don't give a shit?' Tom asks True suddenly.

'I want him to think I don't give a shit,' True says fiercely.

'Why? This is killing him.'

'He looks fine to me. And I'm sure Adele is picking up the pieces.'

'He says you don't answer his letters. You don't answer his calls. All you want to talk about when you see him is the kid,' Tom continues, his jaw set.

'His letters? What? A Post-it saying, "Be there at four for Guy"? They are so inspiring.'

'What do you expect? The guy is played out.'

'The guy brought this on himself,' True says. 'Not that this is any of your business, Tom. I should actually thank you for not telling me he was seeing Adele behind my back.'

'I didn't think anything of it. I didn't think it meant a damn thing. I still don't, True.'

'Well, that's why you and Hank get along so well, Tom,' True says, scooping up her papers and briefcase. 'Do tell Adele, when you next see her that, sad as I am about it, we are having to make some cutbacks, and that her books will no longer be required. She can seek her fortune elsewhere. And thanks for helping me get solvent again. It'll help Hank in the long run. Ta.'

True sails for the door.

Her bravado spent, True sits in the parking lot at the office of their lawyer, where she has made an appointment, because it is on the way home. Elizabeth's words play on her mind, like a piano piece all in minor key. True gathers her bearings, applies powder in the rearview mirror. The she walks in and greets the attorney. She briefly, and with no small humiliation, explains what has happened, that she wants to change her power of attorney to her mother, and that she would like the attorney to prepare an offer of some kind of financial settlement for Hank, as well as requesting that he make no claims against her preexisting estate.

'I don't have to,' the gnomish lawyer says mysteriously.

'I want you to,' True explains. 'You were right.'

'But you, perhaps, were not. Mister Bannister came here several days ago and asked me to prepare a document relinquishing all claim to your property, now and in the future, and informed me of his wish to contribute to the support of Guy Lemieux Bannister and any other children of this marriage.'

'He did?' True asks.

'Here it is,' the lawyer proffers a folder.

True does not open it, but again must sit in the car for a very long while, in the lawyer's secluded parking lot, until her hands stop shaking sufficiently for her to drive safely. Hank has done this.

But what has she done?

HALLOWEEN IS APPROACHING, and play rehearsals are now nightly, with only a month left before opening night. True is ragged. Though Kathleen is doing her utmost to train new employees, the flux, with the loss of regulars who have enlisted or gone home to their origins, is staggering. When she drives Guy to rehearsal, as often as not, she finds herself dozing in a chair, listening to the beautiful music as if her own personal angel chorus were serenading her from a distance. One night, the door is left ajar, and True hears Kitt Reuter-Foss sing

Nancy's song, 'As Long as He Needs Me,' and when Kitt comes out, wearing the tattered barmaid's dress she makes glorious, True is in tears. 'What's wrong?' Kitt asks.

'Nothing, nothing at all,' True tells her. 'Except that I have never heard anyone sing so beautifully in my entire life. You must be . . . I don't see opera . . . you must be a star, and I never knew . . .'

'Hardly. Tell my agent. I'm the perennial Suzuki to Butterfly.'

'But surely, on Broadway . . .'

'You bet I'd do it. I'd love to. But you make less on Broadway than in opera. Guy's got a hard road ahead of him. So do my girls, my daughters.'

'You have children?'

'Two daughters, one little, one almost out of college, who have the real voices in the family . . .'

'You can't be old enough to have a teenager.'

'Well, it's a sad story. I was an unwed mother in sixth grade.' Kitt places the back of one hand against her forehead. 'Please, don't share my shame with anyone.'

'Oh dear,' says True. 'Oh my God.'

'Get out of here! You believed me? No, I'm forty. Married my sweet college sweetie. He's at home now, directing the church choir, and the city choir, and the theater choir, and the swing choir. But let's talk about Guy, he's got the poise, and, if he works at it, he could have a voice, and he can act, and when he gets his growth spurt . . . look out! And unlike some I could mention . . .'

'Like who?'

'Oh me, I've got a big mouth.' Kitt opens her mouth. 'See?' She sings a high 'E' above 'C' and Beatrice calls, 'Ladies!'

Ellery, in his rags as Fagin, opens the door of the rehearsal room. 'Darling True. Are you sleeping well out here? I just passed and heard your delicate snore, which I assume arises from your delicate condition. Miss Kitt, I regret to inform you, you are required to be murdered now . . .'

'I keep forgetting that part,' True murmurs. She hears Conor singing the heartbreaking 'Where Is Love?' and as Kitt leaves, she pipes up, 'You want to come to dinner some night? Not at my house; I wouldn't put anyone through that, but at my husband's restaurant? It's great, Cajun food. I'm sure he'd let us.'

'The guy with the crutches, that's your hubby?' Kitt asks.

'Well, yes, he is.'

'You don't sound sure.'

'It's nothing,' True begins, then glimpses something open and calm in Kitt's eyes that makes her say, 'Actually, it's something. We're separated. But that doesn't mean we can't go to the restaurant. We're still friends.'

'Well, yum yum. I mean the Cajun food of course. Not the fella. Heh. Heh. It's a bitch that you're having problems. But listen, once he lays eyes on whoever's taking up space in there, I think things will have a way of healing themselves. At least, I hope so. I truly do.' She takes True's hand, 'I act like a ninny, but I will pray for you. It's hell being apart from the one you love. Well, I must go and die. I'll take you up on that offer. I've been living on Ramen noodles.'

'Do.' True stretches, and seeks a softer bench. It has become her habit, when she drops Guy off, to stretch out for a catnap, even on nights like this, Saturday, when Hank will pick their son up after the long rehearsal is over, and deliver him the following afternoon for another marathon. Somehow, tonight, the faraway daydream of the music and the pipes of the children's voices make a particularly potent lullaby. Through her doze, she sees Genevra exit the backstage, one of her three little blondes in tow ... 'Oh Genevra,' she calls. 'Thank you for sending the mittens for me to see. I apologize for not getting back to you yet.'

'It's just as well,' Genevra says. 'I'm sorry, but my husband thinks that we need to concentrate on relief work for now. Making warm things for the widows and orphans here and abroad, in our missions. We have missions even in Iran. So I won't have time. But thank you.'

'Okay,' True says, 'I understand.' She has sent money to the Red Cross herself, but this is humbling, so much more personal.

She is glad she had decided against the mittens in any case. Her *husband* has decided. Franny is right. Genevra is a Stepford Wife. Then, Genevra, who has been heading for the door, turns back. 'And True, I have to tell you. I had to scold Guy tonight. He was ... I'm afraid he was frightening some of the other children.'

'Oh dear, well, he would. I'm sure whatever you said did the trick.'

'He was drawing pornography. With Con's pencils.'

'My word! What kind of ... ?'

'Well, he drew ... I guess he'd better tell you himself. And he

345

threatened to hit Conor if he told. So I said, there'll be no hitting. He told some story about Conor biting him, but Conor has never hit or bitten anyone, even his little sisters, thank God. We just don't permit violence. We don't even have a television.'

'I see, well, I will speak to him. Thanks, Genevra. But you know, I'm sure Guy didn't mean anything by it. He's ten. Boys will be . . . vulgar. Still, thanks.'

'Don't mention it. They all get kind of out of hand back there. And Conor's not used to that kind of roughhousing.'

'I see.'

Genevra bustles away, and True lies back down on her bench, and is asleep within a minute, until she feels Guy shaking her shoulder. 'Mama? Mama?' True sits up. Guy's eyes are swollen and raw-looking.

'I told you to use cold cream, Guy, to take off that stuff. It only takes a moment, and now you've got your eyes all sore . . .'

'I used cold cream.'

'What's the matter, then? Are you having allergies from the dust? We should get you tested . . .'

'Mama? Let's get out of here right now. We can go back for Dad to pick me up after everyone else has left. He'll wait.'

'Of course, he'll wait. What's wrong, Guy?'

'Right now, Mama, please.' They walk out into the street, where the only light on is from Expresso Yourself, the tea shop next door, where college students study until the wee hours. 'Mama, let's get a cup of tea.'

'Herbal tea. And no, you need to get to bed. No late movies with Dad tonight.'

'How about hot chocolate? It helps you sleep.'

'This once.' They enter the steamy, aromatic golden hive of the teashop, but even before they sit down, Guy is tugging her sleeve.

'Mama, I'm scared of her. I didn't mean to do anything wrong.'

'Who? Oh, I know. Missus Cahill. She told me all about it.' Guy stops, his whipped cream dissolving, and stares at her.

'She told you?'

'Yes, she told me. And I don't want you drawing any more naughty pictures, kiddo.'

'It was just balls, Mom. We had this cartoon character, Kevin and me, called Big Balls Man. It didn't hurt anybody. But then, Conor

346

said he was going to tell Beatrice, and I said no, don't you dare, she'll yell at me, and I grabbed his arm, and he bit me.' Guy holds out his arm, and there is an angry welt, with neatly spaced and outlined rows of teeth.

'That's going a little far.'

'So I want to quit, Mom.'

'Quit? Quit the play?'

'Yeah, because she's going to get me. She says I'm going to go to hell, Mom.'

'*What?*'

'She says I'm going to go to hell when the country is blown up.' Guy is crying harder now, and True knows it is not the pain of the bite. She gulps a mouthful of her green tea, searing her tongue. 'And he says . . . Mama, you have to promise you won't tell . . .'

'What, Guy?'

'You have to promise first.'

'I will not promise.'

'Promise. Promise me you won't tell her I told you. She said if I told you, then I was an evil little tattletale.'

'Guy, hold on. You and I are best friends, right? We tell each other everything. Remember when we didn't, and Dad's, Hank's knee got wrecked?' Guy nods. 'So that was a big lesson. So whatever anybody tells you, and I don't mean every dirty joke Brendan or Fenn tells you, I mean big things, that scare you so much you want to quit the show you've been practicing for two months, you have to tell me, no matter what.' Guy is crying so hard the students have turned to stare. 'Let's go outside,' True suggests.

'Well, she said . . .'

'She said.'

'She said I was a spoiled little rich brat and that she bets I have my own home computer and I told her I didn't, that I play on the office computers, and she told Kevin, why did he have a computer, and he said for school, and she said we were all spoiled little rich brats. But then she said . . . I told them Dad had adopted me, I was telling Kevin, and she said . . .'

'What, Guy, what?'

'She said, do you know why handsome young men like your so-called dad marry fat old women like your mom? For their money, that's why. And she says all the kids and all their moms and dads say that. And that's why he left you. Because you're so old and gross. They say, True lost her toy . . . guy . . . something.'

'Her boy toy?'

'Yes, and that Dad doesn't really love me, that he's going to forget about me since he dumped you, and take off with a pretty girl who's his own age. And I said, don't say that, my dad loves my mom; they're friends, but they're having problems. And she said, that's what you think . . .' But True is already running, with Guy lolloping behind her, pleading for her not to go back into the theater. At the stage door, Conor is standing alone, sucking a lollipop, so pale and translucent-looking he really does appear as underfed as the character he is playing. True's mother's core almost turns her, like a barricade, from what she knows she will say.

'Where is your mother?' she asks.

'I don't know,' he says, and points at Guy. 'He drew a bad picture.'

'And you bit him. Don't you ever bite my kid again, you hear me? Or I'll let him bite you back. And he has teeth like a piranha.'

'Don't, Mommy, please,' Guy begs her, on the edge of real hysteria.

'Where is your mother? Flying around the roof on her broom?' Shrugging, Conor points into the dim recesses of the backstage. True, who now thinks that if she could see herself, her skin would have tightened over her face like plastic wrap, that she would see a mad mask of True, not herself, is surprised, when she wrenches open the swinging door, that it remains on its hinges. 'Genevra?' True calls into the dusky darkness. 'Beatrice? Genevra?'

Beatrice and Genevra, along with several other mothers, are gathered around a list on a clipboard. 'We were just discussing the potluck, True dear,' Beatrice says.

Quietly, so as not to frighten Beatrice, True says, 'Genevra, don't ever speak to my child again.' She watches with satisfaction as the color drains like spilt milk from Genevra's face. 'Do you understand me? If you have issues about my family or my family's life or problems, you bring them to me, do you hear me? Not to a ten-year-old child, who's so afraid of telling me that he wants to quit the show.'

'Quit the show?' Beatrice asks, confused. 'What's the matter?'

'She is the matter!' True cries. 'She told my son that his father married me for my money, do you know that? She told my son he was going to hell. And that he'd be evil if he told.'

'And he is, the lying little shit,' Genevra says. Her husband steps out of the shadows, carrying Conor's small parka, and takes True's shoulder.

'What my wife said is true. I've observed it. Guy is a trouble-maker. And I don't want my wife upset,' he says sternly. 'Your boy has a tendency to cause trouble . . .' The man raises a palm like a traffic cop. 'You just need to settle down, lady. Talk like a civilized person.'

'If you don't want me to knock you on your ass, you take your hand off my shoulder,' True tells him. 'I may not be able to do it, but I will try. I'm stronger than I look, fat old pregnant and deserted woman that I am. Did she tell you what she said to my boy?'

'She had to reprimand him. There's no discipline back here, among the wilder children . . .' says Conor's father. 'Con is used to a gentle, supportive environment, not a zoo!'

'Wait,' Beatrice interjects. 'Wait, I never said anyone was to discipline the children except myself. I never . . .'

'Next he'll be starting fires, and grabbing the girls' underpants, oh yes, Guy, we know all about how you lit the big electric torch and hid somebody's underpants,' Genevra goes on, as Guy cowers behind True.

'You self-righteous bitch!' True cries. 'Leave him alone! Beatrice, I love you dearly, but I won't have my son tormented. I know what you're saying about fires. He lit the candle-lighter. Once. Call the cops!' The release of tears will not come to her; she is so angry that she does not even stop to consider that she is exposing the baby to the worst possible violent noise, that he will probably get colic as a result and have to have immediate postnatal psychotherapy. 'Let them have it! Have it all! If what she says is true, if this is how people talk about me, I don't want my son to be a part of any of it! And if Hank were here, he'd feel the same way.'

'I need you to leave my wife alone, and I mean it,' says Conor's father, his chest in True's face. 'You might have money, but that doesn't give you the right to bully her!' He takes another step closer. But then, he seems to reconsider and falls back. True wonders if her bared teeth have really frightened him; but then she half-turns, and sees Hank behind her.

Guy runs to him, and slides his arms around Hank, burying his face under Hank's leather jacket. 'Daddy,' he says, 'they told Mom . . .'

'I heard,' Hank says, very quietly. 'I stayed in the hall until I heard

349

the whole thing.' He looks evenly at Conor's father. 'Where I come from, a man doesn't talk to a pregnant woman and a child that way. Be smart, my brother. Don't let the crutches fool you.'

'True, dear, none of this is making any sense,' Beatrice says. 'Genevra. Let's talk this over calmly.'

'Talk it over yourselves. I'm out of here,' True says, taking Hank's arm, forgetting she has no rights to it.

'And he wouldn't get his fancy roles, either, if his mommy didn't buy them for him!' Genevra shouts after them, as they turn to leave, True opening the backstage door for Hank. 'Everybody knows that. He can't sing. He can't dance. He's a joke.'

'Genevra!' Beatrice rears back, shocked.

But they are all out the door, True and Guy now crying, both stumbling, looking like a parody of two drunken clowns. They stand in the street. Finally, True says, 'She's the one who's a joke, Gee. She's a big, fat liar. You know you have talent. You have a smile you can see a mile away, honey. You know that.'

'I wanted to be the Dodger. I was having fun,' Guy wipes his eyes.

'And you will be,' Hank tells him. 'Now, settle down. Don't let her get to you so bad. And True, you settle down. Or you won't be able to drive.'

Guy asks, 'When we get in the truck, can we turn on the radio?'

'Yes,' Hank says, turning to True. 'Are you going to be all right?'

'I'm fine now,' True says, as the Cahills troop by, staring straight ahead and smiling smiles that, to True, look derived directly from Revelations. 'I'm really fine. Thanks, Hank. You have a way of coming along in the nick of time, huh? Make sure he gets to talk to you about it,' she advises, of Guy, who has already got the truck virtually pulsing with the radio blasting idiot tunes about hunkering down for the night, gonna love you all right.

True feels she is encased in glass, the passing world a reel of scenery. She wants only to see her own driveway, her own bed. As she leaves, she rolls down the window and calls, 'I was about to lose it back there. I think I *would* have hit the guy.'

'I don't doubt that for a moment, True. But worse yet, I think the prick would've hit you back, and you come up to about here on him,' he touches his throat. 'You crazy turnip. I didn't really hear everything she said, sweetheart,' Hank says, 'but I knew it was bad when I heard your rebel yell.'

'Well, you'd have yelled, too. She accused Guy of threatening to hit her son, when in fact, Conor bit Guy – I should get him a tetanus shot. And then she proceeded to tell him . . . things about fat old women. Meaning me.'

'So you got crosswise of some crazy stage mother who's jealous of you.'

'Jealous?'

'Of your business. Your home. Your good life. Your good kid. Our good kid. Hers is probably really the spoiled little shit. She names it, she claims it.'

'What about my beauty? Think she's jealous of that? And the fact that I'm an unwed mother at forty-three?'

'Probably.'

'You're certainly the biggest bullshitter in town.'

'Hey, I'm a hero tonight. I like this. I like it when we get a chance to talk. Even if it takes a crisis. I miss being your friend.'

'Mmmmmmm.' Hank does it again. He almost makes it, then says precisely the wrong thing.

But then, he pulls the truck closer. They could almost touch. He says, 'What I really wanted to say is the real reason I stood out there in the hall, listening to you.'

'Which was?'

'It reminded me of the first time I met you. The night you got stuck in the snowbank and . . .'

'And?'

'And I remembered your face when you came struggling up the hill. And why I fell in love with you, right at that moment, when you were wet and dirty and had blood on your face.'

'Why?'

'Because I thought you were the bravest woman I ever saw.'

'You did?'

'Yep,' Hank says, benignly. 'And tonight was like that. The way you were then. Maybe you needed me that night, but I think you'd have figured out a way then, too. You wouldn't have let Esa die. And you sure were holding your own tonight. You're a warrior, True. I guess that's some comfort, given how things are, knowing you don't need me. And there I was, back then, thinking you all insecure. I guess the only thing that made you insecure was me.'

But I do, True wants to say, giving Hank a crooked smile and

351

Guy a big thumbs-up as she rolls up her window. *I need you and I want you to come home. Say something, anything, that will let me tell you.* She is about to open her mouth when Hank says, 'You know, True, I don't want you to find this out from someone else. I'll tell you myself. Adele is staying with me part of the time, only platonically. She's not like you, kiddo. She feels so lost; she's scared to sleep with the light off. I think it helps her just having someone in the house. And she likes the daylight exposure for drawing. Don't worry, she won't ever be around Guy. She's got a girlfriend who stays with her on weekends who's taking a seminar at Harvard. I figured, given the way you feel about me, you wouldn't mind.'

A warrior, True thinks, sharply cornering onto Queen Anne Road and letting her eyes flood. Wouldn't mind? How can he believe this? Of course, of course, he does, but why? It is impossible. First to be dashed for your weakness . . . and then, for your strength. And by the same man, who once seemed incapable of misunderstanding her.

That night, the eagle mother raises her great wings and strokes into her dreams.

BEATRICE IS THE first person to call after it is decent, in Cape Cod terms, to make a phone call, which means it is eight-thirty in the morning. 'True, darling, I must speak to you about last night.'

'Oh Beatrice, I'm so ashamed of myself.' True has already decided she will not get out of her bed at all today. She has arranged the comforter and the pillow so that she is entirely covered, except for her nostrils.

'You have nothing to be ashamed of. That woman's behavior was outrageous.'

'She has a different set of values.'

'Well, she has a different set of values that she has no right to impose on other children. And I want you to know, I never gave her any authority to discipline any of the children. Only I or Laura have the authority to make a child sit down if he's being out of line . . .'

'Was Guy out of line?'

'He and Kevin were drawing naughty pictures. Laura told him to stop and he did and he said he was sorry and threw them away. He did nothing any normal ten-year-old wouldn't do. We didn't think a thing of it. Now, that little Conor . . . he's already bitten

352

two people, and pinched one of the dancers on the leg during the bar number . . .' The hideous little gator, True thinks. 'And I want you to know that Genevra has been told that she must not come backstage anymore during the rest of the production. It is she who is frightening the children. And not just Guy.'

'Okay. But I don't want you to think I'm the cause of all this. Do you know, Beatrice, about Hank and me . . . ?'

'Darling, anyone who has seen you and your sweet husband together, or seen him with Guy, knows that you have a real marriage based on love. No matter what is going on now.'

'No, Beatrice, that is, yes, we do have a great love for one another. But we are parted. It's the saddest thing in the world. But part of what she said was true.'

'What she said was vicious,' Beatrice retorts. 'So no part of it can be *true*. Whatever about it has a grain of fact, I don't know or care. I have never heard anyone else say anything like that. But it still must have hurt you terribly.'

'No,' True says. 'I tried to ignore it.' She takes a deep breath. 'Yes, it hurt me terribly. It made me feel more lost and more a figure of mockery than I did before.'

'Oh, my dear True, you must promise me that you will do exactly what you first said, ignore those words, and try to work things out your own way, and that you will not, under any circumstances, withdraw Guy from the show.'

'Okay.'

'And lastly, True, I want you to promise me one more thing. Will you do that?'

'Yes, Beatrice. Of course.'

'I want you to promise me that you'll tell Guy this. That he has far more talent than his mother has money. In exactly those words.'

'That's one of the loveliest things I've ever heard anyone say, Beatrice,' True says, sitting up in bed. 'Thank you.'

'It's only true,' Beatrice replies, and True gets up, refreshed, and forgets, for an instant, the space in the bed beside her. But then she hears the sounds in her early-morning house, of nothing at all, and Gyp quietly noses under her hand. So I will speak to him, True thinks – because in the end it does not matter who is wrong or who is right, because he *meant* no harm. Addled as it seems, he *meant* no harm. She leaps up and rummages through Guy's desk, and finds

Hank's number. She dials. On the fourth ring: 'If you wish to leave a message for Hank, Adele, or Guy, please do so.'

No time wasted. No inappropriateness spared.

There is nothing on earth that would make True leave a message at the tone.

It is Isabelle who brings the newspaper with the headline above the fold, 'No More, Please, for Mom of "Oliver"?' It's just the *Herald*, but the first paragraph reads, 'The mother of the young actor who plays the lead in Cape Family Theater's lavish production of the musical *Oliver!* has been banned from her volunteer duties backstage, allegedly because other parents complained when she tried to intervene in acts of violence. 'My son was being tormented by older children,' Genevra Cahill of Hyannis explained Tuesday. 'And naturally, I felt protective of him. He is the youngest child in the cast. He is only seven, though he has a great deal more experience with theatrical work than most of the other children, for whom this is a hobby. For Conor, it's a gift from God, a life-work.'

'Indeed,' the story continues, 'Conor Cahill is no stranger to acting, he has been featured in *The Summer Lads*, a film about the Chatham Athletics, made before the tragic death of T. J. Karavos, and several commercials for Friendly's restaurants. "The bigger kids are mean to us," Conor told the *Herald*, "and their moms were mean to my mom."

'CFT Board President Hilary Robin told the *Herald*, "There have been problems with some of the parents and some of the children. We are addressing these issues by issuing a list of guidelines, so that parents and young actors fully understand the time commitment and the rules of conduct required for being a part of our productions. They are stringent, and the children, as well as the adult cast members, are required to behave as professionals."

'But Genevra Cahill says that her son has participated in his last CFT production. "We are a Christian family, and we had grave doubts about Conor appearing in a play that had so much violence as a part of it," she said, referring to a scene in the musical, which will be featured at the Boston Civic Opera House as well as Radio City Music Hall during the Christmas season, during which the character Nancy, portrayed by renowned vocalist Kitt Reuter-Foss, is beaten by her brutish lover, Bill Sykes. "More importantly than that, though, we were shocked and saddened to learn that parents who have more money and influence with the theater are given special treatment."'

True throws down the newspaper.

'This is wonderful,' she says. 'Guy is going to feel as though he's some kind of outlaw.'

'Write a letter to the editor,' Rudy suggests angrily. 'You shouldn't let them get away with that, True. You didn't do anything wrong.'

'I did, though,' True admits. 'I called her names and . . . I lost it.'

'Well, the little shit *bit* Guy for Christ's sake,' Rudy continues. 'Why don't we take a picture of Guy's arm and show that to the *Herald*?'

'Let's just forget it. Thank God they didn't mention my name or my company. I could just see "Baby Company Owner's Son Abuses Tiny Christian." Let's leave it alone.' The baby taps, genuinely taps; it is for sure not indigestion this time, as if to remind True there are other priorities than press coverage.

But by the end of the week, Conor Cahill had been withdrawn from the show, and Beatrice is madly scrambling for a replacement. There is a follow-up story in the *Herald*, quoting Genevra as saying that her 'conscience could not permit' her to allow her son to continue to be involved in such a dangerous atmosphere without 'my personal supervision.'

WHEN HE RETURNS home from school, Guy indeed feels horrible. He hasn't needed to see the newspaper. Everyone has already told him, and made a guessing game out of whose mother is the one getting the shaft.

In subsequent days, he begins to complain, each night before rehearsal, that his stomach aches.

'It's nerves,' True tells him. 'You're nervous. Who can blame you, after what that nasty lady said? And Dad being gone? And everything. The whole world is nervous. Don't worry, Gee.'

'Aren't we Christians, too?' he asks one morning at breakfast. Blue half-moons cup his eyes.

'Of course you are,' Kathleen tells Guy stoutly.

'Just not as good of ones,' Guy replies.

'In God's eyes, everyone is good,' Kathleen tells him.

'Even the terror guys?' Guy asks.

355

'That you have to ask God,' Esa replies, stopping in the kitchen to grab half a bagel, 'but no, honey, so far as I can tell, God doesn't put up with that.'

'How about the newspaper guy who wrote all that stuff?'

'Now *he* was just being dumb,' Esa says cheerfully, grateful to be off the huge subjects. 'You can't blame anybody for that. Dumbness is inherited. Like blond hair.' Guy laughs. His cheeks pink up.

But the next night, Guy tells True that the windshield on Hank's truck has been smashed as it sat in the back parking area. 'I know they did it,' Guy tells True. 'Dad won't say.'

'I wish now I *had* punched out his lights,' True says.

'Dad should have punched out his lights,' Guy says. 'Or hit him with his crutch.'

'Now *that* would have made some headlines.'

'Dad has girl's underpants in a drawer at his house,' Guy says, smiling.

'Maybe he likes wearing them for a change of pace,' True suggests. She feels like vomiting.

'Oh, Mom, you're such a goofer. You know he bought them for you! He just didn't give them to you yet! Ever heard of a surprise?' Guy says, punching her on the arm. 'Let's go upstairs and listen to the baby brother make a heartbeat.'

HANK MEETS TRUE in Boston, for a screening ultrasound. She feels she owes him this. Under the modesty of the cotton drape, the doctor manipulates the tool, and what first appears to be the radar representation of a cyclone shows up on a television screen. But then, the obstetrician shows them how to see the fetus, and miraculously, suddenly, as clearly as if they had been watching dolphins in a pool, they see the bottom of a foot, a push, a swish. 'He's swimming!' Hank exclaims.

'Yes, he is,' the doctor agrees. 'Now, you can't feel that, Missus Bannister.'

'I can, though,' True says. 'I can feel it.'

'It's early to feel. But,' she adjusts the machine, clicks, and measures, 'you are sure you got your dates right? You may be a bit further along, based on the size I'm seeing here. But these things are imprecise. And you've been through this before.'

356

True is mesmerized by the sight of the perfectly formed foot, pushing off, already swimming away from her. She remembers, at that moment, that this is her husband's birthday.

NOVEMBER

YOU'RE MY PUMPKIN!

Everyone thinks of Halloween as pumpkin season, but in early America, it was Thanksgiving when the big, orange squashes were the center of attention. Our wooden pumpkin is a puzzle and shape sorter, with a hat, a triangle mouth, and a big smile. Inside, pumpkiny little mitts and earmuffs to warm small parts as chilly days set in. And you'll love the Blessings Balm that smells of cinnamon and spice, but keeps your hardworking hands feeling like they've been dipped in silk.

As SOON AS the tickets are printed, True selects three, positioned two rows back and slightly to the right of where she will sit, with her family, for the opening of *Oliver!* at the Cape Cod Family Theater. They will be for Hank and for his parents.

The show opens at the local theater the night after Thanksgiving. Then in December, there is a week at the Civic Opera House in Boston, and after that, a return to the Cape Cod Family Theater for two weeks, with a final and triumphant two days at Radio City. The children in the cast are mad with excitement. True wishes the Bannisters could see Guy perform in New York.

But no one wants to go to New York anymore. She will drive her own small posse there, herself, if the seat belt still fits around her.

True pushes the seat control all the way back, heaves herself into the Volvo, and drives to Truro early on a Friday afternoon, hoping to catch Tom so she can drop the envelope off before Hank arrives. But just as she rounds the turn from the highway, she sees his truck.

True's unwashed hair is gathered into a band and crammed under a Red Sox cap. She is wearing the Eileen Fisher red elastic-waist pants, with the elastic stretched to the breaking point, and one of Hank's lesser dress shirts, left behind, with only the top three buttons closed. Her feet have overlapped her normal shoes, and she usually wears, with special poignancy, the red rubber garden clogs in which she was married. Measuring her, the obstetrician asks if True is absolutely sure she became pregnant in early July. Exasperated, True affirms it. Was she absolutely sure the larger of the two violet lines was the darker of the two in the ovulation kit? True cannot be absolutely sure about that; but she is reasonably sure. She does not say she found the ovulation kit impossibly confusing, both times she tried using it. She does tell the doctor that they had never taken precautions before they tried specifically, and that her period in June had been odd and spotty, a fact True had attributed to age and stress.

'Well, many women bleed a little at implantation of their eggs,' the doctor says. 'And so either you're having a fine broth of a girl or boy, as my grandfather would say, or your dates are off. Or maybe all this is fluid. I've seen ultrasounds I swore were ten-pound babies, who came out at six-three, so who knows?'

True's private belief is that she simply has been drowning her sorrows in cinnamon scones, and the mound rising under her shirt owes more to dough than gestation. She doesn't know the psychology behind it; but she does know women eat sorrow and men swill it.

The best part of the looming month ahead, with its holiday coziness and its impossible emptiness is that True will not be spending all of it alone.

Douglas, Esa's husband, has received an offer from an adventure-travel agency, to take a group of grad students to Utah for a month during the holiday break. Unaccountably, with the possibility of disease and destruction in every subway door, and the possibility of explosion at the ignition of every engine, the trip is going forward.

Esa explains that they need the money too much, as they wish to offer to purchase their cottage. Doug also reasons that Dinosaur National Monument and its ongoing digs are not on any major terrorist hit list. The group is driving cross-country in three vans, so Isabelle feels more comforted, knowing Douglas, and not some nervous pilot, will be at the wheel.

'I feel as though I'm coming home!' Esa says. 'I'll miss him like crazy, but at least I'll have you!' She pauses. 'That was kind of a stupid thing to say, wasn't it, True? I'm sorry.'

'It's okay, Esa,' True tells her, 'I feel the same way. I'll miss *him* like crazy, too, but at least it won't be so bad if I have you to talk to.'

So, now Esa is living in the spare bedroom. Given that the consuming events in her life are peeing and struggling for breath when she bends over, True feels safer knowing another adult is in the house. That the other adult is one she trusts with her life is another boon.

Except for the night of the altercation at the theater, she and Hank have spoken only in passing, like an elderly and cursorily hostile married couple who confine their conversation to an exchange of condiments. Their last real conversation, on True's porch, seems to have laid bare too many emotions, and his revelation about Poor Adele's insecurity ('Protect the rest of us from the weak, for they shall inherit everything that isn't nailed down,' Isabelle said when True told her of this) has left True with no strength even to mourn.

With regret, she realizes she may have turned a corner. There will be no more night drives past the little cottage on Princeton Circle, hoping to catch a glimpse of her husband passing the window. No more deliberate hangup calls before the beep – after all, who wants to hear Adele's smug chirp anyhow? No more nights on the flat rock at Ridgevale Beach, at first hugging her knees and then hugging whatever part of herself she can still clutch: True has surprised herself by learning to reflect. No more lonely midnight drives to listen to the reggae man at Nauset. True has learned, late in life, the value of solitude and reflection; but she resents the price tag.

Hank has politely asked, last time he called, whether he may still take Guy on his food-delivery rounds, if they fall after school on Mondays, and True has given permission. He has continued to coach Guy in the basement workout room. About Guy, they chat like the civilized divorced, who have worn all the tread from their marriages in pitted ruts and have ended the charade. 'After the run of the show, it will be okay to keep him overnight every other Friday and Saturday,' True tells Hank. They will share Sundays, even perhaps, if they can manage it, do some things together with Guy. That is how little each of them cares, or pretends to care.

So long as Hank can seem to see her in the way he would see a

360

road-construction sign, as a minor irritant that does not really factor in his life, she will bloody well do the same thing. For her part, True has no idea what the ordinary routine is for separated couples. She could ask Franny. She knows Franny is waiting, with open hands, for her to ask her any class of advice, trivial or of major import; but True's reticence is daily mortared more securely by her pride. After that first burst of vulnerability, brick by brick, the wall she once thought something in her never loved is rising against her will. Through an entire craft show, at which both of them have purchased multitudinous holiday gifts, including, in True's cart, magic wands for Maman Winston, a ballerina music box for Win, and a cigar tray in the shape of an alligator for Gus, she and Franny have managed not to discuss Hank to any significant degree. True feels keenly caught in her own net. How can she not speak of this? How can she? It is both too trivial, a speck in the bloodied eye of life in the general world, and too overpowering, a fiery log thrown through her own window. Franny, with the flexible grace she has always managed to bring to any situation, has begun to refer to True and Guy – when she asks about plans, or issues invitations – as she did before True was married.

She loves Franny more than ever for respecting how fragile is her reserve.

True summons that reserve now, and walks into the restaurant. The first things she sees are the new chandeliers, which she suspects are from Louisiana, raindrops and slivers of crystal on arms of gilt. And table lamps where once there were candles, table lamps in the shape of the lampposts in the Vieux Carre. The whole place looks more spruce and seductive. True is proud of Hank, as she runs her hand over the tablecloths, sage and cream-colored, lightly damasked with sea creatures.

'True,' Hanks says, surprising her, walking out of the back room, wiping his hands on his apron. He has been cutting meat. He looks like hell, she notes, with satisfaction for which she loathes herself. He looks as though he has cancer.

'Boy, this looks great, Hank,' True says jovially. 'The place looks new. You, on the other hand, don't look so hot.'

'Thanks,' he grins. 'I've been giving a lot of time to the place, trying to coax people back in.'

'They'll come. They're stunned, is all. Wow, Hank. You're thin as my finger,' True says, with a sudden sympathy that is not feigned.

This is my husband, she thinks. *This is my husband.* 'What the hell?' They both look down at her finger, where she still wears her silver ring, embedded in rolls of plummy, swollen flesh. In past weeks, True has developed carnival fingers and toes and ankles. But she will not allow the ring to be cut off. True puts her left hand behind her back, and proffers the tickets with her right. 'I bought these for your mom and dad and for you. I didn't know if Win and Matthew or whatever . . . I can get more . . .'

'Matthew's so over.' They laugh. 'Couldn't stand Win's stardom, y'know? Or even the idea that she might try for it. He was a callow fellow.' A third literary reference, even though it does refer to a show tune, True notes, and bites her lip, hard.

Had she ever really done what Hank accused her of, treated him as unlettered, funny-talking? Expected him not to know important dates or books or lyrics? Had she done that in unknowing looks and deeds until he felt diminished? Had she wanted him, once, for his jeans and genes alone?

How meager that seems. She would give her molars to hear him talk now, to fill their house with his drawl, his double negatives, his unquenchable snort of laughter. He tells her kindly, 'Ma and Daddy can't wait. Win's definitely coming, but she's going to drive over. She says you can't imagine how it is in New York. Seeing it on TV isn't like *seeing* it . . .'

'She lives on the West Side, though?'

'In a women's hotel! They have a curfew!'

'Win!' They both grin. 'Imagine her signing out for the evening . . .'

'Yep. The little wild thing.'

'I'll have to get another ticket. I will.'

'I'll pay you.'

'That's okay.'

Silence falls like a drop drape, almost with a sound and a shudder.

'How's Maman?'

'Good.'

'Well, okay, I'm off,' True tells him breezily.

'Oh,' Hank says then, glancing away, 'I . . . I'm having Thanksgiving dinner here, and I'd love it if you and Kathleen would come. I was sure you'd let Guy come. You already knew my folks were coming because I'd said so in my . . .'

'Oh, sure. I figured they'd come anyhow. Despite . . . whatever. At least they'll get a good dinner. Won't have to eat the slop that Kathleen and I make.'

'I'm sure you make a very good turkey, True. Didn't y'all invent Thanksgiving, you Puritans?'

'We did indeed. And yes, I make a pretty mean turkey. Wonder Bread left out three days so the stuffing is dry as a bone. My brother loves it. He wouldn't eat it when he was a little boy, until he found out it had bread in it. My brother once ate a whole loaf of toast . . .' She is babbling. She stops. 'Guy has a rehearsal that night. Beatrice is a barbarian.'

'I'll drop him off right after we eat. So, Dog is coming?'

'Yep, and Esa. Douglas is in . . . digging away for pot sherds, you know. Actually, it's dino bones this time. And Rudy and Keith. We'll have a . . . full table.' She stops again. 'Did I ever cook a meal for you, Hank?'

'I don't recall.'

'Must have made a big impression.'

'Well, now, hold on. I seem to remember something with noodles. Yes. Stroganoff. Without the Strogan. Mushroom Stroganoff.'

'Ahhh, yes. Franny's Cooking Lite recipe.'

'It was good.'

'Well, thanks.'

'Yeah.'

'Okay. See you. Say hi to Tom.'

'Say hi to Esa, and Rudy and . . . everybody. How's the baby, huh? Pretty good?'

'Well, growing like some kind of alien. I've gained five pounds this month. Esa says I'm secretly a Wisconsin heifer, a milking machine. We start the ol' labor classes in two weeks.'

'We do.'

'Yeah,' True says gently. 'Esa and me. She's going to coach me. I didn't think, under the circumstances . . .'

'Right. Well, it suits you. You look young and . . . bright. Nice.'

'Yeah. That's nice of you. I'm trying to figure out which outdoor gear store to go to for a tent to wear to the show's gala.'

'Just wear that velvety thing that has the loops on the side you used to catch up and hang around the loops. To make drapes? Only don't use the loops.'

'That's a great idea. The ruby thing?'

'Right.'

'Okay, I will.'

'And lots of rhinestony jewelry. Be a showboat.'

'Well, I'll be a boat of some variety. 'Bye, Hank. Eat something, for Christ's sake. This isn't like you. Go play darts with someone.'

'Did you mean that nasty?'

'No, I really didn't. I meant that caring. Get back to normal.'

'I haven't been . . . well, eating, in the usual sense of the word.' He leans against the counter, triggering a domino fall of memory.

'Mmmmm,' True says, feeling magnetized, lured, literally leaning back on the heels of her boots to combat the sensation. *Do you want to know, True tells him, without speaking, how many times I've watched, flattened against the bedroom wall, when you pick up Guy and the dog? How many times I've turned to run down there and sing at the top of my lungs, anything? Sing, show a little faith, there's magic in the night? Sing the Come Home Hank Blues? How many times I've had to dig my fingernails into my hands so I didn't run and grab you? How I whipped my crotch at night until my fingers were achy and still couldn't come, thinking of you and your shoulders? How many nights I've sat on that cold fucking beach while the fog swallows the rocks, wearing the coat you left on the hook, that still smells of you? How many times I've driven past that damned house, after midnight, praying I'd see your truck, relieved when I did, then thinking, hell, you could have another woman in there, much less Adele, though of course, you wouldn't trample on her feelings. You could be having a private party with favors like only you offer, like you did with me? How many times I've lifted the receiver to call you, how many times I have called you, and listened to that wretched message? How many nights I've been sure you'd call me? Do you think, my beloved, my dark beloved mockingbird finally out of its cage, that we were really never in the cards, nor in the stars? And that this is actually better for you? And probably even for me?*

True thinks all these things. She turns her back, tips her BoSox cap, and walks out the door. By the time she hits her driveway, her turtleneck is wet enough to wring out. She is a simp. 'So you saw Hank,' Esa says.

'Yep. He's fine. Thin. We were very cordial.'

'You're sick, True. You love this guy. You love this guy so much. What prevents you from some kind of rapprochement? What makes you like this?'

'If I were you, Esa, I'd be running to Truro right now. I'd be running in bare feet down that highway. But I'm not you. And he wanted to go, Esa. He wanted to. Or he wouldn't have done what he did.'

'He didn't want to be *let* go. "Freed," as you put it. He told me . . .'

'You've talked to him.'

'Only about four million times. When he calls.'

'I never knew he called. I mean, other than when we've exchanged information.'

'Well, I never knew he called either, until I passed by once when Kathleen had picked up the phone. She's got the right intention, I guess. She doesn't want to hurt you by mentioning it, but he calls all the time, and talks to Guy.'

'That's different.'

'He always asks for you first.'

'He does?'

'I hear Kathleen say, "She's not in," even if you are. And I know he wants you back. I know.'

'Did he say so?'

'His voice did.

'Why don't you have a meeting, like? I could suggest it . . .'

'We already did that, Esa. Remember? And it was . . . the kindest thing anybody's ever done for anybody. But now, it's too late.'

'It's been *a month*, True. You are so dramatic. That's so not *too late*.' Isabelle stares at True, and goes still. Then she says, 'You want it this way, don't you? You're relieved.'

'I'm relieved it's over, at least.'

'I mean, you never really thought it would work.'

'That's what Hank said. No, I guess I wanted it to work but I thought it wouldn't.'

'So you gave up out of the gate.'

'No. I still haven't . . . given up.'

'So what about my idea?'

'I'll think about approaching him. I guess there's nothing to lose. But it hurts my pride. So badly. I didn't do anything wrong.'

'But there's so much in the balance. Guy. The baby. Your happiness.'

'I'm happy,' True says. 'I'm really not unhappy. It's as if he passed through my life so quickly . . . it's almost like he was never here. It's as if he were a great movie I'll never forget.'

'At least think about discussing it. In a hopeful way. Promise.'

'Well, I'll think about it when I have time. I am starting a business, and gathering inventory, and considering daily signing away my life to Elizabeth and the bank, and preparing Guy for his first real role . . .'

'You're such a busy bee you can't call the man you love?'

'That's me,' says True, meaning to sound light, sounding instead bitter.

THE THEATER IS massive, two, three thousand seats. True has not been inside the opera center since she and Peter attended a performance of the American Ballet Theatre, a Christmas gift from his parents, and that had been so long ago that Baryshnikov was still dancing to Frank Sinatra tunes. Angels clasp hands around the interior of the dome, and men in tuxedos and women in floor-length rustling chiffon enter the ruby-draped boxes. The set, which Beatrice has described for True, both revolves and slides, from the interior of the thieves' den, which is out on the thrust stage, to the tavern where the children will sing 'Thank You Very Much' with Nancy and where she later will die at the hands of Bill Sykes. When it revolves, it is the London street. True has never gone to see one of the full dress rehearsals, not wishing to spoil a moment of this night for herself. She wears her New Orleans skirt, covertly unzipped in back, under a velvet jacket, and Franny has coiled her hair into a twist. Franny and Steve are somewhere in the house, but True can't see them. The house lights blink for the first warning. Ten minutes. The Bannisters are not yet there.

Thanksgiving has been a quiet, odd affair. Keith's artichoke dip was a big success, but True is not sure the turkey hadn't had the dreaded pink bone, though everyone assured her (as heartily as if she had a terminal illness) that it was moist, well-cooked, and prime.

Kitt, who had after all never gotten her meal at That One Place, and who has been living in the Witherspoon Guest House so long she had told True she feels she has acquired Witherspoon genes, was

366

invited and showed up with so many presents of various sizes and colors it seemed Santa had arrived prematurely. There were soft sleep mitts for Baby X or Y, drawstring pajama pants in manly checks for Guy, wrist warmers for True – who'd once mentioned how she liked to ski cross-country, but hated snow up her cuffs – a Santa hat for Gypsy, and a shawl for Kathleen.

'Where did you get these?' True asked, her acquisitive merchant's eye overwhelming her good manners. 'They're beautifully made.'

'I made 'em,' Kitt told her, wrapping her tiny self in one of True's aprons. 'With these fake-fingernailed little paws here. Give me gravy to make. I'm so homesick for my kids – they come tomorrow – I want to make gravy for all America.' She spun around, 'You got a piano, True? Yes, you have a piano. A nice clavinova. I'll sing for my supper.' Of Guy she asked, 'Want to come home with me to Wisconsin for a semester? I'll whip you into shape. You'll be singing on Broadway by next year. Got pretty girls there who always wanted a little brother. They'll make a fuss over you.' Guy nodded vigorously. He has seen pictures of Kitt's two bewitching daughters, one only a year older than he.

'I think he'll be sticking around to meet this fella here,' True patted her belly. 'He's not supposed to show up until late February or even March. But Guy wants him to be a New Year's baby! He wants to be on TV, and get all the free diapers.'

'Well, before I leave the endlessness of this endless run, I will give you the name of a good teacher in Boston for Guy. There's no one around here. He's just about at the end of the boy-soprano period,' Kitt said.

'Will I get taller?' Guy asked.

'Yeah,' Kitt said. 'And you'll get armpit hair.'

'Oh, shit,' Guy said, blushing and covering his mouth; but everyone except Kathleen laughed.

Guy had been too nervous to eat much at all, too eager to show his *grand-père* all Gypsy's tricks. He is a splendid pup, who already will lie and stay at a movement of Guy's hand, watching his eyes eagerly for the next permission. He dances. He covers his nose with a paw when Guy says, 'Fart,' though this has not been a trick they practiced at home. True suspects Hank and his crew of French outcasts.

Afterward, in a moment of dish-rinsing, Kitt said, 'Well, everyone else is afraid to ask, but I will. How goes the separation, and why don't you just call it off? Not that this is any of my business. But I do have to tell you, Guy is miserable. I mean, we're all miserable, sort of, the world being what it is, but when Guy sings with Michael, the little boy who replaced Conor, to make Michael's voice stronger on "Where Is Love?", those are real tears, True.'

'Oh, God. Oh, Christ.'

'Why not a holiday truce? I read a book on marriage that said if people *behaved* as if they were happy, they could almost actually achieve it. I almost divorced my husband once. And this is the love of my life. The one man who ever touched this ivory bod. It was my first real starring role at the Met, only my second-ever Suzuki in *Butterfly,* and he chose to go to his high-school reunion instead. He really wanted to go back to his dumb egghead high school and brag that his wife was a diva from the dairyland . . .' Kitt grouses.

'But he was proud of you! And you were furious?'

'You have so much guts, True. I'd never do what you're doing alone. I can't imagine having a baby, at our age, and running a business. Look at this . . . look around you. All you've done.'

'All you've done . . . doesn't make a dent in . . . what you are, and right now, I don't feel much like a success,' True says.

'So you should reconcile. I saw you two together on the night of the Bitch Invasion. The man loves the ground under your feet.'

'You don't know me, Kitt. I'm wicked bad when I get going . . . maybe I never deserved . . .'

'What is this "never deserved"? A man who marries an older woman, a woman of our age . . .'

'Speak for yourself.'

'. . . Is a person. A mensch. And because of whatever it is he doesn't know that you can't teach him, you give up after, what, a year?'

'Six months.'

'Shame on you. Unless he's done something unforgivable.'

'It . . . was something else. But he's a great dad to Gee, and he'll be a great dad to this person.'

'You don't know the gender?'

'I had the test to see if it had all its marbles, but at the last minute, I decided, no, I want to be surprised. Knowing seemed too mod-ren, as my friend Franny would say.'

The dishes finished, Kitt then sang, as everyone else gathered on sofas and pillows. She sang 'As Long as He Needs Me,' an aria from *Figaro,* and then, with Guy, 'Consider Yourself.' When she took requests, Keith asked for 'Over the Rainbow,' and nearly wept at the last quivering pure flute of her vibrato.

At last, Kathleen, to True's surprise, asked, 'Can you sing "My Funny Valentine"? That was our song, my husband's and mine.'

And so she did, a husky, languid version that seemed less to True a pledge of long-claimed lovers than a prelude to their parting; and Kathleen, by the chorus, was dabbing her face, punished by her champagne and her memories. Kitt then left 'to put cucumbers over my eyes,' and, moments later, True heard the engine of the red truck.

'Dad's here,' she told Guy. 'Run and get Gyp and your things.' Hank waited in the drive, idling the engine. She could see the outlines of Hank's head and Gus's pompadour.

Once Guy and Kitt were gone, the house deflated noticeably. Esa's father showed up, late and unexpected, complaining of fog in Boston. Kathleen insisted on preparing him a full plate of leftovers, and sat sipping champagne with him as he ate. Afterward, Dog and Rudy and Keith watched bowl games with Kellen.

With the realization that she has finally grasped the full significance of her own name, True at last prepared to walk her mother back to her cottage. But Kellen took her arm instead. 'I've made up the sofa bed for you,' Kathleen said, hiccuping. 'I'm afraid I drank too much.'

'So you knew he was coming, even though Esa didn't?' True asks.

'Oh, sure, Katie knows everything about me, don't you?' said Kellen, draping his own huge coat around Kathleen.

'Good night, True. I'm . . . sorry.'

'Don't worry about it. Take four aspirin,' True advised her. 'Just don't fall.'

'I don't mean that,' Kathleen said. 'I mean about being too . . . mistrustful of men.'

'Well, I don't know what to say to that, Mom. And I think it's the bubbly talking anyhow.' Kathleen wobbled over her doorsill, shaking her head mournfully.

True was the last one awake to hear Gyp and Guy come home. Guy tapped at her door. 'Can I sleep in here?' he asked. 'I feel crummy.' True nodded. Guy asked then, as he had not before, 'Will Dad come back soon? Is he ever going to be done thinking us over?'

And True answered, 'I don't know.'

'Can I ask him?' Guy wanted to know.

'You can ask him anything you want, darling. But I don't think he knows the answer. But I do know that he's not moving away, even if you go visit Grandpa and Grandma L. at Christmas, and he's not . . . like getting papers to divorce us, me, I mean. He's a muller, that's what Aunt Franny says. It takes Dad longer to think things over.'

'Why don't you ask him to go bowling and try to be good at it this time?'

'You sound like Esa.'

'You could.'

'Yeah, but he's mad at me, and I was sure mad at him. And before that, I think he was mad at me for a long time, in a way I didn't know about. And now, I think I'm mad enough for both of us.'

'I'm never getting married. I'm going to date only big stars, like Kitt.'

'Kitt's a little old for you.'

'Well, you were a little old for Dad.'

'Right-o!' True says. 'Now let's go to sleep.'

HER CONFESSED AGE aside, the next night, at the theater, when Kitt comes onstage, she does not look a day over twenty-five. The long red fall attached to her hair, and her low-cut and ruched barmaid's dress, have made her the seductive, tender, fun-loving, and forlorn Nancy, mother of urchins, beloved of the satanic Bill.

At the moment Guy makes his entrance, in his silken cockeyed top hat, True glances back and sees Clothilde and Win, waving madly, and Hank, his eyes riveted on their son. True waves, and watches Hank mouthing the words Guy sings beautifully, drawing a roar from strangers. He embodies the Dodger, the brave, lonely little Cockney, her son, tiny on the stage, before strangers, strangers in furs and diamonds. She sees Holly and Addy in the front row, Holly's hands clasped at the sight of her daughter, Amity, who also is a dancer in the play, Fenn wildly applauding his sister. She then sees Holly lean over and kiss Addy on the neck when the big street scene concludes. And she wishes she could clasp hands with her

370

husband, and experience in its fullness the glory of this instant. At the intermission, she finds her way to a bathroom high near the balcony, and hides out in a stall, while beautifully dressed women come and go, one whispering, to True's concealed glee, 'Well, the child with the top hat isn't from the company. I've heard he's a professional. Built like a little fireplug.'

When the performance ends, to four curtain calls, True fights her way through the crowd to kiss Kitt and Beatrice, hug Holly and Franny, and finally, to find Guy in Hank's arms. She runs to Clothilde, who is all business. 'We will find time to have coffee, yes? I have all tomorrow.'

And then Hank hugs her around the shoulders, and congratulates her, and Dog makes a funny attempt to hoist Guy on one shoulder, and True is forced to make polite chat. 'These are . . . Hank's parents, Gus and Clothilde, and this is my mother . . . and my assistant's father, Kellen . . .' Kellen, True notices, is again wearing her father's old tweed sport coat.

There are minutes that feel as though they are not, could not possibly be, the aggregation of sixty seconds. A second is a long time. There are minutes that last up to forty-eight hours; and these are the sort of minutes True passes during the moments her families, lost and found and lost, stand in the foyer of the theater together. Whole hours, and lives, can be encapsulated in such minutes. There is no Scottie Pippen card, but a bundle of twelve yellow roses from *Grand-mère*, and one red one for luck. *You smell like vanilla cookies . . . because you love me.* If he asks her now, she will come; she will lie with him in the bed of the pickup. *The possibilities are endless . . .* She will dash the wall of her pride with an arm as fierce and wide as an ocean-side wave. She reaches out, her hand animated by its own will, and takes Hank's arm. They smile conspiratorially. True draws in a breath, filled with the perfume of minks and flowers.

But he says, 'He's something else.'

And she says, 'He worked so hard. And you worked so hard with him. He owes this to you. To you and Kitt.'

It is as if not Kathleen, nor Gus and Clothilde, but she and Hank are Guy's grandparents, their exaltation over Guy at a remove, a gentle remove.

'Come home to our house. We have cake and punch!' Guy cries.

'Bud, it's a long drive,' Hank says, 'but I promise to come and get you tomorrow, so you and *Grand-père* can have a game of chess.'

'I have a show tomorrow at three,' Guy says, his lip trembling. True sees his effort to get it under control. Damned if he'll ever permit himself to look a sissy before his father.

'But I'll come before, in the morning, when you wake up,' Hank says. 'Now, give me a big fat hug, and sign that little girl's program over there. She's waiting on you.'

Clothilde mouths: 'Tomorrow.'

And Hank's family departs.

True feels desolation like an esophageal ache, a mouthful of hope she cannot swallow.

'Truly, I'm going to hit the road,' Dog says. 'I love you, Sis. Is there, goddamn it, is there anything I can do here? Your business okay and all? The shit's hit the fan all over the place, huh? I was surprised people weren't patted down out there . . .'

'They were,' True says. 'Didn't you see all the National Guard guys? Kids. In uniforms. Like he'll be in ten years.'

'Hope to Christ this isn't still going on in ten years.'

'Hope.'

'True. Jesus, I thought you guys, you and Hank, were doing fine. I'm so sorry, Sis. Why in the hell did you let him adopt Guy if you were going to split up?' Dog is all but wringing his hands. He looks like the outsized basketball lunker he was. 'Why in the hell did you decide to have a kid right away? Do you want me to talk to him? Anything? Whatever?'

Dog has not asked a single question True can answer, nor, so far as she can see, for which there is any answer at all.

'It wasn't as though things deteriorated steadily, honey,' says True. 'One day, something clicked, and I realized I didn't know Hank.'

'If you need to talk . . .'

'You'll be the first one I call.'

Guy pops up, 'Isn't anybody coming for punch and cake?'

'Well, sure, you dope. You're the star. Esa and Granny and Rudy and Keith.'

'I mean, like regular people . . .'

'Everybody has to go home. Unkie and Auntie have to get their Christmas tree tomorrow, and you know, maybe we should get us a Christmas tree early for once . . .'

'You mean, just us. Get the tree?'

'Yeah.'

'You couldn't even drag it. The doctor said you're not supposed to reach for the high shelf even.'

'Rudy'll help me. He's got a great eye for trees.'

'Come on over to Amherst,' Dog urges. 'We'll go to Sandy's and cut down trees, like we used to when we were kids.'

'I would, but he's got shows.'

'Well, you were something else, Gee,' Dog concludes, holding his nephew close and staring at True with beseeching eyes over her son's head. True shrugs.

Guy, after chattering endlessly on the adrenaline-of-his-performance high, suddenly falls asleep just after they cross the Sagamore Bridge. And neither Kathleen nor True has appetite for cake; so Esa and the others sit up talking and eating, and True watches the clouds cross the moon, and the moon reappear, recognizing for the first time that the 'face' on the man in the moon looks like a fetal form, gently curled. She watches until she can no longer distinguish between the moon and the clouds, and then between her sleep and her wakefulness. She does sleep, but she does not rest. Sometime, in the early hours before dawn, she gets up and removes the picture of her and Hank, on their wedding day, from her bedside bookshelf. She does not throw it away, but takes it into the closet and places it tenderly, face down, in the cedar box.

As she is a coward, and fearful that her affection for Clothilde will convince her to make choices from her unruly heart instead of her pragmatic head, True invites Franny to come for coffee, along with her, the following morning. Franny is off, it being a Saturday; but she won't agree until True promises to 'You should pardon the expression, talk turkey to me.'

For what seems like the thousandth time, True gives her spiel: It was doomed. It was unwise, unlucky, unlikely, unfortunate. Franny gets into the passenger seat and helps True buckle. 'There's something missing,' she says then.

'Well, I guess you were right all along. I was too insecure to match him at first. You fantasize about marrying the sexy young guy, then you do, and you feel like Methuselah.'

'But you got over that.'

'I think there'd been too much damage by then. I expected too much, too soon, in every way. He felt trapped.'

'And so Adele was really only the straw that broke the camel's back.'

'Yeah,' True admits. 'She seems so . . . last week, outdated as blue eye-shadow. She's not a factor now. Even though he's living with her.'

'He's what?'

'Yeah, isn't that a pistol? Oh, Franny, I was ready to give it up, take him back if he'd come, and then Adele *moved in* with him. I wasn't going to tell you this. I was too humiliated. She goes home on the weekends to Cambridge; but she's "too lonely" to stay there during the week.'

'Oh, well. That's a hanging offense. Have him hit. I'll pay for half.'

'I'd never hurt him. He and Guy . . . at least Guy and Mister Lucky in here will have a real daddy. It's just going to be an eccentric setup.'

'Well, now I know I would have thrown Steve out on this count, baby or no baby, new marriage or old. But, there's this. When I married Steve, I had options.'

'What, Mikey Nunzio? Teddy Moore?'

'Hey, Mikey took me to the winter formal at Annapolis. When you walk under the cross swords with a guy . . .'

'Bullshit.'

'I still say, the point is, I had options.'

'I have . . . options.'

'You don't have as many options as I . . . as we had, when we were twenty-five.'

'You can't think of it that way.'

'You have to think of it that way,' Franny says, putting her hand on True's arm, so she can't shift the car into reverse and back out. 'At our age, we have options that include . . . well, Evan, and the funeral director, and the guy who works for TerminCo who's doing the research on cockroaches . . .'

'The one in the *Herald*. Who's studying whether the males put their feelers up or down when they're sexually stimulated. The one who said he was looking for his mate, too. Oh, Jesus, Franny.'

'Yeah, imagine getting your feelers up with him. These are our generations, True. The unmarried men of our generations. Men who want to retire at fifty and take slow walks in matching windbreakers and put their feet on the coffee table and watch auto racing on TV . . .'

'Or play golf. Twice a week.'

'Or *watch* golf on TV. On Sundays.'

'That might be the final insult.'

'With soft little bellies. And Sansabelt pants. And persistent hair growth on their shoulders.'

'Franny, this isn't necessary. And it's making my skin crawl.'

'Or clippers for their nose hairs.'

'Evan didn't have nose hairs.'

'How do you know?'

'Of course there are women.'

'Oh, that would make a nice change for Guy. From Mister Macho to Mistress Lumberjack.'

'When I was dating all the bad men in America, I considered a woman. It was not an unattractive idea. No fighting over which movie to go to, double your wardrobe . . .'

'What stopped you?'

'I'm not gay, for one thing . . . and you would have to pitch as well as catch . . .'

'Yes.'

'But, and this is the hard part, the bad thing about men is also the good thing about men. They're not always talking. Even if you might want them to talk more when you want them to, they aren't talking all the time. There are times when even I don't want to talk things over. If you were with another woman, she would sense what was bothering you and want to talk about it and you'd want to talk about it and . . .'

'Go on . . .'

'That's what Hank says,' True admits.

'Which brings us back to Hank. True, he has flaws, maybe lots, and maybe you have things to work out. But you love him. And he's Guy's father. You said it. He's Guy's *father*. He's *this* baby's *father*. You got Guy to accept him, and you're having his child, and now you're letting him go. And fifteen minutes after you got him.'

'*Got* him?'

'Not as in entrapment. As in manna from heaven. I mean, it's like you don't realize the significance of the fact that you're pregnant!'

'Cut it out, Franny!' True glances down in feigned horror. 'Oh, my God, you're right! I *am* pregnant! What am I gonna do?'

'True, don't horse around at a time like this. Tell him come home, all is forgiven. Or at least, all can be forgiven if you two work hard at it.'

'Oh, go on. I'm tired of this, Hank being a great boon to poor True in the last gas station before the desert. Hank did his fair share of . . . dumb things. I don't mean like beating me. But real things, that can't be fixed. Not without real work, which he wouldn't be willing to do. All that . . . *talking*, Franny. Just what you mentioned. Sometimes you have to. Hank hates the talking part. He's a dumb kid. He's a nice, cute, smart, talented . . . dumb kid.'

'He is not. He's a smart . . . kid. And he is a good person. He's a hard worker. He's honest. And I've known you twenty-two years, and I know how you looked when you met him . . .'

'That was lust. Lust makes you inspired. You can't tell yourself from the other person. You want to crawl into him.'

'That is also love.'

'Franny, he wants to be free. He's said it in a thousand ways. He was always ambivalent. If he wasn't ambivalent, where are the Hallmark cards? The late-night calls? Drunken e-mails?'

'None?'

'No. Franny, none. That, at least, I expected. When I didn't get them, I knew. And we're going to be late. My soon-to-be-ex-mother-in-law is going to think I stood her up.'

'Think this over at length, True.'

'I'm trying to. And trying not to. I cry so much I'm dehydrated.'

'Plus, you are an excellent bitch.'

'You're a bitch, too.'

'But I wasn't a bitch when I was first married.'

'Well, I wasn't a bitch either when I was first married, to Peter. I never turned a word in his mouth. Now, I'm a grown woman. I have opinions. I have . . .'

'Rage. Half a lifetime's worth. Which you turn on him. You dared him to . . . do . . . something awful.'

'Okay, I did. But he should have known that people do that . . . they dare people to prove how much they love them.'

'You demanded proofs.'

'People do that,' True sighs. 'Most people. Insecure people. Stupid people, which *is* most people.'

'Honey, I didn't mean it that way.'

'I can take it, Franny. I'm in the gifted class for eating crow now. I'd do that if he'd give a sign. Whatever I did wrong early on, I've taken it back four hundred times. And didn't you snap out on Steve, at first? Don't you still?'

'Sure, I do. But we've been married twenty years. And Steve's used to me. And I'm never as bad as you. Listen to me.' True jerks her hand away and starts the car. 'You *are*. You know how to sharpen the arrow and dip it in curare. You do. But hello. He's no match for that venom. You're mad at him because other women look at him, which you should be proud of . . .'

'No, I'm not! I was, but now I'm mad at him for being an utter fool. Why is it all about I should be proud of Hank? He should be proud of *me!*'

'Isn't he? He acts like he is. We all see that! Do you have to blind yourself to that? Would that be the Kathleen gene telling you not to make so much of yourself?'

'No, for corn's sake, Franny, if he'd just admit himself wrong, and willing, I'd be all over it. I want an admission that he was wrong! Is that so wrong?'

'You know, it isn't. That's the least you deserve.'

They have pulled up in front of Expresso Yourself, and can see Clothilde, inside, her silver hair drawn back in a knot, her silver-ovaled fingers crossed before her on the table, as she gazes down into her cup of tea. She looks up and holds out her arms as True enters.

'You remember Franny,' True says. 'My friend.'

Clothilde says, 'What a pleasure to see you,' but she does not look as though she is pleased. She looks discomfited. 'True,' she says softly. '*Est-ce que okay discuter de quelque chose avec . . . ?*'

'*Oui*,' Franny answers, '*True est ma bonne amie. Ma meilleure amie*. And French was my minor.'

'I'm sorry to have forgotten my manners,' Clothilde says. 'It's unforgiveable. *Cela ne sa dit pas*. I am sorry, Franny. But these are such . . .' she places her hand against her breast ' . . . hurtful matters.'

'Were you nervous, flying?' Franny asks companionably. 'My

husband and I are going to San Diego in January for a family reunion, and I'm just not confident that I'll feel up to it.'

'Oddly,' Clothilde begins, her slow, musical voice making every commonplace sound formal, theatrical, 'not. I have never been a confident flier, and when the children were small, and my husband went to South America, I would be distraught until he was home safely. But now, I think it feels like a slap in the face to those dogs. Like an act of defiance. Like True,' she smiles widely at her daughter-in-law. 'A baby! Just like Maman said!'

'And probably that very night, if not before.'

'Is French your first language?' Franny asks Clothilde then.

'*Mais* no!' says Clothilde. 'I'm not fluent. I have simply lived around Hank ... I mean around Gus, for so many years, and for so many years his mother has lived in our house.'

'Does that work out?' Franny asks.

'You'd have to meet Winston,' True smiles.

'Well, it always works out. There isn't any choice,' Clothilde shrugs. 'In ... where we come from, only a dog would put a parent in a nursing home.'

'Guy threatened me with that a couple of months ago,' True says, almost laughing. 'I can't imagine where he ever even heard about it.'

'He's angry with you,' Clothilde says seriously. 'He does want his dad back. And he does not understand why you won't talk to Hank or answer his letters.' True feels fury crackle and lick.

'Well, Ma, that was a thing Guy said before Hank and I were married. And there have been no letters, and no phone calls, except the most polite ones over Guy's visits. And Guy's a child, and doesn't understand all the elements of adult emotional tangles. And I don't want him to. If he did,' she adds, her voice crisp, 'he might be more angry at Hank than at me. Hank is living with Adele; did you know that?'

'*No!*' Clothilde cries. 'That is impossible.'

'Yes, and he says they are only friends, but as you can imagine, this is intolerable ...'

'Of course ...'

'And whether or not it is friendship or protectiveness from him, it is love from her, and if it were not, why is he not exhibiting the same protectiveness toward his own wife and baby and son?'

'I did not know this! Hank said nothing.'

'He's ashamed,' True says, 'and rightly so.'

'On the other hand, he has tried so hard to make it up to you,' Clothilde begins.

'He has not, not at all,' True says. 'Perhaps he thinks he has.'

'I suppose so,' Clothilde says. 'Yes, he would.' Damn the woman, thinks True, she *would* understand.

'I imagined Hank had told you everything,' True then says.

'We thought he had,' Clothilde says.

'And I'm sure he's as upset as I am.'

'He is, but he says he does not want to come back. He does not think love should be forced,' Clothilde says sadly.

True feels a spurt of nausea, but she answers, 'I think he's right.' Usually, she cannot picture Hank's face complete for more than a fraction of an instant, but now she sees him plain, in his blue chambray shirt that winter night at the bar. As detailed and lingering as a portrait in oils. *It feels good to win.* There is a perimeter of comfort around her misery in knowing that someday she may well hate Hank, or at least feel the indifference she feels when she thinks of Evan, indifference rimmed with a slight irritation, as if even Evan's memory is a waste of disk space.

Franny speaks up, 'I don't think he's right or you're right. Missus Bannister.'

'Clothilde.'

'Clothilde, you didn't see them at the beginning, as we did. That was not a love that was forced.'

'I forced Guy on him,' True admits.

'You did not. He loves Guy very much. And True, we want you to know that, whatever should happen, we want Guy to remain a part of our family, and, if it can happen, you, too. And definitely this *cher* enfant. We want this not to be *adieu,* but au revoir.'

'I want that, too, for Guy, and for this small angel,' True says, as kindly as she can. 'I want this baby to know her Bannister people.' She sees the genuine bewilderment in her mother-in-law's face, and wishes it were permissible to lay her head in Clothilde's lap. But knowing, also, that sides have been chosen, as they must inevitably be, and that Hank is Clothilde's boy, just as Guy is hers, she would say nothing differently, do nothing differently.

'I must get back,' says Clothilde, 'and return to you your son.

He is full of tales of buried treasure, guarded by phantom black panthers, and he swears he and Gus will find this pirate treasure. Our flight is at five. Will you let him come to us, sometime, True?'

'Of course.'

'He is so talented and . . . so dear.'

'Yes, he is.'

'And I think to lose two fathers . . .'

'Please, Clothilde, please, Ma, don't make me feel worse about that than I do.'

'Of course. I so hoped that my son . . .' Clothilde says. 'Perhaps he should come back to where he was born, because . . . but it would be so difficult for him to see Guy then, and the baby will be small for a long while.'

'Is everyone just giving up?' Franny asks desperately. 'Where's Harold Pinter?'

'We are all such vulnerable spirits,' Clothilde says, gathering up her shawl. 'It is so cold up here, True.'

'We say it helps you keep well.'

'Good-bye, True, *chère, ma belle. Toujours.*'

They hold each other for a long moment, and then Clothilde, after shaking Franny's hand, slowly leaves, bending her head to the wind.

DECEMBER

ROCK AND ROLL, LITTLE SNOWBALL!

A sparkly soft-sculpture snowball zips open to reveal a host
of seasonal surprises: a deer with a rack of soft felt antlers,
a snow family of Mama, Papa and child, and an evergreen
tree with a raccoon peeping out. There's a hat with racing
deer and evergreens, even a saucy tree-shaped tassel on top.
And tucked deep inside are scarves of cuddly fleece, one
sized for baby and one for Mama, to complete the celebra-
tion.

THE FIRST WEEKS of December are crowded with things True has not
felt the urge nor energy to accomplish until there is almost no time
left to do them.

She compels herself to do them now. She is running out of time.
At her last checkup, the obstetrician had expressed some concern
about True's blood pressure. 'You want to take it easy,' she'd said.
'We don't want to be looking at kidney problems.' Indeed, some
protein had turned up in her urine sample. 'The only cure for pre-
eclampsia is to end the pregnancy, you know. That is, deliver the
baby early, for the baby's health and yours. And we don't want that.
Not yet.' She writes on a prescription slip, 'BED REST OR HOSPITAL,'
and smiles. 'Tack this up on your corkboard at your office at the
same time you get someone to put a cot in there so you can lie down
for a couple of hours every day. Just so you don't forget to take
five. That's hard at this time of year.'

Feeling virtuous and wronged, True asks Esa to ship the presents
she has purchased for Hank's family. She has shopped extravagantly,
compensatorily, for Guy, getting him the radio-controlled glider he

has longed for, a leather bomber jacket like Hank's, and a weird sort of rocking chair and unicycle combined, which can pedal its operator backward, forward, and upside-down. She ships a rabbit-skin hat with flaps to Kellen Merton, and takes pleasure in thinking of him wearing it as he tends to his green heifers and checks his trees on frigid mornings. For each of her staff members, she has asked a local silversmith to create charms of the Twelve Times Blessed logo, a box from which stars and teddy bears spring, encircled by the words of the company name. For the women it is a charm pendant, to be worn as a necklace or an anklet; for the men, a lapel pin. She has also given each one a sample box of the prototype of First Year Away, though the business itself will not go up until the following May, in time for graduations and August departures: True has worked hard on planning it, thinking as she selects each item, would Hank have liked this? Would he have chosen this? It is a small, pounded-tin locker, suitable for storing books or CDs, with a clasp lock. Each box contains a pair of luxurious handknit socks, so soft True wanted to bathe in the shipment box; a jar of soothing chest rub (far superior to Vicks); a packet of teas; half a dozen hermetically wrapped oatmeal-raisin cookies the size of True's hand; and oddly but fittingly, the CD of lullabies that always goes into the first Blessings box.

They are soothing, the familiar melodies disguised by clever arrangements and orchestrations. On her first night at college, feeling odd and restless, fully five miles from her mother's house, but frightened by the exuberance and sophistication of the other girls, she'd longed to be again a child in the house of imitation Delft lamps, with its kitchen that smelled of ironing spray and creamed corn. She would have liked to fall asleep in her narrow iron bed to a lullaby CD, even as her dorm mates planned a raid on the Teke house for the following evening.

Only providence and reclusiveness had led her, on her third night, to happen on Franny in the study lounge, her head buried deep in Tolstoy. 'I'm a scholarship student from Montpelier, Illinois,' Franny announced. 'And I'm bored by bullshit Sally, bullshit Tracey, and bullshit Linda.' True could have wept from relief. She still more or less feels the same way. On impulse, she has a medallion and prototype made for Franny, who has promised to be her labor coach, since Isabelle thinks she might pass out, and it does not seem proper to True for her and Hank to share this event alone together.

For these few, she has had the logo pins and charms crafted in gold, and added a ruby to the medallion for Rudy, and a diamond for Esa, Franny, and Kathleen, making the little symbol a real piece of jewelry. For her mother, she also buys a long, reversible coat, blue as a sapphire, cashmere on one side and a lovely, crinkly waterproof stuff on the other.

At the last minute, she has a pin made for Hank, too, and wraps it with the prototype. She hopes it will not offend him or make him think she considers him an employee, nor seem too personal from an ex-spouse. She worked at the note to enclose. It first read, 'This demo is yours more than mine. I hope you like it. Let's talk about what you will realize from this if it works.' She first signed it 'Love, from True,' then tore that up; then wrote 'All best, True,' then tore that up; then wrote 'Hope and joy, from True.' She stumped over to the Packin'Mall herself, on her increasingly elephantine legs, and mailed this package, leery of the comments anyone might make, under the circumstances.

'Looks like someone's going to have a special present under the tree,' the woman behind the counter teases, putting out her hand to touch True's belly. Obligingly, like a trained dolphin, the baby rolls.

'Not for a couple of months yet. This is a Saint Paddy's baby. Well, maybe sooner than that. A four-leaf clover. My older son was born on Saint Patrick's Day, too.'

'Gosh,' the woman says. 'Wouldn't that be something? I have four. And you're big and carrying low for six months.'

'Six and a bit,' True tells her. 'Happy holidays.'

'Happy holidays. To both of you.'

At an impromptu little ceremony, with champagne and petit fours, True gives her office staff their gifts. Vivien and the packers love the prototypes; and Harris, a retired policeman newly hired into the office, who always wears a sports jacket to work, puts his lapel pin on right away.

'Beats the light-up Christmas tree the missus got me,' he grins.

'All this,' Rudy announces, upon receiving his, 'feels like a conspiracy to make me cave in to being an adult. This pin seems to presuppose that someday I'll have lapels. Little X in there makes me feel the same way. Pretty soon, we're going to be having a dress code and funky Fridays and stuff. What happened to the old office we used to have, Truly Fair? Where everything was a mess and we were all on the verge of breakdowns all the time? I liked that.'

'We cleaned it up, Rude,' she says. 'We have to be on our toes. It's hard times. And I have to be a good girl. I have to be an extra good girl, because I'm a pregnant, old, practically single lady.'

'Well at least the war means we won't be moving to San Diego,' Rudy pouts. 'Keith doesn't want to be anywhere nearer a coast. I have pointed out that we currently *do* live on a seashore. But he thinks an alien seashore would be even more threatening.'

'That's the best present you could have given me. I can't say I'm sad, Rudolfo,' True comforts him. 'I want you here. Especially now. It's going to be difficult for me.'

'I know, and I'm glad I'll be here, too. Plus, True, there are plenty of people who don't have any jobs at all, and I'm lucky to have mine, which I happen to love. And, of course, Truly Fair, I never did want to leave *you*, personally. With Keith's income, we're doing fine, and it's enough to make you crazy, the collision of the guilt and the gratitude.'

'It is. Imagine how I feel. So happy about this inside me, so sad about everything outside me.'

'It's hard times all around.'

'You can say that again.'

'It's hard times all around.'

True smiles.

'Are you over him?'

'No. I'm not even divorced from him.'

'You swore to me in this very room that you or any woman could recover from a dump by a guy in twenty-one days. You and Esa. You called it the twenty-one-day plan. White wine, Joni Mitchell's "Blue" albums . . .'

'I'm hardly in shape for a wine-guzzling binge. And I can't stop long enough to listen to a whole record, or my feet swell up. That seems so long ago. But I did say that, didn't I? I don't know, Rudy. Maybe he's the love of my life. Or maybe I'm just so senile I don't remember the others.'

'Well, Keith is the great love of my life, and we've been together six years, but I still think I could recover if he dumped me.'

'He didn't dump me. I dumped him. We dumped each other. Or maybe I just wanted to get there first . . .'

'I know the feeling.'

'And I'm . . . recovering. Don't count me out. Look around you. I'm taking care of business, and working overtime . . . And I've been very good about displaying my rotund self about town. I don't seem embarrassed, do I?'

'No, and that's great. But are you, really?'

'Really, I feel like I have a big, fat, red "A" on my chest. As though I've done something wrong that I haven't.'

'Eeek, that's lousy. You do a good imitation of normal, though. As if you have out-of-wedlock kids every day.'

'Well, that's definitely the impression I'm trying to give. I'm glad it's working.'

'Is this how . . . you're always going to be, True?' Rudy asks then.

'Fat?'

'No. Quiet and nice? I hate you like this.'

'Oh, I imagine I'll get up to my old tricks someday.'

'Remember when you threw the printer out the window?'

'Yeah.'

'Remember when you told the baby-sled maker to shove the runners up his ass?'

'Yeah.'

'I love you, but I can't stand being around you. You're so much more . . . peaceful and gentle than you ever were. But you're about as fun as altar guild meetings at my mother's.'

'I'm sorry. Must be hormonal.' True stops. 'No, to tell you the truth, Rude, what I want to do is scream and tear my hair some nights. But I can't, so I don't. I think of him ten hours a day. I lose my glasses, and my car keys. I stand in the middle of the room, and I forget why I'm there.'

'Not going left, not going right.' Trust Rudy to find a way to work in Stephen Sondheim.

'That's it. Was he just being kind? Or am I losing my mind?'

'If I weren't gay, True, I'd marry you. We'd have a Baby Adam, and . . . and maybe a Baby Ruth.'

'You know, Esa once told me she'd marry me if she *were* gay. It was when we were stuck in the snowbank. The night I met Hank. If it weren't for that darned gender preference, I'd be the most sought-after bride in town.'

'Well, I meant it, Truly Fair.'

'I know you did. And I take it as a compliment. Rudy, you're one of the most decent people I've ever known. You're wicked handsome. And you would, you will, make a great dad.'

'Keith says I'd make a great mom,' Rudy says ruefully.

'That's a compliment. What a great dad is, Rudy, is a great mom with a penis.' Rudy laughs, and True thinks of Hank kissing Guy on the cheek outside the trailer where the old horse trainer kept his string of Mardi Gras lights.

'I'm sorry we can't come to the New York performance, True.'

'It's okay Rudy. We're going to drive, and stay in a hotel. Guy wants room service and Nintendo.'

'It's just that . . . Keith thinks Radio City could be the next target.'

'Yes, I'm sure the Rockettes have always been an offense to fundamentalist Muslims.'

'That's better, True. You sounded like you for a moment.'

'That's good. I'm glad.'

'Well, now you don't anymore.'

'Rudy,' True says, 'I'm doing my best.'

KATHLEEN IS SORTING the mail one morning while True, lying on her cot, apologizes to a customer whose November Blessing arrived late, promising to include a special quilt as a bonus in the next package to make up for the lapse. As she puts down the phone, True spots an envelope with familiar handwriting. She watches as Kathleen slits the top and sets it aside. She gets up.

'Give me that one, Mom,' True says. Kathleen gives her daughter a measuring look, and hands her the envelope.

It is a letter from Hank, or rather a card.

'Dear True,' it reads. 'It's obvious, from all you've said and done, and what you haven't said or done, that you think we're on two tracks that are never going to reconnect. Okay. I won't beat a dead horse. I've said my piece over and over. You don't accept it. But don't even think that you're going to keep me out of my children's lives. Wild horses won't drag me away from Guy and the baby. So, whatever you have planned, don't plan on that.' It is signed, 'As ever, Hank.'

Finally, the other shoe has dropped.

'What did he say?' Kathleen asks, looking down at the pile of mail.

'He said he loves me above anything in the world and he regrets every harsh word he ever said to me and he wants desperately for me to reconsider,' True answers.

'Oh?' Kathleen looks up. 'And you believe him?'

'He said nothing, Mom. Nothing at all,' True confesses.

'That's what I thought. You're better off, True.'

'So it would seem,' True muses. She strokes Hank's signature once, then rips the card in half, then in fourths, and throws it into the shredder bin.

THE NEXT SATURDAY, when Hank comes for Guy, True coolly tells him she would prefer Guy didn't go out with Hank until after the run of the play was over.

'He's been looking peaked,' Hank says, reluctantly agreeing.

'Well, he's tired out. It's a demanding part, and . . . however you feel, I know what's happening with us is responsible for some of how he feels.'

'That has to be right. But True, I've been wanting to ask you, would it be possible for him to come with me to my folks' house – not for Christmas, I don't mean that, but for the week between Christmas and New Year's? New Year's is really fun in Louisiana. They have fireworks, and all, and a parade.'

'I'll think about it,' True tells him. 'It's kind of close to . . . you know what . . .'

'Two months! Or more!'

'Well, right. But there was a kind of prior plan for him to go to his other grandparents in Montana that week. I don't know that I'd be okay with him flying anywhere alone right now.'

'Oh, I'd be with him. I'd pay for it.'

'I thought you went home for Christmas.'

'No, I'm going to hang out here, try to keep the place open, and I have . . . well, some friends asked me over for Christmas Day.'

'Good,' True says. 'Tom? Adele?'

'No, just some friends. Up north.'

'I see.'

He leaves, and True thinks, I said nothing of what I have wanted to say. I said nothing. I could have said, look, you're not doing so great, and I'm fairly miserable, and we were doing fine until the Adele thing, so why don't we talk about that, and Guy's terribly worried, and maybe we're giving up too soon, and there's this baby like the white elephant attached to my middle that neither of us talks about? Why, she thought, do people leave titanic matters unspoken, and allow the glue to dry out until their lives fall apart? She has seen this happen in hundreds of movies; it must be the human condition. But is it hers, particularly? Is she programmed to hold back, always hold back, except with Guy, some nugget of emotion, some unconfided truth? Never before, not until these last days, not even with Esa, not with Franny, has she allowed herself to speak unleashed – she has, in fact, drawn a line around herself even those nearest to her know better than to cross.

As she looks up the number for Guy's pediatrician, True thinks of her mother's saintly parsimony after their father's death, of how she seemed to count each pea she doled onto her and Dog's plates, how she'd discouraged, with a slight shake of her head, second helpings of anything. No wonder True, once free, had reveled in food to the point of gagging, downing pints of ice cream, bags of greasy chips in her dorm. Were all widows this way? She had not been. At her lowest ebb, she had never made Guy feel as though he were a burden, extraneous, or had she? No. She and Dog have called themselves first generation, first-generation sane.

Why had her mother not held her, taken her and Dog into bed with her at night when they both heard her sobbing through the thin walls of the house in Amherst? Why hadn't they felt permission to run and comfort her? Kathleen had admitted of no comfort.

True thinks, now I admit of no comfort. I assure everyone that I'm just fine, doing better each day. I go through my routines calmly and precisely. I go to my Lamaze class unselfconsciously with Franny. I tell everyone who isn't my closest friend that I don't mind. And why am I consoled by their believing such an outright lie?

True calls the doctor, tells the nurse about Guy's weariness, and makes an appointment with the pediatrician, who prescribes some iron pills and a mild antibiotic for what looks like a developing ear infection, but confesses she remains puzzled. She asks about stress at home. Forcing herself, True admits to it. The doctor says stress could be a factor, but that if Guy hasn't perked up significantly by the weekend, she'd like a blood count. 'Go ahead and do it now,' True insists.

'No,' Guy says firmly. 'I'm not getting stuck until I have to. I'll get better.'

Still, Guy complains nightly of stomach pains and exhaustion. True reasons that with school, and the play now running at CFT every night, he is overtaxed. She confers with the principal, and, several times each week, allows Guy to sleep late, then make up the homework for classes he has missed.

Tonight is Monday, and That One Place, like almost all the restaurants in town except the chains, is blacked out, some for the rest of the winter.

But tonight is the town bonfire, an ancient and peculiar tradition the origin of which no one seems to quite know. Everyone gathers on Hatter Beach, and, in a rock ring that has been in place as long as True can remember, piles driftwood, firewood, unpainted chairs, a stack of combustibles twenty feet high. Every year, some stalwart citizen suggests calling off the whole business in the name of safety or pollution, but it somehow perseveres. The chief of the fire department does the honors, and everyone brings potatoes to blacken in the fire, which they later eat with the salt and vinegar shakers provided by the ladies from Saint Thomas More. For some reason, children seem to love this ritual, the beginning of the Christmas season, and Guy, though he looks nearly wizened to True, blue smudges under his eyes, begs to go with her for at least a short while. 'I don't want to stay for the choir singing and stuff, Mommy,' he says. 'It would just be weird to miss the bonfire.'

So, at six P.M., she and Esa bundle Guy and themselves up and set out for the beach, blankets in the back seat of the car. As they drive, the first tentative dry snowflakes begin to melt on the windshield. Guy is charmed. 'Maybe we'll have real snow for Christmas, Mom,' he says. 'Real snow, not like a little in the ditches.'

'We did last year,' Isabelle says. 'Remember? We thought it was going to snow forever.'

At the beach, the three of them gather on their blankets. Isabelle is glowing with excitement. In just days, Douglas will be home, and they will have their first Christmas together in their new little home. True tries not to extrapolate. She will go from the thought of Douglas and Isabelle's reunion to imagining how she and Hank might even now be planning their own first Christmas, as well as a perky nursery for Brewster or Chloe, Gwynevere or Emory. True has done nothing for the baby, partly out of fear or superstition, except to buy a Moses basket to keep beside her in her own wide bed. She has to keep her thoughts narrow and her eyes straight forward, or she will collapse into self-pity. Somehow, it seems that the hovering depression might leak into the baby's personality, rendering her joyless, scrawny of feeling.

There are probably two hundred or more people around the fire ring at Hatter Beach. Once the first plume of flame rockets up, with its shower of cinders and shadows, True spots Hank, with a man and a woman, standing across from them. She knows he does not see her; but she can see that his hands are shoved in his pockets, and his layers of sweatshirt hoods are shoved back from his head; he is laughing at something the man has said. The woman is not Adele.

This is why she cannot ask Hank to reconsider, because of her fear that he will tell her he is doing well, coping, healing. That he is actually, now that he recognizes it, happier. What will she do if he says this? Crumble? Throw over her manifest blessings after the one lost? She is taking no chances. The recompense for conditional love is damage control.

Watching Hank, she sees him for the first time with an objective eye. She has never understood movie-star divorces; the beauty and excitement alone would, she has always believed, compensate for any failing short of infidelity or battery. But now, she knows she can see Hank not as entirely beautiful or beatific. She can see him as a man whose nature only appears to be easygoing, because he enlists in events only if they have a great chance of making him look good.

True looks at her very own Hank and feels . . . nothing.

She is passing a dangerous landmark. Shortly after this thought crosses her mind, Hank, fittingly, gets lost in the crowd.

After the bonfire, Guy throws up his burned potato, which does not distress True, since she thinks blackened tubers drenched in vinegar would unsettle anyone's stomach.

When he gets up in the night again, vomiting, she takes his temperature. A hundred and three. Her mother has always taught her, and this wisely, that a fever is nature doing its work, and that to treat a fever of less than one hundred and two in a child is defeating the intended biological strategy. But Guy looks funny. She takes his temperature again, and it is still a hundred and three. His skin is clammy, the color of turned buttermilk. She gives him Tylenol, tries not to be a big sissy, and waits, lying beside him in his bed, as his fever breaks and he dissolves in sweat, soaking the sheets. It does not seem right, but wouldn't the pediatrician, who has known Guy since circumcision, know? She'd called it a bug. No more. Exhaustion.

Still, by morning, he seems again well, if wan, and True figures he's passed a bug through his system. 'My belly is so sore, Mom,' Guy tells True. 'When I talked to Dad, he thought I pulled a groin muscle dancing. I might have a hernia.'

True has not thought of this. With Guy's performance bag, his music, and jazz shoes shoved in the back seat, she drives him to the urgent-care clinic in Harwich, where the doctor says he can see Hank's point of view. 'The pain he's indicating is on the wrong side for an appendix,' the young man explains. 'It could be a hernia, but he's not in enough pain for that, or that's what I'd suspect from the kinds of things he's doing. I think you're right; it's a bug. Force lots of fluids into him and get him rested up.' But Guy needs to caper all over the CFT stage that night as the Artful Dodger.

Yet, after the performance, Kitt approaches True.

'What's the deal with our fella here?'

'He's just worn out, I think. Maybe a little anemic. I haven't been watching out for his vitamins and diet the way I should be.'

'You know, from having two kids, it's just . . . he has sick eyes.'

'I know what you mean.'

At two A.M., Guy wakes again, dry-heaving. True comforts him with cold cloths and ginger ale, which he also vomits. He lies in her bed, Gypsy thoughtfully laving his face with his rough tongue. 'I'm going to call you in tonight,' True tells Guy.

'Fine,' Guy says.

'Let your understudy have a chance.'

'Fine,' he repeats.

This, more than anything physical about Guy's languor, ratchets up True's foreboding. Guy is not the kind of person who, having worked for and won his part, would surrender a second of his reward, his applause, the braided little girls in red-velvet scalloped dresses who ask him to sign their programs as if he were a real actor. Less than a week remains before they take the show to New York, and Guy has been working hard on polishing every comic piece of footwork and business in his performance, his dad having told him that real agents sometimes come to performances such as the one CFT is giving. If he were not past caring, Guy would haul himself up from the bed, as he has so many times, and in an hour would transform himself into a gamboling, grimacing little Cockney.

She calls him in. Beatrice and Laura diagnose exhaustion and a stern case of nerves over the upcoming New York date, coupled with the anxiety all the children are feeling since September. They are all in a hall of mirrors.

ON THE NIGHT of December 17, the last night the show will go up in the theater in Chatham, Beatrice hosts a preperformance benefit gala, intended to seduce donors. True dreads it, but must attend. Though he has still had periodic bouts of nausea, Guy insists he is well enough to perform. The previous night, he had slept fourteen hours.

She literally pays Rudy, lapels and all, to squire her among the donors whose checks will make next year's shows and sets a reality. True wears black velvet pants, suitably balloony, and the satin shirt in which she was married, over a generous vintage camisole Isabelle found somewhere, as she can button only two of the buttons.

Elizabeth Chilmark and her husband are among the guests, as are the moneyed many of the year-rounders.

'You look well, True,' Elizabeth says, when they meet at the bar. 'You look remarkably fit and content.'

'Well, I have few alternatives, Elizabeth,' True replies.

Elizabeth smiles fleetingly. 'Well said,' she agrees.

'You look well, also, Elizabeth; you're thinner, but it suits you,' True says. Elizabeth has always been slender, but now she is concave.

'I've been taking advantage of my new leisure to walk more,' Elizabeth says. 'I'm absolutely sure that is a contributing factor. I like ... the winter air. I like it very much. I spend ... too much time inside, of late.' They have briefly and perfunctorily made their transaction – True regretful but thankful, Elizabeth cheerful but resolute. She has said to expect a memo about new ideas for Twelve Times Blessed. True reckons that these suggestions will be good ones, and must stifle her resentment.

At the silent auction hall off the main room where the gala is being held, True and Rudy glide among the pricey, spicy items, a certificate for a Blessings package among them, True turning sideways to make her way down the aisles. She bids on a lovely yellow blanket bordered with the old quote about 'All things wise and wonderful; all creatures great and small.' Rudy bids fiercely on a mountain bike, but is continuously outbidden by the carefree upbidding of the square-headed son of a local fish baron, who probably spends the cost of such a bike each month on beer. True impulsively buys an opal necklace, because the gold rope that surrounds the molten, fiery-green stone reminds her of the design of her wedding ring. Just as the bidding closes, she marches back to the table and, with a stroke of her pencil, vanquishes the squire's son, winning the mountain bike for Rudy.

'You didn't have to do that,' he says, embarrassed.

'I didn't want him to have it, but now you have to promise to bike to work, and get all buffed,' True says, 'and you have to pay me back what you bid before I made up the rest. The rest is a gift.'

'Yes, Mom,' Rudy agrees. 'That's my True. The ever prudent.'

'Look what you get from imprudence,' True admonishes him, and lays her head on his shoulder.

Beatrice approaches True just before the performance, pulling her aside.

'Darling,' she says. 'You must know how miserable we all are about your . . . your trouble with dear Hank. As happy as we are about . . . your . . . condition. And if anything that happened here had anything to do with that, oh True, of course I mean the former, not the latter . . . I am sorry from the bottom of my heart.'

'It wouldn't have changed a thing,' True says, throwing her arms around Beatrice's tiny waist, as Beatrice struggles to encircle a portion of True's girth. 'You are a marvel, and you have given Guy the very thing he needed to sustain him.' When she pulls back, she sees tears in Beatrice's eyes.

'I know Guy hasn't felt well, but we all think it's the . . . strain,' she says.

'Oh, Beatrice, that makes me feel so . . . terrible,' True says, and begins to cry in earnest. Fortunately, everyone in the crowd is from Chatham or Harwich, and would never dream of having the bad manners to notice, so True retreats to the ladies' room until the house lights blink twice.

Franny, Steve, and Angelique sit next to Rudy and True. 'You can smell the money in here,' Franny says, sotto voce, as the lights blink out, 'the diamonds are brighter than the footlights.'

'Can I feel the baby?' Angelique asks, with touching girlishness. True places her hand on the place she has determined most likely for action, and Angelique is rewarded with the cunning shudder of hiccups.

'You mean it has hiccups just like we do?' Angelique asks, hushed.

'It does,' True replies, taking Angelique's hand, its nails green-enameled, with red-star decals, and covering it with her own.

'I want us to have a baby, now,' Angelique tells Franny.

'Wait three years, move out, and have one yourself,' Franny suggests pleasantly.

'No, I mean you and Dad.'

'They don't just hiccup, they also throw tantrums and go to college,' Franny informs her.

'We'll see,' Steve smiles, nuzzling Franny's neck so sweetly True must turn away.

And then the overture begins.

To True's amazement, people stand to applaud when Guy finishes singing 'Consider Yourself,' and True is so flushed with pride she has to cover her face with her hands. He has never looked stronger, nor more starved and desperate and mischievous. He has never sung with more gusto. She hates it, but she also has to pee. Lumbering past Franny, she ponderously makes her way up the grade of the aisle. When she returns, she decides to stand until after the big barroom number, when Guy must kneel and roll Oliver over and over his back, because then, there will be an intermission. She can see better if she stands, as well. She slips through the darkness to stand behind the rail of the main-floor tier.

Over and over rolls little Oliver, whence Guy is supposed to spring up and quick-step around him to take Nancy's hand, after which the two of them do their little do-si-do.

But Guy does not get up.

True takes a step forward, her hands gripping the rail, her belly bumping the cold gold. It is as they say. She is as frozen as if she were dreaming.

Guy remains at first crouched on all fours, then lowers himself, splayed, prone, onto the stage; he reaches up for Kitt, and in horror, she rushes out to the rim of the theater's thrust stage.

'This is not part of our performance,' she shouts. 'We need a doctor. Is there a doctor in the house?'

There are twenty.

People crowd the aisle as True tries to shoulder them aside, running as best she can for the stage.

By the time she gets there, True glimpses his understudy, lip trembling, pick up Guy's hat and tumble it onto his own head. The music begins, uncertainly, then stops. Beatrice glides out onto the stage, wringing her hands, and announces a ten-minute intermission, as True runs down the stairs, through the labyrinth of backstage hallways, and finally reaches the back alley just as Ellery hands her son into the arms of a paramedic. The ambulance is already open, and two other medics are opening a stretcher, as if it were a folding chair.

IN THE EMERGENCY room, the surgeon, who introduces himself as Peter Oudenhoven, has handed off his tuxedo jacket to a nurse and donned a white, short-sleeved smock and cap. True kneels on the cold ER floor, at Guy's head, stroking his hair, pulling up the blankets an intern has thrown over her shivering son. 'Let me feel around here a bit,' Doctor Oudenhoven suggests. 'Hope my hands aren't too cold. In fact, let me run them under some warm water. That was quite a show-stopper . . . Gil?'

'Guy,' True tells him. 'I know you. You're Joy Hook's husband, aren't you?' She feels a sting of embarrassment, remembering the first fight she and Hank had ever had, at Joy's coffee shop. 'It's such a small place . . .'

'I am. I think we've met. Been having some bellyache?' asks the doctor. Guy nods. 'Let's get you into a room and up on the table. Okay, I'm going to push lightly on some places, and you tell me where it hurts, okay?' Guy nods. 'Any vomiting?' Guy nods. 'Fever?' Guy nods. When the doctor's hands gently palpate his lower left abdomen, Guy howls like a raccoon in a fight.

'Please, please please don't touch that again, hell,' he cries.

'We need a CT scan, Missus . . . Dickenson.'

'Bannister,' Guy breathes softly.

'We need to see what's going on in there, in that bowel area,' says the doctor.

'Are you going to be his doctor?' True asks. 'You just got up out of the audience . . .'

'I have privileges here, and I like to see a case through. It's my old Marine ethic.'

'Are you . . . can you handle this?'

The doctor smiles, though not condescendingly. 'I'm a general surgeon,' he says.

They have ridden through the night in the rocking, bumping ambulance, lights and sirens running, paramedics inserting a line in Guy's small hand to begin running saline, on radio orders from Cape Cod General, in Hyannis. Cars weave off to the breakdown lane, as True has pulled over so many times in her life, wondering what was happening inside the lighted windows of ambulances, where she can glimpse heads and swinging racks of equipment, wondering whether someone was leaving the world or entering it. Kathleen has taught Guy to hold his breath for luck when an ambulance passes, and hold onto a button when a funeral procession goes by, and has also told him that an ambulance going at an ordinary speed, running only lights but not sirens, contains a dead person – that these are like the ambulance that carried Grandpa Bert from his car wreck once they fished him out of the stream, like the ambulance that brought Guy's daddy to the morgue from the side of the road. What surprises True is how the vehicle boats and bangs like a panel truck. 'Don't these things have shocks?' she asks a young paramedic.

'People are always surprised by that,' the young man tells her shortly. 'These aren't Cadillacs, ma'am.'

Now, as True begins to follow Guy's rolling bed down the hall to the imaging lab, she is stopped by a nurse. 'Your sisters are in the waiting room,' she informs True.

'I don't have . . . know why,' True thinks, catching herself at the last moment. Telling Guy she will be back in seconds, noting how his eyes roll away from her as she speaks, True slips off her low heels and lollops in stocking feet down the hall to the ER waiting room, where she finds Holly, Addy, Franny, and Steve, in evening dress. The other denizens of the room, mothers rocking croupy toddlers, are staring with frank amusement.

'We told them we're his aunts,' Franny explains. 'They said they wouldn't give us information otherwise. Can we go back there?'

'I don't think so,' True equivocates. She wants them all to stay, but she knows it will be hours before anyone knows what is the matter with Guy. 'He's about to have a CAT scan.'

'Maybe he has an impacted bowel. Angie had an impacted bowel once,' Franny suggests.

'That would be a relief,' True says. She opens her arms to hug them all briefly. 'Where is my mother?' she then asks.

'She didn't feel able to drive and there wasn't any room for her in the car,' Franny apologizes. 'But I'm going to go get her when I drop Angie off. Angie and Clainey are in the car, bawling. Do you want Kathleen here?'

'No,' says True. 'Yes.'

'Do you want me to call Hank? Or Esa?'

'Yes. Both of them. Hank first.'

'True, you look funny,' Franny says.

'I'm sweating, is all, from running,' True answers, but Franny has already summoned a nurse, who makes True lie down on an ER bed while she fastens a blood pressure cuff around her arm.

'Lie on your left side, Missus . . .'

'Dickinson,' says True. 'Why?'

'It can help the blood flow more freely and takes stress off the fetus,' the nurse replies. 'The danger with pre-eclampsia is that sometimes it means that the placenta is inadequate.'

'What a terrible way to put it,' Franny snaps.

'I mean, sometimes the fetus doesn't get enough nourishment, despite the way it would seem, with all the fluid buildup,' the nurse goes on.

'But no one said I have pre-eclampsia,' True tells the nurse.

'Your doctor didn't? You don't take meds?'

'No,' True insists. 'I'm just upset and swollen. I'm over forty. It happens.'

'I don't know,' the nurse purses her lips. 'I spent five years in labor and delivery . . .'

'Look at your hands, True,' Franny says, with a delicate horror. True looks down. In what seems minutes, her hands have become filled surgical gloves, seemingly made of cartoon rubber instead of skin, her ring swallowed in an unlined, pale-blue bratwurst.

'I . . . I don't know when this happened,' True says. 'They were swollen, but not like this.'

'See?' the nurse says. 'What I told you? It's often sudden.'

'I *guess*,' True says.

'Can I cut that off for you?' the nurse asks. 'It's not looking good . . .'

'Yes, do,' True asks, suddenly feeling the constricting pain. Her ankles are loaves of distended flesh.

The nurse slips through the impossibly imbedded band of silver with a sturdy-toothed surgical scissors, snapping the silver band – the same one that, before sizing, was so large it only fit True's thumb. The relief is stunning. Her hand tingles, as with warmth after frostbite. She rubs the horrid, gelid dent.

'I can't find Hank anywhere! This is his wife and child!' Franny cries, bursting in.

'He should have thought of that earlier,' True replies. Even now, she can manage to locate and mine her vein of bitterness. 'I don't mean that how it sounds, Frannywoman.'

'Well, I'd be pissed, too! Esa's on the way, though.'

'All I thought was . . . that we could rely on him even as a friend. That I wouldn't have to look for him. Franny, he's spending Christmas with some friends, and for all I know, they're in a ski lodge somewhere. Tom won't even know, I'll bet.'

'Keep thinking. I'll keep trying out there. Esa will be here,' Franny says.

'I have to go,' True tells the nurse. 'My little boy is very ill.'

'Well, it's a little better,' the nurse cocks her head to one side, listening to True's blood beat, 'and your pulse has slowed.'

'I'll take it very easy,' True promises.

'Wait!' the nurse cries, as True sets off down the hall. 'Do you want your ring?' She trots to drop the sundered band in True's palm. True places it in her shirt pocket.

'Where is my son?' she asks the nurse, who nods at a hallway.

'Turn right,' she tells True absently, disappearing behind another curtain.

Guy is actually poised at the mouth of the white cavern of the CAT scanner, gowned and positioned. 'Mommy,' he says, 'I thought you left.'

'No, I went to get my blood pressure taken! Isn't that funny? I'm not even the one who's sick!' Guy smiles faintly, and True thinks of the oven the witch primed for Hansel and Gretel. 'May I stay in here while he is scanned?'

'No,' Doctor Oudenhoven apologizes, glancing at her stomach. 'Obviously. But you can wait right outside and look in through the glass. Radiation.'

'You need to drink this, Guy.' A nurse hands Guy a glass of what looks like diluted milk. 'Most people think it tastes sort of like lemonade.'

Guy takes a tentative sip. 'It *tastes* like salt water. Can you put some sugar in it?'

'No,' says the nurse, 'and you have to try to drink it down quickly, so it can guide the doctors watching. It lights up inside you. Most people think it tastes like lemonade.'

'*Most people* must be pretty dumb,' Guy chokes.

'You need to drink it fast,' the nurse insists, unshakeable.

'I'll glow in the dark?' Guy says, with an authentic but stuporous show of curiosity.

'Sort of.'

'I'll try,' Guy takes a deep breath and holds his nose and swills down the liquid. Within seconds, he is throwing it up on his paper gown.

'That's okay, that's okay,' the nurse says. 'Some of it may have stayed down. How 'bout we give it another try?'

'How 'bout you just let me die?' Guy asks.

The nurse cleans Guy up, and consults briefly outside the room. 'Doctor says that might be enough,' the nurse says, a form of address, especially in the third person, which has always chewed True's nerves. Doctor Oudenhoven returns.

'We don't have time to wait,' he says.

'Will you cover up his . . . genitals?' True asks.

'We'll do the whole thing the right way. It doesn't take nearly so long as you think, Missus Bannister.'

It takes as long as a three-course meal. For what seems like hours, the doctor simply seems occupied with chatting on the telephone, probably ordering pizza, as Guy lies flexing and pointing his toes. By the time True has gone for water, paced, checked the clock, recovered her shoes, peed seven times, and finally slumped down onto the tacky carpet with her back against the wall outside the door, Franny has returned, with Starbucks coffee and a blanket. 'They keep this place like Labrador,' she complains. 'I got a feeling you might be spending the night.' Kathleen, Franny explains, is too distraught to come to the hospital. 'She says this makes her think of your father . . .'

'Oh piss,' True says. 'That's so lame. How dare she intrude her thirty-year-old anxiety into her grandson's illness?'

'I actually told her something like that,' Franny says. 'But she was afraid . . . True, she's an old lady. She was afraid Guy would die if she came, I think.'

'Well, I'm grateful for that analysis, Miss Freud. Kathleen and Hank both off the hook now. My mother will be telling everyone how she nearly collapsed herself . . .'

'Yeah, you know, it figures. Some people are afraid of hospitals.'

'And others are afraid of commitment.'

'Anyway, I'm here. I'm more useful,' Franny reasons.

'What do you think is wrong with him, Franny?'

'Maybe he really does have a deep-seated immaturity.'

'God! I mean Guy!'

'I think he has a hot appendix.'

'Why?'

'Because he's been sick for weeks, and when Steve had a crummy appendix, they said it "smoldered" for weeks and that it could have burst.'

'What happens if an appendix bursts?'

'Well, that would be not good, because the infection would spread.'

'And?'

'He'd be real sick. Speaking of which, what was wrong with *you* back there?'

'Nothing. My blood pressure went up. Because I freaked. I have pre-pre-eclampsia maybe. But they have medicine for it.'

'No, they make you go to bed, period,' Franny says. 'My sister Patty had it.'

'That's not what my doctor said,' True goes on. 'Anyhow, it's not life-threatening.'

'It is if it goes so far you get seizures. It can kill the baby and you,' Franny says. 'And even if it doesn't go all the way, it can be dangerous.'

'I mean the appendix! The hot appendix! The appendix! One world at a time, sweetie!'

'No,' says Franny. 'That's not.'

The doctor emerges. 'Well,' he says, 'I was right.' The intern stands behind him, nodding. 'Guy has suffered a ruptured appendix. That means we need to get him down to the operating room right away and clean this up, fast. Mary here,' True notices a nurse standing behind her, 'will give you the permission slip for you to sign for the surgery, and she'll bring you over to the registration desk to deal with insurance and such . . .'

400

'Well, I want to go with Guy,' True says, scribbling her name on the bottom of a form.

'You can go as far as the anteroom, while we get him ready.' Guy is wheeled out into the hall, and speedily, two male nurses begin running down the hall, wheeling the cart like a Grand-Prix racer.

'Why are they in such a rush if it's not life-threatening?' True asks.

'I didn't think his appendix had really ruptured, or I wouldn't have said anything,' Franny bites her lip.

True turns to the doctor, 'It isn't, is it? Life-threatening?'

'The appendix burst . . . some time ago, which makes this a little more urgent,' Doctor Oudenhoven explains.

'Some time ago?' True asks. 'An hour ago?'

'Oh no. Days ago.'

'How can you tell?'

'By what we see on the pictures. But we can't be sure until we get in there, and that's why now, I have to go . . .'

'What does this all mean?'

'It means that the gunk . . .'

'Define gunk,' True demands.

'The contents, the toxic . . . he may have gangrene, Missus Bannister, and some necrotic tissue of the bowel that we'll need to get out . . .'

'Define necrotic.'

'Well, dead tissue.'

True stumbles back. She trips and sits down hard, on her butt, on the edge of the heat register. 'Let her stay there until she's ready to get up,' says the nurse, whom someone calls, 'Mary!' sounding faint and far away. 'Do you feel light-headed, Missus Bannister?'

'No,' True tells her, though she indeed feels faint and has a headache that makes her temples feel physically bruised. 'Did I sign the form?'

'Yes,' Mary tells her, 'and now all I have to do is get your insurance card.'

'I don't have it. I had my evening purse. He was in a performance.'

'Oh, we could tell that from the makeup and the clothes. We didn't think he normally dressed that way,' Mary laughs.

She *laughs*.

'Can't you . . . just find us in the computer or something?'

'Have you ever been in this ER?'

'Many times, and recently, with Guy and my husband.'

'Okay, then, we're set. But you still have to sign him in . . .'

'Not until I see him.'

Franny helps True to her feet, and half-supports her through the corridors, following arrows that direct them to signs that direct them to mazes that direct them to elevators that direct them to more signs that point to the operating room. Inside a door that declares NO ADMITTANCE, True sees Guy on his table, nurses opening his gown and applying soap and iodine to his belly. She pushes open the door.

'I'm his mother.'

'Mommy,' says Guy. 'Will this hurt?'

'You'll be asleep. It might hurt a little after, but they'll give you some painkiller and you'll sleep and Mommy will be right here.'

'Are they going to cut my stomach?'

'Yes. But not much.'

'And take out the appendix?'

'Yes.'

Guy asks, 'Is Dad out there?'

'Yes,' says True. 'He's on his way.'

'Okay.'

'Guy, Gee, Gee,' True leans over the head of her son. 'It's going to be all right. All well. I promise.' The nurses gently wipe away her unwanted tears that drip onto Guy's face, as they sponge off his makeup.

'What were you doing? Late Halloween?' asks one.

'I'm an actor,' Guy tells them, and True bends double and sits down on the floor.

'Please, please take care of him,' she tells the nurses.

'Get somebody to take care of her,' says the charge nurse. 'Ma'am, you can't be doing gymnastics.' A large woman helps True to a reclining chair. She can see Doctor Oudenhoven beyond a wired window, carefully and slowly scrubbing his arms, a nurse placing a paper cap on his short silver hair.

'Please, please, this is my only child,' True calls.

'For the moment,' the nurse smiles. 'Don't worry. He's gonna come through this like a champ.'

'Please, oh please,' True calls, as Guy is wheeled away, a blue mesh cap snapped over his hair.

These are the words that are being repeated, in Urdu, in Spanish, in German and Turkish, in one-story concrete-block hospitals with six beds, and fourteen-floor hospitals with ten thousand beds, hospitals at the end of dirt roads and on the most illuminated corners of urban streets, by mothers and fathers and grandmothers. All the words, prayers and pleas, pleadings and incantations, float upward, and converge. The products of weeping that sometimes accompany the words also meet, and salt the ground.

AN HOUR LATER, Kitt arrives, still in full stage makeup as a barmaid with blood on her forehead. 'Where is he?' she asks. 'The nurse out there tried to get me a wheelchair but I said it was just good makeup. You should have seen her back away . . .'

'He's in surgery,' True says. 'His appendix burst. I feel like hell . . .'

'You look like hell,' Kitt says.

'No, I mean I feel like hell I didn't know.'

'You consulted his doctor, True. Twice. His doctor didn't know.'

'The pain was on the wrong side for an appendix,' Franny puts in, 'because it had already burst. When it burst, it didn't hurt so badly.'

Kitt turns pale. 'They're doing everything . . . you shouldn't go to Boston?'

'He's in good hands, I think,' True answers, rocking, rubbing her arms. Kitt leans down and unlaces her worn jazz shoes and removes her shawl.

'Here, this will keep you warm, and the shoes are all busted up, so you'll be comfortable if you have to stand. It's a long night you have ahead of you. If I didn't have to go pack, I'd stay with you.'

'Kitt, thanks,' True says.

'I love you,' Kitt says unexpectedly. 'You raised a great kid. And I'll be back. I'll see you again. Couple of days. Put your feet up, True. Come on. Where's Hank?'

True shrugs. 'We can't find him.'

'He'll turn up,' Kitt says. 'As soon as he finds out.'

True and Franny have taken turns peeing, a dozen times. True believes she has peed the equivalent of Puget Sound. The TV in the

403

waiting room jabbers incessantly – the children watching cartoons until the adults grouse and switch to CNN. A postal worker in D.C. has died from the inhalation form of anthrax. A man with a videotape of the gentle-eyed, ascetic man in robes who has possibly engineered the ruin of the world, a videotape made in December, in which he explains his plans to demolish the World Trade Center, has been detained in Strasbourg. The children, whose grandparents have had heart attacks, beg to switch back to Nickelodeon. The adults agree, and complain that the coffee has run out. When the telephone rings, everyone leaps to their feet. The caller is Kathleen. 'He is in surgery, Mom,' True explains. 'They say he will be fine. He has a ruptured appendix.'

'I knew that he didn't have flu,' Kathleen mutters, 'or a strained groin muscle.'

'Yeah,' True agrees, drumming her nails, deciding to chew them off.

'Well, is there anything I can do?'

'You could come over here.'

'It's snowing.'

'Okay, then you can walk the dog and feed him. And you can pray.'

'True, I am praying. Rudy wants to know, do you want some food?'

'No thank you. But tell him he is sweet.'

'Well you have to have food for the baby. So I'm going to have him bring you a tuna-salad sandwich.' True feels her gorge rise. 'And Isabelle is on her way.'

'I know. Did Hank call?' Kathleen doesn't answer, seems to be speaking to someone with the receiver covered. 'Did Hank call?'

'No,' Kathleen says, after a pause. 'I think Isabelle called him.'

'Did you call the Lemieuxs or . . . oh forget that.'

'Are you holding up, True? Rudy can bring you over some different clothes.'

'In the morning.'

'Well, all right then. I'll call Ellen and tell her to pray, too . . . in fact, I can activate the prayer chain . . .'

'Don't do that.'

'Why?'

'It makes it seem like code red in heaven. I don't want God to take this all that seriously, as if he were dying.'

404

'Okay. Good night, True.'

After she hangs up the receiver, a man in the room announces, 'People come off respirators all the time. They're weaning my mother off right now. It's not true that once you're on a respirator, it's forever.' A ferrety woman in a black raincoat nods. When True looks up, Doctor Oudenhoven is standing in the doorway, looking his age, which True assumes to be about sixty. He nods his head and, with a gesture of his hand, invites her into the hall. True turns to Franny, but Franny is cuddled on her coat in a corner, gently snoring.

'He's in recovery.' But as True turns to run, the doctor places a dry hand on her arm. 'When I was a young surgeon, in the service, I was told that if you asked a surgeon to name his five most complicated cases, each one of those would involve an appendix. In other words, when we got in there, Missus Bannister, there was a great deal of work to do. There was gangrenous tissue, and pus everywhere, and he is a very lucky boy to be talking to the nurses right now. I don't want to scare you; what I want to emphasize is that he will probably have a long recovery. Come here,' he gestures to a tiny office labeled QUIET ROOM, and sits down. 'What we did, beyond, of course, removing the appendix, was mop up as best as we could the products of that rupture. Now, if he were only a little younger, like five, we'd have lost him. And if he were an adult, your age, we'd have lost him.' Something in True's face evidently alarms him, because he says, 'Missus Dickenson . . . Missus Bannister, calm down. We would have, but we did not. He has such a strong little immune system, he's going to do very well; we can anticipate that . . . maybe ten days from now, on strong doses of antibiotics and fluids, we might see him go home. Maybe even by Christmas, if he bounces back remarkably.'

'Ten days? In the hospital?'

'I hope, Missus Bannister. And I will say that I have seen young people bounce back and get the packing removed from the incision . . .'

'The packing . . . ?'

'We don't close the incision. Guy still has an open wound, packed with gauze, that will continue to leach out whatever might still be bubbling around in there. When we're sure his cell count is normal, we'll take out the packing and then sew him up . . . or perhaps not.

We might send him home with an open incision and just let it keep draining, and we'll teach you how to tend to that . . .'

'Why?'

'Because the other possibility is that some people develop a pocket, a sort of abscess, from the infection.'

'And then.'

'And then we'd have to open him up and take that out, too, or in the best case, withdraw it with a needle guided by an ultrasound.'

'Oh. But he will be well, eventually.'

'The next twelve hours will be a big indicator.'

True reels. 'You mean, there's a chance that Guy could still die?'

'I don't think that's the case. But he did have a very short time before . . . these kids. They are so strong. They go on like dead men walking. The pain must have been excruciating. And the way he was moving around on the stage . . .'

'How long would it have been before he got really sick?'

'He is really sick.'

'How long would it have been before he . . . ?'

'There's no way to estimate that, Missus Bannister.'

'Try.'

'It could have been two hours. Or three hours. It could have been an hour.'

'Hours?'

The doctor nods.

'Hours? An hour?'

'Certainly no more. Maybe less. I'm very grateful, personally, that I was there,' says Doctor Oudenhoven, and does not appear surprised when True takes his hand and holds it against her cheek.

THE FIRST WEEK of Guy's hospitalization passes nearly in silence. He moans, and presses the red button on the machine that dispenses morphine. It can be pressed every ten minutes, and when her son does not reach for it, True presses it herself. He is dragged out of bed to sit, to try to jump-start bowels and metabolism. There are moments when he awakes.

He asks, 'Will I have a scar?'

'Yes,' True admits sadly.

'Oh, that's good,' Guy sighs. 'I wanted a scar.'

'Look at all your cards and things,' True encourages him.

She has finally, after three days, and only while Esa sat watching Guy sleep, showered and changed out of her crusted, bloody, stinking evening outfit, into a T-shirt and sweatpants with an expanded panel. So that she can lie on her left side, the nurses have wheeled a second hospital bed into Guy's room. Her obstetrician has visited, and done an exam, the curtain pulled discreetly between True and her son, and pronounced True 'not sick enough to admit but probably just as well here as anywhere else.' Rudy has repeatedly brought her croissants and hummus, having thrown her mother's tuna salad out at the beach, where he says he hopes no mammals will die of it. She still wears Kitt's jazz shoes. They comfort her. Guy scans the wall of letters, the stuffed figure in ragged pants and a top hat the cast has sent, the bushel of balloons, so large they could loft Guy from the room, sent by her staff. Beatrice has given Guy exquisite chocolates that only the nurses can stomach, and Elizabeth has had cabbed over an entire porcelain New England village with lights and figures. Dog has brought a BB gun, for which True will slug him when she sees him. He calls Guy, promising a surprise that will be there with bells on, at Christmas, and challenges Guy to figure it out.

'The surprise is fine; the gun goes.'

Guy tries to dicker. 'But it's the rule, Mom. If someone gives it to you, you can't say no, even if it's something your mom wouldn't get you. It's part of my heritage, like Dad says.'

'No guns. Now of all times. This isn't some play-game of Southern honor. There's a real war happening, baby.'

'I know. Remember when Daddy was going to go? It's just an ol' BB gun. Gyp and I can run in the woods and shoot trees and rocks.'

'Or Gyp . . .'

'Mommy! I promise I'll never shoot a bird, Mom. Or a kid, or you. Dad did it.'

'Dad grew up in another time and another place.'

'Can I shoot it at Grand-père's?'

'Oh, sure,' True says wearily, 'and how do you propose to get the gun there?'

'You can travel with guns, if you have a permit.'

'Jesus, Guy, how can you be thinking of this now? Nobody on this green earth can travel with guns now. Nobody.'

On her way home after the New York performances, Kitt drops

in to say good-bye. She leans over Guy, the tip of her bright red mohair scarf tickling his nose.

'I'm telling you, get up out of that bed and come home to Wisconsin with me,' she says. 'I can wrap you up. This is your last chance. My girls will make a big fuss over you. You can watch TV all day. R-rated.'

The two women hug. 'I feel I've found a friend in you, True. And Guy is something special. And I . . . I wish you love. I suppose the best Christmas present you could have is this skinny guy right here and that little gold nugget in there.' Guy smiles, and kisses Kitt fervently. 'Next time, you'll be Louis and I'll be Anna, okay, babe? Shall we dance, on a bright cloud of music, shall we glide? Or you'll be the young prince! It's a puzzlement! Huh?' Kitt promises, 'You ain't seen the last of me.' When Kitt leaves, True somehow feels that a great dam has been broken, that nothing will any longer be forbidden to flow over and to claim her. She sits on the bed and cries until she is drained, and her nasal passages are as sore as if she's swum underwater for hours. It is all so very real, and she is so wicked sick of bawling. She should by now be a husk, instead of a water balloon.

Rudy has brought a spud gun, for when Guy feels fit enough to shoot at the cork board, and a fart cushion, and a Christmas tree from Guy's Montana grandparents, decorated with white lights and white mice. Rudy has phoned the Lemieuxs himself. 'It's kind of a Republican tree,' Rudy says. 'Why didn't they come to see him?' Why, indeed, True wonders? But, of course, they still think she is married. They would not have wanted to make an abrupt appearance. And there is the war.

One day, Kathleen comes to sit for the couple of hours it takes True to go home and get her toiletries, reading to Guy from *The Jungle Book*, the part he loves best, about Mowgli returning to the human village and leaving his wolfen brothers. Kathleen has promised to leave only to use the washroom or get a bite to eat while Guy is napping. When True returns, both her mother and her son are lightly snoring.

Rather than wake them, True attempts to sort the growing pile of gifts and cards, so she and Guy can pass the time writing thank-you cards.

Then, True discovers a WWF Wrestling video and a race-car magazine. At the same moment, Guy awakens. 'Hi, Mommy,' he yawns.

'Did Unkie send these?' she asks Guy.

He looks away. 'No,' he says.

'Who are these from?'

'Dunno,' Guy says. 'Maybe Ellery. Here's Esa!'

Isabelle, her eyes elderly within, belying the big smile on her face, kisses Guy and says, 'You sure know how to get attention, you stinker. You didn't even see me last time I was in here, you were so drugged up. If I didn't have to go home for Christmas now, I'd get you out of that bed and tickle-torture you.'

'Did you send these over for Guy?' True asks, as she hugs Esa. Esa does that same funny thing. She looks away.

'Nope,' she says, and seems relieved when a nurse enters the room.

'Come home soon, Guy, we miss you,' Isabelle whispers, and takes from her huge trash bag a full case of regular Coke and an electronic elf, which sings, in the voice of Judy Garland, 'Have Yourself a Merry Little Christmas.' She also tells him Granny is taking good care of Gyp and Ed, but that Gyp lies on the foot of Guy's bed every night, and that Ed would do the same thing if he could.

True stares at the WWF video, wondering.

Daily, just as True wanders down the hall to get a coffee, Doctor Oudenhoven comes in and checks Guy's incision and his chart. She never, ever catches him, can never ask why Guy's packing stinks like a charnel house (True has never smelled a charnel house, but she has smelled a dead deer and her imagination can supply the link). It is something she asks the day nurse, Anna, a tiny, exquisite Latina girl, and the night nurse, Nigeria, who is anything but tiny but has the most delicate braids True has ever seen. True cannot take her eyes off the crystal beads. 'Why does it stink so?'

'You should ask the doctor,' Nigeria advises.

'I never see a doctor,' True complains. 'They wait for me to leave the room and then dart in, like spies.' Nigeria laughs. 'Are you from Nigeria, Nigeria?' she asks then.

'No, Brooklyn.'

'Was your mother from Nigeria?'

'No, Brooklyn.'

'Why are you called Nigeria?'

'Why are you called True?'

'I was born on Valentine's Day.'

'Well, my mother and father wanted a genuine African girl, I guess. I don't know. But I'll page you up a resident, and we'll ask him about the stink.'

The resident is perky, delivered straight from a prime-time hospital television show, where all residents are reed-thin and have perfect haircuts. 'Yikes,' she says. 'It does reek. Doctor Oudenhoven must not have much of a sense of smell. On the other hand, what's oozing out of there is evil stuff, so I suppose it could be normal. Tell you what. I'll call him and ask if I can change the exterior packing and do a little cleanup.'

Ten minutes later, what True had looked forward to as a mercy has blown up into a nightmare. Guy is screaming, digging his nails into his mother's hands, as the resident slowly, gently withdraws the endless layer of bloody, unspeakably stained and slimy wadding. 'Stop her, Mommy! I'm fucking dying! Stop her, please stop her.'

'Push the morphine button,' the resident instructs True, her tension palpable.

'I'm pushing. I pushed it when you started. Can't you get him a shot? Please, get him a shot.'

'We don't want to give him too much . . .'

'Doctor,' True scans the glossy name tag, 'Gideon. He's in intolerable pain. And how is it going to be when you put that stuff back in?' Absorbed in cleaning the open-mouthed edges of the wound, as Guy screams, Doctor Gideon at first does not answer. Then she stands up, puts her hands on her hips, and rings for the nurse. 'Ten mil Valium,' she says, and minutes later, Guy is only moaning, as the packing is replaced, the dressing secured. True's entire body is drenched with sweat.

As they watch him drift into sleep, Doctor Gideon says, 'Can I ask you a silly question? Actually two questions, one silly?'

'Sure,' says True.

'Are you the rich lady, the one who has the doll company?'

'No,' True answers. 'I'm not rich, and I have a baby company.'

'Oh, then . . . why? Oh, right. She's on the medical floor.'

'Who is?'

'The doll-company lady.'

'Elizabeth? Elizabeth Chilmark? She's in the hospital?'

'Yes.'

'I . . . what happened to her?'

'She . . . well, you ask her, huh? I'm not supposed to say things . . .'

410

'Okay.'

'How about that other question?' True nods. 'Are you on any meds for that swelling? How far along are you?'

'Almost seven months. My doctor says just to take it easy and stay off my feet.'

'Well, then, do it. You look like a two-pound baby waiting to happen. I'm not kidding. Get in that bed and get a stack of pillows under your feet and have them monitor your blood pressure every time they do his. And drink water. And have them get a fetal heart rate . . .'

'I have my own,' True says.

'You have your own?'

'Paranoid. I almost miscarried.'

'Okay. Well, at least you'll get attention. Since it's Christmas, anyone who can be wheeled or dragged out of here is gone . . .' True thanks her. She looks at her watch. It is Christmas Eve. She wonders if Hank is looking up at the same gray sky, shedding its feathers.

THAT NIGHT, AS Guy sleeps, True gets up and wanders until she finds the medical floor. She asks for patient Elizabeth Chilmark.

'Two-two-three,' a nurse mutters, not looking up from her computer.

There is a tiny but exquisite beaded lamp lit next to Elizabeth's bed, and her bed is covered with a soft, white-down quilt. Though her head is turned away, she appears to be awake. 'Elizabeth?' True whispers.

'How is Guy?' Elizabeth replies, without turning her head.

'Better. May I come in?'

'Of course, True,' Elizabeth turns her head. Her lips are blue.

'What happened to you?'

'Nothing.'

'I mean, why are you in the hospital?'

'I have leukemia, True.'

'What? Why didn't you tell me?'

Elizabeth waves a manicured and skeletal hand. 'Why would I?'

'Well, I suppose . . . we weren't really . . .'

'I don't mean I wouldn't have told you. But it's not common knowledge.'

'Are you in remission?'

411

'No.'

'Are you having . . . something?'

'I'm waiting for a bone-marrow transplant candidate. When one is available, I will go into isolation. As I have no children, and no siblings, this represents a difficulty. I have to wait until something comes from an anonymous donor . . .'

'I'll give you my bone marrow.'

'Thank you, True. But you have your hands full now. And the test requires the withdrawal of blood and then, I believe, marrow from a hipbone. It's extremely painful and requires isolation . . .'

'I don't care! And what about Isabelle, and my mother, and Rudy? And your husband, and what about all your friends?'

'My husband has been tested, and one of my employees, and my niece, but they were not good matches.'

'I see. But if you found a match, that would be essentially . . . ?'

'Yes, a cure.'

'How long have you known about this?'

'Two years,' Elizabeth says. 'At first, the chemotherapy worked beautifully. But not eventually.'

'Shit!' True says. 'Elizabeth, shit! You should have told me this long ago. I would have donated bone marrow!'

'I didn't need it long ago. Anyone who wants to donate bone marrow to me is welcome to. I'm not a stoic, True. I'm not looking forward to dying.'

That night, when True speaks to Rudy about the Blessings – all have gone out, and on schedule – and wishes him a merry Christmas, she tells him of Elizabeth's illness, and Rudy sets about compiling a list of everyone he knows who might be willing to be tested as a candidate for Elizabeth's savior.

CHRISTMAS IN A children's hospital ward is not a recommended experience.

Even the tentatively religious are moved by the choirs of nurses who wander the nearly empty halls, holding lit candles, singing in angel voices about the baby in the barn. Laura, CTF's stage manager, brings Guy a veritable Santa's bag of toys, paints, books about black holes, stuffed animals, and a three-foot greeting-card caricature of Guy as the Dodger drawn by Ellery and signed by all the cast.

True offers Guy some chicken soup, so foul-smelling she wouldn't permit the dog to eat it, and an iced can of Coke. He sips eagerly, but vomits it up a few minutes later. He tries again, and keeps a few sips down.

'You've got to push those liquids,' says the night nurse who has replaced Nigeria for the holiday. His name is Russell.

'He throws them up.'

'Well, you have to keep trying. I'll get him something for the nausea. Time to walk, pal.'

This is an excruciating daily marathon, which began two days after the surgery, watching her sturdy, husky little dancer hobble in his socks down the hall, supported by his IV pole and the nurse. Guy gets to the end of the hall and, spent and ashamed, begs to go back. True notices, just at the moment Guy does, that the back of his gown is open, revealing his shrunken rear end. She has forgotten the robe Granny brought from home. But it is no matter. No one, save the sobbing baby in the next room, whom True is forbidden to rock because she is 'spoiled and contagious,' according to the day nurse, is there. 'Once around,' Russell says. 'Come on, or you're a weenie.' Guy finally makes it back, yellow with exhaustion, pees into the hat on the toilet so his urine can be measured, pees less urine than he did into his diaper as an infant, and collapses on the bed.

'I want to see wrestling,' he whispers. But in less time than True can load the tape, he is snoring.

'Russell,' she asks the nurse, turning over the tape. 'Did you see anyone besides my relatives come in here?'

'I don't know your relatives,' he says. 'I'm a floater.'

'Did you see a guy with black hair come in here yesterday?'

'I saw a guy in a leather jacket,' he tells her. 'Who just looked in when you were both asleep. Then he left. But he comes in all the time. I see him in the lobby. That your brother?' This could have been Rudy. And yet Rudy had been wearing a buff-colored parka when he'd come in previously. Only one person she knows wears a leather jacket *toujours*.

But if it were he, wouldn't he have . . . spoken? Kissed his son?

After the dinner hour, True switches on the television and locates a Midnight Mass telecast from . . . someplace where it is midnight.

Kneeling by Guy's bed, she tries to summon the words she has repeated on this night every year since she could speak. It is like

413

dialing a telephone number one cannot remember, by picturing one's fingers making the motions on the face of the receiver. Easily, it comes. 'And it came to pass in those days, that there went out a decree from Caesar Augustus . . . and Joseph went up from Galilee, into Judea . . .' she knows she is dropping words ' . . . to be taxed with Mary, his espoused wife, being great with child. And so it was that, while they were there . . . she brought forth her firstborn son, and wrapped him in swaddling clothes, and laid him in a manger; because there was no room for them in the inn. And there were in the same country shepherds, keeping watch over their flock by night. And, lo, the angel of the Lord came upon them . . .' She stops, and lays her head on her arms.

'Go on,' Guy says sleepily, 'I like that part.'

'Well, the angel said, "Fear not, for, behold, I bring you good news" . . .'

'Good tidings,' Guy corrects her. 'Geez.'

'"Good tidings of great joy, which shall be to all people. For unto you is born this day in the city of David a Savior, which is Christ the Lord" . . . and suddenly, there was with the angel a multitude of the heavenly host . . .'

'What's the heavenly host?' Guy asks. 'More angels?'

'Backup angels. The chorus.'

'Oh.'

'At least I assume. And they were praising God, saying, "Glory to God in the highest and on earth peace, good will toward men."'

'You left out whole parts, Mom. Like the wise guys. And the Frankenstein and myrrh.'

'I'm not all there, Guy. I'm not right in my noggin'.'

'I never thought I'd spend *Christmas* in a hospital.'

'Ain't my idea of fun, either, sweetie,' True says.

A volunteer from United Way brings Guy a candy cane and a teddy bear.

'This is pretty babyish,' Guy says, after the volunteer has left, after he has politely thanked her. 'Should we give it to Baby Carr?'

'We'll keep it for our baby. I sent Baby Carr a present.'

'I'll bet he's one now. He'd think it was totally baby.'

'Sweetie, a one-year-old is still a baby. You were still a baby when you were one. And two, and almost three. You're not even anywhere near grown-up now. Our baby will be a little baby for a long time.'

414

'What are we going to name it?'

'What do you want to name it?'

'Hank. Hank Peter Bannister. Hank Peter Guy Bannister.'

'Oh. I thought maybe Big Nose.'

'Mom, don't make me laugh. It kills.'

'Or Stinkpot. You'll have to change the dipes, you know. I'm too busy for that. I'm a working girl.'

'No way! I'm not changing diapers. That's not in my job description.' Guy pauses, 'Mommy?'

'Ummmm?'

'Where's Dad?'

'You mean in heaven.'

'No, Dad now. He was just here a minute ago. Or maybe an hour ago.' A chill runs down True's spine.

'I think he's with *Grand-mère* . . . or with his friends, skiing. He didn't know this was happening, Gee. And I told him he couldn't have you over until after the show . . . I told him he couldn't have you at Christmas.'

'Thanks a lot, Mom! So you let him go away without coming to see me?' Guy's voice, its broken belief, is beyond enduring.

'I'm so, so sorry, Guy. We've tried to call him. I don't know if Esa reached him. Tom couldn't find him. And he was going to go to Louisiana anyway, and I told him you couldn't go because you had to go to your Grandpa and Grandma L.,' True improvises. 'It's not his fault. He would be here right away . . .'

'Or maybe he's just fricking dumb.'

'No, he isn't,' True says.

That night, after speaking on the telephone with her brother, True watches the snowfall and sees in the parking lot a lone red truck. Squinting, she makes out the grille logo, and thinks she can tell that it is not a Dodge but a Chevy. Mulling over the bars where the ginger water is served and the naked girls who leave nothing to the imagination dance, and how, in her hunger to have Hank's child, she had ignored that foolishness and seduced him, True wonders what Hank might be doing precisely now. *Laissez bon temps roullez.*

Maybe he *is* just fricking dumb. Maybe a guy who thinks air guitar is a real instrument is an air person.

Guy wakes in terrible pain at midnight, and there is another shot, and just as he falls asleep, lab technicians arrive, switch on all the lights, and commence to take vials of blood. 'This is going too far,' True says. 'You're going to exsanguinate him. He can barely drink anything. His pediatrician thinks he's in danger of an electrolyte imbalance. He's going to get brain damage.'

'We have to keep looking to see if the cell count . . .' Of course, to these white coats, he is blood, as he is a brain to the neurologist, an emergency to the cowboy intern. There is no dealing.

'Let them do it, Mom, and get it over with.' True gets up to hold Guy's hand. She is so exhausted she can barely stand.

'Forget it,' True says. 'I don't give you permission.'

The technician blinks. 'I have orders.'

'Ask the doctor to come and tell me himself. Tell him it's against my religion. I just changed it.'

Later, as they wait, hands clasped, for the pain meds to find their targets, Guy murmurs, 'I think maybe I want to die, Mommy. I can't stand this much longer. I can't throw up anymore. Mom, I'm gonna die anyway . . . at least I'd see my real daddy.'

True jerks her hand away and slaps Guy across the face.

She then looks in wonderment at her stinging palm, and she shouts, 'Guy Lemieux, don't you ever, ever, ever say that again! You say that again, and I'll get up and walk out that door and I'll leave you here alone. I won't come back until it's time to pick you up. I swear to God I will!'

'You hit a sick kid! You *both* hit me. You and . . . that ugly bass turd Hank! When I tried to save his life by breaking his leg. He practically slugged me.'

'I'll hit you again, if you say one more word about dying, one more word . . .' and then she is on her knees, 'Gee, Gee, please don't die. Listen, listen, if you don't die, I'll buy you anything in the world you want. What do you want more than anything in the world?' Guy cautiously opens one eye.

'I hate you,' he says.

'Me, too,' True agrees.

'A horse.'

'You know we can't get a horse. Where would we put him? The garage?'

'Maybe a laptop. The orange kind.'

'Okay. I'll get you a laptop. The best they've got. Right now. I'll call them right now, how about that?'

416

'Mommy, you can't call right now. It's Christmas Eve.'

'Well, they might be there. They work all the time. Look, the doctors are here. Police are out there. Maybe computer people are too.' She dials information, then an 800 number and, sure enough, a nimble young man is happy enough to sell her the tangerine model with its own handle, and a color printer, and several very violent games. 'You don't deliver tomorrow?'

'UPS does. It costs . . .'

'I don't care. Get it here as fast as you can.' True turns to Guy, 'See? Must have been MacSanta.'

'Thanks, Mom.' She turns her eyes from the fingers of mottled red welt forming on his cheek.

'Guy, I'll never hit you again.'

'I know.'

'But you can imagine how scared Mama is . . . I thought you were having a vision.'

'I was.'

True stiffens. 'Of what?'

'Forget it. Go to sleep, Mom,' Guy says. 'Turn off the pope. I would hit you if you died, too.'

But True does not sleep. She clasps her knees and squeezes herself onto the heater, next to the window, where a sky of white cloud on amethyst occasionally shreds to disclose, only for a moment, a star. She remembers driving with Guy, once when he was maybe seven, and how she had spotted two stars that seemed to be ping-ponging back and forth in the sky. 'Look Guy,' she'd pointed. 'A flying saucer. Or a satellite. Or shooting stars.'

'Or maybe astigmatism,' Guy had replied, and True had thought with amusement, this is his first grown-up conversational joke.

True has no idea what frequency God is on tonight. But she looks hard at whatever star is revealed at a given moment, as if it were a button she could press, and prays, 'They say You had a son. I don't think You treated him well.'

She forms her hands, a hollow to cover her face, and goes on, 'You let him die when he cried for You. You made him essentially a suicide pilot for Your . . . Your glory. I don't think it would have been worth it to me. I don't respect You for it. But I know You believed it was right. That much I know. Did You regret it? Did You care? Were You . . . proud? At least, if all this is true, You got him

417

back. He was with You that very day. He went right to Your right hand, where he sitteth. And, even before that, You had all Your heavenly hosts. All Your heavenly Pips. I only have Guy. I have this one son, like You did. You took my father, and Peter, and Hank. They say You watch the sparrows, so watch me. If You are my Father, don't take my child. I'll give up sex or food, or my life, or my bone marrow, or anything demanded of me. I'll give up Hank for good. I'll never get over vanity, but I can live with being old and ugly. I'll give up my looks. I'll give my money away.

'Please spare this one. Even if You take away the one inside me. Please spare this one.'

TRUE IS ASLEEP, cat-curled on the foot of her bed, at ten A.M. on the day after Christmas, once the tide of yet more carolers and candy-cane bringers, who have awakened all the patients, has ebbed. Something in the atmosphere of the room changes. She opens her eyes. A man in a black overcoat and black hat stands in the doorway. At first, she thinks she must be dreaming, that the angel of death, whom she has unambiguously invited by lipping off to God, would not wear a fedora.

But the man asks, 'Are you True Dickinson?'

She thinks then, divorce papers.

I am being served. He is a bass turd. As sensitive as a bass turd.

'Yes?' Or is this . . . the truant officer. 'I've called school twice,' she murmurs, dazed. 'Of course, they're on break.'

'I am Norris Mitchell, of Mitchell and Tate. I represent the estate of Elizabeth Chilmark.'

'Elizabeth?' True sits up. A lawyer perhaps. Forms for a donor. Perhaps they have settled for her after all, though her genetic profile, revealed by her blood draw, matches Elizabeth's on only three of the possible six indices. This, the physician who spoke with her explained, is at least more than most of the general public, but they would try to do better, for four or five of six, to lessen the chances of rejection.

But the man quickly says, 'I am so sorry that I have to tell you that Miz Chilmark died yesterday morning shortly before six A.M.' True stands up. 'It was peaceful. She was asleep, and in no pain. But I am here, True, because it was Miz Chilmark's wish that I deliver this to you personally. He holds out an envelope, addressed in Elizabeth's firm copperplate handwriting. Her personal stationery.

418

As a gesture of love and faith, Elizabeth has written, in a short note, she wishes True to accept as a bequest the restoration of Elizabeth's shares of Twelve Times Blessed. True's debt is cancelled. '*I hope*,' the note concludes, '*this letter finds Guy well and strong. I appreciate your gesture, True, your courage and perseverance. And your many kindnesses. Your friend, Elizabeth.*'

True holds the letter on the flat of her hands like a small live bird, like a chalice. Elizabeth's generosity is unexpected and magnanimous beyond anything True would have suspected.

Still, after the man leaves, she raises her eyes and addresses the ceiling, 'I want You to know, if this is closing a door and opening a window, I am not signing on. It's no deal.'

JANUARY

BRAND-NEW YEAR, BRAND-NEW LIFE

Let the good times roll with a molded poly snow globe, filled with glittering New Year symbols, from stars and moons to golden horns and flutes, which plays not just 'Auld Lang Syne' but also 'The Skye Boat Song' and 'Pachibel's Canon,' and which cannot be overwound. It comes inside a golden-quilted keepsake treasure chest (suitable someday either for baseball cards or earrings), with a champagne candle for you, and a little figure toy that's a whole new 'twist' on Father Time!

SINCE GUY HAS come home, weighing only eighty pounds and walking with a rightwise hitch, True has made brief office appearances but spent most of her time tutoring and playing with her son.

He is weary but game; she is wearier.

As promised, her brother had arrived with bells on. When Guy was released from the hospital, two days after Christmas, Dog had hired a four-horse hitch with a suitably Victorian-looking driver, swathed his wife and daughters, Guy, True, and Kathleen in fur robes, and had them driven all over Chatham, a tableaux with lights shimmering, bells jingling. Alerted in advance, friends waved from their doorsteps. 'Welcome home, Guy!' 'Way to get better, Guy!' 'Guy, looks like you're riding in style!'

The doctor has forbidden school for at least three weeks, as he does not wish Guy to risk further complications from the possible infection of an open incision. Even a sore throat at this juncture could have mortal consequences.

His teacher has not taken this news especially graciously. 'He's already missed *a lot* of school for those performances,' she tells True, 'and I've heard he was out sledding! And moreover, I've had students come to school in casts, wheelchairs, even with IV poles!'

'The performances had nothing to do with the appendix,' True reminds her mildly. 'And those other children? I'll bet those kids had chronic illnesses.'

'They did,' says the teacher. 'Serious illnesses. Like . . . leukemia.'

'But Guy has a *critical* illness, and if he comes to school and gets sick from somebody's sneeze or cough, I'll sue the school district, and you personally, and the public health department, and everyone else I can think of,' True says, even more mildly.

'Well,' the teacher relents, 'I'll send home his work.'

'And it's required by law for you to provide him a tutor.'

'I'll put in a requisition.'

This, True knows, would take at least until Guy's thirteenth birthday to actually go through. So they conspire to whip off all the assignments in the first week, dropping the capitals of Asian and South American countries down onto maps as meaninglessly as alphabet macaroni into soup. They spend the rest of the time surfing the 'Net on Guy's new laptop, or playing 500 rummy at the kitchen table. This, True reckons, is mathematics.

Every time True wins a point, Guy is compelled to sip at ginger ale or try to master a mouthful of pudding. Each time, he gags, but True persists, her mother's fear overriding her mother's natural revulsion at subjecting him to such dreary indignity. Hydration and Guy's sodium levels, matters that scarcely ever crossed True's mind except on the hottest day among the dunes, are now daily anxieties, are vital issues, his pediatrician has warned. Guy has to relearn appetite, like a baby. As if he intuits Guy's frailty, Gypsy lies protectively at his feet. When Guy throws his ball, he cunningly brings it back, but then crosses his paws over it, gallantly sparing his friend's stamina. Since Guy came home, Gyp has never returned to True's bed. True considers the folly of letting a child with an open incision sleep with a dog, but figures it is safe so long as Gyp stays outside the coverlet.

Guy doesn't return to her bed, either. He says he is afraid that his mother will toss, and hurt his cut, or that he will toss and hurt the baby, and that at last to sleep in a soft double bed that smells of him and Gyp, instead of alcohol, starch, and blood, is like being in heaven.

The day after Guy's arrival at home, True hears the red truck crunch onto her driveway, and her heart stutters. Hank throws back the front door, banging the knob against the plaster. 'My guy!' he cries. 'You're home at last! How are you? At least they can't keep me out of here! You look like hell!'

'So do you!' Guy cries gratefully, leaping up, then stooping with the clutch of pain. 'Where have you been?'

'Sit down there, honey. Let me see your cut!'

'Okay!'

Guy pulls up his shirt, and Hank dashes quickly at the corners of his eyes as he beholds the ugly red mouth, with its crusted yellow lips and the rubber tubing True must clean with sterile gloves each day before she changes his dressings, as taught by the home-nursing coordinator. 'Oh, my son, my poor baby, you went through so much! True, you don't look so hot yourself – what's with the hands? Are you supposed to be swollen like that?'

'Glad you could make it, Hank,' True tries to keep her voice flat, but it is riddled with the shrillness of her unspent anger. 'I had everyone but the state police look for you. I called your cell phone. I called Tom. Esa called Adele. My mother . . .'

'Your mother! Stop right there, True. Your mother said I was not to call the hospital under any circumstances, that you had given her express orders that I was not to visit the hospital. She apologized. She said she knew how hard it must be for me, but that she had to go along with your instructions . . . not that I cared. I went anyway . . . I went every day.'

'She did not say that. Hank! Please don't insult me. Please don't try to cover up. You went off resorting for Christmas. It's okay, but don't be an ass about it.'

'Sorry, *ma petite*. Tom found me in Vermont with these two buddies before Christmas, and I bombed back as fast as I could, *in fact*. I was in Vermont because it was no Christmas for me, without my children or my family, True, so you can just shove . . . sorry, Gee. I thought there was a chance you'd relent and let me have Guy part of the time. My parents were set to come before he got sick. Then, I lurked around that hospital parking lot like a fucking pervert, trying to get in and see my child,' Hank says roughly. 'I'm sorry for swearing, Gee. But, say, come to think of it, True. What the hell do you care? Where do you come off asking me my whereabouts? My

422

son, yes, I can see Gee needed me. I'll always hate myself that I didn't just face you and walk right in there and demand to sleep in there like you did. I have an equal right. I was trying to keep the peace.'

'Why?'

'I thought you might give me some credit for it. But you? Not you. True Blue True, the Ever-Righteous. You never answered my letters, or tried to get in touch with me. Why do you give a damn where I was?' Hank's face is purple. Guy fixes on one, then the other face, as if viewing a tennis match.

'Your letters? You mean that single epistle – we're two trains on different tracks? What kind of answer was I supposed to give to that? You made it clear what you wanted. The kids. No part of me,' True retorts. 'Let's get Guy to leave the room while we discuss this.'

'I don't want him to think I'd desert him, though you'd probably like that,' Hank begins.

'I certainly would not like that,' True sighs.

Hank glances at her face, at her girth, and his voice gentles, almost crooning, 'Wait a minute. Maybe I misunderstood.'

'Look,' True says, 'I didn't expect you to be so blunt in your note, that's all. Out of the blue. After how . . . civil we'd been since you left.'

'Yeah, civil,' Hank snarls, newly affronted. 'That is the specialty of the house on Stage Harbor Lane. No matter how you really feel.'

'Give me a break, Hank. I just spent about two weeks in the hospital with a desperately sick kid; and I am not so hot myself, in case you can't tell. I'm ill, and I should be in bed, or this baby is going to come way too early, and neither of us wants that. I really felt snubbed by that note. I'd never given you any reason to think I'd deprive you of access to the children, so why would you threaten me?'

Hank looks genuinely baffled. 'The last note? What did you expect me to say? Keep on begging my ass off? What about the rest? I wrote you pages. What about the phone calls? You never called me back, even before Guy got sick. Never once. Nor after. Even when I came up there.'

'I never saw you. The nurses never saw you.'

'They saw me. They talked to me. That big dark girl with the beads? And the guy? You were asleep. Guy talked to me.'

423

'Did you leave things for Guy?'

'A couple of things.'

'He didn't know.'

'Yes, he did. He said, "Hi Dad," a couple of times, but I don't know if he thought he was dreaming or not. He was all glassy-eyed.'

'I never got a letter from you, Hank. I never got a call. I'm telling you the truth.'

'You got messages.'

'I did not. Only when Esa said you'd called for Guy.'

'What about from your mom?'

'None.'

'Well, then she forgot to tell you. Or she neglected to. After he got sick, I called Isabelle every day, and she told me everything, and I came over to the hospital ten times, but half the time I was afraid to do more than look in. I thought they'd throw me out. I begged Kathleen to let me see him. I begged Esa to let me talk to you.'

'This doesn't jibe. If you called Isabelle, why didn't she tell me? And come to think of it, why didn't you just walk right up? You said you thought of it,' True thinks she must have dropped a stitch. None of this makes sense given the Hank she knows – brash, insouciant, all but incorrigible – especially with strangers.

'And have you take off on me in front of him? Kathleen said you were furious. She said you had the idea that stress had contributed to Guy's illness . . .'

'I never said that! I wouldn't have thrown you out. You have to think better of me than that.' True's disgust is as sudden as her exhaustion. She whispers, 'And you're lying. I should know that if you're talking, you're lying, Hank. Esa would have told me. Why you're bothering to lie, now, is beyond me.'

'Kathleen said she would fire Isabelle. That's what Esa told me. She vowed she would fire her if she did anything to further upset you or Guy.' True tries to remember the times she'd asked Esa, often sharply, to leave off about Hank. She remembers Esa's dozens of failed pleas and ruses to cajole True into calling Hank. If Kathleen still can intimidate her forty-three-year-old daughter, how much more a twenty-six-year-old girl? 'Wait. You said my *mother* would fire Isabelle?'

'Yes, she said she has power of attorney for you now.'

'She does, since you left, but . . . this makes no sense. I can't see

Esa not coming to me. On the other hand, this is not a situation she's ever faced, and she really needs her job now. I wasn't open to the suggestion. But why would my mother . . . ?'

'Here's what I thought. You can hate my guts, True, but to keep me away from him when he was . . .'

'When I was dying, Mom!' Guy breaks in. 'And I did see you, Dad. Lots of times. And I did think I was dreaming, Dad, because you'd just go "shush" and disappear. I was really mad at you.' Guy's visions, True thinks.

'Well, I didn't mean it!'

'She slapped me,' Guy says softly.

'She slapped you? What was that about, True?' Hank demands.

'You're attacking me? For slapping him? Mister Macho? Who said his father fought duels in his spare time?'

'Oh, bullshit, True.'

'Well, don't make me out like a child abuser. You're the one who got him to jump off . . .'

'I told you he wanted . . .'

'Shut up, both of you!' Guy shouts weakly.

'Tell him why,' True says. 'Tell him why I hit you.'

'No reason,' Guy shrugs.

'No *reason?* He said he wanted to die so that at least he could see his real daddy.'

Hank kneels down. 'I'm your daddy, Guy. I'm not your real daddy, but I don't give a damn about that, and I'll bet your daddy in heaven wants you to have a daddy here, too. And if it wasn't for Mom, I'd be here with you right now.'

'Leave me out of this,' True orders.

'If it wasn't that Granny was so scared I'd upset you or something . . . Granny at least gave you my cards and my presents, right?'

'No!' Guy is shocked.

'I sent you OP shirts and a metal detector, and *Grand-mère* sent you waders, your size, and *Grand-père* sent you his own chess set! The Civil War one. And a coat for the baby. And this whole layette Maman crocheted. Where are they, True?'

'I'm sure I don't know. I didn't hide them. They aren't here.'

'Where's Kathleen?'

'Wait, wait, wait. I'll work this out. Just visit him now that you're finally here. Can I leave him with you for a moment?'

'I think I can handle that, True. You can trust me if you go into another room and leave me with our son,' Hank deadpans. Then he asks, the words tumbling out, 'May I touch the baby first?' True thinks of Hank and Adele, perhaps reading before a little fireplace, perhaps starting a beach bonfire, and shakes her head, once, sharply. Hank's face stiffens, and he jerks as if she's slapped him. 'Let me touch my baby, True. Please.'

She softens, and points to a bulge, 'What we have here is a foot.'

Hank touches True's T-shirt with a fingertip. She nearly laughs. 'No, Hank! Not like you're touching a hot stove! You have to give it a little push there, or he's not going to notice you.' Hank pushes harder, and the baby kicks him back. 'Oh, my God,' Hank says.

'There. Now I'm going to go talk to Kathleen.'

With a stride that would have done Himmler proud, True sets off for her office. She does not think she will strike her mother, but the notion is a satisfying and propelling impulse. Kathleen is on the telephone. True scribbles a note on the desk pad.

She will wait for her mother in the kitchen. To join her for tea. ASAP.

As if to share True's indignation, the baby rolls, like a whale breaching.

GUY IS NAPPING, and Hank has left a note promising to return the next morning, when True finally phones her mother and asks her again to come up from the office and join True for a cup of tea.

'I asked you to come up,' she says, when Kathleen strolls into the kitchen, 'an hour ago.'

'I've been too busy, since you haven't been in the office, or at least, not at full capacity,' Kathleen says, no fool she.

'Make an exception,' True says. 'We really need to talk.' Kathleen sighs.

'What can you possibly want that's so urgent?' Kathleen asks. 'Is Guy ill?'

'Guy's fine. He's sleeping. Hank was just with him.'

'Oh, I'm sure he's *fine* then. What do you need?'

'Sit down, Mother.'

'All right,' Kathleen says. 'You said tea. Where is the tea?' True flips the switch on her electric kettle. 'It's a bitter day. Clean through to the bones. I should move to Florida.'

'That's not a half-bad idea.'

'I'd never move to Florida.'

'I know, Mother.'

'Too many ancient, wobbling . . .'

'I know, Mother.' True prepares each of them a cup and a matching saucer. She sits down. 'Now, tell me why, and don't bother to make up anything, not that you would, why you never told me that Hank called me, asking to speak to me personally, not just to arrange a visit with Guy, or that he sent me mail, or that his family sent presents to Guy, and why you prevented him from coming to see Guy in the hospital and threatened to fire Isabelle.'

'Are you still on that kick?'

True thinks her eyeballs will explode from within. '*Kick?* Mother, I asked you why you invaded my privacy and kept my son from his father . . . and I want an answer. Now.'

'His father?' Kathleen sniffs, and nods at True's abdomen. 'And *his* father?'

'I don't care what you think of Hank. But Guy wanted his *father*. He might have recovered sooner if he had Hank to comfort him . . .'

'That was no father,' Kathleen says again. 'That was no father.'

'That's not for you to judge.'

'Well, you're no judge.'

'I can't believe what I'm hearing.'

'You were so sex-crazed and eager and lonely, panting like a dog. You'd have forgiven anything,' Kathleen says. 'I heard you, all those nights, moaning in your room.' True can see herself rising from the chair, catching Kathleen by the shoulders, and shaking her until the teeth rattle in her head.

'You listened to me cry and never came to try to comfort me?'

'I didn't think you'd want it known that you were falling apart. I respected your right to your solitude. Would you have wanted me to come in?'

'No,' True admits. 'I would have felt ashamed, I suppose. In front of you. I'd have felt you were ashamed of me. But I don't know why. You're my mother. I should have wanted to tell you how terribly sad I was.'

'You had a right to be sad. That man made a fool of you in front of this whole town.'

'Stop that, stop it now. I want to know only one thing. Where are my letters? Where are Guy's gifts?'

'I saw Elizabeth gave you back your company.'

'You looked at the letter.'

'Open on the hall table, True. You made no attempt to hide it. Very classy of her. She was a very well-mannered, decent woman.'

'She was. Now, you be one. Tell me where my letters are.'

Kathleen is agitated. She twists her fingers in her pockets and locates a linty mint, which she delicately brushes off and swallows. 'True, if you upset yourself, your blood pressure is going to go up.'

'I'm not upset, Mother. I'm determined.'

Kathleen sighs. 'As for the gifts, you can have them. I didn't open them. And I didn't bring them to Guy because I just thought it would be harder for him in the end. And for you. The reminders. They're in the safe in the office.'

'Okay, I'll get them. I'll give them to Guy when he wakes up. In case you don't realize it, the Bannisters love Guy very much. They love him whether Hank and I are together or whether we're not.'

'Yes, they seem very affectionate. They throw it around.'

'Mother, that's so mean-spirited, even for you. *They are that way*. It's not a show. And don't change the subject.'

'Ah, yes.'

'I *want* my letters!'

'Be sure you do, before you ask.'

'What the hell is this, Mother? Some scene from a Daphne du Maurier novel? Get off your high horse and stop trying to manage my life like some Gothic retainer. What're you going to do next, burn up the curtains? Why wouldn't I want my letters?'

Kathleen drains her tea.

'I have to go get them. They're in my hall table. Then, go ahead and read them. And fall for the big, fat line everyone falls for, be a fool.' She storms out the door, unlocks her door as True watches her through the window, marches back, and then drops two bundles of letters at True's feet.

'You know I can't pick those up, Mom.'

Kathleen stoops and hands True the slimmer bundle. Slowly, True opens the first letter, dated a week after Hank left home.

Dear Wife,

I'm prideful and foolish, and I'm prepared to regret everything I've ever done to hurt you. I can explain better in person than in writing. Please give me a chance. You may hate me, but at least we can talk. Can't we talk? I'll wait for you Monday at Comfort and Joy's. How about six?

Hank

And then the next.

Dear True,

I know now that you are furious. Beyond furious. I've seen you furious. I know this is more. I know you are determined that you will never forgive. But I have to try.

You have a right. I don't blame you. I did wrong. I don't need my mother to tell me that, though, believe me, she has. And more than once.

I have to explain. Please give me a chance. Nothing is like it seems. It's as if it all started to spin out of control and I couldn't stop it. Yes, I could have stopped it. But I didn't feel I could.

At first, I wrote to Adele because I felt sorry for her. I didn't initiate the correspondence. She did. And it never seemed to matter to anyone before if Adele would call or write. I thought this was the same kind of thing. I didn't realize what she must have been feeling about our marriage. I was gullible. But I also guess I liked the idea that she couldn't get over me. She always said no one could ever take my place, that I ruined her for other men. It was an ego thing. I feel like a fool about it now.

And then, when she kept on writing, I didn't know how not to answer her. She was so desperate the sicker her mom got. Her grief was like a web. It was palpable. It reached for me and grabbed me. I never thought she was using that grief to get to me in a way that wasn't possible anymore. Before, Adele would drop into town, and we'd have dinner and

429

whatever, and then off she'd go again. It was as if I was the one thing she could count on always being there for her.

When she drove up here the first time, on the way to New Hampshire, I was happy for her. She seemed to care about this guy, though she said she'd never love him the way she loved me. That was freaky. I tried to beg off. I tried to explain that I couldn't see her. Then, the thing with this Dave was over, like almost before it started. Clearly, he caught on to something about Adele way sooner than I did. She was hysterical. I honestly thought she'd kill herself, and her baby, after he ditched her. That's when she came to the restaurant.

And I still told her, I have a wife. I love my wife. I love my son. We're having a baby. And she cried and said, what about all those years, Hank? You mean you could love her more in six months than you loved me in six years? I was terribly sorry for her. You would have been sorry for her, if you'd seen her. But I said, when you find the one for you, you'll know. You'll know just like I did. I told her the truth. The time we could have been together is past. And finally, she said she understood. But she still wrote me, dozens of e-mails, begging me to answer. And I would try to answer one or two, just tell her I was still her pal.

Then, when Marie was dying, I thought you would understand. That this was the end of it, that she would stop clinging to me. I never knew, when I came home that day, that you'd be sick. And I had already decided not to go, when I went into the shower, with your mother standing there, when you went at me. And the fool in me just rose up. I wouldn't let any woman tell me my business. I thought of all the times I felt like that when we were first married, that you were the boss and I was just some guy you let hang around.

And I did the worst thing I ever did in my life. I left you alone there.

Oh, True, I'm not a begging man. I've never begged. But I would beg you on my knees if you would forgive me for that mistake. It was cruel and mulish and hard-hearted. I turned that truck around five times to come home, but then, I'd think, she threw me out. She threw me out, and I'd go on. All I did the whole time I was in Cambridge was think of you, and how

I'd make it up to you. All I did was worry, thinking I'd kill myself if I got home and our baby was gone.

Then I got home. And I wanted to throw my arms around you. And you told me to pack. You threw me out like a piece of garbage. You wouldn't hear a word I said. It wasn't your fault. I know how it looked. But I could have told you, it was never that way.

The least you could do was stand in front of me and tell me that what we had wasn't real to you. That it wasn't something you never felt before in your life. Tell me that the way you looked at me at Esa's wedding wasn't filled with something you can't put words to. I can't put words to it.

But you knew me, I'm sure of it. As you never knew any other man. And I loved you with everything I have in me.

I still do, True. I still do. I still do.

I didn't have sex with Adele that night. I would never have dishonored you that way.

I want to be your husband all my life. I want to live with you in peace. If you think I need a shrink, I'll go to a shrink. A man can change, if he has will enough. I can change with you. My daddy says it. He says I've lost the dearest jewel in my life, and he's right.

Please come to the restaurant, any time. We can talk. I know you'll see my side of it. I've made a lot of mistakes. Big ones. Number one was behaving like I did about our child. How selfish and immature I was with Guy. I'd let him rip the shirt off my back and use it for a kite now. True, I can't eat and I can't sleep. I've got a lot to answer for. But I can spend the rest of our lives proving to you that I never, ever meant to hurt you. If it's a sin to be stupid, then I'm a sinner. But I want to touch you more than I want heaven.

Your loving husband, Hank Bannister

It is Hank in every line, but True cannot believe he has written it. A man who can seem so ebullient, so quick with the gesture, and yet so abstruse when it comes to hard answers has laid his full hand on the table. True cannot unravel the ball of yarn back to the first knot. She cannot site the exact place where two quirky people planted

431

a flag on the crest of their unusual circumstances, and no sooner having pledged, began to slide. She cannot sort out which of her foibles prompted Hank to throw up barriers, or which of his barriers unleashed her claws.

But these words might have prevented all of it, once. They might never have parted, then been forcibly held apart, by circumstance and duplicity. Holding these pages, she is weighted by terrible tenderness and poignancy. She wipes her spilling eyes with the insides of her shirt cuffs. How must she have seemed to him, how callous, how shallow, ignoring this naked a supplication?

And yet these words on a paper do not erase all they have done and said, the myriad small and large wounds never healed.

But it cannot be too late. She can make him understand. He has made her understand. If there is time, there must be hope. There must be.

She opens the other letter, written later, more desperately.

True,

If I have been a fool and a child, I am sorry. I'm not a writer. I don't have a gift for words. But I love you still. I still want to live with my wife and my son. I miss my boy. Please reconsider this choice. Love cannot be forced, but when you threw me out, I could not bring myself to apologize. We share this awful pride, you and me. Let me tell you about the hours I've spent walking that beach, looking up at the lights in the house that was my home, where I spent the happiest days of my life as a man.

I never thought I was getting back at you, through Adele, for the small way you made me feel. About my role in your life. Like I was just another of your servants. Now I see that I was. I see that it wasn't you who made me feel that, it was me. You kept saying you weren't good enough for me. I kept thinking I wasn't good enough for you.

You know everything. Books, business, history. I knew nothing but how to make shrimp on rice. I act like a bigshot to cover that up. Oh, True, maybe you never should have loved me. But you did, True.

You did love me. I know it.

432

I might be undeserving of that love, True. But we got over all the rocks. Didn't we? The horrible hard parts, the fights, the hurt I caused, all the fears you felt. We beat them all. We did what they all said we couldn't do.

How can you give that up? I can't say I don't understand why you don't want me. But whenever I see you, I don't miss the longing in your eyes. I don't know if it's for me or just for the future we were supposed to have, that didn't work out as we planned. I ask Guy, and he says you're just waiting for the right time to let me come home. He says you're teaching me a lesson. Teaching me a lesson? That sounds like my wife. My Puritan.

Maybe that's too forward. I shouldn't be presuming to make jokes.

Do you want me to wait forever? I would say that I would wait forever, if that would give me hope. I'm here. I'm waiting.

I'll say one more thing. Guy tells me you cry. He tells me you sleep in my shirt. Oh, the fucking shirt! Why didn't I see what I was doing? Your poor face, your hard work.

Why didn't I give you praise when you were unsure? Why did I mock it?

I guess because I was so insecure myself. Insecure? Hank Bannister? Mais yeah. Like Perry. I had to show everyone. The slinky girls. The motorcycle. But I was nothing but air inside a suit of clothes.

I never showed anyone anything inside me to anyone but my kin. And then you. Mostly to you. I guess I never thought there was a damn thing inside, 'til you saw it. You brought out the best in me and I spurned it.

You told me you were mine. Bébé. You told me you were MINE.

When I see you, you're not cold. You're not mean. You're like you'd be with an old friend. But I don't feel that way. I don't feel like you're my old friend. It kills me. I want what we had. Yes, all the mess. All the complications. All the noise. I even miss Kathleen.

At least think this over. For Guy's sake, and the baby's, if not for us. I won't let you down. You have no reason to believe me. But I will not. I swear it. You can count on me forever.

This sounds like a stupid country-western song. There are some things you just can't say without sounding corny.

Hank

Her mother has stood, erect and motionless, while True reads. True raises the letter between them, like a torch. 'Why in the name of everything human did you do this, Kathleen?'

Kathleen answers, 'Didn't you love the part where he said he missed me?' She smiles, a smile wrung by malice, and something else. There is an animal scent in the room. A wild taint.

'Don't you dare say one word about him in my house, Kathleen. Not one word.'

'Don't call me that,' her mother snaps.

'I can't call you "Mom" right now. I feel as though I'm standing here with a stranger.'

'Well, I suppose now you're going to run over and ask his girlfriend whether you can see him.'

'That's ugly, Kathleen,' True says. 'But yes, if I could, if he would listen, if you haven't made that impossible, that's approximately what I would do. I'd walk there, if I had to. How could you think these letters were anything but sincere? How could you have failed to see how much he regretted what he'd done? There's something about . . . you. You're . . . scared, aren't you? You're scared by what you did? I'm going to pretend I didn't hear what you just said. I'm going to give you a chance to be good to me.'

'Before you go running, there's something else I want you to see,' Kathleen says grimly. 'I should have showed you these months ago, but I had my own privacy to think of.'

'*Your* privacy! How dare you mention your privacy? After you've invaded my life, done your best to derail my life?' True takes the bundle of envelopes Kathleen holds out to her. They are yellowed, furled with age. She lifts them and shakes them in her mother's face. 'What are these? Dad's letters? You want to prove to me what a real man says to his wife? Here's a news flash! I don't care! I don't want to read them! I'm sick of hearing about Bert Dickinson. So far as I can tell, he never went to a ballgame with Dog, and he never came to a play I was in, and I guess you two had something huge I never quite got the hang of, but I wouldn't have wanted a life with a guy

434

who was gone more than he was there, and was gone even when he *was* there! You know that, Mom? I have no memories of Dad, except for him telling us to read the damned yearbooks! Why do you think that is? I don't think he was much of a father. Maybe you shouldn't have had kids. Maybe he didn't want us . . .'

'If you'll stop raving, you'll see that those are not your father's letters to me,' Kathleen says quietly. 'Look at them, True. Look at them very carefully.'

'Why? What would they mean? How would you like it if your life was scanned by someone else without your knowledge? As if someone were watching you with a hidden camera?'

Kathleen says nothing.

'Come on, Mom, how would you like it? Answer me, Mom!'

'Listen to what I said. They're not from your father,' Kathleen says. 'If you look at them, you'll see what I mean, and why I did what I did. Because I did want children. My children have been my whole life, True. I had no other life. Look at them, True.'

'Who are they from?'

'They're *to* your father. He never saw them, either.'

True looks down at the bundle in her hands. All these letters are open-flapped, dated 1959, 1963, 1965. The handwriting is fat and flowery, like a middle-schooler's. Each small letter 'i' is dotted with a heart or a star.

'Go ahead. There were a dozen times when you were a young woman I wanted to tell you about this, but I never . . . I couldn't bring myself to do it. You might as well know now.'

'I don't want to hurt you, Mother. Take these.'

'No.'

'Take them. They're yours. If we both do something awful, it's only going to make it worse.'

'You can't make it worse. That's already been done.'

Robbie,

says the first letter,

Did you get in big trouble when she called and the hotel clerk said Mr. and Mrs. Dickinson had just left for dinner? Oh, I hope you didn't. But in a way, I hope you did. Then, it can

435

*all be over, the hiding and the lying. How are True and
Augustus? The pictures you sent make him look very bright
and tall. I am dying of love for you. And I can't wait until I
see you again. Your girl forever, Barbie.*

True walks slowly up the stairs, Kathleen behind her, close and silent
as a breathing shadow. True sits down on her bed. The baby break-
dances. She lies back and draws a huge breath. She peels open another
letter, which is only lightly stuck in one corner, one of the old-fashioned
red-white-and-blue striped envelopes with a ten-cent stamp, and reads:

Robbie, darling,

    *I'm afraid our friend hasn't come to visit. And neither have
you. For a whole month! Not that I care. I'll just find myself
a man who looks just like James Dean and leave you in the
dust. Oh, no, would I ever do that? You're the smartest, kindest,
dearest man I've ever known. Everywhere I look – at 'our'
yellow vase, the shelves you built, my rocking chair, I think of
how much you give me. But the worst thing about all this is
that we can't have a baby of our own. Why not? Why not,
since you spend half your time here anyway? Didn't you ever
see that movie, about the amazing Mr. Pennypacker? Maybe
you have more love than one roof can hold, too. Robbie, I'm
sure I'm not p.g. But I like to think of you worrying about
me. I like to think of you kicking off your shoes, even if your
socks are stinky – how does that woman wash, anyhow? She
must not use fabric softener. And I'm reading the new year-
book. It's the most. Love you, Barbie.*

True's mother is standing in the frame of the bedroom door. 'If
he ever got a single one of them, I never knew. It's easy to take mail.
No one really goes looking for it. It's even easier in a house like
this, in constant chaos.'
'My house is not in chaos. Who is this?'
'Bert's woman.'
'Dad? My dad had a mistress?'
'If you want to call it that.'
'Well, these don't read like the letters of a prostitute.'

436

'Take my word for it, True. She was a slut. I am telling you the God's honest truth here. She was someone to whom he sold encyclopedias. And they did it on that first day. She just wrote him a check and they went right to bed. Or so I assume. I don't even know why she bought the encyclopedias. I doubt whether she could *read*. After I found out, I never slept with him again.'

'But, Mom, you loved Dad so much,' True says, her anger merged with a horrible pity. 'You loved Dad with all your heart. What about all those dances at the Moose Lodge? How could you bear it? How did you find out?'

'Well, you see right there. She sent the letters right to our *house*. She used to put the return address as World Book, Incorporated, but I knew that World Book corporate offices didn't write in violet ink, and like a retarded child. So I started to open them. To steam them open.'

True remembers the night of Hank's envelope of photos, and Kathleen's glittering eyes.

'It must have broken your heart. Mom, you kept this all in. Did you tell Ellen? Did you tell your priest?'

'I told Father Adams. He said that I must pray and hope and fight for my marriage, for your sakes and the sake of Bert's soul. This was what I believed, too.'

'But there was more to it.'

'I wasn't going to let her have him, was I?' Kathleen's eyes brim, horrified.

'I . . . I have no idea.'

'A divorce? This was the 1960s, and not the Sixties you think of when you talk about such things, True. The real 1960s, not peace and love beads. I had never known anyone except Lena Livowitz who'd been divorced. And that was because her husband had another wife in Lynn. I wasn't going to let her have Bert's savings, his pension, other children, a life with the man I'd gone to as a virgin . . .'

'God and Christ.'

'Don't curse.'

'Well, Mother, you must admit . . .'

'I know that you are shocked. I kept meaning to tell you and Augustus. But what did it matter? He was dead. He loved me. He never loved her. I believe that. I know that. But I could see that this man, this Hank, was going to do the same thing to you . . .'

'Mother, no.'

'A younger man? The way he looked at Esa?'

'Esa?' Laughter bubbles up from True like a reflux. She cannot stifle it. 'Esa?'

'At everyone! I saw him looking. And when he left you, and spent the night with that slut . . .'

'I don't think Adele is a slut, but that's neither here nor there . . .'

'You know he would have! You know he would have left you in the end, however it happened! Broken! You'd have lost everything! I still don't know what you'll lose in the divorce! He called you from that woman's apartment, True. I looked at the Caller ID! And then, when he found out you were expecting, he acted like the cock of the walk!'

'That's . . . that's sometimes how it was, right.'

'And how many times did my Bert call me from her house? In that same way, do you see? Her keeping quiet as a mouse? Or laughing at me?' Kathleen rummages among the contents of the bundle. 'Look, look! Here's a picture of her!' True sees a piquant, tiny woman, swathed in a cheap fox coat, a seductive smile, eyes cast sideways in a parody of desire. 'Do you think she is beautiful?'

'No, Mommy. You were much more beautiful!' True, her head pounding, fireworks before her eyes, can still reflect that she has never had such a long and intimate two-way conversation with her mother, over anything except finances and the abuse of library books. 'You are still beautiful.'

'I am. I mean, I was! I was the prettiest girl in Amherst, besides a few. And he took me from my father's house. I wanted him. Yes, True, I had to marry him . . .'

'You were pregnant with Dog?'

'No, but I'd let him . . . do that. And once I had, I was lucky he did marry me.'

'Jesus.' True glances down at one of the open letters. *I'm knitting you a sweater, and I don't have any measurements but my arms. I hope it's good enough. You have those broad shoulders. I can't wait until you come back next time, until you take me dancing at the Big Pine in Madison . . .*

'Why didn't you ask him about it? Why didn't you face him?'

Kathleen hesitates. 'Because then he would have had an excuse to leave.'

'Where did she live?'

'Wisconsin.'

'That's a long way.'

'It was his territory. East of the Mississippi.'

'Does Kellen know this?'

'Kellen is the first person on earth to ever know this. He did some checking for me. He found out where she is. She's still alive. She is married. She has children. Kellen looked it all up.'

'And you never told Dog a word of this.'

'God, no.'

'I still don't get it. How could he know she was sending letters to him and not be terrified you would find them?'

'He didn't care, I suppose. I couldn't exactly bring up the letters, could I? Over dinner? In front of you children? Alone in our bed? I thought that if I kept them, and he asked for a divorce, I could use them as evidence of desertion. But he never asked for a divorce, and he never mentioned any letters. And after you were born, we never had relations.'

'You said that. Mom, I don't want to know any more about that.'

'So it didn't matter. He was on his way home from her when he died.'

'So it was Chappaquiddick.'

'What?'

'Dog and I . . . we always thought something was . . . funny about Dad's death. About how we never really heard very much about it. We just carried on . . .'

'Everyone did, in those days. You weren't supposed to talk to children about the dead parent. That's what the mortician said.'

'But if she was in Wisconsin . . .'

'She was here! She was here, visiting, that summer. *Visiting*. She had a house in Harwichport.' True is mystified, horror and fascination a seductive brew.

'I could have seen her. When I was out there, baby-sitting.'

'I was afraid that you would.'

'But I wouldn't have known her, Mother. How would I have known?'

'Yes. I thought she might . . . approach you.'

'It doesn't matter. I'm sorrier than I can tell you. Mommy, you made this plaster saint out of Dad for us, for the whole world, and he was just a weasel who cheated on you all your life.' She pictures her parents, getting out the Christmas ornaments, slicing the Sunday roast, perhaps him fastening the clasp of her necklace before Casino Night at the Moose Lodge, circling, for a decade, the big elephant leering and swaying in the middle of the living room. She imagines them driving in their car, commenting on the weather, the price of children's shoes, the illnesses or births among their circle of friends.

Her mother bursts out, 'How could I face it? How would that have made me look? If I'd admitted it? Poor Katie, couldn't hold on to her man. Do you think I'd have kept my friends? Kept any self-respect? I would have looked the way . . .'

'The way I do now, Mother. I know that's what you mean. But I don't care, Mother. I don't agree with the way you think of me. Though I have felt terribly humiliated. It's phony humiliation though. I just shook the dice and lost. That doesn't make me a fool. Or, it doesn't make me so much a fool as I feel. Have . . . Mom, have you ever talked to a doctor about this?'

'You mean, a psychiatrist?'

'Yes, because what you did with Hank . . . this was very not . . . it was overly . . . it was nuts.'

'Not if you think about it.'

'Yes, if I think about it. I haven't even begun to think about it. When I think about it, I'll think it was even more outrageous than I do now.'

'She came to the funeral, True! She came to Bert's funeral! I saw her. I saw her look at me. She was fat. Not fat. A stout woman. By then.'

'But that was thirty years ago, Mother. You didn't speak to her?' True is aghast.

'I wanted to. I wanted to say, "Give me what belongs to me. Everything he gave you, every scrap of paper or piece of jewelry." I don't know if she even worked, True. He could have paid her rent. I would never have known. Bert carried the checkbook. Bert paid the bills.'

'I think you *should* see a psychiatrist. You have been carrying this around way too long. You still have a long life left, Mom. If you're going to . . . live, you might as well try to get over this. What you lost, and what you did to . . . me.'

'What would a psychiatrist tell me? That I was overprotective of

440

my only child? I mean, my only daughter? Who was in the same trouble I was in, so long ago?'

'Were we in the same trouble? I don't think that we *were* in the same trouble. Hank made a lot of lousy calls. But so did I. I was afraid. And . . . maybe a doctor would say that you let fear get the best of you, your whole life. I don't know,' says True. 'Wait until Dog hears about this.'

'Don't tell him, please,' Kathleen pleads. 'He'd lose respect for your father.'

'I'm going to tell him, Mom. Unless you threaten to hang yourself from the linden tree. He deserves to know. It's his life, too. And now that we're on the subject, stop treating Dog like the crown prince and me like Cinderella. Why spare his feelings and not mine?'

'It will break his heart. He respected his father. And he was only twelve. Still, if I were going to kill myself, I'd have done that a long time ago. Don't think I didn't consider it. I pictured Bert finding me dead. Him knowing. But it just was not worth that. I didn't want her to have you,' Kathleen says fiercely.

'Thank goodness for that. She doesn't sound like the sharpest pencil in the box, Mom, if that's any comfort. You're a far more literate woman, with much more class. And I'm sure Dad knew that. But I *am* going to tell my brother, and Hank, and Franny. And it will stop there. I promise. And Mother, I'm not going to fire you.'

'What?'

'I'm not going to fire you, but I'm throwing you out. No, no, not like you think. I'm going to buy you a cottage. Somewhere else nearby here. I am! Because I want to still love you, and I want to still work with you. And I still want Guy to have a grandmother and I want my mother. But I don't want you to monitor my life. I don't want you to pull my strings. There may be times I'm away when Hank or Esa want to stay in that guest house, and that was all it was ever intended to be. Or I might need a baby nurse who'd like her privacy to stay there. Anyhow, I intend to have a life again, Mom. And you should, too. You should . . . go on a date. Live your life.'

'Go on a date!'

'The judge asks you . . .'

'At my age!'

'You *practically* date Esa's father.'

441

'That's ridiculous. And if you want me to move, fine, True. I'll just call Augustus and then . . .'

'Okay.'

'You would let me, wouldn't you? You mean this. Despite Guy's feelings. And my new grandchild. You'd let me move. Alone.'

'I mean it. I never meant anything more. It's what we have to do. I want sole custody of my life.'

'You are cold, True. I don't know how you became so cold.' True doesn't answer, but puts her arms around Kathleen's stiff little shoulders, and feels through Kathleen's sweater the sharp outlines of her shoulders, and the profound droop of her defeat.

'SONOFABITCH. HOW DID we sense it?' Dog asks, later, on the telephone.

'Children do,' True tells him. 'They sense everything. We picked it up like a virus. We were such little goodie-two-shoes. At least I was. And you were a dumb basketball bouncing goofy kid, practically. We were so obedient, Doggie. We were so . . . we tiptoed. We were overdoing it. Because we could see she was hurting. She wasn't just a stick. She was miserable. And trying so hard to put on a show.'

'It really was Chappaquiddick.'

'It really was.'

'How old would Dad have been when he died?'

'What? Forty? Forty-two?'

'Well, at least he had some happiness.'

'She didn't. Mom didn't.'

'Maybe she will now.'

'I told her she needed to get some counseling,' True tells him.

'Oh, I'm sure she'll do that, True. And maybe she'll take over the chairmanship of General Motors.'

'She could. She could have done . . . so much. Had so much. And she didn't, because it wasn't done. In her world, it wasn't done.'

'Yeah. What kind of man must he have been?'

'I think there were a lot of men like him then. President Kennedy, for one. Did you ever cheat on Linda?'

'No. I thought about it once, a long, long time ago. Right after college. We were high-school sweethearts, True. And I thought I should have at least one chance . . . but no. I would tell you, if I had. True, life is endlessly perplexing. But you got your company

442

back. And now you know Hank tried so hard to reach you. Does that matter to you?'

'It might have, once. I think the moment's passed now. We'll talk about it. By the way, Mom might come to live with you sometimes.'

'Whoa there.'

'Either that, or I'm buying her – no, *you* and I are buying her – a little house. I don't want her so close, where she can have such ready access to me and my every move. If I ever have a life again. Don't worry, I'll pay for most of it, Doggie. But you're going to have to chip in. You have enough money. You have time. Or you'll make time. You're going to have to find the place. I'm going to be a new mom over here. You're part of the sandwich generation, brother mine. And you haven't even tasted the mayo.'

Dog sighs. 'I can't have a real conversation with Mom.'

'No one can have a conversation with Mom. Though I think I just did. It was surreal.'

'I pictured you two having discussions about books, making plans for the business, listening to music . . .'

'Oh, it was *so* like that, Dog. You must be on drugs. Send some over. Yes, she's just finished calling me a sex-crazed, deluded old hag.'

'I'm sorry, Sis. That you had to swallow that. I knew she was hard to take, but not like that. Well. I'll do more. Linda will. I wish I'd been there for this. I should have been. I could have driven up.' Dog pauses. 'And if I'd known what she did to Hank and you . . .'

'Well, I could hardly have invited you to the occasion. The opening of Pandora's box.'

'At least Guy's better,' her brother offers.

'Yeah, but I'm not so hot . . . I have pre-eclampsia.'

'What the hell is that?'

'The short answer is, high blood pressure and so much water in me I feel like the *Titanic*. It somehow keeps the babe from getting enough of what it needs.'

'Better see to it quick, then.'

'I will. I love you, bro.'

'I love you. The sonofabitch.'

'Who?'

'Hank. I mean, I blame Mom, too. But there's the fact. He caused this.'

443

'No, Doggie. I'd love to agree with you, because a part of me is still royally pissed at Hank, too, but there was also so much about him I never understood, and maybe that he didn't understand until . . . we lost each other. But stress has nothing to do with it. Nothing. That's an old wives' tale. Even if I am an old wife.'

The letters Kathleen has shown her, however, had done their intended work, planted the seed of the bitter fig. She is afraid to write, afraid Adele may open her letter, or, if she mails it to the restaurant, it may be opened by one of the staff, or the accountant. She thinks of marking it 'PERSONAL,' but that is all but an invitation.

And what if he simply rejects her?

What if she has left him too long with head bowed?

That afternoon, before she sees her obstetrician, True mails Hank a card in care of the restaurant. She is careful with her phrasing. She writes:

Dear Hank, I'd like to talk with you soon. There still are many things we need to decide. At least, I hope there are. Things that haven't yet been decided. And I have something interesting to tell you, which may help explain why I gave it my worst at every possible juncture. I know you're very busy right now. So don't think of this as a summons. But whenever you can make time, please be in touch. Please. True.

BECAUSE OF HER condition, the new obstetrician, a charming Asian woman about True's age, has ordered that True's blood pressure be checked every two days, and the fetus monitored at the same time. Both can be done not in Boston, as True has feared, but closer to home, at Cape Cod General, in Hyannis, where True will deliver. 'I can tell you this,' the doctor says. 'You really can't predict fetal size from an ultrasound, no matter what anyone says, but her, er . . . or his development looks good. The size looks good. So we know the baby is growing, at least.'

Esa, who accompanies True to the appointment, in the role of the husband, learns to read True's blood pressure with a home unit. 'It's not just a job, Truly Fair, it's an adventure,' she says cheerfully, as she marks the morning, noon, and evening numbers on a chart each day. True's pressure hovers at around one hundred and fifty or sixty over ninety-five, not yet terrifyingly high, but concerning.

True gets out of bed to shower, to sit at her desk for brief periods, until her head begins to thump and to whirl. Then slowly, stopping at every riser on the staircase, she returns to her bed and her elevated foot pillows.

A week passes, then two. True feels as though she is swimming in dreams, lights and sounds that are not real jigging before her eyes. Pain at her brows and temples scoffs at Tylenol. She sleeps and wakes, and sees Hank's face, near, up close over hers, the sky above Mount Washington behind him, his lips parted, his eyes thirsty and embracing. She reaches down to touch her ring and finds it gone. She remembers, then. Another seven or eight weeks of this trance? True cannot feature it.

She drifts and sleeps, sleeps and rises to use the bathroom. This time, she tries to read, Anne Morrow Lindbergh. But she cannot. She must go, but the pee will not come, an extraordinary sensation. She walks back and forth between her bed and the window. She tries again. She cannot go. True lies back down, having splashed her face. Anne Morrow's words dance a hornpipe before her eyes. She closes them to sparklers on her eyelids. *Hank's back, in his soft blue chambray shirt. Hank, flying through the air on the stunt bike, his grackle-black Indian hair grown long, blown back. Clink, the coin on the floor of the blue, blue tomb. Hank's hands on her belly, tickling; her breasts beat and tingle.*

She reads, forgets what she reads, and speaks on the telephone to Larry Sornberger, who says that he is fashioning her a cradle, gratis. She thanks him sweetly. He says it will be made in the old style, with a foot rocker and a handle that can be reached from the bed, to rock the babe when he awakens.

There comes a day when she cannot rise even to shower.

True's head no longer hurts, but feels as though it is expanding. If she could see herself, she would see a vast, stretched rubber mouth and a forehead elongated as in a plane of funhouse mirror. A fish-eye lens has replaced her own good eyes. Her hands, splayed before her, do not seem to be hers, nor even human. She reaches for her bedside scissors, and poises them to puncture her own swollen upper arm, just above the top of her wrist, and stops herself a centimeter before the sharp blade pierces her skin. She would rejoice to see the liquid gush out, freeing her, shrinking her, giving back her sense of her body's own reality. *Hank, she calls out in silence, think of me.*

She has no time left.

True lifts the phone and dials her office. 'Esa,' she says, 'I need to go to the hospital.'

SHE LIES ON her side in her bed, with its bottom cranked to raise her feet, and imagines flying. Like the mother eagle, True can see down, from high above. She can see her mother bustling about her cottage, packing, raging. Crying? Is *Kathleen* crying? Or is this an old memory of a movie, a movie like *The Wizard of Oz?* Dog is there, his hands too large, large beyond competence. Dog will see to matters. She sees Hank, down below Kathleen, on Ridgevale Beach, with pale, small Guy walking quietly at his side and Gypsy romping. She is more dizzy than she would have thought it possible to be without a snootful. She is dizzy, whirling while lying still. She curls on her left side, a monitor like a bellyband on a horse circling her girth. What have they put in the IV that drips into her hand? Surely, nothing that could fill her with more fluid. It is perfume. It is grape-fruit juice. It is heart's blood.

'*Her pressure is one-sixty over one-ten . . . and there it goes, it's fluctuating . . .*'

'*The fetus is showing some signs of distress . . . no, maybe just deprivation . . . oxygen? Not for the baby, for her?*'

'*The diastolic is rising . . .*'

'*. . . to the placenta?*'

'*Every day is a good day. Let's hold off and watch . . .*'

'True,' Franny says soothingly, 'I'm here.'

True wakes suddenly, fully. 'Franny, how long have I been here?'

'Three days, honey.'

'I think they keep me doped.'

'I think they should.'

'Are you here because I'm in trouble?'

'I'm here because they think they're going to induce your labor, True.'

'Induce my labor?'

'Yes.'

'Wait,' True reaches to buzz for the nurse. 'They're confused. It's way too soon.'

446

'They've done antistress tests on the fetus . . . she seems as ready as she can be. You knew that the risk of prematurity . . .'

'The baby will die! Where is Hank? I want Hank!'

'He's coming,' says Franny, as the nurse comes bustling in. It is not Nigeria. True wishes it could be Nigeria.

'We're going to prep you and move you into the labor and delivery suite, Missus Dickinson . . .'

'Missus Bannister. It's too soon. What day is it?'

'It's the seventeenth of January.'

'That doesn't make any sense. The baby is due March fifth.'

'Doctor thinks that the risk to the baby and to you at this point outweighs the risks of prematurity . . .'

'I want my baby to live!'

'Missus Dickinson . . .'

'Bannister,' Hank says. 'She's my wife. I'm Henry Bannister.' Hank is immaculate, in white shirt and chinos, his hair still wet.

'Folks, we've seen more premature babies do extremely well. After the first few days, she'll be out of the woods. We'll watch her breathing, and monitor her closely for a brain bleed . . .'

'Her brain? No, I'll wait. I'll just wait.'

'You can't, Missus Bannister.'

'Mom,' Guy says, his voice a tremor. 'Is our baby going to die?'

'No,' True says. 'Come here and hold my hand, Gee. Our baby is going to be fine.'

'I brought you your doll. Look what Esa put on it.'

On the back of the doll, given her so long ago, in a makeshift carrier, is now a papoose, a little face wrapped in layers of burlap. 'Rudy made her. See her little black hair?'

True is absorbed in looking not at the papoose but at the doll's face. She has never before seen it so plainly. It is not, after all, a reject, a prototype for Chris Evert Lloyd. It is, instead, vintage, this doll model made over into the image of True, in her sweatshirt and jeans. It is the original Saint Joan, from the days when True first began her work at Elizabeth's Heroines, before the decision to cut the doll's hair short, in the soldier's style Joan wore most of her years as a general and as a martyr at the stake. This doll, with long hair, is a collector's item, at least, and almost a relic. There is a remote possibility that it is only coincidence that Elizabeth chose this doll to give to Rudy as the model for the caricature of her former

447

adjutant. But it would be difficult to believe. Elizabeth did nothing without due consideration, and was entirely aware that her dolls might one day form part of a Smithsonian exhibition on twentieth-century home life.

True thinks of the living Joan, centuries ago, her testimony re-created, in language children can understand, in the book that accompanies the doll, *If I am in a state of grace, I would hope that I should remain so, and if I am not, I would hope that I shall be.* An unlettered child, dirty and imprisoned, alone, terrified and bullied, in her filthy scarlet gown, knowing full well she had scant hope of ever growing up, or falling in love, or bearing a child, or even looking up unchained at the blue French sky, she had reached out, before her cruel inquisitors, for courage. Nothing has ever been different, now or then, in the world. I have lost what seems to have been the great love of my life, and what absolutely was the grand passion. But most people have lost more. I have almost certainly lost the possibility of ever having another child. But perhaps this one will be safe. If she is not, I will make her well. I am strong. And so, True thinks, the center of my life is intact. It will be intact. And it is not beauty, not my talents, nor even my son alone, nor this child, but an abiding courage, to see life through in a murky world, so that life might offer its own occasions for grace. The doll beside her on the pillow, True allows the nurses to roll and lift her cumbersome self onto a rolling bed. Even as she lies there, the nurse hangs a new drip.

In what seems moments, but which, True can tell from the shift of the sun outside her window, are, in fact, hours, she begins to writhe with cramps.

The cramps build steadily, then begin to roll, wavelike, in timeless cadence.

'Do you need something for the pain, Missus Bannister?'

'Do you mean an epidural? You betcha!'

'That's my True!' Hank says. He has donned a blue net, not different from the one he wears to cook. 'My wife isn't a stoic about pain.'

'I am,' True says. 'But . . . I want to do this thoughtfully and gently, and not strain.'

She begins to drop, down a rabbit's hole, her lower body detached, even while visible to her, her belly's clenching and softening, a marvel of machinery.

'. . . *valium?*'

'*Ninety percent effaced . . . six centimeters . . . we need to be thinking of a Cesarean, Mister Bannister.*'

'Franny?' True cries. 'Franny?'

'I'm here.'

'I want to push.'

'Not yet, True, not yet. They're talking it over.' True thinks of the endless discussions over Guy's CAT scan. Oh, good, she thinks; the baby will be ready for preschool by the time they're finished . . .

'Now, wait, we're at nine centimeters . . . give her a moment . . .'

'Hank?'

'I'm here, sweetie.'

'Do you see the baby?'

'Not yet.'

'Is he handsome?'

'Not yet, True. Wait now, wait . . .'

'Take a deep breath, Missus Bannister,' the kindly Asian doctor instructs True, from a distance. 'Take another . . .'

'Franny, are you holding my hand?'

'I'm holding your hand, True, and Guy is holding your other hand,' Hank says calmly.

True struggles for a clear moment of consciousness. 'Whose hand is Franny holding?'

'My own!' Franny calls.

'I'm gonna yak,' Guy says faintly. 'This reminds me of my appendix . . .'

'I'll take you outside,' Franny offers.

'How long have we been here?' True asks.

'Four, no, five hours,' Franny answers. 'I'll get Guy some food.'

'We just got here!' True cries out. 'I have to clean his incision . . .'

'I did that, at home,' Hank tells her.

'You did?'

'Yes, it's fine.'

'Did you put the bandage back on? Is that Esa?'

'She just peeked in. There, wave to her.' True lifts one hand, lets it drop.

'She'll be fine,' Hank tells Franny firmly. 'I'm here. Now, I'll be with True. Okay, True, let's do this . . .'

'I can't remember *anything*. From last time.'

'This is a new time. You don't have to remember anything. Except that I love you and we're having our baby. All you have to do is what they tell you.'

'Take a deep breath, Missus Bannister, and now . . . push!' True writhes and puffs, and Hank grips her shoulders and gently but firmly, presses down with both his big hands. Franny returns.

'Are you comfortable with the nurse and your friend holding your legs?'

'Is my son . . . home? Is my son at school?' True asks.

'He's outside, and he's fine,' Franny says. True relaxes, and potent potions make her drift.

'Each of you take one leg . . . now, take a deep breath and . . . I see dark hair; I see the baby's . . . we're crowning . . . one more push, Missus . . .' True glances down on her splayed, slick, and pulsing self and sees a tiny dolphin girl, a mermaid child, come sliding into the doctor's hands. The tiny mermaid is whisked away, before Hank even can cut the cord, which a father and not a nurse should do; and True strains to see as the doctor instructs her, 'Now, we'll push out that placenta . . . we're not done here yet.' But my baby, True insists, her mouth making no sound, as a great, sucking sliding mass emerges, the doctor's firm hand pressing down on her abdomen. 'There . . . there we go.' My baby, True asks, watching the white rumps of the assembled team gathered around the bassinet at the corner of the room, moving, reaching, measuring, lifting . . . through their elbows and waists she sees a thick shock of wavy dark hair. Adam or Isabelle, Brewster or Gwynevere, Chloe or Ian. Crying, crying in good, strong, indignant resentment at being thrust from the safe floating world that was her own.

Is it a girl? Is it a boy? True asks. Her mouth makes no sound.

'MISSUS BANNISTER?' SAYS the doctor. 'Are you awake?'

'Yes,' says True. 'I'm ready.'

The mirth in the doctor's face lets True breathe. 'I've already spoken to your husband. We are very, very encouraged. You baby is four pounds and ten ounces, which at this point of gestation is quite large indeed, and breathing well, unassisted, and the Apgar scores were eight at birth and nine at five minutes! What do you think of that, huh?'

450

'I'm very happy, but . . .'

'So as soon as we perform the standard tests, and as soon as you can get the weight up over five pounds, we can look at perhaps going home, unless something untoward develops.'

'Doctor! Is my baby a boy or a girl?'

'Oh, Missus Bannister. I'm so sorry. Didn't you see her? It's a girl! It's a beautiful, olive-skinned little girl!'

'A girl?'

'Yes, a wonderful little girl. The best jaw and lips! A kissy mouth.'

'Has Hank . . . has my husband seen her?'

'And held her. And so has your son.'

'Will you bring her to me?'

'I'll bring you to her.' True goes into the washroom, fluffs her hair with wet fingers, brushes her teeth, and pees for such a long and ridiculously delicious interval it is nearly orgasmic. When she steps on the scale, she has lost twenty pounds. Her hands, while still swollen, again have lines at the knuckle. Pre-eclampsia, the doctor has said, gradually simply disappears on its own, and no one quite knows why it happens or to whom it will happen. Even age, though it is more common among mothers past forty, is no sure predictor. True then allows herself to be wheeled down the hall to the special-care nursery, where she searches the bank of Plexiglas beds for the baby she is certain she will recognize.

'You see,' the doctor says. 'There are larger babies in there than your little mite. Those are the babies in trouble. Who have breathing issues, or heart defects . . .'

'She doesn't have those.'

'Not so far as we know . . . she's a corker, but I'm afraid she doesn't look much like you.'

'I guess her father has very bossy genes after all,' True smiles. 'She's part Creole.'

'Well, that explains it,' the doctor beams, as they round the door. 'Premature babies who have the very best lung development are African-American and female. Guess you got lucky with that bossy gene.'

'You don't have to wheel me all the while, you know. You're . . . don't the nurses do this?'

'Normally. But when I had my son two years ago, my sister gave me Twelve Times Blessed.' The two women exchange a private smile. Then the doctor says, 'There she is . . . oops, looks like she's just getting her flannel back on . . . that's a special heated bed, and unless we wrap her in thermals, you can't really keep her out too long . . .'

But the doctor's voice is tuning out, like a distant radio. True watches her daughter's arms flail and wriggle, her tiny chapped red feet drawing up calisthenically.

She would know her anywhere, on any street on any planet. She has known her all her life, and before her life began, and before life itself began . . .

'Elizabeth Brewster Bannister,' True says, bending over her daughter's flossy, huge head, her little, muscled, skin-covered sticks of arms and legs. She is half-baked, no eyebrows, no fingernails, but a full set of essential parts. Her eyes are great and dominant, already brown. 'Brew Bannister, my daughter. Hello.'

TRUE AND HANK lie together on the hospital bed as True nurses.

'You didn't name her that for me? Just because I wanted to?' Hank asks, using the outside of his forefinger to stroke the baby's cheek.

'I'm so lucky you were part Creole; I think that's what saved her,' True says.

'One thing I did right. But about her name.'

'Hank, I love her name. It means a great deal to me to call her after Elizabeth, my contribution, and the name you loved. We're gonna be a team, aren't we, sugarheart? True and Brew, you and me against the world. And, Hank, you were great in there. How come you're not always like that?'

'How come *you're* not always like that?'

'I'm best in a crisis.'

'Guess I am, too. And I never had a baby before.'

'You still haven't.'

'You know what I mean. You rise to the occasion.'

True knows that fathers can sleep overnight, and on an impulse asks Hank, 'Do you want to stay . . . with us? They let the fathers stay, you know.' His face brightens, but then Hank shakes his head.

'Guy needs me, kiddo. He's at the house.'

'With *Adele*? My son is with *Adele*?'

'True, it's a school day. He wanted to go to school, even though

452

he was up half the night. Bragging rights, I guess. Surgery and a new sister. He won't be home for an hour, and Esa's meeting him there. I think he's feeling a little neglected, after being a celebrity last month.'

'You got to get in there quick in this family, to get your fifteen minutes.'

'Yeah, he said to me last night, "You know, Dad, I almost died." I think I should be with him.'

'He'll be fine. I'll get Esa to stay overnight.'

'True, he'd rather be with me. If you're worried about Adele, she's not there anymore.'

'You mean, not today.'

'I mean, not at all, not anymore.'

'Why not? I thought you two had a nice thing . . .'

'I don't really want to talk about this now.'

'Oh fine, Hank! I'll just cater to your wish for defuscation. Then just leave. Esa will stay with Guy . . .'

'All right! All right! I asked Adele to find a roommate. I was waiting to answer your letter until she did. And she has now. You won't believe it. She went to New York with . . .'

True's heart flickers. 'Why?'

'Why was I waiting?'

'Yeah.'

'I didn't want her being in my space to get in the middle of anything we talked about.'

'Why did you ask her to move?'

'That was the other reason I held off getting together with you. She was getting . . . too involved.'

'How do you mean?'

'She was getting too involved with me, making assumptions . . .'

'That you were going to be a couple?'

'Yes.'

'And you're not.'

'No. We never would have been.'

True gently transfers Elizabeth Brewster to the other breast, feeling with gratification her strong, satisfying tug. How can a baby, full seven or eight weeks early, be so strong? She would have been a monster, the doctor has said, a nine-pounder easily. It is as though she were describing a bass. 'I'm sorry, Hank.'

453

'You are?'

'Well, yes. I didn't want you to put Adele out just on general principle. Her ... what happened ... it was only the proximate cause of the end of us. I read the letters. I know how much anger was there. And how much genuine promise. It was all so confusing to me. I think you believe I was guilty of more wisdom than I ever was. At first, when I finally got hold of your letters, I wanted to call you and ask you to move back home that night.'

'I wish you had,' Hank says softly.

'But then, when you didn't follow up on my note, I thought, I'm reading more into this than was there. He meant that then, but he doesn't mean it now, and he doesn't know how to tell me. And I was so sick . . .'

'Oh, True,' Hank tells her, gently pushing back her hair, which is gloriously, freshly washed, for what True feels is the first time in months. 'What a mess. The first thing you have to know is that my silence didn't mean I want this to be the end of us.'

'You don't? Oh, Hank, I . . . I don't, either. And it's not only the pain medication. Or the hormones. Or this beautiful little thing here. I don't want this to be the end of us, and I've been as stiff-necked and foolish a Yankee as you ever called me.'

'So you want me to come home?' Hank looks aggrieved, not relieved.

'I do, so much. I always have.'

'Thank God. I mean it; I prayed. Because for all those weeks, I didn't know. I would never have moved in with Adele, and nothing would have ever happened, if I had known there was even a chance we could begin to restore our family. But you see, I didn't know. I thought of you tearing those letters up and laughing at me. Then, I come to learn about Kathleen keeping the letters. I was hurt and I was mad.'

True thinks she has heard something that zings and crackles around the room like stray voltage.

She shakes her head, and her nipple slips out of Brew's mouth, and True is forced to chuckle at the baby's watery, breast-milk moustache. She tries to reconfigure her position; but Brew is clearly sated. Instantly, with a chesty little double sigh, she collapses into sleep. 'Nothing would have happened? You mean you never would have let Adele stay with you? But the pregnancy? You said she felt so alone. I know how she must have felt. I had Esa, and Rudy, and my mother . . . and Guy, or I'd have, I'd have given up. It was just like you said. My crew.'

Hank looks past her, out the window where a corner of the beam of a nearby lighthouse at Hyannisport circles, circles, sweeps.

'Hank?'

'I slept with her.'

'You had sex with her?'

'Just once.'

'Did you . . . use protection?'

'She's pregnant, True. It wouldn't have mattered.'

'You had sex with Adele?'

Hank jumps off the bed to close the door, and then literally gets down on his knees next to the bed. True rings for the nurse. 'I think she's a little chilly, do you mind taking her. She's out like a light. I can bring her back in later,' she struggles to control her voice, as the nurse deftly folds Brewster into her blanket, not much larger than a table napkin.

'True, listen. I thought you didn't want me. You never returned my calls; you never answered my letters. You sent me these little business notes . . .'

'You were married, Hank, with a pregnant wife,' True says flatly. 'Separated, yes, but how you could be so profligate? And also expose yourself to . . . whatever her asshole boyfriend might have had?'

'Don't trot out the big words, True. You're not really Emily Dickinson . . . and I had a test.'

'Oh, so you did think of your own safety. Okay, no big words. How could you be such a horny fucking toad that you had to fuck Adele while I was carrying our child, and almost losing her, in the bargain? That plain enough for you, you fucking twit?'

'Well, if I weren't married to the ice queen, who couldn't forgive Christ for crying in the garden . . . no, True, no, wait. You're right. I'm just barking because I'm ashamed. You're absolutely right. I shouldn't have done it. But I was so lonely, after you, after us. I just wanted . . . a little touch, a little life.'

'I've heard that, Hank! I've heard it all before! Shame on you! *Shame* on you!'

'Please, True, I swear to you on the baby's head, it didn't mean anything to me . . .'

455

'Why do men say this? Why is it supposed to be a source of comfort to me that you screwed a woman who loves you – *to whom it did mean something* – that it didn't mean anything to you? Doesn't that make you even a bigger shitheel?'

'I never thought of it that way.'

'You never think. You don't think, you don't think! We could have been ready to start again . . . you could have taken our baby home with me!'

'I still will.'

'Of course,' True says. She will not cry. She lifts her chin, knowing how absurd she must appear. 'You are her father. You will always be her father. You will take her home with me and then you will go home and you will see her anytime you wish to.'

'Can't you forgive me?'

'Why did you tell me? Answer me that. Why did you even tell me?'

'You said there were supposed to be no secrets between us.'

'You told me to soothe your own guilt, Hank. You told me because you felt guilty, and you wanted me to take it away. Well, I won't. I refuse. I won't be the mother who blesses you. Now, I have to think of this for the rest of my life. No, I don't, I can't. I don't know if I ever can forgive you. When did you do it?'

'At least more than a month ago. Before Christmas.'

'That's not more than a month ago.'

'Just once. One day, when she was crying, and I put my arms around her. And then she was all . . . you know.'

'Yeah, I unfortunately do know. Get out of here! Get out of this room,' True begins to shout, but lowers her voice. She has never hated anyone more. She realizes she has never truly hated anyone.

'I still want to take care of Gee,' Hank counters.

'That's fine,' True says. 'Just leave. Leave me alone now.'

She watches him as he shrugs into his leather jacket.

'Will you go on seeing her now?' True cannot stop herself from asking.

'I don't know. If I do, it will only be out of friendship,' Hank says. 'I will never marry her. I will never be her lover. I don't want to be. It wouldn't be good for her, or for me.'

'Especially her,' True says, biting her lips. 'Of course, what you just said was that it wouldn't be good for her or for you. Not for me, or for Brewster or Guy.'

'Obviously, I meant that. It would insult our love. I'll wait forever, True.'

'Forever? Was six weeks forever? That's how long you waited! If you meant it would insult our love, why didn't you say it? You didn't mean it. You were thinking of number one,' True is sickened to admit that what she is saying may actually be the case. She cannot comprehend such callousness. And she had hoped, she had so hoped, upon those letters!

Hank tries again, 'Please, listen. I'm flustered. I'm saying all the wrong things, and you're picking me apart as fast as I say them. I used to think this was all your fault, that you watched me, that you were always ready to find fault, that you couldn't bear anyone having a say in your life because you were too used to being in charge. But I was a dumb kid,' Hank tells her. 'I was a dumb kid and I was conceited. No woman ever challenged my ways. I can change. I swear I can change. I was dumb. I'm still dumb.'

'And *I* was a dumb kid,' True replies, regret softening her rage. 'An overgrown kid. When I met you, I was about a tenth-grader in the class of human relations. Never learned how to be normal with a guy. I came by *that* naturally. Given the way it went, the leap I took marrying you, I'd probably have been half buggy anyhow. But not so much as I was. That was . . . an artifact of my personal history. One I didn't know about. Like, if archaeologists found a statue with the hands broken off, a thousand years from now, they'd probably think human beings had evolved past needing hands. You see what I mean?'

'Not really. But hey, you probably learned that in sophomore year. I was a seventh-grader. That was probably history, too.'

'Sixth-grader,' True smiles. 'I guess I thought if I won you, it would make me a pretty girl again. A girl. All those years with Peter. They seemed to have been lost. I wanted to be like those girls in your envelope.'

'You saw those? I figured that's how you must have known about Mount Washington. But I was scared to bring it up.'

'I wouldn't have opened it. It was my mother's idea to look in the envelope. I wouldn't have wanted to know, do you see?'

'I do. And I wish I never had to.' Hank's eyes are liquid, but he bluffs a joke, 'Well, you're a piece of work. And I think you're

457

a big fibber. I was *at least* in junior high emotionally. I should have . . . known more than I did. Stuff I sort of didn't want to know.

'And I thought that if I married you, I would be a better man, that I could confer responsibility on myself . . .' Hank adds.

'Without passing go . . .' True says.

'Skipping all the boring steps.' Hank grins. 'That's *moi, bébé*.'

'Well?'

'Please think this over, True. Just think; don't make any hard decisions. Take it easy, True. I'll be back tomorrow to see the little bug, and to drive you home. When Brewster is ready to come home, I'll drive you both. And True,' he adds, with an abstract fondness, as if speaking to an old pal who's developed a bald spot, 'you were the prettiest girl in school.' True shakes her finger at him, as she nods.

'Oh Hank,' True abruptly calls. He takes a step toward her. 'No, go ahead, I'm fine.'

'Just first tell me what you meant in your note,' Hank bargains.

'Oh, yeah. It seems a thousand years ago. It's a long story. About the day you came over to see Guy, right when he got out of the hospital? Something happened between my mom and me. But you remember what you said a long time ago? Why I don't trust? Why I think I'm . . . unable to be, oh, I guess they'd say unguarded, in the women's magazines . . . well, forget it. It doesn't matter.'

'I want to hear it.'

'Well, the short version is that my mother . . . look, sometime, I'll tell you about it. Maybe it doesn't mean as much as I thought it did.'

'Tell me anyhow.'

'Someday. If it matters. Good night, Hank.'

'I'm going to stop by and kiss Brew before I go.'

'Good,' says True.

After what she imagines to be a long enough interval, she gets out of bed to go and see Elizabeth Brewster, and as she does, she catches sight of Hank walking away, toward the elevators. Has he seen her? She thinks he must have. She waits for him to turn and wave. He does not. He does not look back at her. She watches hungrily, analyzes his walk, still cocky, the way he turns up the collar

458

of his leather jacket. Between a mother and wanted child, love is an unceasing spring-fed river that runs only one way. Between adults, especially if they are of different species, man and woman, love is a series of questions. True has asked all the ones that allowed for multiple choice. The easy ones. Their age difference, her appearance. As for the essay questions, her blue book had been handed to her when the time for the test had run out. Her forms had already been completed, the circles neatly and fully penciled in. *All we know of heaven,* True thinks in the words of her wise, eerie, isolated ancestor. *All we need to know of hell.*

LATE THAT NIGHT, after feeding Brew, True phones Franny. 'I hope it's not too late. Did I wake you?'

'No,' Franny says. 'I was watching TV. How's the little peach?'

'Peachy. Were you fooling around? You sound winded.'

'You wish. I was watching TV on the treadmill.'

'I . . . have to talk to you.'

'Is she going to be okay?'

'She's fine. She's practically perfect. She's gained, like, an ounce or two. They say she'll come home maybe in a week.'

'Oh, True. You dodged a big bullet.'

'Tell me.'

'What did you want to talk to me about?'

'Say you and Steve separated and he had a fling with another woman.'

'I'd forgive him,' Franny says instantly. 'I'd forgive him every day for the rest of his life, and make sure he knew it. That's my pattern. I wouldn't want to give him the chance to go out and find happiness elsewhere and look back at this event and say it was a foible of his youth.'

'Now, say the woman loved him.'

'Say she did. That's not my lookout. If it was a fling.'

'Franny, my dad had a mistress,' True says, looking up at a panel just inside the door of her room, a plaque that reads IN MEMORY OF OUR ANGEL, ANNAMARIE. *Clink went the coin on the tiles of the floor of the crypt.* 'Franny, I found out night before last that my father cheated on my mother. He had a mistress all the time we were growing up.'

'I'm not surprised,' Franny says.

'You aren't?'

'No, it explains a lot,' Franny goes on. 'Kathleen's fascination with men. How she flirted and flirted and needed so badly to be attractive, but then never wanted to follow up on it. And it also . . .'

'What?' True asks.

'It explains a couple of other things. About someone else I know.'

'Mmmmmm. I love you, Franny.'

'I love you, too. And I know we're not talking about Steve and a potential fling he might have had while we were theoretically separated. So let's have the weather report.'

'He slept with Adele,' True admits, the words almost impossible to bring forth. 'He really *slept* with Adele. During this time. When she was staying with him . . . for the view. For her *drawings*.'

'You knew she would try as hard as she could to get him to come back. She never gave up. Not even when she was with the other fellow, I don't think. But, True, don't . . . please don't go batshit up there. You'll dry up your milk.'

'I'm not. I'm shattered. Still, I sensed this. I knew this, I can almost *feel* the day he did it. But I owe it to the baby and Guy to stay calm. The worst is, when the baby was being born, I felt that he was with me, that he was truly *with me*, Franny.'

'He was.'

'He couldn't have been. Not if he'd done that.'

'He's a man, True. He did that, and he filed it. You don't even count the fact that he didn't have the information that your mother was keeping him away from you. He thought that was all coming from you. Or not coming from you.'

'Still.'

'Still. I'd be furious. I'm not defending him.'

'Good, because he doesn't deserve it.'

'Well, you have to decide. I take it he's desperately sorry. He's not taking an attitude.'

'No, he's genuinely, desperately sorry. He wants to come home.'

'Are you going to let him?'

'I would, Franny. I would in a heartbeat. If I thought I could forgive it. If I thought I could get that drug that lets you experience things and then forget them in a fraction of a second.'

'Versed.'

'Right. If I thought I could let him touch me and know that he wasn't thinking of her.'

'Did you ever think – just wait and hear me out – that while he was touching her, he was thinking of you?'

ON A WARM Saturday of January thaw, True bundles Elizabeth Brewster into her fancy stroller and takes her and Guy for Brewster's first walk in downtown Chatham. They can barely get down the street for all the attention. Irene Riggins from the Candy Corral comes out to admire the baby extravagantly, to give Guy fudge, and comment on how wonderful Guy is looking; and how well True is looking, the picture of fitness already. Then, the women from ShoeBiz all flutter around the carriage as True tries on a pair of walking shoes. 'Let me touch her. Look at that olive skin! She'll never need makeup,' says Missus Curry. On impulse, True buys the shoes, though they are outrageous, and in red. They are, she figures, investment shoes. She will be doing a great deal of solo strollering. It is the same at The Eccentric Yankee. Mollie cradles Brew, and gives her husband Tim a mournful look. They have four children, the youngest only three. 'Leave, True. You are Satan,' Tim teases. 'She's absolutely gorgeous. And her brother looks in the pink.'

As they pass the Children's Garden, True catches a motion of something familiar from the corner of her eye. She turns, and sees Hank handing Adele down the steps. Adele is holding a paper shopping bag, and is great with child, her cheeks pinked and her hair, longer, caught up in a tortoiseshell clip. Because she cannot levitate, nor run out into traffic, True must keep walking. Simple physics dictates that they will meet precisely as Adele and Hank reach the end of the flagstone path.

'Dad!' cries Guy, running into Hank's arms, as if he had not just seen him for breakfast earlier that morning. True, nursing, had watched from her rocking chair behind the bedroom curtain as Hank opened the truck door and Guy, almost entirely chipper again, hopped inside.

'Hi fella,' Hank says softly. 'Hi, True. Adele, I want you to meet – well, you've already met my wife. And I want you to meet my daughter, Elizabeth Brewster Bannister, the First.'

'And the last,' True smiles. 'How are you, Adele? Ready for all this?'

'Actually,' Adele dimples, 'I am. Has Hank told you that David and I are back together? David, the baby's father?'

461

'No, Adele, that is wonderful. I must send you a Blessing,' True says. 'And I send you a blessing, too. Really.'

'I have to thank you, True. And to apologize to you. I was outrageously needy with your husband.' True is shocked and touched by Adele's bluntness. 'And after you had given me my real start. I think I lost it when David and I parted and then Mom died. I'm so very sorry. He has been a good friend. He continues to be. This,' she holds up the bag, 'is his wedding gift to us! A christening gown for whoever this person is.'

'Adele,' True replies gently. 'You were the one who made those beautiful books. I should thank you. Good luck.'

As True prepares to resume her walk, Hank puts out a restraining hand. 'Adele, do you mind if I have a moment alone to talk to True? This is going to be our only conversation for a while. And I have private things to say. Do you mind very much?'

'No,' Adele says. 'Of course not. Hank, give me your keys. I'll go warm up the truck.'

As Adele walks away, her pregnancy invisible from the back, Hank reaches down and scoops up his daughter, who delights him by yawning like a kitten. 'I meant to ask you, True, do you still want to talk to me? Now that it's all out, over, said and done?'

'The answer is something like yes but I shouldn't want to. Does that compute?'

Guy is listening avidly. Hank notices and asks, 'Guy, can you go get me a toffee crunch over there? I got me a hungering.'

'I know that trick. You want to talk to my mom.'

'Who wouldn't want to talk to a pretty blonde with a cute baby?'

Guy sighs, 'Okay. Gimme the money.'

'You're still too skinny, Gee. You get yourself one, too.'

'Chocolate would puke me. I just had fudge.'

'Then get yourself a sucker, or get your ear pierced. If you hate chocolate so much, then, next week, when I come to dance, I'll bring Jell-O.'

They both crack up. Clearly, this is an inside joke.

As Guy leaves, Hank tells True, 'He told me that when he was in the hospital, he had every kind of Jell-O known to man. He says he'll never be able to look Jell-O in the face again.'

'Yeah, and it has pig epidermis in it. I read in school!' Guy calls back.

'I love pig epidermis,' Hank replies loudly. 'And quit lyin', Guy. You know you do, too. We like a nice, stuffed pig epidermis with a side of blood sausage, huh?'

'Don't make me laugh,' Guy pleads, clutching his belly. 'It still kills if I laugh too hard.'

'Well, you better start laughing, 'cause next week, we're going to do a *pas de bourée* or two. Assemblé. And start stretching. *Grand-père* says you don't want to form adhesions . . . scars, inside there.'

Guy holds up his hands pleadingly, and addresses the sky: 'Haven't I suffered enough?'

True sees the attachment between them, invisible and tensile as fishing line. She loves Hank more than she can bear without looking away, for this alone, this gift to her boy.

With him across the street, Hank rolls his shoulders once, turns up his collar, and says, 'So, I know what's coming. You thought it over, and the gist of it is, you want me to go.'

'Your car's running.'

'I mean, go . . . go. For good. Not talk about it again. That's what I wanted to make sure of, privately, before I went.'

'Well, okay, yes. I do want to talk about it again. As soon as we can,' True admits. 'I can't get it off my mind. Not for a moment.'

'Nor me.'

'Then, Saturday? After Guy and you work out?'

'Suits me down to the ground. I'm glad to hear you say it.'

'Give Adele my best. I *mean* that. This is less her fault than yours.'

'I will. She's moving. To New York.'

'Wow.'

'Well, you got to live where your man lives.'

'I guess so,' True replies, elaborately adjusting Brew's bunting.

GUY MARCHES UP out of the basement, sweat dripping from his chin. 'He hasn't changed,' Guy mutters. 'It's okay if you don't get back with him.'

True has to laugh.

'Don't sit close to me. I probably stink,' Hank says, following Guy up, using his T-shirt to wipe off his own arms and chest.

463

'It's okay. You never smelled like bad stink. Just like salt and fish,' True says.

'Kathleen's got wash on the line. Wonder how long this weather will last.'

'Yes. You know, she's in the middle of some monumental stuff. She's moving.'

'She is?'

'To her own little cottage. In Harwich, we think, Dog and I. And she's going to Wisconsin, you know. Yes. On a plane. To visit Esa's pop. In April.'

'Huh.'

'Pretty amazing, don't you think? I suggested she have one date, and she's going cross-country!'

'True,' says Hank, getting up.

'You going? I thought we were going to talk . . . the baby's asleep.'

'Can I kiss you?'

'Yes,' True says, and slips against his hot skin, and lets her head drop back and her mouth open into his, turning and searching, as if to find a way that she can get closer to him than the tissue of their skins permits. 'I love you so, Hank. I had to keep you . . . distant. I had to. That was my shield. Like you said. Civility when all else fails. It never was a case of not loving you.'

'And I love you. You're my wife. You're my heart, True.'

Both of them hear Guy turn the shower on, and simultaneously, Brewster's sharp cry. She is awake, her light coverlet kicked loose, her reed new legs with their brand-new plump curvature, furiously beating the air. Hank scoops her up and begins to sing, 'She's as sweet as Tupelo honey. She's an angel of the first degree . . .'

'That's what I used to sing to Gee,' True tells him. 'She loves it. I don't think it's going to do any good now, though. She's hungry, I'm afraid.'

'Go ahead.'

True opens her blouse, expecting Hank to turn his eyes away. He does not. 'You did the hard part without me,' he says, so sadly.

'No, the hard part's ahead,' True tells him. 'I don't know if I'd want to do that without you.'

'But you . . .'

'Well, I have an idea.'

'It couldn't be worse than wanting my wife, watching her nurse

464

my child, and knowing I have to go home to an empty shack.'

'I don't think it is,' True says, sweeping a strand of her hair behind one ear.

'Don't do that,' Hank requests sharply.

'What?'

'Put half a piece of hair behind your ear. It's . . . just that it's my favorite thing you do. Don't do it now, in here. In our room.'

'Okay. I'm sorry,' True says, secretly joyous to have seen how candidly her mere motion has affected him. 'Here's my idea. I want you to go steady with the children. I want you to see them every day. I want you to be their father anytime you want.'

'Oh. I hoped for that. I thought this was about us. So it isn't.'

'It is.'

'Well, then. What about me and you?'

'You may ask me out.' Her words sound starched, prim as a paper collar. This isn't how she meant for this to unfold.

'Ask you out.'

'And we'll date.'

'We'll date? We'll date, or we'll go places like friends with the kids?'

'No, we'll really date,' True says. 'And after a month or so, if you still want to, we'll . . . we'll make love, if we can. And then we'll do it again. And maybe after a few months, we'll go on a trip . . . does this sound okay so far? You know, I'm kind of making it up as I go along. I thought about it for nights, and I'm still winging it. There's no book about this, Hank.'

'I know. I know it's an unusual situation. But . . . okay, say we date, and all this leading up to . . . ?'

'I can only tell you what I hope. What I hope is . . . that we'll see what we are, Hank, what we really are. If we can have that . . . bond we thought we caught sight of, once upon a time. Do you think that's possible? Do you think we might not have to change, except for the fatal flaws, to have to learn how to genuinely trust each other?'

'I trust you.'

'But I don't trust you right now. And I want to! I love you so much that I can't have anything less than the real thing with you. You said the same thing. And don't you think you really *do* need to learn to trust me, too?'

'How do you mean?' he asks.

'Everything you said, when you left. That I have no respect for you. That I think you're – a boy toy. Equipment.'

'I was mad, True,' Hank looks away, shamefaced. 'I don't really think that.'

'A tiny part of you?'

'Maybe . . .' Hank concedes, but reluctantly. 'But that can change, and why does it have to take months? It didn't take months before!'

'I hope it doesn't! I want it to be tomorrow! Look, maybe we can learn to overlook what we can't change. And then never stop. The way we should have before we got married.' True stops, and breathes out slowly. 'Like, I know we'll have a fight. We'll have a fight, and we'll sing if it gets too bad. We'll cook dinner together. We'll talk about movies and read books to each other. I know, it sounds boring, but we've had too much of the other way.'

'No, you're speaking gospel. A life without drama. I could be all over that.'

'Okay, so you agree. We'll try. We'll . . . figure it out. And if we figure it out, then we'll . . . get married.'

'True, we're already married.'

'We'd have to do it over. Or I couldn't believe it. You broke it, Hank.'

'So did you. For better, for worse,' he reminds her.

'Forsaking *all* others,' she reminds him.

'Let's do it over now. We know all that, *bébé*. We know everything.'

'That's what we thought once, my dear, my love. And look what happened . . .'

Hank points to Brewster. 'Yeah, look what happened. I'd say that's not so bad!'

'It isn't. She's wonderful, our lucky star. If only she were the only thing that's come from this. But, at first, Hank, I thought I'd just run. I'd never see you again. But I couldn't do that. So I tried to think, how can we try? How?'

'And?'

'This was the only way I could think of to try that I wouldn't be so resentful I'd ruin it for both of us.' True puts her hand on Hank's forearm, and looks at her hand, the shape of it, resting there. 'If I ruin it, I'll break my own heart. Because maybe, someday, if I tried

466

hard and kept busy, I could look back and stand to lose the angry, selfish, pouty little shit of a guy who walked out of here.' She stops, so long that Hank almost speaks. But then she goes on, 'But if I lost the man who wrote those letters, the letters I almost didn't see, I'd be losing the mate of my life.'

'You won't lose me.'

'I know. I do know,' True says. 'I *believe* that. I have to *see* it.'

'Do we have to get divorced first?'

'Hank, don't horse around. I'm doing the best I can. I don't mean *legally* get remarried. I mean, make the vow. To each other . . .'

'In front of people?'

'Maybe. Maybe at the Elvis chapel in Vegas. This time forever. I have to know if you really can be a forever kind of guy, knowing all it means. See, even by your agreeing to wait, I'll know more than I knew before.'

'That's true. Because if you knew me, you wouldn't question that I'd wait. We still don't really know each other, deep down. I thought about that a million times. It was like we got on a roller coaster, and it was as much as anyone could do simply to hold on. Too much has happened, that . . . got in the way. But I think it'll be hard to wait. Especially for some parts.'

'Some features of the plan might be in place sooner than others. But the sugar on the top shelf tastes sweeter.'

'I think you're a hard woman.'

'I am a hard woman. I have to be. If I'm not, I'll do what I want to do with all my heart, just pull you down right here on our bed and . . . make a mistake that would be the end of us. I know how bad I can be. I know how vengeful and vulnerable, and you do, too! Hank, do you think I want this? I want more than anything else in the world to say, you go get your suitcase; I'll go get a pizza; we'll all get in bed with the baby and Gee . . .'

Hank's mouth works, his lip uncontrolled. 'How can you do this?' he pleads.

'Because I want this to last so bad. I love you so bad. And the thing you did, it's still too new in my mind. It's like a snake that would bite me. It would bite us. I have to see it like you see it. As a detour in the road. As a stumble that has nothing to do with us.'

He sighs deeply. Then, he looks down at her and grins. 'Okay. Miz Dickinson, when may I call on you?'

'Mister Bannister, I would be charmed. Let's see. Just so I don't leak through my blouse, as I am indisposed, you see, in a delicate condition, shall we say, three P.M. a week from next Sunday?'

'I'll be here to drive you.'

'Oh, but we must take my car. I have so much trouble, sir, getting into trucks because of the stitches betwixt my limbs, you see . . .'

'And what would you like to do, ma'am?'

'I thought, well, since by then I will be able to lift more than ten pounds, I might like to go bowling.'

'Bowling, you say? Well, I must warn you, Miz Dickinson, I am an accomplished bowler. And I am not given to mercy.'

'Oh, do not show me mercy, Mister Bannister. I am a competitive person. I like to win. I always get what I want. And so, Mister Bannister, I will kick your ass.'

'We'll see about that.'

'Oh, yes we shall,' True answers, and smiles up after kissing Brew's head. 'We shall see what we shall see.'

May 5, 2002
Port St. Lucie, Florida

The Deep End of the Ocean

Jacquelyn Mitchard

The international number one bestseller.

'Watch your brother,' says Beth Cappadora to her seven-year-old son Vincent. Only minutes later she turns again and asks, 'Where's Ben?' It's the moment that every mother fears: for three-year-old Ben is gone. And no one can find him. Despite a police search that becomes a nationwide obsession, Ben has vanished, leaving behind a family that will be torn apart with anguish. Until, nine years later, a twelve-year-old boy knocks on their door – a boy who does not know them, but who will irrevocably twist their lives a second time . . .

'A blockbuster read . . . a rich, moving and altogether stunning first novel. Readers will find this compelling and heartbreaking story - sure to be compared to *The Good Mother* – impossible to put down'   *Publishers Weekly*

'So well observed and perceptive it's hard to shy away from . . . masterfully paced . . . A story of one family's slow tumble back into light'   *Los Angeles Times*

'*The Deep End of the Ocean* burns itself into the memory line by line. It is by turns lyrical and startling, brilliant. I wish I had written it. Ms Mitchard is blessed with a surplus of raw, vigorous talent'

KAYE GIBBONS, author of *Charms for the Easy Life*

0 00 649909 0

A Theory of Relativity

Jacquelyn Mitchard

A tragic accident, an orphaned one-year-old and a bitter struggle that will break your heart.

For Gordon McKenna and his parents, the only way they can survive the loss of their beloved sister and daughter, Georgia, is to prepare to devote themselves heart and soul to the care of her baby girl, Keefer. But another family feels the same way and, as Keefer becomes the focus of a fiercely fought custody battle, the limits of love, and its capacity to heal, are tested again and again.

ISBN 0 00 713985 3